— The —
KINGDOM
and the **CROWN** VOL 1

FISHERS
OF MEN

A NOVEL

GERALD N. LUND

ENSIGN PEAK

First printing in hardbound 2000
First printing in paperbound 2006

Visit us at EnsignPeakPublishing.com

This is a work of fiction. Characters described in this book are the products of the author's imagination or are represented fictitiously.

Library of Congress Cataloging-in-Publication Data

Lund, Gerald N.
  Fishers of men / Gerald N. Lund.
    p.   cm. — (The kingdom and the crown; v. 1)
  ISBN 1-57345-820-1
  ISBN-10 1-59038-667-1 (paperbound)
  ISBN-13 978-1-59038-667-5 (paperbound)
  ISBN-13 978-1-60907-949-9 (paperbound)
1. Bible. N. T.—History of Biblical events—Fiction. 2. Jesus Christ—Fiction.
  I. Title.
PS3562.U485 F57 2000
813'.54—dc21   00-056281

Printed in the United States of America
LSC Communications, Harrisonburg, VA

10   9   8   7   6   5   4   3

PREFACE

Jesus of Nazareth.

Messiah. Redeemer. Savior. The Lamb of God. The Son of God.

No other single life has so profoundly changed the course of history and influenced humanity.

Thousands upon thousands of books have been written and are still being written about his life and teachings.

Some of the greatest artistic masterpieces in art, literature, and music have been inspired by him.

Even our basic division of time into two great eras is marked by his birth.

Numerous wars have been fought in his name.

Christianity today, with its hundreds of different churches, is the largest of all world religions. More than half of the world's population is at least nominally Christian.

The book that contains the story of his life and the most complete summary of his teachings is the bestselling book of all times. For instance, the American Bible Society alone has distributed more than five billion Bibles since its founding in 1816; and it has translated at least portions of the Bible into more than five hundred languages.

With all of this, it isn't hard to understand why my decision to write a historical novel set in New Testament times was not made lightly. In addition, it would be folly to assume one could write a novel that would embrace all interpretations of the faith and please all Christians, or even a small portion of them. And yet it is fascinating to think about those first days. . . .

To wonder what it must have been like when there were no "Christians."

To try to imagine how it must have felt when the word first began to leap from mouth to mouth about a carpenter from the obscure village of Nazareth.

To sit at his feet and hear his new and astonishing doctrines for the first time.

To stand just feet away from him and personally witness as he healed the sick, gave sight to the blind, restored the crippled and maimed, raised the dead.

And perhaps most important, to ask oneself the question, "How would I have responded if I had been there?"

The following brief observations may be helpful to readers as they begin *The Kingdom and the Crown*. Writing a novel based on the life of Jesus Christ as told in the New Testament created some interesting challenges and dilemmas. My commitment in writing historical fiction has always been to represent both the history and the time period as accurately as possible. In this case, that became a particularly challenging task. In the first place, we are two thousand years removed from that time. Second, the only dependable historical record we have of the life of Christ and those he influenced is found in the New Testament. And the four accounts written by Matthew, Mark, Luke, and John were never meant to be histories or biographies. They are eyewitness testimonies of his life and ministry. This leaves many of the details required by a novelist woefully lacking. A third challenge comes in interpreting what those events and teachings mean for us today—a question that has been answered in a thousand different ways.

Without trying to suggest that my answer to that very difficult question is the right one, and without trying to "convert" the reader to my way of thinking, here in brief summary are some issues I wrestled with and how I resolved them. This, I hope, will help the reader better understand the story contained in this book.

There are now dozens of "versions" or translations of the Bible in English alone. Which text to use when presenting the teachings of

Jesus posed a dilemma. The King James Version (often called the Authorized Version) is still the queen of all translations, not only in the numbers sold but in its influence on other translations and the art and culture of our civilization. Therefore, I chose to use the King James Version as the text I would follow.

Whole books have been written on the exact date of Christ's birth, with the greatest consensus placing it between 7 B.C. and 4 B.C. However, our calendar assumes he was born in 1 B.C. Since this is a novel and not a scholarly examination of this question, I have chosen to use 1 B.C. as the base for dating in the novel. I did this simply because most readers will find it easier to think of Jesus as thirty years old in A.D. 30, rather than having to mentally add or subtract dates.

By the same token, though the Hebrews had their own calendar with different names for each of the months, and even though the primary characters in the novel are Jews, I chose to use the Julian calendar, which gave us the names of the months we still use today. Again, this allows the reader to know what time of the year it is when a date is given.

The cultural setting of Israel in New Testament times was very diverse. The common people in the Holy Land spoke Aramaic, but their scriptures were in classical Hebrew. Latin was the language of the Romans, but Greek was the *lingua franca,* or the language that was spoken everywhere in business and commerce. To accurately portray this diversity in the dialogue between characters could be very tedious. So while I remind the reader from time to time of this fact, I have deliberately avoided trying to be perfectly consistent because such an approach would soon become confusing.

In a similar vein, the problem of names becomes a challenge as well. *Jesus* is the English form of the Greek, *Hee-ay-sous.* In Hebrew the name was *Yeshua,* which is the same as the English form of the Old Testament *Joshua. Moses* is actually *Moshe* (MOH-sheh) in Hebrew.

John is *Yohanan*. After some internal debate, I determined that I would use what "felt" authentic for fictional characters but stay with the more recognized forms of the names of actual people. So in the novel it is "John the Baptist," not "Yohanan the Baptist." It is "Jesus of Nazareth," not "Yeshua of Nazareth." One fictional character is named Moshe, but I never refer to the Law as "The Law of Moshe," even though in actuality that was Moses' name in Hebrew. This does create a few places where we have Jewish people explaining Hebrew names, which of course they would not have done. While it may not be entirely logical, I hope it lessens the confusion for the reader.

The name of God in the Old Testament is written with four consonants—YHVH. No vowels are given in the original. The King James translators and other versions have rendered this as *Jehovah* (the Y often becomes J in English). In recent times it has become more common to translate this as *Yahweh* or *Jahveh*. I chose to follow the more traditional form given in the King James Version.

The New Testament gives us four records or testimonies of Christ's life. The four Gospel writers wrote to different audiences and had somewhat different purposes. Much of the material is common to more than one author, but each account has unique elements as well. Many scholars have attempted to create a "harmony" of Christ's life, putting the recorded events in a logical order of occurrence. Few of these harmonies agree in every respect, and even the four Gospel writers do not agree on some minor details. A historical novel generally follows the sequence of events as they occurred. In this case, that is impossible to determine with complete accuracy. Therefore, while I have tried to follow the basic structure of Christ's life—not taking things from late in his life and putting them in the first days of his ministry—in many cases it really doesn't matter exactly when certain events happened. I therefore took some minor liberties in the sequencing of events and combining some of his teachings.

However, I did not feel free to take liberties with *what* Jesus taught.

Though some minor changes in punctuation and sentence composition were necessary to put his teachings into dialogue form, I have not changed *what* he said. It is my firm conviction that what he said is sacred. We are free to interpret those sayings for ourselves but not to alter them as they were given. It was not possible in the novel to have Jesus say only what is recorded in the New Testament. The gospel writers did not record the casual, day-to-day interactions that surely were part of his life. But I kept these "fictional conversations" to a minimum and never used them to have Jesus teach something that is not part of the scriptural record.

It has been my privilege to travel to the Holy Land more than a dozen times, the last visit being in the summer of 2000. As part of that experience my wife and I have made numerous friends who are Israeli and Jewish. Through such associations and through my studies, I have become a great admirer of Judaism, its rich traditions, its long history, its symbols and rituals. These have not only profoundly influenced Christianity, but they still carry significant spiritual meaning today. I am not Jewish, but I have tried to accurately portray Judaism in all its richness and diversity. If I have fallen short of doing so accurately and sensitively, it is because of lack of personal experience, not lack of respect and admiration.

I have used notes at the end of each chapter to accomplish two purposes. First, the notes provide some information that will be helpful to the reader but that does not naturally fit into the flow of the novel. Second, I have given scriptural references so readers can easily find the original accounts in the New Testament and read them for themselves.

In conclusion, I must say that I have worried long about whether this "picture" of Jesus, and those who first heard and accepted him, appropriately represents reality. I have the greatest reverence for Peter and Andrew; James and John; Mary, the mother of Jesus; and all the other real people who were part of those foundational years. The scriptural record simply does not provide the detail needed to have them become fully fleshed-out characters in the novel. It is my deepest hope that in giving them personality and character, I have not misrepresented what they actually were and the contribution they made to the history of Christianity. That is especially true of the Savior himself.

People in the world have many different feelings about Jesus. Some say he was a great teacher but nothing more. Others accept him as a prophet but not divine. Some modern Bible scholars question the miraculous elements of his life, assuming they were added by later generations of Christians to enrich the story and heighten Christ's stature. But many millions have believed and do now believe that he was literally the Son of God.

It will quickly become clear as one reads this novel where I stand. I accept the scriptural record as true. I believe with a totality of heart that the four Gospel writers were men of honesty and integrity and that they accurately portrayed what actually happened. I believe Jesus was the greatest man to ever live on the face of this earth. *And more!* I believe and accept the testimony of these first Christians who saw him nailed to the cross and then three days later saw and felt his glorified, resurrected body. This was what changed their lives forever. This was what changed the history of the world.

One day in northern Galilee Jesus asked his disciples, "Whom do men say that I am?" Two thousand years later, Peter's answer still rings with power. His answer also perfectly reflects how I feel about Jesus of Nazareth and how I have tried to portray him in this book. Peter answered and said, *"Thou art the Christ, the Son of the living God"* (Matthew 16:13, 16; emphasis added).

Alpine, Utah
July 2000

LIST OF MAJOR CHARACTERS

The Household of David ben Joseph, Merchant of Capernaum

    David: Simeon's father, 46[1]

    Deborah bat Benjamin of Sepphoris: Simeon's mother, 44

    Simeon: Second son of David and Deborah, ardent Zealot, 21

    Ephraim: Simeon's older brother, 25, married to Rachel

    Rachel: Ephraim's wife, 22

    Leah: Simeon's sister, 15

    Joseph: Simeon's youngest brother, 10

    Esther: David and Deborah's granddaughter, daughter of Ephraim and Rachel, 4

    Boaz: David and Deborah's grandson, son of Ephraim and Rachel, almost 2

    Aaron of Sepphoris: Deborah's brother, Simeon's uncle, a dedicated Pharisee, 39

The Household of Mordechai ben Uzziel of Jerusalem

    Mordechai: Miriam's father; leader of the Sadducees, member of the Great Sanhedrin of Jerusalem, 42

    Miriam bat Mordechai ben Uzziel: Mordechai's only daughter, 18

    Livia of Alexandria: Miriam's servant and friend, 20

The Household of Yehuda of Beth Neelah

    Yehuda: Simeon's friend and partner in the Zealot movement, a farmer, 24

---

[1] Ages are given as of A.D. 30.

Daniel: Yehuda's younger brother, also a farmer, 22

Shana: Yehuda's sister, 17

Other Prominent Characters

Jesus of Nazareth: Carpenter and teacher, 30

Mary of Nazareth: Mother of Jesus[2]

Marcus Quadratus Didius: Roman tribune, 25

Sextus Rubrius: Roman centurion, about 50

Moshe ben Ya'abin: Bandit and thief

Pontius Pilate: Procurator of Judea

Azariah the Pharisee: Leader of the Jerusalem group and titular head of the Pharisees, 50

Simon Peter: Fisherman, one of the Twelve Apostles called by Jesus

Andrew: Simon Peter's brother, one of the Twelve

James and John: Sons of Zebedee, partners in fishing with Peter and Andrew; both apostles

Matthew Levi: A publican in Capernaum; called to follow Jesus, also one of the Twelve

Amram the Pharisee: Leader of the Pharisees in Capernaum, about 50

Nicodemus: A leading Pharisee in Jerusalem, member of the Great Sanhedrin

Gehazi of Sepphoris: A leader of the Zealot movement, mid-50s

---

[2]Ages for actual Bible characters are not given here since they are not known (other than the age of Jesus), though suggestions about their age may be included in the novel itself.

GLOSSARY

NOTE: Some terms which are used only once and defined in the text are not included here.

Adonai (ah-doh-NAI)—Literally, Hebrew for "my lords." Because of the reverence with which the Jews held the sacred name of Jehovah, or Yahweh, they substituted *Adonai*, meaning in that case "the Lord." The translators of the King James Bible (and some other versions), out of respect for that practice, wrote in LORD in all but one or two places where Jehovah was found in the Hebrew version, writing it with small capital letters to distinguish it from the use of the word *Lord* (the singular *adon*), which referred to a person of respect. See, for example, Psalm 110:1, where both uses of *Lord* is found.

bar mitzvah (bar MEETZ-vah)—Literally, "a son of a commandment"; the ceremony whereby a Jewish boy at age thirteen becomes an official adult in the religious community.

bath or *bat* (BAHT)—Daughter, or daughter of, e.g., Miriam bat Mordechai, or Miriam, daughter of Mordechai.

ben (BEN)—Son, or son of, as in Simeon ben Joseph or Simeon, son of Joseph. An Aramaic translation of *ben* is *bar*, as in Peter's name, Simon Bar-jona, or Simon, son of Jonah (Matthew 16:17), and *bar mitzvah*.

Beth (BAIT; commonly pronounced as BETH among English speakers)—House of, e.g., *Bethlehem*, House of Bread; *Bethel*, the House of God.

caligulas (ca-LIG-yoo-lahs)—A sandal with short spikes in the soles worn by most Roman soldiers.

christos (KRIS-tohs)—In Greek, "anointed one"; in English this becomes "Christ." The meaning is the same as the Hebrew *meshiach*.

chuppah (KHOO[1]-pah)—The canopy under which a couple are married in the Jewish faith.

Diaspora (dee-ASP-or-ah)—Literally, "the dispersion," meaning the scattering of the Jews among all nations; first begun after the fall of Jerusalem to Babylon in 587 B.C.

gehenna (geh-HEN-ah)—A Latin word derived from the Greek *geenna*, which comes from the Hebrew *ge-hinnom*, which literally takes its name from Ge Hinnom, or the Valley of Hinnom, where piles of refuse burned without ceasing. *Gehenna* refers to the world of spirits or the world where the dead go.

goyim (goy-EEM)—Gentiles, literally in Hebrew, "nations," a word used for anyone not of the house of Israel, or in modern times, one who is not a Jew; singular is *goy*.

matzos (MAHT-zos)—Unleavened bread, especially that used during the Feast of Unleavened Bread and with the Passover meal.

menorah (commonly, men-ORE-rah, but also men-ore-RAH)—A candlestick; usually refers to the sacred, seven-branched candlestick used in the tabernacle of Moses and later in the temples.

meshiach (meh-SHEE-ach)—In Hebrew, "anointed one"; in English, "Messiah"; same as the Greek *christos*.

mezuzah (meh-ZOO-sah)—Literally, in Hebrew, "doorpost"; the small wood or metal container with scriptural passages inside fixed to the doorposts and gates of observant Jewish homes in response to the command in Deuteronomy 6:9.

minyan (meen-YAN)—A "quorum," the minimum number of adult males (which is ten) required to carry out official worship services.

mitzvah (MEETZ-vah)—"Commandment," the Hebrew word for all the requirements God places upon his obedient children.

---

[1] The CH sound in Hebrew is a throaty guttural, pronounced like KH together but with air coming through the throat.

Pesach (pe-SOCK)—The Hebrew name for Passover.

peyot (pay-OHT)—The long side curls worn by strictly observant Jews in obedience to the commandment in Leviticus 19:27. In Hebrew *peyot* literally means "edge" or "corners."

phylactery (fil-ACT-ur-ee)—The Greek word for *tefillin*; comes from the concept of a safeguard or amulet.

praetorium (pree-TOR-ee-um)—Official residence of the Roman governor or procurator or other high government official.

publicani (poo-blee-KHAN-ee)—Latin for "public servant"; the publicans of the New Testament were hired by Romans to serve as the tax assessors and collectors in local districts.

seder (SAY-dur)—From the Hebrew word for "order." The Passover meal is often called *seder*; there the various prescribed foods are laid out in a specific order.

Shabbat (sha-BAHT)—Hebrew name for the Lord's day; the source of our word *Sabbath*.

shalom (shaw-LOWM)—"Peace," used as a greeting and a farewell.

Sh'ma (sh-MAH)—Sometimes also *Shemah*; from the Hebrew imperative for "hear!" One of the most solemn declarations of faith for a religious Jew; it is said every day and, if possible, is the last prayer of the dying. Comes from Deuteronomy 6:4, "*Hear*, O Israel: The Lord our God is one Lord."

Talmud (TALL-mood)—A collection of sacred writings and commentaries written by learned rabbis and Hebrew scholars of the Torah over many generations.

tefillin (the-FEE-lin)—From the Hebrew word for "prayers"; the small boxes affixed either to the forehead or the left bicep by observant Jews in keeping with the commandment in Deuteronomy 6:8. Inside are pieces of parchment on which are written scriptural passages.

Torah (TORE-ah)—The writings of Moses; the first five books of the current Old Testament.

yeshiva (yeh-SHEE-vah)—A Jewish school, one that particularly emphasizes the study of the Torah and the Talmud.

Yom Kippur (yam kee-POOR)—The "Day of Atonement," the most sacred of all Hebrew holy days; it occurs in the early fall in our current calendars.

Pronunciation Guide for Names

Readers may wish to use the common English pronunciations for names that have come to modern times, such as David. The Hebrew pronunciation is for those who wish to say them as they may have been spoken at the time of the Savior. Any such pronunciation guide must be viewed as speculative, however; we simply do not know for certain how Hebrew names were pronounced in antiquity.

Abraham—In Hebrew, ahv-rah-HAM
Anna—ahn-AH
Azariah—ah-zeh-RAI-ah
Bethlehem—English, BETH-leh-hem; Hebrew, BAIT lech-EM
Beth Neelah—BAIT nee-LAH
Bethsaida—English, BETH-say-dah; Hebrew, BAIT sah-EE-dah
Caesarea—see-zar-EE-ah
Capernaum—English, ka-PUR-neh-um; Hebrew, kah-fur-NAY-hum
Chorazin—khor-ah-ZEEN
Daniel—dan-YELL
David—dah-VEED
Deborah—deh-vor-AH
Ephraim—ee-FRAI-eem
Esther—es-TAHR
Eve—hah-VAH
Galilee—English, GAL-leh-lee; Hebrew, gah-LEEL or gah-lee-YAH
Ha-Keedohn—ha-kee-DOHN

Jairus—Some think the Greeks would have pronounced each vowel, therefore, jay-AI-rus. More commonly it is JAIR-yus.

James—Same as Jacob, or yah-ah-KOHV in Hebrew

Jerusalem—ye-roosh-ah-LAI-eem

Jesus—Hebrew form of the name is Yeshua (yesh-oo-AH), which is the same as the Old Testament *Joshua*; Greek form is hee-AY-soos.

Joachin—yo-ah-KEEN

John—Hebrew form of the name is Johanan (yo-HAH-nahn).

Joknean Pass—yohk-NEE-an

Joseph—yo-SEPH

Kidron Valley—English, KID-rohn; Hebrew, kee-DROHN

Kinnereth—English, KIN-ur-eth; Hebrew, keen-ohr-ET

Leah—lay-AH

Menachem—meh-NAKH-em

Miriam—meer-YAM

Mordechai—mor-deh-KAI

Moshe Ya'abin—mohw-SHEH ya-ah-BEEN

Mount Hermon—hur-MOHN

Mount Tabor—English, TAY-bur; Hebrew, tah-BOHR

Phineas—feh-NEE-as

Ptolemais—TOHL-eh-mays

Rachel—rah-KHEL

Samuel—shmoo-EL

Sepphoris—seh-PHOR-us

Shana—SHAW-nah

Simeon—shee-MOHN

Simon—see-MOHN

Tabgha—tab-GAH

Yehuda—yeh-HOO-dah; other forms, Judah or Judas

PROLOGUE

I

14 OCTOBER, A.D. 29

The waters of the Sea of Gennesaret—or Kinnereth as the Galileans called it in their breathy, guttural Aramaic—were usually a deep blue-green, but under the leaden winter sky, the waters were a slate gray. The basin in which the lake rested looked like a huge bowl with brown sides and a gray bottom. Even then, it provided a stunning backdrop for the men of the second cohort of the Tenth Legion Fretensis. The line of about two hundred men had just crested a long ridge where the land dropped off sharply to the waters far below. The first of what the Jews called "the early rains" was drizzling from the sky, and the soldiers moved along with their heads down, enduring one more miserable day as they had so many before it. And yet the bright red capes, the gleaming brass helmets, and the dull glint off the Roman broadswords provided a sharp splash of color in an otherwise dismal landscape.

In the reckoning of the Julian calendar, created by Julius Caesar almost a hundred years before, it was the fourteenth day of October in the fourteenth year of the reign of Tiberias Caesar, or the seven hundred and eighty-first year since the founding of Rome. In the reckoning of the Jews, it was the third day of the month of Marchesvan, in the three thousand seven hundred eighty-ninth year since the coming of Adam, who in their myths and legends was the first man on the earth.

Marcus Quadratus Didius, newest tribune in the tenth legion, shook his head. Was there nothing that these Jews did like other peoples? They even had their own way of reckoning time. He brushed aside the sudden irritation and reined his horse aside to watch his men approaching four abreast.

As the first rank moved past his position, the cohort's standard straightened, the long pole with its red banner and its glittering golden eagle at the top snapping into position. There was a stiff breeze coming up from the lake, and the flag crackled briskly. The brilliantly dyed fabric was embroidered in gold with the four letters SPQR. Almost without thought, his mind formed the words *Senatus Populusque Romanus*—the Senate and the Roman people. And that stilled any thoughts of the intransigent Jews. Here in a single symbol was embodied all that he stood for, all that had brought him so far from his home and that would keep him here for the next several years.

Though not a single pair of eyes so much as flicked in his direction, almost imperceptibly heads lifted, chins tucked in, shoulders squared as the men passed by their new commander. It was a stirring sight, and he felt a sudden thrill of pride shoot through him. He was only a month out of Rome, and he was still struggling with a growing conviction that the gods had played a cruel and terrible joke on him by making the province of Judea his first command.

He leaned over and patted the neck of the sorrel mare, feeling her chafing impatience to return to their rightful place at the head of the column. But there would be time enough for that. Now he needed this. This was Rome! This was the pulse that throbbed from Britannia to Libya, from the Pillars of Hercules to the Euphrates River. Fifty million people, frontiers of over four thousand miles, twenty-five Roman legions marching in disciplined ranks throughout the length and breadth of it, making possible *pax Romana*, the Roman peace. Who would not be stirred to think he was part of that heartbeat, part of the greatest empire in the history of the world? Sennacherib of Assyria, Nebuchadnezzar of Babylon, Cyrus and Xerxes of Persia, even Alexander the Great—all would have stood in awe to see what Rome had created.

Marcus straightened, surprised at the depth of his own emotions. His father was right. The emperor was not Rome. No one man— though powerful beyond belief—could sweep aside the essence of the empire. It was the empire that mattered. It was the empire that welded scores of peoples and dozens of tongues into one vast unity. The emperors came and went, but the empire endured!

The clear green eyes darkened as Marcus thought of Pontius Pilatus, or Pilate, as the people called him, current procurator of Judea and Marcus's own direct commander. Pilate was a Roman official, an appointee with full power to represent Roman authority in this part of the empire. Haughty, arrogant, more likely to act on impulse than through careful deliberation, Pilate was typical of many of the procurators and legates who governed the various provinces. He was more inept than some, less corrupt than many. But he did the job, and it was clear that for the moment Tiberias Caesar was satisfied with how things were going in Judea. So let the governor strut and posture and throw his power about. Marcus would carry out his commands without question, for in discipline and obedience lay the secret of Rome.

Marcus lifted the reins, preparing to dig his heels into the mare's flanks and move out ahead of the column again, when he saw that

Sextus Rubrius, his senior centurion, had stepped out of position a short distance away. He was not watching his men pass by but rather stared down at the lake below, his rough-hewn features dark and moody. Marcus nudged the horse forward until he came up beside him.

"Worried?"

"Yes, sire, somewhat."

"Why? Surely you've been sent out to assist in collecting taxes before."

The veteran noncommissioned officer, who was about the same age as Marcus's father, looked up. He seemed to sense that Marcus's question was sincere. After a moment's thought, he spoke. "Yes, sire, I've been asked to collect delinquent taxes before. But this is the Galilee. There is a saying among the men, sire. We say that if the Jews are the tinderbox of Rome, then the Galileans are the flint that strikes the spark."

"Really?"

"Yes. I was stationed here in the Galilee for some of the eight years I have been here in the province. I learned that Galileans are born with a sword in their swaddling clothes, suckled with the milk of rebellion, and weaned with a spear."

Marcus started to chuckle, then, seeing Rubrius's expression, let it die. So that was why Rubrius had mustered a full maniple for this assignment. Marcus looked down to where, far below them, the roofs of Capernaum stood waiting, barely visible through the mists of rain. Capernaum contained an important customshouse on the great highway that ran from Alexandria to Damascus, and Marcus knew that the procurator kept a small garrison of legionnaires in the city to see that the duties owed to Rome were collected properly and without difficulty. He had wondered why Pilate had asked them to handle this problem. He looked at Rubrius. "Did you actually live in Capernaum?"

"Yes."

Marcus reined his horse around. "Good. Let's hope you didn't antagonize them too badly."

He gave a sardonic grin. "Yes, sire. I hope so too."

II

A Roman legion was made up of ten cohorts. A fully staffed cohort consisted of three maniples, which had two centuries each (companies of a hundred men). Thus a battle-ready legion had about six thousand men, not counting auxiliary troops. Typically, however, in peacetime conditions, a cohort might drop to as low as half their full strength. When Marcus Quadratus Didius had, two nights before, received his orders from Pontius Pilate to go to the Galilee to help collect overdue taxes, Marcus had been a little surprised. The Romans hired local tax collectors who collected most assessments. While it was not uncommon for them to occasionally ask for some muscle to back them up, usually the local garrisons did that. Puzzled, Marcus had sent orders to assemble one maniple, or about a hundred men. The next morning when he went to the assembly area he found that Sextus Rubrius had obeyed his order but had brought the maniple up to full strength, giving them double that number. When Marcus had raised one eyebrow, his senior centurion had only grunted, "We're going into the Galilee, sire."

But now that they were here in Capernaum, Marcus understood a little better. He had been here in the Jewish province for only a month, but he was already used to the baleful stares and the open hostility that greeted a Roman whenever he was out among the people. But here it had been more like acid on the flesh. One could feel the contempt pouring from the doorways and every shop. The fact that the four families who were in arrears were wealthy and powerful only added to the tension. And finally, Marcus had understood. These families were being extorted heavily by the local publican and had refused to pay. Pilate would receive a healthy cut of what they brought in today, all under the table of course. The local soldiers could never have done it. Fortunately, they had made their first three collections without undue incident, the families realizing what a full maniple of soldiers meant. He was tempted to jibe Rubrius a little for being overly cautious, but then decided he would rather have that in his centurions than cocky overconfidence. And he had to admit, even he was glad that he had two hundred men behind him.

He shook his head. These Jews and their belief in one god—no, one *true* god to the exclusion of all others—was still baffling to Marcus. He had heard about their strange religion before he ever left Rome, but he had put most of it down to wild exaggeration. One god? That was incomprehensible to Marcus. The Roman pantheon was a bewildering collection of gods and goddesses. Selfish, capricious, foul of temper, driven by lust, these divinities of Rome were very ungodlike. Which one would you pick as *the* god? Even if they had chosen the three brothers—Jupiter, Neptune, and Hades, who between them ruled the heavens, the seas, and the world of the dead—Marcus could have understood that, but one god who ruled all? And to believe in that one god so passionately?

"I find the whole thing still quite incomprehensible."

"What's that, sire?" Rubrius asked, looking up at him.

Marcus realized he had spoken aloud. "These Jews and their religion."

The centurion removed his helmet and began to wipe the drops of rain off against his tunic. "Odd as it may sound, sire, once you come to understand how they feel, it does have a kind of strange attraction about it."

That brought Marcus up. Did he detect a note of admiration there? But the older man didn't notice. He went back to scanning the rooftops above them. The street was narrow, and an enemy could easily launch stones at them from the roofs on either side of the street. The men were strung out now, no longer four abreast, but going two by two and staying close to the houses. Rubrius turned his back to his tribune. "Do you know the story of Judah, or Judas, as we say it, of Gamla, here in the Galilee, sire?"

Marcus nodded. He had been briefed on that shortly after his arrival. Some thirty years before, Quirinius, a new legate in the province of Syria, of which Judea was a part, had called for a census. This counting of people and property was done for purposes of assessing taxes. *Publicani*, or publicans, contracted to raise the assessment in each district. Anything they could get beyond what was assigned, they kept as their "salary." It was the Roman way and was a very efficient way to tax a vast empire. But by its very nature it encouraged widespread corruption. Many of the great fortunes in the empire had been made by the publicans, drawn from the sweat and blood of the people in their districts. The system was particularly hated by the Jews. Not only did they feel the injustice of the extortion and heavy financial burden placed upon them, but they were also angry that the taxes went directly to the support of the Roman emperor. With the coming of the Caesars had come the idea that the emperor was divine, one of the gods. Therefore, the Jews saw taxation as a direct support of idolatry and a tremendous affront to their religion.

Thus, when Cyrenius called for the census, the Jews revolted. Spurred by a charismatic leader named Judas of Gamla, the whole of Galilee rebelled. Judas told his followers that if they had any faith in their god, they would show forth their *zeal* for him by fighting against any and all forms of paganism, even by the sword if necessary. This had struck a deep chord in the fanatical Jews, and they took upon themselves the name of Zealots. It had taken three full Roman legions to finally put the rebellion down. Judas and about two thousand others had either been killed in the battle or crucified afterwards.

Unfortunately, their defeat hadn't stamped out the Zealot movement. The people weren't in open rebellion at the moment, but the hot coals still glowed just beneath the surface of the whole society.

"Well," Rubrius went on, his eyes moving everywhere as he spoke, "we go now to the home of David ben Joseph, a merchant. He is one of Capernaum's wealthiest citizens and is greatly respected here. He is one of the few moderate voices among the Galileans."

"Good."

Rubrius shook his head. "His wife's name is Deborah." When Marcus didn't respond to that, he added. "Deborah was a famous woman general in Israelite history. She led the people in battle against their enemy. She was very fierce, very courageous."

Marcus was watching him closely, trying to read what lay behind the words.

"Are you saying—?"

"Judas of Gamla was Deborah's uncle."

"Ah," Marcus said slowly.

"We will need to be very careful, sire."

III

Marcus stood in the spacious courtyard of David ben Joseph, leading merchant of Capernaum, and remembered the words of his centurion. The naked hatred in the eyes of the family was like a hot poker thrust against his flesh. The four of them—the mother, a daughter, and two sons—stood in a tight knot at the edge of the courtyard facing the soldiers who had thrust their way in a moment before. A fountain murmured softly just behind them. Though she was slender and a full handspan shorter than Marcus, no queen could have stood more regally than Deborah, the wife of David. There was not the slightest trace of fear in her, though there were four quaternions—sixteen men—with drawn swords around her. Her head was up, her back stiff, and her fists clenched, and she did not shrink back from the legionnaires. Suddenly "zeal" took on a new meaning for Marcus. He could see it smouldering in her eyes, and now he understood why Rubrius had doubled the number of men and warned them to be especially alert.

Deborah's daughter—probably fourteen or fifteen—stood just behind her, luminous dark eyes frightened but also angry and resentful. Already taller than her mother, the girl was surprisingly fair of complexion. According to Rubrius, though, that was common in the Galilee.

The youngest son—about ten, Marcus guessed—stood apart from his mother and sister, hands on his hips, legs hardened into tight muscular knots, valiantly trying to stare down the intruders. On a man that stance would have caused the hairs on the back of Marcus's neck to prickle a little. On a boy it was almost amusing. And yet somehow Marcus felt a sudden grudging admiration. Someday, the gods willing, he would raise such a son as this.

But it was the oldest son that Marcus watched most closely. He had moved slightly ahead of his mother and sister, letting Marcus clearly know that he was the one they would have to deal with today. The moment he had seen him, Marcus felt instant wariness, like entering a room and suddenly sensing someone was standing in the shadows. Probably near twenty—only a few years younger than Marcus himself—his arms were powerfully muscled and bronzed by the sun. Like his sister, he was fair of complexion. His eyes were light brown and quite wide set. He was also clean-shaven, which was surprising. The beard was highly esteemed among Jewish males, and most boys began growing a beard as soon as they passed puberty. A full, carefully trimmed beard was a mark of wisdom and maturity. To see a young Jew as clean-shaven as the Romans was not unheard of, but it was unusual.

But Marcus's thoughts stayed on the absence of a beard for only a moment. The young man was a picture of hostility. His eyes were hard pinpoints of glittering contempt. His fists were up, clenched tight enough to show the knuckles gleaming white.

Suddenly Marcus remembered something that Rubrius had told him on the ride over from Caesarea. He still found this to be incredible, but Rubrius swore that he had been there and witnessed it with his own eyes. One of the Jews' ten laws, the "ten commandments" as they called them, forbade the worship of graven images. The Roman battle standards often carried carved busts of the emperor, which therefore were a great affront to the Jews. When Pontius Pilate arrived in Judea, he had determined that he would show these stubborn Jews that their new governor was not about to coddle their foolish attitudes. That was not hard for Marcus to believe. He had already learned that Pilate had an ego the size of the Circus Maximus in Rome.

When Pilate sent a garrison of soldiers from Caesarea to Jerusalem, he commanded them to carry the standards with the bust of the emperor on them. His only concession was to send them into the city by night. By morning, word had spread, and the whole city was in an uproar. Thousands of Jews came down to Caesarea to protest. They came to the *praetorium* and virtually laid siege to the governor's palace. For five days and nights they entreated Pilate to withdraw the offensive images.

But what happened next was what caused Marcus to marvel. According to Rubrius, on the sixth day the governor lost his patience. He invited all of the Jews into the hippodrome, the stadium where the chariot races are held, and had them surrounded by legionnaires with drawn swords. "People of Judea," Pilate had shouted, "we have not harmed your religion. This is matter for us alone. Accept the standards or die now!"

As one, the multitude lay on the ground and bared their necks. Humiliated, but realizing that he couldn't begin his reign with a massacre, Pilate backed down, and the standards had been removed. Now as Marcus looked into the face of this young Jew who stood defiantly before him, he believed it. Here was one who was baring his neck in his own way at this very moment.

With a slight motion of his head, Marcus motioned Rubrius forward. His centurion was the only man in the cohort who could speak fluent Aramaic. As Rubrius began to speak to the mother, slowly and patiently, Marcus nodded to himself. Rubrius was like an ox in both body and temperament—slow, methodical, not easily shaken from his task. And yet he was powerful, full of strength. The Jews could not bait him, nor did he taunt and ridicule them, which, next to knucklebones and dice, was a legionnaire's favorite pastime.

Marcus glanced around. All sixteen of the men he had brought into the courtyard with him and Rubrius were fully alert. The rest of the maniple was stationed outside at both ends of the long street that led to the merchant's house.

As the centurion finished, the woman responded with a quick stream of Aramaic. Marcus caught the word for "my husband" two or three times and the name Damascus, but the rest was a blur. He was studying the language, but it was mostly still a bewildering babble.

He spoke quietly in Latin. "What is it, Rubrius?"

The soldier did not turn his head. "They do not have the money, sire."

Both Marcus and Rubrius stiffened as the older son took a menacing step forward, thrusting his face toward Marcus. "My mother said that my father is in Damascus obtaining the money and will return soon." He spoke in flawless Latin, with none of the Jewish tendency to let the final consonants hiss off into nothingness. Marcus was surprised, but then understood. Greek was the common language of business throughout the empire. Latin was the language of the Romans. A successful merchant would be well advised to speak both languages in order to carry out his business. Then Marcus had a sudden intuition that the young man had deliberately spoken in Latin so that all of the legionnaires would perfectly understand his defiance.

Marcus touched Rubrius on the arm. The centurion moved back, but one hand had grasped the hilt of his sword and Marcus sensed that his sergeant was strung as tight as a bow. That tension was communicated to the men who were in the courtyard with them, and they too were stiff, holding spears and swords more tightly.

"I am Tribune Marcus Quadratus Didius, commander of the second cohort of the emperor's tenth legion. We are here under the direct orders of Pontius Pilatus, procurator of Judea, to collect the taxes owed by your family. We mean you no harm and wish no trouble."

The young Galilean spat on the tiles. "Pontius Pilate is a pig!"

As one man, every soldier stiffened, their swords coming up. Marcus flung his hand out, freezing them in position. The boy's mother had reacted with equal speed, clutching at her son's arm. "Simeon!" It came out as a hiss, but Marcus saw that her reaction was not so much that of fright, but rather that she knew this was not the place for foolhardy bravado. Good, perhaps there was some sanity behind the fanaticism that burned in her eyes.

The young man jerked free from her grasp, and she turned quickly to Marcus. "Your tax collector knows my husband could not raise the assessed sum in so short a time. He also knows that my husband has every intention of paying it, in spite of the fact that it is nothing short of the most blatant extortion. There would be more honor if a man broke into our home and stole from us at the point of a sword."

The son named Simeon spoke again, his voice strained with bitterness. "Absalom the publican sucks the life blood from his own people. He is a pig, and the governor who supports him is a pig, and I spit on their names!"

Marcus whirled at the slap of sandals on the pavement. "Stand!" he barked sharply. "The first man who moves without my express command will bend over the scourging tree until there is not a shred of skin left on his back. Now hold your ground!"

He turned back to the defiant young Jew, not waiting to see that his men grudgingly obeyed, their faces ugly with anger. "What is your age?" Marcus asked, amazed that his voice held a quiet calmness and was under perfect control.

The boy did not so much as flicker.

"My son is twenty years of age, soon to be twenty-one," his mother answered in halting Latin. Marcus nodded.

"That is old enough to man the oars of a slave galley or to fill the buckets in the Egyptian copper mines. One day in either place would teach you that a sharp tongue is an expensive luxury, my young friend."

Simeon responded with a sneer of disgust, but again his mother cut him off by grasping his arm sharply. Then she spoke to Marcus. "I do not disagree with my son's assessment of Absalom. He is a thief and a robber. How Rome, which professes such nobility of purpose, can support such extortion is another question. However, my son has not yet learned the wisdom of controlling his tongue."

Marcus was amazed. It was—what? Not an apology. In fact, there was an insult in her words as well. But she had acknowledged that she accepted his superior position in this circumstance. She did not want to provoke him.

Marcus took a deep breath, then spoke firmly, slowly enough that she could follow his Latin. "I do not know this Absalom the publican. We are not here at his behest." Which was not completely true. They had come because Pilate had sent them. And Pilate had sent them because Absalom, Rome's hired tax collector, had complained—and had offered a tempting cut in order to get what he wanted.

"We have collected taxes from three other families today without incident. Like the others, your husband was given a week to raise the necessary money. Now I am asking you. Do you have the ten thousand shekels?"

She straightened slowly, and Marcus saw again that the fires that lit the Zealot movement were not reserved for Galilean men alone. "So," she answered sadly, "you would be party to this thinly disguised plunder?"

Marcus tried not to flinch in the face of such utter contempt. "I do not sit as a judge in these matters," he said. "I am only a soldier who has orders that he must obey."

"My husband went to Damascus to raise the money. He said he would be back as soon as possible. He told all of this to Absalom. My husband is a man of his word. We expect him soon, and then you shall have your precious taxes."

Marcus hesitated, moved by the honesty in her face. There was no doubt but what she spoke the truth. But with equal clarity he knew exactly what awaited a young tribune who returned to Caesarea with three successes and one excuse. Nor was he comfortable waiting with his troops here in Capernaum to see if David ben Joseph was a man of his word. He had already seen Pilate's reaction when someone did not perform as expected, and Marcus had sworn that he would never be a target of such rage.

He took a deep breath, then shook his head. "I am sorry," he said quietly. He glanced at Rubrius who seemed to be staring right through the family at the walls of the large home behind them. "By decree of the governor," Marcus said slowly, "we are empowered to confiscate all of your property and possessions in order to fill the assessment."

He hesitated as the family gasped, then went on, not meeting their eyes. "I am also authorized to arrest your family and sell you as slaves to help pay off this debt. However—"

At that moment, Marcus Didius made a serious error. He was not proud to be part of this, and in consequence, he had decided to be magnanimous and forgo taking them prisoner. He was watching the woman, hoping to see that his leniency might soften her in some way. And that was a mistake. There was a blur of movement out of Marcus's eye; then an arm of iron sinew clamped around his throat. He was jerked around hard, and instantly he felt the sharp prick of a dagger through his tunic at that spot just below the rib cage where his leather breastplate ended.

"Stand, or the tribune dies!" Simeon shouted. As one, the legionnaires had lunged forward. The command, barked in Latin, froze them in mid-stride.

"Simeon, no!" The mother fell back, shocked at the sight of her son holding a Roman officer prisoner.

"You will not be taking any slaves today," Simeon hissed into Marcus's ear. Then he gave one quick guttural grunt. The younger son leaped forward, looking up at his brother, the young eyes wide and frightened. Simeon barked another sharp command in Latin to the soldiers. "Stand clear of the stairs!"

Sextus Rubrius hovered near his commander, sword out, waiting for an opportunity to strike. He swung around. "Move!" he bellowed.

Half-dazed, the soldiers shuffled away from the wall where stone steps led from the inner courtyard to the roof. Without looking down at the ten-year-old, Simeon snapped out a quick stream of Aramaic. Like a stone flung from a sling, the boy raced across the courtyard and scrambled up the stairs. In the time it took to realize what was happening, he was gone. The boy had been sent for help. That galvanized Marcus to action.

To give a legionnaire better grip on gravel or stone while on the march, the Roman quartermaster issued each man a pair of *caligulas*, a thick leather sandal studded with short iron spikes in the sole. Most officers of the equestrian class refused to wear them, preferring a smooth sole for the stirrups. From the time of his enlistment, Marcus had ignored the jibes of his fellow officers, determined he would wear what his men wore. Now as his captor dragged him toward the stairs, shouting at the women to come, Marcus raised his right foot and then jammed it downward, raking the spikes across the bare shin of the Jew.

The scream of pain nearly broke his eardrum, but Marcus was hardly aware of it. He hurled himself backward, simultaneously throwing out both elbows to push the dagger's point up and away from his ribs. He and Simeon crashed heavily to the paving tiles, Simeon hitting with a sickening thud. Instantly Marcus rolled clear and moved into a crouch, his sword out. But Rubrius was quicker. He leaped past Marcus, sword arcing downward. The Jew scrambled back, dagger up to ward off the blow, but the sword snapped the blade like a dried reed and slashed into the young man's tunic. He screamed and crashed back to the floor again, blood streaming from his chest.

"Simeon!" The mother flung herself toward her son.

Dazed by the swiftness of what had happened, Marcus watched her throw herself down beside her son. The girl also dropped beside her wounded brother. Marcus slowly straightened, breathing hard. He stumbled back, groping for the fountain as a wave of dizziness swept over him. Rubrius was instantly at his side. "Get me a cloth," Rubrius bellowed at the nearest legionnaire. Marcus stared at his centurion in bewilderment. He was only now aware of a searing pain along his right forearm and the sticky warmth engulfing the hand that held his sword. He stared at the gash, half a handspan long, not sure how he had gotten it. Only slowly did an understanding come. He had not completely escaped the slashing dagger. Rubrius gently took the sword from Marcus's hand, wiped the blood from it on the skirt of his own tunic, then slid it backhand into Marcus's scabbard.

One quaternion moved around Marcus in a protective circle. Another had closed around the two women and Simeon, swords drawn and ready even though any threat was now gone. Marcus saw another squad of four had gone over to block the stairs that led to the roof. Wonderful, he thought. Now that the boy was gone, they wouldn't let anyone else disappear on them. He shook his head, struggling to think, fighting to decide if he was doing all he should to make sure they were protecting themselves.

A man came forward with a flask of water and a length of cloth. Rubrius snatched them from him. "Here," he said, taking Marcus's arm. "We've got to stop the bleeding until we can get you to the surgeons."

Marcus glanced down. His whole lower arm was covered in blood, and it was dripping from his fingers to the courtyard tiles. "No surgeons. I won't have those Greek butchers touching it."

Rubrius grinned. Hardly a soldier in all the legions felt differently. It was far safer to face the heat of battle than to submit oneself to the knives of the army surgeons. The centurion went to work, moving swiftly but efficiently. He poured the flask of water on the arm, scooped another from the fountain, and repeated it a second time. He peered at the wound, then began to wrap the cloth around Marcus's arm, binding it tightly. "You'll have a nice scar to impress your future wife."

"Thank you," Marcus said through clenched teeth. "I've been hoping for such a thing."

Rubrius chuckled. With the arm wrapped, he took out his dagger, cut off a length of rawhide thong from his scabbard, and tied the bandage on tightly.

As he finished, Marcus turned and looked to where the mother worked frantically over her son. She had torn a large piece from her robe and was pressing it against the boy's chest. "Is he dead?" he asked quietly.

Rubrius shook his head. "No, sire. But he is bleeding badly." He guessed what Marcus was thinking. "If we try to take him, he will die immediately. If we leave him, he will die shortly." He took a quick breath. "If you're up to it, sire, I would recommend we make our departure."

Marcus gave him a quick nod.

"What about the women, sire?" the leader of the quaternion asked. "Shall we bring them?"

Deborah, wife of David the merchant, shot to her feet, the front of her robe now stained with her son's blood. "You will have to kill me to do it," she said in a low voice.

When Marcus hesitated, the squad leader, barely glancing at the woman, frowned deeply. "Sire, they have resisted arrest."

Too tired to wrestle with another moral dilemma at the moment, Marcus waved his good hand. As the soldiers stepped forward, Deborah lunged to the left, diving for the broken dagger that lay on the courtyard tiles. She never stood a chance. Two soldiers pounced on her, driving her to the ground. The sister dodged in to help but went right into the arms of two more men. Kicking and screaming, the women were dragged back from the wounded Simeon. In moments their wrists were behind their backs, bound tightly with cords. Realizing that struggle was only making things worse for them, the mother said something, and both went quiet.

Something in the expression of Sextus Rubrius caught Marcus's eye. "You don't approve?" Marcus said.

Rubrius turned, a little surprised that he was being observed. "Sire, the boy has gone."

Marcus swore. He had forgotten about the boy. He swung on the nearest two soldiers. "After him!" he shouted.

Rubrius jumped forward. "Sire!"

The soldiers, who had started to move, abruptly stopped.

"Yes?"

"With the tribune's permission, sire."

"Speak."

"In this country, the rooftops are all connected. You can go almost anywhere in the city without coming down to the streets. The Jews call it 'the road of the roofs.'"

Feeling light in the head, Marcus wasn't sure what Rubrius was saying.

"Sire, the rooftops here are what the alleys of the Palatine Hill are to the thieves and whores of Rome. Only the very strong or the very foolish venture in after them."

"I see." Marcus nodded to the two who were at the base of the stone steps. "All right, let him go."

Rubrius spoke again. "Sire?"

Marcus turned to him fully now, sensing the urgency in his centurion.

"We would be well advised to forgo searching the house."

There were cries of dismay from the men. Looting was a legitimate way to supplement a soldier's meager income, and the spaciousness of the courtyard and the fineness of the house promised a lucrative day indeed. Though Marcus had never liked the practice, he accepted it as one of the realities of life.

"Explain!"

His centurion did so in a rush of words. "The boy was sent for help, sire. David is a prominent man in Capernaum. He is widely respected. I think it would be wise if we formed the cohort and left immediately for Tiberias."

Marcus rarely heard Sextus say anything in a hurry, and that alarmed him as much as his words. "Even with a full maniple?" he asked grimly.

"With the Galileans, if this gets out of hand, a full cohort could be cut to pieces."

That settled it. There was not one shred of cowardice in this centurion of his. "All right! Form up the men. Put out guards front and rear of the column. Bring the women. Leave the young man to die."

This time Rubrius stirred but didn't move.

"What?" Marcus almost shouted it at him.

"Sire, prisoners will only slow us down."

His eyes narrowed. He had a sudden suspicion that his centurion was more concerned about the prisoners than he was about getting away quickly. His jaw tightened. "No! They come with us."

"Yes, sire." There was no more hesitation. Rubrius began barking orders in staccato fashion. Though the disappointment at the loss of booty was clearly evident in the men, the soldiers sprang instantly into action, the clatter of their sandals rattling on paving stones. The two women were led away, the daughter sobbing hysterically. The mother tried once more to break free and get to her dying son, but she was dragged back.

Taking a deep breath, Marcus straightened and moved slowly to the outer gate of the courtyard. He waited for the others to go through, then stopped for a moment and turned around. The newest tribune of the Tenth Legion Fretensis looked at the body, seeing the blood seeping slowly onto the tiles. Earlier that day he had gloried in the power of Rome. Now he felt slightly sick.

There was a noise behind him. He turned to see Rubrius holding the gate open for him. There was considerable anxiety on his face.

Wincing at the pain, Marcus stepped out into the street. Waving help away, he pulled himself up into the saddle, then wheeled his mount around. He didn't wait to see if the cohort was coming. He spoke softly to his horse and started off, feeling the cold October rain against his face.

IV
15 OCTOBER, A.D. 29

They were up at dawn at the insistence of Sextus Rubrius. Marcus's arm ached like fury, but he too wanted to be out of the Galilee. The rain had stopped during the night, and as they moved out of Tiberias, the sun was just rising above the eastern hills of Gadara, turning the surface of the lake into a blinding mirror. They took the road that led directly west from Tiberias, climbing steeply up the western hills to the Galilean highlands. This was not as good a road, but it meant they did not have to head back toward Capernaum to connect with the main highway. At Rubrius' recommendation, they would go almost due west to the port of Ptolemais. There the two women would be turned over to the slave auctioneers and shipped off to Rome. That route also bypassed Sepphoris and the other Zealot hot spots. It was longer but considerably safer.

It was a hard climb for men in battle dress, but Rubrius wouldn't let them slack off in their readiness even though they were out of the city. But the men were rested, and they were anxious, and that gave strength to the march. By the third hour of the day they had rejoined the main road, and by midday they were approaching Mashkanah. From that point on, the forest began to thin out and they would be in open country the rest of the way to Ptolemais. As they stopped at a stream for a brief, cold meal, it was obvious that the men were beginning to relax. There had been no sign of any trouble, not from the rear, not from the advanced scouts. Rubrius, however, did not relax. He allowed them only ten minutes' rest, then drove them on. He would not be completely comfortable until they were back down on the coastal plains where the Zealots had little or no influence.

It was less than half an hour later when Rubrius raised his hand. Marcus pulled the mare up, squinting in the bright sunshine. Up ahead about a quarter of a mile, six of the advanced guard were coming back down the road toward them. They had three men between them, marching them out in front at the point of their spears.

"What is it?" Marcus asked, resting his arm on his leg to ease the pain.

Rubrius shook his head, peering first at the oncoming trio, then around at the surrounding hillsides. The trees were scattered, and the pines were giving way to oak and thick patches of bushes. Suddenly Rubrius stiffened, leaning forward.

"What?" Marcus said, straightening.

"That's David ben Joseph," Rubrius said.

"Who?" And then as he heard a cry behind him, he knew the answer to his question. The woman and daughter had seen who was coming too. There was a choked call from behind him. "David!"

Marcus turned in the saddle. "Watch them," he said to the men who had the two women contained in a hollow square of marchers. The girl was weeping for joy now. The mother was standing with her shoulders thrown back, her face filled with triumph. Then he turned back. He felt a little chill as he saw Rubrius searching the countryside on both sides of them now. "What does this mean?" he asked in a low voice.

"I'm not sure," Rubrius grunted. Then he turned. "Look alive back there," he called in a low voice. "Keep a sharp eye." It wasn't necessary. All up and down the line, the men had their hands on their swords or gripped their spears tightly. They were looking around nervously.

As the party approached, Rubrius moved forward. He stopped a few feet away from the approaching group, and the soldiers stopped too. "David?" Rubrius said. "What are you doing here?"

"I want to talk to your tribune, Sextus."

Marcus's mind was still sluggish from the shock and loss of blood of the day before, so it took him a moment to realize that his centurion had called this Jew by name and the Jew had used the centurion's given name.

Rubrius turned to Marcus, raising a questioning eyebrow.

"Bring him forward," Marcus answered. Then to the man he said, "Are you alone?"

"I have my two servants with me."

As the merchant came closer, his two servants came up with him. Both carried bulging leather bags.

From behind Marcus the woman suddenly cried out, "Oh, David. They've killed Simeon."

David's eyes seemed to take in everything all at once—his wife and daughter, now roped together, the sullen look on the faces of the soldiers who guarded them, the rest of the column, now on full alert.

"Simeon is still alive," he said. His eyes lifted to Marcus. "Barely."

"Blessed be our God," Deborah cried. Then in a rush, she went on. "They came for the taxes, David. I told them you would be back soon. They wouldn't listen." Her head jerked up to stare at Marcus. "This tribune wouldn't believe me."

"And so you tried to kill my son?" David asked quietly.

Rubrius stepped between the merchant and Marcus. He shook his head. "Simeon was a fool, David. He let his temper override his wisdom. He attacked the tribune with his dagger." His head came up a fraction, and what he said next came very softly. "It was I who struck him."

David took that in, then raised his gaze to Marcus once again. For a long moment, the two of them stood there, their eyes locked, taking the measure of one another. What Marcus saw was a man in his early forties, strong of feature and with compelling, powerful blue eyes, eyes that showed no fear. He also saw understanding in David's eyes, as if what Rubrius had said helped explain a great deal to him. Then David's gaze dropped to look at Marcus's bandaged arm.

He nodded slowly. "I saw blood in my courtyard, Tribune. I see now that it was your blood as well as that of my son."

"Sextus was right," Marcus said. "Your son was a fool. We did not come to your house seeking trouble."

"I told you my husband would come," Deborah cried. "Why wouldn't you give us more time?"

David barely seemed to hear. His eyes never left Marcus's face. "My son is like a spirited stallion, and it is difficult to rein him in." His eyes flicked to Sextus Rubrius for a moment, then back. "However, he *has* been reined in by the swift action of Sextus here. The physicians are not yet sure he will live."

Again it struck Marcus as odd that this Jew should refer to a

Roman centurion in such a familiar fashion. Then he remembered that Rubrius had lived in Capernaum. Had these two become friends in that time? Could that be? A Roman soldier and a Jew friendly to one another?

David went on, speaking carefully now. "It is possible that my son shall forfeit his life for what he did." There was a sudden challenge and pleading in the blue depths of his eyes. "Is that not sufficient payment for the wrongs committed yesterday?"

Marcus straightened. He looked at Rubrius, but the leathered face of his centurion was unreadable, so he went on. "Your payment was due. You were given fair warning."

"I was delayed in Damascus. It takes time to raise ten thousand shekels." He half turned. "But I have your payment with me."

The two servants held out the bags and shook them softly. There was the rattle of coins.

David waited until they came up beside him, then turned back to face Marcus. "Ten thousand shekels for my"—there was suddenly bitter mockery in his voice—"*assessment*," he said. "I have brought an additional tenth of the assessment as a penalty for being late."

Marcus had to fight back letting the surprise show on his face. A thousand additional shekels? That was a concession of no small proportion. And yet . . . "Your son interfered with the legal duties of a Roman official. That is a crime punishable by death."

"It is," David said gravely. "And Rome is famous for its justice."

Marcus's eyes narrowed, but he detected no sarcasm this time. The older man seemed to mean the words exactly as he had stated them.

The merchant went on, quietly now, but in great earnest. "But Rome is also known for other *pietas*—what you call the virtues— honor, duty, courage, respect for family."

This time Marcus couldn't help himself. His eyes widened in surprise. From the time he could understand his first words, his father and grandfather had taught Marcus about the *pietas*, the Roman character, the virtues that made Rome great. Did this Jew know of such things?

"I see in your eyes," the merchant went on calmly, "that unlike some of your countrymen you have not only been taught in the way of the *pietas,* but you have not forgotten them either." There was a long pause. "I deeply regret that my journey was delayed to the point where this terrible thing has happened. But you have your taxes now, with penalty. And while your blood stains my house, so does that of my son. Justice has been done. Let us be done with it."

Marcus took another deep breath, keenly aware now of the throbbing pain in his arm and the numbness in his fingers. When he didn't answer, he saw David's eyes narrow slightly.

For a moment Marcus thought the man was going to offer him more money, but he didn't. He simply waited, his eyes looking deeply into Marcus, perhaps searching for the virtues he seemed so sure were there. It was good the Jew did not offer more. A thousand additional shekels was an important concession, a just penalty for being overdue. More than that, however, would have constituted a bribe. And while his countrymen—including the governor under whom he served— might be famous for accepting, indeed, even demanding, bribes, Marcus Quadratus Didius, oldest son and heir of Antonius Marcus Didius, was not. An attempt to bribe him would have been deeply offensive to Marcus.

"And what if I simply seize you and put you in bonds along with your wife and daughter?" Marcus said, curious now. This man was no fool. Surely he had considered this possibility. "Then I have the taxes, the penalty, *and* you."

David seemed thoughtful. Then without warning, he gave a piercing whistle. Marcus started as the hillsides on both sides of the road suddenly came alive. Men stepped out from behind trees. What seemed to have been bushes suddenly rose up and became men with branches tied to their heads and backs. Stones that seemed too small to hide a fox now revealed men on one knee with bows drawn and arrows nocked. There were a hundred. Then two. Then three.

A cry went up and down the Roman line. Soldiers spun around, whipping out their swords, dropping their spears to the level. Rubrius fell back, grabbing his sword to stand beside his commanding officer.

Finally silence descended on the site. David, who hadn't moved at all, spoke again, his voice more conversational than challenging. "I have no desire for a confrontation. All I wish is to have my wife and daughter returned to me and the whole affair forgotten."

"You would attack a Roman column?" Marcus cried, still stunned, but feeling anger.

"I have no desire for a confrontation," the merchant said again with great patience. "All I wish is to have my wife and daughter returned to me." He motioned to his servants, and they took one step forward and laid the two bags of money on the ground. "You have your taxes and a penalty. Roman law and justice have been satisfied. Let us be done with it."

Marcus was fuming, and yet he couldn't help but marvel. The man was as calm as a sleeping child. Finally he looked down at Sextus Rubrius.

The centurion nodded quickly. "Say the word, and we shall fight our way clear, sire."

"But?" Marcus was learning to read the subtle nuances of his centurion's face.

"As he says, we do have what we came for," Rubrius said carefully. He took a quick breath and lowered his voice. "We could distribute the extra thousand shekels among the men," he said. "It would serve in lieu of the looting they had to forgo."

Marcus also understood what lay behind his words. "Let me use the penalty money to keep the men happy, and word of this will never reach the governor's ear."

The newest tribune in the Tenth Legion Fretensis turned back to the man standing in front of him, suddenly tired beyond anything he had ever felt before. Was the glory of Rome worth a bloodbath here? David ben Joseph might be calm, but Marcus knew with absolute certainty that this was not a bluff. If Marcus chose to gratify his Roman pride at this point, slaughter on both sides would surely result.

He straightened to his full height, letting go of his wounded arm so both hands hung down at his side. "Yes," he said to David. "Let us be done with it."

David ben Joseph inclined his head, his eyes filled with gratitude. "Thank you, Tribune. I was right in what I saw in your face." He turned around and raised both of his hands. "The Romans are to have safe passage out of the Galilee," he called in a loud voice. "We are done with it."

As quickly as they appeared, the men began to melt away. Marcus watched for a moment, then turned again in the saddle. "Let the women go," he said wearily.

CHAPTER NOTES

In a passage of scripture read by millions every Christmas season, Luke wrote: "And it came to pass in those days, that there went out a decree from Caesar Augustus, that all the world should be taxed. (And this taxing was first made when Cyrenius was governor of Syria)" (Luke 2:1–2). That seems to be the same census, or enrollment for purposes of taxing, that led to the beginnings of the Zealot movement in Palestine as noted here. The Roman spelling of the legate's name is Quirinius. Wherever possible, people were enrolled in the city of their family's origins. Thus Joseph and Mary, who were of the house of David, left Nazareth and went to Bethlehem, which was the city of David (see Luke 2:4).

The reign of Pontius Pilatus, or Pontius Pilate as we know him, as procurator of Judea began in A.D. 26. He served in that position for ten years. The story of his attempt to force the Roman standards on Jerusalem and the ensuing showdown with the Jewish people is told by Josephus (*Antiquities of the Jews*, xviii.iii.1.2).

CHAPTER 1

CHILDREN'S CHILDREN ARE THE CROWN OF OLD MEN; AND THE
GLORY OF CHILDREN ARE THEIR FATHERS.

—*Proverbs 17:6*

I

20 MARCH, A.D. 30

David ben Joseph stopped for a moment in the courtyard, listening for any sounds in the house. "Deborah!"

There was no response. He walked swiftly over to the main door to the house. Out of long habit, he reached up and touched with the tip of his fingers the *mezuzah* that was mounted on the door frame; then he pushed the door open. "Deborah?"

He heard the soft slap of footsteps on stone; then Phineas, their chief household servant, appeared in the upper hall. "Mistress Deborah is not here, sire."

"Oh? Do you know where she is?"

He shrugged. "She said only that she would be gone about an hour."

"Thank you, Phineas."

"Would you like me to go find her, sire?"

"No, that's all right. I'll check over at Ephraim's. It's nothing urgent."

"As you wish, sire."

"What about Leah?"

"She went with her mother, sire."

"Phineas?"

"Yes, sire?"

"How many years have you worked for Deborah and me now?"

"Six years, sire."

"And how many times have I said that you don't have to call me *sire*, that you can call us just David and Deborah?"

There was no change in the man's expression. "More times than I could count, sire."

David shook his head. "Just David is fine."

"Yes, sire." He bowed slightly and retreated back down the hall.

As David shut the door again, he stopped at the fountain in the courtyard and bent down to wash his face. It was still just the beginning of spring, but it was warm today and the swiftness of his walk back from the seashore had left him perspiring.

Straightening, he wiped his face off, then stopped. His eyes had fallen on a dark stain on the marble tiles. He sat back, leaning against the lip of the fountain. Now his eyes picked up the other place. Here the stain was not as prominent, and it was made up of several smaller splotches. His eyes half closed as he tried to imagine the events of that terrible afternoon five months before. They had scrubbed at the bloodstains on the tile and removed most of them. They had hoped a winter of rain—and even one brief, rare snowstorm—would eventually take the rest away, but it had not. A month ago David had offered to have the tiles ripped out and replaced, but to his surprise his wife had said no. It would serve as a grim memorial of Rome's terrible legacy, she said, a reminder of why the Zealots would continue their resistance until every Roman was driven from the land.

David's eyes clouded as he thought about this one corner of his wife's mind that he had not been able to penetrate and change. Deborah had been fourteen when her uncle, Judah of Gamla, had risen up against the call for a Roman census. Along with the rest of her family, she had joined in the rebellion, running food to the Zealot armies, secreting messages through the lines, risking her life on a daily basis. By the time of Deborah's fifteenth birthday, Judah and another of her uncles had been killed in battle. A third brother—Deborah's father—and three of her cousins had been crucified while the rest of the family had been forced to watch. That winter, still on the run, Deborah, her mother, and her younger brother had hidden in a cave, rarely with the benefit of a fire, throughout the winter. Before spring came, her mother had died from consumption and Deborah was left to be mother and father to ten-year-old Aaron.

Deborah was a gracious and cultured woman. She had a gentleness and patience about her that always drew others to her. With her two grandchildren she was tender and warm, a delight to them, and they adored her. Very few ever saw that tiny piece of her that was as cold as the snows of Mount Hermon and harder than tempered steel.

David sighed as he stood and started for the gate that led into the street. Ironically, it was Simeon who had inherited that particular part of his mother's nature. Deborah was close to all of her four children, but there was a special bond between her and her second son. Her tragedy became his tragedy; her vows became his crusade. And what had happened to Simeon right here in this courtyard had only solidified that determination into an implacable, rock-hard desire for vengeance.

David understood Simeon's anger, just as he did his wife's bitterness. Even now, when he thought about how close they had come to having Deborah and Leah sold off as slaves, it left him weak and trembling. Every day, even now, five months later, David offered thanks to God for his help in freeing his wife and daughter before the unthinkable had become reality. Every day he thanked God for sparing the life of his son. The vivid scar across Simeon's chest was a constant reminder to David of how close they had come to losing him. But Simeon did not dwell on how fortunate they had been, how great the mercy of God was in their behalf. Simeon brooded over what might have been more than what was. He kept the image of his mother and sister tied in bonds at the forefront of his mind. It was like fuller's soap, eating at him, corroding his inner soul, deepening and fueling his hatred for everything Roman.

David sighed again, pushing all of that from his mind, and exited the courtyard.

II

David and Deborah's oldest and only married child lived just four doors up the street from their own house. David knocked on the door once, again paused for a moment to touch the *mezuzah* that was on this doorway as well, then walked right in. "It's me," he called.

"In here, Papa."

At the sound of Rachel's voice, he turned and went into the back of the house where the kitchen was. His daughter-in-law was at the table, shaping fat loaves of bread with her hands for eventual placement in the stone oven behind the house. Her apron was covered with flour, and there were a couple of smudges of it on her face. He went to her and kissed her on the cheek. "Granmama is not here?" He used the name that Rachel's eldest child always used for her grandmother.

"No. She and Leah took Esther and Boaz for a walk down by the water."

"Oh." His face showed his disappointment. "I was just down that way and didn't see them."

Rachel shrugged. "That's what she said."

He sat down on a bench, then looked around. "Is Ephraim at the storehouse?"

"Yes." She smiled. "Isn't he always?"

There was a deep satisfaction in David's eyes as he replied. "He loves it as much as I do."

"I know." Rachel rubbed one cheek with the back of her hand, adding another spot to the others. "I'm glad."

David nodded. How fortunate he and Deborah had been in choosing this young woman for their oldest son. It had not been a hard decision for them. Rachel's parents were weavers, and David marketed their blankets and robes across all of northern Galilee. Ephraim and Rachel had been close friends from the time they were small, and Ephraim had instantly agreed when David proposed that an arrangement be made with Rachel's family. He frowned. "I wish we could pour a little love for merchandising into Simeon's head."

"Oh, don't despair," Rachel smiled. "Simeon is still young. When he gets a wife and children, he'll settle into the business just fine."

"I hope you're right. And we're working on that, by the way."

She looked up in surprise. "Shana?"

He nodded.

"Wonderful!"

"Don't say anything to Simeon yet," he said. "He and I have talked about it, and I think he is about ready to agree to it, but not quite yet."

"I won't."

Just then they heard voices at the front of the house. David turned. "There they are now."

"Look, Mama!" Four-year-old Esther came through the door into the kitchen, holding out a cluster of pink flowers in her tiny hand. Her eyes were wide with excitement, but as usual, her face was grave and thoughtful.

Rachel brushed the flour off her hands and went to her daughter. As she reached her, Leah came in, holding Boaz, who was not quite two, in her arms. Deborah was right behind them. Leah put the boy down, and immediately he waddled over to his grandfather and climbed up into his lap.

David nuzzled his neck with his beard. "Hello, young Boaz."

Boaz giggled and pulled away. David looked up at his daughter. Leah was fifteen now and looking more like her mother every day. "Where is Joseph?" he asked.

Leah shrugged, and Deborah answered for her. "Where is Joseph any time? Out practicing with his bow and arrow with his friends, probably." When she said it, there was pride in her voice.

David frowned at that. His youngest, just ten years of age, was smitten with a bad case of hero worship, and his hero was his older brother. Simeon was renowned for being an outstanding bowman. He was also excellent with a sling and could throw a dagger and split an apple at thirty paces. Only Yehuda could best him in a battle with staves, and though David had never seen it personally, he knew that his son was also a master with the Roman broadsword. It was one thing to have a boy desperately trying to emulate those skills; it was quite another to have that boy subtly encouraged to do so by his mother.

"What kind of flowers are they?" Rachel asked her daughter, sensing the sudden coolness in the room.

Esther turned and looked at her grandmother for help.

"Cyclamen," Deborah said.

"Yes," Esther told her mother.

"They're beautiful," Rachel said. "Let's get some water for them."

David watched Esther as her mother got a bowl down, filled it with water from the pail, and set it on the table. One by one, as carefully as if she were handling bird's eggs, Esther began putting the flowers in the dish, placing each one with great precision. Through it all, her expression never changed.

Esther was not only a source of great delight for David, she was also a continual fascination for him. He called her his little sphinx. Whereas Boaz was always giggling and laughing and teasing and singing lustily to himself, Esther was much more quiet and reserved. It was not that she was unhappy. She could sit quietly, playing with this or that, humming to herself softly in perfect contentment. But she rarely let her emotions show on her face. Even people she knew well were hard-pressed to get a response from her. As they tried everything possible to draw her out—complimenting her, pulling faces, tickling her, offering her sweets—she would only watch them gravely with those enormous dark eyes, her face as if it was carved from stone. If she knew them really well and if they were very good, they might win just the tiniest wisp of a smile around the corners of her mouth. If they were strangers, they didn't exist. She would ignore them as completely as though they were invisible.

David and Deborah saw her almost every day, and so she was completely comfortable around them. She called Deborah "Granmama" and David "Pampa," which had been her first attempt at pronouncing his title. It had so delighted him that even now when she was four and could say grandfather clearly, he encouraged the use of the original. For them the smiles came easier, though it would have been an exaggeration to say they came frequently. But when they did, they lit up her face like a thousand lamps. It had become a goal with David to get at least one full smile from her every time he saw her.

He marveled at how different two children could be. Boaz was already starting to string sentences together and was as bright as a silver denarius. Esther, on the other hand, had hardly said a word until she was three. It had worried Deborah for a time that she might have some kind of problem, but it had never concerned David. She hadn't talked early because she didn't need to. She was a master at communicating her desires with gestures and a few basic sounds. Then at three she had suddenly started talking in whole sentences. When David played with Boaz, teasing or tickling him, he would shriek in delight. When he did the same with Esther, she would often stick out one finger and shake it at him, as though she were the schoolmaster and he the child. He adored them both, but Esther was especially endearing to him.

Leah went over to the table beside her sister-in-law and began to help with the shaping of the dough into loaves. Boaz slid off David's lap and went over beside her. "Me?" he said, holding out a hand. Leah pulled off a small piece and handed it to him.

Esther looked up and saw David watching her. She smiled shyly at him. He stood and went over and sat down beside her, studying the pattern she was creating in the bowl. He nodded his approval. "They're like little crowns, aren't they?" he said.

There was a quick bob of her head.

"They are almost as pretty as you," he teased. That did it—the smile spread from her eyes all across her face. On seeing that, he shook his head. "No, on second thought, I don't think there's anything in the whole world quite as pretty as my little Esther."

She giggled, looking up at her mother. Rachel was watching with soft eyes. "I agree with your grandfather."

Deborah came over and sat down on the other side of Esther, reaching out to touch her hand. "She chose these all by herself, Pampa."

"You found those down by the beach?" he asked. Usually cyclamen did not grow by the water but preferred the meadows and rocky places of the Galilee.

Deborah shook her head. "We didn't go down to the lake. We went out to the east of town. The grass and the flowers are just coming into bloom now." Then she gave him a strange look. "Are you helping Rachel bake bread?" She reached up and brushed flour from his tunic.

Rachel saw it and laughed. "That's my fault," she said.

David chuckled. "My favorite daughter-in-law—"

"Your only daughter-in-law," Rachel cut in quickly.

"My favorite daughter-in-law loves me a great deal, but not enough to let me help with her baking."

"Good," Deborah said, patting his cheek, the previous moment of tension now gone. "I was worried there for a moment." Then a thought occurred to her. "Were you looking for me?"

He nodded. Then seeing that Esther had finished putting all of the flowers in the water, he held out his arms. She moved over and stood beside him, snuggling in against him. David looked at Deborah. "I was over speaking with Andrew and Simon."

"And how was the catch last night?"

"Excellent." He hesitated. "But we weren't talking about the fishing."

"Oh?" There was a thriving fishing industry along the shores of the Sea of Kinnereth, and Capernaum was one of the most active towns in that industry. One of the more profitable aspects of David's merchant business was his partnership with two of the families of fishermen. He purchased their catch each day, getting it to the markets in town while it was still fresh, and packing the surplus catch in casks of salt. These were sold to the caravans that moved up and down the *Via Maris*, or Way of the Sea. This great Roman highway that led from Egypt up into Syria and beyond was an important trade route in this part of the world, and there was always a ready market for salted fish. Fish from the Sea of Kinnereth was eaten even in Rome. Simon and Andrew, who were brothers, were two of his partners. James and John and their father, Zebedee, were the others. Originally from Bethsaida, now Peter and Andrew lived here in Capernaum. The partnership between the two fishing families and David and his family had proven to be profitable for both sides.

"They've just come back from Perea," David explained.

"Perea?" Leah spoke up. "What were they doing down there?"

"They went down to hear a man named John." He paused to see if that registered. "John, whom they call the Baptist."

"John the Baptist?" Rachel broke in. "I have heard of him. My mother was telling me about him just yesterday. They say great multitudes go out into the wilderness to hear him and to be baptized by him."

"Yes," David said, pleased at her response. "He is creating a great stir. Andrew says that he teaches with tremendous power and that his message is for all men."

Deborah was suddenly wary. "He's not another self-proclaimed Messiah, is he?" If he answered yes to that question, that would end the conversation right there for her.

For thousands of years, Israel's prophets had foretold the coming of the "Anointed One." In Hebrew, the title was *Meshiach,* or the Messiah. In Greek, an anointed one was *Christos,* or the Christ. This Anointed One was to come in the latter times as Israel's king and deliver her from her oppressors. In recent years, with the hatred against Rome growing rapidly, the feeling that the time had finally come for the arrival of the Messiah had swept across the land. There was a great sense of expectation everywhere. In Deborah's mind this hope had become almost a national obsession, and that obsession had led to tragedy more than once. Time after time this or that leader would rise up, and the people would flock to him, believing he was the Promised One. Usually what that meant was that he led the people in a revolt against Rome. And therein lay the tragedy. So far it had always ended the same. The Roman lion was pricked by the "Messianic spear" until it rose up in fury. Then the so-called Deliverer would be caught and the rebellion crushed. That was why Deborah kept telling Simeon to be patient. The time would come when they would be strong enough to take on the legions, but it was foolhardy to do so before they were strong enough to succeed.

David was shaking his head. "Actually, Andrew said that some priests and Levites came out from Jerusalem to see John. They asked him straight out if he was the Messiah. He said no, that he definitely was not."

"Really?" she said, relieved. "Well, that's a change—a preacher with a following who says he isn't the Promised One."

David reached inside his tunic and withdrew a small piece of parchment. "Do you recognize this?" He handed it to Deborah.

The lines were written in his hand in black ink. She read swiftly. "'The voice of him that crieth in the wilderness, Prepare ye the way of the Lord, make straight in the desert a highway for our God.'" She handed the paper back to David. "Of course I recognize it. It is a passage from the prophet Isaiah."

"I want to see, Pampa," Esther said, taking the parchment from her grandfather and peering at it. Seeing nothing she could understand, she handed it back.

"And how do you interpret it?" David asked his wife.

She thought for a moment, but Rachel didn't hesitate. "It's my understanding that this person crying in the wilderness is thought to be a forerunner for the Messiah."

Leah jumped in as well. "That's what I was going to say too."

"Who is a forerunner for the Messiah?"

They all turned as Ephraim came into the room.

"Abba!" Esther cried, pulling away from David and running to her father. Boaz also darted to him.

Ephraim, David's oldest son, was twenty-five years old now. He and Rachel had been married for almost six years, seven if you counted their betrothal. He swooped both of his children up, then staggered as if he would collapse under their weight. Esther giggled, and Boaz shrieked at the top of his lungs.

After a moment he set them both down and gave each an affectionate swat across the bottom. "Go out and play for a bit," he said. "I want to talk to Pampa and Granmama."

"See my flowers, Abba," Esther said.

Ephraim went over to look and made appropriate noises. Satisfied,

Esther took Boaz by the hand, and they went out into the small court-yard behind the house.

"So what is this about the Messiah?" Ephraim asked.

David handed him the parchment. He read it and handed it back. "Yes, I agree with Rachel and Leah. There will be a forerunner for the Messiah."

"I think so too," David said.

Now Leah came in again. Though she was the youngest in the room, she was an adult. David and Deborah were already talking about finding the proper husband for her in the next two or three years. "I heard the rabbi talk about this one day," she said. "He said that the imagery is drawn from when a king comes to visit another country. It would be an embarrassment if the king's party were unable to get to where he was going, so as part of the preparation for the royal arrival, the hosting king sends out his workmen to prepare the roads. They fill in any places that have washed out, repair the bridges, smooth in the rough places."

"Yes," David said. "That makes the meaning all the more signifi-cant, doesn't it?" He took out a second slip of parchment and handed it to Ephraim without speaking.

His son took it and read aloud: "'Behold, I will send my messen-ger, and he shall prepare the way before me: and the Lord, whom ye seek, shall suddenly come to his temple, even the messenger of the covenant, whom ye delight in.'"

David sat back as Ephraim passed it to the three women to read. "Essentially this says the same thing. Only this time it is the prophet Malachi speaking. So he too foretells of a messenger who will prepare the way for the Messiah."

Deborah handed the parchment back. "What is all this about, David? Why all the sudden interest in this forerunner?"

He looked around at all of them. "So you agree that there will be a messenger who prepares the way for the Messiah?"

They all nodded.

David retrieved the other parchment, then sat down again. His eyes were somber. "This John, that they call the Baptist? He says that he is the forerunner."

Now the bread was forgotten. "He said that?" Rachel asked slowly.

"Yes. Andrew says that John claims that *he* is the voice of one crying in the wilderness, that he is that messenger."

Deborah gave a low exclamation of surprise. "He used those exact words?"

"That's what Andrew said."

"But," Leah said, as surprised as the others, "that would mean that the coming of the Messiah is near."

David nodded, very serious now. He looked at Deborah. "It's been thirty years now."

She started slightly, knowing instantly what he meant.

"Thirty years from what?" Ephraim asked.

David shook his head and changed the subject. "If this John is the forerunner, then the Messiah may already be here." He let that sink in before going on. "Andrew says that John seeks nothing from those who come to hear him. He is not after money; he is not after position. He lives very simply in the wilderness. His raiment is a camel's coat and a leather girdle. He eats locusts and wild honey. But he calls on everyone to repent. If they do, he baptizes them for the remission of their sins. When the Pharisees and the Sadducees came out to see him, he called them a generation of vipers and warned them that the ax is laid at the root of the tree and that they had better repent if they don't want to be hewn down."

Ephraim grinned broadly. "He said that to them? I like this man already."

Leah was troubled. She looked at Deborah. "Do you think he really could be the forerunner, Mother?"

She hesitated, watching her husband's face. "Andrew is about as practical a man as you can find. I wouldn't think he would be easily deceived."

"Exactly what I thought," David said eagerly. "I think it warrants looking into."

She nodded, not prepared for what he said next.

"I want to go to Bethabara."

Deborah visibly jerked. "What?"

"I thought that Ephraim and Simeon and I could go. We need to make contact with the date plantations down in Jericho anyway, make sure they're still going to fulfill their contracts with us this year. We could go and hear this John for ourselves while we're there."

Ephraim looked a little dazed. "But Father, there is so much to do right now."

"I know, but nothing that can't wait a few days." He turned to his wife. "By the way, where is Simeon?"

Her eyes dropped. "He left this morning."

"Left?" David said. "For where?"

"The Zealot council asked him to provide an escort for the Jerusalem delegation to the meeting in Sepphoris."

David grimaced. "That! They really are going through with it?"

"Yes. The Great Council in Jerusalem asked for the meeting. The Zealot council has agreed to at least hear what they have to say." She was obviously uncomfortable telling him this. "As a member of the local Sanhedrin here in Capernaum, you have been assigned to represent our city. So you can't go anywhere until after the meeting."

"I don't want to go to Sepphoris."

She smiled thinly. "You know that you don't have a choice, David."

"It will just turn into a verbal brawl." He looked at his son. "You could give those Zealot leaders a talent of gold and ask them if they thought it was of any value, and they would argue about it until the Great Sea turns to mud."

"David," Deborah warned.

He held up his hands. "I know, I know. We'll go." He looked at Ephraim. "That's supposed to be held in three days. We'll bring Simeon back with us, and the three of us will head for Bethabara right after that."

Ephraim shrugged. "All right." He had sensed the tension between his parents and decided to move on to something else. "One thing is for sure."

"What's that?" David asked.

"If this forerunner is a voice crying in the *wilderness,* John certainly qualifies. I don't even know where Bethabara is."

CHAPTER NOTES

The scriptures cited here by David come from Isaiah 40:3 and Malachi 3:1.

In Deuteronomy 6:4–5, what is perhaps the most significant scripture in the Jewish faith admonishes the House of Israel to hear and remember that the Lord their God is one Lord and that they should love him with all their heart, soul, and might. This is known as the *Sh'ma,* from the first word of that passage in Hebrew. Immediately following those verses, the Israelites were told to keep these words in their heart and to "write them upon the posts of thy house, and on thy gates" (v. 9). The *mezuzah* (literally, in Hebrew, "doorpost") was developed in response to that commandment. Tiny scrolls of parchment on which were written the passage from Deuteronomy 6 and another passage from Deuteronony 11:13–21 were inserted into a small case or tube and attached to the doorposts and gateposts of the home. The Hebrew word *Shaddai* (the Almighty) or sometimes just the first letter of that word (the letter *shin,* which looks somewhat like the English *w*) is usually carved or embossed on the outside of the *mezuzah.* It is not known whether that was the case in biblical times or not. It became traditional to touch the *mezuzah* each time one entered or left the home as a constant reminder of the commandment to love God and serve him.

CHAPTER 2

WHOEVER THROWS A STONE STRAIGHT UP,
THROWS IT ON HIS OWN HEAD.

—Ecclesiasticus 27:25

I

22 MARCH, A.D. 30

Miriam bat Mordechai ben Uzziel came awake with a start, her eyes trying to focus in the semidarkness. Vaguely it registered in her mind that the low ceiling above her head was some kind of rough fabric. To her left, a crack of light revealed a flap of the same fabric. She squinted against the half light. Where were the polished marble walls, the intricately carved olive wood panels that adorned the ceiling of her bedroom? Raising her head slightly, she groped for the trans- parent curtain of the finest Egyptian linens that surrounded her bed, but there was nothing. There was no window with its magnificent view of the Temple Mount, no ebony tables, no teakwood chests bought by her father at exorbitant prices from the caravans that came from far to the East.

Then in one instant memory returned. She dropped back to her pillow with a soft groan. She was not in Jerusalem, and this was not her father's palace in the upper city. It was a small tent, hastily erected in the dark of night, and they were somewhere in the hill country of Samaria. She groaned again. There would be no leisurely breakfast of melon spears, no apple nectar chilled overnight in the cool waters of the cistern, no dates from the plantations of Jericho stuffed with honey and chopped almonds. Worst of all, there would be no bath drawn by Livia, no scented rose water, no oils to protect her delicate skin from the blazing sun of the central highlands.

Miriam rubbed her arms, stretching lazily, focusing, trying to remember what had awakened her. The only sound was that of Livia's deep, even breathing from the smaller bed near hers. Her lips drew into a tiny pout. If her father and Azariah the Pharisee were starting to break camp at this hour, they would find a full-scale revolt on their hands. Miriam was a person of the night, often staying up well into the third watch to read or to tally up her father's books. She could be irritable and petulant if awakened too early.

Wondering what time it was, she peered up at the ceiling of the tent. Light was visible, but it didn't seem to be full sunlight yet. So they were about to begin the first hour of the day. She had hoped that they would not leave until the third hour at least. That was more to her liking. She had hoped for that but did not expect it. There was need for haste. She understood that. Tomorrow's meeting with the rebel leaders from the Galilee would have the utmost consequences for Judea, for the most difficult of times now lay upon them. The very fabric of the nation was in jeopardy, and much of that danger lay in the stubborn nature of her own people.

It seemed like there were squabblings and disagreements and distrust on every side. The Judeans looked down with patronizing scorn on the "crude and unlearned" peasants of the Galilee. Jerusalemites strongly believed that anyone who lived outside the environs of the Holy City was worthy of their pity. The hatred Samaritans and Jews harbored for each other stretched back several centuries. The Idumeans, Arabic descendants of Esau, were viewed by all other

Judeans as thieves and murderers. And of course, then there were the Gentiles, who were viewed with distaste and distrust by all the others. Even the very name her people used for their country showed their attitude toward the Gentiles. They called Israel *Ha-eretz*, "*the* land." The rest of the world was covered by the faintly condescending phrase "outside the land."

It was no different in their religion. The Jewish nation was hopelessly divided and subdivided into groups that viewed each other with considerable suspicion, if not open contempt. There were the wealthy and aristocratic Sadducees, of which her father was one of the leading elders. They controlled the office of high priest, which gave them control of the temple and its enormous revenues. The Pharisees were by far the most popular sect, with many among the common people supporting their views even if they were not willing to endure the endless minutia and stultifying rituals the pharisaical way demanded.

Closely allied with the Pharisees were the scribes. Often Pharisees themselves, the scribes were the lawyers of Israel, the experts in the Law. Unlike the Gentile nations, in Israel the Law was the Law of Moses and therefore was scripture as well as legal code. When Israel was taken captive to Babylon six hundred years before, the people gradually assimilated into Babylonian culture. When they were freed seventy years later to return to their homeland, Aramaic had become their daily tongue and they no longer spoke nor read classical Hebrew. Since the scriptures were written in Hebrew, those who could read and understand it formed a new professional class.

Miriam laughed softly to herself. At fifteen, to her father's utter horror, she had flirted with Pharisaism for a time. Though she loved her father deeply, she was honest enough to see that the religion of the Sadducees was mostly outward show, a cloak to be worn on Shabbat and other holy days, but otherwise kept in the chest where it could not inconvenience anyone too greatly. But to the scribes and the Pharisees, religion touched every aspect of life—not only touched but shaped and molded and formed it. She had hoped that their totality of commitment would somehow satisfy the vague inner longing she was feeling, but she had quickly changed her mind. With the commitment came a rigid obsession with minutia and an unbending demand for exacting ritual. Miriam had been raised by her father from the time her mother died, when she was six. She was the pride of his life, and he doted on her without shame. She had not only been given an education far beyond what other women and many men of her nation received, but also she was raised with a great deal of independence. So she found the rigidity of the Pharisees admirable but terribly stifling.

Miriam sighed, thinking of the meeting tomorrow. Then there were the Zealots. These too claimed to be a religious party, but their ideology was fanatically militant. They would defend God and his law by violence and rebellion. Accommodation with Rome or any other pagan power was eschewed with the deepest of passion. The frightening thing was that some of the Zealots were determined to stop those more moderate from themselves from that accommodation too. "The friend of my enemy is my enemy as well," was a favorite saying among the Zealots.

This was why she was here in a tent before the sun was up, wondering what she was going to find to eat this morning. It was the Zealots who had brought this crisis upon them. Amid the wild melee of clashing ideologies and fiery passions, Miriam and her father and Azariah the Pharisee moved north, hoping to form an alliance between the Zealots and the main parties of Judaism so as to avert war with Rome. If they could not make that alliance, life might become grim indeed. Once before, the Zealots had almost brought about the destruction of their nation. As the old Persian proverb said, "When the elephant is angered, everyone in the grass gets trampled." These rabid patriots could and would destroy the fragile equilibrium that her father and the Great Council was holding together.

So in a rare show of unity, the Sadducees and Pharisees who sat on the main Sanhedrin, the Great Council of Jerusalem, agreed to send two representatives north to try to strike a treaty with the Zealots. It said much about her father that he was the one designated to lead the delegation, with Azariah as the second ambassador. As chief rabbi of the Pharisaical party of Jerusalem and thereby titular head of all the Pharisees, Azariah was as different from her father as the forested glades of Dan were from the barren wastelands of Beersheba. Azariah wore the *peyot*, the side curls, in keeping with the Pharisaic interpretation of a commandment given in the book of Leviticus that said to never cut the corner of your beard. Her father and his associates, who didn't think that was what the scripture meant at all, found the whole concept of *peyot* irritating and embarrassing. Azariah went through elaborate and meticulous washings before every meal and after touching anything that might spiritually defile him. Her father mocked this ritual unmercifully, challenging Azariah and the other Pharisees to show him in scripture where such fastidiousness was required by Moses.

And yet it didn't surprise Miriam that Azariah had been selected for this mission. The chief Pharisee was a pompous, strutting old brood hen, but he was shrewd, with a mind that ran swifter than a fox with a firebrand tied to its tail. He would not be the only man with the *peyot* at the conference table tomorrow, and he would see to it that the Pharisees were properly represented in whatever decisions were made. He had absolutely no concern about whether anyone liked him or his peculiar Pharisaic habits in the process.

Her head jerked up sharply as a soft whistle sounded outside. She came up on one elbow. This, she realized with a start, was the sound that had awakened her. She remained motionless, straining to hear. But once again there was nothing but Livia's soft breathing next to her.

Aware of a sudden chill, Miriam slipped out of bed and moved quietly to the flap of the tent. She opened it a crack and peered out. She had been right. The sun was not yet up, though she could see that in only a few minutes it would be. For a moment the brightness half blinded her. Then a quick movement off to one side caught her eye. Beyond the tent shared by her father and Azariah, the donkeys were munching on wisps of grass. A tail flicked, and for a moment Miriam thought it was that which had caught her eye. But a few rods farther on, near a large oak tree, something moved again. It was Joab, her father's steward and chief servant. He was beckoning urgently to someone out of Miriam's line of sight.

Alarmed, Miriam darted to her bed, threw on her outer robe, then dropped to the small chest that held her things. Pawing quickly, she found the stubby dagger that was a gift from one of her many suitors. In an instant she was at the back wall of the tent slashing at the stitching. The steward of a rich man's house had a great deal of trust, and Joab had more than most. But Miriam did not like the man. His studied servitude seemed strained to her, and his fawning never touched his eyes. To whom was he beckoning at dawn in the wilds of Samaria? She put one eye to the slit. What she saw froze her blood. More than a dozen men were slipping down the hill toward the camp. Their hands were filled with drawn swords or bows and arrows.

In two leaps she was at Livia's side, shaking her roughly. "Livia! Wake up! The camp is under attack!"

Miriam whirled, found her sandals and jammed her feet into them, then spun back around. Her servant girl was wide awake, her eyes large and frightened, the long honey-blonde hair in wild disarray.

"Joab has betrayed us!" Miriam hissed. "I must warn Father!"

Miriam burst from the door of her tent and ran directly into the arms of a tall bearded man. As he grabbed her and yanked her around, pinning her arms to her side, she screamed out. Joab had hired half a dozen men to serve as their escort to Sepphoris. This man was one of them. Miriam had found them all repulsive and stayed clear of them as much as possible. She didn't even know this man's name.

"Ha!" the man crowed triumphantly. "The bird flies from the nest into the net." His mouth pressed against her ear. "You must learn to look more closely when you peek from the door of your tent. You give yourself away."

Another person appeared from behind the tent. He was another of those hired by Joab. Miriam felt her heart plummet as she realized that Joab's betrayal was complete.

The second man leaned forward, thrusting his face so close to Miriam's that she could smell the foul odor of wine on his breath. "Tell me," he leered to his comrade, "do you hold her tightly so she will not flee or because you like the softness of her body?" He threw back his head and cackled hideously. His head snapped forward again, and he grabbed at her arm. "Let me have a turn guarding the little bird."

Miriam spat directly into the pockmarked face. The man recoiled as though struck by a ball of molten lead, but the other hooted in delight. "Stand back, or the bird will peck out your eyes."

But the first man was not laughing. His eyes were murderous, and the mouth, almost hidden in the tangle of black beard, was twisted and ugly. He slowly wiped off the spittle with the back of his hand; then he pulled a dagger from his belt. "Our beautiful mistress has no respect for her servants," he muttered. "Let us teach her who is master now."

For a moment, Miriam nearly screamed again, but then the sight of the gleaming blade brought sudden recollection to her. Though her arms were pinned by the powerful grip of the taller man, her forearms were free and she still held her dagger in her right hand. Her hand jerked up, then down, plunging the steel into the flesh of the man's upper leg. He shrieked with pain, and Miriam was free. She whirled to face her second captor.

Stunned surprise instantly turned to pleasure. "So the bird has claws," he breathed. "Excellent. I shall cut them out."

He lunged at her, knife flashing. But he had taken too much wine, and he moved like a cow heavy with calf. Miriam side-stepped easily, her own dagger coming up. The man lumbered to a stop, staring first at her, then stupidly at his hand. It no longer held his dagger, and the back of it was red with blood.

"Miriam! Watch out!" Livia's sharp warning, hissed from behind her, spun Miriam around. Half a dozen men came running up. They slid to a stop at the sight of the two wounded men and the woman with blazing eyes and flashing dagger.

Breathing hard and holding the blade high, Miriam moved quickly to put her back to the tent wall. Livia, still clad in her sleeping robes, stepped out of the tent to stand beside her mistress. Pale with fright, she nevertheless stood shoulder to shoulder with Miriam and faced the ring of men that was rapidly swelling in numbers.

There was a hoarse cry of rage, and the circle gave way. The servant who had first grabbed her limped forward, swearing incoherently. As he passed through the encircling men, a tall, lean man with the face of a ferret grabbed the back of his tunic and jerked sharply. His feet flew out from under him, and he hit the ground hard.

The others roared with laughter. "Let him go!" cried one. "I'll put ten shekels on the woman."

At the sight of the ferret—clearly the group's leader—the second man stopped short, clutching his hand to stop the bleeding. The other servant got back to his feet, his eyes filled with hate—not for Miriam now but for the man who had pulled him down.

"The dead are worth nothing to me," the ferret snarled. "I told you that the women were not to be touched." There was a grunt of disgust. "I have no use for bread soggy with wine. Be gone!"

"What?" the first man cried. "What about our share of the spoils?"

The ferret-faced man didn't bother to answer but turned back around to face Miriam. Something snapped inside his pickled brain. With a cry, the second man retrieved his dagger from the ground and lunged forward. Quick as he was, the man standing next to the bandit leader was quicker. Miriam gasped as a sword flashed. The heavy metal butt caught the attacker just below his right ear, and he went down like a stalk of wheat beneath the blade of the scythe.

The leader looked at the man's partner. "You have until I count to a hundred to get your friend and be gone or you shall both get more than your share of the spoils."

Trembling, the man grabbed at his partner's arm and helped him to his feet. They shuffled away as the other men jeered and kicked dust on them.

The bandit leader turned to Miriam. "You will drop the knife now."

The words didn't register. Things had happened so swiftly.

"I said that you will drop the knife now."

Miriam looked up, bringing the dagger up higher.

"Eliab!"

A short man with glittering black eyes stepped forward, nocking an arrow in his bow. He drew it back to the point. When the arrow leveled it was pointed directly at Miriam's chest.

Somewhere in the back of Miriam's mind, Livia's horrified gasp registered. But she didn't turn. With a great effort of will she forced herself to meet the gaze of the ferret. She gave a quick, almost imperceptible shake of her head and stepped in front of Livia. "The dead are of no worth to you, remember?"

The man threw back his head and laughed in delight, revealing badly discolored teeth. "Now I see why you have never married and why Joab so willingly betrays you." He chuckled again, then sheathed his dagger and folded his arms. Eliab released the pressure on the bow and returned the arrow to its quiver and also stood back to wait.

In a moment Miriam understood why. From her father's tent there came a muffled shout, then brief sounds of struggle. The flap of the tent opened, and Joab came out. Behind him four men with drawn swords herded her father and Azariah the Pharisee toward them.

"Bring them here," the tall one called, his eyes never leaving

Miriam's. The ring of men stepped back as the prisoners were brought inside the circle. There was a quick look of relief from her father when he saw her; then he was jerked around to face the bandit leader.

"You are Mordechai ben Uzziel the Sadducee, member of the Great Sanhedrin of Jerusalem?"

Miriam's father just glowered in defiance. The dark eyes of the bandit leader lifted briefly to those of the chief steward. Joab nodded. "This is he."

"I am Moshe Ya'abin. Perhaps you have heard of me?"

Mordechai's eyes widened perceptibly. Behind him Azariah gasped. His side curls bounced and danced as his head jerked in surprise. Then the Pharisee instantly recovered. "Who has not heard of the beast who feeds on the blood of his own people and terrorizes all of Judea?" He spat in contempt.

Ya'abin's mouth twitched slightly in what Miriam supposed was meant to be a smile. "We all engage in plunder, Azariah of the Pharisees. You and Mordechai here simply go about yours with a little more refinement than we do."

He motioned with his head toward Miriam. "This is your daughter?"

Miriam started, but again it was the chief steward who provided the answer with a quick nod. Ya'abin did not turn but kept looking at her father. "I will begin to count. If the knife is still in your daughter's hand when I reach three, you will die." He seemed faintly amused.

Eliab once again began to nock his bow.

"One . . ."

Miriam's shoulders sagged as the dagger plopped softly in the dust.

"That's better." He turned. "Eliab! Watch the two women. You are not to touch them unless they attempt to escape." The black eyes looked Miriam up and down appreciatively. "If they do, you are free to do with them what you will."

Livia gave an involuntary shudder as Eliab stepped forward, lust naked in his eyes. Catcalls of encouragement rang out from the circle of men. But now it was Miriam's father who had found his courage. He leaned forward against the grip of his captors, his voice low and trembling with fury. "If you so much as touch my daughter—"

Ya'abin gave the older man a long, almost amused look. "Where is the money?"

Mordechai hesitated for only a second, then laughed derisively. "Only a fool travels in these times with money on his person."

Miriam watched sadly. It was a brave show, but even from where she stood she could see the nervous tic at the corner of her father's mouth as he tried to meet Ya'abin's stare.

"He keeps it in a bag buried in a hole dug beneath his bed," Joab said quickly.

Miriam's father lunged at Joab, breaking free, his fingers aimed for his throat. "You dare to betray me!"

Even as the guards leaped forward and seized Mordechai again, Joab fell back, his face white.

Ya'abin roared in delight. "I don't think your master is pleased with you, Joab." The laughter died as suddenly as it had erupted. "How much does he have?"

"I am not sure," Joab blurted. His eyes momentarily flitted to the disappearing figures of his two hired henchmen. There was a quick nervous flick of his tongue. "He brings funds from the Sanhedrin to bribe the Zealot leaders. It is in gold. Perhaps as much as five thousand shekels."

Ya'abin turned to his men. "Bring the money to me. Anything else in the camp is yours."

It was like setting a pack of dogs loose on a downed ox. Howling and shouting, Ya'abin's men raced through the small encampment. Tents were slashed open even though nothing prevented them from going through the front flap. Saddlebags were ripped apart, baskets and barrels smashed or overturned. They snatched at everything in sight and, like the dogs they were, snarled at the slightest encroachment on their territory. Their leader seemed oblivious to it all as he waited. In a few moments, two men came from Mordechai's tent straining under the weight of a thick leather bag bulging with coins. At the same moment, Miriam heard Livia's quick intake of breath. She turned to see a heavily bearded man in a filthy tunic run from their tent, swinging a golden necklace, the only piece of jewelry she had brought with her.

Miriam shook her head in quick warning to Livia, then whirled to face Joab. "For years I have told Father that he had taken a serpent into his bosom."

The chief steward took one menacing step toward her. "And for years I have awaited this moment with great anticipation. I have endured your icy contempt and haughty superiority. Now I will be present when you are sold to the Parthians. They are men who know how to make a woman meet their every whim."

"Ya'abin!" Miriam's father was not intimidated by the men who still held him tightly.

The robber leader turned slowly to face his captive.

"I am a wealthy man. My household will pay handsomely for our release. Far more than the Parthians can pay."

Ya'abin gazed out across the camp where the looting and plundering were in full sway. Finally he nodded thoughtfully. "One would be a fool not to have thought of that."

Joab's head jerked around.

"And whatever else may be said of Moshe Ya'abin, let it not be said that he is a fool."

He snapped his fingers, and Eliab reached inside the folds of his tunic and withdrew a parchment scroll. "You shall draft a letter and sign it with your own hand. We shall send a messenger to Jerusalem. When they have returned with the money, you shall be freed."

Joab lunged forward. "No!" He thrust his face next to Ya'abin's. "You promised them to me. I must have time to appropriate his estate."

Ya'abin's dark eyes narrowed slightly, but when he spoke, his voice was calm, almost conversational. "Joab, my friend, I spoke of being a fool. Anyone who trusts another is a fool. A man who trusts a thief is the greatest fool of all."

"You can't do this!"

"To the contrary. As long as I do not bother the Romans, Pontius Pilate, our esteemed Roman governor, doesn't much care what we Jews do to one another." He laughed. "And if he does, where shall he look to find us?" Without noticeably changing tone, the voice took on the sudden menace of Eliab's nocked bow. "Since you have been of service to me, friend Joab, I will tell you what I shall do. I will allow you to leave now along with your two associates. It will be three days before your master is released and can begin searching for you. That should give you a comfortable head start."

"Flee quickly," Miriam spat, as Joab rocked back, suddenly white. "My father may someday tire of searching for you, but I never will!"

"I will hunt you down to the ends of the earth, Joab!" Mordechai said, still trembling with the outrage of being betrayed by the one he most trusted.

Beads of perspiration had formed on Joab's lower lip and trickled into the neatly trimmed beard that hid his mouth. He looked at Ya'abin, then at Mordechai.

Miriam's father turned to Ya'abin. "I will add a thousand shekels to the ransom if you send him back to Jerusalem with us."

Again Ya'abin threw back his head and hooted as Joab paled even more. "Surely, O great leader of the Sanhedrin, there must be some honor, even among the dishonorable." His voice instantly became as hard and cold as the blade of a sword. "Unless, of course, Joab were to try my patience and lead me to believe that he did not appreciate the great generosity of Moshe Ya'abin in letting him leave now."

Joab hesitated only one instant, then turned and fled, his long robes clutched up around his knees. Ya'abin's men roared with delight as he scrambled away like a beetle with hot olive oil on his tail.

Ya'abin looked around at the faces of the other men Joab had hired, his eyes hard. "Do any of the rest of you feel I have treated your employer unfairly?"

No one moved.

"Good." Still chuckling to himself, Ya'abin turned and handed the scroll to Mordechai. "You will go over there beneath the tree and write."

To that point the voice of Moshe Ya'abin had been pleasant, but as he turned to face Azariah the Pharisee it turned raw with undisguised contempt. "You too, Pharisee. You hide behind your long robes and pious prayers and your dancing side curls, but you are as avaricious and corrupt as any man in the camp. You too shall pay for your freedom."

He handed the parchment to the man guarding her father. "See that they both sign. I think twenty thousand shekels for father and daughter should suffice. Ask five for the Pharisee. Only his own family would think he is worth that much."

He swung around to face Miriam even as Azariah began to sputter. "Meanwhile, I would like to get better acquainted with this woman who talks and fights like a man."

The color drained from Miriam's face as Livia clutched at her arm. Mordechai spun back around, his mouth hard. "No!" he cried. "We are paying for our freedom."

Azariah shook his fist at Ya'abin. "God will smite you if you add this horrible curse to your many other crimes."

Ya'abin gave a short bark of laughter. "God has overlooked many opportunities to smite Moshe Ya'abin for his terrible deeds. Perhaps he will do it again today."

"Blasphemy!" Azariah cried in horror.

Eliab aimed a kick at Azariah, who barely leaped aside in time.

"You are a most unreasonable man, Mordechai ben Uzziel," Ya'abin said, giving Miriam's father a tiny, hard smile that sent chills up Miriam's back. "The choice is simple. You may have your daughter back in a few minutes, only slightly soiled, or you may have her back in small pieces. Which would you prefer?"

Mordechai stared in horror for what seemed like an eternity. For a moment Miriam thought he was going to try to attack this awful man, but Mordechai ben Uzziel had sat at too many heavily laden tables, drunk too many goblets of Syrian wine, ridden too many times around the streets of Jerusalem in a litter carried by his servants. Finally he gave a strangled cry. His face crumpled, and he looked away.

Still completely calm, Ya'abin turned to the man with the parchment. "Make it twenty-*five* thousand for the Sadducee and his daughter." He jerked his head, and a dazed Mordechai and a muttering Azariah were driven at sword point toward the large oak tree near the center of the camp.

Ya'abin turned to face the women. Livia threw her arms around Miriam and started to cry, but Miriam pushed her away gently and faced the robber squarely. "You *will* have to cut me to pieces before I submit to you." Her voice was trembling, but more with fury than with fright.

"Eliab!" Ya'abin tossed the heavy bag of money to his lieutenant. "Watch this and the servant girl. If I am undisturbed, you may have your pick of the two when I am done." Ya'abin's hand flashed out with the speed of a striking adder and seized Miriam's wrist.

But one wrist was not enough. Miriam erupted into a clawing, kicking fury, tearing at his face, arms, and shoulders like a demon. The terror that had paralyzed Livia snapped at the sight of her mistress in battle. She leaped onto Ya'abin's back to tear at him from behind. A stunned Eliab stared for a moment, then dropped the bag and hurled himself into the fray. But he was a moment too late. With the roar of a wild bull, Ya'abin spun around, hurling Livia off his back. She crashed heavily, her head striking the tent pole. There was one sharp cry; then she slumped to the ground and lay still.

Ya'abin whirled back, and with all the force of a powerfully muscled arm, he caught Miriam full across the face with the back of his hand. She bounced off the wall of the tent and pitched face first into the dirt. Instantly, Ya'abin was over her. He grabbed her hair and yanked her head back hard. Miriam felt a sharp pain at the corner of her jaw, but dazed as she was from the blow, it took her a moment to realize the point of his dagger was pressing into her skin hard enough to draw blood. He thrust his face next to hers, the black eyes filled with murder. Blood was starting to ooze from two ugly scratches on his left cheek.

"Now my angry wildcat," he hissed, "we shall see who is the master here."

He yanked her up, and pushed her past Livia's still body. Miriam caught a glimpse of an ugly welt on the side of her servant's head and saw that Livia's face was as pale as death. Eliab, finally galvanized into action, stood awkwardly with his sword, wavering between the fallen woman and the captive one.

Ya'abin lifted the flap of the tent with one foot, keeping the dagger up hard against Miriam's jaw. But just as he was about to push her into the waiting semidarkness, there was a soft whir followed by a dull thudding sound. It was almost lost in the noise of the looting of the camp, but Eliab's gasp was sharp and distinct.

As both Ya'abin and Miriam whirled and gaped at him, Eliab staggered back, clutching wildly at the feathered shaft that had buried itself in the front of his shoulder. His eyes were filled with shock and surprise as he looked at his leader. "I've been hit," he exclaimed. Then his legs buckled, and he sank slowly to his knees.

II

Ya'abin reacted with incredible swiftness. In one movement he jerked Miriam around, using her body as a shield. He grabbed Eliab with his free hand and dragged him to his feet, all the time screaming, "Attack! Attack!"

In the final stages of looting the camp, his men reacted with equal speed. Spoils were dropped, weapons snatched as they dove for cover. Beneath the oak tree where they had been taken to write the ransom letters, Mordechai and Azariah scrambled behind the massive trunk. Those guarding them sprang into a crouch, swords and bows drawn, their heads jerking sharply as they looked around.

Ya'abin and Eliab reached the cover of the sheltering branches, and Ya'abin shoved Miriam hard toward her father. He snatched up a bow and a quiver, dropping to one knee. "Ithamar! Shaul! Cut down the tents so we have a clear field of fire."

Two men stood. Before either could move, that same soft whisper sounded. Ithamar screamed and fell back, clutching at an arrow buried in his upper thigh. Shaul promptly forgot about his leader's orders and dove behind a pile of baskets and boxes.

"Stay down!" Ya'abin screamed, moving back even more into the circle of his men. He was raging now and swung around on Eliab, who was rocking back and forth, moaning as he pressed against the spot where the arrow protruded from his shoulder. "I told you to leave men on the ridge to cover us!"

"I left two," Eliab shot back, clenching his teeth. "They must be down."

"Someone's coming!" The low cry from one of the men brought them all around with a jerk. The man was pointing up the hill into the rising sun, where they could see the dark figure of a man striding down the path toward the camp.

"I can easily take him," said the man next to Ya'abin, raising his bow. He pulled back the arrow until the feathers of the shaft caressed his cheek. The tip moved slowly, settling in on the dark figure just coming into bowshot.

Miriam tensed and prepared to spring. Whoever that was coming down the hill, he had saved her from Ya'abin. She would not see him die without warning.

But at that moment the man stopped.

"Hold!" Ya'abin commanded softly. "He stands directly in the sun. Let him come into range."

But the man remained where he was, raising his hands to his mouth. "Ya'abin!"

The call came floating down to them, clear and challenging. Ya'abin started. Who knew that it was his band looting the camp? He straightened slowly, resting one hand on the shoulder of the bowman.

"Put down your weapons. We have no desire for a massacre. If we did, your two men would be dead now and not just wounded."

Ya'abin took a step forward. "Identify yourself or die!"

The man gave a soft hoot of derision, barely discernible, then raised one hand into the air. "I have two dozen bowmen."

The thieves stiffened noticeably, glancing around the hillside in fear.

"For a man of such fearsome reputation, Ya'abin," the voice continued, "you have left yourself in a terrible field position. We can hit any and every man without showing ourselves."

"He's bluffing," the bowman cried.

The raised arm suddenly dropped. From three different directions came the soft hiss of shafts flying, followed by the solid whack of metal tips biting deep into the bark of the tree trunk. Everyone beneath the tree jumped, then stared at the arrows trembling softly just inches from their faces.

Miriam almost laughed aloud when she saw Ya'abin's twisted face. The setter of the snare was trapped himself. His eyes darted back and forth, uncertain, filled with fear.

The figure above them raised his arm again. "The next volley is for you, Ya'abin. Drop your weapons, and you have my oath that not a man will be harmed."

Ya'abin stared for several more long seconds; then suddenly his shoulders sagged, and he turned to his men. "Lower your weapons."

The bowman cursed softly as he let the bow spring back, and he returned the arrow to its place; but the other men jumped eagerly to obey, dropping their swords and daggers, flinging aside bows and quivers. Then they stood with hands held clear of their bodies so the unseen marksmen could see they were in total compliance.

Miriam turned and flung herself into her father's arms with a sob of relief. He swept her up, holding her tight, and she was suddenly aware that he was trembling almost as violently as she was. Behind her the steady crunch of sandals came closer. She straightened and turned to see their deliverer.

If the man's intent was to make a dramatic entry, he fully accomplished his purpose. Every eye in the camp was fixed on him. No one moved. The only sound, besides the confident stride, was the soft rustling of the oak leaves above their heads. But the intruder seemed unaware of the reaction he was creating. His stride was unhurried and confident, like the supple grace of a leopard padding through a thicket of trees. He wore a sleeveless, knee-length tunic, leather sandals laced around ankle and calf, a short sword in a scabbard on his right hip, in the style of the legionnaires. Powerful muscles rippled under skin burned metallic brown by innumerable days spent in the open. His head was bare, his hair neatly trimmed and touched with sun-bleached highlights of gold. To her surprise, he was clean-shaven. Had he been in uniform, he could easily have been mistaken for a Roman soldier.

As the man came under the shade of the oak and stopped a few feet in front of Ya'abin, Miriam's eyes widened in surprise. She saw the face of a young man, not much older than herself. And he was almost certainly a Galilean, for though deeply tanned, his skin was fair, his hair light brown, almost blond. She had also heard in his voice the more guttural accent of the northern parts of her country. The eyes were almost sand colored and were touched with flecks of emerald green, like the waters of Kinnereth. She also saw that Ya'abin was a full palm width taller than the stranger. That too surprised her, for he had seemed so tall striding down toward them.

He let his eyes move slowly from man to man, resting briefly on Azariah and Miriam's father, but stopping only when they met Miriam's. The face softened. "Are you all right?"

She nodded, involuntarily touching the tiny cut on her jaw and her bruised face. "Yes," she murmured. "Yes, thank you."

There was a faint smile, a quick nod; then the eyes continued their probe of the camp, finally stopping on Ya'abin.

"Who are you? What do you want?" Ya'abin's bravado had noticeably slipped.

Without turning, the man called out loudly. "Yehuda! Leave the others and come down."

About a hundred paces away, from behind a clump of brush that didn't look big enough to hide a young boy, a large man slowly straightened, archer's bow still up and ready. All eyes turned to him except for the Galilean's. He continued to watch Ya'abin steadily. As the big man walked swiftly down to join his comrade, the bandit leader brought his eyes back to his attacker.

Ya'abin finally regained a little of his courage. "Have you come for a share of the spoils?"

The Galilean's voice cut in hard and cold. "You are to be more despised than the Romans, for you are a parasite that lives on the flesh of your own people."

"We can make an arrangement if—"

The man's mouth clamped down. "My oath protects you to the edge of the camp, Ya'abin. Thereafter I consider myself duty bound to kill you and the vermin that run with you."

"There is plenty for us both," Ya'abin cried. "This is Mordechai ben Uzziel, one of the richest men in Jerusalem. The Sanhedrin will pay handsomely for him and his daughter."

The second man moved up alongside the bronzed Galilean. He was broad shouldered and powerfully built, with jet-black hair and a full beard of the same color. He spoke, his voice a deep rumble of contempt, his accent betraying that he was likewise Galilean. "Does the sparrow beg the eagle for a piece of the carcass?"

"Be gone!" the Galilean said to Ya'abin in a voice made all the more menacing by its softness.

Ya'abin was sputtering. "Our weapons. You can't send us away with nothing."

"When we are gone you may cower back like the dogs you are and retrieve them," Yehuda said. "But take heed. We shall follow you until the sun has reached its zenith. Any man who turns back before then will die."

To Miriam's surprise, the Galilean turned to face Eliab, who still clutched at the arrow in his shoulder. "It is not a barbed tip," he said. "You may pull it out without fear of tearing the flesh."

Eliab looked startled, then grasped the shaft and jerked, gasping as he did so. The arrow came out easily and he flung it aside, pressing his fingers against the wound again. He looked sick, the corners of his mouth pinched, his eyes somewhat glazed.

The young rescuer pointed to one of the other bandits. "Help the other man that is down." As the man stood slowly and started for the man writhing on the ground with an arrow in his leg, the young man swung back on Ya'abin. "Go!" he said softly. "The cup of my patience is nearly drained."

Ya'abin hesitated, but his men didn't. They broke into a shambling retreat up the hill, looking nervously at every bush and tree they passed. Their leader gave one last look of pure hatred, then started after them. As he got a safe distance away, he turned his head. "We shall meet again, Galilean," he screamed. "Then you shall learn that Moshe Ya'abin cannot so easily be thrust aside."

If he heard, the young man gave no sign. Miriam stood and

stepped toward him. "My servant girl has been hurt." She pointed. "May I go to her?" At his quick nod, she hurried past him.

The Galilean turned to Miriam's father and Azariah. "We must hurry." He motioned with his head to Mordechai. "Go through the baggage. Find any food that has not been ruined by these wild dogs." He turned. "You, Pharisee. Get some water and help with the girl." Without waiting, he and Yehuda stooped down and began collecting the weapons of Moshe Ya'abin and his men and tossing them into a pile.

In a half dozen quick steps, Miriam reached Livia and dropped to the ground beside her. As she lifted Livia's head, sudden tears sprang to her eyes. She was breathing! The face was ashen white and an ugly blue-black lump protruded from the left temple. But she was breathing!

A moment later Azariah hurried up with a goatskin water bottle and dropped beside her, for the first time seemingly unaware that he was kneeling on contaminated Samaritan soil without a mat. Miriam tore off a piece of her inner nightclothes and held it out. He soaked it with water, and she began gently bathing Livia's face.

"Praises be to God; blessed be his holy name," Azariah breathed fervently. He reached up absently and fingered one of his side curls. "The Lord has delivered us out of the hands of the oppressor."

Miriam shot him a sharp look. "A few of those praises could be directed at the Galilean. He took a deadly risk for us."

"Aye," Azariah agreed soberly. "How close we were to tragedy."

Miriam shuddered, then concentrated on Livia. She moaned, then stirred slightly.

Azariah suddenly lowered his voice. "But could it be that we have been rescued from the jaws of the rat only to fall into the paws of the jackal?" he whispered.

Miriam looked up in surprise.

"Did you not hear the big one's comment about taking spoils from the eagle?" He clucked his tongue in despair. "We have been delivered from one group of godless outlaws only to fall into the hands of another."

"If so," Miriam snapped, "I will gladly take the jackal." The Galilean's first spoken words had been to inquire after her welfare, and she sensed his utter contempt for what Ya'abin had been about to do to her. Let him rob them. Let him hold them for ransom. There would be no dagger at her throat and no glittering eyes raging with lust. She was sure of that and would not let a muttering Azariah steal her immense relief.

Livia moaned again, and her eyes fluttered open, though she stared blankly, not recognizing Miriam.

"She is coming out of it." The deep voice next to her elbow startled Miriam. The big man, Yehuda, had joined them without a sound and was looking at Livia with concern. Half of his face was lost in the thick tangle of black beard, but warm brown eyes peered out from beneath shaggy brows.

"She tried to save me," Miriam said softly, gently bathing the ugly wound on Livia's head.

He nodded. "We saw it from the hill." There was a deep sadness in his voice. "We could not shoot for fear of hitting one of you. It was a brave thing you both did."

Livia turned her head slowly, recognition returning. "Miriam!" She clutched at Miriam's robes. "Those men—"

"They're gone, Livia," Miriam soothed. "They're all gone now."

The pale blue eyes lifted to stare at Yehuda, fear still clouding them.

"These men saved us. Ya'abin is gone."

"She needs water," Yehuda said, taking the goatskin from Azariah and dropping to one knee. He put the spout to Livia's lips as Miriam lifted the girl's head. Livia drank eagerly, then struggled to sit up. Yehuda put a massive hand behind her back and smiled his encouragement.

A noise behind her caused Miriam to turn. The young Galilean and her father had joined them. In one hand, her father had a blanket tied into a sling filled with food. The halter rope of one of their donkeys was in the other. The Galilean looked down at Livia. "How is she?"

"She is awake," Yehuda answered, standing up to tower a full head over his companion. "She will have a great headache, I think, but she is fine."

"Then we must leave." He turned to Miriam. "We shall prop your tent up enough for you to enter. Take her inside and change into traveling clothes quickly. Leave everything else."

Azariah was up instantly, spluttering like a boiling pot. "Leave everything? Why?"

"Ya'abin is still out there," Mordechai said. "Aren't we safer here?"

Yehuda helped Livia up. She stood unsteadily for a moment, clutching at his arm. He smiled down at her. "We really must hurry, for, you see, our leader here is a shameless liar." The smile slowly faded. "We do not have two dozen men. Besides us, there are only three others!"

"Only five!" Miriam and her father had spoken as one.

"Yes," the Galilean said. "In less than an hour Ya'abin and his dogs will be out of the hill country and will know that only one man follows them. Then he will return very swiftly."

That was enough to spur Miriam on. As Yehuda stepped to the tent pole and lifted it enough to allow entrance, Miriam and Livia went into the tent. The four men stood there, awkwardly, not speaking; then suddenly Mordechai started. He was staring at the ground, just beyond where Eliab had dropped to his knees after being hit with the shaft. The Galilean saw his look and turned. There on the ground, where Eliab had dropped it, lay the money bag. For a moment no one moved; then with a leap Azariah pounced for it. But the

Galilean was quicker. In one quick movement he had it. He swung back around to face Mordechai, hefting it thoughtfully.

Azariah's face had turned a furious red, but Mordechai just looked steadily at the young man before him. "You saved our lives," he said evenly. He glanced at the tent door, his eyes suddenly shining. "And my daughter. What you did for her . . . " His voice had gone suddenly gruff, and he shook his head quickly. "Take what you will."

The Galilean hefted the bag again. "How much?"

"I told you!" Azariah snapped. "I told you they were no better than Ya'abin."

Mordechai ignored him, still meeting the gaze of the other. "About six thousand shekels."

The Galilean suddenly tossed the money bag, catching Mordechai so completely by surprise that the heavy weight hit him in the chest, knocking him backwards and making him drop both the food and the donkey's lead rope.

The Galilean's head bobbed slightly, his sand-brown eyes faintly amused, faintly contemptuous. "We shall ask a tenth. Half for this morning's work. Half for delivering you safely to your destination."

Both Sadducee and Pharisee gaped at him. The Galilean turned slightly as he realized that Livia and Miriam had come out from the tent behind him and were watching.

He turned back to Mordechai. "Yehuda and the others have families, or we would not ask that. Agreed?"

Mordechai ben Uzziel shook off his stunned amazement. "Gladly! I will pay twice that for what you did for us this morning, and that again if you escort us to the Galilee."

The other shook his head quickly. "Such shameless wages would only corrupt my men."

Yehuda chuckled deeply. "We might even be accused of plunder."

The young Galilean swung around to Miriam. "Can you walk?"

"Yes, of course, but—"

"We are not taking the horses. But we have one donkey. Your servant can ride for a time."

"We are going to walk?" Mordechai said in dismay. "Wouldn't the horses be faster?"

"They leave too clear a trail to follow. We'll cut them loose. They'll make their way back to Jerusalem."

Yehuda turned and in one gentle swoop had Livia off her feet and onto the back of the donkey. "Will you be all right?" he asked kindly.

Livia, still pale and drawn, nodded.

The Galilean thrust the donkey's halter rope into Miriam's hand. "We must go." He started away.

Miriam stepped into his path, blocking the way. "Wait! You have done us—" she stopped. "*Me!*—a great service, and I do not even know your name."

"Yes," Mordechai added quickly. "By what name are you called?"

For the first time, a full smile played at the corners of the young man's mouth, crinkling around his eyes as well. "The Romans call me 'criminal.'" He glanced at Azariah. "The Pharisees call me 'infidel' and are horrified that I do not wear a beard and the *peyot*. Yehuda here calls me 'the crazy one.' And Moshe Ya'abin? I suspect he is calling me things which it would be better not to repeat in the presence of women."

With that he stepped around Miriam and started back up the path down which he had strode so confidently less than half an hour before.

CHAPTER NOTES

In the age of the Bible, time was marked by the natural rhythm of light and darkness. Each twenty-four-hour period was divided equally into day and night, and each of these were divided into equal twelve-hour blocks. The rising of the sun marked the beginning of the day and its setting the beginning of night. This made their "hours" distinctly different from ours in that the length of the hour would vary from season to season, being twelve shorter periods in winter during the day, and twelve longer periods in summer for the day, with the opposite for the night. Since the Holy Land is somewhat closer to the equator, this variation was not as great as it would be in more northern latitudes.

If we think of sunrise as occurring on the average about 6:00 A.M., and sunset about 6:00 P.M., then it is easy to calculate the time as given in the New Testament. The third hour would be between 8:00 and 9:00 A.M. The end of the sixth hour would correspond to our noon. The eleventh hour would begin at 4:00 P.M. and the twelfth at 5:00 P.M.

Probably from their strong military tradition, the Romans divided the night into four "watches" of three hours each. By New Testament times the Jews had adopted the Roman way of referring to nighttime hours. Thus, the first watch would be from about sundown to 9:00 P.M. The last, or fourth watch, would be from about 3:00 A.M. to sunrise (see Fallows, 3:1661–2, 1714).

In Leviticus 19:27, the Law reads: "Ye shall not round the corners of your heads, neither shalt thou mar the corners of thy beard." Most scholars agree that this was a prohibition against a practice found among the heathen religions, which made cutting the hair or shaving the beard in peculiar ways part of their religious rituals. Today some of the most strict of the Jewish groups interpret this to be a literal commandment and never cut their sideburns, that is, the place where the beard and the hair join. Thus they develop long side curls, which are called *peyot* (Hebrew: "edge," or "corner"). Though no mention is made of the wearing of the *peyot* in the New Testament, the author has assumed the practice was observed among the stricter sects of the Jews at that time as well.

Many Galileans were indeed fairer in their complexion than most of the other inhabitants of Palestine. After the Jewish captivity in Babylon and their subsequent return, Galilee was left mostly to the Gentiles (see, for example, Isaiah 9:1). Only about 150 years before Christ was it resettled by Jews, and even then there continued to be a heavy influence of fair-skinned people there.

CHAPTER 3

THE DEEPEST RIVERS FLOW WITH THE LEAST SOUND.

—*Quintus Curtius Rufus*, Alexander the Great, *VII.iv*

I

22 MARCH, A.D. 30

With a great sigh of relief, Miriam sank wearily onto the grassy creek bank, slipped off her sandals, and thrust her burning feet into the deliciously cool water of the stream. The Galilean, who was scanning the valley floor from whence they had just come, spun around at Miriam's audible groan of pleasure.

"Not here!" he said sharply. Then, seeing the stab of disappointment on her face, his voice softened and he raised his arm to point. "Follow the stream up a hundred paces, and you'll be in the trees. We'll rest there."

Miriam's father was instantly to her side and helping her up. "Come, my dear. Just a few more steps." Azariah the Pharisee likewise moved to her and took one arm.

Miriam jerked away, aware that the Galilean was watching with what looked like a touch of mockery in his eyes. She replaced her sandals, trying not to wince at the pain. She straightened and started away, determined not to limp. This tenderness in her feet was a surprise to her. She walked all the time in Jerusalem. Unlike her father, Miriam was embarrassed to be carried about in a carriage. Besides, she loved the Holy City. Her father spent long hours involved in the management of the Great Council, so Miriam had much time on her hands. Unless the weather was terrible, she took long walks every day, exploring every corner of the rabbit's warren of streets and alleys and narrow marketplaces. So it came as a shock that in the last hour the bottoms of her feet were starting to grow very tender. True, the pathways and trails they had been following were not paved, but even then . . .

Moving slowly, Miriam followed the stream to where it bubbled from a large outcropping of rock at the base of the steep hillside. The scattered oak and tamarisk trees gave way to a stand of pines that provided a deep and welcome shade. As they left the hammering sunshine, the smell of the pine needles was deep and rich. Miriam started, suddenly aware that two men were there near the spring. It was the other two who served with Yehuda and the Galilean. She didn't know their names. They had trailed the group at some distance, watching their back trail. Now suddenly they were here. One of them came noiselessly over. He gently took the donkey's halter from Miriam, helped Livia slide down, then pulled the willing animal over to the creek and tethered it where it could reach both water and grass.

The two men drank quickly, then moved away again, disappearing into the trees. To stand guard, no doubt. Since leaving the camp this morning, they had seen no more sign of Moshe Ya'abin, but it was reassuring to Miriam to know they were not taking any chances.

She turned as Yehuda came up and spoke. "We shall rest here. We must wait for Daniel."

Miriam's father grunted. "Is he the one making sure our robber friend does not follow?"

"Yes. He is also my younger brother."

Livia seemed anxious. "Do you think there was more trouble?"

Yehuda was quick to shake his head. "No." Then he gestured

toward the small stream. "We have about an hour. Rest. I shall get some food." He moved away.

The four of them sat down, and once again Miriam removed her sandals. She grasped her ankle and pulled her foot around so that she could examine the bottom of it. What she saw was no great surprise. It was deep red, and a large blister was starting to form on the ball of her foot.

She heard a soft intake of breath and turned to see Livia staring. Livia had ridden the donkey all day and therefore had not been on her feet. Miriam warned her off with a quick shake of her head and thrust both feet into the water. She sighed in pleasure as the burning sensation instantly stopped.

An audible groan came from the other side of her. Her father was removing his sandals, a pair carefully crafted from the finest Antiochan leather and which had cost him more than fifty shekels. Earlier in the day, the first time the Galilean and Yehuda had allowed them to stop, her father had wisely wrapped his feet in cloth. Now he was biting his lip as he unwound the cloth, and as he got to the last layer, Miriam saw a dark stain. Then she gasped as he removed the cloth. The bottoms of his feet had already blistered and then burst.

He closed his eyes as he put his feet into the stream, and she saw his mouth pinch a little at the pain. She reached out and laid a hand on his arm. The ample girth beneath her father's robes bore silent witness to the softness of the life he lived, and yet he had not once complained.

He smiled grimly, patted her hand, and closed his eyes.

A movement caught Miriam's eye, and she turned. Yehuda and the young Galilean were kneeling beside the blanket they had filled with food, breaking off chunks of bread and slicing off pieces of cheese. Miriam smiled faintly. How different these two were. Yehuda was the gentle bear. She guessed that if he ever became aroused, he would be fearsome to contend with. Otherwise, he was of quick humor and gentle manner. She liked him very much.

The Galilean was an enigma. At the camp he had shown a brief flash of gentleness, but she had seen little of it since. He had driven them relentlessly for the better part of the day, allowing only brief stops until now. He was silent, aloof, almost withdrawn.

She dropped her eyes again when the two men stood and started toward them, conversing in low tones. To her surprise the Galilean came directly to her. He held out a piece of bread and a thick slab of cheese. "I'm sorry. There can be no fire."

As she took the food, he retrieved some dates from the bag and handed those to her as well. Yehuda gave Livia an equal portion.

Miriam took the offering gratefully. "A stream and a hearty appetite are better than a fire."

That seemed to please him, and he murmured something in assent. Yehuda broke the loaf of bread into great chunks and passed it to Mordechai as the Galilean sliced off more cheese for them. Her father held the food out to Azariah, but he did not see it. He was staring out across the valley below them.

"Are we out of Samaria?" Azariah demanded.

The Galilean's eyes hardened, but his face remained impassive. He nodded. "Yes. This stream comes from Ein Harod."

"If this is the Spring of Harod," Yehuda added, in case they weren't sure exactly what that implied, "we are at the base of Mt. Gilboa, which means we left Samaria some time ago."

Azariah's eyes raised heavenward, his one hand reaching up to grasp one of his side curls, as was his habit. "Praises to the Holy One of Israel; blessed be his name." He flung off his outer robe, strode to the creek, and began washing himself with meticulous care.

As Miriam watched, she realized that the fact that Azariah had agreed to the shorter route through Samaritan territory said as much as anything about the gravity of the meeting that would be held tomorrow. The bitter rivalry between the Jews and the Samaritans had begun centuries ago, when soldiers from the conquering armies of Assyria stayed on to garrison the land. They intermarried with the poorest class of the people who had not been taken captive. According to the Jews, the Samaritans mixed the true worship of Jehovah with pagan influences and therefore were rejected by God. To this day, Samaria, which occupied the central highlands between Judea and Galilee, was seen by the Jews as a slice of foreign soil stuck into the heart of the Holy Land, and it galled the Jews unendingly.

Many Judeans, especially the Pharisees, believed that any contact with the Samaritans, or even with the soil on which they lived, brought spiritual defilement. So when traveling to the north, instead of taking the direct route through the heartland of the country, they went east from Jerusalem down to Jericho, turned up the valley of the River Jordan, and finally cut back into Galilee above Beth Shean. This bypassed the hated Samaria and Samaritans altogether. It also added a full day to the journey, which, as far as Miriam was concerned, was way too much hate.

Miriam turned and saw that the Galilean watched Azariah as well, his face a picture of disgust. He started slightly when he realized Miriam's eyes were on him. Straightening, he became instantly brusque. "Eat! When Daniel comes we must leave. We still have some way to go before nightfall." With that he took the rest of the food and started over into the trees to join his other two men.

Yehuda watched him go, then turned to Livia. "Are you feeling better?" he asked.

Livia's head dropped slightly, and red spread quickly across her cheeks. "Yes, thank you." The knot on the side of her head had gone down somewhat, replaced by a large, ugly bruise on her temple. Yet even in the shade of the trees, Miriam could see that her face was still somewhat pale.

"Good," Yehuda rumbled. Then with a look that also mirrored his disapproval, he glanced at Azariah, still deep in his ablutions, shook his head, and moved away. He stepped across the creek easily, then dropped to one knee and scooped up water in one hand in order to drink. Finished, he went to join his other companions for their meal.

Miriam turned and smiled at Livia, who blushed all the more deeply under her gaze. She almost teased her servant about her obvious embarrassment, but then decided it might not be appropriate. None of these four men wore a ring on their index finger, nor did they have the armband that also signified either marriage or betrothal. Those tokens were not universally worn, but they were common enough that Miriam had just assumed none of their rescuers was married. Yehuda's open interest and solicitousness for Livia supported that idea, but she wanted to be sure before she encouraged Livia in any way. And yet, as the rabbis summarized the stages of a man's life, eighteen was the age given for marriage. All four of their rescuers were in their early twenties —Yehuda was probably the oldest, twenty-four or twenty-five, she guessed—and it would be a little unusual if none of them was married.

And then she suddenly realized she didn't really care one way or the other. She was terribly tired. Her feet hurt, and the smell of the bread made her realize that she was ravenous. She ate hungrily, then drank deeply from the stream. It was not melon spears and chilled apple nectar; nevertheless, it tasted as good as anything she had eaten in a long time.

II

Miriam opened her eyes slowly. For a moment she was disoriented; then she saw Yehuda, the bear, a few paces away, stretched out flat on his back, his chest rising and falling slowly. Azariah, chief of the Pharisees and member of the Great Sanhedrin, was propped against a tree a little farther on, his head back and his mouth open in the fulness of his beard. His snoring made a soft raspy sound. She turned her head the other way. Her father and Livia were also stretched out, nestled on a thick bed of dead pine needles. Just a few paces away from her, the Galilean sat beside the stream. Another man sat beside him—one they hadn't seen before. So this must be Daniel. As he turned his head to speak to the Galilean, she saw the clear resemblance to Yehuda, although he was definitely younger, about the same age as his leader. Then as she realized what Daniel's presence signified, she groaned inwardly. They would be moving again soon.

Miriam turned on her side, laying her head on one arm, and studied the man who had saved her from Moshe Ya'abin. This morning he had walked into the camp like a lion—regal, confident, dangerous. It was not surprising that Yehuda and the other men, all of whom seemed older than him, should accept him as their leader. One sensed a supple power beneath the lithe, easy grace of his movement. There was also a sureness of purpose, almost to the point of implacability.

Her eyes narrowed as the light caught him across the chest and shoulders. The way he was bent over left his tunic open to the waist. She squinted a little, peering more closely. Starting just below where his tunic had left his skin white, she saw an angry red slash, standing out so vividly against the whiteness of his skin that it shocked her. She shuddered inwardly, only barely able to imagine what had made such a terrible gash in the flesh. It was at least two handspans in length and straight as an—she stopped herself. She had been about to say straight as an arrow, but now she knew the better metaphor. It was as straight as the edge of a sword.

Then he leaned back, and the scar was gone.

A noise behind her made her sit up. Yehuda was still flat on his back, but his eyes were opened, watching her. "That's Daniel."

"Yes, he looks like you," she whispered, mindful that the others were still sleeping.

He nodded gravely. "Not everyone is born with such good fortune."

She clamped a hand over her mouth to cut off the laugh that had exploded from her.

He grinned lazily. "My mother was some woman," he said earnestly. "Can you imagine producing two such handsome devils?"

She laughed softly, in control again. "No. She must be very proud of you."

His grin faded. "She died several years ago now."

"I'm sorry."

He waved that away with his hand, obviously not wanting to say more. Then his eyes moved back to the two men downstream from them. There was clear affection in his eyes now. "Look at him, would you—hanging on every word. You'd think it was Simeon who had been father and mother to him instead of me. He never—"

"Simeon?" Miriam said in surprise. The Galilean actually had a name?

Yehuda looked surprised. "Of course. Had we not spoken his name before now?"

She shook her head.

"Sorry. That is Simeon, son of David of Capernaum, though some of us prefer to call him *Ha'keedohn*."

Miriam jerked bolt upright. "The Javelin? Simeon is the Javelin?"

Yehuda laughed, a deep rumble in his chest. "So you have heard of Ha'keedohn?"

She sat back, staring. Ha'keedohn, the Javelin, was the name that was most frequently mentioned of late in the Great Sanhedrin in Jerusalem. He was the worst of what the Zealot movement was capable of producing. A charismatic leader. A fearless fighter. Daring. Bold. Reckless. So bitter was his hatred against everything Roman that they said even the most hardened rebels spoke his name with a touch of awe. It was men like the Javelin who were the reason for the meeting in Sepphoris.

She leaned back, her mind still reeling. Then she realized that Simeon and Daniel were staring at her. Evidently they had heard her burst out, though she hoped they had not heard her words.

Seeing that Yehuda was awake now as well, the two stood up and came over to join them. She realized that her face was hot as he looked at her curiously.

"Isn't this where Gideon destroyed the Midianites?" she asked to cover her embarrassment.

"Yes. This is 'Ein Harod,' the Spring of Trembling."

She nodded. One of Miriam's favorite stories from Jewish history, recorded in the book of Judges, was the story of Gideon. Called by the Lord to help throw off the yoke of the Midianites, Gideon sent out a call to the twelve tribes for men to join the army. More than thirty thousand soldiers had answered that call. The Lord told Gideon that was too many, that he wanted Israel to know the victory belonged to the Lord and not their own force of arms. When Gideon invited those who so desired to return home, twenty thousand immediately left. Miriam loved that part. Better to identify the fainthearted then, than in the heat of battle. But the Lord said ten thousand was still too many. When they reached a small brook, the very brook where they now were, the Lord told Gideon to watch how the remaining men got a drink. If they set aside their weapons and lay flat on their stomachs, they were to be rejected. If they dropped to one knee and scooped up water in their hand, all the time watching for possible attack, they were chosen. Of the original thirty-two thousand men, only three hundred were retained, but with that three hundred a great battle was won that night.

Miriam explained why she had asked her question. "I thought of Gideon when I saw Yehuda stop to drink at the stream earlier."

Simeon's eyes flicked to his friend.

Miriam turned to Yehuda, glad for this diversion. "You didn't lie down," Miriam said to him. "You scooped up water in your hand, just like Gideon's men."

"It is a good thing," Simeon growled, "for when Yehuda lies on his stomach it takes a windlass and a team of oxen to get him up again."

Miriam swung back in surprise. Though his face was still sober, the sand-brown eyes were laughing at his friend. He was actually making a joke!

Adjusting the quiver he was using for a pillow, Yehuda winked at Miriam and then closed his eyes again. "When the puppies yap at the heels of the bull, only the puppies are impressed by the noise."

Livia had sat up beside Miriam. She clapped her hands in delight. "Well said," she exclaimed.

Yehuda turned and gave her a warm smile, pleased with her response.

"Please," Simeon pleaded, flashing a startlingly boyish look at Livia, "don't encourage him. The only thing about Yehuda that is as large as a bull is the size of his pride."

Yehuda closed his eyes again. "The pup is fortunate that the bull is contented and full."

"And unable to get up," Daniel said dryly. Before Yehuda could retort to that one, Azariah the Pharisee suddenly woke up. He straightened, clearing his throat. Mordechai ben Uzziel also rolled over and sat up. As suddenly as it had come, the humor in the man they called the Javelin was gone, and the bowstring tautness was back. He watched with narrow eyes as the Pharisee went to the stream and washed carefully before reaching for more of the food.

Everyone was aware of the sudden change of mood except for Azariah, who was humming some tuneless melody to himself as he munched on a large slice of cheese.

Finally Simeon let his eyes come back to Miriam. This time she did not flinch under the probing gaze, but met it steadily. "We have moved with much haste since this morning," she said softly. "I fear we have not properly thanked the five of you for what you did this morning."

He shrugged, but she wouldn't let him brush it aside. "Each of us has much to be grateful for." She felt an involuntary shudder as the searing memory of Ya'abin's hot breath on her neck hit her. "I, most of all."

He nodded soberly; then the humor touched his eyes again. "Actually, I think it is Ya'abin who owes us a debt of gratitude. Once inside that tent, I don't think we could have saved him from you any longer."

She flushed, realizing that what she saw on his face was genuine praise.

Yehuda finally got up to a sitting position, but it was his brother who spoke. "Had we delayed any longer," Daniel said, he too with admiration in his eyes, "there wouldn't have been a man left in camp without a mark from your dagger."

Miriam felt a little thrill of pride. She understood that these men did not give praise lightly. Then the humor in Simeon's eyes went out again as sharply as a candle blown by the wind. He turned to look at Miriam's father. "Why do you bring women with you into the countryside when it is common knowledge that men like Moshe Ya'abin roam unchecked?"

Her father reared back a little, caught completely off guard by the swiftness of the change and the bitterness in the accusation. When he spoke, his own voice had a touch of asperity in it. "Who I travel with and why is my affair. We hired those extra men to guard us. If it hadn't been for my steward's treachery—"

"My father didn't want me to come," Miriam cut in quickly, irritated by the sudden switch in mood. "But I serve as an informal scribe to the Great Sanhedrin, and they asked that I come in that capacity." Which was not completely true. As a scribe Miriam could write almost as fast as a person could speak, and so she had done much work for her father, some of which included his responsibilities on the Great Council. When she learned he was going, she asked to come. He had refused, noting there was a slight chance of danger. But she hated it when she was alone, and besides that, her father had business in Caesarea after they finished their business in the Galilee. She loved Caesarea and the beaches surrounding it. So while in most matters the will of Mordechai ben Uzziel was unbending, in this case he had finally surrendered to Miriam's insistence, learning that he had raised a daughter with a strong will of her own. That was when he had asked Joab, the steward, to hire six additional men to guard their party on the road north. As if that was enough!

Simeon suddenly looked bored with such foolishness and looked away. To Miriam's surprise, Livia cleared her throat nervously, wanting to speak. Simeon turned back. She brushed at a strand of the blond hair that had picked up a pine needle. "I also thank you," she said nervously. "When I think what could have happened to mistress Miriam, I—"

"And to you as well," Simeon snapped.

"To all of us," Mordechai broke in smoothly. "We are most grateful that you happened by at such a fortuitous time."

The Javelin and his men quickly exchanged glances. Miriam caught it and suddenly understood. "You didn't just happen by, did you?"

Yehuda grinned but didn't answer. Daniel shook his head slowly.

She turned to Simeon. "Did you?"

There was an almost imperceptible shake of the head.

Surprisingly it was one of the other two men who spoke next. "We followed you from the moment you left the Hill of Samuel, north of Jerusalem. We knew Ya'abin was in the area but did not expect betrayal from within your own camp. He was in control before we could stop him."

Azariah had forgotten his food and was likewise staring at their rescuers. He spoke to Simeon. "But why were you following us?"

He didn't answer. Yehuda stood up, brushing the needles from the back of his tunic. "It is a dangerous time to travel in Judea. The men of Sepphoris thought it would be well if you had an escort."

Mordechai's head came up sharply. "Sepphoris? You know of that meeting?"

Again Simeon just watched them, not answering. Miriam was tempted to turn to her father and blurt out, "Do you know who this is? This is Ha'keedohn, the infamous Javelin." But she held her peace. She wasn't sure if Simeon had heard what Yehuda had told her. If not, she didn't want him to know that she knew.

And then her father seemed to accept the fact that he wasn't going to get an answer. He nodded, looking at Simeon. "However it came about, we are grateful for the consideration of your leaders in sending an escort. And I, along with my daughter and her servant, offer my thanks to you for your timely intervention in our behalf. I will tell your leaders as much when I see them tomorrow."

Simeon half listened, absently rubbing a spot on his left calf with his other sandal. Miriam's eyes followed the motion, then stayed locked there when he lowered the foot again. Here were more scars. These were nothing like the one on his chest, but they still made her shiver a little. Three parallel lines ran vertically down his leg from just below the knee almost to the ankle. It looked as though a huge cat had raked her claws down his shins and left him permanently branded. This young lion had seen his share of conflict.

Simeon was suddenly impatient and looked at Livia. "We have about three more hours before we reach the place where we stay the night. Are you strong enough to continue that much longer if we keep you on the donkey?"

"I am fine now. I can walk."

Yehuda stepped forward and once again lifted her as though he were lifting a bag of goose feathers and plopped her atop the donkey. "If Yehuda says you are to ride, you shall ride."

Simeon looked curious now. "You are not Jewish, are you?"

Livia was startled by the question and looked down. "She is Greek," Miriam answered for her.

The bronzed rescuer swung on her sharply. "Do you view your slave as an ox who cannot speak for herself?"

Miriam recoiled as though she had been slapped. "No, I . . . "

"She is a woman! A person! Let her speak for herself."

"I know what she is!" Miriam shot back, stung deeply. "And she is not my slave, only my servant."

"Only my servant," he mimicked sarcastically. He swung back to Livia, cutting off Miriam's retort. "How did you come to be a *servant*?" The last word was spoken with heavy mockery.

Livia ducked her head, biting her lip.

"Well?" he demanded.

"My parents were slaves to a wealthy Roman patrician in Alexandria. When he lost his fortune through foolish business dealings, we were sold to pay his creditors."

Miriam stared at the pale girl standing next to her. Livia was two years older than Miriam, and Miriam's feelings toward her were more like that of a sister than a servant. Her father had brought her to their house five years ago, and in all that time Miriam had assumed her family to be dead. She realized with a stab of guilt that she had never really asked.

"Where is your family now?" the Galilean persisted, gentle now as he addressed her.

Tears welled up and trickled down her cheeks. "I don't know," she whispered.

Simeon's face was like flint as he turned on Miriam. "Moses made the selling of another human being punishable by death. So today we pious Jews let the Romans do the unacceptable for us."

"She's not a slave," Miriam said, realizing how weak it sounded even as she spoke.

He shook his head in disgust. "If you lash a burden on a donkey, calling him a horse doesn't make the burden feel any lighter."

He spun abruptly and started away, the disgust clearly written on his face.

Mordechai, Azariah, and, surprisingly, Yehuda all began to speak at once, springing to Miriam's defense, but it was Livia's voice that cut through them all.

"I was not finished speaking!" she cried.

Simeon of Capernaum stopped; then in the sudden silence, he turned slowly back around to face her. Livia brushed at her cheeks angrily, then took a deep breath. "Mordechai ben Uzziel purchased me in the slave markets of Alexandria five years ago. On the day of the purchase he gave me my freedom."

"That's right!" Mordechai said. "I gave her the papers too."

"You freed her to be your servant?" the Galilean cried. "Hail, O noble Mordechai!"

Mordechai was slapping at his leg angrily. Not many in all of Judea dared speak to him in that tone. "I don't care what you did this morning, young Simeon. You will not—"

"Please!" Livia said sharply. "May I finish?"

Mordechai was shocked into silence. Around the house Livia barely raised her eyes to meet his glance, let alone speak to him. But Livia did not wait to see his reaction. She whirled back to face the Javelin.

"This morning . . . " She took a deep breath. "When that filthy animal grabbed Miriam, in one instant I knew that—" She turned to Miriam. The tears spilled over and ran down her cheeks, and she made no effort to hide them. "I knew that I was willing to die for her if necessary. She is my family now and . . . "

Her voice broke, and she dropped her chin. Stepping forward,

Miriam touched her arm, her own eyes suddenly burning. Livia raised her head to meet the gaze of the man confronting them. "And when Miriam stepped in front of me to shield me from the man with the bow, I also knew that she was willing to give her life for me."

Again her voice caught. She stopped, bit her lip, staring at the ground. Then her head came up proudly. "If that is what it means to be a servant, then I accept it gladly, for it is something I never had when I was a slave."

Miriam threw her arms around her, crying openly now too. Livia's words had touched her more deeply than anything she could ever remember. For a long moment they clung to each other, then finally pulled apart and faced the Galilean together.

But all anger had left him now. He nodded, looking at Livia. "I understand," he said quietly. "I'm sorry." His eyes moved to Miriam and held hers for a long moment. She could still see the anger lying just below the surface, but she also thought she could detect a touch of shame there as well.

Then he swung around abruptly to Yehuda. "We must go," he said. "Daniel, you take the lead now. I'll watch our back trail." Without waiting for an answer he strode away, out of the trees and into the bright afternoon sunshine, setting his face to the north.

Daniel cleared his throat, breaking the awkward silence. "Get your things."

The other men with him looked a little sheepish, and they all three moved away together. The gentle bear Yehuda sighed and shook his head. "I'm sorry," he said, speaking to Miriam. "Our friend Simeon has many devils that roost in his rafters. Sometimes he forgets to drive them away."

"I would say that the devils are more in his heart," muttered Azariah.

Yehuda stiffened, instantly cold. "What would you know of his heart?" he exclaimed. "You don't even know your own heart, Pharisee. Don't try to judge the heart of another."

Miriam looked away. She had to press her hands against the sides of her skirt, so hot was the indignation and shame burning inside her. Earlier, she had thought of this man as the lion, and so he would continue to be—strong, solitary, almost majestic in his aloofness. But Ha'keedohn was the better title. He was hard, unbendable, cold as sharpened steel. Or maybe he would just be Simeon. Simeon the brave but ill-mannered Galilean.

She felt a touch on her arm and looked up into Yehuda's enormous brown eyes, now saddened. "If it makes you feel better, it is a rare thing for Simeon to apologize."

"He didn't apologize to *me*," she blurted. "He apologized to Livia."

His smile was slow and sorrowful. "So you weren't watching his eyes then?"

Miriam's head came up, and her eyes widened. She *had* seen something there.

Yehuda shrugged and turned to the two representatives from the Great Sanhedrin. "Come," he commanded. "We have much farther to go before you can rest."

CHAPTER 4

THE STROKE OF THE WHIP MAKETH MARKS IN THE FLESH,
BUT THE STROKE OF THE TONGUE BREAKETH BONES.

—Second Epistle of Pontianus

I

22 MARCH, A.D. 30

The rabbis had a saying: "Judea is wheat, Galilee straw, beyond Jordan, only chaff."

As the little column of weary people made their way through the verdant countryside of the upper Galilee, Miriam thought of that statement and shook her head. How like the arrogance of those in Jerusalem. Whoever had come up with that was more clever than wise. The latter rains, those that came in the late winter and early spring (as opposed to the first rains, which came in the late fall and early winter), had left the entire landscape bathed in brilliant greens. The grass alongside the pathway was as high as the donkey's belly. Entire hill-sides were a riotous splash of color, as though someone had punched holes in the rainbow and it had spilled its dazzling load across the fertile earth. One narrow valley had been so filled with wildflowers it was as if they were fording a river of scarlet as they passed through it.

They were not together any longer, but spread out over about a quarter of a mile. The two whom Miriam did not know by name were in the lead now. With their destination nearby now, they were striding eagerly out ahead. Azariah the Pharisee came along just behind them, astonishing everyone with his tireless ability to keep pace with the younger men. About fifty paces behind those three, Miriam's father hobbled along by himself, leaning heavily on a thick walking stick he had found somewhere along the way.

Miriam understood only too well why he hobbled so badly. She could no longer distinguish individual sources of pain on the bottoms of her feet. Though she hadn't looked, she was sure they were one large mass of blistered flesh now. And if hers were like that, what must her father be suffering?

Daniel followed close behind her father, watching him to make sure he was going to make this last few hundred paces.

Directly in front of Miriam, Yehuda walked ahead of the donkey on which Livia still rode, holding the halter rope. Though he was half a head taller than any of the other men and probably outweighed Simeon by half again, Yehuda moved with effortless ease, swinging along as though they had come only a few paces, rather than many miles.

And what of his brother Daniel, Miriam wondered. He had followed Ya'abin for who knew how far before he doubled back to catch up with the rest of them. How many miles had he walked today? But like his older brother, he showed no signs of tiring.

As for Miriam, she followed wearily along behind the donkey. She had stayed close to the animal all afternoon, reaching out to hang on to its tail from time to time if the trail got particularly steep. Somewhere behind them, Simeon was bringing up the rear. Or Ha'keedohn, she corrected herself. That was still so astonishing to her that she had to rehearse it again and again in her mind. She had heard his name mentioned so many times by members of the Council that she had half expected him to be taller than Goliath and more fearsome than a battering ram.

She didn't turn to see if he was still in sight. Sometimes he was; other times he disappeared.

"Are you ready?"

She lifted her head. Yehuda had slowed his step, walking backwards now as he looked at his two charges. They were coming around a bend where the path hugged the side of a hill. It was opening up into another of the small mountain valleys that seemed to be everywhere up here.

"Ready for what?" Livia asked, craning her neck to try to see around him.

"Are you ready for a sight that will leave your eyes dazzled forevermore?"

Livia's laugh filled the air. Even Miriam managed a smile. His enthusiasm was as boundless as his endurance. Then she smiled even more. Without thinking, the Greek word had come to her mind: *enthousiasmos*. From *en-theos*, literally meaning to have a god within you. Though she realized that Livia was partially bringing this exuberance out in Yehuda, it was also his natural zest for life. Enthusiasm was a fitting word for Yehuda the Zealot.

The big man saw her smiling. He wagged his finger at her. "Oh, daughter of Jerusalem," he intoned, "after what you are about to see, you shall never be satisfied with your drab and lifeless city again."

Miriam laughed aloud. "Are all Galileans so shameless?"

Still walking backwards, Yehuda half turned his head to see where they were, then stepped to one side, giving a grand flourish. "Behold my humble home, the village of Beth Neelah."

About two arrow shots away, nestled in a lush cradle of pines and oak, the simple houses of a small farming village were bathed in the last rays of the setting sun. Built of the white limestone that was so common in all of the Holy Land, the buildings glowed like golden brooches fastened on a tapestry of royal green. Miriam stopped, her breath drawing in. For a moment the burning pain in her feet was forgotten. She heard Livia give a soft "oh."

Yehuda hooted. "I warned you now, did I not?"

"It is lovely!" Livia exclaimed, slipping off the animal's back as it came to a stop. She moved over to stand next to Miriam.

"It is, Yehuda," Miriam agreed. "It is beautiful." Her eyes took the sight in, and she felt a quiet peace come over her. "Beth Neelah," she mused. "The House of Joy. A name as lovely as its setting."

Suddenly aware of someone's presence behind them, Miriam turned and saw Simeon just coming around the bend behind them. When he saw the three of them there, he shook his head. "Ah, Yehuda, are you touting the glories of the village again?"

"But of course," he said happily.

Simeon sighed in mock weariness and spoke to the women. "If he could put Beth Neelah into goatskin bottles, he would try to sell it to every person who walked by."

"Aye," the big man answered, "and what a simple way to make a fortune."

"Is this your home too?" Miriam asked, pleased to see that his mood seemed to have improved again.

For a moment Simeon seemed startled by the question, but then he shook his head. "No, I am only an adopted son."

Then she remembered that Yehuda had told her that Simeon was from Capernaum, down on the shores of the Sea of Kinnereth. "The rest of us are from here," Yehuda explained when it was clear Simeon wasn't going to volunteer any more information, "but Simeon has been cursed to dwell in the lowlands." He gave his friend a pitying look. "It is a lovely little place, but . . . " He turned and looked at his village as if the view said it all.

"You make more noise than a ram's horn," Simeon responded.

"Stop your trumpeting and let us get these people to a place where they can stop at last."

"Of course," Yehuda said, not in the least bit deflated by his friend's pretended sourness. "Come, let me introduce you to our village."

Miriam started to smile, then had to remind herself that this bantering was going on between a Zealot warrior and Ha'keedohn, one of the most virulent of the Zealot leaders. It was so foreign to her expectations that she was still having a difficult time assimilating it. She had come expecting—what? she wondered. Men more like Ya'abin? Men who hid behind masks or beneath hoods?

Without thinking, she stepped forward, putting her full weight on the ball of her foot. She gave a sharp cry and nearly stumbled. Livia reached out quickly and grabbed her arm.

"What is it?" Yehuda said, moving in beside her.

"It's nothing. I—" She glanced at Simeon. "My feet have grown a little tender, I fear."

"You ride the rest of the way," Livia said, taking her elbow more firmly. "I'm fine now."

Looking down so that the two men wouldn't see the tears of pain that had sprung to her eyes, Miriam shook her head. "We're almost there."

"Miriam, really. You ride. My head is fine now."

Miriam shrugged off Livia's grasp and started up the trail, fighting with every shred of willpower not to wince. Out of the corner of her eye she saw Simeon nod in Yehuda's direction. Suddenly she was swooped upward, Yehuda's fingertips nearly touching as his massive hands encircled her waist. He set her gently on the back of the donkey and took the halter. "The Javelin has spoken." He grinned. Yehuda apparently found it hugely amusing that Miriam had been so shocked to learn that Simeon was the infamous Ha'keedohn.

They had barely started again when a noise drew their attention. The lead ones in their party were just approaching the village and had been sighted. A cry went up, and almost instantly the place erupted into life. Children raced out, whooping and shouting. A dozen dogs followed right on their heels, barking furiously. In a moment the women and older girls appeared, their high-pitched voices echoing off the hills. Miriam saw one woman plow into the two lead Galileans and throw her arms around one of them. Then another figure broke loose from the group, waving and shouting. Waist-long black hair streamed out behind her as she careened down the path. She raced past Miriam's father and blasted into Daniel. Miriam could hear her squeal as he lifted her and spun her around. But the moment her feet touched the ground again, she was off once more. Now she left the path to take a more direct route. She came toward them like a young gazelle, leaping over stones and darting through the brush.

"Shana!" Yehuda dropped the halter rope and ran forward. They met a moment later, and the young woman flung herself across the last several feet into his outstretched arms. For a moment it looked as though the slim figure would be completely crushed in the awesome bear hug that encircled her, but there was no cry of pain, only a breathless, "Yehuda! Yehuda!"

Livia and Miriam looked at each other, a little taken aback by the ferocity of the welcome. Was this the answer to the question as to whether Yehuda was married? But finally he pried loose the arms that were locked around his neck and, with a giant grin, turned his attacker around to face Miriam and Livia. "Shana, I want you to meet some-one." His pride in presenting Beth Neelah had been evident before. It was nothing compared to what they saw on his face now. "This is Miriam bat Mordechai ben Uzziel, daughter of one of the most impor-tant men in all of Jerusalem. And," he turned slightly, "this is Livia of Alexandria."

Livia flushed even as she smiled, and Miriam sensed how deeply it pleased her that Yehuda had not added, "and maidservant to Miriam."

The big man put his arm around the girl's shoulder. "And this is my sister, Shana."

Shana nodded in greeting. *Of course!* She had the same enormous brown eyes that made Yehuda seem so gentle. Now those eyes were filled with unabashed curiosity as Shana slowly scrutinized the two women before her.

Yehuda nudged her a little. "That was Mordechai, the important man of whom I just spoke, that you nearly knocked down as you ran to greet Daniel."

"Oh." Shana didn't seem at all contrite. She was still eyeing Miriam and Livia. She was perhaps a year or two younger than Miriam, and though clothed in simple Galilean homespun, she was remarkably lovely. Her facial features were flawless and set in equally flawless skin. She had a girlish freshness that only heightened the loveliness of the woman. There was no mistaking her relationship to Yehuda, since she was a replica in miniature.

After a moment she lifted her head. There was an instant transformation. "*Shalom*, Simeon," she said softly, her eyes lowering behind thick dark lashes.

"Peace to you also, Shana. How are things with your house?"

Miriam watched half in surprise, half in amusement at the change that had so swiftly transformed the breathless, eager girl into a demure and shy young woman. Shana's eyes studied the rocks on the pathway with meticulous attention. It was hard to believe this was the same person who just moments before had tumbled down the hill with such wild abandon.

"Things are well, thank you." Her head came up, and she gave Simeon a dazzling smile. It was clear that the rest of them had been totally forgotten.

Yehuda cut in now. "Come! We are tired and hungry and nearly home. We have guests, Shana. We must show them why our village is called the House of Joy."

II

Among the Jews it was always said that one "went up" to Jerusalem. While Miriam knew that was literally true, since the city sat astride the central Judean highlands between the Great Sea on the west and the Sea of Salt on the east, the phrase implied far more than a topographical change. To go to Jerusalem was to ascend—emotionally, intellectually, spiritually. The populace of the city looked down with condescension on those Jews so unfortunate as to dwell outside the Holy City. Surrounding Judeans were viewed with a slight touch of pity, but tolerated, for they at least had the common sense to live close to the city of God. But the Galileans? The urbane and worldly wise Jerusalemites spoke of them with barely disguised contempt. They were peasants—not only ignorant and unlearned but, what was infinitely worse, content to stay that way. Their slaughter of the Aramaic language was the constant butt of ridicule. A common joke among the Judeans was that if a Galilean asked for a lamb, one could not tell whether he asked for *immar*, a lamb; *chamar*, an ass; *hamar*, wine; or *amar*, wool.

With a touch of shame, Miriam realized that to the Jerusalemite, the Galilean was slow, oafish, crude, and earthy. Occasionally one might hear a Jerusalemite admit, but only with some reluctance, that the Galileans were also known for their warmhearted openness, their unrestrained hospitality, and their uncompromising honesty. They were men of the soil and the sea, and this kept them much more in touch with the deeper values of life than their urban cousins. They had also traditionally furnished the fiercest warriors in Israel's battles.

As Miriam sat near the fire in the open square of Beth Neelah, she admitted to herself that she had been guilty of these feelings towards

Galileans. Now she was envious. Perhaps it was because they had not been confined to the twisting, garbage-strewn ruts that passed for streets in Jerusalem. They had not had to learn to deal with the sophistries of the street vendors, who could change the weights on their scales with the swiftness of a master magician. Nor had they been forced to learn the intricate and endless hypocrisies of conversation that filled the homes of Jerusalem's finest. Maybe that explained their openness and their love for life.

The whole village—about three hundred souls—had made the occasion of the return of Simeon's men and their guests into a minor festival. The four native sons were given a family's welcome, and Simeon had clearly been right when he said he was an adopted son of the village, for he was welcomed as warmly. But to her complete surprise, the four strangers from Jerusalem were accepted without restraint. Though simple, the food had been carted out without measure. Roast lamb, dates, olives, grapes, fresh vegetables—the makeshift tables groaned with the load. Again it was with a twinge of guilty conscience that Miriam wondered what it would have been like had the situation been reversed and the Galileans visited Jerusalem.

Even sour Azariah the Pharisee had been noticeably impressed to the point that his muttered grumblings about the events of the day finally ceased. The excellent wine had mellowed his crusty exterior, and he became warm and expansive. Half the village gathered around him now as he told story after story, leaving them laughing uproariously one moment and in tears the next. Miriam was amazed to see this side of Jerusalem's leading Pharisee. She suspected that not many in the Great Sanhedrin knew this Azariah.

At that moment Shana reappeared, winning a ripple of approval from the crowd. She carried several timbrels, a sistrum, and a wooden flute. Instantly the villagers spread out across the square, and in a moment the area was cleared. Shana thrust the flute into the reluctant hands of her brother Daniel, then passed out the other instruments to waiting women. A hush descended over the square, and for a moment the only sound in the night was the crackling of the fire. Then Daniel put the flute to his lips and began to play.

At first he played without accompaniment, his eyes closed, his face a flickering mirror of the firelight. The sound was haunting, almost hypnotic in its lonely melancholy. Then gradually, almost imperceptibly, there was a subtle change of mood. The tempo increased and the sadness gave way, first to happiness and then to joyful abandon. Shana began to beat the circular timbrel with its metal rattles against her leg. Soon the other women joined, the strumming of the sistrum blending in. Quickly now, the beat became more powerful, almost impelling, causing the body to respond without conscious thought.

Suddenly Yehuda was on his feet, followed almost instantly by a dozen others. He faced Shana, who was now beating the timbrel rapidly with the tips of her fingers in a counter rhythm to the others. With great soberness Yehuda's feet began to move in time to the music. Like the music itself, the dance was completely extemporaneous and unrehearsed, but it was as though Yehuda's feet and Daniel's fingers were attuned to the same inward sound. And the villagers were connected to that same invisible source, for they followed Yehuda's lead with precise execution and effortless grace, the men on one side, the women on the other, as was the Jewish way. Miriam watched, fascinated. This too was the way of her people—spontaneous music, the improvised dance—but rarely had she seen it performed with such flawless execution.

Livia was sitting beside Miriam. She leaned over and whispered into her ear. "Look at your father."

Here was a second surprise for Miriam. A short distance away, across the fire from them, Mordechai ben Uzziel was clapping his hands rhythmically in time with the beat of the timbrels. The lines of weariness, so evident earlier, had vanished. He was smiling broadly and obviously enjoying himself. Miriam had not yet told him that their rescuer was none other than Ha'keedohn himself. She had started to while they were eating supper, then decided that she did not want to ruin what was proving to be a very pleasant evening.

"I think he would be up dancing were it not for his feet," Miriam smiled.

"Yes," Livia agreed. She turned to look at the dancers. "And how does Azariah do it? He has walked as far as you and your father."

Miriam shook her head as she turned and watched the small, round figure of the Pharisee. He had the skirts of his robe pulled up slightly, and with his side curls bouncing and bobbing, he kept in step, as agile and quick as any man in the circle. "He must walk everywhere in Jerusalem. I don't think he has raised so much as a single blister."

"He is like a young boy. It is hard to believe it is the same person."

Miriam's head turned slightly. Not far from where her father was, Simeon sat with his two men and their families. "It is interesting," she mused softly to Livia. "Yehuda and Daniel and Azariah dance. My father wishes to. But Simeon sits. It is almost like the music has not even touched him."

Before Livia could respond they were both startled by a figure looming over them. It was Yehuda, smiling down at them. "You have escaped the hands of Moshe Ya'abin," he said, his breath coming quickly from his exertions. "Is that not reason for celebration?"

"Indeed," Miriam answered with a smile. "But unfortunately my feet have danced over too many pathways for one day."

Yehuda's face fell, and he instantly dropped to one knee to examine her feet. There was a quick intake of air, and he gave a low whistle. "No wonder you walk with pain in your eyes. We must put something on them or you will have infection tomorrow. I will have Shana get it."

"No," Miriam said, aware now that Simeon was watching the interchange. Then more softly she added, "It can wait until after the dance."

Yehuda hesitated, then nodded. He turned to Livia, who was suddenly staring at the fire with intense concentration.

Miriam smiled. "*Your* feet are not blistered, Livia."

She looked down at her hands, her fingers twisting at her sash.

"Well?" Miriam persisted. "Does your head still hurt?"

"No, but I—" Her eyes flicked to Yehuda then dropped again, and she colored even more deeply. "I have not danced for many years."

"Aha!" Yehuda cried, grasping her hands and pulling her up. "Blistered feet are an acceptable excuse. Leaden feet are not. Come! I shall teach you."

From the dancing villagers came a warm cry of approval, and the women quickly made a place for Livia in the line. The pace of the music slowed as Yehuda boomed out instructions, and Shana took Livia's hand and began to walk her through some steps. Miriam watched, first in pleased amusement, then in growing thoughtfulness. Perhaps it had been years since Livia had danced, but either she had danced a great deal in her youth or she had an abundance of natural talent. Very quickly, to the delight of the villagers collectively and Yehuda in particular, Daniel brought the music back up to full tempo, and Livia was one with the others.

This was a night for new insights, thought Miriam. Azariah enthralling the crowds with his stories, then dancing like a young boy. Her father clapping his hands in time to the music. Livia, dancing like a sprite.

Miriam jumped slightly. A figure had moved over to stand in front of her. Her dark eyes widened as she looked up and saw who it was.

"I didn't mean to startle you," Simeon said.

"Oh . . . I was just watching the dancers." Her voice trailed off, and she looked away just in time to see Shana miss a step and flash her a sharp look. It was an unmistakable signal. "Stay away." But Miriam was trying to cope with the fact that Simeon was standing there, watching her steadily. She didn't have time to worry about Shana.

He dropped into a crouch directly in front of her. "How are your feet?" he asked. He was between her and the fire, which left his face in deep shadow and impossible to read. Nor did his voice give any clue. Was he compassionate? angry? irritated?

"I . . . They'll be all right," she murmured. "They just need a rest." She started to draw her feet back up and under her, but he reached out quickly and grabbed an ankle. Before she had time to react, he was probing at them gently. She winced, biting her lip. As he gave a low whistle, she looked up at him. "I walk all the time in Jerusalem. I don't understand why they are so tender today."

"Thirty miles?"

"What?"

"Do you walk thirty miles in one day?"

He was closer now, and she could see his features more clearly. They were not angry or irritated, only filled with gentleness.

"Is that how far we came?" she murmured.

He nodded. "I'm sorry. We had to be sure we were clear of Ya'abin."

She shuddered. "I would walk sixty miles to be clear of him." Then, suddenly aware that he still held her ankle, she pulled it away, and he sat back on his heels. At that moment one of the young boys came trotting up, a small clay jar and some thick folds of cloth in his hands.

Simeon nodded, and the boy squatted down next to Miriam's feet. "This will help," Simeon said. Then to the boy he added. "Be gentle. Her feet are very bad." Then to Miriam he said, "This is Adar, Yehuda's nephew."

Miriam wrinkled her nose as Adar swiped out a smear of dark brown, foul-smelling paste on his fingers. "What does it do?" she asked.

Adar shrugged, smiling shyly. Simeon answered for him. "Deadens the pain, fights the infection, toughens the skin." He flashed her a quick look. "It may hurt a little."

It didn't hurt a little. It hurt a lot, so much so that Miriam had to dig her fingernails into the dirt to stifle the cry that welled up in her throat. The boy worked swiftly but with surprising gentleness. "You can cry out if it helps," he said.

"I wouldn't dare," she muttered between clenched teeth.

Simeon's eyes widened slightly. "Why not?"

Because I don't want you to think that I am a soft and coddled woman of Jerusalem. But aloud, forcing a lightness into her voice, she said only, "It might throw the dancers off their step."

His eyes narrowed, and he gave her a long, scrutinizing look. Gratefully, the paste was now taking effect, and the pain diminished rapidly once she had endured the searing agony of having it smeared on. Finally Adar finished and sat back on his heels. "There."

Miriam took a deep breath and tipped her head back, letting her long hair brush the ground. She was aware that both Adar and Simeon were watching her, but she didn't care. A delicious numbness was stealing across the soles of her feet, and that was all that really mattered. "Oh, that's wonderful!" she sighed. "I can't believe how quickly it works."

Simeon nodded, then to the boy motioned with his head toward where Mordechai was sitting. "I think her father is also in need of treatment." Nodding, Adar handed Simeon one of the folded cloths, then left them and walked over to Mordechai.

"Thank you," Miriam said, watching as Adar began working on her father's feet. "His blisters are worse even than mine."

"This will fix them."

"What is it, anyway? It smells terrible."

Simeon tore the cloth into two equal strips, then handed them to her. As she started to wrap them around her feet, he smiled faintly. "Fuller's soap, tanning acid, myrrh. It is also mixed with a touch of camel's milk and three measures of powdered pomegranate seed."

Miriam's head came up slowly, and she just stared at him in disbelief. "Really?"

"It is a secret formula that has been in Yehuda's family for generations. It's good for blisters, sunburn, toothache, leprosy, and gout. It can also be used for softening saddle leather, killing scorpions, greasing the winepress, or—"

"Stop!" Miriam cried, breaking into laughter. Could this be the same man who just a few hours earlier had lashed at her for keeping Livia as a servant?

A tiny smile finally cracked through his somberness, and he looked steadily at her until she regained her composure.

"You don't know what's in it, do you?" she finally said.

"Am I so transparent?" he said sadly.

"I'm afraid so."

He turned to watch the dancers. Miriam finished wrapping her feet, then looked over at him. The firelight played on his face, softening the line of his jaw and smoothing the chiseled features. She dropped her eyes quickly when he turned back, then let her gaze move to Adar, who was just finishing his administrations to her father's feet. The young boy looked up, saw her watching him, and flashed her a quick smile.

"Adar obviously thinks a great deal of you," Miriam said, returning his smile across the fire.

Simeon turned to look, and she could see the muscles along his jaw soften. "He is at an age when he is easily impressed."

Miriam didn't think that was the only explanation but didn't say anything. In the shadows she could see the top portion of the terrible scar across Simeon's chest, and she noted again the three parallel scars down his one leg. When a man carried badges such as these, she thought, it was no wonder that the eyes of young boys were wide with adoration. She was tempted for a moment to ask about them, about what terrible thing had happened to leave him so marred, but of course she didn't. She finally settled for a safer question. "Do you have other family?"

He nodded. "I have a younger brother the same age as Adar. His name is Joseph, after my grandfather. I also have a sister, Leah. She is fifteen, just two years younger than Shana. She and Leah are best of friends. And then I have an older brother who is married with two children."

"And your father is a merchant in Capernaum?"

He gave a quick nod. "He and my mother will both be at Sepphoris tomorrow."

"Oh." Then the impact of his words hit her and her eyes widened. "In Sepphoris? At the meeting?"

He stood abruptly. A smile was on his lips, but it had a certain grimness to it. "Yes. My father is a member of the local Sanhedrin in Capernaum. He will represent our city with your father and Azariah. My mother will accompany him."

She was staring, completely astonished. "So your parents are leaders in the Zealot movement as well?"

He gave a short, mirthless laugh. "My father would not agree with that assessment. In fact, he would vehemently object, but my mother would take it as a compliment." Now he turned sardonic. "It's hard to believe, isn't it? On the outside we Zealots look just like normal, ordinary people, not the fierce barbarians that we really are?"

She flushed instantly. He was not angry, but there had been a slight edge to his jibe. "I—" Still reeling, she decided to change the subject. "A woman is allowed to sit in on the meetings in Sepphoris?"

"*You* will be there," he reminded her with a touch of irony.

"I will sit in the back corner and record the proceedings. You sound as though your mother will be a representative at the table."

For several seconds he just stood there and looked at her, and now she could feel the coldness returning. "Does the name Judah of Gamla mean anything to you?"

That caught her off guard, but she immediately nodded. "Of course. I assume you refer to the Judah who was a priest somewhere up here. About twenty-five or thirty years ago, in partnership with a Pharisee named Zadock, he started a revolt against Rome when the Syrian legate called for a new census. As I understand it, he was the founder of the whole Zealot movement. Is that the Judah to whom you refer?"

"It is."

"Then I know of him. Who doesn't? Why do you ask?"

Again there was a long pause, as if he hadn't made up his mind whether to say more. Then he went on quietly. "Judah of Gamla was my mother's uncle."

"What?" she blurted.

"Her father and mother, another uncle, and three cousins—all in addition to Judah—were either killed in the war, captured and crucified by Quirinius, or died while being hunted down like jackals."

Miriam's mouth was open a little. She had thought she had gone beyond surprise when she learned that Simeon was the Javelin.

"As a fifteen-year-old girl, my mother fought the Romans along with the other surviving members of her family." Again there was that mocking smile. "I think she will not be asked to leave if she comes to the meeting."

Miriam didn't know what to say. Here again was this stark contradiction. The Zealots were tearing the nation apart, throwing them into a crisis of national concern. Could they really be the same people she saw now—the likeable Yehuda and his brother, the lovely Shana, and the rest of the warmhearted villagers of Beth Neelah?

He watched her, seemingly amused at the reaction he had triggered.

"And while I am expanding your education, there is probably something else you ought to know."

"What?"

"Did you wonder where the parents of Yehuda and Daniel and Shana are tonight during all this celebration?"

"I—" While they had been eating, Livia had noted that the brothers and sister didn't seem to have any other immediate family here. Then she realized what he was suggesting. "Not them too?"

Simeon nodded gravely. "Though not directly related, Yehuda was named for Judah of Gamla. His father also fought in the rebellion. Though he escaped that initial defeat, he was killed about ten years ago when his band was ambushed and caught by a Roman cohort in the Jordan Valley. The Romans tortured the men to try to learn the names of other resistance leaders. When they refused to betray their companions, the Romans crucified them, then took their wives and children and sold them into slavery."

Miriam closed her eyes, feeling sick. Simeon's words were slamming into her like missiles from a catapult. Yehuda had told her his mother was dead, but . . .

"On their way to Ptolemais, where they were to be put on a slave galley headed for Rome, Yehuda killed one of the guards and got away with Shana and Daniel. He was fourteen years old. Daniel was twelve. Shana was seven. Yehuda learned later that his mother and younger brother never made it to Ptolemais. They don't know if they were executed as punishment for the escape, or if they died under the shock of it all."

Miriam sought for something to say. She felt as if she had just swallowed a powerful emetic and was going to throw up.

Any anger in Simeon was strangely gone. Instead there was a deep, lingering sorrow now in his voice. "You can rest for most of the day tomorrow. We won't leave for Sepphoris until afternoon. It is only two hours from here." His eyes held hers for a moment, dark and gloomy in the firelight. "But for tonight, enjoy the welcome of this simple village. I fear that tomorrow you shall learn just how truly far apart Galilee and Jerusalem really are."

CHAPTER NOTES

Beth Neelah is a fictional village but is pictured by the author to be in the general vicinity of Jotapata, Sepphoris, Nazareth, and Cana in the hill country west of the Sea of Galilee. All other places mentioned thus far in the novel are actual places from that time period.

The common unit of distance in New Testament times was the Roman mile. The Roman mile is somewhat shorter than our modern statute mile, the former being 1,620 yards, the latter 1,760. In most places in the novel, the difference doesn't matter and the term *mile* is used without trying to be exact to either.

Judah (or Yehudah in its Hebrew form) of Gamla, a town in northern Galilee, is credited with being the founder of the Zealot movement. The Zealots' beginnings seem to have been triggered by the census taken by Quirinius around the beginning of the Christian era. We know from contemporary historians such as Josephus that Judah and many in his movement were eventually caught by the Romans and killed but that others in his family carried on the Zealot tradition he started (Brandon, pp. 634–35).

CHAPTER 5

HE HAS PLACED BEFORE YOU FIRE AND WATER;
STRETCH OUT YOUR HAND FOR WHICHEVER YOU WISH.

—*Wisdom of Sirach 15:16*

I

23 MARCH, A.D. 30

"Simeon, wake up!" Joseph shook his older brother roughly. "Wake up!"

It said a lot for how safe Simeon felt in Beth Neelah that he was not instantly awake and reaching for his sword. When the last dance of the night before had been finished and the fire had died down to glowing embers, Simeon had taken his bedroll down to the far end of an olive orchard. He had no wish to be bothered by someone still loquacious from too much wine. There beneath the stars he promptly fell into a deep, untroubled sleep. He now rolled over, staring up at the face above him.

"Joseph?" He rubbed his eyes. "What are you doing here?"

"Mama and Papa are here. I came with them."

He rose up on one elbow with a jerk. "Here?"

"Yes. They arrived a few minutes ago. Papa wants to speak with you."

Simeon threw back his blanket and tied his tunic around him. He noted that the sun was still behind the hill, though out in the valley to the west of them the land was bathed in full sunlight. That meant his parents could not have come from Capernaum this morning. That was a six- or seven-hour walk from here. They had to have come to Cana or one of the other nearby villages last night. He wondered why. His mother had said only that they would meet him in Sepphoris at the Zealot council.

He threw back his bedroll and reached for his sandals. As he laced them up, he looked at his youngest brother. "Will you roll up my stuff and bring it up to the house?"

"Can I shoot your bow, Simeon?"

He smiled and ruffled Joseph's hair. "If you promise to get everything back to the house, we'll go shooting after we eat."

"Great!" Then he pointed. "They're at Yehuda's house."

II

When Simeon came around the corner of the home where Yehuda and Shana lived, his father and mother were both waiting for him outside. His mother gave a low cry and ran to meet him. He held out his arms and gave her a vigorous hug. "Good morning, Mother."

"*Shalom*, Simeon." She kissed his cheek. "Are you all right? Yehuda said you had some unexpected trouble."

"Yes, but nothing we couldn't handle."

"Good morning, Son."

Simeon released his mother and grasped his father's outstretched hand. "*Shalom*, Father."

"Yehuda said it was Moshe Ya'abin." His father's face was grim.

"Yes." Simeon frowned. "I'm going to recommend to the

brotherhood that we send someone after him and the others like him. They run at will in Judea, and the Romans do nothing. It is our people who are being bled by that swine."

Just then Yehuda came out the door. He reached up and touched the *mezuzah*, then came on, smiling at the sight of the reunion.

"Where's Leah?" Simeon asked his mother. "Didn't she come with you?"

Deborah nodded. "Of course. She is in with Shana. She and I are going to stay here for a couple of days and visit with Naomi."

Simeon started to nod. Naomi was his mother's widowed cousin; she had come up to Beth Neelah to live with her daughter after her husband died. Then he remembered and looked at her more closely. "But what about the meeting?"

David answered for her. "There's not going to be any meeting."

"What?" The exclamation had come from both Yehuda and Simeon.

David blew out his breath in disgust. "There was a major clash in the Council yesterday. The Sepphoris leadership sent word down that they don't want the group from Gischala included. They say they are too radical. That, of course, infuriated the Gischala leaders, and they convinced the towns of Chorazin and Bethsaida that if Gischala wasn't included, then none of them would come. So they canceled the whole thing." He threw up his hands. "If our people could ever just once unite—truly be one—we wouldn't need a Messiah to deliver us. The Romans would have no choice but to leave."

Simeon couldn't believe it. "So after all of that—going all the way down to Jerusalem, taking on Ya'abin, coming thirty miles in one day so the delegation would be out of danger—now the meeting is canceled?" He exhaled in disgust. "What is the matter with these people?"

"The delegation from Jerusalem is not going to be pleased to hear this," Yehuda said. "Why didn't they decide this three days ago?"

There was no good answer to that, so David said nothing. He let them fume for a time before he went on. "It's just as well," he said.

Simeon snorted softly. "I agree. I have never thought trying to make an alliance with Jerusalem was a wise move."

"That's not what I was referring to," David said.

Simeon finally turned to him. "What?"

"I brought your mother and Leah and Joseph up here for a visit because I want you to go to Bethabara with me and Ephraim."

He was bewildered. "Bethabara?"

"Yes, down in Perea. It's not far from Jericho."

Deborah came in now, amused. "It's such a famous place that none of us have ever heard of it before."

"What's in Bethabara?"

His father seemed suddenly hesitant. "We need to go down to Jericho and see to the date harvest contracts anyway."

Simeon looked at his mother, sensing his father was stalling for some reason.

"Just tell him, David," Deborah said.

He nodded and began. "There's a man preaching down there. He's called John the Baptist."

Yehuda stirred. "I've heard of him. They say great multitudes are going out to hear him."

"They are," David answered.

"Not another self-proclaimed Messiah!" Simeon cried.

Deborah laughed. Those had been almost her exact words. How like her was this son of theirs.

David gave Simeon the same explanation he had given her, then told him quickly about John claiming to be the forerunner of the Messiah.

Simeon's eyes narrowed. "Do you think that's really possible?"

"Andrew and Simon were very impressed. They are convinced he speaks the truth."

Deborah was watching her husband now, her eyes soft. "Your father is determined to go see for himself," she said to Simeon. "Simon and Andrew are not easily swayed by foolish prattle. I find it hard to believe that it could really be, but—" She became quite firm now. "I don't want your father making this journey down into Judea alone, Simeon. Once you leave Galilee, the roads are no longer safe." She looked away. "Particularly with the likes of Moshe Ya'abin around."

"We need to go to Jericho anyway," David stressed again.

Simeon shrugged. That was true. He was skeptical about this John, but on the other hand, if he really were . . . The implications of that were staggering. He turned to Yehuda. "How about it?"

His friend shook his head. "Daniel and I have left Shana to care for things too much as it is. I'd better stay."

That wasn't unexpected. He turned to his father. "When do you want to leave?"

"Now."

"You mean *right* now?"

He nodded. "Shana and Leah are preparing food for us. We need to stop in Capernaum and get Ephraim, so the sooner we start the better. Your mother and Leah and Joseph will come back tomorrow or the next day. Yehuda will send someone from the village with them."

"All right." Simeon turned to his mother. "You'll have to tell our visitors from Jerusalem what's happened."

"That pompous old Pharisee will burst a blood vessel, I'll wager," Yehuda said.

"It's Mordechai the Sadducee who's in charge of the delegation," Simeon explained. "He's the man with the real power." Then he had a thought. "They're going to need an escort back to Jerusalem."

Yehuda grunted. "Mordechai told me that he has business in Caesarea after the meeting. I guess Daniel and I could see them safely to the coast. The Roman presence is strong there. They'll be all right after that."

Simeon grinned wickedly. "I thought you had to stay here. Volunteering to escort them wouldn't have anything to do with that young woman servant, would it?"

Yehuda cuffed him on the shoulder. "How would you like to go to Bethabara on a stretcher?" he growled.

They all laughed at Simeon's pained expression.

"Go see to the food, David," Deborah said. "Since you're taking my son away from me again, I want to spend a few more minutes with him."

Her husband nodded, and he and Yehuda went back into the house. Simeon turned immediately to his mother. "I'm surprised you are as positive about this John as you are," he said.

She grew thoughtful. "Andrew has convinced your father there is something to all of this." She shrugged. "And who knows? Andrew and Simon are not ones to be blown off their feet by any little breeze."

"True." There weren't many men who were more conservative and solid than those two brothers.

Deborah put her arm around his waist and began to walk with him. "Your father believes that the Messiah is the answer to all the problems that lie before us. If he would come, then it would not be up to the Zealots to rise up and overthrow Rome."

"Unless it is *by* the power of the Zealots that he rises up and overthrows Rome. His armies have to come from somewhere, and Father seems not to have considered that."

Deborah seemed to sense his thoughts. "Your father is a wise man, Simeon. I wouldn't want you to think that because I have doubts about this, I don't respect his judgment. It *is* important that we continue to watch for the Messiah. It's just that—" She stopped to collect her thoughts. "Every generation since the ten tribes were taken captive by Assyria has thought theirs would be the one to see the Messiah finally come. It seems almost unbelievable that it really could be ours."

"True," he answered, "and yet someday he will come, and that generation will probably say exactly what you just said."

"I know. And you are right. When he does come, he is going to need the brave and the faithful to stand with him, sword in hand."

"I want to be one of them."

She smiled sadly. "It frightens me terribly, but I want that for you too. It would be a way to bring our family justice after all these years, to give some meaning to the sacrifice my mother and father and others in the family made. And yet, when I think of things like yesterday with Ya'abin, my whole body goes cold with fear for you."

"The death of your family is not the only debt waiting to be paid," he said bitterly.

She sighed, suddenly feeling very tired. "Nothing permanent happened to Leah and me, Simeon, thanks to your father. And your wound is healed now. It's time to forget about vengeance for what happened that day."

He shook his head, quick and hard. "When I think of how close you and Leah—" He stopped, his eyes so cold now that it frightened her a little.

She laid a hand on his arm. "To be a true Zealot means that we are filled with faith and with courage. It does not mean that we are consumed with blind anger."

He barely heard her, and she decided there was something else he should know. "Simeon?"

"Yes."

"There is another reason why this trip to Bethabara is important to your father."

"What is it?"

"I'd rather he tell you. It's something that he has not spoken of to you before."

"Oh?"

"I think it's time you knew. Just wait for the right moment, and then ask him to tell you about Bethlehem."

"And that's it?" he said, smiling now. "You're going to make me wait after dangling a piece of bait like that in front of me?"

She smiled softly. "Your father is a brave man, Son. Because he is not filled with the same passion as you and me doesn't mean that he lacks the courage to do whatever is required."

Simeon looked surprised. "I've never doubted that."

"Ask him about Bethlehem," she said again. "It will help you understand why he is so driven to hear this John and see if he is the forerunner."

"I will," he said. His mood had lightened again. "I promised Joseph that I would take him out shooting this morning. Will you tell him why I can't?"

"Yes." Then she cocked her head. "Yehuda tells me that the daughter of Mordechai ben Uzziel is very beautiful."

He looked at her sharply. "What is that supposed to mean?"

She shrugged innocently. "That was just what he said."

"She is the daughter of Jerusalem's richest and most powerful Sadducee. Did you think you raised a fool for a son?"

She shook her head sadly. "No, unfortunately, you have never had the luxury of being a fool. But is she as beautiful as Yehuda says?"

He laughed. "You told me once that your father raised you to be a Zealot first and a woman second. Are you asking this question as a Zealot or as a mother?"

She nudged him gently, smiling a secretive smile. "This early on a beautiful spring morning, I think it is all right if I am a mother first, don't you?"

He chuckled and gave her a squeeze, then instantly sobered again. "As you said, Miriam is the daughter of a rich and powerful man, Mother. She probably spends more on perfume than the village of Beth Neelah spends on food in a year. What more is there to say?"

That seemed to satisfy her, and she started walking slowly again. "And what of Shana, Simeon? She is as lovely as the lilies of the valley, and you would not have to worry about how much she spends on perfume."

Simeon laughed softly. "Mother, you are incorrigible."

"Well, you are twenty-one now and not even betrothed yet. The rabbis think you are rapidly becoming a danger to society."

"You just want more grandchildren."

She nodded immediately. "Other people my age have half a dozen or more by now. I have only two because my second oldest son seems to be afraid to marry."

"I'm not afraid. It's just that—well, for one thing, Shana is only seventeen."

"The age when most young women marry," she said pointedly.

"I know. And I like Shana. Very much. She would make a good wife."

"Would or will?"

He hesitated. "It is not much of a life to be married to a Zealot, Mother. You know that as well as anyone."

"Shana is a Zealot to the core. She and Yehuda and Daniel have paid the price. She would never stand in the way of what you are doing." She hesitated. "Do you know why I oppose a marriage between Leah and Daniel?"

He stopped dead. "I didn't know you did oppose it."

"Well, it's not in the formal stages yet. Leah is only fifteen. But I have discouraged it when Yehuda has brought it up with your father."

"Why?"

"Because she has your father's gentle heart. She weeps when she sees a bird with a broken wing. Being the wife of a Zealot would be very difficult for her."

Simeon nodded slowly. "I think it would destroy her."

"But not Shana," Deborah said. "She is very strong."

He was thoughtful now. "She's very much like you in that respect," he said.

"So why do you continue to hesitate? You are ready. She is ready, Simeon. All you have to do is watch her eyes whenever your name is mentioned. It will still be another year before you are wed."

"I know, but—" And then he stopped. His mother was right. The battle with Rome could drag on for years. Would he go without a family all that time? If he had to choose, a woman like Miriam was only a passing fantasy. Shana would not only support him in his life of opposition against Rome, she would be a good wife. She too was beautiful. She was a good friend and companion. He finally looked at his mother. "No, you are right. Shana would make a good wife."

One eyebrow lifted. "Would or will?" she asked again.

He laughed at her, shaking his head. How he loved this gracious and wonderful woman, with all the depth of soul that she possessed. "She *will* make a good wife," he answered.

She grabbed his arm. "Do you mean that?"

"I do."

"Enough that I might speak to your father about it?"

He hesitated and then plunged. "Yes."

"Wonderful." She took his arm, very happy now. "Now," she said with sudden impishness, "if only we can convince Shana that you are not such a brute."

He laughed, and she laid her head against his shoulder. They walked on slowly, enjoying this moment together.

III

Mordechai ben Uzziel was fuming. "Is there nothing we can do?" he demanded of the woman who stood before him. "Why didn't your husband stay here to help us? They say that he commands great respect among the Zealot leaders."

"He does," Deborah of Capernaum said evenly. "But I am sad to say that some of our fellow Galileans have bones in their head that are thicker than a weaver's beam. Even a man of my husband's stature cannot pierce through that. He tried to reason with them yesterday and failed, even though he did not agree with the meeting to begin with."

The daughter of Mordechai ben Uzziel suppressed a smile. Miriam liked this Deborah, mother of Simeon. She was as slender as a reed, but there was nothing but pure sinew inside.

Azariah exploded. "So just like that, there is no meeting? We have come a long distance and faced much peril." There was a little shudder. "I even consented to come by way of Samaria. And now they simply refuse to meet with us?"

"This is most disturbing," Miriam's father agreed. "Most disturbing."

"If you knew much of the Zealots," Deborah said quietly, unperturbed by the anger of these two luminaries from Jerusalem, "you would not have put yourself in such peril in the first place. You seek what you call accommodation with Rome. Well, we don't use such a fancy word. We simply call it surrender. We call it a pact with the devil. Here in the Galilee, we believe that if you take an adder into your bosom, no matter how good the reasons may be, one of you will die, and it will likely not be the adder."

"Now listen—" Azariah began to sputter, his angry movement causing his side curls to bob wildly.

Deborah went on calmly, cutting him off. "Even if today's meeting had not been canceled, you would have gone home with your bag still heavy with gold and your agreement unsullied by the mark of a pen."

"What does a woman know of such matters?" Azariah snapped.

Deborah's eyes narrowed. "A woman knows that it will be her sons whose blood is spilt trying to win back what those in Jerusalem trade away in order to maintain their velvet thrones and marbled halls."

Azariah didn't even give her the satisfaction of a reaction. He looked at Mordechai. "I say we go to Sepphoris in any case. We have the funds. Let those fools from Gischala and Chorazin stay away if they wish. They will find out soon enough what they might have had if they had not been so stubborn."

Yehuda had stood back with his arms folded while Deborah had explained the situation to their guests. Now the big Galilean spoke for the first time. "For strangers to venture alone into Sepphoris in times such as these is a good way to prove once and for all who is the greater fool here."

"And you won't take us?" Mordechai asked.

Yehuda shook his head. "Not unless you are invited. I am not a fool either."

"Then we have come for nothing."

Miriam turned to her father. "Perhaps if we wrote a letter and sent it." She looked to Deborah. "Would you be willing to carry it for us?"

"If they won't receive Mordechai or myself," Azariah harrumphed, "they won't receive a woman."

Miriam turned slowly, her eyes turning glacial. "Must you be so—" She searched for the right word. "So like yourself, Azariah? There is no need for rudeness."

He ignored her. "I say we go to Capernaum," he said to Miriam's father. "I am good friends with Amram, leader of the Pharisees there. He has told me secretly that if we fail in Sepphoris we perhaps could make other arrangements that would still be profitable."

Mordechai's temper snapped. "You heard the Great Council as well as I, Azariah. We are authorized to make no agreements save the ones they have already approved."

He turned to Deborah. "I apologize for my associate's manners. Would you consider taking a letter to Sepphoris in our behalf?"

Deborah glanced at Yehuda, who nodded. Then she spoke, "We will. I make no promises, for I think your request will fall on deaf ears.

But if that is your wish, then I know it would be the wish of my husband that we at least try."

"Thank you." Ignoring the protests coming from Azariah, Mordechai turned to Miriam. "Get your writing things. I would like to do that immediately."

IV

"You do not find the Zealot way at all to your liking, do you?" Deborah asked.

Miriam looked up in surprise. "I—" She thought quickly. What Simeon had told her last night about his mother still left her feeling strangely confused. And yet Miriam too was frustrated that they had come so far and at such risk only to run into a wall of stone. She took a quick breath. "I do not agree with what Rome stands for, nor with what they do. But neither do I believe that blind faith can offset the power of an empire. If we do not make some accommodation to reality, there will be no more Zealots or Sadducees, or Judea or Galilee or anything else."

Deborah nodded, watching as Miriam carefully sprinkled a dusting of fine sand on the ink, let it absorb the liquid for a moment, then blew it away.

Miriam rolled the parchment up carefully, then held the stick of red wax over the flame of the candle that burned on the table beside her. When it was soft, she pressed the sealing wax over the edge of the paper, then immediately took her father's signet ring and pressed his mark into the wax. She blew on it, making sure it had hardened, then handed the scroll to Deborah.

When she realized that this woman wasn't going to respond to her comment, Miriam almost let it go, relieved in a way that her own answer had not brought a stinging rebuke. But something inside her could not let it pass.

"May I ask you a question?" she said, putting her writing materials back in the bag.

"Of course."

"A few minutes ago you spoke of mothers whose sons may spill their blood trying to make things right. Doesn't it concern you—" She caught herself. Of course it concerned her. Miriam had no wish to sound arrogant or condescending. She started again. "And what if you send your sons to war and it all proves to make no difference? What if it is a war that we cannot possibly win?"

Deborah slipped the scroll inside her robe. She started to turn, still not answering, then thought better of it. "May I tell you a story?"

"Yes."

"Not so very long ago, a family who lived near here was visited by Roman soldiers, come to enforce an unjust tax assessment. Even though everyone, including the Roman officer, knew that this assessment was terribly unjust, the direct product of a corrupt system upheld by Rome, no one was willing to take a stand against it. No one dared stand up to the *Roman way*." She spit out those last two words with complete disdain. "The father had gone to raise the money but had been delayed in his return. The family explained all of this to the soldiers, but even though he believed them, the Roman officer would not give them an extension."

Her voice had gone very quiet now, and Miriam leaned forward, watching her closely, hanging on every word. At first she had thought it was going to be a parable or allegory of some kind. The Galileans were famous for those. But now she knew she was hearing a description of an actual event.

"The officer ordered the house and all that the family owned to be seized and the mother and her children to be sold into slavery."

She looked directly into Miriam's eyes. "It was fruitless to resist.

There was no way anyone in this family could make a difference. There were well over a hundred soldiers either in the courtyard or outside in the street. There was no way that family could possibly win. None."

Miriam colored as she realized Deborah had deliberately chosen to use Miriam's own words.

"But one of the family decided that he had to act. He didn't consider the danger. He didn't stop and add up the numbers or calculate the possibility of winning. He decided to do what was right, not what was safe. He was wounded terribly that day. It nearly cost him his life, in fact."

Miriam was suddenly aghast. "I saw Simeon's scar," she whispered. "It was him, wasn't it."

Deborah's eyes were glistening as she looked out the window of Yehuda's small home. "Another man came the following day and confronted the Romans. It was foolish and stupid. There was no way that he could change the mind of Rome, and yet he did. He freed his wife and daughter and saved them from an unthinkable fate."

"I'm sorry," Miriam said, for the first time beginning to understand what made the Zealots so frightening to the Jerusalem leadership, and for the first time wondering if her father and the others were right in what they were doing.

Deborah's eyes came back and held Miriam fast. "Tell me, Miriam of Jerusalem. If you were to ask that family if blind faith is a foolish thing, what do you suppose they would say?"

Miriam couldn't answer and had to look away.

Deborah's eyes softened as she lifted the scroll. "Thank you. I will bring a response from Sepphoris as soon as possible." She made as though to leave, then stopped again. "Do you know why my son wears no beard?"

Caught completely off guard by the question, Miriam could only shake her head. "I had noticed," she mumbled, "and wondered."

"It is so that he can enter Tiberias or any other Gentile city and pass himself off as a Roman." She bit her lip. "Do you know what that does for me as a mother? To know that he walks into the lair of the lion and tweaks his whiskers?"

Miriam nodded numbly, pummeled by the pain in Deborah's eyes.

"Well, I am the one who told Simeon to go clean-shaven because that's how strongly I feel about what must be done."

Miriam was staring at her writing materials. She could not bear to meet Deborah's burning eyes. "I'm sorry," is again all she could manage to say.

As she started for the door, Deborah stopped for a moment beside the table where Miriam sat. She breathed deeply. "That smells wonderful," she said with a tiny smile. "What perfume is it that you wear?"

Surprised, Miriam looked up. "It—It's from Ephesus. They call it the Rose of Diana."

"It's very lovely." And with that, Deborah of Capernaum went out the door, leaving the daughter of Mordechai ben Uzziel to stare after her, deeply regretful that she had been so foolish as to speak her mind in this matter.

CHAPTER 6

BUT THOU, BETHLEHEM EPHRATAH, THOUGH THOU BE LITTLE
AMONG THE THOUSANDS OF JUDAH, YET OUT OF THEE SHALL HE
COME FORTH UNTO ME THAT IS TO BE THE RULER IN ISRAEL; WHOSE
GOINGS FORTH HAVE BEEN FROM OF OLD, FROM EVERLASTING.

—Micah 5:2

I

23 MARCH, A.D. 30

Simeon and his father took the road that led northeast out of Beth Neelah. They passed through the village of Cana, then began dropping swiftly down the sides of the "bowl" in which the Sea of Kinnereth nestled. As they moved down the narrow road that snaked its way back and forth from the tops of the ridges to the shores of the sea, they looked directly down on the city of Tiberias. Located at the site of some hot springs that sprang from the mountainside on the western shore of the lake, Tiberias was the most Gentile city in this part of Galilee.

Built by Herod Antipas, son of Herod the Great, and named for the emperor as a way of gaining favor with Rome, the city had very few Jewish inhabitants. Though he did not know it at the time he began construction, Antipas chose a site that covered part of an ancient burial ground. In the Torah any contact with a dead body was said to defile a person. When the Jews learned that the city was being built on a graveyard, all but the most secular of them refused to live there.

That Jewish attitude was fine with the Romans and the other Gentiles. Tiberias was one of the few places a Roman citizen could walk down the streets without feeling a thousand eyes of hate raking over him. It was also a beautiful city, built largely of marble and stone in the finest Roman style. The Herods were masters at currying favor with the emperor.

Simeon and his father often visited the city, which was about ten miles south of Capernaum, because a prosperous part of their business was bringing in the supplies needed to keep a city running. The more devout of the Jews would not sell directly to Gentiles because they believed that contact with the *goyim*, or Gentiles, as they called all non-Jews, defiled them. Simeon's father viewed that as ridiculous. Defilement came in many ways, but not through interaction with a non-Jew. So David had set up contacts with various merchants in Tiberias—a butcher, two different bakers, a spice monger, a sandal-maker, and the city's largest supplier of woven goods. He brought in the raw materials they needed and in turn helped them market their finished products not only in Tiberias but in the other towns up and down the shoreline of Kinnereth. The residents of Tiberias were pleased because they liked the quality of the Jewish products, and the Jews that David represented were pleased because they had access to a profitable market without having to compromise their strict standards by dealing with the *goyim* directly.

Leah loved Tiberias and begged to go whenever her father went there. Simeon did not like it at all. In the first place, one could hardly walk a dozen paces without meeting Roman soldiers, a sight that always made his stomach knot up and his flesh crawl a little. The other problem was that Simeon always felt like the inhabitants of the city reacted to the few Jews they saw with one of three emotions—faint condescension, open disdain, or idle curiosity. Each of these three attitudes irritated Simeon so deeply that he always came away angry, so he stayed out of the city as much as possible.

As they came to the junction where the road turned right to Tiberias and left to Capernaum, they turned left, but the sight of Tiberias got David started talking about business. He reviewed the things in Tiberias that needed attention to keep their business running smoothly. That discussion lasted well past Magdala, and only as they approached the little village of Kinnereth did the conversation finally lag.

Simeon waited until he was sure his father was really finished, then spoke. "Father."

"Yes, Son?"

"Mother said you have something to tell me."

One eyebrow lifted. "She did? About what?"

"She said I should ask you about Bethlehem."

His step slowed.

"She said it would help me better understand why you feel so strongly about going south to see this John the Baptist. She said it was time I knew about it."

He said nothing for several moments, then finally nodded.

Simeon grinned. "I didn't think a father was supposed to keep dark secrets from his children."

If he heard, his father made no sign. His eyes were far away and his expression quite solemn. Simeon's smile faded. "What is it, Father? Can you tell me?"

His eyes focused again, and his head slowly bobbed once or twice. "I think your mother is right. It is time that you know."

The sun was high now, and along the shores of the lake the air was hot and humid even though it was still only the end of the month of Adar, just past mid-March as the Romans reckoned the calendar. It was common knowledge in the empire that the Sea of Salt, or the Dead Sea as the Gentiles called it, was far below the level of the Great Sea, the Mediterranean. But outside of the Holy Land, few knew that the Sea of Kinnereth, the Sea of Galilee, was also below the level of the Great Sea, some six hundred feet below that level, if the Roman mapmakers and engineers could be trusted. So even though the temperature in the highlands had been pleasant, at these lower elevations it was getting oppressive, and both father and son were sweating as they walked briskly along.

David pointed to a large fig tree off to one side of the road. "Let's stop for awhile. We're making good time."

"Good." Simeon was very curious now. It would be better to hear this, whatever it was, without being interrupted by someone they knew passing them on the road.

Together they moved over into the deep shade and found a place where the grass was thick and soft. They sat down facing each other and got settled. Now that he had decided to go ahead, David seemed anxious to do so and began immediately.

"What I am about to tell you, I have not spoken of for many years now, except with your mother." He paused, then added. "This happened thirty years ago next month, during Passover season."

"So you and Mother were not married yet." Simeon hadn't really made it a question. He knew that his parents were soon to celebrate the twenty-ninth year of their marriage.

"No. We were betrothed. We had been for almost a year by then, but we didn't marry until the following spring." He paused to collect his thoughts for a moment, then went on. "I used to tell everyone I met about it. I was so excited, so on fire with it. In fact, I felt I had an obligation to do so. But then—" He sighed. "As the years passed and nothing more happened, people began to give me strange looks, or openly scoff. I felt this was too sacred to be treated in such a manner. Once your grandfather died, I—"

"Grandfather was there too?" Simeon cut in, not sure what any of this meant.

"Yes. And your cousin Benjamin." He began to rub his eyes. "When the years became decades and nothing more happened, I began to wonder if I had misunderstood or—" He sighed yet again. "So I decided I would not speak of it openly anymore until I knew more."

"What?" Simeon said, thoroughly puzzled now. "What happened?"

His father looked suddenly sheepish as he realized he had gotten lost in his own memories. He leaned forward and began. "As you know, my father's sister, your great-aunt Sarah, married a Levite. As you also know, the various orders of the priesthood have responsibility for supporting the temple rites. Now that Jerusalem has grown so large, and with tens of thousands coming into the city for the annual feasts, it takes many people to support the operation of the temple. The various courses of the priesthood are responsible for all the practical aspects of keeping the temple operating—cutting wood, purifying the sacred oil for the great *menorah*, preparing the sacrifices, baking the shewbread that is put in the Holy Place each Sabbath."

"Yes." Simeon didn't understand all the complexities of the various courses of the Levites, but he knew that it took literally thousands to do all that had to be done.

"Well, one of those courses is responsible for caring for the animals that are used in the sacrifices. With all of the various offerings—the sin offerings, the trespass offerings, the thank offerings, the daily sacrifices—keeping sufficient sheep on hand is a major task as well. Your Great-Uncle Seth belonged to that order of the Levites who were in charge of the temple flocks, which were tended around Migdal Eder, the fields just north of Bethlehem."

Again Simeon was nodding. His Uncle Seth and Aunt Sarah had both been gone for several years now, and Simeon's memory of them was somewhat blurred, but he knew it was considered a great honor that there was a Levite in the family who served the temple, even though only as a shepherd.

"Our family always went down to Bethlehem and celebrated the Feast of Unleavened Bread and the Passover with Uncle Seth, Aunt Sarah, and Benjamin. They had enough room for us, and Bethlehem is only six miles from Jerusalem, close enough that we could participate in the celebrations at the temple. With hundreds of thousands of people coming to Jerusalem for Passover each season, it is very difficult to find lodging of any kind, so we considered ourselves fortunate."

His face softened in a gentle smile. "It was wonderful. Of all the cousins, Benjamin and I were the closest. He was only a year younger than me, and he and his family would always come to the Galilee in the summer and spend time with us as well. We were more like brothers than cousins."

"I think of Benjamin and Esther more like an uncle and aunt than as my cousins," Simeon agreed. "Of all your family, they are my favorite relatives."

"Yes, I know. Ephraim feels the same. That is why they named little Esther what they did. Well, anyway, in this particular year I was sixteen and Benjamin was fifteen. Our family arrived in Bethlehem a day or two before the Feast of Unleavened Bread was to begin. It was the usual hectic rush. My mother would always help Aunt Sarah clean house and make sure every speck of leaven was removed. They would shop together in the markets to get the *matzos* bread, the bitter herbs, and all the other things we needed for the *seder* meal. It was hectic but a wonderful time.

"One of the things I always enjoyed the most," he went on, "was that Father and I would go out and tend the sheep with Uncle Seth and Benjamin. It's usually lambing season at Passover season, so we would go out and sleep in the fields with them and help make sure none of the newborns was lost." He flashed Simeon a smile. "For a boy who spent his life in the city as the son of a merchant, the shepherd's life seemed wondrous to me."

None of this was new to Simeon. Benjamin and Esther had moved to Jerusalem, but Simeon had often heard his father talk about those earlier times.

Now his father's voice grew soft as the memories came back to him. "This year at first seemed no different from any other. It was Uncle Seth's turn to spend the night out in the fields. He asked my father and me and Benjamin to help. Benjamin and I stayed behind at the house for a little while to help Aunt Sarah do some things, so we were alone as we started out of the city to find my father and uncle.

"Like every other night during Passover, the city was an impossible clog of people. Every street was thronged. You could barely push your way through. You could hear a dozen languages as you made your way, and take in every smell imaginable. It was wonderful.

"Then—" He stopped and his eyes half closed, as though he was picturing it in his mind. "As we made our way along, we were passing this *khan*, a *caravanserai* near the center of Bethlehem. Every place of lodging was full; every room within twenty miles of Jerusalem had long since filled and filled again to overflowing. But this was a large *khan*. We could see into the great center courtyard as we passed. It was filled with camels and donkeys, chickens, pigs, cattle, boys selling food, men taking cages of doves to sell to the temple officers. Around the courtyard people were camped in every vestibule, their cooking fires filling the air with smoke."

He smiled. "For a young man used to the quieter life of Capernaum, it was a grand sight. But anyway, we were passing by this *khan*. Benjamin and I were laughing and talking and not paying much attention to what was going on around us. Then as we passed the door of the keeper of the *khan*, I noticed a man and a woman there, inquiring about lodging. I guess that's why I noticed. I can remember thinking, 'You've only just come to Bethlehem and are looking for a place to stay? Don't you know anything about Bethlehem at Passover time? Everything has been completely filled now for more than a week.' I can remember feeling sorry for them, because from what we could see of the woman's face, she looked like she was sick. I heard her husband say something about needing to find a place where she could rest."

Even though it was a simple account of simple things, there was something in his father's tone that had Simeon completely attentive. He didn't say anything, not wanting to interrupt his father's flow of thought.

"Well, we immediately forgot about them as we went on. Soon we were out of the city and joined my father and Uncle Seth. It was a glorious night. The stars never are quite as bright around Jerusalem as they are up here because of the lights of the city, but they were still beautiful. I remember that Benjamin and I spent a lot of time looking for stray lambs that night, those that were abandoned by their mothers at birth. If you don't get them back to the ewes right away, the mothers won't nurse them anymore."

Simeon's father looked at his hands. He turned them over as if seeing something there he hadn't seen before. "I'm not sure what time it was," he went on, "probably sometime in the second watch. Benjamin and I had fallen asleep, I remember that. My father and Uncle Seth were talking quietly."

He stopped. For a long time he was silent, his eyes down and his face hidden. Just as Simeon was about to prod him by saying something, he began again, but now his voice was very soft and filled with a strange wonder. "I heard my father cry out, and I leaped up, thinking that a wolf or perhaps a thief had come in among us. To my astonishment, a brilliant light was illuminating the whole landscape around us. It was as though it were midday right there where we were."

Simeon felt a little chill run up the back of his spine. "Like midday?"

"Yes. At first I threw my arm across my face. It was too bright to look at. Terror shot through me, and I couldn't so much as cry out. I didn't know what was happening, and it frightened me deeply."

He looked at his son, his eyes wide and filled with a touch of that amazement he had felt thirty years before. "Then I heard a voice. It was like nothing I had ever heard before. 'Fear not,' the voice said."

"A voice?" The chills were coursing up and down Simeon's back, and he felt suddenly cold.

"We were all on our feet by then. I was ready to bolt. Then I looked directly at the light." He paused. "And I saw a figure there."

Simeon felt frozen in both time and space. His eyes were locked on his father's features.

"It was an angel, Simeon. An angel of the Lord, standing there in all of his glory. 'Fear not,' he said again, 'for I bring you good tidings of great joy, which shall be for all people.'"

David took a deep breath, his eyes never leaving Simeon's. "Our minds were reeling, of course, but his words penetrated our hearts like a shaft of fire. 'For unto you is born this day in the city of David, a Savior, which is the Messiah, the Lord.'"

That brought Simeon's head up with a snap. "The Messiah?" It was almost a gasp.

"Yes. The angel said that Christ, the Anointed One, had been born that very day."

Simeon felt like all the blood had drained from his head. He leaned back on his arms to steady himself a little.

"Then he told us that there was a sign by which we would know this babe. We would find him wrapped in swaddling clothes—"

Simeon nodded. It would have been a surprise to find a newborn that hadn't been wrapped up tightly with the long strips of cloth mothers used to keep newborns snug and secure in their cribs.

"—And lying in a manger."

"A *manger?*"

"Yes. That's what the angel said. He will be wrapped in swaddling clothes and lying in a manger. Not a crib. Not a bed. Not a cradle. But in a manger."

"The Messiah of the world born in a *manger?*" Simeon was incredulous.

David nodded slowly, letting Simeon take it all in. When he finally seemed ready, he went on. "As we stood there marveling, suddenly we saw a vision. The heavens opened, and we saw with the angel, a great heavenly host. They were praising the Lord and saying, 'Glory to God in the highest, and on earth, peace and good will toward men.'"

He stopped, and Simeon saw that there were tears in his eyes. "Oh, Simeon, the very thought of it even now makes my whole body tingle with joy. It was the most glorious thing I have ever heard."

Simeon closed his eyes and began to rub at them with his fingertips. Mentally it felt as if he had just stepped in front of one of the great battering rams they kept at the Antonia Fortress in Jerusalem. Finally he opened his eyes and looked at his father.

"You can see why I don't speak of this with just anyone," David said. There was a half smile. "First of all, it is very sacred. Second, when I did tell others, many thought I was mad."

Simeon wasn't sure what to say, how to respond. Finally, lamely, he asked, "So what did you do?"

"Well, that's the rest of the story. The moment the vision closed and we regained our senses, we turned to each other and said that we had to go to Bethlehem and find this wonderful thing that the Lord had made known unto us." He laughed shortly. "You know, to this day I don't remember what we did with the sheep that night. Did we just leave them? Did someone stay behind to watch them? I cannot remember."

"But you went to find the baby?"

"Yes. And we didn't go to the palaces of Jerusalem. We didn't go to any of the finer houses in Bethlehem. We went to a stable. In Bethlehem, as you know, the hills are honeycombed with many limestone caves that are used as stables and sheepfolds. Well, this was one of those. And there in the stable we found the babe and its mother."

"And he really was in the manger?"

His father nodded slowly. "Yes. They had him wrapped in his swaddling clothes, but they had no bed, so they had made a place for him in the hay, there with the animals."

"But why in a stable?"

That look of wonder filled his father's face again. "That was the second shock of the night for Benjamin and me."

"What?"

"When we finally found the place and went in, we—" He stopped, and again the tears overflowed.

"What?" Simeon asked again, unable to wait a moment longer.

"It was the couple we had earlier seen looking for a place to stay. That's why the woman looked sick, Simeon. That's why her husband said she needed to lie down. It was her time. She was heavy with child. And there was no place for them to stay."

As Simeon marveled at what his father was saying, David sighed. "I've wondered since if the keeper of that *khan* didn't take pity on them. Can you imagine having a baby in the middle of a *caravanserai*, with no privacy, with all the noise and tumult and crowds? Maybe it was the innkeeper's stable. I don't know. But that's where the birth took place."

Without being aware of it, Simeon was shaking his head. "That can't be."

"Why?" his father asked, already guessing what Simeon was going to say.

"The Messiah is to be our king, Father. A king isn't born in a stable!"

David's eyes were somewhat amused. "So the angel was wrong, is that it?" Before Simeon could answer, he waved that comment away.

134

Now he sighed, a sound of deep stirrings within him. "Actually, I have pondered long on that, Simeon. For thirty years I have wondered about it."

"And?"

"I don't know. If I had heard this in any other way, my reaction would have been exactly like yours." His head came up. "Why a stable? I don't know. But I do know what I saw and heard that night. That knowledge burns like an unquenchable fire in my breast."

He grew thoughtful now. "There is a more important question than why the stable."

"What?"

There was a long silence, then: "It has been thirty years now, Simeon. Thirty years! Why haven't we heard anything more? Why hasn't he come?" His eyes took on an anguished look. "Where is he now, Simeon? Where is that Messiah who was born in a stable and cradled in a manger?"

Simeon was staring at him. His father was right. That was by far a more pressing question. Where was this Messiah, if that's what he was?

"If John the Baptist is really the forerunner for the Promised One," David concluded, "then maybe he will know where he is."

II

When Simeon and his father reached Capernaum, they immediately sent one of the servants for Ephraim and began packing what they would need for their journey. But they had not been home for half an hour before they heard someone banging on the gate of the courtyard. "I'll get it," Simeon called to his father.

When he opened the gate he was surprised to see Andrew standing there. A fisherman's best time for fishing was during the night, and they typically arrived back with their catch just at sunrise. They would sort the fish, hang out their nets to dry, then go home to sleep for the better part of the day. It was not yet the ninth hour of the day—still mid-afternoon—and the sun was still high in the sky. This was prime sleeping time for them.

"*Shalom,* Simeon."

"*Boker tov,* Andrew. Good afternoon."

"Did your father return with you?"

"Yes. We arrived just a short time ago. He's inside. Come in."

They padded silently across the courtyard and into the spacious home, both pausing to touch the *mezuzah* as they entered. "Father," Simeon called as they shut the door behind them. "Andrew is here."

A moment later David appeared, smiling broadly. "Andrew! How good see you. Simeon and I were going to stop by your home in a little while. We are preparing to leave for Judea and wanted to get some directions on how to find Bethabara."

"I thought as much. That's why I've come."

"Oh?" He motioned to their guest, and the three of them moved over and sat down around the table.

"There is no reason to go now."

David's eyes widened. "Why not?"

"John is in prison."

Both father and son rocked back. "Prison?" David cried.

The fisherman was grim as he nodded quickly. "As I told you before, John has been fearless in denouncing evil. He calls everyone to repentance. Pharisees, Sadducees, Jews, Gentiles. For example, when some publicans asked what they should do, he told them to exact no more than that which was appointed to them."

"Now that would be refreshing," Simeon said dryly. "An honest publican?"

Andrew went on. "Even some Roman soldiers came out to hear him. When they asked what they should do, John told them to do violence to no man, to accuse no man falsely, and to be content with their wages."

Simeon was taken by surprise. "You didn't tell me that, Father." He turned to Andrew again. "He really said that to the soldiers?" If so, that *was* remarkable. By law a Roman soldier could impose his will on the people at any time. He could compel them to give him their cloak if the weather was cold. He could make them carry his pack and march with him for up to one Roman mile. If a soldier made any kind of accusation against a person, no proof was required to substantiate it. Either the person paid whatever the soldier demanded or the accused could be beaten or dragged off to prison. It was the way many soldiers supplemented a legionnaire's meager income.

"Yes, Simeon. It's as I told your father; John is remarkable. This man is different."

"If he is telling Roman soldiers they have to repent, no wonder they threw him into prison."

"It wasn't the Romans. It was Herod Antipas."

They all turned at the sound of the voice. There at the door to the room stood Simeon's uncle, his mother's youngest brother. Simeon stifled a groan. Aaron ben Benjamin, a Pharisee from Sepphoris, was Simeon's personal nemesis and the one thing over which Simeon and his mother clashed regularly.

"*Boker tov*, Aaron. Good day," David said getting to his feet. "Come in." Simeon knew that his father didn't find his brother-in-law all that wonderful either, but unlike Simeon, he had long ago accepted the fact that he was a relative—Deborah's only remaining family member—and so welcomed him warmly and treated him with respect. "What brings you to Capernaum?"

"We heard that Azariah, leader of the Pharisees in Jerusalem, was coming to visit Amram here in Capernaum. Several of us from Sepphoris were invited as well. I would never miss an opportunity like that."

"No," David said dryly, "I don't imagine you would."

If he caught the quiet jab, Aaron gave no sign. He came across the room and, without waiting to be invited, sat down. "Good afternoon, Andrew."

"Hello again, Aaron. It's been a time since I last saw you."

They shook hands; then Aaron turned to his nephew. There was no mistaking the change in his voice when he said simply, "Simeon."

"*Boker tov*, Uncle Aaron."

"What is this about Herod Antipas?" Andrew asked of the new arrival.

"It was Herod who had this John arrested, not the Romans."

"Because of Herodias?" David asked, guessing now what was coming.

"Of course," Aaron said with just a trace of smugness. It pleased him to know something that his brother-in-law did not.

Simeon tried not to frown. This was what bothered him most about his uncle. It was the arrogance, the disdain for the unwashed—which was everyone who didn't know as much as Aaron—his supercilious condescension that he made little effort to hide. These attitudes were all too common among the scribes and the Pharisees, but Aaron had raised them to a high art. Simeon almost chuckled aloud as he remembered a comment his father had once made after Aaron had left them. It was one of the few times he had ever heard his father say anything negative about his brother-in-law. "Aaron was born with a very high opinion of himself," he said, "and he has greatly increased his birthright."

"Yes," Aaron was saying, "Antipas lusts after Herodias. The fact that she is his brother's wife makes no difference. So Antipas divorces his own wife and sends her home to her father. As for Herodias, she has probably engineered the whole thing because Antipas controls a more lucrative kingdom than Philip, so why not change husbands and move up a step or two?"

"The Herods are like poisonous snakes in a field of tall grass," Andrew said, knowing that what Aaron said was very likely true. "It is not safe to walk anywhere when they are around."

"The difference here," he went on, "was that unlike everyone else, the Baptist didn't gossip about the marriage of Antipas and Herodias only behind closed doors. He condemned them both loudly and publicly."

"Yes, he did," Aaron said. "He is courageous; you have to grant him that." It was a grudging admission, and that irritated Simeon. He decided to say something.

"According to Andrew, who heard him on more than one occasion, John spoke against all corruption courageously. Including the pompousness of some religious leaders."

As was intended, Aaron instantly bristled. "Even fools can be courageous, Simeon."

David's hand shot out and grabbed Simeon's arm before he could respond. "All right, that's enough." He looked at Aaron. "I was asking Andrew some questions about John. If that is of interest, you may stay and *listen*." There was a soft emphasis on the last word. Then without waiting for a response, David turned back to Andrew.

"What a bitter disappointment. I really wanted to hear John for myself."

"If you want to learn more," Aaron said tartly, "why don't you come to those who have been trained in the Law?"

Simeon hooted openly. "Because we are not interested in learning how to count leaves on a sprig of mint or determine how many times you have to wash your hands before a meal."

Simeon's father swung on him. "I said that's enough, Simeon."

"Yes, Father." Simeon nodded, embarrassed that his father had been forced to correct him twice in front of his business partner. And yet, that jibe about fools and courage had not referred to John alone; it was meant for Simeon, and both of them knew it.

David shot Aaron a warning look as well, then continued talking with Andrew. Simeon was only half listening now. He was glad his mother wasn't here, for she would have gotten angry with him. How could two people from the same family be so totally, so completely different? Deborah, daughter of Benjamin of Sepphoris, had been orphaned when she was not quite fifteen years of age. Aaron had been ten at the time, and Deborah had become his mother. That tragedy had only deepened Deborah's conversion to the Zealot cause, but somewhere along the way, Aaron had chosen a different path.

It did have a kind of perverse logic to it, Simeon had to admit. The Pharisees believed that Israel had first gone into bondage to Babylon because they had turned away from Jehovah in the reckless worship of false gods. The fact that they were still in bondage some six hundred years later was proof, in the minds of the Pharisees, that God was still not pleased with them. The Zealot answer was to be more courageous in standing up for God's cause, even resorting to violence if necessary. The Pharisaical answer was to bring their lives into stricter compliance to the Law. Then God, pleased at last, would intervene in their behalf. He would be their Deliverer.

One day after a particularly hot interchange between uncle and nephew, David had taken Simeon aside and tried to explain all this. The fact that Simeon's mother vigorously defended Aaron did not mean that she agreed with either his philosophy or his choices. In fact, she strongly disagreed with that philosophy, but she was still more mother than sister to him, and Simeon's clashing with his uncle would only alienate him from his mother. Since then, Simeon had tried to hold his tongue, but sometimes Aaron could be such a—

He shook his head, unable to find a word that adequately described the man who sat across the table from him now, fuming at the imposed silence. His thin face and narrow-set eyes made him look like a pouting child. He was balding from his forehead back, and his beard, light brown and with a touch of red, was thin and uneven. That was a surprise, because his *peyot*, his side curls, were thick and dark brown, literally curling as though they had been wrapped around a hot iron and pressed into that shape. They bobbed gently now as his head moved back and forth to follow the conversation between David and Andrew. With an inward sigh, Simeon focused again on what his father was saying.

"The main reason Ephraim, Simeon, and I were going to Jericho was that I wanted to ask John about the Messiah. If John really is the forerunner, as he says he is, then perhaps he would know if the Messiah has come."

Aaron leaned forward, his mouth working. "This John is not the forerunner that Isaiah foretold. I know that he claims to be, but—"

David turned slowly, his eyes cold now. "Aaron, I'll say it one more time. Andrew and I are having a conversation. If you would like to listen, you are welcome to stay. But I already know how you feel, and I'm sure I'll have additional opportunities to hear about that, so please, let Andrew speak."

Aaron sniffed disdainfully and got to his feet. "If you are not interested in truth, then perhaps I shall go speak with my sister."

"Mother is still in Beth Neelah," Simeon said, surprised but pleased at his father's tartness. "She and Leah won't be home until tomorrow or the day after."

David's voice was kinder now. "You've had a long journey, Aaron. There is food in the kitchen."

"Thank you." He stood and flounced away, obviously in a huff.

David blew out a long breath. "I'm sorry, Andrew. What I was trying to say was, if John is the forerunner, do you think he knows if the Messiah has come?"

"He has," Andrew said quietly.

David's head came up slowly. Simeon was also staring at the fisherman.

Leaning forward, Andrew went on eagerly. "That's the other thing

I have to tell you, David. While I was there last week, John kept speaking about the Messiah. Or at least we all assumed it was the Messiah he spoke of. He kept saying that there was one among us whom we did not know, whose shoe latchets John wasn't worthy to unloose. Knowing the reverence in which we all hold John, that was a startling statement, of course. Everyone pressed him to know who it was, but that was all he would say."

His face glowed with excitement. "Then the very next day, a man came to where John was baptizing. The moment John saw him, he stopped speaking. He stared at him in such wonder that we all turned to see who it was."

David was holding his breath. "Yes? Yes?"

"John raised a hand and pointed at him. 'Behold the Lamb of God,' he said in tones of greatest reverence, 'who takes away the sins of the world.'"

Simeon leaned forward. "Did he call him the Messiah?"

David gave his son a sharp look. "Let Andrew tell it, Simeon."

The fisherman smiled at his friend's earnestness. "No, he didn't say anything about the Messiah, at least not then." He turned back to David. "To our surprise, the man came forward—"

"Who was he?" Simeon cut in.

"Simeon!" his father said with a scowl.

Andrew chuckled. "His name is Jesus. He is from Nazareth, the son of a carpenter named Joseph. They say that Jesus too is a carpenter."

Not waiting to see Simeon's reaction to that, Andrew went on. "So this Jesus came forward and asked John if he would baptize him. John was shocked. You could see that, even from where we were. 'But I have need to be baptized of thee, and you come to me?' he said. But Jesus insisted, saying to John, 'Suffer it to be so now, for thus it becomes us to fulfill all righteousness.'"

Simeon stirred but at another fierce look from his father held his tongue.

"So John took Jesus down into the river and baptized him. It was nothing unusual, very much like all the other baptisms John was doing." Andrew stopped, his eyes focused on something beyond David. "That is, until he finished."

"What?" Simeon said, forgetting the other question he had been about to ask. "What happened then?"

"John looked surprised, almost startled. He was looking up, over and above the head of Jesus, and then he got this most wonderful look on his face."

"What was it?"

Andrew shook his head. "We weren't sure. Not then, anyway. Later, John told a group of us that as Jesus came up out of the water that he, John, saw the Holy Spirit descending on Jesus as if it were a dove."

Complete silence filled the room as Simeon and his father both stared at the fisherman. "He actually saw the Holy Spirit?" David finally asked in awe.

"No. He saw a dove, which was the sign of the Holy Spirit's presence." Now he leaned forward, very earnest. "But that's not all. John said that he had been told that when he saw the Spirit descending upon a person, that person would be the one who had come to baptize not just with water, but with the Holy Ghost as well."

"But did he say if this Jesus was the one?" Simeon blurted. "Did John say this man was the promised Messiah?"

"No," Andrew said slowly. "He didn't say that specifically." Then he shook his head. "That doesn't matter, Simeon. He didn't have to say the exact words. That's what he meant."

That's what you think he meant. Or hope he meant.

Andrew's words broke into his thoughts. "The next day we were with John again. We were listening to him teach. Then this Jesus of Nazareth came by again. To my complete amazement, the moment John saw him, he said again, 'Behold the Lamb of God.'"

"What is that supposed to mean?" Simeon asked, quite perplexed. "The Lamb of God?" To his surprise, his father wasn't trying to stop him now. It was like Simeon was asking the very questions that David also had.

"I am not sure," Andrew said slowly, "but at that moment, I knew John was telling us that here was the man we should follow. That he was the one who had been promised would come."

He looked at Simeon squarely, challenging him to disagree. Simeon looked away, strangely disappointed. He had felt his hopes surge there for a few moments. Then another thought struck him. He started to put it into words, when again they were interrupted.

"He isn't the Messiah. He couldn't be."

They all turned. Aaron was standing at the entrance to the hallway that led to the back of the house. How long he had been there, none of them knew.

"Aaron," David said in warning.

But Andrew waved him off. "Why do you say that?" he asked.

"You say this Jesus is from Nazareth?"

"Yes."

"Then how can he be the Messiah?"

"I'm not sure what you mean."

"Do not the prophets say that the Messiah will come out of Judea, out of Bethlehem?"

Now Andrew saw where he was coming from. "Yes," he said slowly.

"Not from the Galilee?"

"No, from Judea."

Simeon was watching his father, remembering his powerful experience of some thirty years before in Bethlehem. Again, David seemed content to let Aaron now ask those questions that were troubling him as well.

Aaron went on quickly. "And he is a carpenter? the son of a carpenter, you say?"

"Yes."

Aaron uttered a soft laugh of contempt. "Can a carpenter from Nazareth be the Great Deliverer of our people? Does he have an army? Does he meet with the leaders of the people and unite them beneath his banner?"

Andrew watched him steadily for several seconds, then finally spoke. "I don't understand all things, Aaron, but I do know this. This man is unlike anyone I have ever known."

Simeon could no longer contain himself. "But Aaron's point is well taken," he said. "If he is the Messiah, the Anointed One, he has to be more than some obscure craftsman from a village that isn't even mentioned in the writings of the prophets."

"Exactly," Aaron said.

Andrew ignored Simeon's uncle and turned back to Simeon and his father. "I will only say this. After I had spent a whole day with Jesus, I returned to the place where we were staying and found my brother Simon. 'We have found the Messiah, the Christ,' I told him."

"What did Simon say to that?" David wondered.

"He wanted to see for himself. So I took him to meet Jesus."

"And was he convinced?" Simeon asked, curious now too. Simon, Andrew's brother and partner, was about as practical and pragmatic a person as Simeon knew.

Again a peculiar light came into Andrew's eyes. "When Jesus saw Simon, Jesus looked at him for a long time and then said, 'Thou art Simon, son of Jonah. Hereafter, you shall be called *Cephas*, or *Petros*.'"

"A stone?" Simeon replied. "He said that Simon would be called a stone?"

But David had caught a point that had passed right by Simeon. "Did Jesus know that you and Simon are the sons of Jonah?"

Andrew shook his head. "No."

Aaron strode across the room now, clearly agitated. "That is common knowledge here in Capernaum," he snapped. "Anyone could know that."

Andrew shrugged. "Perhaps." Then he turned to Simeon and answered his original question. "How did Simon react to all of this?" His eyes bored into Simeon's. "Simon immediately decided that he would become a disciple of this man as well." There was a soft laugh. "We've already started calling him Simon Peter, Simon the Rock."

David's thoughts were only half with the other two in the room. "If we went south, do you think we could find this Jesus of Nazareth and see him for ourselves, even though John is in prison?"

Andrew shook his head immediately. "Jesus is not down in Judea any longer. He's come back up here."

David's head lifted sharply. "Really? Where?"

He shrugged. "He was in Bethsaida the other day. I would guess he's gone back to Nazareth by now. That's his home."

David felt a great surge of disappointment. They had passed within a short distance of Nazareth on their way down from Beth Neelah just a few hours ago. They could have gone there so easily.

Simeon's voice cut into his thoughts. It wasn't very often that he and his uncle saw eye to eye on things, but Aaron had made a telling point. "Father, think about it. Can it be possible that the Messiah would come out of Nazareth?"

Andrew smiled slowly, a tolerant, patient smile. "Simon Peter and I have a good friend from Bethsaida. His name is Philip. Jesus asked Philip to be a disciple also. He agreed to do so immediately, just as Simon and I have done."

Simeon nodded politely, not sure what that had to do with his question.

"Then Philip told an associate of his about Jesus." He looked at Simeon more closely now, and there was a faint smile. "The associate, whose name is Nathanael, reacted exactly as you have Simeon. 'Can any good thing come out of Nazareth?' he asked."

"A very good question," Aaron said quickly.

Andrew ignored him, as did Simeon. "And what did your friend Philip say to that?" Simeon wondered.

"What Philip said to Nathanael, I now say to you and your father, Simeon." He turned to Aaron. "And to you as well, Aaron the Pharisee."

"What is that?" David asked.

"If you want to know about this Jesus, come and see."

CHAPTER NOTES

While scholars do not agree as to the exact time of the Savior's birth, it is generally accepted that it did not take place on December 25, as we now celebrate it. This date was fixed much later, and the birth was attached to a Roman festival, probably to give it wider acceptance. Generally, shepherds would not have been out with their flocks by night in the winter. The most likely time for them to stay with their flocks would have been in the spring, during lambing season. If the birth of Christ occurred in connection with the Passover season, when huge numbers of pilgrims came to Jerusalem, that would explain why Luke wrote that "there was no room for them at the inn" (Luke 2:7). He might also have written, there was no room for them anywhere.

Though the word *inn* conveys to Western readers the image of a quaint English cottage or tavern by the roadside, we are indebted to Frederic Farrar for a description of an Eastern *khan* or *caravanserai* (meaning, a place where caravans stop for the night): "A khan is a low structure, built of rough stones, and generally only a single story in height. It consists for the most part of a square enclosure, in which the cattle can be tied up in safety for the night, and an arched recess for the accommodation of travellers. . . . A large khan . . . might contain a series of such recesses, which are, in fact, low small rooms with no front wall to them. They are, of course, perfectly public; everything that takes place in them is visible to every person in the khan" (Farrar, p. 33).

Thus, while the innkeeper of Bethlehem is often depicted in Christmas stories and pageants as a heartless man who sends a woman in need away, it is possible that he or someone else took pity on Mary and found a place where she could give birth out of the public eye.

M. R. Vincent makes this comment about Migdal Eder: "There was near Bethlehem, on the road to Jerusalem, a tower known as *Migdal Eder,* or *the watchtower of the flock.* Here was the station where shepherds watched the flocks destined for sacrifice in the temple. . . . It was a settled conviction among the Jews that the Messiah was to be born in Bethlehem, and equally that he was to be revealed from Migdal Eder. The beautiful significance of the revelation of the infant Christ to shepherds watching the flocks destined for sacrifice needs no comment" (Vincent, 1:142; emphasis in original).

The tradition that the stable was actually in a grotto or a cave, and not in the more traditional wooden structure we see pictured in so many Christmas scenes, is very old. Justin Martyr, who lived in Palestine within a hundred years of Christ, identified a cave as the place where the nativity took place (see Farrar, p. 34). The current Church of the Nativity in Bethlehem is built over just such a grotto.

The account of Andrew's becoming a disciple of Jesus and of giving Simon the name of Peter is found in the first chapter of the Gospel of John.

CHAPTER 7

ONE SWORD KEEPS ANOTHER IN THE SHEATH.

—Jacula Prudentum

I

26 MARCH, A.D. 30

Miriam, daughter of Mordechai, member of the Great Council at Jerusalem, felt her spirits lift. Their light carriage was passing southward along the *Via Maris*. The great highway ran in a straight line across the flatness of the coastal plains. Less than a mile to the west of where they now rode, Miriam could see the blue water tipped with white where the waves were cresting just offshore. This was the massive body of water which the Romans, with their usual practicality, called "The Sea in the Middle of the Land," the *Medi-terranean*, but which most others called simply the Great Sea.

It was a beautiful spring morning, and the breeze off the sea was gentle and pleasant. Meadows and byways were a riot of brilliant color following the latter rains, the spring rains. Yellow groundsel and crown daisies carpeted great stretches of the land. The purple blooms of the milk thistle, cushioned in their spined bases, lined the roadway. Not as profuse but equally beautiful, the brilliant reds and oranges of the Persian crowfoot, a member of the buttercup family, added their splash to the overall scene. Birds were singing in bush and tree, and Miriam thought that if it weren't for the rattle of the carriage, they could have heard the soft humming of bees.

These were the Plains of Sharon, beloved of her people for untold generations and one of Miriam's favorite places in all the land. She had been a little awed by the spectacular vistas of the upper Galilee, but here everything came together in a soothing, harmonious wholeness that was exactly what she needed after the horror, frustration, and aggravation of the last few days.

About a furlong away, between them and the beach, Miriam could see the construction project currently undertaken by the Roman governor, Pontius Pilate. She had heard about the great aqueduct that would eventually bring water to Caesarea, some twenty-five miles from the heights of Mount Carmel. The project had generated so much opposition and controversy that Miriam expected the aqueduct to be a blight on the land and an affront to the eye. But instead, she was pleasantly surprised. Pilate was using native stone, the same used in buildings all over the land of Israel, and the overall effect was actually pleasing to the eye. Here the aqueduct was probably twice the height of a man, running mile after mile in a perfectly straight line. Its graceful stone arches dipped and rose with the land, but the top—which hid the plastered water channel—remained straight as an arrow's shaft. She knew it had to have a constant downhill grade to carry the water to the city, but to her eye it looked perfectly level.

"Who but the Romans?"

She turned to her father in surprise. She had thought he was asleep, but he was watching her as he also looked out the carriage at Pilate's project. Off in the distance, about half a mile ahead of them, they could see the end of the aqueduct, where the crowds of men were erecting scaffolding to continue the project's southward run.

"They are quite the builders, aren't they," Miriam agreed.

Mordechai nodded. "They say there is a place in Aquitania where they have built an aqueduct that runs for more than thirty miles, crossing steep gorges and narrow ravines. Yet in all that distance, it has a total drop in height of no more than forty-five or fifty Roman feet, or about thirty of our cubits."

Miriam shook her head. That was incredible. "I heard they have so many aqueducts coming into Rome that they bring as much water to the city as the Tiber River itself."

"I believe it," Miriam's father said. He was gazing out at the passing aqueduct with some soberness. "Only fools would think they could defeat a people who make their own rivers and bring springs of water to their very doorstep."

Miriam looked at him sharply. Was that what had kept him so quiet and moody since they had left Ptolemais early this morning? He had been in a dark mood ever since learning that the meeting in Sepphoris had been canceled. His failure to reestablish that contact through the letter sent by the hand of Deborah, Simeon's mother, angered him all the more. He had said little all the way from Beth Neelah to Ptolemais, the Roman port north of Mount Carmel. And he had done little more than grunt at her and Livia and the hired driver since leaving this morning.

Miriam decided not to pursue that line of conversation. Old fussy Azariah was no longer with them—he had gone to Capernaum and would make his own way home—and she didn't need anyone else darkening her mood. It was a glorious day. The birds were singing, the flowers were everywhere in rich profusion, they were going to the city which, next to Jerusalem, was Miriam's favorite in all of Israel. She began to hum softly, determined to turn her mind to other things.

II

Say what you would about Herod the Great as a man, Miriam thought, no one could ever belittle him as a builder. During his almost forty-year reign, the man had used the enormous wealth generated within his kingdom to undertake a construction effort like few except the Caesars themselves had ever done. Whole new cities had been started. Old ones were totally reconstructed. One stronghold after another had been created or strengthened in a large ring around the land. His enemies said it was because he always wanted to be close to a fortress when his people turned against him. There was Machaerus, the Herodium, the majestic mountaintop fortress of Masada overlooking the Sea of Salt. In Jerusalem he had changed the entire face of the city. He built a beautiful indoor theater in the city and a great outdoor amphitheater just outside the walls. A royal palace near the Jaffa Gate in the Upper City was as much fortress as it was palace. He reconstructed the citadel at the north end of the Temple Mount and named it the Antonia Fortress for Marcus Antonius, or Marc Antony as he was more commonly known, who at that time was his Roman patron. And that was to say nothing of his most breathtaking project of all, the reconstruction of the Second Temple, a project that was still going on after nearly fifty years and that provided major employment in the city. It had become proverbial now: "He who has not seen the buildings of Herod has never seen anything beautiful."

Of course, Caesarea was nothing compared to the Temple Mount, but it was still an incredible building project of its own. The coastline of Israel was remarkably smooth from the Nile River on the south to Mount Carmel on the north. Joppa was the only harbor of any consequence for several hundred miles, and it provided little shelter from the storms that roared in off the Great Sea. So Herod had decided to remedy that situation. At an ancient site called Strato's Tower, he began construction of a new city. Always mindful of whose patronage kept him in power, he named the city Caesarea, in honor of Augustus Caesar. Completed after twelve full years of intensive labor, it was a beautiful coastal city, with a magnificent temple built in honor of Caesar and a spectacular amphitheater that overlooked the blue waters of the sea.

What was most incredible, however, was the artificial harbor. Herod had brought massive stones from quarries that were a considerable distance from the city, put them on barges, and, one by one, dropped them into the sea, thus creating a giant breakwater that extended a furlong or more out into the water. Lesser men looked for natural harbors that provided a haven for ships. Herod built his own, creating the most important seaport between Alexandria and Tyre, and added even more to his immense wealth as his custom agents taxed the goods brought there by ships from all over the Roman Empire.

Miriam breathed deeply, smelling the sea and tasting the salt on her tongue as the breeze stiffened in the late afternoon. Her father, seeming to have had his own mood brightened by hers, laughed at the expression on her face. "You would think you were smelling the winds blowing out of heaven's gate."

"Oh, Papa, I love the sea. I love this city. Everything is so beautiful and so clean."

He laughed again. "I think I could take you to parts of Caesarea where you might change your mind about that."

"Don't tell me," she said quickly. "I don't want to hear it."

"Spoken like the daughter of Alexandra of Lydda. You are your mother's offspring, that is for certain."

"Well," she said, half defensively, "I know that there is squalor and filth in the world, but do I have to have it placed before my eyes?"

Their carriage rounded a corner and started down a broad street that led toward the center of the city. "Look," Mordechai said, pointing. "There is the Praetorium."

Miriam had recognized it too. "I see it," she said in excitement.

From behind them, Livia was leaning forward, taking everything in eagerly. She had not come with Miriam on a previous trip and so had never been in Caesarea. "Is that where the procurator lives then?" she asked.

"Lives and rules," Miriam's father agreed. "It is his palace and the seat of government."

Miriam could already see that there were several Roman legionnaires at the massive gate to the complex. "Do you think they will let us in?" she asked. "They say Pilate is very distrustful of his Jewish subjects and keeps a close guard at all times."

"I hadn't thought of that," her father answered gravely. "What shall we do if he doesn't give us audience?"

She thought he was teasing her, but Miriam wasn't sure. Her father was a powerful man in Jerusalem, but most of that power lay in his position with their own people. Romans, and especially Roman governors, didn't seem to take much stock in the political maneuverings of their subject peoples.

"Well, if worse comes to worst," he said, watching the soldiers now as well, "we can always find lodging at the Inn of the Golden Lion."

Miriam decided that maybe he wasn't just teasing her after all, that he really wasn't sure if they could get in to see the governor. "That will be fine with me." The inn, which was really more of a lavish guest house for travelers of substantial means, was only a stone's throw from the beach. A walk along the water's edge, even with her tender feet, would be the appropriate end to a pleasant and enjoyable day.

As they approached the Praetorium, the soldiers saw that the carriage was going to pass them by. They were instantly alert, and a centurion in full armor came forward quickly, holding up his hand. Their carriage driver, a man who had hardly spoken a word since they had left Beth Neelah, pulled the team of horses to a stop, lowering his eyes to the ground.

"State your business," the centurion said gruffly as he came up to them, one hand resting on the hilt of his sword.

"Mordechai ben Uzziel of Jerusalem, requesting an audience with the governor." He glanced quickly at Miriam as if to say, "Well, it's worth a try at least."

The man came to full attention, and his arm slapped at his chest in a brisk salute. "Yes, sire. We've been expecting you." He turned and waved some men forward. "The governor has requested your presence for dinner. In the meantime, may I escort you to your quarters so that you can rest and freshen up?"

Mordechai bowed his head slightly, a tiny smile playing at the corners of his mouth. "That would be most kind of you, centurion. Thank you."

As the soldiers sprang to get their baggage and Miriam and Livia climbed down from the carriage, Miriam pulled a face at her father. "You knew all along?" she mouthed.

He laughed in pure amusement. "One is never sure about such things," he said softly, "but one can always hope."

III

Pontius Pilate rose from his marble chair the moment the servant opened the door and showed Mordechai ben Uzziel and his daughter into the spacious hall. Everyone else in the room stood as well, and every head turned in their direction. Pilate didn't move from his place beyond the head of the long table—that would have been seen as a sign of weakness—but the fact that he did not remain seated showed astonishing respect for a non-Roman. Once again Miriam had to fight to keep her face expressionless. Her father was being welcomed as though he were another procurator.

Mordechai took Miriam by the elbow and guided her forward. He had warned her that it was not appropriate for her to smile or acknowledge the other guests until they had paid their respects to the governor. She moved gracefully, aware that every eye in the room was following her movements, even more than those of her father.

Finally, as they were just a few steps from the throne—for it was more than simply a chair—the procurator stepped forward, hand extended. "*Shalom*, Mordechai ben Uzziel. Welcome to Caesarea." To Miriam's surprise, he greeted them in Aramaic. He spoke with a heavy accent, but he spoke easily and clearly. And then she wondered why she should be surprised. Pilate had been here now for more than four years. That was plenty of time to learn the language of his subjects.

He was dressed in a white toga, every fold meticulously arranged— by a slave, Miriam was sure. On his feet were sandals of fine leather with gold trim on the latchets. He wore a plain gold bracelet on his left arm and a thick ring on one little finger. Other than that he was the picture of elegant simplicity, which was the Roman way.

"Thank you, Your Excellency," her father said in Latin that was not nearly so assured as Pilate's Aramaic had been.

Pilate waved a hand. "Please. We feel comfortable conversing in your language."

"Thank you. I do better in Greek if that is more to your liking."

"Aramaic is fine."

"Thank you." He touched Miriam's elbow and brought her forward. "May I present my daughter, Miriam." He smiled. "Her Latin is much better than mine."

Pilate took her hand and spoke in Latin. "We are pleased that you were able to accompany your father, Miriam of Jerusalem. Welcome to the Praetorium."

"Thank you, Excellency," she answered back in the same language.

"The beauty of your palace outdoes the wonders of your city. It is an honor to be invited to sit at your table."

Pilate brought up her hand and kissed it briefly, then looked at her father. "You are right, Mordechai. Her Latin is nearly flawless." Then to Miriam he added, "You are more lovely than I had remembered from our previous meeting."

Miriam blushed with pleasure. She felt a little bewildered by the warmth of the greeting. It had been about two years ago that her father had taken her to a banquet hosted by the Great Council of Jerusalem in honor of the governor. She had been introduced to the procurator and his wife in a reception line, along with many others, but they had not sat at their table. She had met him only one other time, again very briefly, at a ceremony that was part of the Festival of Purim just a year ago. She had doubted he would even remember her.

"We thank you, Excellency," Mordechai said now. "Thank you for extending this invitation to us."

Miriam had to fight not to turn and stare at him. Pilate had extended this invitation? Her father hadn't asked for an audience. That took her completely by surprise.

Pilate turned, and a woman stepped forward. "May I present my wife, Fortunata Cassandra Drusus Pilatus."

Miriam had already recognized her from their previous meetings. She bent one knee and bowed her head slightly. "We are honored by your kind hospitality, madam."

She accepted the greeting with a smile and a quick curtsy, but said nothing. Fortunata Pilate was dressed in the same simple elegance as her husband. Like his toga, her outer dress was of glistening white and delicately draped around her shoulders and arms. She wore a filigreed gold necklace and matching bracelet and a band of gold with a row of small emeralds in her hair, which was piled high atop her head. It was a style that her father told her had become quite popular in Rome now. Where her husband's features were coarse and weathered, Fortunata's were fine, almost fragile, and her skin milky white. It was well known in Jerusalem that the governor's wife hated the unforgiving Judean sun and went to great lengths to protect herself from it. She rarely ventured out with him when he went on his trips of state.

Pilate took Mordechai's elbow and turned him. Standing just behind the table, not quite at the head, was a Roman officer in full dress uniform except for the red-plumed helmet, which was sitting on a bench in one corner. "Mordechai, this is Tribune Marcus Quadratus Didius, commander of my garrison here in Caesarea. Marcus, this is Mordechai ben Uzziel, leading member of the Great Sanhedrin of Jerusalem."

"Sire," the officer said, coming to attention with a sharp snap of his heels. He brought one arm up across his chest in a salute. "It is a pleasure to greet you."

"And you as well, Tribune," Mordechai said easily. He started to turn to Miriam to bring her forward, but the officer was ahead of him. He took one step forward, made a sweeping bow, then took Miriam's hand and kissed it briefly, as had the governor. As he straightened, he was looking directly into Miriam's eyes. What she saw on his face took her aback a little. It was evident surprise and open admiration.

He was a strikingly handsome man. His hair was dark and slightly curled, a pleasant contrast to the brilliant red of his cape and the polished brass of his breastplate. His eyes were a deep green and filled with both curiosity and intelligence. His cheekbones were high and prominent, his nose definitely Roman, his mouth firm and yet pleasant. Yes, definitely a striking figure of a man.

"The governor told me that the daughter of Mordechai ben Uzziel was lovely, but—" He spoke to Pilate without his eyes ever leaving her. "I'm sorry to contradict my commanding officer, sire, but I fear you have not done the lady justice with your words."

Pilate laughed, then shook a finger at her in mock severity. "Watch this one, Miriam. He is as quick with his tongue as he is with the sword."

Miriam realized that she was blushing even more deeply and finally looked away. "Thank you," she murmured. Then her eyes lifted and met the officer's. "It is easy to slip on a tongue that is too smooth."

Pilate's wife clapped her hands in pleased surprise. "Well spoken, Miriam." She turned to Marcus, still chuckling. "You shall have to watch yourself, friend Marcus. I think you have met your match."

Marcus, laughing softly, gave her a grudging nod, but the brazen admiration never left his eyes. Miriam was keenly aware that those eyes did not leave her as the governor and his wife took her and her father around the circle and introduced them to the rest of the guests.

As they finished, Pilate and his wife assigned them their places at the *triclinia,* the long couches or divans placed around the table. It was customary for the Romans, just as it was for the Jews, to eat in a semi-reclining position, leaning on one elbow, with their feet extending outward from the table. The *triclinium* got its name from the fact that it was wide enough for three people to recline on the same couch. Pilate and his wife were alone on one couch at the head of the table. Mordechai was placed to Pilate's right on the first *triclinia*—another mild surprise for Miriam, for this was the place of honor—with Miriam beside him. It was less of a surprise to Miriam when Marcus took his place beside her, though she could not tell if that had been Fortunata's plan all along or if she had changed her mind when she saw the reaction of the tribune to the daughter of Mordechai of Jerusalem.

Miriam decided she didn't care. This was going to prove to be a very interesting evening.

IV

It was not surprising that Miriam found many of the Roman customs and practices strikingly different from her own, even peculiar in many ways. That was to be expected from two cultures that were so dramatically different. But one difference she found more amusing than annoying was the fact that the Romans always had to have entertainment as part of a proper dinner party. For her people, conversation was its own entertainment. Once the prayer of thanks was offered over the food at a Jewish dinner, the room would virtually explode with talk that ran the gamut from courteous to heated, from exploratory to accusatory. It was far more stimulating and invigorating than any imported entertainment might be.

Tonight's dinner had shown just how different the two cultures were. Throughout the evening the mood had been solidly respectable and consistently dignified. As the slaves began bringing out the sumptuous courses of food, another slave—obviously trained for this very purpose—stood off to one side and recited poetry. Not many listened, but out of respect for the poet—not the slave—all conversation was kept subdued. The poetry had been followed by a vocal soloist, who sang ballads and love songs accompanied by two musicians with flute and lyre. When they began, all conversation stopped. Then as the last of the food was cleared away and the wine brought out, a professional storyteller began regaling them with amusing stories and anecdotes. He was so entertaining that, though it didn't seem to be expected as it had been during the singing, again all conversation virtually stopped until he finished.

Miriam could tell that Marcus Quadratus Didius had hoped for more opportunity to talk to his companion at the table. And she was a little disappointed as well. As the governor stirred and it was obvious that the dinner was coming to an end, it surprised her when Pilate turned to his tribune.

"Marcus?"

"Yes, sire?"

"Mordechai and I have some matters to discuss. I think our lovely guest might enjoy a tour of the palace and the grounds."

Marcus looked momentarily startled, then instantly smiled. Not many commands from the governor were as pleasant as this one to carry out. He got to his feet and offered a hand to Miriam. "Unless you are too tired from your journey?"

She shook her head quickly and allowed him to help her up, being careful not to put too much weight on her feet all at once. Her blisters were healing nicely, but she still had to be careful. "I would very much like to see the Praetorium," she said to Pilate. "I was most impressed as we arrived today."

"Good." He gave a dismissive wave of his hand, and Marcus took Miriam's elbow. Fortunata saw that as her signal as well and started shepherding the rest of the guests toward the large doors at the end of the hall. The procurator then signaled to one of the slaves, who quickly secured a flask of wine and two golden goblets and took them into a small atrium off the main hall.

As Miriam and Marcus reached the door, Miriam glanced back in time to see her father and the procurator already in deep conversation as they left the room together. And it was then that she realized that there was a part of her father's life that she did not know and probably never would. One thing was clear to her now, however. Though he had been disappointed that the meeting with the various Zealot factions had not come about, he had not seemed terribly upset. That had puzzled her. Now she realized that being here tonight was the real purpose for their trip and not some half-hearted attempt to make an agreement with a bunch of Galilean rebels.

V

Pontius Pilate slouched back in the cushioned seat of his chair, sipping at his wine as he looked at Mordechai ben Uzziel over the top of the goblet. The slave had retreated quickly and shut the door behind him, leaving them alone.

"We are men with much on our minds," Pilate said as the door closed. "Shall we not waste any more time?"

Mordechai nodded, pleased with the bluntness. He was in no mood for small talk and disdained those who felt that it was necessary as a prelude to business. "Agreed. As I mentioned to you earlier, the rebel leaders had a falling out among themselves and refused to come to the meeting. Therefore, our attempts to buy an alliance with the Zealots came to naught."

"Not a great surprise."

Mordechai laughed shortly. "Not at all. We have a saying among our people. If you have three Jews, you will have four opinions."

It took a moment; then Pilate hooted. "Now if that is not a grand description of your people, I've never heard one."

Mordechai's face remained bland, even though without knowing it, the governor had just insulted him. "Well, in the case of the Zealots, if you have three Zealots, you will have at least ten opinions, maybe more. They are hardheaded, extremely passionate about their cause, and so independent they can't even get along with their own kind."

"No wonder they call them *lestai,*" Pilate said in disgust.

The Sadducee from Jerusalem leaned forward. "I understand why, officially, you call them *lestai*—bandits, brigands, or criminals. But that is misleading. These are not like the bands of robbers that infest some areas of Judea." He pulled a face, remembering his experience with Moshe Ya'abin three days before. "Those are the true *lestai*. But it would be a mistake to think of these Galileans in the same way."

Pilate's eyes narrowed. He didn't like being told he had made a mistake, especially by a Jew. But he also knew that this man was not criticizing him directly. "Why a mistake?" he asked.

"There is a story in our history, at the time when our people had come out of Egypt. As you know, one of our Ten Commandments says, 'Thou shalt not commit adultery.'"

Pilate snorted softly in derision. "Another one of your beliefs that the rest of the world finds most strange." There was a salacious grin. "And far too restricting."

Mordechai ignored the subtle dig. He smiled smoothly. "Not all view it with quite the same fanaticism as do others." They both laughed knowingly.

"Anyway," Mordechai went on, "while our ancestors were wandering in the wilderness, one of the men committed adultery. That displeased our God very much, and he was about to bring down his wrath upon the people. But a man named Phineas was so outraged that he took a spear and ran both the man and the woman through. The record states that God's wrath was turned away and Israel spared because—and I quote now—'Phineas was *zealous* for God's sake.'"

Pilate sat back slowly and began to nod. "And thus the Zealots of today."

"Exactly. In our language, the word used in that scripture is *kahna'ah*. Those who exhibit such passion and zeal for God's cause today thus call themselves the *kahna'im*. The Greek translation is *zelotays*, or Zealots."

"And the point of all this?" Pilate asked, not disrespectfully. It was clear that Mordechai was not just filling him in on trivial details.

"If your soldiers go against these Zealots thinking they are only trying to run a group of common criminals to ground, they will be sadly misled. These men are passionate believers that what they do is God's will. They are not only willing, but they view it as part of their mission, to use violence—even murder if necessary—to throw off all pagan influence. And giving their life to the cause only brings them greater rewards in the life to come."

Pilate rested his chin in one hand, thoughtful now. "So you are saying that these people are religious fanatics."

"Yes. The worst kind of men to deal with."

Pilate sighed softly. "Yes. Indeed. The very worst kind."

Mordechai wondered if Pilate was remembering his clash with the Jews when he tried to bring the Roman standards into Jerusalem about four years before, but he said nothing.

Pilate formed a steeple with his fingers now, staring through them out the window at the palace courtyards where torches flickered and danced in the evening breeze. Finally his eyes came back to the leader of the Jews from Jerusalem. "And the Great Sanhedrin was trying to make a pact with these Zealots?" he asked in a very soft voice.

Miriam's father instantly saw the danger that lurked beneath that mild tone. "If the procurator will permit, I should like to speak frankly."

"I would find that most refreshing," Pilate responded, folding his hands in his lap. "Most refreshing."

"As you may have heard, Your Excellency, the Great Sanhedrin of Jerusalem is made up of about seventy of the country's most respected leaders, who represent the various sects of our faith."

"Yes."

"Well, as you may also know, there is within the Great Council another, much smaller council. Very few know of this body of men."

Again there was a slow nod. "The real power behind the throne, as we say in Rome."

"Exactly. There are five of us. I went to Sepphoris officially representing all of the Council. But in actuality, I had a more pressing mission from this inner council."

Now Mordechai had the procurator's full attention.

"You must understand clearly the position of this inner council, Your Excellency. There is no one in all of Israel who is more convinced than we are that the worst possible thing we can do for our people is to try to break off the yoke of Rome."

"Go on."

"Our plan was to publicly arrange an alliance with all the Zealot factions. Once that was secured, we—the inner council—hoped to call a second meeting of all the Zealot leaders within the month. Secretly, I was authorized to come to you with the details of that second meeting."

There was a strange light in Pilate's eyes. "I see."

"Do you?" Mordechai asked, emboldened by the eagerness he saw there.

"Yes. If the Roman eagle was to swoop down on an unsuspecting pack of dogs, the leadership of these *lestai*—or rather Zealots, as you say—would be wiped out in one stunning, decisive blow."

Mordechai sat back, deeply satisfied. It was a pleasure to deal with men who thought not just tactically, but strategically.

"And," Pilate continued, nodding with obvious admiration, "the rich and powerful of Jerusalem would no longer have to worry about a small group of fanatics bringing down the full wrath of Rome upon their country."

Lifting his own goblet, Mordechai drank deeply, then lifted it in a salute. "It would solve that and many other problems, Excellency."

Once again silence filled the room as Pilate considered all the implications of what he had heard. When he finally stirred, his brows were knitted into a deep frown. "And now? You have told me that you failed to get the Zealots to even agree on a place and time to meet the first time."

The eyes of the wealthy Sadducee narrowed into two hard, cold points of black light. "If the fox is too clever to walk into the snare, what do you do?"

Pilate gave him a malicious smile. "You run him to ground."

Mordechai nodded thoughtfully. "That is one alternative. But you had better have a very fast horse if you wish to do that."

"And the other alternative?" Pilate asked.

"You put a morsel in the snare that the fox simply cannot resist."

VI

As they finished their walk through the meticulously groomed gardens of the governor's palace, a thought began to stir in Miriam's mind. For the first hour, she had been completely charmed by the handsome young tribune. In between his pointing out the features of the building, constructed by Herod after the pattern of the sumptuous palaces on the Palatine Hill in Rome, Miriam had plied him with questions. This was not just a way to maintain a comfortable conversation. She really was pleased to have an opportunity to learn more of the Roman culture and traditions. Miriam had some of the natural biases of her people against all things heathen, but through the eyes of her mother, and especially her father, she had also learned that there was much that Rome brought to the world that was worthy of study and emulation.

Marcus seemed pleased at her genuine interest. He spoke of his family in Rome, of their vast estates and yet the basically simple life led by his father. His younger brother and only sibling was also a tribune, currently with the Sixth Legion Victrix in Spain. Marcus spoke of him with evident pride and affection. Then gradually, with her encouragement, he began to speak of his own first campaign in Germania. There he had fought against the wild-haired Celts, fiercely barbaric tribes that were "madly in love with the very thought of war." He told her how the Celtic kings would be killed by their own people when they grew too old to lead in battle or if they could have no male offspring. The Druid priestesses would watch the death struggle and read the patterns in the blood to determine how the tribe should be ruled next.

It was when he spoke of how bitterly the Celts resisted being taken as slaves that the idea first struck Miriam. As they stopped beneath a palm tree whose fronds were silhouetted in the soft moonlight, Marcus indicated a bench beside a lily pond, and they both sat down. She waited a moment, then took a quick breath. "Tribune Didius?"

"Yes?"

"May I ask a question of you?"

"Of course."

"I—I am not sure if it is appropriate. I do not wish to give offense."

"I find that hardly possible," he said nobly. "Ask on."

"As you know, the Hebrew law does not allow us to own slaves."

"One of the few things we Romans could learn from your people."

She bit her tongue. The arrogance was so natural as to be almost innocent. These Romans. She didn't think Marcus was even aware of how condescending he had just sounded. She ignored it and went on, more slowly now. "I have a servant girl named Livia. You haven't met her."

"I saw her with you as you came into the courtyard this afternoon."

So he had been watching even then. She smiled. "She was once the slave of a Roman nobleman in Alexandria. When his fortunes turned, she was sold to help pay his debts. My father purchased her as my servant and gave her her freedom."

"I understand." There was a twinkle in his eyes. "And does she receive a wage from you then?"

Miriam stopped at the unexpected question. "Well, no. She dwells in our house and eats at our table. She wants for nothing."

"As do the slaves at our villa," he said solemnly.

Strangely, the image of Simeon flashed into her mind at that moment. "*Only* a servant," he had said when she had tried to explain that Livia was not a slave. The disdain in his voice had cut like a lash.

She rushed on, a little flustered now. "The rest of her family were sold as well. She has no idea where they are now."

"A too frequent tragedy that is one of the unfortunate consequences of the slave trade. I am proud to say that my father goes to great lengths to keep our slaves together with their families. In fact, it is my father's policy that if one of our women slaves bears three children, her work on the farm is reduced. If she bears a fourth, she is granted her freedom, for she has blessed our house greatly."

Miriam looked away, appalled once again at the callousness that lay behind the innocence. She thought of the elegant and lovely Deborah, mother of Simeon and Leah, being dragged off to spend their lives in hard manual labor, and it made her want to hold her stomach and cry out in pain. She was growing more uncomfortable with this talk of slaves and servants with every minute, but her desire to get an answer was stronger than ever. "I have heard it said that you have people in the empire who—" She stopped, not even sure how to say it. "Who make a living trying to locate slaves for others."

"Oh, yes." Now he saw where she was going with this. "We call them professional slave hunters. Normally they are employed to find runaway slaves and return them to their masters, but I have heard of cases, especially in some of the outlying provinces, where wealthy freedmen have hired slave hunters to find members of their family who were captured in battle."

"Are there records kept of such transactions then?"

"Of course. In fact, we have elected civil officials we call *aediles*, who, as part of their duties, are responsible to see that careful records are kept of all such transactions, just as they would be in the sale of other property. That way the buyer is not cheated."

Miriam looked away for a moment, chilled to the core of her being. Here was a part of the Roman culture that she would never feel comfortable with. How casually he spoke of "property." But now that she had come this far, she felt compelled to finish. "Do you personally know of any such men?"

"Slave hunters?" He shook his head. "No. Usually they are quite unsavory characters." Seeing her disappointment, he hurried on. "But I'm sure I could locate one. I have a centurion here who can answer just about any question I put to him. Would you like me to try to find such a man and have him look into it for you?"

She hesitated at that. What would her father think if he knew she was trying to locate Livia's family? And for that matter, what would she herself do if by some remarkable chance she found them? But the instant she asked, she knew. The shame she felt three days before as she realized that not once had she ever wondered about Livia's family lay heavy upon her. If her father refused to help purchase their freedom, Miriam would draw from her own funds. Her father had been paying her handsomely for her work as a scribe for him. He had also designated a healthy sum as part of her inheritance and invested it along with his own funds. Miriam was not wealthy, not in the sense that her father was wealthy, but she had considerable means of her own now. And she had full control over a good part of them.

Marcus was waiting for an answer, so finally she took a quick breath and nodded. "I would appreciate that. I can get you what information is known. It would mean a great deal to Livia if we could find out what happened to them."

"I'm sure it would." Now there was obvious respect in his eyes. "In that sense, you do for your servant what few Romans would do for their slaves."

Embarrassed now, she stood. "Thank you, Marcus. You have been a most congenial host and guide."

"Never has the mantle of duty laid so lightly upon my shoulders," he said gallantly.

"I am weary." She could feel the throbbing starting in the bottom of her feet again. "And Father says we must leave early to return to Jerusalem."

"The governor has assigned you an escort to see you home safely. Alas, I am off to Joppa to inspect our garrison there and will not be able to accompany you. But the centurion of whom I speak will command the maniple. He will see to your comfort."

"Thank you."

He hesitated, then took her hand. His eyes were more black than green in the moonlight, but they searched her face with eager hope. "But the governor has asked that I take a full cohort to Jerusalem for the Passover season, which begins next week."

For the first time, he seemed unsure of himself. "Would it be possible that I might call on the home of Mordechai ben Uzziel? I will speak to your father of this, of course."

Miriam wasn't really caught off guard by his request. She was woman enough to see the interest in his eyes. But . . . did he not sense the vast gulf that lay between them? She had wanted to learn more of these Romans, especially more about one as young and handsome as this tribune. But could she ever push away the coldness she felt as he talked so casually of slaves and slavery? She was the daughter of a Sadducee, one of Jerusalem's privileged aristocracy. There would be no horror when a Gentile came into their home, no ritual cleansing after he left. That had nothing to do with it. The question for her was—

She realized with a start that he was watching her, the first signs of disappointment showing in his eyes. She also realized at that same instant, that even as she and Marcus stood here in the moonlight, her father and the procurator of all of Judea were meeting together inside the palace. This Roman tribune was second in command to the governor. If she said no . . .

She forced a bright smile. "It would be a pleasure to show the tribune around our home," she said. "It is nothing in comparison to the Praetorium, of course, but—"

"It would be my great honor to have that privilege," he cut in, not trying to hide his relief.

"Then I shall look forward to seeing you again in Jerusalem," she murmured. And to her dismay, she realized that at least one part of her really meant it.

CHAPTER NOTES

The brief summary of Herod the Great's tremendous building projects captures only a small part of what he did in his four decades as ruler. Even now, two millennia later, archeologists and architects still marvel at what he wrought. Many sources describe this great building effort, but Schürer's summary is comprehensive and concise and includes a description of Caesarea's artificial harbor (see pp. 138–42).

It is known from numerous sources that slavery was a common social institution throughout the Roman Empire. In the city of Rome itself, it is thought that one in every three persons was a slave, or about 400,000 in number (Carcopina, p. 65). Slaves came from several sources, such as children sold by their families who were in abject poverty, criminals guilty of capital crimes, people who could not pay their debts, and those captured by pirates or kidnappers (this last category, of course, was similar to the situation of the African Blacks of our own age). By far the greatest source of slaves, however, was war. When a town was conquered, the population was considered part of the spoils of war. Sometimes the wealthier citizens were allowed to pay a ransom for their freedom, but the rest were taken as slaves. It is said that during the successful campaign of Julius Caesar in Gaul from 58 to 51 B.C., his victories generated more than a million slaves (Shelton, p. 163).

CHAPTER 8

WHO CAN FIND A VIRTUOUS WOMAN? FOR HER PRICE IS FAR
ABOVE RUBIES. THE HEART OF HER HUSBAND
DOTH SAFELY TRUST IN HER. . . .
STRENGTH AND HONOUR ARE HER CLOTHING;
AND SHE SHALL REJOICE IN TIME TO COME.

—*Proverbs 31:10–11, 25*

I

1 APRIL, A.D. 30

For a little village like Beth Neelah, any unusual event—birth, *bar mitzvah,* betrothal, marriage—was a time for joyous celebration. But in this case, it was the most important event to happen there in a generation. In the first place, the family of David ben Joseph, successful merchant of Capernaum, was known throughout all the Galilee and was highly respected. That alone would have been unusual enough. But within the village itself, the family of Yehuda the Zealot was also greatly esteemed. His family had lived in Beth Neelah for five generations. He was not only a prosperous farmer, but his courageous escape from the Romans as a boy in his teens, and his exploits with the Zealot band of Ha-keedohn since then, made him a local champion. And Shana was no less beloved in the village. With her two brothers gone with the Zealots so often, the villagers had taken her as their own and considered themselves almost as her parents now. And if all of that was not enough, to have the bridegroom be the Javelin himself made the whole thing absolutely perfect. Simeon had made for himself a reputation known throughout all of the province. The villagers, who usually viewed outsiders with some reserve, had fully accepted him as one of their own.

Little wonder, then, that on this day the village began to overflow with people long before sundown. They came from Nazareth and Sepphoris, Cana and Jotapata, Dabaritta and En Teena. There was also a significant number who had come up from Capernaum to be with the family of David ben Joseph on this day of celebration. They brought food and gifts and their bedrolls, for this celebration would last through the night and well into the next day.

David ben Joseph brought his entire family, of course, including Ephraim and Rachel and their two children. Phineas, their chief household servant, accompanied them to help in the celebration. They arrived about mid-afternoon, having left Capernaum long before the sun was up. Some of the young boys had been sent out to watch for them, so by the time they reached the village, a crowd was there to greet them. The noise was deafening. Men called out their congratulations to Simeon and to his father. The women and girls launched into a shrill ululating cry of joy, peculiar to that area of the world, that could be heard for at least a mile.

Immediately, Deborah, Leah, Rachel, and the two children were taken to Yehuda's house, where Shana was waiting. A neighbor took Esther and little Boaz so that Rachel could be free to help her mother-in-law. There was no sign of Shana, of course. To be seen by Simeon at this point would have been unthinkable. David, Simeon, and Ephraim were met by Yehuda and Daniel and taken to the house of their cousin on the outskirts of the village. He had graciously moved out and given over his house to the bridegroom for the celebration. Young Joseph, because he was only ten and had not yet had his *bar mitzvah*, could have gone with the women and children, but when told that, he wrinkled his nose and said he would stay with the men, where he belonged. The two groups did not see each other for the rest of the day.

At sundown the women who were the formally invited guests began arriving at Shana's house. There Deborah took over the role of Shana's mother. Shana sat on a stool in the center of the room, smiling and responding graciously when comments were directed to her, but otherwise she remained silent. This was a time for everyone else to speak and for her to listen.

"How beautiful she is," one would say. "Oh, yes. Look how dark and lovely are her eyes." "Her skin is like milk." "Have you noticed what slender fingers she has?" "Yes, you should see her milk the goats. Her fingers fly so quickly, they are almost a blur." "And have you seen her dance?" "Ah, yes, she is like a dove's feather in the evening breeze." "She is one of the most skilled in pressing out the olive oil." "She chooses only the finest of leather bottles for the wine." "Though Yehuda gets the credit," an older woman said, "it is really Shana who makes the wine that is desired in all of upper Galilee." "It doesn't matter at what time Yehuda or Daniel come home, the house is always in perfect order." That comment was directed at Deborah so she would know what kind of daughter-in-law she was getting. So was the next one: "She is as slender as a reed, but the women in her family have never had any trouble bearing children. There is no need to worry on that account." At that, Shana blushed furiously.

As the evening wore on, the wedding dress was finally brought out. Shana was beaming with pride as she unfolded it and laid it across the table. Yehuda had gone down to Capernaum and purchased the material himself. She had worked on it with meticulous and loving care since the betrothal had been arranged. It was a long, one-piece robe of Egyptian linen dyed the color of a summer sky. The sleeves came to the wrist but were open and hung down several inches from her arms.

A veil was required in the ceremony, of course, and this one was of the same color but so fine as to be transparent. The headband was of white twisted linen trimmed with silver, and Yehuda had bought a sash to match.

The women stood around her in a circle with their backs turned while she put the clothing on. When she said she was ready, the room was filled with exclamations of awe and much clapping of hands. The light blue set off Shana's olive skin, dark eyes, and jet-black hair to perfection. The sash showed the slenderness of her waist. Leah said it all when she gasped, and her hands flew to her mouth. "Oh, Shana!" she exclaimed. "Simeon is going to think he's seen a vision."

For the next while, Shana had to stand in the center of the room, again without speaking, while everyone walked in circles around her and admired both the dress and how it made her look.

Next came the adornment. The use of cosmetics was an art that only the older women knew and which Shana's young friends watched with great eagerness so they could learn how it was done. Only the wealthy city-dwellers wore cosmetics regularly. Here in the country, the oils and the powders were kept carefully stored away and brought out on only the most special of occasions. These they were using today would be part of Shana's dowry, a gift that showed she was prepared to be a wife. The art lay in applying the cosmetics so that they enhanced Shana's natural loveliness but did not call attention to themselves. While it was being done, she was warned no less than a dozen times that when she slept tonight—if she slept tonight!—she had to lie on her back all night long so she didn't smear any of it.

Through it all, the women chatted and visited, laughed, ate sweet-meats, and drank a light wine. Step by step they prepared Shana for what was about to come. From time to time, someone would bring in some flowers, and the women would braid them into Shana's long dark hair. Gifts were also brought. When the gifts were coins, they were sewn into a cloth headband in such a way that they dangled in front of her forehead, testimony to all that this woman did not come to the marriage without means of her own. This was the beginning of her dowry. Other things—a hand-knit shawl, a set of painted pottery bowls, a blanket, a winter cloak—were set in the corner where Simeon and the men could later admire them.

Finally, after almost two and a half hours of this womanly activity, the jewelry was brought in. Leah and Rachel, as future sisters-in-law, caused a great stir when they presented Shana with a delicate necklace made of tiny gold links with three brilliant red carnelians that hung at her throat. Then a hush fell over the room. Shana went to a cupboard in the room where she slept and brought back a small wooden box with a brass clasp that held the lid shut. Everyone crowded in as she opened it. Inside were two earrings, simple silver rings with no other adornment, and three matching bracelets. These items were probably not worth more than three or four shekels if sold in the marketplace, but Shana took them out with a look of deep reverence on her face. This jewelry had belonged to Shana's mother and grandmother. When the Romans had swooped down upon the Galilee, Shana's mother had wrapped the box in goatskin and buried it in the olive orchard, even as the legionnaires raced through the village looking for her and her husband. Before she had been torn from her children, she had whispered to Yehuda that these were for Shana. Over the years Shana had taken them out and looked at them many times, but she had never worn them, vowing that she would save them for this special day.

She slipped the bracelets on, two on her left wrist, one on her right. When she went to put on the earrings, however, her fingers were trembling so much that Leah had to step in and help her. When Leah was finished, one by one the women came to Shana, took her in her arms, and held her for a moment. Rachel and Leah were third and second to last in the line. Deborah was last. There were tears in her eyes as well now.

"Dearest Shana," she whispered, "I am so happy for you tonight.

But no happier than I am for myself and for my son. Welcome to our family."

II

As the sun went down and darkness came on, the scene at the house of Yehuda's cousin was similar in many ways, and yet significantly different as well. The house was so filled with men that there was not enough room for all to sit down. In addition to his own family members, several of Simeon's Zealot band were there to congratulate their leader. David and his chief servant, Phineas, brought out Simeon's clothes, which had been carefully packed for the trip. He quickly donned them, as exclamations of praise rang out all around. His tunic was made of finely woven cotton and was a dark brown. His outer cloak, however, was a bright gold with scarlet and royal blue embroidered patterns on the front of it. His hat was round, made from padded silk with a cloth that fell down the back and covered his neck. The hat was a bright red and also trimmed with gold embroidery. The brightness of the colors were symbolic of the joyousness of this occasion. A pair of knee-high sandals made of a soft and supple leather from Bashan was a gift from his father. Ephraim provided him with a golden brooch that held his cloak together at the throat.

As was happening with the women, the evening was spent in paying tribute to Simeon and his family. Unlike Shana, however, Simeon was fully expected to participate in the conversation. Simeon's father shared stories of his childhood. Ephraim recounted how many times he had gotten his "little brother" out of trouble while they were growing up, and won a delighted hoot when he suggested that he was still doing it. Daniel and Yehuda touted Simeon's courage and leadership, recounting some of their exploits as a Zealot band. To Simeon's great relief, the two brothers remembered that Simeon's father was present and kept the stories relatively tame.

When they finished, Yehuda, more emotional than he had intended to be, raised a goblet of wine and said in a husky voice how proud he was to have Simeon become his brother-in-law. That was the first of many toasts that followed.

Yehuda, who was serving two roles tonight—as Shana's "father" and as Simeon's man of honor—gave the formal tribute to the bridegroom and his family. He had set it to poetry, which, to Simeon's surprise, was really quite well done. In several places Yehuda's quick wit and irreverent sense of humor shone through, and the assembly laughed uproariously. Once he had them in a lighter mood, Yehuda began to describe, with great solemnity, some of Simeon's peculiarities—his grave intensity, his stern impatience with shoddy performance, his habit of rubbing at his scar with the tip of his thumb when he was deep in thought, how his voice broke into raspiness when he was excited and began to shout out commands. It was so perfectly done and with such a complete deadpan that Simeon, holding his sides, finally had to beg him to stop. Finally, as the second watch was drawing to a close and the hour of midnight approached, Simeon's father stood up. The room quieted quickly. The goblets of wine were set aside, and an air of expectancy filled the room.

"Simeon ben David?"

"Yes, Father?"

"It is time for the *erusin*. Are you ready?"

"I am."

Simeon stood now as well. Yehuda, as "friend of the bridegroom," came and stood by his side. Ephraim and young Joseph fell in directly behind them, and the others began forming a double line. David gestured to his son. "Then let us go. The bride and her attendants await us."

By the door a long table was filled with small hand lamps. These were small round containers, comfortably held in the palm of the hand. Made of baked clay and pinched on one end to hold a wick made of braided cotton or wool, each was filled with a small amount of olive oil, enough to burn for about an hour. Beside the table in a large stone pot were several torches, smeared with pitch on one end and standing ready. Once everyone was in place, David went to the fireplace, where a small fire had been kept burning all night. He took a long reed from the mantel and lit it. Cupping his hand over the flame as he walked, he moved to the table and one by one lit the lamps. As he did so, Yehuda came over and took a lamp to each person. All got one except for those in the front of the line. When he finished, he took his place again beside Simeon. Through it all, no one spoke. The mood now had become very solemn.

Once he was sure everyone had a burning lamp, David tossed the reed onto the fire and moved to the large pot. He took one of the torches, lit it from the fireplace as well, and then went quickly to the door. He opened it, touched the *mezuzah* briefly, then stepped outside so as to keep the torch's black smoke from blackening the ceiling.

A cry went up. "Here they come!" "There's the bridegroom!" "It's time!"

A large crowd of both men and women were outside the door, waiting for this very moment. David stepped aside, holding his torch high. The night was black—the moon was not up as yet—and the stars as brilliant as flashes of sunlight off the water. Now the procession inside the house came outside as well, each of those first in the line stopping to touch the doorpost, then grabbing a torch as well. One by one, David lit their torches as they came out, and soon the street was filled with flickering firelight.

As the rest of the guests came out of the house, the people crowded around. Each person there also carried a tiny clay lamp in his or her hand, though none of them were lit. Now the guests held out their lamps, and fire was passed from lamp to lamp until all were lit.

Not waiting for the rest to finish, the first guests started away, moving up the street that led back into the village. Up ahead, doors were opening on every side. People had heard the cries and knew it was time. As David took his place on the other side of Simeon, the procession of light started forward. Now the crowd surged in all around them, the joyful cries were continual, and the women again began the warbling cry of celebration. Up ahead, those who were out in front of the procession held out their lamps for the newcomers, who were appearing on every side. Every individual carried his or her own lamp and thrust it out eagerly. A river of fire appeared to be moving slowly out ahead of the wedding party. At every door the cry was renewed: "Make ready for the bridegroom! The bridegroom cometh!"

III

Simeon well knew that in ancient Israel, during the times of Abraham, there were typically three stages in the process of "taking a wife"—the arrangement for the marriage, which was usually done by the two families; the physical transfer of the woman to the home of the bridegroom's family, especially if they were separated by some distance; and finally, the consummation, or actual cohabitation as husband and wife. Father Abraham sent his most trusted servant to Haran to find a wife for Isaac. After meeting Rebekah at the well and being deeply impressed with her, the servant then went to her family and gave them gifts, which they accepted. This was the *erusin,* or the formal betrothal. The servant then returned to Canaan and brought Rebekah with him. Rebekah lived with her future mother-in-law in her tent. This was the transfer of her person to her husband's home. After an appropriate time, she moved into Isaac's tent, and the marriage was consummated.

Though they lived some distance apart, there would be no change of dwelling for Shana yet. Things had now changed. As Israel became settled and no longer nomadic, the process of marriage had evolved into two formal acts—the betrothal and the marriage, and only in rare cases did the bride change her home prior to the formal wedding. Once the *erusin* was performed, a woman became *arushah*, or "the betrothed one." It literally connoted that she was "a desired woman." The couple were then considered to be married, even though the bride would not live with her husband for at least one year. This allowed time for her to prepare herself to be a good wife and to accumulate more dowry and for him to become financially independent and prepare a home. So binding was betrothal that there were only two ways to dissolve it—with a written bill of divorcement, or through the death of one of the two parties.

Thus, though it would be another year before they became man and wife in the fullest sense, on this night Simeon knew that he was becoming the bridegroom and Shana the bride. And the village of Beth Neelah was in a state of great joy and celebration.

IV

As the hours dragged on, the women's conversation in the home of Yehuda the Zealot began to lag. All of the compliments had been given, all of the praises sung, all of the advice and counsel that Shana needed—and more!—had been doled out. The food and the wine, though in no way taken to excess, were taking their toll. Bodies grew weary, eyelids became heavy. The only sound in the house now was the quiet whispering between Leah and Shana. Shana still sat on her stool in the center of the room, and Leah sat on the floor beside her.

All around them, women and girls were leaning against the walls or curled up on rugs on the floor. Most were asleep.

Near the door a long table was filled with small hand lamps. At the moment, Deborah was moving along the table with a pitcher of olive oil, making sure every lamp was filled to its limited capacity and that the wicks were sufficiently long enough to burn while the oil lasted. Finished, she turned and looked at the two girls and smiled softly. Shana was two years older than Deborah's Leah, but that made no difference to them. They had been friends for years, and Deborah knew they had been hoping and planning for this night long before Simeon had ever decided that Shana was the woman he wanted to marry.

Suddenly Deborah cocked her head. Leah's head came up. For a moment their eyes met; then Leah jumped up and went to the door. She opened it quickly. Deborah hurried to her side. Now the sound was unmistakable. It was the high, wavering shriek of women expressing their joy. Some distance away, they could see flickering light illuminating the branches of the trees on the far side of the village.

Deborah spun back around. Women were already stirring and sitting up. Shana was on her feet now, smoothing down her dress and straightening her veil and headband. "He is coming!" Leah cried. "Hurry. He is coming!"

Deborah took three steps to the small fireplace, found the reed waiting there, and lit its tip. Now all of the women were up, fluffing their hair and brushing off their robes. Deborah moved to the table and began to light the lamps. The moment one was lit, Leah picked it up and handed it to one of the women. It was passed from hand to hand until the room was filled with light and each woman had a lamp of her own.

Deborah blew out the reed and set it down, then moved over to Shana. "Are you ready?"

Shana nodded, her eyes reflecting the dancing lights and her own radiant joy. "I am."

Deborah slipped an arm through Shana's right arm, and Leah, who was "maid of honor," slipped her arm through Shana's other arm. The others fell in behind in a rough line. Now the sound was not only noticeably closer but swelling rapidly in volume as people all over the village joined in the oncoming procession.

As the women moved out into the night, it was no longer dark. Not only were their own lamps providing light, but hundreds upon hundreds of lamps and candles were being lit all across the village. People were on the housetops and lining the streets, all of them crying out the news. "Here he comes! Here comes the bridegroom!"

V

Traditionally the betrothal ceremony took place in the home of the bridegroom, but due to the unique circumstances of Shana's family, the family of David ben Joseph had decided to hold the ceremony in Beth Neelah instead of Capernaum. But Yehuda's little cottage was far too confined to hold the crowd that had gathered that night. Because of that, the *chuppah*, the canopy, had been set up in the town square. Even then it was barely large enough to accommodate everyone. Tables laden with food for the all-night banquet which would follow lined one side of the square. Fortunately, it was a beautiful, warm spring evening, with the stars forming their own brilliant canopy overhead.

Both arrivals were carefully timed. Deborah led the bridal party directly to the square. Shana and Leah took their places by the left side of the *chuppah*. The other women stepped back, holding their lamps in front of them and singing softly. Some distance away, the men moved slowly, taking a circuitous route through the streets of the village and even into the olive orchards, making sure the bridal party would be in place when they arrived at the *chuppah*. Their procession was like a huge serpent, spangled with lights, weaving its way sinuously in and out of the streets of Beth Neelah.

When the men arrived at the square, their procession came to a stop. All of the shouting and the warbling also stopped, and a great quiet fell over the village. David and Yehuda handed their torches to Ephraim and Daniel, then escorted Simeon over to stand on the right side of the canopy, where Rabbi Nahum stood waiting. Beth Neelah had its own synagogue and part-time rabbi, but Rabbi Nahum of Sepphoris was Shana's uncle and would perform the ceremony.

Neither Simeon nor Shana had yet looked at each other, as was the custom.

The rabbi stepped forward, smiling broadly. "Simeon, son of David of Capernaum, we are here on this solemn occasion to betroth to you Shana, sister of Yehuda and Daniel of Beth Neelah. Is this not correct?"

"It is."

"Do you have the *ketubah?*"

"I do." His father moved forward again, holding out a small parchment scroll. Simeon took it and handed it to the rabbi. Rabbi Nahum untied the ribbon, unrolled the scroll, and read it carefully. Then he turned and held it up for all to see.

"This bill of betrothal, which in accordance with the Law, outlines the financial obligations of the bridegroom to his bride and the conditions under which those considerations shall be delivered. Also in keeping with the Law, the bride's representatives signify that she is a virgin, clean and pure, and that she is willing to become the wife of Simeon of Capernaum and serve with him faithfully for the remainder of her life."

He turned to Yehuda. "Have you, serving in the role of Shana's father, read the *ketubah?*"

"I have."

"And do you certify that the conditions outlined therein have been or shall be met?"

Yehuda turned and indicated the table that was set up not far from the canopy. It was filled with the presents Simeon's family had brought up from Capernaum—three full donkeys' worth. Most prominent was the exquisitely carved, highly polished oak chest. This would provide Shana a place for the items she would now begin collecting for her marriage. "I do so certify," he said loudly. "Simeon of Capernaum has been most generous, and we thank him and his family."

"You will then sign the *ketubah* and witness that it is acceptable. We shall have to have another witness as well."

Daniel moved up quickly. The two brothers went to the table and both signed their names to the bottom of the parchment. They rolled it back up and tied it again with the ribbon, then handed it back to Rabbi Nahum. With great solemnity, the rabbi turned to Simeon. "The *ketubah* has been examined and certified as acceptable." He handed him the scroll, and Simeon put it into a fold of his robe.

Rabbi Nahum turned back to face Simeon. Again the crowd grew very quiet. "Simeon of Capernaum, it is now time for the ceremony of *kiddushin*, or holiness. I remind both you and your bride of the sacred nature of what you are about to do. *Kadash* means that something is holy or sacred. When a man gives property to the temple, it becomes *kiddushin*, or consecrated to God. It is holy and can no longer be claimed by anyone else as their property. Do you understand that?"

"I do," Simeon said.

"With this betrothal, Shana becomes *arusah*, your espoused wife. She too is now *kiddushin*. She is forbidden to all other men and is consecrated to you, and you to her. Do you understand that as well?"

"I do."

He turned and looked at Shana. "I do," she said clearly.

The rabbi nodded in satisfaction. Then he turned to Yehuda and nodded. Yehuda and Daniel moved over to stand beside Shana. Simeon's father moved up beside his son, and Deborah came over to stand beside him as well. Her role of escort for Shana was now completed. She was now Simeon's mother. Together they led him beneath the canopy and then stepped back.

Yehuda took Shana's arm and, moving slowly and with great dignity, he escorted her to the canopy as well. Leah, as the first maid, followed closely behind. Yehuda brought Shana to stand on Simeon's right side, and then he stepped to his left side, now serving as Simeon's man of honor. Leah took her place on the opposite side of the canopy as the maid of honor.

The air was filled with great expectancy. What would happen now was based on traditions thousands of years old. Yehuda had brought Shana to Simeon because when Adam and Eve were married, God served as Eve's escort "and brought her unto Adam." Shana was placed at Simeon's right hand because in the Psalms it said, "Upon thy right hand, did stand the queen."

The young couple turned and faced each other. For the first time Shana looked up fully into Simeon's face. Though she did not smile—this was a time of great solemnity—her eyes were dancing with happiness. Then she slowly lowered her head and Simeon carefully reached out and lifted the veil that covered her hair and dropped it in front of her face.

As he lowered his hands again, a cry of joy exploded from the crowd. Two thousand years before, when Rebekah was brought to Isaac, as recorded in the book of Genesis, she covered her face with a veil prior to her meeting with him. The "covering" of the bride was the signal for the crowd. As one, they shouted out, invoking the same benediction that Rebekah's family had pronounced when she had been betrothed to Isaac. "Blessed be our sister. Be thou the mother of thousands of millions, and let thy seed possess the gate of those who hate them." The sound reverberated off the stone buildings and faded away into the pine-covered hills that towered over the village.

When it was quiet again, Simeon reached into the folds of his robe and withdrew the parchment scroll. "Shana, sister of Yehuda and Daniel of Beth Neelah, with this *ketubah* and the money that is promised therein, you are now betrothed to me in accordance with the laws of Moses and of Israel." He extended the scroll, and she took it gravely. She held it in both hands for a few moments; then Leah came forward and took it from her to hold until the ceremony was complete.

Deborah was nodding. This was a custom she liked very much. The prenuptial agreement was a great protection to the bride, and this is why the scroll was given directly to her. In the first place, it was a way of showing that the future husband was capable of caring for his wife and family. More important, where the Law of Moses allowed a man to divorce his wife without her consent, the *ketubah* was a woman's protection. It guaranteed a financial settlement in the case of either death or divorce. In effect, it also served as a deterrent against hasty divorces.

In the writings of Jeremiah the prophet, it is said that a woman shall "compass" or go around a man. This was interpreted to mean that a woman should court a man, but here it would also be taken literally. Shana began a slow circle around Simeon, pronouncing the three expressions of betrothal given in the writings of the prophet Hosea. "I betroth me unto thee forever." She circled him once. "I betroth thee unto me in righteousness and in judgment, in loving kindness and in mercies." She completed the second circle. "I betroth thee unto me in faithfulness, and thou shalt know the Lord." As the last words were spoken, she completed the third and final circle.

Rabbi Nahum stepped to a small table on which sat a silver goblet and a pitcher of wine. He filled the cup, lifted it high, and intoned the traditional benediction over wine. Then he offered a second benediction. "To him who sanctifies his people Israel by the rite of the *chuppah*, or the canopy, and the rite of *kiddushin*. Amen."

"Amen!" everyone present echoed.

The rabbi moved to the canopy and handed the cup to Simeon. Watching Shana gravely over the top of the cup, he took one swallow. Then, holding the cup in both hands, he gave it to Shana. "With the sharing of this wine, we signify the sharing of our lives in this betrothal."

"Amen," Shana said solemnly. She took the cup and also drank one swallow.

"You may now kiss as husband and wife," Rabbi Nahum said, taking the cup back.

"*Mazal tov! Mazal tov!*" Good luck! The guests burst forth as Simeon lifted the veil and for the first time ever, gently kissed his new bride.

CHAPTER NOTES

Much of what we know about betrothal and marriage customs at the time of Jesus comes from Talmudic tradition. However, the Talmud, which in Judaism is the most sacred collection of writings after the Bible, was not put into written form until sometime after the destruction of the temple in A.D. 70. Therefore, it is difficult to determine how much of what is written there describes the practices at the time of Christ. Some things can be dated with some certainty, however. For example, there is evidence that the *ketubah*, or prenuptial contract, dates back to at least four hundred years before Christ.

The author relied heavily on the Talmudic descriptions in writing this chapter (see Bloch, pp. 23–34, who provided the greatest help). However, because all customs cannot be dated with precision and because even the Talmud does not contain sufficient detail to fill in every niche a novel may require, the author also took liberties in creating some of the details given here. Normally the betrothal period was for twelve months. If the marriage was arranged while the girl was quite young, the waiting period might last for several years until she reached maturity. When it was a widow who remarried, the waiting period was limited to thirty days.

CHAPTER 9

TEN MEASURES OF BEAUTY CAME INTO THE WORLD; OF THESE,
NINE WERE TAKEN BY JERUSALEM.

—*Rabbinical Proverb*

I

3 APRIL, A.D. 30

The home of Mordechai ben Uzziel was located in the Upper City,
on the eastern shoulder of Mount Zion. It was just three houses down
from the house of Caiaphas, the current high priest. The Upper City
was the home of Jerusalem's wealthy and powerful, and every home
was palatial. But the home of Mordechai ben Uzziel was exceeded in
both space and cost by only two others in the city—the house of
Caiaphas, and that of his father-in-law, Annas. Annas had placed
Caiaphas in the powerful office of high priest when the Romans made
him step down from the office some years earlier. Between them, they
had controlled the office for more than thirty years now. They were
without question the most powerful men in Judea. It would have been
a serious lapse in judgment for Mordechai to have built a home more
pretentious than theirs, even though, if the truth be known, he was
richer by far than either of them or perhaps both of them together.

As Miriam stood at the window of her bedroom looking out on the magnificent view of the Temple Mount below, now bathed in the first rose pink of sunrise, she thought about her father and his immense fortune. Her eyes moved to the north where she could see the smoke from a thousand morning cooking fires smudging the still air. And she wondered about the inequity of life, as she had so many times before.

Whenever Miriam walked through the other quarters of the city, she came away feeling guilty and filled with a deep and troubling question. What had she done to deserve her station in life? Why was she wrapped in luxury beyond what the poor could even imagine? What had they done that had brought them forth in such squalor and misery?

It was a question she couldn't discuss with her father. The Sadducees held strictly to the writings of Moses, and in the writings of Moses there was no specific mention of either a premortal or postmortal state of existence. Therefore the Sadducees denied that there would be a resurrection and said that the soul perished with the body at death. Miriam didn't believe that. Couldn't believe it. She believed that the writings of the other prophets were inspired of God as well, and they definitely spoke of both a premortal state and of resurrection after death. She and her father had gone through some flaming battles over theology, and finally Miriam decided it wasn't worth it. She clearly was not going to change his mind, and she wasn't going to let him change hers. So they had backed off into an unspoken neutral zone that neither violated.

Once again this morning, she had the strong conviction that birth could not simply be an act of sheer random chance. But why was she so fortunate? She didn't know. What she did know was that at this Passover season, when she always felt increased gratitude to the Lord, she wanted to raise her face to the sky and shout, "Blessed art thou, Adonai, our Lord. I thank Thee for everything."

There was a soft knock at the door. "Come in," she called, without turning around. At this hour it could be only one person.

The door opened and Livia came in, her bare feet making no sound on the marble tiles.

"Good morning, Livia."

"Good morning, Miriam. So you are awake?"

"Yes. I've been up for some time already. Is Papa ready for breakfast?"

"He's gone."

Miriam turned in surprise. "Already?" Her father was a person of the night, often not even coming home until long after sundown. So rising early was not his usual habit. And this was the Week of Unleavened Bread, which preceded Passover. It was traditional for them to eat breakfast every day together during this greatest of all the festivals.

"Yes," Livia answered. "He said to tell you he was sorry. He got word late last night that he is to go to the Antonia Fortress to meet with that Roman tribune this morning. Something to do with a message from the governor, he said."

Miriam felt a little leap inside her. So it was true. Marcus Quadratus Didius had come as promised. She wasn't sure whether to feel elation or anxiety. She had begun to wonder if he had forgotten all about his promise.

As if she had spoken it aloud, Livia answered her question. "Your father said to tell you that the tribune will be dining with us this evening. He wants you to supervise the servants when they go to the market today so that only the finest food is purchased and prepared."

Again there was that little flutter inside her; then a thought struck Miriam. She smiled. "I wonder how Marcus Didius will view a meal where only unleavened bread is served."

Livia was ready with an answer. "Your father mentioned that. He said that he wants you to get some bread that is leavened to serve to him."

Shocked, Miriam stared at Livia. "He wants me to bring leavened bread into the house?"

Livia gave a quick nod.

Miriam moved back and sat on the bed. When the Lord told Moses to deliver the children of Israel from Egypt, he gave strict instructions that for one full week no leavened bread be eaten. But more than that, the Lord commanded the Israelites to put all leaven out of their houses. Leaven, or yeast, easily spoiled. Leavened bread quickly turned moldy; whereas *matzos,* or *un*leavened bread, could last indefinitely. The rabbis had interpreted the prohibition against leaven during this time as symbolic of spiritual corruption. Thus, in every Jewish home across the empire, to prepare for the Week of Unleavened Bread and *Pesach,* or Passover, which followed it, families made a ritual of going through the house and discarding any leaven or anything that had leaven in it. This was done with great solemnity, for the Lord had said, "Whosoever eateth leavened bread from the first day until the seventh, that soul shall be cut off from Israel."

Her father and the rest of the aristocracy that made up the Sadducean class didn't pay much attention to all of the formalities the Pharisees wrapped around the festivals, but this was one even they observed. She and Livia had gone through the palatial home just three days before, purging every cupboard, carefully sweeping out even the crumbs that had fallen on the floor.

"I won't do it," Miriam said.

"Miriam!"

"I don't care what Father says. We are not bringing leaven of any kind into this house. Not this week." And then she brightened. "I'll explain it to Marcus. Surely he won't be offended by our determination to observe our traditions. It's not like we're going to ask him to eat frogs or something terrible like that."

Livia frowned. "Actually, the Romans do eat the legs from frogs."

Miriam gave her a sharp look, hardly believing it, but not really thinking that Livia would tease her about something like that.

Then she pushed aside all thoughts of what her father would say when she disobeyed him. She stood and walked swiftly to the oak chest that half filled one wall and threw open the doors. "Can you come with me and help, Livia?"

The servant's eyes widened in surprise—as if she had to request her permission! "But of course."

Seeing her look, Miriam stopped. "What?"

Livia shook her head. In the last few days Miriam's attitude toward Livia had changed noticeably. Where before she commanded, now she asked. Where before she told Livia what needed to be done, now she consulted her, sought her opinion, even in important decisions. And it was not just a surface courtesy. She seemed to really want to know.

The change had been evident enough that at dinner the previous evening, Mordechai had twice given Miriam sharp glances when she spoke to Livia so openly. Miriam, of course, hadn't noticed, or if she did she had ignored them. Had the words of the Galilean Zealot about Livia being a slave so stung her mistress? That was when the whole change in her behavior had begun. Or was it that horrible experience with Moshe Ya'abin? Something had happened that day, Livia knew, that had been very significant for the both of them.

Well, Livia thought happily, it didn't matter. All she knew was that she and Miriam were becoming more friends than associates, more sisters than servant and master, and she was happier than she had been for many years.

Miriam pulled down a dress made of the finest Egyptian linen and held it up. It was a soft blue and provided the perfect contrast for her long dark hair and dark eyes. "What do you think?" she asked.

"For shopping?" Livia laughed.

Miriam was momentarily flustered. "I thought if we left right now we could go up on the Temple Mount first. You know how I love it up there, especially during feast days. I love to see people from all over the empire."

"That would be nice," Livia answered. She loved going up there as much as Miriam. She didn't like the crowds, but the temple complex was so awe inspiring, so lifting to her spirits. "Then, yes. If we are going to the temple, that dress is one of my favorites."

"Good!" Miriam twirled around once, humming softly to herself.

"You wouldn't be thinking of going by the entrance to the Antonia Fortress on the chance that you might see your father and the tribune, would you?" Livia teased.

Miriam waved airily. "One never knows where one's feet might take her."

II

Jerusalem, or *Yerushalaim* in Hebrew, sat squarely astride the hill country of Judea. As Miriam and Livia started down from the Upper City, Miriam took it all in, loving this view of her home city. Under the Jebusites, the city occupied only Mount Ophel, a narrow ridge that divided the Kidron Valley from the Tyropoean (or Cheesemakers') Valley. When King David made it the capital of his new kingdom a thousand years earlier, it spread northward onto Mount Moriah. On Mount Moriah David's son and successor, King Solomon, built the first temple. Over the generations the city had ebbed and flowed across the surrounding hills and valleys.

Now with a population approaching two hundred thousand, in addition to Mount Ophel and Mount Moriah, it also covered Mount Zion on the west, went as far as Mount Scopus on the north, and included two villages on the Mount of Olives to the east. These were

Bethphage, or the House of Unripened Figs, which was right near the top of the ridgeline, and Bethany, the House of Dates, a little down the eastern slope. Both villages were now considered to be part of the city.

The temple of Solomon was supposed to have been a magnificent structure, built on the very spot where Abraham was said to have brought his son Isaac to be sacrificed. Six hundred years before, the Babylonians had destroyed that temple and sacked its treasures. When Cyrus, king of Persia, decreed that the Jews could return to their homeland seventy years later, they were granted permission to rebuild the temple. This was done under Zerubbabel, but the second temple was a mere shadow of its former glory.

Then came Herod the Great.

Thoroughly hellenized and romanized, Herod nevertheless wanted to do something that would keep his Jewish subjects at least somewhat pacified. The Herods were Idumeans, a cousin tribe that was looked upon by the Jews as being only one slight step above the detested Samaritans. Herod's father, Antipater, had thrown his armies into alliance with Rome in battling with the hated Parthians to the east and had won himself a small kingdom as a reward. Using all of his shrewdness and cunning, a marriage to the royal Hasmonean family, and every other device that would propel him forward, Herod had eventually become king over all the province of Judea. His subjects hated him with unrestrained passion and feared him even more. He was brilliant, a gifted ruler, utterly ruthless, and completely without morals. Murder and betrayal were common stepping-stones to achieving and maintaining power in this age, but Herod raised such tactics to new heights. Even as he solidified his power with Rome, he estranged himself further and further from his Jewish subjects.

Then in the eighteenth year of his reign, he hit upon an idea that even his most virulent enemies could not demean. The temple built by Zerubbabel was an embarrassment. Herod's own palace near the

Jaffa Gate and many of the mansions in the Upper City were more glorious than the house of the Lord. Assuring the religious leaders that he would allow them to supervise the reconstruction at every hand so that no scriptural laws were violated, he began one of the greatest of all his construction projects.

First, he built massive retaining walls and hauled in enough fill to extend the temple platform to more than ten acres, or about twice its original size. In essence he took the narrow ridge top of Mount Moriah and made it like the top of a table. The temple itself and its immediate courtyards, magnificently wrought of Jerusalem limestone and marble, were completed in eighteen months, without any interruption of the daily sacrifice.

But this was only the beginning. He built a huge complex of court-yards, plazas, colonnades, staircases, gates, and bridges. He constructed covered galleries on three sides of the platform, but along the south end of the platform he constructed what he called the Royal Stoa, but what the people immediately called Solomon's Porches. Larger than the temple itself, this was the crowning piece of the project. One hundred and sixty columns of solid stone were quarried and brought to the site. Massive monoliths, the columns were fifty feet high and so large that it took three men with outstretched arms to encircle one of them. Putting them in four rows of forty columns each, he constructed a covered colonnade that filled the entire south end of the Temple Mount. This was left open on the north side, providing access to the great plaza that surrounded the temple.

Always given to the grandiose and the lavish, Herod provided some spectacular entryways to the complex. The main entrance on the west was over a bridge that spanned the Tyropoean Valley to the Upper City. It was almost half a mile long and supported by arches more than a hundred feet high. On the southwest he created a massive staircase that opened into Solomon's Porches. On the south, where the original royal city of David had once been, the north end of Mount

Ophel was cleared and a great plaza created. Here the towering walls were pierced by two entrances, one a double gate, and the other a triple gate that led through tunnels up into Solomon's Porches as well. On the east facing the Mount of Olives was the Golden Gate, an entry thought by many to be so beautiful and so wondrous as to give a special blessing to any who entered there.

Since Miriam and Livia were coming from the Upper City, the shortest and easiest way for them to go onto the Temple Mount would have been to cross the great bridge and enter through the west gate. But unless she was in a hurry, Miriam preferred the southwest entrance. Her feet were completely healed now, but she was determined that never again would she be found vulnerable to her own softness. Since returning to Jerusalem, she and Livia took long walks every day. Climbing the great staircase, which had more than three hundred steps, was the ultimate test of their endurance.

As they finally reached the top, entering the coolness of the colonnade, the two women stopped to catch their breath.

"Do you want to rest here for a moment?" Miriam asked through her labored breathing. It was going to be a warm day, and she could feel the beads of perspiration forming on her forehead.

"It's up to you," Livia said automatically. She was leaning against one of the massive columns and taking deep breaths.

Miriam's mouth pulled down as she gave Livia a warning look.

Apparently remembering the new order of things, Livia corrected herself quickly. "No, I'm ready to go on if you are."

Miriam straightened. "I am." She looked around. "Let's walk down to the apse and see if the Council is in session." On the east end of Solomon's Porches, a large semicircular room had been built that was known as the apse. Here the Great Sanhedrin met to conduct their business. That was a ruse, of course. The Council did not meet on holy days, but it was unlikely that Livia would know that.

Livia poked at her. "Yes, perhaps your father will bring the Roman officer to the assembly."

Miriam blushed, a little chagrined that she was so transparent. No Roman would be invited to attend the Sanhedrin, but she had wondered if her father might show Marcus where they met. It was an impressive sight. "I didn't get to say good-bye to Papa this morning, that's all," she finally murmured.

"Of course," Livia said. Miriam was grateful Livia hadn't pointed out that those days when Miriam got to say good-bye to her father were more the exception than the rule.

They started moving eastward, working their way through the throngs. Though it was still early, Solomon's Porches were already crowded, and Miriam knew that by midday the porches would hold a veritable crush of people. At festivals the population always swelled dramatically. But this was the beginning of Passover. The population of Jerusalem had probably quintupled in the last few days as Jews from all over the empire had come to observe this greatest of all the feast days.

Before they even reached the apse, Miriam could tell nothing official was going on. It was too noisy, too chaotic. The Great Sanhedrin was authorized by the Romans to keep their own group of temple guards—soldiers, in actuality—who were always nearby to keep order when the Council was in session or when its members were there talking informally. As they drew closer, Miriam could see that there were no guards present.

Disappointed, she changed directions. "They're not there," she said to Livia. "Let's go to the market."

Miriam headed for the Court of the Gentiles, as the great open plaza on the Temple Mount was known, a route that would take her around the east side of the temple, not the shorter, more direct route to the west gate. "You wouldn't be going to the marketplace by way of the Antonia Fortress would you?" Livia asked wryly.

Miriam eyed her quickly, trying to decide if she could successfully protest her innocence. Then she laughed in surrender. "One never knows where one's feet might take her."

III

Mordechai ben Uzziel approached the two guards standing at the great double gate that blocked the entrance to the Antonia Fortress. Seeing his bold approach brought them instantly to alert. They stiffened, their spears coming forward so they could bring them into play in an instant if necessary.

"I have an audience with Tribune Marcus Quadratus Didius," he said in a low growl, which only made his Latin sound worse. He found their wariness both amusing and irritating.

"Are you Mordechai the Jew?"

"I am Mordechai the Sadducee," he snapped, "member of the Great Council of Jerusalem."

The one nearest to a small wooden door beside the gate saluted and turned. "The tribune is expecting you. Follow me."

Good, Mordechai thought. It was right that word had been left with the watch at the gate. It showed that Pilate was taking all of this seriously. Then the guard saw the package Mordechai was holding and hesitated.

Mordechai understood immediately. "It's an extra tunic." He unwrapped it and held it out for the man to see.

"Thank you."

They entered the vast courtyard, and the legionnaire turned sharply to the right, headed for the main hall. Mordechai stopped. "I will wait here."

The man looked at him in surprise, then shook his head, a little disgusted. Evidently he had dealt with these Jews before. "Yes, of course."

As he walked away, Mordechai looked around. The rest of the temple complex was built on the narrow ridge of Mount Moriah. On three sides the walls built by Herod rose from steep hillsides, providing a natural defense. But on the north the ridge leveled out, making the entire complex vulnerable to attack from that quarter. With his usual eye for fortification as well as beauty, Herod had built a massive fortress on the northwest corner of the mount and named it for Marcus Antonius, who at that time was in ascendancy in the Roman power structure.

Mordechai smiled to himself. His people hated Herod with undiluted passion, but he would have loved to have met the man. When Antony was defeated at the Battle of Actium by Octavian, the man who would go on to become Augustus Caesar, Herod was caught in the embarrassing position of having backed the losing side. But with the adroitness of a cat dropped from a window, Herod switched loyalties and landed neatly on his feet. While Antony slunk off to Egypt to commit suicide with Cleopatra, Herod threw his powerful armies behind Octavian and helped him consolidate his power in the east. For that, he was given the kingship he so desperately wanted.

The Antonia Fortress was just that. Built of heavy stone masonry that could withstand battering rams for many days, it had four great towers on each corner to give its defenders a clear field of fire against anyone trying to besiege it. It had its own cisterns and several large storehouses built into the walls, where enough food to sustain a cohort for several months was stockpiled.

You couldn't help but admire a man that shrewd, Mordechai decided. Not only was the fortress an important defense against any attack from the vulnerable north side, but Herod had been clever enough to attach it to the Temple Mount itself. He knew as well as anyone that if there was ever going to be trouble with the Jews, it would likely begin right here. Thus the Romans kept a garrison stationed here all the time, a garrison that was greatly strengthened during festivals like the present one. One sign of trouble and the legionnaires could pour out into the great courtyards and deal with it before it got out of hand.

He heard the crunch of *caligulas* on stone and turned. Tribune Marcus Didius was coming toward him, the guard following directly behind.

"Ah, Mordechai," he said. "Thank you for coming. I was hoping it wasn't too late for my message."

To Mordechai's relief, he spoke in Aramaic. It wasn't as fluent as Pilate's, but for being in the country only six months, it was surprisingly good. "There is no need for an apology."

"Good. Come, I have some breakfast waiting in my quarters. We can talk there."

Mordechai hesitated, looking away.

Marcus instantly understood. "Oh, yes. The contamination factor." It was said with dry humor.

"I find such practices highly offensive," Mordechai said smoothly, "and hold no such feelings about Gentiles myself. To think that simply being in the presence of a non-Jew somehow defiles a man is so ridiculous as to require no further comment. However, there are those on the Council who would use the fact that I ate at the table of a Roman officer, especially during Passover, as a weapon against me. I apologize for the narrow-minded bigotry of some of our people."

Marcus nodded. It was a point well made. "I understand. Even in the Senate of Rome we have those who watch eagerly for any excuse to pull down those who are stronger than themselves."

There was a quick flash of gratitude in Mordechai's eyes. If Marcus had insisted, he would have had no choice. "Shall we walk in the courtyard as we talk?" he asked, motioning toward the gate.

"Yes. This is my third time here in Jerusalem, and yet the press of business has kept me from seeing your great temple. I would like that."

Again Mordechai hesitated, choosing his words. "I have no wish to offend, Marcus, but—"

Marcus had started toward the gate. He stopped and turned back. "I am not easily offended, Mordechai. Say on."

The Sadducee withdrew the tunic from the package. "The temple courtyards are crowded today with the Passover. The people are used to seeing the soldiers, but a Roman officer walking around in full uniform will draw many stares. There is no danger, of course," he added quickly. "I just wondered if you might be more comfortable with this."

Marcus looked at the tunic, then at Mordechai. "I understand," he said, taking it. "Thank you." *I also understand that it will draw less attention to Mordechai the Sadducee if he is not seen holding close conversations with a Roman officer.* But Marcus said nothing more. He removed his helmet and unbuckled his breastplate and handed them to the guard. "Put these in my quarters."

Suddenly Sextus Rubrius appeared from nowhere. Seeing the look on the centurion's face, Marcus started to explain. The centurion waved it off. "I agree with Mordechai. It would be better this way."

With that Marcus began to don the tunic. When they were finished, they moved to the small door and stepped through it to the outside. A moment later, Sextus came through as well. Marcus looked at him in surprise.

Sextus grinned faintly. "I'm just going to walk around," he said.

But when they started off, Mordechai saw that the centurion fell in at a discreet distance behind them, his eyes constantly moving, taking in everything.

Marcus saw it too and grunted to himself. He would regret seeing Sextus Rubrius posted back to Capernaum after Passover was done. He had come to value the wisdom and courage of this particular officer, but so had Pilate, and Capernaum was an important outpost. When the time came for Marcus to be transferred to a new post, he would see if there was any way to take Sextus with him.

It surprised Marcus to see how many people were out and about already. It was barely the second hour of the day, and the sun was just now flooding over the eastern walls to illuminate the courtyards, but they were already heavily thronged. Judging from the dress he saw, many were obviously from other provinces, some from distant parts of the empire. He heard snatches of strange languages all around him.

"It is a requirement of the Mosaic Law," Mordechai said, noting where Marcus was looking. "If at all possible, every Jew comes to Jerusalem for Passover each year, even those in the *Diaspora*."

"The Diaspora?"

"Yes, the Dispersion. After our people were taken captive into Babylon, many began to settle in various parts of the world. Up until that time we had been all right here in our land, so we called that natural migration the Dispersion."

"And your people are expected to come here for Passover even from distant places?"

"Supposedly. In reality, some come only once or twice in a lifetime, but if they can manage it, it is expected that they will come." He looked around. "The Council estimates that the normal population of Jerusalem, which is about two hundred thousand, swells to as many as a million during *Pesach,* as we call Passover."

"Then it is no wonder the governor increases the size of the garrison at this time."

Mordechai nodded. That was just the opening for which he had been waiting. "Your message said you bring word from the governor."

"I do," Marcus said, moving a little closer and lowering his voice. "He received your plan and heartily approves. If you can deliver the Zealot leadership, Pilate agrees to all of your conditions."

"Including the increased judicial powers for the Sanhedrin?"

"Yes."

A surge of elation shot through Mordechai. It was going to work. "Wonderful."

"He wants to know the name of the man you will use to set this all up. He says he must give his approval for that as well."

Mordechai stopped. Marcus stopped as well and turned to face him. "There is too much at stake to have something go wrong," the tribune said.

"There is too much at stake to have a name whispered in the wrong places," Mordechai shot right back.

That was basically an insult, Marcus thought. This Jew was suggesting that either he or the governor could not be trusted. But he also understood the concern in Mordechai's face. This was an extremely delicate matter, one that could do irreparable damage to Mordechai's person and the Sanhedrin as well. "Pilate authorized me to tell you that no one but me will hear that name from you, and no one but him will hear that name from me. But he insists that he know."

"So he does not trust my judgment?"

"Pilate does not trust anyone's judgment but his own," Marcus said blandly. "That is what makes him such an effective governor."

Mordechai began to walk again, very slowly now. After several paces, he spoke, choosing his words with great care. "I understand the governor's concern, but you must understand my position. Even in the inner circle, no one but me knows the name. They have approved the plan, but not even they know who I will choose to carry it out. It has to be this way. One unguarded whisper and it could bring us all to ruin. Utter ruin! You cannot comprehend the disaster that would be."

Marcus said nothing for a moment. In fact, Pilate had instructed him to push hard to find out who Mordechai would select as his instrument of treachery, but he had given him some leeway if Mordechai balked.

"I haven't yet talked to this person. He may not agree."

"Once it is set, then will you give us the name?"

Mordechai shook his head adamantly. "I cannot. You must help the governor see why that is so."

Again Marcus was quiet for a time. Then: "Do we have your word that you will keep us informed of every other detail?"

"Every one, *if* I have your solemn word that only the two of you will hear them. Again, all things must be done with the greatest discretion."

"We understand. That goes without saying."

"Good."

"How soon will you make contact with this man?"

"Soon. During the festival." There was a short laugh. "Assuming that your soldiers don't see him first and he ends up in the cells of the Antonia waiting crucifixion."

Marcus raised one eyebrow. So the man was wanted by Rome. Pilate would be pleased to hear that. The Zealots were not going to trust anyone who wasn't an avowed enemy of Rome. He thought about asking another question, pressing for more information, but sensed that Mordechai was now wishing he had not said even that much.

Suddenly they heard a shout. "Father!"

They turned. Through the crowd they could see a woman waving frantically, pushing toward them.

"Miriam?" Mordechai said in complete surprise.

Now Marcus could see her clearly. She was smiling and waving her arm. He laughed. Perfect! He had planned to ask Mordechai about his daughter once they finished their business.

The older man shot Marcus a quick look. "Everything is set then?" he said in a low voice. "I am free to proceed?"

"Yes."

"Good." The somber expression gave way to a smile as he turned to greet his daughter.

Marcus grinned as he saw Miriam stop, her mouth opening in surprise as she only now recognized who it was in the simple brown tunic walking with her father. He lifted a hand. "*Shalom*, Miriam."

CHAPTER 10

FOR THE ZEAL OF THINE HOUSE HATH EATEN ME UP.

—*Psalm 69:9*

I

3 APRIL, A.D. 30

"Wait, wait," Marcus said, holding up his hands in surrender. "Start over again."

Miriam cocked her head and gave him a stern look. "Please pay attention, Tribune. It was you who said you wanted to learn about the Temple Mount." She smiled. They were speaking in Latin, at her insistence.

He laughed. "Yes. Yes, I did. But I didn't realize I would have to think so hard."

The two of them stood at the east side of the temple, near what was known as the wall of partition.

"Think of the Temple Mount as a vast table," she began again. "The whole tabletop is the Court of the Gentiles. It is the largest of all the courts, as you can see. We call it the Court of the Gentiles because anyone can come into it, even those who are not of our faith."

"The *goyim*, as you call us," he said with a sardonic smile.

Surprised that he knew the term, she nodded. "Yes. It's unfortunate that some have turned that word into a term of derision, but it literally means 'the nations.' So a *goy* is only someone of a nation other than Israel."

She stopped, watching his face. That seemed to satisfy him, so she went on. "So in the Court of the Gentiles, anyone and everyone—Roman, Nubian, Parthian, Egyptian—are welcome as long as they are willing to act with some reverence and decorum."

"I understand."

"Good. Now in the center of the tabletop is a series of platforms built one upon the other. The first and largest platform, the one you see right before us, is five steps higher than the main court. This raises the temple and the courts around it above the rest of the Temple Mount and clearly defines the area where Gentiles are not allowed to go. That is why they have built this wall or partition all the way around it."

She reached out and touched the marble partition in front of them. It was about chest high and made of thin sheets of beautifully decorated and highly polished marble. These were held in place by marble pillars about four or five feet apart, with openings allowing passage at regular intervals. "We call it the *soreg*, or wall of partition. It is a way to clearly mark the point where Gentiles can go no farther."

"On pain of death?" he asked dryly. He took a step forward and reached out with his finger and began to trace the letters carved in the stone. Written in both Greek and Latin, the inscription he touched read: *No foreigner is allowed within this balustrade and embankment about the sanctuary. Whoever is caught therein will be personally responsible for his ensuing death.*

Miriam watched him, searching for a way to explain.

He turned. "If I were to step through there"—he was pointing at one of the entrances—"would I really put my life in peril?"

He was half teasing, but the very thought made her shudder. "Yes,

Marcus. If they knew you were a Roman, there would be an instant riot. You would be dead in moments."

It pleased him that in her earnestness she had called him by his given name for the first time. So he decided to prolong this obvious concern. He half turned until he saw the glint of Sextus Rubrius' helmet in the crowd. "My loyal centurion would rush in to save me," he said. His face was sober, but his eyes were laughing at how serious she had become.

Miriam turned as well and saw the other soldier who had been shadowing them the whole time. She had already recognized him as the man who escorted her and her father from Caesarea to Jerusalem a week or so before. "Then he would die too," Miriam said quietly. "It is a law that the Emperor Augustus gave us permission to enforce. Protecting the sanctity of the temple from defilement is of the utmost importance to us."

Now all humor went out of him. "Yes, I know. I was briefed expressly on this peculiarity when I arrived in Judea."

She looked at him for several seconds, sensing that her comment had offended him.

He reached his hand over the top of the partition. "Does putting my hand over the wall defile your religion as well?" Then he shook his head, half speaking to himself. "I must say I find it surprising that the emperor would give you that kind of authority."

She decided that the only way out of this was to treat it lightly. "But it is God who gives us the authority," she said sweetly. "The emperor only validates it."

He laughed, pleased that she would not be bested by him. "I wonder if anyone has ever told Caesar that." He lifted his head, shading his eyes from the blinding reflection of the sun off the golden walls of the temple. "So, we are here in the Court of the Unclean. What comes next?"

They stood close together, the crowds swirling around them and paying them no attention. In addition to the centurion, who hovered unobtrusively nearby, Miriam could also see Livia not far away. When her father suggested that Miriam take the Roman officer on a tour of the Temple Mount, Miriam had considered sending Livia to do the shopping without her. Then she realized that act might be interpreted by Marcus as being too bold on her part. Without being asked, Livia moved away, but she tried to stay within sight of Miriam so as to keep things appropriate and proper.

The Passover crowds had increased dramatically now, spilling out from the temple courtyards following the morning sacrifice, so Marcus and Miriam stayed close together. To her surprise, until the last few moments, she had found him in a teasing mood, and their conversation was filled with light banter and gentle jabs at one another. With his uniform covered by the tunic, there were times when she forgot she was in the company of a Roman gentleman and a commanding officer in the tenth legion.

Grateful to be off the subject of the wall of partition, she pointed at walls behind the partition, which towered above them. "Well, as you can see, the temple and the inner courts are all enclosed as well. Three large gates lead into the first court, which is called the Court of the Women."

"Because only women can enter there?"

"Oh no, but women can't go beyond there except to make a sacrifice. Also, there's a place in that court especially for women to worship, and that also gives it its name. It's beautiful inside. It too is surrounded by ornate columns, though they are not anywhere nearly as grand as the porticos around the Court of the Gentiles."

He nodded, his eyes taking in the walls and buildings that were in front of them.

"On the west side of the Court of the Women is a beautiful curved stairway that leads to the Nicanor Gate. It is called that because its set of massive, ornately carved bronze doors was donated by a very wealthy

Alexandrian Jew named Nicanor. They open onto the Court of Israel, where the men worship. On the west side of that court is a low balustrade which allows people to look into the Court of the Priests. There only those who are priests and Levites are allowed to enter."

She stopped to see if he had any questions, but he only nodded. "So in a way, permission to enter becomes more and more restricted as you move in toward the temple. In the center of the Court of the Priests is the great horned altar on which we offer our sacrifices."

"To your one God," he said. "What is it you call him again?"

"His name is sacred, so we most often call him *Adonai*, Lord, so that we don't use his name too frequently. But his name is formed by four Hebrew letters—YHVH—which is a Hebrew root meaning 'to be' or 'to exist.' When Moses, one of our ancient prophets, asked God by what name he should be called, he said, 'I am that I AM. Tell the people that I AM sends you.'"

"Hmm."

He seemed intrigued, so she decided to add one more thing. "In our faith, we believe that there is only one god in all the world who can actually say, 'I am. I exist. I live.'"

If he heard that, he gave no sign. "And the temple is in the Court of the Priests?"

"Yes, it stands on the western end of that court. It was built of the most carefully cut marble blocks—Herod brought in only the finest of stonemasons from Phoenicia. Then these blocks were covered with gold plating. It is glorious. As you can see, when the sun shines upon it, it is so dazzling that one can hardly bear to look at it. It bathes the whole Temple Mount in golden light."

"I'll wager there are some who can barely stand to look upon that much gold without being overwhelmed by covetousness."

Miriam didn't smile. "The temple has been sacked by conquerors more than once."

"So what is it like inside?" he asked.

She hesitated for a moment. "Within the temple itself, there are two main rooms. The first is called the Holy Place. Inside that room is a table on which we put what we call the shewbread, bread that is baked especially as an offering to God. There is also an altar for burning incense in connection with the morning and evening prayers and also the great *menorah,* the sacred candlestick or lampstand. All of these are also made of gold."

"Ah, yes. Sextus Rubrius told me about that candlestick. He says it is massive."

"They say it is taller than a man and has seven lamps, signifying the perfect light of God's Spirit. It is always kept burning and provides the only light inside the temple."

"They say?" he repeated. "You mean you've never seen it?"

She smiled and shook her head. "No one is allowed into the temple except the priests, and they can go only into the Holy Place. The second room, which is half the size of the first, we call the Most Holy Place, or the Holy of Holies. It is divided from the Holy Place by a veil on which are embroidered *cherubim.*"

"Cherubim?" She had used the Aramaic word and not the Latin.

"Yes, what you would call angels. They represent sentinels who stand guard and protect the entry to Deity."

"And your people can't go into this Most Holy Place? That seems odd. I thought a temple was supposed to be a place of worship for all those who follow that god."

She shook her head. "No one enters the Holy of Holies except the high priest himself, and then only once a year on the Day of Atonement, what we call *Yom Kippur.*"

Marcus stared at her in amazement. The building she was describing towered above the inner walls, rising to a height of a hundred and fifty feet or more. It was a magnificent structure, worthy of any Roman deity and more. "Only one man goes inside and then only once a year?"

She shook her head. "I was talking only about the Holy of Holies. The priests go into the Holy Place every day to burn incense, and they change the shewbread each week. But entry through the veil into the Most Holy Place, yes, only the high priest and only once each year. And that happens only after he goes through a careful ritual of purification."

He blew out his breath. "You have a very strange religion," he said. But it came out without malice and sounded almost half like a compliment.

She decided she wanted to help him better understand. "Actually, there are two things that make us seem strange and also make us unique from other religions."

"What?"

"Symbol and ritual."

He thought about that for a moment. "Isn't that what makes all religions what they are?"

"In a way, yes. But it is so much more to us." Then she had a thought. "How old is the Roman Empire now?"

Surprised by the question, he turned to look at her. "The empire itself? That's hard to say, but the traditional founding of Rome was more than seven hundred years ago."

"That is a long time for one people to maintain their identity," she said.

"Yes, it is." He hadn't really thought of it in that way, but that was an interesting perspective.

"Well, our people have maintained their identity for almost two thousand years now. How do we do that? With symbol and ritual. That is what holds us together. That is what gives us our identity. Take our *mezuzah*, for example—the small metal or wood cases you see mounted on the doorways of every home and gate in Israel."

"Yes. I notice that your people reach up and touch them each time you go in or out."

"That's right. Those cases contain a tiny parchment scroll on which are written some passages from the Law. Basically it tells us that we are to love God with all our hearts. A *mezuzah* may be very plain, or it can be very ornate. What matters to us is what it symbolizes."

"Which is?"

"Every time we leave our house, we touch it to remind us that we will live the Law and keep the commandment to love God while we are outside of the home. And each time we return, we touch it again to remind ourselves that inside our homes, the Law and our love of God will prevail there as well."

He was nodding slowly. "I see."

"And I'm sure you have seen our men as they come from morning prayers with a strange black box on their foreheads and on their arms."

"Ah, yes, the *phylacteries*."

"That's the Greek word. We call them *tefillin*."

"I've wondered what they are for."

"If you don't understand the spiritual realities they represent, they may seem very strange. But they are similar to the *mezuzah*. Inside the *tefillin* are tiny compartments. Here again, passages from the Law are written and placed. Can you think why we would do that?"

His brows furrowed momentarily, then straightened again. "Because that puts the Law always in front of your eyes."

"Good," she said, deeply pleased. "It also represents that the Law is always forefront in our minds. The *tefillin* on the left arm is placed on the biceps so as to be close to the heart."

"Ah," he said again. "I understand." Then his expression turned more dubious, and he waved one hand at the towering building in front of them. "So your temple is only a symbol?"

"*Only* a symbol," she said softly. "Is it true that your soldiers swear an oath on the standards of your legions?"

Surprised, he nodded. "Yes, it's called the *sacramentum*."

"An oath for which they are willing to give their lives?"

"Without hesitation."

"But why? The standard is only a gilded eagle, or it contains a small bust of your emperor. What does that bust cost? Two sesterces? Maybe three? That seems like a silly thing to die for."

He watched her, liking the intensity in her eyes, the animation of her face.

"Why are you laughing at me?" she said suddenly, jerking him out of his thoughts.

"I wasn't laughing. I was admiring."

She looked skeptical. "Admiring what?"

"Your logic. Your way of reasoning." *You!* But he didn't add that last word out loud. "All right, your point is a good one. I shouldn't have said *only* a symbol. I agree. Symbols can be very powerful."

She was pleased that he had conceded, or more important, that he agreed with her. She decided to make one additional point. "The temple, though it is a marvelous structure, is only a symbol of a greater spiritual reality. We say it is God's house, but it is only a shadow of what it must be like in God's real home in the heavens. Each courtyard is a few steps higher than the previous one to signify that we are always ascending upwards to God. The cherubim embroidered on the veil inside the temple represent to us that God is so holy, so sacred, that there must be guardians to prevent the unclean and unworthy from entering his presence." She smiled to soften her intensity a little. "And I'm not just talking about Gentiles here. That's why no one but the high priest is allowed inside. The whole purpose of our faith is to become worthy enough to enter God's presence someday."

She stopped, a little breathless, surprised at how passionately she was trying to help him understand. When he did not turn but continued to let his eyes roam over the temple, she gave a little laugh of embarrassment. "I'm sorry, I didn't mean—"

He swung on her. "Don't apologize."

"Well, I didn't mean to sound like I was trying to convert you to Judaism."

"I didn't think you were, not in any way." He stopped, searching her eyes. "In fact, you did make me a little envious."

She was taken aback. "Envious?"

"Yes. I have to wonder what it would be like to feel so strongly about religion."

She didn't know what to say to that. He obviously meant it, and now she saw that he was a little embarrassed by his openness.

He took her by the elbow. "Come," he said. "I've heard much about the Royal Stoa. Take me there."

II

They strolled leisurely in the deep shade of the great portico letting the crowds surge around them. For now Miriam was content to let him see the grandeur of these columned halls without her commentary. She was relieved to be off the topic of religion and back on safer ground.

"This is magnificent," he breathed, his head tipped back and looking at the massive stone columns with their Corinthian caps and the roof that was fifty feet above their head. "No wonder they call it the Royal Stoa."

"Actually," she said with a half smile, "we call them Solomon's Porches."

"Solomon?"

"Yes, he was a king of Israel about a thousand years ago. He built the first temple here."

"So why do you find this amusing?"

"Poor Herod. This reconstruction of our temple was perhaps his greatest achievement, his most magnificent project, and yet his name is nowhere to be found on it. Your people call it Herod's temple, but we never do. We call it the Second Temple. And calling these the Royal Porches suggest Herod's name to us. So we call them by Solomon's name, even though he had nothing to do with them."

"In Rome's eyes Herod was a good ruler, a good administrator."

"Yes, we know. But he was an evil man, Marcus. He killed his wife, two of his sons, and several others of his immediate family. He was ruthless and brutal. For example, just before his death, there was a rumor that what we call the Messiah, our Deliverer, had been born in Bethlehem, just to the south of us. When Herod heard that, he tried to find out where the baby was. When he couldn't, he ordered all of the children in the village under the age of two to be killed, just to be sure that he didn't miss him." She couldn't keep the horror from creeping into her voice.

He took that in, his face impassive. "Brutal but efficient," he finally said.

She stared at him, hardly believing he had dismissed her comment with such utter banality. He had already turned and was looking up again and didn't see her expression. Suddenly she was angry.

"Even your own Emperor Augustus is said to have made a clever play on words, using the Greek. He said that it is safer to be Herod's *choiros*, or hog, than it is to be his *huios*, or son."

Something in her voice brought him back to face her. "As I said, he was brutal. Everyone knew that."

"When he saw that he was about to die, King Herod ordered all the Jewish leaders in Jerusalem detained in the Hippodrome with orders that they be executed at his death. That way he was assured that at least someone would be mourning at his death."

"Really!" Marcus said. "I hadn't heard that."

"Fortunately, his sons were wise enough not to carry out his order." She was trying hard to keep the anger out of her voice. "Did you know that even now, some thirty years later, we celebrate the anniversary of

Herod's death as a festival? All mourning, even for the death of a loved one, is forbidden by law on that day."

He reared back a little. "Ho, that's a lot of hate."

"Herod gave us a lot of reasons to hate what he was." She hesitated a little. "The tragedy is that Rome could never see any of that."

"This is not an excuse," Marcus said, sensing that he had somehow triggered something in her, "for I do not condone all that the emperor and the Senate do, but Rome cannot concern herself with every little problem in the provinces. The empire is too huge, too vast. We have to trust the procurators or the local rulers to keep things in order."

Miriam looked away. In that moment the face of Deborah, wife of David ben Joseph of Capernaum, flashed into her mind. "You seek what you call accommodation with Rome," she had said. "Well, we don't use such a lofty word. We call it a pact with the devil."

"Tell me," he said, watching her closely now. "Have I offended you?"

She shook her head after a moment. "No, but I would be less than honest if I didn't say that your words represent the very reason why so many of my people find Roman rule so unbearable."

III

Any light and bantering mood was gone now. They walked slowly, Miriam making brief comments now and then about the architecture or the functions that took place in one part of the complex or another. Marcus would murmur a comment or two, but otherwise walked beside her in silence. By unspoken agreement, they started back toward the Antonia Fortress, where Marcus would return to his duties.

As they came out of Solomon's Porches and started across the

Court of the Gentiles again, Miriam suddenly changed direction. "We don't want to go over there," she said.

"Why not?"

"That's where the moneychangers have set up shop."

"The moneychangers? What do you mean?"

"Well, it is part of our law that each year every person in Israel—rich or poor—must pay a tax of one-half shekel to the temple as an atonement for their sins. The money is used to support the operation of the sanctuary."

He nodded. Almost every temple in the empire collected some sort of fee or tax from its worshipers.

"I assume you are aware of our prohibition against any graven images?"

"I am."

"Well, since many coins carry the image of the emperor or some other ruler, they are not acceptable for the temple treasury."

"I see," he said slowly. "So they have to change their money before they can contribute it."

"Yes. At Passover especially, it becomes a huge business because we have people coming from many different places. Normally the exchangers stay outside the walls, but with the huge crowds they move into the courtyard."

"And these moneychangers charge a fee, I presume."

"Yes. Five percent commission." She frowned. "Or at least that is what it's supposed to be."

He chuckled with soft irony. "So while your religion may strive to make you more holy, in practice your people are much like all the rest of us."

Stung, she didn't know what to say. "The Sanhedrin tries to enforce the five percent, but some men have no scruples." She felt a little guilty at that, for she knew that some members of the ruling council, including her own father, were financing the moneychangers and reaping tremendous profits from the practice.

"I would like to see these moneychangers," Marcus said, changing direction.

She sighed and fell in beside him. This was a part of the Temple Mount she avoided. She didn't like being squeezed in so tightly you could barely move. She didn't like the noise. She didn't like what she saw happening there.

And then she realized something that brought her back to reality. Marcus wasn't just curious. He was a Roman officer reconnoitering his command. He wanted to see what his soldiers were up against if there was any trouble. She turned and saw that the centurion had moved in closer to them now. Their eyes met, and then he looked away. She looked for Livia but couldn't see her.

As they drew closer, the bleating of sheep and the lowing of cattle began to fill the air. He turned to her in surprise. "They let animals in here too?" He cocked his head, suddenly mischievous. "Are they considered Gentiles too?"

On the defensive now, she tried to explain. "The people who come here from long distances want to offer a sacrifice at the temple, but they can't bring their own animals. So they have to buy one here. Normally, these are kept outside the walls too, but—" She wasn't sure how to explain to him something with which she herself was disgusted.

"I see."

He said nothing more as they moved into the chaos of the area. Makeshift fences were propped up to form triangular pens. Some were large enough to hold two or three bullocks or half a dozen sheep. Some were empty, the sale already having been made. In addition to the noise the animals were making, their droppings filled the air with a strong stench, and Miriam put her hand over her nose and mouth. A little farther on, the crowd surged around rows of tables and booths. The noise was deafening. People shouted and yelled as they haggled over prices or the rates of exchange. The vendors banged pans or rang bells to try to attract business to their table. Individuals yelled at each other in order to carry on even a normal conversation.

Miriam and Marcus passed a row of tables piled high with small cages filled with doves. Marcus gave her a questioning look.

"Birds are an acceptable offering for some things," she explained, "especially for those who are too poor to buy a sheep or a bullock."

He took her arm again. "I can see why you don't care for this," he said. "I'm sorry I made you come over here." He steered her in the direction they had originally been headed.

As they started to move away, suddenly a woman's voice shrieked out above the noise. The noise momentarily dropped, and she screamed again. "He's got a whip!"

Instantly cries of alarm went up, and there was a rush of movement. Marcus whirled, going up on tiptoe to try to see what was happening. The noise was coming from where they had been just moments before. They heard a crash, another scream, and the wild bleating of sheep.

"Stay here, Miriam!" Marcus said. He started to remove his tunic, but Miriam grabbed at his arm. "No, Marcus, don't! The crowd might turn on you if they know you are Roman."

He hesitated, then shook his head. He ripped off the tunic and threw it aside. Shouting for people to get out of the way, he plunged back into the throng. Without waiting to consider what she was doing, Miriam darted after him, staying right behind him as he made a path through the crush. Now people were rushing past them in the opposite direction, clearly in a panic.

Marcus turned his head, searching. "Sextus!" he shouted in Latin. "Alert the troops. Put them on standby."

There was an answering shout and the flash of a helmet. Then, suddenly, Miriam and Marcus burst into a large circle where the crowds had fallen back. There was a loud pop, and Miriam's eyes jerked toward the sound. What she saw startled her. A man with a whip held high above his head was driving half a dozen sheep. The whip cracked again. On the far side of the circle, people leaped out of the way, and the sheep darted through the opening.

"Look," Miriam cried in Marcus's ear. "One of the pens has broken."

One side of one of the temporary triangular pens dangled crazily over, leaving a wide opening. Marcus's eyes narrowed in concern. He pulled her tight beside him. For a moment that puzzled her. The sheep were fleeing in the opposite direction. There was no danger to her. Then, in an instant, she understood.

The man with the whip strode over to another pen, this one with three heifers inside. A man in a filthy tunic threw out his arms to try to block the way. The whip came up and cracked sharply in the air above the man's head. The owner leaped aside. Up came one foot of the whip-bearer. He gave a mighty kick, and one side of this pen collapsed as well. He strode into the pen, cracking the whip over the animals' heads.

Now things broke out in pandemonium. People screamed as the heifers raced away, tails high, bellowing wildly. The crowd had to leap aside or be run down.

The man turned to face them. His blazing eyes raked the crowd, then stopped on the owner of the now-disappearing cattle, who wailed and wrung his hands. "This is my Father's house. What have you made of it?"

Several impressions struck Miriam all at once. The man was about the same height as Marcus, but he was powerfully built, with broad shoulders and muscular arms. His tunic was simple, such as was worn by peasants and craftsmen. He wore a beard, and his hair reached to his shoulders, like most of the rest of the men of the working classes. But it was his eyes that arrested her. They were filled with great indignation. They were like hot coals glowing even in the brightness of full day.

For a moment those eyes rested on Marcus, who was poised for action, one hand on the hilt of his sword. If the sight of a Roman officer deterred him, he gave no sign. His head turned in the direction of the rows of tables where the moneychangers were set up. They were on their feet now, hovering over their tables as people fled in terror or came running to see what was happening. A look of deep anger passed over the man's face.

He whirled and moved to the first table in three great strides. The moneychanger saw him coming and cringed, throwing his arms around the pile of loose coins and the bags of money on the table. Down came the whip, lashing the tabletop just inches away from the man's bare arms. He cried and jumped back.

The attacker said not a word. With his free hand, he grabbed one of the heavy bags and tipped it upside down. Coins spewed out, pouring onto the table and bouncing wildly onto the tiles. "Why do you cheat these people in the house of God?" the man shouted at the moneychanger. He grabbed the edge of the table with both hands and heaved upward. The sound of metal coins hitting marble was lost in the crash as the table was overturned.

A roar of approval burst from the crowd as the moneychanger dropped to his knees and scrambled to retrieve his money. Instantly he was joined by a dozen others, grabbing wildly for the loose coins.

Down the row of tables the man went, the whip cracking sharply in the air if anyone was bold enough to step forward to try to stop him. Few did. Table after table was overturned, and thousands of coins bounced across the courtyard. Marcus moved along behind, stepping over and around the people who were on their hands and knees now, shouting and yelling as they clambered frantically for the money on the tiles.

One of the moneychangers saw Marcus's uniform and darted over.

"Aren't you going to stop him?" he shouted. "He's robbing us of our money."

"Leave him alone," a man beside them shouted. "Look! He's not taking the money. He's giving it back to the people. It's the money-changers who are the robbers."

Miriam turned to see who spoke, but the man was already melting away into the crowd, not wanting to give the Roman soldier a chance to respond to his taunt. But she realized with a start that the heckler was right. The scourge-wielding attacker had not picked up a single coin. He was hurling thousands of shekels to the ground, but he paid no heed to the money itself. This was not robbery; it was white-hot anger, fury against the extortion that filled this corner of the Temple Mount.

Miriam felt a tug on her arm and turned. Livia was there beside her. "Are you all right?" she cried.

Marcus turned and saw who it was. "Get Miriam out of here," he commanded. "There's going to be trouble." He started to draw his sword.

Miriam jerked free from Livia's grasp, then reached out and pinned Marcus's wrist against his side. "No, Marcus! Don't draw your sword. Look at the crowd. They are delighted with what is happening. If you try to arrest him, they'll turn on you."

He pulled free, but now there was hesitation. Her eyes were plead-ing. He had no idea how fragile this situation could be. Her people were so emotional. The slightest spark could set them off. "I'm not the one in danger, Marcus. You are." She turned, pointing to the melee around them. "Listen to them. They love what this man is doing. If you try to stop him—"

She stopped as she realized the man with the whip was coming straight toward them now, the whip swinging back and forth at his side. Marcus took a quick step in front of the two women to protect them, but the man with the blazing eyes walked right past them, not even seeming to notice they were there.

They turned. Five feet away was the table piled high with the cages of the doves that Marcus and Miriam had passed just minutes before. The merchant was wailing piteously, holding up his hands. "Please! Please, don't!" he begged.

The man stopped, and Miriam could see his chest rising and falling. The whip was tapping ominously against his leg. There was a sudden hush, and then the attacker spoke. "Take these things out of here," he said in a tight voice. "Why have you made my Father's house a house of merchandise?"

"Who are you?" the seller of doves cried. "By what authority do you interrupt our business?" But even as he spoke he began removing the cages with the birds and stacking them on a small, hand-drawn cart behind the table. There was no answer from the man who stood before him in terrible silence.

At that moment two of the temple guards, soldiers employed by the Sanhedrin, burst out of the crowd and into the circle of surrounding onlookers. They looked around at the chaos.

"It's him!" one of the moneychangers shouted, pointing. "He overturned our tables. He's stealing our money."

"He broke my pens and set the animals free," another voice cried.

One guard rushed forward, his spear held at the ready. "What do you think you are doing? You are under arrest."

The man with the whip straightened to his full height and faced the guard. There was not the slightest indication of fear on his face. "This is the house of the Lord," he said quietly. "These—" his hand swept out in a gesture that took in all of the merchants and their places of business—"these have made it into a den of thieves."

"Yes!" a woman cried. "He's right. Leave him alone."

Instantly the crowd took up the cry.

"Arrest the thieving moneychangers," a man shouted. "Leave this man alone!" called another. As one, the crowd drew the ring in tighter, anger on their faces.

The guard with the spear looked around anxiously, then quickly stepped back beside his companion. The spear lowered. Only a fool could miss the mood of the people. The merchants and money-changers who profited from the simple piety of the pilgrims were deeply resented. The attack on them had hit a responsive chord.

"We had better report this to the Council," the one guard said to the other. His companion nodded, his eyes darting back and forth with real fear now. They backed away, then plunged through the crowd to the jeers and catcalls of the people who let them through.

A little dazed by it all, Miriam turned back to see what this angry avenger would do next. To her astonishment, he was not where he had been just seconds before. "Where did he go?" she exclaimed.

Marcus and Livia whirled back as well. Like Miriam, they had focused on the humiliating retreat of the guards. Now all three searched the faces of the people around them. But the man with the blazing eyes was nowhere to be seen. He had pushed into the throng and disappeared.

Marcus grabbed Miriam and Livia by the arms and gave them a gentle shove. "My soldiers may be coming," he hissed. "There could be trouble. Now go! Your father will have my head if something happens to you."

This time Miriam didn't resist. If the legionnaires intervened, there was indeed real danger. "Be careful," she said, touching Marcus on the arm, the previous tension between them now forgotten. Then she took Livia's hand, and the two of them pushed their way into the crowd, heading for Solomon's Porches and away from the Antonia Fortress.

CHAPTER NOTES

From the writings of early rabbinical sources and contemporary historians such as Philo and Flavius Josephus, and also through extensive archaeological excavations in Jerusalem, we have a remarkably detailed picture of the great temple complex built by Herod the Great (see, for example, Edersheim, *The Temple*, pp. 42–60; Schürer, p. 141; Ritmeyer, pp. 25–53).

The temple complex was an engineering as well as an architectural marvel. Some of the stones used to build the massive retaining walls that formed the Temple Mount are huge. For example, one stone carved from a single piece of limestone has been found in the lower courses of the western wall. It is forty-six feet long, ten feet wide, and thought to be ten feet thick. Its weight is estimated to be more than four hundred tons! (see Zimmerman, p. 41).

There were two cleansings of the temple, one at the beginning of the ministry of Jesus and one at the end (see John 2:13–16; Matthew 21:12–13). Elements of both have been combined here.

The *mezuzah* was explained in an earlier chapter. The phylacteries, which are mentioned in Matthew 23:5, or *tefillin* as they are called in Hebrew, come from a core passage in the sixth chapter of Deuteronomy. After giving the great command to love God with all their hearts, the Israelites were commanded to keep these words in their hearts and to "bind them for a sign upon thine hand, and they shall be as frontlets between thine eyes" (v. 8).

CHAPTER 11

LEGEM NON HABET NECESSITAS.
[NECESSITY KNOWS NO LAW.]

—St. Augustine, Soliloquium, 2

I

3 APRIL, A.D. 30

As they stood in the deep shade of the portico, taking a moment to recover their breath before descending down the great staircase, Miriam scanned the courtyard where they had been a few moments before. The commotion had died down now, and she could see the spears of the legionnaires above the heads of the crowd. The spears were all close together, suggesting that the soldiers were back in formation. The crisis was over.

"Who was he?" Livia asked in wonder.

Miriam didn't have to ask who "he" was. "I don't know. He was a Galilean."

"How do you know that?"

"Didn't you hear his accent? Yes, he was definitely a Galilean." She shook her head, remembering his eyes. "I have never seen such rage in a man before."

To Miriam's surprise Livia shook her head.

"What?"

"Anger, yes; rage, no."

"Didn't you see him overturn those tables?"

"I did. But if he was in a rage, why didn't he overturn the tables with the doves?"

Miriam reared back a little, startled by the unexpected question.

"Well," Livia said, seeming a little defensive now. "When he came toward us, I thought he was going to overturn those tables too. You could see that he was still very angry. But he didn't. Why?"

"I—" Miriam hadn't even considered that fact before. "I don't know."

"If the cages were thrown to the ground, what would have happened?"

Miriam began to nod slowly. "The doves would have been injured. Some even killed perhaps."

"Yes!" Livia said in wonder. "He was inflamed with anger, but he had not lost control of himself. Not for one minute."

Miriam's eyes widened. Livia was right, and that was remarkable. Then she remembered something else. "Did you hear him? Twice he called it *my* Father's house. He was so angry because of what was going on in 'my Father's house.' What do you suppose he meant by that?"

Livia was silent for a moment, then shook her head. "I don't know."

"I want to know who he is," Miriam said. "He was magnificent."

Livia stared at her. "Magnificent?"

"Yes! Didn't you feel it? I hate this aspect of Passover. They turn the Temple Mount into a dung heap. Everyone in the city complains about the graft and corruption, but we stand by and do nothing." She took a quick breath, a little surprised at her own passion. Then she rushed on. "Well, *he* didn't just stand by and do nothing. Why didn't anyone stop him? He was only one man in a multitude. Not even the armed temple guards dared confront him. I call that magnificent."

Livia slowly bobbed her head. "Yes, I guess it was. It was really remarkable."

Miriam turned and looked back to where they had been a few minutes before. "I want to know who he was."

"And how are you going to find that out?"

As Miriam turned back, an idea came. "Marcus will know. He will find out about him." She smiled, and there was a trace of sorrow in it. "And Marcus is coming for dinner tonight. I will ask him." Then she straightened and turned. "We had better go."

As they started for the portals that led down to the great western staircase, Miriam looked back over her shoulder one more time. "I'm going to find out who that man is and thank him," she murmured. "He was magnificent."

II

Gratefully, the tension that had developed between Miriam and Marcus while discussing Rome and its policies regarding its client states seemed to be forgotten. Marcus was warm, witty, and seemed to feel quite comfortable in the home of Mordechai ben Uzziel and his daughter. Miriam soon found herself relaxing and enjoying his company once again.

And yet. Back in the corner of her mind she could not shake the faint disquiet. She found him to be a compelling and attractive person, perhaps one of the most charismatic men she had ever met. Though none of the men she knew personally treated Miriam with disrespect—she was too wealthy for one thing, and her father was too influential for another—more than one man of her acquaintance had that she's-a-wonderful-woman-*but*-she-is-a-woman attitude always lurking just below the surface. She did not sense even the slightest touch of that with Marcus. He treated her with great respect and spoke with her as though she were his equal.

On the other hand, he was thoroughly Roman. Everything Miriam had ever seen of the Roman personality had been from a distance. She had heard the Roman psyche discussed and analyzed, but for the first time it had been her privilege to walk right up next to one of the Roman nobility, supposedly the best that Rome could produce, and be allowed to peek inside his soul and mind. And what she saw there was chilling. He had dismissed the deaths of young children with three words that both condemned and praised Herod in the same breath—"brutal but efficient." Savagery was brushed aside as the incidental side effect of running an empire. Slaves were referred to with the same indifference one used when talking about pieces of furniture or shovels and rakes. She couldn't even think of a word to describe what it was that had shaken her so deeply. Callous didn't do it. He was refined, intelligent, genteel, cultured. *Casual.* That was the word she had finally come to. The thing that bothered her most about Marcus Didius was how casual he was about things that she held to be of enormous importance.

To her surprise, she found herself comparing Marcus to Simeon the Javelin. What a contrast! It was ironic that she had met two such unusual men in the period of four days. Both were powerful personalities and natural leaders. Both were strikingly handsome. The irony lay in their being complete opposites. Marcus was outwardly warm, charming, and immensely likeable—but what she glimpsed inside was deeply unnerving to her. Simeon, on the other hand, was cold, aloof, bitter, and used his tongue like the point of a sword. And yet, beneath the surface, she had caught a glimmer of a very different person. Whether or not that other person ever fully surfaced or not she would never know, but . . .

She pushed her thoughts away and focused on the conversation between her father and Marcus. They were discussing the current status of chariot racing in Jerusalem, a sport that had become quite popular since Herod the Great had completed the Hippodrome south of the Temple Mount some years earlier. It had become the sport of favor with the Jewish elite, and Miriam knew that her father bet heavily on his favorite drivers and teams.

There was something else on Miriam's mind, and she listened politely, waiting for an opportunity to change the subject. When they went on and on, the conversation now being directed by Marcus as he talked about the greatest chariot races of all at the Circus Maximus in Rome, Miriam finally decided she would not wait any longer. At the first momentary lull in the conversation, she broke in. "Marcus? Were you able to find out who that man today was?"

Marcus frowned, and not because of the interruption. He had not planned to bring up the subject of what had happened at the temple this morning. He didn't want Mordechai to know that his daughter had been that close to a potentially deadly situation. He shook his head. "No. We inquired, but the people weren't very cooperative. I'm not sure they knew either."

Mordechai had gone very still. He was looking at Miriam with narrow eyes. "What man?"

"There was a disturbance today in the Court of the Gentiles. A man with a whip—"

"I know all about that. The question is, how do you?"

Miriam realized her mistake even before she saw the warning in Marcus's eyes, but now it was too late. "As the tribune and I were walking around looking at the temple, we happened upon the scene."

Mordechai swung on Marcus. "You were there?"

Marcus nodded. "I was. We were a few feet away when we heard a commotion. I saw most of it."

"Marcus made Livia and me leave," Miriam said quickly.

Her father barely heard. "You were there, and you didn't stop him?"

"I was alone," he said evenly. "I sent my centurion to alert the troops, but then the man was gone again."

"The crowd was very ugly, Papa," Miriam said. "They were cheering the man on. It would have been a mistake to try to stop them. Especially alone."

She was surprised to see a flash of irritation pass through Marcus's eyes. Though unspoken, the message was clear and unmistakable. *Enough. Say no more.* He spoke to her father. "It was not a general insurrection, and we have strict instructions to leave internal affairs to your Council to handle, unless they cannot." There was an obvious jab there, and Marcus pushed it home in case his host had missed it. "Your temple guards were there. Aren't they charged with maintaining order and security on the mount?"

Mordechai gave a disgusted grunt. "They were afraid of the crowd." He seemed mollified now and ready to change the subject.

"Who was he, Father?"

He waved a hand. "Some itinerant teacher from the Galilee. His name is Jesus of Nazareth."

That seemed to interest Marcus. "From the Galilee? He wasn't a Zealot, was he?"

Mordechai quickly shook his head. "No, they say he is a carpenter. He's come down for the Feast of the Passover and has been teaching on the Temple Mount these past few days. He's won himself a small following."

"Well, he won a lot more than that today," Miriam said. "It was remarkable to watch him."

The corners around Mordechai's mouth tightened perceptibly. "I thought you said you and Livia left?"

"She saw just the first part," Marcus answered smoothly, "then I sent her and the servant girl away." Then once again, in what Miriam was learning was his style, Marcus turned the conversation and put her father on the defensive. "So did *you* bring charges against the man?"

"No. Several of us on the Council found him later in the Court of the Women. We questioned him for a time, demanded to know by what authority he interfered with the business of the temple."

"That is not part of the business of the temple, Father," Miriam broke in. "You know what those moneychangers are doing. It is a travesty."

"Miriam, that's enough." It came out quietly, but his anger was barely contained. "The moneychangers operate with the permission of the Sanhedrin. Yes, there are excesses, but they are not interlopers to be driven out by someone with no authority."

"And what did he say?" Marcus asked, wanting to deflect what he saw happening here.

Mordechai was fuming now. "We asked him to give us a sign of his authority. He is a madman. Completely insane."

"Why do you say that?" Miriam asked, unable to contain herself although she knew that she had nearly crossed a line with her father that was dangerous to cross. "He was angry at what he saw happening there, but he certainly didn't seem like a madman."

"No?" he barked. "Well, when we asked him to give us some sign of his authority, he said, 'Destroy this temple and in three days I shall raise it up again.'"

"What?" Marcus blurted. "He actually said that?"

"Really?" Miriam said, as shocked as Marcus.

"Yes. We've been building this complex for forty-six years, several years even before I was born." He shook his head, thoroughly disgusted. "And he says he can rebuild it in three days? He's mad, I tell you."

"Then why didn't you arrest him?" Marcus asked quietly.

There was silence. Finally, Miriam's father sighed. "A lot of his sympathizers were in the crowd. The Council feared that we might start a riot if we tried to arrest him. And besides, we couldn't get any witnesses to testify against him. They said he hadn't stolen any of the money."

Miriam stirred, but Marcus cut her off. "He did not. Not while I was watching."

Her father muttered something that Miriam missed, his brows deeply furrowed.

"What did you say, Father?" Miriam asked.

He glanced at Marcus before he looked directly at her. "I said, this is a man we are going to have to watch very carefully."

III

Mordechai saw Marcus out to the gate of his courtyard, where Sextus Rubrius and a squad of four legionnaires were waiting for him. As the Romans marched away, he motioned to the servant who waited at the main entrance to the house. The man trotted over.

"Tell Miriam that I have some business with Caiaphas and not to wait up for me."

"Yes, Excellency."

Mordechai waited until the servant had gone back inside; then he went to a pot that was hid behind an olive tree and reached inside. He drew out a long hooded robe made from dark brown material. Slipping off his own outer robe, he put the other on, becoming all but invisible. Looking around to be sure he was alone, he slipped through the gate out into the street. He didn't turn to the left, however, which would have taken him to the house of Caiaphas. Instead, he turned right, pulling the hood up over his head. Then he hurried along, staying close to the buildings.

At the next street, he turned right, then right again. Five minutes later he was at Zion's Gate, which led through the south wall of the city. He stopped and waited a few moments, watching, but the hour was getting late and only one man with a donkey loaded with firewood came through. Satisfied, he walked swiftly through the gate and out into the night.

Circling around the south side of Mount Zion was the Valley of Hinnom. As he began to feel the path drop sharply, Mordechai could see the dull glow of smouldering fires down below him. At the same moment he smelled the foul stench of burning garbage.

The Valley of Hinnom, or *Ge Hinnom* in Hebrew, gave its name to *Gehenna*, the world of departed spirits or the world of the damned souls. Though theologically this was a concept that Mordechai and the other Sadducees rejected, he had to admit that if there were some kind of hell after this life, the image of Gehenna was a vivid one. The Valley of Hinnom was Jerusalem's garbage dump. From time to time someone would bring burning coals or hot ashes along with their garbage, and the refuse piles would catch fire. Except in the rainy season, the fires would burn for weeks, even months, fouling the air and providing the perfect symbol for the fires of hell that would torment the souls of the wicked forever and ever.

He smiled wryly. It was his own private little joke that this should be the meeting place tonight. It was the perfect irony.

He rounded a bend in the path and passed a large outcropping of rock. Now he could feel other eyes upon him. That was good. He expected nothing less. At the far end of the rock, he stopped, pulling back his hood. Then he settled down to wait.

He had figured it would take about half an hour before his "guest" would know for sure that he came alone and this wasn't a trap. In reality, it was a full three-quarters of an hour. Mordechai was half-pleased—none of them could afford sloppiness at this point—and half-irritated, for he prided himself on being punctual. But finally he heard the soft crunch of footsteps on the path, and then saw a dark shape standing about twenty feet away from him.

"*Erev tov.* Good evening," Mordechai said easily.

There was a barely perceptible nod. "I have three bowmen with arrows trained on your heart. If you plan to betray me, then also prepare to say the *Sh'ma*, for you shall never leave this place alive."

"If I planned to betray you, you would never have made it this far safely."

The figure stepped forward, stopping now just five paces away. "I'm listening."

Mordechai began to speak in a low voice. He spoke for almost five minutes, not pausing for questions or comments. When he finished there was a long silence. He smiled in the darkness. It was always so satisfying to sense when the bait was being taken.

"And what am I supposed to do while the Romans take the Zealots?"

"I am surprised that the fox would ask the weasel how to suck eggs."

There was a muffled laugh in the darkness.

Mordechai reached inside his robe and withdrew a leather pouch. He bounced it softly in the darkness, making the gold coins clink audibly. "Half now, half when the job is completed."

"All now," came the quick retort. "We would both be fools to meet again. Ever."

"Agreed." Mordechai pulled another bag from his cloak. He had assumed as much, but it was always worth a try to start with less. He didn't worry much about this man keeping his bargain. There was the heavy smell of booty in this deal, enough to keep this man to his bargain. When the fox realized that he was wrong, it would be far too late.

"How many others know of this?"

"Two on the Council besides myself, the governor, and a Roman tribune."

"Too many. It doesn't take a thousand tongues to lose a battle."

"Only five in all know of the plan. Only one knows your name. Myself."

"Not even Pilate?"

"No. He asked, but I refused. I have as much to lose in all of this as you do."

"You have only your reputation at risk here. You may think that is as valuable as my life, but it is not. Swear by the temple that no one but you knows about me."

Mordechai wanted to laugh. As if that romantic notion of what made an oath binding would make a difference. "I swear by the temple. I swear by my head. No one but me will know who you are. I suggest you be just as careful on your side of things. The tongues that lose battles can be on both sides of the line."

Again silence. Finally. "When?"

"At least a month, maybe longer. This is going to take some time to arrange so that all appears perfectly natural."

"Good. That's how it must be. By the way, no decoy."

"What?"

"These Zealots are fanatics, but they are not idiots. Either that Roman column is completely legitimate or they will smell a trap."

"I don't know what the governor will say to that. Some legionnaires might get killed."

There was a snort in the darkness. "You think Pilate cares about that? Just tell him if he wants to end his problem in the Galilee, it has to be the real thing."

"You make it difficult. Do you think I can just tell the Romans what to do?"

"Yes, if the Romans want what you have badly enough." There was a momentary silence, then a soft hoot in the darkness. "You think I worry too much, don't you?"

"The idea crossed my mind."

"Do you know the story of the fox and the lion?"

"No."

"This is told by the great Roman poet Horace. The lion was sick and asked the fox to come and administer to his needs. When the fox arrived, he did not draw close but stayed his distance. 'But why are you so frightened?' the lion asked. 'Because,' said the fox, 'on my way to see you, I saw many footprints leading this way and none coming back.'"

Mordechai laughed in spite of himself. "So, who is the fox here, and who is the lion?"

The man gave an answering laugh; then, suddenly, he moved across the space between them. His hands reached out and snatched the two purses from Mordechai's hand. "Then it's done."

He leaned closer, peering at Mordechai in the darkness. There was a quick intake of breath. "*You?*"

Mordechai nodded. "Yes. Surprised?"

"But why? Of all men, why would you choose me?"

"Because," Mordechai said with only the barest trace of sarcasm, "I needed a man I could trust."

Moshe Ya'abin threw back his head and roared. Then as silently as he had come, he disappeared again into the night. "Give us twenty minutes before you leave," he called back. "And give my best regards to your beautiful daughter for me." There was a cackling laugh.

"I will see you in *Gehenna* first, my unsavory friend," Mordechai muttered. "Enjoy your gold while you can."

IV

4 APRIL, A.D. 30

"He must be stopped!" Azariah the Pharisee was on his feet, punching the air with his fists. "We cannot have any more of this."

Miriam's father blew out his breath in disgust. He sat beside the chair of Caiaphas, the high priest, four seats away from where Azariah was pontificating. "You have control of more of the temple police than anyone else on the Council," he snapped. "Wasn't it your men who had him at spear point yesterday, then turned tail and ran away like two puppies facing a lion?"

He turned to Caiaphas and under his breath added, "The old hypocrite."

Miriam, who sat in a small vestibule behind her father at the rear of the apse, was making a private record of the proceedings so her father could review it later. She heard the comment clearly. She wanted to smile. It was always interesting to watch the sparks that flew between the Pharisees and the Sadducees during the meetings of the Great Sanhedrin in Jerusalem.

"Mordechai knows as well as the rest of the Council what happened yesterday," Azariah shot back. "The people were in an uproar. They were pleased with what this man was doing. And that was the problem."

"And why shouldn't the people be pleased?" That came from Annas, father-in-law to Caiaphas. "We lost about four or five thousand shekels yesterday, thanks to this Jesus. It was as though the people had stumbled and fallen down a gold mine."

"Well, whatever the reason," Azariah muttered, "the guards could have started a riot if they had pressed ahead with the arrest."

"And so now, when this Jesus has doubled the size of his following," Caiaphas said sourly, "now you want us to fix what your people could not do yesterday."

"The temple police do not represent the Pharisees alone," a voice said quietly. "They represent all of the Council."

Miriam leaned forward to see who was speaking. It was Nicodemus. Miriam had always liked and respected this member of the Council. Like her father, he was a man of great means, but he was a Pharisee and one of the more moderate voices among the rulers. Unlike his fellow colleague, Azariah, Nicodemus did not speak up very often, but Miriam had noted that when he did his was a respected voice, even by her father.

"Whether the two guards acted wisely or in fear," he went on, "is not worthy of our debate. The question before the Council is, what shall we do now about this Jesus of Nazareth?"

"That is not a question," Azariah snorted. "He must be stopped."

Now Zarak, another Sadducee and one of the more powerful voices on the Sanhedrin, came in. "And how do we do that? It is the time of the feast here in Jerusalem. That is always a dangerous time. The multitudes can easily be aroused and break out in riot."

"Why are we saying he must be stopped?" Nicodemus answered. "We have teachers and rabbis come onto the Temple Mount all the time and try to get people to listen to them. We don't try to stop them."

Caiaphas leaned forward, peering at Nicodemus coldly. "None of them have braided themselves a whip and taken it upon themselves to drive out the moneychangers without authorization."

"None of them claim to be miracle workers, either," Azariah cried out.

"I have inquired about that," Nicodemus replied. "Jesus himself does not claim to be a miracle worker, but others are saying that with their own eyes they have seen him do remarkable things—heal the sick, give sight to the blind, and so on."

Azariah was livid. Here was one of his own party directly opposing him on the Council. "People are starting to say that this Jesus is the Messiah. Do you know what that means? Is that what you want?"

That sent a ripple of shock through the assembly. Miriam sat straight up in her chair, listening intently now. The Messiah? Here was a whole new development.

Nicodemus seemed to have been caught completely by surprise by that as well. "Who is saying that?" he said.

"The people! The mobs. That wild man, John the Baptist."

Nicodemus sat down slowly. He turned to the man seated next to him. "John said that?" he said, looking almost bewildered.

One man near the end of the long table jumped to his feet. He was newly appointed to the Sanhedrin, and Miriam didn't know his name yet. He was a scribe and therefore likely aligned with the Pharisees. "Our esteemed chairman notes that the overturning of the tables of the moneychangers was not authorized," he said tartly, "but perhaps it was necessary. Allowing those people into the temple itself is an outrage."

That did it. The whole Council erupted. Men were on their feet shaking their fists, yelling and shouting and bellowing. Miriam sat back and set her pen down. There was nothing to record out of this melee, but she was secretly pleased that someone had finally said it. It was the Sadducean party that controlled the priesthood and therefore all of the temple revenues. Therefore it was the Sadducees who had lost most heavily when the Galilean had driven the merchants out of the temple courtyards. Several on the Council clearly objected to that blatant merchandising within the temple precincts, whether or not they agreed with the actions of the teacher from Nazareth.

Then she turned and looked at Nicodemus. He was watching the pandemonium around him but seemed oblivious to it. His eyes were troubled, his face filled with questions. He wrote something quickly on a small piece of parchment and handed it to a man two seats down from him. Curious, Miriam watched to see what his reaction might be. There was too much noise to hear anything now, but she kept her eyes fixed on the second man. He read the note quickly, then looked at Nicodemus and nodded firmly. She couldn't get it all, but she clearly saw his lips form the words *John the Baptist*.

V

5 APRIL, A.D. 30

Miriam slipped through the wall of partition, past one of the signs that warned all Gentiles to go no farther, and climbed up the five stairs to the top of the first platform. That put her about three feet higher than the rest of the Court of the Gentiles. She went up on tiptoes, searching the crowded square for any signs of an assembly. Seeing nothing, she slowly came back down the stairs and rejoined Livia. She shook her head.

"It's the last day of unleavened bread," Livia said. "Perhaps he won't come to the Temple Mount today. Many people are staying home getting ready for Passover tomorrow."

It was a gentle rebuke, and Miriam understood it for what it was. They had guests coming for Passover. Even though Miriam's mother had died some years before, her younger sister still came from Joppa with her husband and four children and stayed with them at Passover each year. One was a cousin Miriam's age. They would be arriving sometime this afternoon. "We'll leave shortly, Livia. There will be time to get everything in readiness."

"Why are you so set on finding this man?" her servant asked. "Is this an assignment from the Council?"

Miriam was aghast. "No, Livia! I have no official role with the Council. And if my father knew I was trying to find Jesus and listen to him, he would be furious. No. No one on the Council knows anything about this."

To her surprise, Livia seemed relieved.

"Is that what you thought?" Miriam asked. "That I was doing this for the Council?"

Livia looked away. "Well, you came home yesterday, and all you could talk about was how angry the Council was about Jesus. Then this morning, the moment your father leaves, you come up here and start looking for this Jesus."

"No, Livia! After what happened the other day with the money-changers, I want to hear this man for myself. They say he has been working miracles. Some even think he might be the Messiah."

Livia merely nodded. Not being Jewish, that didn't electrify her like it had Miriam. "I'm glad, Miriam," she said. "I would like to hear him too."

"Let's go around to the north side of the temple. We can see the rest of the courtyard from there."

They stayed near the wall of partition, making their way slowly through the throngs. Suddenly Miriam stopped. She went up on her toes again. "There's Nicodemus."

"Who?"

"Nicodemus. He's the one I told you about, who spoke up in defense of Jesus." She grabbed Livia's hand. "Come on."

As they drew close, Miriam hesitated. Then seeing that the member of the Council seemed to be alone, she stepped forward. "Excuse me. Nicodemus?"

He turned; then his eyes widened in surprise. "Miriam?"

"Good morning."

He looked around quickly, acknowledging Livia with his eyes but obviously looking for someone else.

"May I speak with you a moment?"

He nodded, clearly wary. "Concerning what?"

"Jesus of Nazareth."

He visibly started, and again his eyes darted past her.

"My father knows nothing of this," she said quickly. "He would be angry if he knew I was asking."

He took her by the arm and moved over to the wall of partition where there was an open space with no one close by. Livia followed behind. "Why *are* you asking?" he asked suspiciously.

She too looked around to make sure no one was watching or listening. "Because," she said quietly, "Livia and I were there when Jesus drove the moneychangers out."

"You saw it?" he asked incredulously.

"Yes. Most of it."

"And?"

Miriam shook her head, remembering. "He was magnificent," she whispered. "He was so angry because of what those people were doing. He kept talking about how they were polluting his Father's house."

He seemed to relax a little now. "That's what I heard too."

"Have you heard him teach?" Miriam asked, eager now.

Again he was suddenly tense and looked around quickly.

"I want to know, Nicodemus. I promise I will tell no one that I have spoken with you."

He considered that, searching her face carefully. Though he had not been directly involved in Miriam's brief interest in Pharisaism, as a leader of the Pharisees in Jerusalem, Nicodemus had known about it. When she had determined it was not for her, unlike some others, he had been kind, telling her that he understood. Perhaps it was the memory of that experience that helped him make up his mind. "Come," he said.

Including Livia now, he walked quickly around to the west side of the temple, where the crowds were the thinnest. He moved over into the deep shade of Solomon's Porches. Though the main portico was on the south end of the Temple Mount, a narrower porch—only two columns deep—ran around most of the rest of the Court of the Gentiles. The west side, opposite the entrance to the temple court-yards, usually had the fewest people. He went to a spot behind one of the pillars and motioned for them to sit. When they did so, he sat down as well. He faced them, which, Miriam noticed, also turned his back to the main courtyard so he would not be easily identified.

Once settled, he seemed hesitant again. When he did speak, his first words completely stunned Miriam. "I went and saw Jesus last night," he said.

She just stared at him. Livia, who had said nothing at all since they had begun speaking with him, leaned closer.

"Yes. I went by night," he said, with a touch of shame in his voice, "because I was afraid someone might see me. You know what the Council would say to that."

She nodded gravely. With the current mood of the Council, he could easily lose his seat on it.

"What did he say?"

"Well, it was most strange. I wasn't sure how to begin, so I didn't really ask him a question. I just said, 'Rabbi, we know that thou art a teacher come from God: for no man can do these miracles that you do, except God be with him.'"

Miriam nodded. That was very much along the lines of what she had been thinking. If the stories were true, then . . .

"And then he said the strangest thing. He said, 'Verily, verily, I say unto you, except a man be born again, he cannot see the kingdom of God.'"

"Born again?" Livia exclaimed, apparently so caught up that she forgot herself. She looked away quickly, murmuring an apology. Neither Miriam nor Nicodemus even noticed.

"That's almost exactly what I said," the Pharisee went on. "'How can a man who is old like me be born again?' I asked. 'Am I supposed to try to enter again into my mother's womb?'"

"How strange!" Miriam said.

"How did he answer you?" Livia said, seeming to realize that Miriam did not expect her to hold her peace.

Nicodemus leaned forward, his eyes troubled. "He looked right at me and said, 'Verily, verily, I say to you, Except a man be born of water and of the Spirit, he cannot enter into the kingdom of God. That which is born of the flesh is flesh; and that which is born of the Spirit is spirit.'"

"Of the water and the spirit?"

"Yes, that's what he said."

Miriam looked at Livia, deeply puzzled. Livia shrugged.

"I guess I looked as troubled as you do," Nicodemus said with a faint smile. "Jesus then compared it to the wind. He said we can feel it blowing and know that it is there, but we cannot tell from whence it comes or where it is going. He said that is what it is like for those who are born of the Spirit."

Miriam was quiet now, deep in thought. Finally she looked up. "Did he explain what he meant?"

The member of the Great Sanhedrin looked a little chagrined. "No. I was so perplexed that all I could think of to say was, 'But how can these things be?' I mean, we know that a proselyte to Judaism is immersed in water in the ritual bath as a symbol of his entering a new life, and we say that he has been born again. But—" He rubbed his hands across his eyes. "But he didn't just talk about this happening to Gentiles who become Jews. He said *every man.* Can he really mean that we, the children of Abraham, must be baptized of water and the Spirit before we can enter the kingdom of God? That's when he looked right at me—or through me!—and said, 'Are you a master of Israel and don't know these things?' he asked."

Miriam winced, feeling the pain that must have caused this good man.

"He wasn't angry or anything. It was almost as if he was surprised that I would be asking him questions like this."

"And what did you say to that?"

"Nothing. He told me that if he had taught me earthly things and I couldn't understand them, what would I do if he taught me of heavenly things?"

"I want to hear him," Miriam declared suddenly. "Do you think he might be in the temple today?"

He shook his head. "That's why I came, but I haven't found him."

"I am troubled," Livia said. "You speak of being baptized. In Greek, *baptizmos* means to immerse in water."

"Yes," Nicodemus said. "That's what John the Baptist was doing. He would take people into the River Jordan and baptize them."

"Yes, I have heard that," Livia said. "But what is baptized with the Spirit?"

"This was the question I asked myself over and over," came the reply.

Miriam's mind was working furiously. "Maybe he is saying that every one of us, Jew, Gentile, believer, nonbeliever must be immersed in God's Spirit as well. But why?"

No one spoke, letting her continue to think aloud.

Remembering what she had said to Marcus about symbol and ritual, and how the power of the symbol lies in what it represents spiritually, she began to nod. "Being immersed in the water symbolizes that we have our sins or impurities washed away."

"Yes," Nicodemus said eagerly, "and if that happens, you could say that we are in a state of . . . ?" He left the question hanging for her to finish.

Both women looked blank. Finally, Miriam nodded her head.

"Innocence. If we are pure, we are innocent, are we not?"

"Yes."

"Or you might say," he said, speaking very slowly, "we become innocent *again*."

Miriam was blank for a moment; then suddenly her eyes widened. "Like when we were born."

He sat back, satisfied now. "Now think about what Jesus told me."

It was Livia who drew in her breath now. "So if we are baptized with water and with the Spirit, it is like we are being reborn to become clean and pure and innocent."

"Yes," Miriam whispered. "Because unless we are clean and pure and innocent, we cannot return to live with God, who is clean and pure and innocent."

Nicodemus smiled, his eyes soft now. "That is what I came to as well. It feels right to me," he said. He gave a sorrowful smile. "But what do I know? I am only a master in Israel."

With that, he gave a quick nod of farewell, stood, and walked away. But he had gone only a few steps when he turned and looked at Miriam. "You will speak of none of this to your father?" he asked.

She shook her head. "I will not, if you will not."

Again he gave a quick nod, and then he was gone. Both women watched him go, struck by the sadness in the man. Miriam spoke first. "I have never seen him like this. He's a man of great wealth and confidence. But this experience seems to have really humbled him."

Livia murmured an assent. "This Jesus seems to have a strange effect on people."

"I know," Miriam agreed. "That's why as soon as Passover is finished, I'm going to find him. I want to hear him for myself."

"I would like that too," Livia said.

"Good." She took her hand. "Well, we'd better get home and get ready for Passover. My aunt and her family will be here before sundown."

VI

8 APRIL, A.D. 30

Miriam's mother's sister and her family stayed through Passover and two additional days beyond that, so it was not until the third day after their conversation with Nicodemus that Miriam and Livia were able to return to the Temple Mount. It was a sharp contrast to what they had seen before. The huge crowds were mostly gone now. The custodians of the temple had swept the great Court of the Gentiles. And Jesus of Nazareth was nowhere to be found.

By midday Livia returned home, but Miriam made one more swing through Solomon's Porches, hoping to find him. As she was about to leave, she saw Nicodemus enter the portico.

She walked swiftly to him. He saw her coming and looked around nervously. She realized this was neither the time nor the place for another conversation, but she had to know. She made as if she were going to walk right by him, then, as she came up beside him, stopped momentarily. "I have looked for this Jesus to hear him for myself. I cannot find him anywhere."

"He has returned to Galilee."

"No!"

He bowed slightly and moved on. It was as if they had paused momentarily for a greeting. Miriam walked on, turning her face away so that no one would see the disappointment on it. She went to the edge of the portico and stepped out in the sunshine, then stopped, staring out across the vast courtyard.

CHAPTER NOTES

The account of Nicodemus, who is called both a Pharisee and a ruler of the Jews, is found in John 3:1–21. His conversation with Jesus, which was held at night, is drawn from that scripture. His interpretation of that conversation with Miriam and Livia is, of course, an extrapolation of the author.

Nicodemus is referred to twice more in the Gospel of John—once when he speaks up in the Council in defense of Jesus (7:50), and once when he joins the other disciples in helping to prepare the body of Jesus for burial following the Crucifixion, and brought a gift of a hundred-pound weight of precious spices (19:39). He seems to have been convinced early on that there was more to Jesus than being just another teacher, but whether through timidity or some other factor, he probably did not become a full disciple until after Jesus was crucified.

Tradition says that after the Resurrection, he was fully converted to the Savior and publicly declared his faith. The Jewish religious leaders then stripped him of his office, beat him, and drove him from Jerusalem. A man of enormous wealth, as suggested by his gift at the burial, another account says he lost his entire fortune, and he and his family died in the direst of poverty (see Farrar, pp. 166–67).

CHAPTER 12

TRADITION IS A FENCE AROUND THE LAW.

—*Talmud*, Aboth, 3:14

I

20 APRIL, A.D. 30

A week following their return from Judea for the celebration of the Passover, the family of David ben Joseph was surprised when Deborah's brother, Aaron, showed up in Capernaum. He had stayed in Jerusalem a few extra days; then, being a strict Pharisee, Aaron had taken the longer route from Judea to Galilee that bypassed Samaria by going down to Jericho, then up the Jordan Valley. Passing through the accursed land and mingling with the accursed people was unthinkable except in the gravest emergency. Capernaum was a little north of the road that turned west and led to Sepphoris, but it still made for a convenient stopping place, especially when there was free lodging and food to be had. The family assumed that he would stay only overnight, then continue his journey on to his home in Sepphoris. They were wrong.

As usual, his presence proved to be a source of great irritation to Simeon. It had nothing to do with the fact that Simeon's younger brother Joseph had to move into Simeon's room to make a bed available for their uncle. Simeon spent half his life sleeping out beneath the stars, so sharing his bedroom was no bother at all. It was much more than that. It was the constant little digs about the Zealot cause. It was his side curls dangling and dancing, as a constant reminder that he lived a higher law. It was his snide comments about Deborah's family not being more observant of the Law—meaning, of course, the Law as interpreted by the Pharisees. It was the constant reminders of his spiritual superiority over the rest of the family, who just never seemed to take their faith quite seriously enough. But Simeon gritted his teeth. One night was not too much for him to hold his patience, especially if it kept peace with his mother.

But in the morning, Aaron didn't go. After breakfast he murmured something about spending the day with Amram and the other Pharisees of Capernaum, and left. That evening Joseph—to his mother's embarrassment—asked Aaron straight out if he would be leaving in the morning. Joseph didn't like sleeping on the floor in Simeon's room. Aaron just laughed and said no, that he wouldn't be leaving then either.

That's when Simeon's irritation began to turn to curiosity. What was going on? Aaron had a family to support. He was a potter of some renown and had a thriving business in Sepphoris. He had not gone down for Passover only, but for the entire Week of Unleavened Bread as well. Not with his family, Simeon noted darkly. They had three young children, and that would have meant that Aaron would have had to spend at least some time in Jerusalem seeing that their needs were met. But he had been gone for almost two weeks now. Why was there no urgency to get back to his home?

After dinner on the third night, Simeon got his questions answered.

II

When the last of the meal was finished, the adults moved to the roof, where the evening breezes were already cooling the humid air. It was customary in the Holy Land for most houses to be built with flat roofs, with parapets around the outside. As the sun settled in the west, the evening breezes would spring up, and all across the land people would go to their roofs to visit and talk. In the worst of the summer heat, many would sleep on the roof rather than in the sweltering house below.

Leah and Joseph had gone over to watch Esther and Boaz and put them to bed so that Ephraim and Rachel could be with the rest of the family. As they found chairs and benches and settled down, Aaron finally revealed his hand. The conversation initially began with David, Simeon, and Ephraim talking about the coming wheat harvest and what it would mean for the merchant business. Deborah and Rachel spoke quietly about other things. Suddenly, without waiting for an opening, Aaron came in. "Did you hear what happened at the Temple Mount during Passover?"

David straightened, trying to bring his thoughts to this new topic. "No. What?"

"About the moneychangers?"

Now David began to nod. "We heard something about some trouble on the Temple Mount, but—" He stopped, his mouth opening slightly. "Was that Jesus?"

Aaron didn't respond. Again he abruptly changed the subject. "I heard that your fishing partners have become his disciples."

David's head came up; then he looked at Deborah. Had she been telling her brother about Simon and Andrew's interest in Jesus? But she was already shaking her head. "I didn't say anything to him," she mouthed.

"So what does that mean for you?" Aaron said with a faint mocking tone. One hand came up, and he began to twirl one of his side curls. "Are you going to have to support them now?"

It was then that Simeon realized that, for some reason he didn't understand, Aaron was trying to start an argument—and for once, it wasn't with Simeon. It was with his father. Now his curiosity deepened.

"In the first place," David said tartly, "they haven't given up fishing. And why should it bother you if they choose to accept the teachings of Jesus? I've been trying to get an opportunity to hear what he has to say too."

Aaron turned to his sister. "Which goes to show that even good men can be fools."

Simeon scowled darkly, angered by the arrogance in the man. But he spoke with a pretended tone of innocence. "When you speak of fools, Uncle Aaron, are you talking about Father, Simon and Andrew, or the Pharisees?"

His mother shot him a look, and his father made as if to speak, but Aaron was too quick for both of them. "Why didn't you include the Zealots in there as well?" he sneered.

"Aaron," Deborah said quickly, "let's not have any arguments tonight."

But David wanted to know. "Was it Jesus who drove out the moneychangers?" he asked again.

"Yes, it was. And he is lucky that he got away before the Great Council had him arrested and thrown into prison."

"That's not what I heard," Simeon said sweetly. "I heard that the temple police were afraid to stand up to him and that the Council didn't have the courage to press any charges."

David and Ephraim turned to Simeon in surprise. "Where did you hear that?" his father asked.

Simeon shrugged. "I was in Jerusalem too, remember."

Aaron sniffed in disdain, then turned to his sister. "I'll be leaving tomorrow afternoon, Deborah."

The others turned in surprise. Simeon had to look down lest his uncle see the relief in his eyes.

"Oh?" Deborah said, obviously caught off guard by his comment as well. But then she nodded. "I have some things I'd like to send up with you for Hava and the children."

"I won't be going directly home," he said. He shot David a triumphant look. "I will be staying at Amram's house to work on some things, and then I am going up to Nazareth in a few days with him and some of the other Pharisees."

David couldn't help himself. "Nazareth?"

There was a gleam in Aaron's eye. "Yes, we have learned that this Jesus has returned home. There's a rumor that he may preach in the synagogue on Shabbat. After that madness he exhibited with the moneychangers, a committee has been formed to look into the whole matter."

"A committee of Pharisees?" David asked, with just a touch of irony in his voice.

"Yes, of course."

"A totally objective committee, I'm sure," Simeon drawled to his mother.

She frowned and gave him a sharp look.

Aaron's mouth turned up in what was meant to be a smile, but the expression came out more as a sneer. "Perhaps you and Deborah should come hear him as well," he said to David. "If you are so anxious to learn what kind of a teacher he is, then you can see for yourself that this man is not the Messiah. He is not a great teacher. He is nothing but an imposter."

But David had barely heard that last comment. He looked at Deborah with excitement. "What do you think? Would you be willing to go up to Nazareth? I could get things in order here before we leave."

Deborah hesitated. She was not at all interested in going to hear this unknown preacher whose name seemed to be on everyone's lips, but she knew how much it meant to David. And besides, she thought, perhaps Aaron was right. Perhaps this was a way to get the idea out of David's mind. "If you would like to go," she said, "then I will go with you."

"Good." David turned to his brother-in-law. " I think we shall come."

"Perhaps after you have seen for yourself that this man is a deceiver and a servant of Beelzebub, you can talk some sense into Simon and Andrew and those other two brothers with whom you are in partnership."

"Simon is no fool," David said, his voice tightening in spite of his resolution not to let Aaron irritate him. "And calling a man that you have never even met a servant of Satan seems to be a kind of foolishness all its own."

But Aaron was enjoying this too much to be angered. "The man has not spent his life studying the Torah as the great rabbis have. How can he claim to be a teacher?" His voice rose in pure derision. "And besides, a Messiah from Nazareth?" He hooted. "You should have spent more time studying the Torah as well, David."

"Aaron," Deborah said tartly, "we all know how learned you are, but that doesn't mean that the rest of us are without any knowledge. You know how I feel when you act like that."

Simeon had to look away so that she wouldn't see his surprise. It wasn't often his mother spoke so pointedly to her younger brother.

"All right," he said, rubbing his hands together, showing no signs of being at all sorry for what he had said. "Let me ask you some questions, David. Let's see if you are as knowledgeable as my sister thinks."

"Aaron, I'm warning you. I won't have this."

"It's all right, Deborah," David said. "I respect Aaron's knowledge of the scriptures. I wish I knew as much as he did."

Simeon jerked forward, annoyed beyond holding back further. "My father's problem, Uncle Aaron, is that he is more concerned about *living* the Law than he is about *knowing* it. Unlike some people I know."

Deborah slapped sharply the bench on which she was sitting. "That is enough! All of you. We will either speak civilly to each other or we shall spend the evening apart." She glared at Simeon, then swung on her brother. "Do you understand me, Aaron? If you want to have a discussion, that's fine, but one more insulting comment like the one you just made to David, and you can see if Amram has a bed for you tonight."

The rooftop was dead silent now. Rachel stared at her mother-in-law in amazement. Ephraim couldn't believe his mother had just spoken like that. Aaron looked as if he had been caught from behind with a sharp blow. David was staring at his wife in wonder.

"Yes," Aaron finally said. "I'm sorry, David. I didn't mean it."

Simeon, still looking at his mother in shock, nodded too. "I apologize as well."

It was David who finally went on. "Go ahead, Aaron. I would like to hear what you have to say. I have never said that this Jesus is the Messiah, though I know some think that he is."

"Do Simon and Andrew?" Aaron asked.

He looked quickly at Deborah before answering. "I think so." He saw her shake her head slightly, obviously not pleased with that answer, and he wished Aaron hadn't been that specific.

"All right," Aaron said. "Let's talk about the Messiah then. Let's start with Isaiah." Now his voice almost took on the attitude of a cantor in a synagogue as he began to intone a memorized passage. "'For unto us a child is born, unto us a son is given, and . . .'" He stopped, motioning for them to continue in his place. "What's the next phrase?"

"'And the government shall be upon his shoulder,'" David answered.

"Yes!" Aaron exulted. "The government will be on his shoulder, David. He is to be our king. Then what does Isaiah say next? 'And his name shall be called Wonderful! Counselor! The *Prince* of Peace!'" He stood and began to pace back and forth, pleased with his point. "Did you hear anything in there about a carpenter?" He leaned over his chair, triumphant now. "Can you picture a king or a prince coming out of Nazareth?" One hand flicked, dismissing the very idea with disdain.

Simeon started to raise a hand, but Aaron rushed on, his face flushed with excitement. "And remember what the prophet Balaam said under the inspiration of the Almighty? 'There shall come a Star out of Jacob, and a Scepter shall rise out of Israel, and shall smite the corners of Moab, and destroy all the children of Sheth.'" He punched the air. "A *scepter*, David. What does that mean to you?"

"Rulers hold scepters," David conceded calmly.

"Exactly! Kings and princes hold scepters. So tell me, what scepter does this Jesus have?" He scoffed. "A carpenter's mallet? A saw? Surely you cannot believe that some peasant preacher from the back hills of Galilee is going to rise up in power and smite all of our enemies."

"I—"

"Listen to the Psalmist, David." He began to quote again. "'He shall judge among the heathen; he shall fill the places with the dead bodies; he shall wound the heads over many countries.' Now there is a Deliverer for you. Simeon and his Zealot friends will be able to put away their swords and stop playing childish games. There will no longer be a need for such foolishness. When we become faithful and obedient, then the Messiah will come and overthrow all our enemies."

Simeon stirred but then remembered the anger of his mother and bit back a retort.

Again there was a derisive hoot of contempt. "Perhaps when we are in Nazareth we shall see the armies that this Jesus has raised.

Perhaps we shall see his great store of arms that he will use to throw off the yoke of Rome."

Simeon had come to his feet, truly angry now that Aaron was speaking in this tone to his father, but David pulled him back down, not even looking at him. He seemed not at all perturbed by Aaron's outburst. "I know there are many other passages just like those you have cited, Aaron."

"Many!"

"I pray that you are right in your interpretation of these passages, Aaron, because then Deborah and I won't have to lie awake nights when Simeon is gone and wonder if he will return to us. I would love to think that a Great Deliverer is coming."

Simeon turned to look at his father. He knew that his father did not approve of the path he was taking, but this was the first he had ever heard him express concern about his safety.

"But let me ask you just a couple of questions if I may."

"Of course," Aaron sniffed.

"Is it not true that the scriptures give us another picture of the Messiah as well? Yes, there is the image of the powerful King who will make us free and govern us in righteousness, but don't the prophets also paint a picture of what some of the rabbis have called 'the suffering servant' Messiah?"

Aaron had stopped his exultant pacing. "Well, yes, but—"

Deborah turned, her eyes wide as she looked at her husband. Simeon was also staring at him in surprise.

"For example," David went on, almost musing now, "Zechariah said something very interesting I think." There was a quick deprecating gesture. "I can't quote it as you do, Aaron, but doesn't he say something like 'Your king is lowly and comes to you riding upon an ass and the foal of an ass'?"

Aaron was clearly thrown off balance by this totally unexpected side of his brother-in-law. "Well, yes, something like that. But that is an image we don't fully understand."

"Don't the rabbis agree this is a passage that refers to the Messiah also?"

"Yes," he admitted.

David looked puzzled. "So I don't understand. When a king wants to signify that he visits another city in peace, he comes riding on a donkey. Why? Because the horse is associated with war—chariots and cavalry—but it's hard to appear very threatening if you mount a donkey and charge the walls." He lifted a hand and moved his fingers in an imitation of the mincing steps of a donkey. At the same time he cupped his other hand to his mouth and called out, "Surrender, you dogs. Here I come!"

Ephraim clapped his hands in delight. "The men would fall off the walls laughing," he said.

Now David swung back on his brother-in-law, and the musing tone was gone. "So how do you explain that, Aaron? Does the Messiah come as the Great Deliverer, or will he come in peace, riding on a donkey? Incidentally," he went on, speaking to his wife and son and cutting off Aaron's response, "Isaiah did call the Messiah a prince, but note that he is a prince of *peace*, not a prince of war."

Aaron's eyes were flashing anger, but David went on calmly. "Or tell me this. How is it that Isaiah, whom you have already cited, tells us that the Messiah will be despised and rejected of men? That he will be a man of sorrows? That he will be wounded for our transgressions? That doesn't seem to fit the picture of a powerful conqueror."

Simeon noted there was no smugness in his father, even though he obviously had Aaron scrambling for an answer. He seemed genuinely concerned. "I wish I did have your knowledge of the scriptures, Aaron, for I have puzzled long over this of late. I have been reading a great deal, and frankly, I don't know."

Aaron's excitement had died noticeably. He was frowning deeply.

"The words of the prophets are like a swift river. It is easy for one who is not used to swimming in deep water to lose one's footing."

Simeon shot forward. "And only you who are properly schooled are strong enough to brave the current, is that it?"

"Don't be insolent, Simeon," Aaron snapped. "The great rabbis say that the oral traditions are the hedge around the Law. They are there to protect us—all of us—so don't mock those who spend a lifetime learning how to erect that hedge."

To Simeon's surprise his mother spoke in his defense. "I don't think Simeon was being insolent, Aaron. In fact, I think it is a fair question. David has raised some troubling issues. Are you going to respond or simply use your greater knowledge as an excuse for not answering him?"

"So now my own sister turns on me?" Aaron cried. "You know that was not what I was saying."

"Then answer David's question. Frankly, I would like to think you are right, Aaron. I want the Messiah to be the Mighty One of Israel. I want him to come out of the morning sun with flashing sword and invincible power, sweeping all of our enemies before him." She looked at Simeon. "I want him to make it so that the Zealots do not have to fight. Knowing that would make the Roman yoke more endurable now. But what of these other prophecies?"

Aaron was pulling at his beard. He was still clearly miffed, but Deborah's challenge could not be sidestepped. "What I meant to say, when I used the image of a deep river," he began, "was that much of the inspired writings are to be taken literally, but sometimes the Lord uses figurative language, imagery that helps us see the truth. For example, just because a king is powerful and mighty doesn't mean he cannot be humble too. After all, humility is one of the qualities of greatness. Perhaps he will be wounded by our lack of faith. Perhaps his sorrow comes because his people are not ready for him."

Simeon could see his uncle's eyes becoming bright again. He liked the sound of what he was saying. "Wouldn't that be a tragedy if the Deliverer comes and we are not worthy to receive him and stand with him? Then he really would be like a suffering servant." He stopped, nodding in satisfaction. "I don't think it is all such a great mystery."

"May I ask you a question, Uncle Aaron?"

He turned and looked at Simeon, suddenly wary. "What?"

"The *peyot* or side curls that you wear. Is it true you have not cut them since the day you decided to become a Pharisee?"

"Of course." He touched them now, curling them around his fingers as he often did.

"And this commandment comes from the Levitical code?"

Deborah was giving Simeon a warning look, but he ignored it, watching his uncle.

"Yes," Aaron said proudly. "The law says that you shall not round the corners of your head nor mar the corners of your beard."

"And that is interpreted to mean this area right here?" Simeon touched the hair directly beside his ears.

"Yes."

"Simeon," his mother broke in, "I won't have you making light of something that is sacred to another person."

He looked at his mother. "I have no intention of making light of anything, Mother. Actually, this is a question that has bothered me for some time."

"I can defend myself, big sister," Aaron said with a smile of appreciation. Then to Simeon, "So what is your question?"

"There are some who say that Jehovah gave that commandment to Moses because in some pagan religions, such as in Egypt, the side curl on a boy was never cut until he reached puberty. Then it was shaved off and offered ritually as part of his dedication to one of the gods."

Aaron nodded, still quite comfortable. "Yes, I know that some believe that."

"Then is it possible that the Lord gave that commandment as part of a prohibition against following after idolatrous practices and that he never meant for that part of the hair to be left untouched by those who are his faithful followers?"

To Simeon's surprise, again his uncle nodded amiably. "Yes, that is possible."

"And yet you don't think so. You think it should be taken literally?"

He fingered the *peyot* again. "Obviously."

Simeon sighed. "Father and I do not wear the *peyot*. Yet you Pharisees do."

"Many people other than the Pharisees follow this practice, Simeon. And not all of those who stand with us, I am sad to say, believe that *peyot* are part of the *mitzvah*, or the commandments."

"All right," Simeon said, thoughtful now. "You interpret the Law literally. Father and Ephraim and I and others do not. Me especially, since I shave even my beard. If we are wrong, then what we do is displeasing to God. Is that right?"

Now there was hesitation, but finally Aaron nodded. "Yes, I believe that your failure to accept God's law, for whatever reason, is displeasing to him."

Simeon's father stirred but said nothing. He was curious to see where Simeon was going with this.

"Do you believe that we want to displease God?"

"Of course not. I believe you are sincere in thinking that the passage has only limited meaning. But sincerity does not make one right."

"Agreed, but I thank you for at least acknowledging that we are sincere. Because you are right. I do not want to displease God. If I really believed in my heart that it mattered to God how I cut my hair, my side curls would be longer than yours, Uncle Aaron. But I just have trouble accepting that interpretation. So here is my question for you. You say that some passages of scripture have to be taken literally and yet others are to be interpreted figuratively. So how do you know which is which?"

"I . . . " He stopped, looking a little perplexed.

"You say that the suffering servant passages are probably symbolic, while passages predicting a Mighty King are literal? What rule do you use to decide when to be literal and when not to? That is the question I have for you. And don't just quote the great rabbinical teachers. My question applies to them as well."

His face darkened instantly. "Don't criticize those who have devoted their lives to studying the Law. The schools are not just social clubs, you know. A price has to be paid before you can answer such things."

Once again Simeon's mother surprised him. "That's all well and good, Aaron," Deborah said quietly, "and we all know that you have paid that price and we have not. So answer Simeon's question. It is a good one. How *do* you know when to be literal?"

He turned to face her, surprised that she was taking Simeon's side on this. "It isn't that easy, Deborah. It's not always a question of logic or common sense. You just know with some things. After a while you just know."

"But I don't just know, Uncle Aaron," Simeon said, shaking his head. "So what does that say about me? Is it just because I am so ignorant of the Law?" His mouth pursed into a thin line. "Or is it perhaps that you have too much learning, that you are relying too much on your knowledge and not enough on inspiration?"

"Now you *are* being insolent," Aaron snapped.

"I agree, Simeon," Deborah said. "We will stop this discussion right now if you can't be reasonable to each other."

"I'm sorry," Simeon said, and he meant it. He really did want to know, and taunting Aaron was not the way to get him to answer.

Aaron's eyes darted around the group. Absently, he smoothed his beard as his mind sought the proper response. Then his head bobbed slightly. "You have asked a thoughtful question, Simeon. May I ask you one in return?"

"Will you answer mine first?"

"This is my answer."

"All right. Go on."

"Do you believe in the power of prayer?"

Simeon's breath exploded softly. "Of course."

"I'm not just talking about the set prayers we offer three times each day. I'm talking about personal prayer, when your heart yearns for help or solace and you turn to God, pleading for his help or for an answer or for comfort. Do you believe in all of that?"

"You know I do. You know we all do."

Aaron nodded, his voice calm now. "And tell me about God, Simeon. Do you believe he is all powerful?"

"Yes."

"That he is all wise and all knowing?"

"You know we do."

"Then why do you pray?"

"I beg your pardon."

"Why do you pray? If God is all wise and all knowing, doesn't he already know what our needs are before we even ask? I mean, do you picture yourself looking up at God and saying, 'I have a problem, Lord,' and having him say, 'Oh, I didn't know that.'"

Simeon was silent for a moment before he shook his head slowly. "No, I believe God knows all things."

"Including the thoughts of your heart?"

Simeon sensed that he was being led into a snare now, but he had no choice but to answer. There was only one answer. "Yes, including the thoughts and feelings of my heart."

"Then why not just sit back and wait for God to give us what he already knows we need? Why do we have to ask?" He turned to the others. "Deborah? David? These questions are for you as well."

"Well, I—" Deborah started. She stopped, trying to collect her thoughts. "For one thing, I want to express my gratitude to God for the goodness of life. It's not just that I want to ask him for things."

"Good, good. But if he knows that in your heart you are grateful, why do you have to say it?"

"Because of what it does for us," David finally said. "It is good for me to give thanks aloud, to tell God how thankful we are for life and for all he does for us."

"Yes, that is part of it, isn't it?" Aaron said thoughtfully.

Simeon's mind was racing. This was an interesting question he had not thought about before.

"But let's focus on the asking part of prayer," Aaron went on. "Why can't we just say, 'Lord, you know my needs. The sooner you can meet them, the better.'"

"Because God is not just there to meet our every whim," Simeon said, knowing he was now doing what he had accused Aaron of doing a few minutes before. He was skirting the real question.

Aaron wouldn't let him get away with it. "Now who is not answering, Simeon?" He turned to Deborah. "You see, Sister, it is not logical. It doesn't fit our notion of common sense. But because it is hard to explain doesn't mean that it is wrong."

Simeon's father was very thoughtful now. "I've thought about this a lot, especially in the last few weeks. It seems to me that God asks us to pray because of what it does for us more than what it does for him."

Aaron whirled, clearly triumphant. "Yes, go on. Tell me why you say that, David."

"For example, when Deborah came close to death bringing young Joseph into the world, I pleaded with the Lord to spare them both. It wasn't that I doubted for one minute that he had the power to do so."

"Yes, yes," Aaron prodded. "Keep going."

David began to nod slowly. "It was because I wasn't sure I was worthy to ask such a thing of him. And so I tried to humble myself. I asked myself what things I might be doing that were displeasing to him, that might prevent me from having sufficient faith to call down his power in our behalf. I promised with all the fervency of my heart that I would try to be better, to do better, so that he would bless me."

"Exactly," Aaron exclaimed. "And that softening of your heart, that mental inventory and recommitment of the heart, *that* is why God asks that we pray to him. He doesn't need our prayers. We need our prayers. It is what it does to us and for us."

He turned to Simeon. "Wearing the *peyot* doesn't make sense to some people. It is not logical. It seems strange and peculiar. To be honest, I am not absolutely positive that it is something that he wants of me." He drew in a breath. "But it is what wearing the side curls does for me that counts, Simeon. It is my way of saying, 'I will do whatever God asks. I will not eat certain things. I will wear certain articles of clothing. I will worship him in specified ways. I will let my hair grow long.' Why? Because he wants me to be different from the world, even if the world laughs and ridicules me for doing so. This is how I show my love and gratitude for him."

He sat back, a little surprised at his own passion.

Simeon was strangely moved. All that he had ever seen of his uncle was the outward rigidity, the arrogance, the superiority. He had just caught a glimpse into his heart, and it was a view that totally surprised him. Simeon turned and saw that his mother's eyes were shining as she looked at her brother. Obviously she saw something there as well, perhaps part of the young boy she had once known.

Finally Aaron turned back to his nephew. "Are there any other questions, Simeon?"

Simeon shook his head. "No. You have answered well, Uncle Aaron, and given me much to think about. Thank you."

CHAPTER NOTES

There are literally hundreds of what are termed "Messianic" passages in the Old Testament. The dualistic picture of the Messiah depicted here is found in those passages, some of which are paraphrased here. With the conquest of Jerusalem by the Romans and their subjection of the people, the idea of the Messiah as a great King and powerful Deliverer rose in popularity during the last century before Christ's ministry (see Mathews, pp. 3–32).

The passages referred to by Aaron include Isaiah 9:6; Numbers 24:17; Psalms 45:6; and 110:1–7. Those referred to by David include Zechariah 9:9, and various verses from Isaiah 53. There are numerous other passages that could be used to support both viewpoints.

The passage that is cited for the practice of wearing the side curls, or the *peyot,* a practice still followed by some of the stricter sects of Judaism today, is Leviticus 19:27.

CHAPTER 13

AND HE SAITH UNTO THEM, FOLLOW ME, AND
I WILL MAKE YOU FISHERS OF MEN.

—*Matthew 4:19*

I

23 APRIL, A.D. 30

"Ho, Simon!" David waved as he shouted, shading his eyes against the blinding glare coming off the water. The sun had just cleared the heights of Gadara on the east of the Sea of Kinnereth, and the two fishing boats were coming straight down the glimmering path it blazed on the still water.

Backlighted by the glare, a figure on the closest boat straightened and turned. Then it too waved, "*Shalom, shalom.* Good morning, David. Come to see how much money you are going to lose today?"

David laughed. "I can see that your boats ride like a feather in the water. That is not a good sign."

Another silhouette joined the first, and Andrew's voice came clearly to him as though he were only a few feet away. "It has been a long and fruitless night, David. You won't be needing any laborers today. There will be barely enough to feed our families."

From the second boat another man waved. "Barely enough to feed one child." It was the voice of James, son of Zebedee, who with his brother John was also in partnership with David.

David bobbed his head, disappointed but not surprised. That was exactly why he or one of his sons usually came down to the shore so early each morning. On some nights of fishing you could put your nets out and hit a school so large that it nearly swamped the boat. The next night in the same place you could troll back and forth all night and come up with nothing. When they were successful, it took four or five men to clean and salt the fish, so David would go to the main square in Capernaum and hire whatever day laborers he needed to help with the catch. But there would be no men hired today. At least not by him. David shrugged philosophically. That was part of life as a merchant.

David turned and looked up and down the shore of the lake. In the early-morning hours there was always plenty of activity along the seashore. The boats usually started returning home about sunup. Their families or associates would be waiting, and each boat became a center of action. The fish had to be sorted and then cleaned. Nets had to be spread out to dry so they didn't get moldy. Sails and nets and rigging had to be kept in constant repair. Occasionally the boats themselves had to be caulked or repaired so they didn't leak.

A loud splash brought David around again. Impatient with their slow progress, Simon had removed his outer robe and jumped into the water. Up to his chest, he took the rope Andrew tossed to him and began pulling it toward shore. A moment later there was another splash, and James had done the same for their boat, though he angled to David's left, where Zebedee was on shore already mending the extra net.

Kicking off his sandals and hiking up his robe, then securing it with his sash, David waded out and grabbed the rope as well. Together, he and Simon pulled the boat up and onto the graveled shore. Andrew stowed the oar and jumped off to join them.

If one knew that Simon and Andrew were brothers, one could see the resemblance between the two of them, but it wasn't that striking. Andrew was the older of the two, approaching his twenty-sixth birthday in a couple of months. Simon was three years his junior. Both had blue eyes with flecks of green and wore their hair to their shoulders and their beards thick and bushy. Simon's was a lighter color, a soft brown that showed highlights of red in the sunlight. Both brothers were powerfully built—an inheritance from their father and from years of fishing—but Andrew was not as broad through the shoulders and was slimmer through the hips. His hands were more delicate, with long nimble fingers that could stitch a sail or mend a net with surprising dexterity. Simon's hands looked like two wooden mallets when they were closed. What they lacked in dexterity, they made up for in power.

David found all four of his partners pleasant to work with and filled with integrity. They were men of the sea, speaking only when they had something to say and then usually with straightforward honesty. In terms of their dependability, there was no shadow of compromise. That was one of the reasons David had sought them out in the first place. That had been seven years ago now. They had worked out the terms of their agreement verbally and had shaken hands. Nothing more had ever been required.

Once they got the boat well onto the beach, the two fishermen climbed back aboard and lifted the heavy net, still dripping wet, and tossed it over the side. All along the beach, frameworks of sticks were fixed to serve as racks for drying nets. Since there was no catch to clean this morning, David knew that Simon and Andrew would use the time to mend their net. Though he had more than enough to do back at home, he decided he would stay for awhile and help. When they went home to sleep, he would then go to his place of work.

With the net hung out to dry, Andrew turned to David. "You went up to Jerusalem for Passover?" It wasn't really a question. The annual pilgrimage was expected of everyone unless there were pressing reasons why they couldn't.

"Yes. Actually we got back a few days ago, but Deborah's brother came to stay with us."

"So did you get to hear Jesus? He taught several days in the temple."

David shook his head in deep disappointment. "I heard that later. I wish I had known. You knew that I went up to Nazareth a couple of days after you told me you thought he was there. But by then he had gone back to Jerusalem for Passover. It seems like wherever he is, I am not; and where I am, he is not."

"Well, now he's come back to the Galilee," Andrew reported. "You should be able to hear him now."

"Back in Nazareth?"

"No, actually he is here in Capernaum. Peter saw him yesterday. Then he plans to return to Nazareth for Shabbat."

"Yes, that's what Aaron said. Deborah and I plan to go up to see if we can hear him."

"Good."

Then something Andrew said struck David. "Peter?" He turned to Simon. "Oh, yes. That was what Jesus called you, wasn't it?"

Simon had stopped at a place in the net where there was a tear the length of his arm. "Yes." He held up the net and shook it at Andrew. "No wonder we didn't catch anything," he muttered. "A boat could slip through that hole."

Andrew nodded and went to the boat, returning in a moment with a coil of the thin hemp rope they used to mend the netting.

"So you're changing your name?" David asked Simon. That really surprised him. Simon was of a strong will, and it took a lot to make him change his mind about anything.

"Not changing it," he said, not looking up. "Just adding to it."

"We like it," Andrew said, completely serious. "Simon Peter. Simon the Rock."

"This Jesus must have had a real impact on you," David said after a moment, watching Simon closely.

Andrew answered for the both of them. "More than you know, David. We are most anxious for you to meet him."

"As am I."

Simon was holding the net tight as Andrew worked on mending the hole. He looked now at David. "As a boy I can remember times when my father would teach me how to do things—how to cast the net, or how to pull in a full load of fish without breaking my back, or how to read the winds and spot a school of fish beneath the surface." His eyes had a far-off look in them. "I can remember marveling as he talked, wondering how he had ever gotten to be so wise."

"Yes." David had known Peter's father well. He was a man of simple means but greatly respected in Bethsaida.

"Well, that's how I feel whenever I hear Jesus speak," Simon went on. "It's like he opens my eyes to see things I've never seen before. I come away marveling, filled with wonder. So if he wants to call me Peter, then Peter I shall be."

Andrew stopped for a moment, looking at his younger brother. Then, very quietly, he said, "Tell David about Cana, Peter."

Simon Peter seemed startled by that and gave his brother a sharp look. Andrew only nodded. David waited, not sure why Simon seemed so hesitant.

Finally Simon Peter nodded. "This happened a couple of weeks ago," he said as Andrew went back to work again, "before Passover." His eyes narrowed slightly as he thought back. "Andrew and I and James and John and Philip were invited by Jesus to attend a wedding of one of his relatives who lives in Cana. During the wedding feast, the host ran out of wine."

"Really?" That would be suprisingly poor planning. Part of a host's duty was to anticipate the needs of his wedding guests.

Peter was frowning. "It was partly our fault. Here we were, five additional men that the host had not expected. Jesus didn't know we were coming until that day, so there was no way to warn the host. But anyway, while we were eating, Mary—that's the name of the mother of Jesus—leaned over and whispered to Jesus that they were out of wine."

"She expected him to go find some?" David said. That seemed a little strange. It was the host that was responsible for seeing that all went well at a wedding feast, especially if he had not planned sufficiently. But then, he thought, if this was a relative, perhaps Mary was helping put on the feast.

Simon Peter was deep in thought now. "I'm not sure what she expected. She just said it very quietly."

"And what did Jesus say to that?"

"He was very gentle," Andrew answered. "He said, 'Woman, what have I to do with thee? My hour is not yet come.'"

David waited for a moment, hoping for more. When it didn't come, he spoke again. "His hour was not yet come? Was it too late to purchase more wine?"

Simon Peter chuckled. "We wondered the same thing. As I have thought about it since, I think Mary was asking for his help, and he gently reminded her that the time for showing forth his power was not here yet."

"Showing forth his power? What do you mean by that?"

Peter ignored the question. "His mother didn't seem bothered at all by his answer. It wasn't like Jesus had refused. It was more of a reminder. She motioned to some of the servants and told them to do whatever Jesus said."

"Go on." David sensed there was much more to this story than just a shortage of wine.

The fisherman's face became a study in concentration. "There were six stone water pots in the next room. These were large, containing two or three firkins apiece."

David nodded. Three firkins of liquid would pretty well load down a donkey. A jar that held three firkins would come to a man's waist.

"Yes. Well, Jesus told the servants to fill them with water."

"All of them?" David blurted. If there were six, that would take several trips to the cistern, even with multiple servants.

"Yes, all of them. We waited while the servants drew enough water to fill them to the brim."

"And then what happened?"

Simon Peter shook his head slowly. "When they were full, Jesus just said, 'Draw out now from the pots and take to the host of the feast.'"

David was incredulous. "He told them to serve water instead of wine?" Under the strict laws of hospitality and the customs of wedding etiquette, to serve water because the wine had run out would be a terrible humiliation.

Andrew leaned forward eagerly. "That's just it, David. Can you imagine? Serving water instead of wine at a wedding feast? We were all shocked when he said it. The servants hesitated, but then they did as he said. They drew a pitcher and went into the host and filled his cup."

The two brothers were looking at each other, as if they were still having a hard time with what they were telling David. David couldn't bear it. "What?" he demanded. "What happened?"

Peter went on quietly. "Remember, the host didn't know any of what had happened. He assumed they had just gotten some more wine from somewhere."

"But *we* knew what it was," Andrew came in. "And the servants knew."

"And?"

Peter continued. "The host took one sip, then motioned to the bridegroom. The room fell quiet, for they thought he was going to give a speech." Simon Peter stopped, looked at Andrew once, who nodded his encouragement, then went on. "'Friend,' the host said to the bride-groom, 'it is customary at such a feast to set forth your best wine at the first, and then when everyone has well drunk and no longer can discern clearly, the poorer wine is brought forth. But we commend you, for you have kept the finest wine until now.'"

David was gaping at Peter. "He thought it was wine?"

The fisherman shook his head slowly. "No, David. It *was* wine."

"But—" He just stared at him. "You don't mean—"

"Yes," Andrew said with half a smile, "that is exactly what we mean. Jesus didn't do anything except to tell the servants to fill the pots. But what went in as water came out as wine."

Reeling, David started to say something, then didn't know what it would be. He reached out and fingered the net, his thoughts tumbling. Simon Peter and Andrew looked at each other but said nothing. Andrew went back to working on the net.

Almost five minutes went by. They finished that tear and moved down to the next, a much smaller one. Finally David spoke. "If people had too much to drink, perhaps—"

Peter looked up. "No one was drunk, David. It was not that kind of a wedding."

David nodded. He wanted to think that Simon Peter was just not being realistic, but these men were not ones to shade the truth. Another two or three minutes went by before David had another thought. "Were the pots used for wine before that night?"

Andrew laughed softly, seeing where David was going with this. "They were water pots."

"Are you sure? Did anyone look inside? Perhaps there was some wine in them before. Stone will hold a residue from the wine."

Peter stopped and laid a hand on David's shoulder. "There was somewhere between twelve and eighteen firkens of water drawn and poured into those stone containers, David. That's enough to water a caravan of camels. Even if those pots had been half full of wine—

which they were not—do you think the host of the feast would have declared it to be the finest wine we had drunk so far?"

There was an enigmatic smile. "I told you, David. We were not drunk that night."

"Then how do you explain it?" David cried.

The two looked at each other for several seconds; then Peter answered for the both of them. "We don't. That's why we call him Master."

II

Once the net was mended, Peter decided that they couldn't simply quit with such a meager catch, so he and Andrew retrieved their hand net from the hold of the boat. Here David was of no help to them. The hand net or "cast net" was made of a fine mesh and was circular, about ten feet in diameter. The edge was lined with lead sinkers, and a line was attached to the center of the net. Holding the line with the left hand, Peter arranged the net in neat folds over his shoulder. Therein lay the skill. An experienced fisherman, and Andrew and Simon Peter were that if nothing else, could send the net sailing outward until its full width almost floated over the water. Then it would settle gracefully and sink to the bottom.

Working about twenty-five paces apart, the two brothers waded out to their waists, then stood motionless. Peter had the net poised and ready. For several long minutes no one moved. All three of them watched the water intently. Suddenly, off to Peter's right, the surface of the water rippled softly.

"Over there!" David cried, pointing.

Peter had already seen it. Moving very slowly, he turned his body until he faced the spot. Even as they watched, the ripples moved southward along the line of the shore. With one smooth sweep of his arm, the net went sailing outward, extending to its full circle. The fish saw the movement and wheeled away, but it was too late. The net dropped, the sinkers plopping softly, and the fish were encircled. Now, moving swiftly, Peter drew on the cord. This pulled the weighted perimeter of the net in tighter, trapping the catch. Andrew moved in quickly to make sure the bottom of the net held their catch as the fish began to thrash wildly. In a moment it was clear that the day would not be a total waste.

III

About half an hour later, as they finished cleaning and putting the catch into buckets of lake water, Andrew stopped and turned. A commotion down the beach had caught his attention. David and Peter turned to look as well. Near the far end of this stretch of fisherman's beach a path left the shore, cutting through the trees to the main road that led to Capernaum. It was there that a small crowd of men, women, and children had appeared, moving toward them.

"Trouble?" David asked, squinting in the sunlight, unable to tell what it was.

Andrew shook his head but didn't speak. He was peering carefully at the crowd. Even as they watched, the group kept moving toward them. Now they could see that the crowd was gathered around one figure who was leading them. They could hear the murmur of many voices and the sounds of people calling out to one another.

Andrew stood, leaning forward slightly. His body was rigid, his eyes fixed on the man who led them. Then he jerked around. "It's him, Peter."

Peter was nodding. "Yes, I thought it was."

"Who?" David asked.

"Jesus."

That brought David to his feet as well. He peered at the group that was moving slowly toward them. All along the beach, people were being drawn to join the crowd.

"Yes." Andrew was transfixed.

They stood there without speaking further. Slowly the swelling crowd came toward them. It was like a magnet being pulled through a pile of metal shavings. As Jesus approached, people stood and went swiftly to join him. Nets were left stretched out on the sand, the sorting and cleaning of fish forgotten for a moment.

Finally they were close enough that David could see the man around whom everyone swirled. He was dressed in a simple robe or tunic of homespun material, the dress common to peasants and craftsmen all over the country. He was taller than David had expected, and had broad shoulders. He moved slowly, holding the hand of a young girl, answering questions, smiling pleasantly in greeting as additional people joined him.

Now it was David who was transfixed. He couldn't take his eyes off him. This was the man who had so occupied his thoughts for the past weeks, and now here he was before him. Suddenly he had a thought. "Do you know how old he is?" he asked Andrew.

The fisherman turned, giving David a strange look. "How old?"

"Yes," David said, eager now. "How old is he?"

"What difference does—"

But before Andrew could finish his question, Peter cut in. "He's thirty years of age. I heard John ask Jesus' mother that same question at the wedding."

"Ah." It came out as a soft sound of wonder from David's throat.

"Why?" Peter asked, staring at him as strangely, as Andrew was.

David didn't hear them. Jesus was now no more than twenty-five or thirty paces away, and David was watching his every move. Three young boys ran alongside, calling something up to Jesus. He nodded and spoke, and the one boy hooted in triumph. Jesus laughed at the spontaneous enthusiasm. For a moment it was as though the four of them were completely alone, sharing a pleasant moment together.

Then he was to them. Jesus stopped a few feet away, and the people around him stopped as well. A hush quickly fell over the group, for it was obvious he was going to speak. But for a moment he did not. His eyes seemed to take in everything—the net with its newly mended spots, the buckets of fish, the fact that Peter and Andrew were wet to their waist.

Finally his eyes stopped on Peter. A smile of infinite softness played around the corners of Jesus' mouth. For a moment David thought he might say something about their catch, but when he spoke, he called them by name.

"Simon Peter? Andrew?"

Both men straightened, their eyes fixed on him.

"Follow me." The smile broadened, and David could see the pleasure in the eyes of Jesus. "Follow me," he said again, "and I will make you fishers of men."

David was astonished. That was hardly what he had expected. He turned, wanting to see the reaction to such a strange comment. To his utter amazement, Andrew dropped the knife he had been using to clean the fish, turned to a bucket of water, and washed his hands quickly. Wiping them on his tunic, he came over to stand beside Jesus. Simon Peter had not budged as yet. He was looking straight at Jesus, his eyes wide and questioning. Then without a word, he turned and walked to where his outer tunic lay beside the net. He put it on quickly, girding the sash around his waist, then walked over to stand beside Andrew.

There was a slight nod from Jesus, as though he had expected nothing less than this astonishing response; then he started forward again. As he reached David, he slowed his step, submitting to David's unabashed scrutiny with calmness. His eyes penetrated David, as if he was looking deep inside him and quietly asking, "Is there anything you would ask of me?" When David's eyes finally fell away, he smiled and moved on.

Drawn as if beyond his will, David fell in with the crowd as they continued on. But at the very next boat, they stopped again. Zebedee and his two sons were all on board their vessel now, mending the large net. Or rather, they had been mending it. At the approach of the crowd, they stopped working as well and were watching intently. Once again the man from Nazareth stopped. Once again there was a hush as the crowd quieted to hear what he said. And once again came those simple words as he looked at the two sons of Zebedee. "Come, follow me, and I will make you fishers of men."

These two brothers were as different as pomegranates and onions. James was the older of the two, being about Peter's age. He was of a more sober mien, thoughtful, reflective, deliberate. John was not yet twenty and looked younger than that. His nature was more open, warm, and friendly to all. Yet in spite of their differences, they were both energetic and strong willed. Now they both turned to their father. But Zebedee was staring at Jesus and didn't see them. As with David, once again the young teacher from Nazareth submitted to the searching scrutiny with calm serenity. Finally Zebedee turned to his sons and nodded. James set the net aside, walked to the bow of the boat and jumped lightly down onto the beach. John followed him without hesitation. As they reached Jesus, he reached out and took James' hand, holding it firmly for a moment. Then he put an arm around John's shoulder, and together they moved off.

David ben Joseph, merchant of Capernaum, watched them until they were a full stone's throw away. Then he turned to his old friend. Zebedee was older than David by almost ten years and had turned the fishing business mostly over to his two sons—the two sons who had just walked away from it without hesitation.

"What will you do?" David asked Zebedee. He wasn't thinking

about what this would do to his own trade in the fish business. He was wondering how Zebedee would make out.

After a moment Zebedee shrugged. "I'm not sure."

IV

"They're going to give up fishing?" Deborah had stopped her sewing and was staring at David in astonishment.

"Not completely."

"To follow after this man? And what is Anna supposed to do? How will she care for her family if Simon is off chasing butterflies?"

His head came up sharply. "You have never met Jesus, Deborah," he said softly. "If you had, you wouldn't say that."

"What?" she cried. "What is it about this man that is so compelling that grown men leave their occupations, leave their families without means of support?"

"I can't explain it. There is something in his eyes. Something in the way he speaks. He's like no one I've ever known before."

She leaned forward, her sewing forgotten. "What are you saying, David?"

He took a deep breath. "I'm not sure. But I am determined to learn more of him."

She shook that off. That was not what she had meant. "What if he had asked you to follow him?" she queried. "What then?"

He was silent for a long time.

"You wouldn't, David! Just up and leave everything?"

"I want you to hear him, Deborah. See him." Then he remembered and became suddenly eager. "Simon Peter says he is thirty years old now."

"That's another thing," she retorted. "Simon is changing his name?"

David remembered how Peter had responded to that. "No, he's just adding to it." Then he said it again. "He's thirty, Deborah. It was thirty years ago this spring when I was in Bethlehem."

Her face softened. "David," she said, her eyes filled with love, "there are many people who are thirty years old now. Do you know what the chances are that it is this particular person?"

"Small," he came right back. "But at least it fits. If he were twenty or forty, then I would know he couldn't be the Messiah." He stood and went over to her, kneeling in front of her. "Will you at least come with me and hear him?"

She sighed, wishing she had not responded as she had the previous night. "I told you I would."

"Good." He returned to his seat. His eyes were wide and filled with longing. "I love being a merchant, Deborah."

That surprised her. "I know you do. So do your sons." There was a soft laugh. "At least Ephraim does."

"It has given me great satisfaction," he went on, ignoring that last comment.

"Yes, I know it has."

"But—" He stopped and shook his head.

Surprised, Deborah peered at him. "But what, David?"

"To be a fisher of men?" His shoulders lifted and fell. "Imagine, helping people come to God, helping them find meaning and joy in their lives."

Deborah's eyes were fixed on him in complete amazement.

He finally met her gaze. "That would make being a merchant seem insignificant indeed."

CHAPTER NOTES

Obviously the four Gospels do not contain any physical descriptions of either Jesus or his disciples, nor do they give any ages for anyone except Jesus, who was thirty when he began his ministry (see Luke 3:23). Therefore, all such descriptions are the creation of the author. Care has been taken, however, to keep the *characters* of real people consistent with what is known about them from the scriptural record.

The story of the changing of the water to wine at Cana is found in John 2.

The fact that Mary felt some obligation to solve the problem when the wine ran out suggests that this was likely the wedding of a relative (see Clarke, 3:526–27; Talmage, p. 144). Farrar proposes it could have been the marriage of one of the immediate family (p. 142). We are told that Jesus had four brothers and a plurality of "sisters" (Mark 6:3), so there were at least six other children. All of these, of course, would have been younger than Jesus. If it were an immediate family member getting married in Cana, it would better explain Mary's sense of obligation when the wine ran out.

Though Mary, the mother of Jesus, is mentioned throughout the Gospels, the last mention of her husband, Joseph, is when Jesus was twelve (Luke 2:42–43). Since it would seem odd to mention his mother at the wedding but not his father if Joseph was still living, most scholars suppose that Joseph had died by this time. Many artists depict him as much older than Mary because of that, but there is no basis in fact for that supposition.

The account of the calling of the fishermen comes from Matthew 4, Mark 1, and Luke 5.

CHAPTER 14

AND HE CAME TO NAZARETH, WHERE HE HAD BEEN BROUGHT UP:
AND, AS HIS CUSTOM WAS, HE WENT INTO THE SYNAGOGUE
ON THE SABBATH DAY, AND STOOD UP FOR TO READ.

—Luke 4:16

I

25 APRIL, A.D. 30

The village of Nazareth sat in a narrow depression in the southern hill country of Galilee. Running for about ten miles from west to east, the Nazareth Ridge rose sharply from the flat richness of the Plains of Jezreel and finally died out in the highlands overlooking the Sea of Kinnereth. Here was pure Galilee—steep hillsides covered with forests of oak, pine, carob, and other trees, spectacular vistas of the valleys to the south, and frequent breezes that kept it significantly cooler than the lowlands around the lake.

After being gone for two weeks to Judea for Passover, Ephraim and Rachel decided that they could not make another extended trip with the children so soon. On hearing that, Leah, who had never enjoyed extended traveling, volunteered to stay and help Ephraim catch up on things. The barley harvest was in full cycle now, and in a week or two the wheat harvest—their busiest time—would also begin. It said much for the urgency David was feeling that he would leave his affairs at this time of the year and go off into the mountains to hear a new teacher. Deborah went also, though somewhat reluctantly. Simeon agreed to accompany them for three reasons: He was somewhat curious about Jesus; he had Zealot business he needed to discuss with Yehuda and David; and, most important, it would give him time to see Shana again, the first opportunity he had had since the betrothal. Deborah was glad for his presence. She hoped that having two united voices might be enough to persuade her husband that Jesus of Nazareth was not the man for whom he had been waiting and watching for thirty years.

Nazareth was not quite twenty-five Roman miles from Capernaum, so David and his family left shortly after sunup on Friday, coming only as far as Beth Neelah, arriving about half an hour before sundown and the beginning of Shabbat. Though he was surprised to see them, Yehuda was delighted and welcomed them into his home. Shana, of course, was very pleased.

Once the Sabbath meal was over, the two families, now legally joined in the bonds of marriage, spent a pleasant evening together. Though it was still almost a full year away, there were many plans to be made for the wedding. It also provided an appropriate opportunity for Shana and Simeon to begin to interact together in their new roles as betrothed husband and wife. To Deborah's relief, other than David explaining to Yehuda's family why they had come up from Capernaum, there was no further talk that night of Jesus of Nazareth.

II
26 APRIL, A.D. 30

In the morning they ate a leisurely Sabbath breakfast—cold, of course, because no fires were kindled on Shabbat—then started out for

Nazareth about the third hour of the day. It was no more than a couple of hours' walk, and this gave them plenty of time to reach the village before services began. To Simeon's surprise, Yehuda decided to come with them. The hill country was buzzing with rumors about this new preacher from Nazareth, and Yehuda said he had been thinking of going to their neighboring village to see for himself. Daniel declined the invitation to join them, but an ecstatic Shana, who had slept little the previous night, also came along. Deborah teased her somewhat about whether her interest lay in Jesus of Nazareth or Simeon of Capernaum.

Simeon smiled to himself as he thought about the night before. He and Shana had not been left alone—that would not be appropriate until the actual wedding—but they had been able to spend several hours together with the rest of the family. Simeon had watched her closely throughout the evening, seeing her through new eyes now. Though he still found the whole idea of marriage a little strange—for him at least—it was confirmed again to him that he had made a wise choice. She was as lovely as a meadow of wildflowers, and the joy he saw in her eyes made her all the more so. She was intelligent, quick of wit, a hard worker in the orchards and vineyards, and anxious to prepare herself to be his wife and mother to their children.

Suddenly he felt a tug on his arm. He looked around to see Shana beside him. She laughed up at him. "You look so sober, Simeon. Are you contemplating a funeral or marriage?"

He grinned at her, marveling at the sweetness of her face. There was nothing here to be sober about, he thought. "No," he responded. "Actually I was thinking about what *you* are getting in all of this. That is sobering."

She moved back over to walk beside his mother. "I shall try to adjust to the idea."

"I wouldn't be too quick to put away his concerns," Deborah said. "You haven't seen Simeon first thing in the morning. He is like a bad-tempered lion waking up from a nap. It is best to give him a wide berth for an hour or two."

"Mother!" Simeon said as Shana hooted in delight.

"It's all right," Shana said to Deborah. "Leah has already warned me about this. Only she said it was more like dealing with a porcupine just coming out of its burrow in the morning."

David and Yehuda roared at Simeon's wounded look. "So this is what the women in my family talk about when I am not around," he said, clearly miffed.

Yehuda looked at Simeon's father as if Simeon were not anywhere around. "I have seen this for myself," he said, "and it is truly fearsome. I did not dare tell Shana any of this until after the betrothal was complete for fear that she would change her mind."

Shana decided to take pity on him. "I am not troubled by any of these reports," she said sweetly, "for after living with Yehuda for all these years, I would find even an irritable lion a welcome improvement."

Yehuda yelped and took a swipe at her. "Well spoken!" Simeon called as she darted away to escape Yehuda. Deborah slipped an arm through Simeon's. "You have made a wise choice, Son," she whispered, watching as Shana easily stayed clear of her brother's grasp.

"I know, Mother. I am very pleased."

They walked on, enjoying the light mood and the beautiful morning together. Then, after a time, David said, "I suppose Aaron arrived at Nazareth last night all right."

"Oh, yes," Deborah said. "I'm sure of that. And long before sundown. You know Aaron. He wouldn't risk violating the Sabbath even by a minute."

Simeon smiled at the gentle barb. His uncle had left Capernaum when it was barely light, a full hour and a half before the rest of them were ready. Deborah had invited him to accompany them and stay at Yehuda's home, but he reminded her with a touch of reproof that while Beth Neelah and Nazareth were not that far apart, it was still more than a Sabbath day's journey, and therefore he had to get to Nazareth before the Sabbath began.

Keeping the Sabbath day holy was viewed by their people as one of the most important of all the commandments. The fourth of the Ten Commandments was very clear about this. "Remember the Sabbath day, to keep it holy. On the seventh day thou shalt not do any work."

The problem in the mind of the scribes and Pharisees was how to define *work*. They had devised a complex set of rules defining what did and did not constitute "labor" on Shabbat. With their usual obsession with leaving no aspect of the Law undefined, they had even gone to such lengths as to warn a tailor against sticking his needle in the lapel of his tunic, lest he forget it and be found carrying his "tools" on the Sabbath day. When they wrestled with the question of whether or not a person could carry any olive oil on the Sabbath, in case it was needed for anointing, they finally determined that it was acceptable to carry enough oil to anoint "the smallest member," which was defined as the little toe of a baby one day old. They had even defined with some specificity what could and what could not be rescued from one's house if it caught on fire on the Sabbath.

One of the more thorny issues the rabbis had wrestled with was how far a person could legitimately walk on the Sabbath day without it constituting work. If you said no walking was allowed, that would eliminate any visit to the temple or synagogue, an equally important commandment. Citing passages from the Torah which stated that the distance from one part of the camp of Israel to the Tabernacle of Moses was two thousand cubits, the great legal thinkers worked it out from there. A cubit was the distance from the elbow to the tip of the index finger. That was roughly the equivalent of one step or pace for a person. Walking a distance of two thousand paces and back was obviously acceptable to the Lord. This came to be known as a "Sabbath day's journey."

Beth Neelah and Nazareth were about four miles apart, much more than what was allowed on Shabbat, and so Aaron and his fellow Pharisees, including Amram, leader of the Capernaum congregation of Pharisees, left early enough to go all the way to Nazareth before the sun went down and Sabbath began. Aaron made no secret of the fact that he viewed David's and Deborah's casual approach to the whole matter with great disapproval.

Simeon blew out his breath softly. This was what was so maddening about his uncle and his associates. He had no quarrel with the basic principle. The Lord had made it clear that the Sabbath was to be a day of rest and worship and not a time to undertake normal travel. And Simeon completely agreed that God expected them to cease their labors. But this taking of the Law and examining it until you had every possibility covered, every trivial aspect defined, every infinitesimal exception protected irritated him to the point of exasperation.

What galled him the most was that even the Pharisees found their own prohibitions too restrictive, so they developed "exceptions" to allow them greater freedom. Simeon compared these to the "loophole" windows found on a fortress. Narrow vertical slits were made in the walls, with a slightly wider aperture at the bottom to allow an archer a field of fire at the enemy below while he himself remained in hiding. But Simeon knew from his own experience that an expert marksman from outside could find one of those loopholes with his shafts and do considerable damage. Thus it was with the scribes. They built this great wall of protection around the Law, but then left loopholes for themselves so they could get around those restrictions that inconvenienced them too much.

The one that pariculary irked him had to do with this Sabbath day's journey. For a person living in a small village like Beth Neelah, or even in a larger town like Capernaum, staying within the limited distance while you moved about town was fairly simple. But in a large city like Jerusalem, this was more of a problem. How had the scribes dealt with this limitation? Well, one of the rules stated that if a person deposited some food in a jar or a bag in a certain place before the Sabbath, that act extended the person's place of "residence" to wherever the food was located. So some of the scribes and Pharisees would have their servants place containers of food in various places around the city the day before the Sabbath. Then the following day they could go anywhere they pleased, as long as they were sure to return to one of the "places of residence" before they went the full two thousand paces.

"You're frowning again."

He turned in surprise to see his mother and Shana watching him with faint smiles.

"You are starting to worry Shana, Son," his mother teased. "Is the thought of being her husband so disturbing?"

He laughed now. "Actually, Mother, I was thinking about Uncle Aaron."

"Oh." Now she frowned. "I don't want you saying anything to him today, Simeon. No arguments."

He held up his hands. "I couldn't think of a better way to improve my day."

III

The synagogue at Nazareth was not much to speak of, though it was larger than Simeon had expected for the village. It was built of stone and designed properly, but it had little adornment. It certainly was not designed for the large crowd that was waiting for the doors to open that Sabbath morning. Evidently, whoever had told Aaron and his associates that Jesus would be here had sent word to others as well. There were three of the leading Pharisees from Sepphoris; two from Jotapata, which was even farther to the north; and several from other villages around. Two men, richly clad in robes that were far more expensive than anything the rest of the people wore, looked to be Sadducees. That really surprised Simeon. He didn't recognize them as being from Capernaum, and he could hardly imagine that they had come up from Jerusalem. Yet out in the small villages, especially in the Galilee, you didn't find many Sadducees. But there these two were, largely ignoring the common people around them and deliberately steering clear of the Pharisees.

Deborah and Shana separated from the men with a nod as they entered the door—no touching between man and woman was allowed in the synagogue—and moved over to the women's section. In all synagogues, seating for men and women was separated by a wooden partition, usually of lattice work. The benches for the women were mostly taken, but it was the men's section that was quickly filling to overflowing. Fifteen minutes before the service began, the synagogue was packed. When the benches filled, people lined the walls two and three deep. All of the shutters had been thrown open, and through the windows Simeon could see even more people crowding around, hoping to hear whatever was going on inside. For a small village, this must have been a shock to the ruler of the synagogue.

Fortunately, David and his family arrived in plenty of time to get seats before they were all filled. Not the front ones, of course. Those were reserved for the most illustrious of the visitors, who were invited to sit beside the ruler of the synagogue and the other officers. Once Simeon was seated, it took a few moments for his eyes to adjust to the gloom. It startled him a little to see that his uncle was seated on the first row, placed between Amram of Capernaum and Hezekiah, leader of the Pharisees in Sepphoris. That said as much as anything about how rapidly Aaron was rising in the ranks of the Pharisaical party. His devotion—or fanaticism, as Simeon thought of it—was paying off.

Simeon felt a nudge against his arm. He turned. His father was looking partly over his shoulder. "There he is," he whispered.

Yehuda leaned forward. "Which?"

"On the fourth row, fifth from the end."

"That's Jesus?" Simeon asked in a low voice.

He didn't really have to ask. Every eye in the synagogue was fixed on the man. Some were even rude enough to point him out to others, whispering loudly. As his father nodded, Simeon studied the man. He couldn't see his face clearly. His head was turned as he conversed quietly with the men on his right. It was clear there was an easy familiarity among the five of them that took the end of that bench, and Simeon wondered if these might be brothers or other family members. The other four men all looked younger than Jesus. Then Jesus turned slightly so that Simeon could see more of his face. He smiled then, not at Simeon, but toward the women's section. Simeon's eyes followed, and through the partition he saw an older woman smiling back. Beside her sat two younger women, obviously her daughters.

Until he had smiled, Jesus had not appeared out of the ordinary to Simeon. His features were pleasant enough but not particularly striking—though his eyes did have an arresting quality about them. His hair was long, down to his shoulders, and his beard full, with just a touch of red in the light from the windows. But when he smiled something remarkable had happened. It was like a lamp had been kindled behind his eyes and illuminated his whole face.

His father had talked about how he had been almost mesmerized when Jesus had called Peter and Andrew to follow him. Now Simeon understood what he meant. He couldn't take his eyes away from him. Jesus' lips moved as he mouthed something to his mother. Then he laughed softly to himself, and Simeon wished he had seen what Jesus' mother had done to elicit that.

A hush suddenly fell over the room, and Simeon's attention was drawn to the front again. The ruler of the synagogue had given the sign that the services were to commence. In addition to the benches that filled the room, there were two primary pieces of furniture in the synagogue—the lectern, or podium, where people stood when they spoke to the congregation, and the "ark," which stood a few feet in front of the lectern and which was a carefully crafted cabinet where the Torah scrolls and other sacred writings were kept.

David leaned over. "Perhaps Jesus or his father helped make the ark here," he said.

Simeon nodded. He had forgotten for the moment that Jesus was a carpenter and that his father had been a carpenter as well. In a village the size of Nazareth, there wouldn't be more than one or two carpenters, so it was very possible this was their work. He nodded again. It was fine workmanship, something appropriate for a house of worship.

The hush became total silence as the legate of the synagogue stepped to the lectern. While the ruler oversaw all aspects of the worship services, it was the legate who always led out. He lifted his arms and began to recite in a deep and most solemn voice the first benediction that preceded the saying of the *Sh'ma*.

"Blessed be Thou, O Lord, King of the world, who formest the light and createst the darkness; who makest peace and createst everything; who, in mercy, givest light to the earth and to those who dwell upon it; and in Thy goodness day by day and every day renewest the works of creation. Blessed be the Lord our God for the glory of his handiwork and for the light-giving lights which he has made for his praise. Blessed be the Lord our God, who hath formed the lights. Amen!"

"Amen!" every voice in the synagogue said in perfect unison.

Without pause he began the second benediction. "With great love hath thou loved us, O Lord our God, and with much overflowing pity hast thou pitied us, our Father and our King."

Simeon closed his eyes as he listened to the words that he had heard more times than he could count. He loved these benedictions that opened the services. Their solemn cadence provided the perfect transition from the outside world to the inner sanctuary of worship.

"Enlighten our eyes in thy law; cause our hearts to cleave to thy commandments."

Suddenly Simeon remembered what his uncle had said a few nights before. "Prayer is for us more than for God." *Yes!* He understood that. That's why Aaron's words had surprised him so. He hadn't consciously thought about it before, but he understood it.

"Blessed be the Lord, who in love chose his people Israel. Amen!"

"Amen!" Simeon said, opening his eyes again.

Next came the *Sh'ma,* that most fundamental and sacred of all Jewish prayers and benedictions. It was the first sentence an infant learned and, if at all possible, the last words on a person's lips prior to death. *Sh'ma, Yisrael, Yehovah eloihaynu Yehovah ehad.* "Hear, O Israel, the Lord our God is one Lord." The *Sh'ma* took its name from its first word, the Hebrew imperative form of "to hear." Made up of three additional passages from the Torah, this prayer, which took no more than a few seconds to recite, embodied the whole of the Jewish faith. It was prayer, creed, affirmation, and testimony all wrapped together in one brief but powerful statement. Every faithful Jewish male spoke it at least twice each day, once in the morning and again in the evening. Women and children believed it and often recited it, but they were not under the same obligation as the adult male.

To hear more than a hundred voices recite it together in perfect unison sent a little thrill up Simeon's spine. This was something that the Romans could never understand, a simple collection of sentences that defined an entire people.

Two more benedictions followed the *Sh'ma,* and then the legate looked around the crowded room. It was time for the *aliyah,* the "going up." He stepped to the ark and opened it. Moving with meticulous care, he unveiled the great scroll that rested within the cabinet.

The temple was first and foremost a place of worship, but the synagogue was first and foremost a place of learning. After the initial prayers came the reading of the scriptures, followed by a sermon or exposition on the scriptures. To be "called up" to read from the sacred writ was one of the most solemn moments of the synagogue service. Any male who had successfully completed his *bar-mitzvah* and become a Son of the Covenant was eligible to read.

As the legate looked around the room, every eye followed his. Who would be asked to read on this day?

"We shall read from the book of Isaiah," the legate said.

And then there was an audible stir. Behind where David and Simeon and Yehuda sat, Jesus had risen to his feet. If the legate was surprised by this, he gave no sign. He picked up the long pointer made of ivory, which was a surprising luxury for a small synagogue such as this, and held it out. As Jesus came forward, Simeon had to smile. The front two rows of worshipers, the Pharisees and scribes who had come for this very reason, were muttering in low voices to one another. As Jesus reached the ark, the legate handed him the pointer, then went to his seat. All sound stopped.

For a moment Jesus studied the writings before him; then to everyone's surprise, he did not begin where the legate had opened the scroll. He turned the spindle on the scroll, his eyes scanning quickly. After a moment he nodded, and the turning stopped. Bending over slightly, he scanned more closely. Then with the pointer touching the parchment, he began to read. His voice was deep, and he articulated each word slowly and distinctly.

"'The Spirit of the Lord is upon me; because he hath anointed me to preach the gospel to the poor.'"

David looked at Simeon in surprise. Simeon raised an eyebrow in question. It was from Isaiah all right, near the end of the book.

"That's Messianic," David whispered.

Now David understood. Jesus had specifically chosen a scripture that was understood by all to be a prophecy of the coming of the Messiah.

Jesus paused, and his eyes moved across the front row of onlookers, who glared at him, angry that he had not read from the place he had been assigned. When Jesus went on, he did so even more slowly than before, pausing to look up after each new phrase. "'He hath anointed me to preach the gospel to the poor. He hath sent me to heal the brokenhearted; to preach deliverance to the captives and for the recovering of sight to the blind; to set at liberty them that are bruised; to preach the acceptable year of the Lord.'"

It was as though every person in the room had stopped breathing. The silence had deepened to the point of almost unbearable tension. The young carpenter slowly set the pointer back in its slot, then closed the lid on the ark. Finally, he looked up. "This day," he said softly, "is this scripture fulfilled in your ears."

The pent-up breath exploded in shock and dismay. Amram the Pharisee shot to his feet. "What!" he shouted. "What did you say?"

"This day is this scripture fulfilled in your ears."

Now people were leaping to their feet on every side of David and Simeon. "Blasphemy!" Hezekiah of Sepphoris screamed, shaking his fist at Jesus. "How dare you!"

Aaron was up as well, his face white with shock. He spun around and looked at David. "Did you hear that?" he hissed. "He claims to be the Messiah." He spun back around, glaring at Jesus. The synagogue was in pandemonium, with everyone on their feet. Small puffs of dust were rising from the floor as people stamped their feet in fury. Simeon was astonished. There was no way to mistake what Jesus had just done—in that Uncle Aaron was right. Jesus had just read a Messianic prophecy, then announced that today it was being fulfilled. There was only one way to interpret that. He looked at his father and saw that he was deeply shaken as well. Then Simeon caught a glimpse of the face of the woman he had assumed was Jesus' mother. Her eyes were wide and frightened as she watched the congregation explode in rage.

"You are Joseph's son!" the ruler of the synagogue shouted.

The legate had leaped forward to stand beside Jesus. He slammed a fist against the lid of the ark, something that was strictly forbidden. "You claim to be the promised Messiah? Outrage!"

Jesus had been looking down, not looking into the eyes of his accusers. Now he lifted his head. The bedlam died away in an instant. "I know what you are thinking. You would say to me, 'Whatsoever things you have done in Capernaum, do also here in our country.'"

He looked around the room, and Simeon was surprised to see what looked like profound sorrow in his eyes.

"Verily I say unto you, no prophet is accepted in his own country." His eyes stopped on the ones who stood in the front rows, their faces dark with fury. "But I tell you of a truth, there were many widows in Israel in the days of Elijah, when the heaven was shut up three years and six months, when great famine was throughout all the land, but unto none of them was Elijah sent, save unto Sarepta, a city of Sidon, unto a woman that was a widow."

The muttering began to rise as the impact of what he was saying hit them. Sidon was a Gentile city. The widow of Sarepta was not an Israelite.

His voice rose sharply. "And many lepers were in Israel in the time of Elisha the prophet; and none of them was cleansed, saving Naaman the Syrian."

"Enough!" Amram roared, his face livid. "He blasphemes the name of God and the name of Israel."

"Away with him!" another shouted.

"Imposter! Deceiver!"

Simeon now saw his own mother's face. She was staring at her brother in shock, and only then did Simeon realize that it was his uncle who had shouted those last words.

"No," a woman cried. "Let him speak."

"Let us hear him," a man from behind Simeon agreed.

But the rest of the crowd overrode any such moderation. The legate of the synagogue grabbed Jesus by the arm and jerked him forward. In an instant the ruler of the synagogue had him by the other arm. "Out! Out of our synagogue!"

"Death to the blasphemer!" a man from behind Simeon shouted.

They rushed at him, and Jesus was surrounded. Hands snatched at his robe. Two men pinned his arms behind him. As they moved forward, another man shoved him hard from behind, and he was prevented from going down only by the press of the crowd. With a roar of triumph, they dragged him toward the door, then poured out of the synagogue and into the streets of Nazareth.

"Come on!" David said, motioning to Simeon and Yehuda.

"What?" Simeon cried. Surely his father was not going to become part of this.

"We've got to stop them. They're going to kill him." He spun around, moving for the door. But they were already too late. The crush of people had completely plugged the narrow entrance of the synagogue. Everyone was fighting to get out, shouting, crying, shrieking. Others pushed in from behind, cutting off any movement from any direction. Suddenly, Deborah and Shana were at their side. "What's happening?" Deborah cried. "What are they going to do to him?"

David shook his head, thrusting out with his elbows to fend off those who were fighting to get through. He arched his neck to see if there was another way out and spotted a door leading to the back of the synagogue. "This way," he shouted. Bellowing like a bull, he lowered his shoulder and hurled himself against the flow. Simeon grabbed his mother and pulled her in behind him. Yehuda did the same with Shana as they also plowed after David.

Even fighting with all their strength, it took another minute to force their way through the pressing crowd and break free. The sound was deafening. Now the angry shouts and furious yells were mingled with screams of panic as people began to be crushed in the stampede for the door.

Once free, David walked swiftly to the back, where daylight

showed beneath a door. "Yes!" He took Deborah's arm and pulled her with him. The others fell in behind them.

In a moment they were outside and felt the rush of cooler air. David didn't hesitate. "Stay here, Deborah. You too, Shana. Come on, Simeon, Yehuda." He leaped forward, heading for the street in front of the synagogue.

The street was a mass of people. David jumped into the air even as he ran, trying to see over the heads. There was no mass, no clot of angry men, just small groups of people fluttering around and talking in great excitement. He grabbed a man and spun him around. "What did they do with Jesus?" he demanded.

The man jerked away, then pointed. "There. They're taking him there."

He was pointing to a spot off in the distance, and David wasn't sure what it was. There were houses, then forest and ridges beyond. "Where?"

But the man had already slipped away. He confronted another. "Where are they taking Jesus?"

This man just shook his head, but a woman heard his question. She turned, obviously greatly distraught. "To the precipice."

David rocked back. "What?"

She pointed now too, and finally David and Simeon and Yehuda saw what she was pointing at. On the edge of town, the Nazareth Ridge rose to a single high point, then dropped off sharply. "They said they were going to throw him off the cliff," the woman said with half a sob.

David spun, grabbing for Simeon's arm. "Let's go!"

But as they crossed the street, they ran headlong into a line of men standing shoulder to shoulder. One of them was the ruler of the synagogue. He held up both hands, and they slid to a halt.

"Let us through," David shouted.

"No. You are not from here. This is not your affair."

"They've got to be stopped," David exclaimed. "You can't do this."

"Go home!" another man snarled. "This is our concern. We know what to do with blasphemers."

For a moment Simeon thought his father was going to hurl himself into the line, and he grabbed him by the shoulder. Yehuda did the same, and they pulled him back. "No, Father," Simeon shouted into his ear. "You can't fight them."

IV

A quarter of an hour later the crowd outside the synagogue still filled the street. They were milling around, waiting for the group that had taken Jesus to return. David's group stood off to one side, speaking in low, shocked tones about what had happened. David was still shaking with anger, and Deborah spoke softly to him, trying to calm him down. On every side the people's conversations swirled around two things—the astonishment at what Jesus had said about himself and the shock of what had happened next.

Then a shout pulled them around. Coming down the street toward the synagogue was a crowd of men, obviously the ones who had dragged Jesus off. The crowd surged forward, but the line of men across the street held them back. The ruler of the synagogue left the line and ran out to meet the returning group. They conversed quickly and angrily. When they finished, the ruler walked back and said something, and the line broke up.

"There's Aaron," David said. Without waiting for the others, he darted forward. Simeon took his mother's hand, and they followed swiftly.

Aaron saw them at the same time. It looked for a moment as if he was going to try to duck into the crowd and avoid them, but he saw that they had seen him and raised one hand in a halfhearted wave.

"What happened?" David cried.

Aaron looked around, embarrassed that David's exclamation had caused several of the returning men to turn and look at them. "It's over," he said, taking David's arm and trying to pull him aside.

David jerked away, then grabbed Aaron's shoulders and shook him. "You didn't—" he gasped.

Aaron's mouth tightened. "I didn't do anything." He stepped back. Now Simeon, Deborah, Shana, and Yehuda came up to them as well. "Besides, he escaped."

"Escaped?" David exclaimed, his shoulders sagging with relief.

"Yes, he slipped out of their grasp and escaped into the forest. There are some out looking for him now, but he's gone."

"Did you try to stop them, Uncle Aaron?" Simeon said, not trying to hide his disgust.

Aaron whirled. "Don't speak to me that way, Simeon. I don't answer to you."

"Even if the man is deluded," Simeon shot right back, "you don't kill a person for that."

Deborah was still partly in shock. "You didn't try to kill him, did you, Aaron?"

"No. I told you that. I didn't take part in that."

"But you were with them," Simeon shot back. "Is that what you Pharisees stand for? Kill anyone who disagrees with you?"

For a moment Simeon thought his uncle was going to strike him, but then he pulled back, his lip trembling. "This is not just any delusion, my arrogant young nephew. This man publicly claimed that he is the Messiah. That is blasphemy! But worse than that, do you know what Rome will do if they hear about this? That someone is claiming to be the Messiah?"

Yehuda spoke for the first time. "Let Rome come. We will be ready."

Aaron was incredulous. "You too, Yehuda? You think this Jesus is the Messiah?"

Yehuda emphatically shook his head. "No. I think the man is mad. But I'm not sure his delusion can do us more harm than you so-called religious leaders are doing."

Aaron started to sputter, but to Simeon's surprise it was Yehuda that his father turned on. "Don't be too quick to judge a man mad, Yehuda. Pharaoh considered Moses to be mad too. Would you condemn a man before you have learned if he speaks the truth?"

Deborah drew in a sharp breath. "David, surely you don't believe what Jesus said? He claimed to be the Messiah."

"It's blasphemy," Aaron blurted, nodding in vigorous agreement with his sister. "Surely you can see that, David."

It was a rare thing to see David of Capernaum angry. Simeon had seen it only a few times in all his life, but now his father spun around to face his brother-in-law, his face white, his hands trembling. "It is blasphemy only if he is *not* the Messiah, Aaron."

"David!" Deborah cried, reaching out for his hand. "Be careful of what you say."

He ignored her, still looking at Aaron. "You have to prove that he is *not* the Messiah, Aaron. Our law says that a man gets a trial, even for blasphemy. How do you and your friends, who claim to have so much love for the Law, justify trying to throw a man off a cliff without a trial?"

He turned away, not waiting for an answer.

They were all shocked into silence. Aaron had never seen this kind of emotion in his brother-in-law. Finally he looked at his sister. "I wasn't part of the group that wanted to throw him off the precipice, Deborah. Amram and I stayed back."

"Did you try to stop them?" Simeon asked. "Did you even raise your voice in protest?"

Aaron flushed. "I don't have to answer to you, Simeon. Now stay out of this."

Deborah stepped between them. "Aaron, you know my feelings. I think what Jesus did in there is shocking. I still can't believe my ears. But in this other matter, David is right. To drag a man out and try to kill him without even a hearing? I never raised you to be part of something like that."

"Deborah, I—"

But suddenly David was back. He was calmer now, though his voice was still filled with emotion. "I have one more question for you and Amram and the rest of the Pharisees," he said.

Aaron hesitated, not sure that he wanted to hear it.

"How far would you say it is from here to the edge of the precipice?" David asked.

Aaron's mouth opened slightly. "How far?" That was the last question he had expected. "I don't know. More than a mile, I suppose."

"More than a Sabbath day's journey?" David asked softly.

The shock was evident in Aaron's eyes. It was something that he had not once thought about until this moment.

David shook his head, and now his eyes held only sadness. "So here's my question, Aaron. Does your tradition allow an exception to the Sabbath day's journey in the case of murder?" Then, again without waiting for an answer, he turned and walked away, leaving Aaron, his face totally drained of color, to stare after him.

V

"Well, are we even going to talk about it?" She spoke as though she addressed everyone, but Shana was looking directly at Simeon. They were nearly back to the village of Beth Neelah now, and since leaving Nazareth they had barely spoken; no one had said a word about what they had just witnessed.

"Shana!" Yehuda warned.

Her lips clamped tight, and she shot Simeon a withering look, as if to say, "Why aren't you helping me in this?" Simeon shook his head. Part of their silence was the result of what had happened in the synagogue. In a lifetime of going to Sabbath worship, they had never seen it erupt into open riot, unrestrained fury, and attempted murder. But deeper than that for Simeon and his mother was what had happened between David and Aaron. There had always been an uneasy truce between David and his brother-in-law. Philosophically, they were as different as calf and chicken. In temperament they were furlongs apart. Normally such deep differences would have led to constant conflict, but for Deborah's sake David had simply made up his mind that he would not battle with Aaron. Though Aaron sometimes deliberately tried to needle David into a reaction, he too had realized that if he pushed too hard, he would lose Deborah's devotion and loyalty. And so for years now, they maintained an unspoken resolve to hold back. That had all shattered in the street in front of the synagogue, and it was going to take some time to sort through the aftermath of what had just happened.

But to Simeon's surprise, it was his father who responded to Shana. He and Deborah were a few paces out in front of the others. He slowed his step and looked at her. "Would you like to talk about it, Shana?"

Shana was surprised at that response but recovered quickly. "I would. I am full of questions."

"Such as?"

"Did I hear him correctly? Was Jesus really announcing that he was the Messiah there in the synagogue?"

Now it was Deborah who nodded, relieved to be talking about it now as well. "Yes, Shana. When he said, '*This day* is this scripture fulfilled in your ears,' I think there's only one way to interpret that. That's what sent everybody into a rage."

"Not everybody, Deborah," David reminded her softly. "There were quite a few people there who were shocked, but not to the point of trying to kill the man."

Simeon spoke up then. "If he is not the Messiah, then in one way Aaron and the others were right. That does come very close to being blasphemy, and blasphemy is a capital crime under our law."

His father stopped dead, planting his feet. "Are you saying that those men were justified in trying to kill Jesus?"

Simeon backed down quickly. "No, I didn't mean that. As you said, the man deserves a trial if charges like that are to be brought forward, but . . . " He shook his head, suddenly tired of it. "I guess I am like Shana. I can't believe he would stand up and publicly say such a thing."

"Unless he really *is* the Messiah," David responded in a low voice.

No one spoke, having too much respect for Simeon's father—but the silence was almost as eloquent as if they had each shouted aloud. After a moment he smiled sadly. "Do you think I do not understand your minds? Do you think I do not see the disbelief in your eyes? Speak! Shana is right. It is time to say what we are feeling in our hearts."

The four of them looked at each other, no one wanting to be the first.

"I see only three possibilities," David said, encouraging them further. "First, he is an imposter. He has deliberately chosen to set himself up as the Messiah even though he knows he is not. In that case, it is blasphemy and should be punished severely. Second, he is mad or terribly deluded. In other words, he truly thinks he is the Messiah, but is not. If that is true, then he should be pitied and helped. The third possibility is . . . " He shrugged. "Well, I don't think any of you are ready to even consider that, so let's talk about the other two."

"I think he is mad," Shana said after a moment. "How could any normal person stand up and quote a scripture and think he was the fulfillment of it?"

Simeon instantly saw the error in that answer. "If he *is* the Messiah, Shana, he would not be a normal person."

"Have you ever known anyone who was mad, Shana?" David asked.

Her head reared back slightly. "Well, yes. We had old Abiathar the beggar here in the village for many years."

Yehuda nodded. "I think he had evil spirits. He was always hearing voices."

Simeon's father looked squarely at Shana. "You were just a few feet away from Jesus," he said. "Did he seem insane to you?"

That caught her back a little, but Shana had a quick mind. "Not at first. He seemed nice. But—"

David turned to his son. "Did you think he was mad?"

Simeon was tempted to hedge or soften it somehow, but he knew his father too well to think he could get away with that. "I don't know," he started, but then he wanted to be honest with himself as well as his father. "No, I didn't. I was watching his eyes. There was something very compelling about him. I didn't see anything that would make me think he was deluded or possessed."

"So?" his father prodded. "Then you think he is an imposter?"

Simeon could see the box now. "No, I'm not sure of that either. But the Messiah? I'm sorry, Father. It is just too incredible. Too unbelievable. He's a nobody, Father. A carpenter from a village that's barely known outside the Galilee."

"Do you have another explanation then? You know that many are saying he works wonderful miracles everywhere he goes."

That part wasn't hard for Simeon to answer. "Rumor flies on wings swifter than a hundred eagles and grows larger with each retelling."

"True," his father agreed. "So what is your explanation? If he is not the Messiah and he is neither mad nor a fraud, then what?"

He tried to meet his father's calm but arresting gaze, then finally shook his head. "I don't know. I want to think some more about it."

"Yehuda?"

Yehuda hesitated, then shrugged. "Not all madness reaches the face and not all evil can be found in the eyes."

David nodded, seemingly untroubled by the bluntness of Yehuda's answer. Deborah knew she was next and tried to deflect the question. "I think that was Jesus' mother sitting not far from Shana and me. Did she look familiar to you at all, David?"

Simeon started. Yehuda and Shana had no idea what she meant, but he did. Memories of what his father had told him about what had happened in Bethlehem came flooding back. He had seen the mother of the Messiah at the door of the *khan*. He had seen her again at the stable that night.

"No," David said, and his voice was forlorn. "But it's been thirty years, and the light was dim that night. I—"

"What's been thirty years?" Yehuda asked. "What night?"

David shook his head. "It's a long story." He stopped, still looking at his wife, waiting for her to answer the question that he had not yet spoken.

Deborah also knew that what had happened today was far too important to try to brush aside or sidestep. So she took a quick breath and said what she felt she had to say. "No, David, I don't think Jesus is the Messiah."

He seemed more thoughtful than disappointed. "I guessed as much."

"I think what happened was unforgivable. I know Aaron was not directly responsible, but I am terribly disappointed that he had any part in it."

"I know. Thank you." Then to her surprise, he reached out and took her hand.

They started walking again, no one speaking for several moments. Then Shana couldn't stand it any longer. "And what about you, David? Tell us what you think."

His head came around, and he looked a little surprised. "Oh," he said soberly. "I don't have any question in my mind. I believe that Jesus of Nazareth *is* the very man for whom I have waited for more than thirty years now."

CHAPTER NOTES

In the Jewish way of reckoning, the day began and ended at sundown. Thus, the Sabbath actually began on Friday evening and continued until Saturday when the sun set again. Incidentally, this is the basis for our practice of having Christmas Eve and New Year's Eve precede the actual day of celebration.

The references to some of the rules surrounding the Sabbath day and what was defined as work comes from the Talmud (see Blackman, pp. 15, 38, 92). For a complete explanation of the "Sabbath day's journey," which is mentioned in Acts 1:12, see Fallows, 3:1501–2. The specific figure of two thousand cubits comes from Joshua 3:4.

Thanks to the rabbinical writings that have been preserved to our day, we know quite a bit about synagogue worship at the time of Christ. Though some of the precise details had to be added here, the description of the services in this chapter accurately reflects a typical Sabbath day synagogue service at that time (see Edersheim, *Sketches*, pp. 267–74).

Luke is the only one of the Gospel writers who records the rejection of Christ at the synagogue in his hometown, but he does so with the details given here (see Luke 4:16–30). The Messianic passage the Savior read from Isaiah is found in chapter 61, verses 1–2.

CHAPTER 15

WHEN JESUS HAD ENDED THESE SAYINGS, THE PEOPLE WERE
ASTONISHED AT HIS DOCTRINE: FOR HE TAUGHT THEM AS
ONE HAVING AUTHORITY, AND NOT AS THE SCRIBES.

—*Matthew 7:28–29*

I
10 MAY, A.D. 30

Deborah was kneading dough on the large wooden table in the kitchen. Esther was kneeling on the bench beside her grandmother. She was covered to the elbows in flour and had smudges of dough around the corners of her mouth from a series of what she thought were undetected snitches. Against her olive skin, the light brown flour looked white.

When David came in from the hallway, Deborah looked up in surprise. "So soon?" she said, wiping at her cheek with the back of her hand. "I thought you were going to spend all afternoon at the storage barns."

"*Shalom,* Pampa."

"*Shalom,* my little angel all in white."

"I not dressed in white," she answered, looking puzzled.

He laughed and walked over and kissed her on the top of her head. Then he looked at his wife. "I just saw Peter."

For a moment she looked blank; then she remembered. Deborah was still not used to Simon's additional name, even though David, Andrew, James, and John all called him Peter or Simon Peter almost exclusively now. "Oh?"

"Jesus is here again. Peter thinks he is going to spend some time teaching the people."

"Oh." This time it wasn't a question, and this time it was harder to keep her voice nonchalant. Since being so violently rejected at Nazareth two weeks before, Jesus had come down to Capernaum and the surrounding towns. So far David had been able to get away only on one or two days to listen to him, for which she was grateful. She returned to her kneading, not watching him anymore.

"Will you go with me?" he asked.

"I go Pampa," Esther said gravely.

"I would love to have you, Esther, but this is for big people."

"I big. Mama says."

He bent down and kissed her again, this time on the cheek, picking up a smudge of flour on his beard. "I know you are, but you would have to sit real still on Pampa's lap for a long time. You couldn't get down and run around or play with your friends."

Her face fell.

"How about if Pampa comes over later and you and I go for a walk down to the beach?"

She squirmed excitedly in his arms. "Yes! Can Boaz come too, Pampa?"

"If it's all right with Mama. We'll ask her."

She wiggled out of his grip and jumped to the floor. "I ask Mama." With that she shot out the door.

He shook his head and turned back to Deborah. "That one is completely unique, isn't she."

Deborah's face softened into a warm smile. "She's a little goat, that's what."

"Why?"

"Yesterday Rachel and I went over to see Tamar. Her baby should be coming anytime now, and we took her some things."

"And?"

"How many times have we had Esther over at Tamar's? She's Rachel's closest friend and neighbor. It's hardly like she's a stranger. But do you think Esther would respond to her? It was like she didn't even know her." She laughed. "We were there for over an hour, and Tamar tried everything to get even a tiny smile out of her. Esther would just look right through her. It was as though Tamar wasn't even in the room."

"That's my little sphinx," he agreed. "Unless you happen to be one of the few she accepts as family, you might as well be transparent."

"It worries me in a way." Deborah's forehead had creased a little.

"No," David scoffed. "That's just Esther."

"But she's so shy and reserved—far more than other children, David. Around strangers she won't even look at them." Then her face softened. "If they try to get too close she sticks that finger out, shakes it at them, and barks out, 'Don't!' as though she were a queen warning off an invading army."

He laughed aloud, knowing exactly what she meant. Even he got that treatment if he began to tease her too much. "Queen Esther," he chuckled. "Ephraim and Rachel were inspired when they named her. But there's nothing to worry about with that one, Granmama. She's a happy child, and her mind is quicker than a darting swallow."

"I suppose," she sighed. Her eyes filled with warmth. "She is the joy of my life, that is for sure."

"And mine," he said. She went back to work with the dough. David watched her for a moment and then said, "So what about going and hearing Jesus today?"

There was a momentary pause in the rhythm of her hands before she nodded. "If you ask me to go with you, David, then I will go."

"It's not just for me, Deborah. I'd like you to hear him and see what you think too."

"I heard him in Nazareth," she reminded him.

"No," he said. "He didn't really teach there."

He moved behind her and put his arms around her. "Suppose Nazareth hadn't happened. Suppose someone came to town and said, 'We have found the Messiah.' Wouldn't you at least go out and see him, listen to what he had to say?"

"Perhaps," she admitted. She sighed, torn between her loyalty to this man she loved and the deep conviction that he was going to be hurt by all of this.

David stepped back away from her. "Before you decide about that, there's something else I need to tell you."

She was struck by the sudden gravity of his tone. "What is it, David?"

"Sextus Rubrius is back in Capernaum."

She stiffened, and her eyes flew open.

"Now that Passover is over, he's been given his old post at the Roman garrison again."

"Does Simeon know?"

"I don't think so. I just saw him this morning."

"David, you know what Simeon will say if he sees you consorting with any Roman soldier, but with this particular centurion—"

"I know," he murmured. "I know. I have been very careful since that day. I have never spoken to him. Sextus understands. He would go out of his way to—"

"I know you think he is a good man, David," she cut in sharply, "but he nearly killed our son."

"Deborah, he was only—"

"No!" she cried. "Don't talk to me about duty. You weren't there.

He reacted out of instinct. He gave no thought to killing a man." She took a quick breath. "Just promise me that you will not continue your friendship with this Roman. For Simeon's sake. Promise me!"

"I promise. It is already over."

She began kneading the dough again, her hands twisting and punching at it like it was suddenly alive and threatening her. He watched her, knowing that he had to be the one to tell her but glad now that it was done with. It was time to change the subject. "Peter told me something I want to share with you," he said after a minute.

She didn't slow at all. "What?"

"Did you know that Anna's mother has been very ill?"

She nodded, her hands hesitating. "Yes. I talked to Anna yesterday morning at the market. She was trying to find something she could give to her mother to break the fever. She was very worried." Then a look of concern filled Deborah's face. "Has her condition changed?"

"Yes."

"Oh, no, David. What? I'd better go and see Anna."

"She's better."

"But she was extremely ill," she said. "Now she's better?"

"Yes."

"But—"

"Peter told me that when they came home at sundown last night, they found his mother-in-law in her bed, barely able to move." He stopped, waiting for Deborah to look at him again. When she did so, he went on slowly. "Peter said they were starting to worry about whether she would make it; she was that gravely ill."

"And now she's getting better? That's wonderful."

"Not *getting* better, Deborah. She *is* better."

Finally Deborah realized that David was saying something more than just reporting on the condition of Anna's mother. "What happened?"

"When Jesus saw her lying there, he went to her bedside and reached out and touched her hand."

Deborah was very still. "Yes?"

"Peter said the instant Jesus touched her, the fever broke. Anna's mother immediately got out of bed and helped Anna prepare supper for them. Immediately, Deborah!"

Deborah just stared at him, not sure she had heard right.

"Yes. The moment he touched her she was healed."

She sat down slowly, the bread dough forgotten. If that was true . . .

"That's why I want you to hear him, Deborah. Jesus is no ordinary man. There is a power in him that is unmistakable."

"David, I—" She stopped and leaned back, half closing her eyes. "I know how you feel about this man. I know how badly you want to believe he is the one you've been waiting for, but I think you are going to be terribly disappointed. I cannot believe he is the Messiah."

"That's not all, Deborah."

It was as though her words had flown right past him. "What's not all?" she asked wearily.

"As they were coming back to Peter's house today, two blind men suddenly appeared in the crowd."

Deborah's head came up, her eyes widening.

"They called out to Jesus. 'Have mercy on us,' they begged."

He stopped as she made as if to speak, but when she didn't he went on. "Jesus stopped and let them come up to him. Then he asked them if they believed he was able to help them. Both of them said yes, they did."

He took a breath, filled with wonder again even in the telling of it. "Then Jesus said, 'Be it unto you according to your faith.'"

"No!" Deborah breathed, knowing what was coming but not able to believe he was going to actually say it.

"Then he touched their eyes with his fingers," David said softly.

Realizing she was holding her breath, Deborah released it slowly. Her mind wouldn't believe it, *couldn't* believe it. "And?" she whispered.

He sat down beside her and took her hands, oblivious to the flour and the dough on them. "They were both healed. Both of them." His voice caught momentarily. "They were blind, Deborah," he whispered. "And now they see."

"David, I—" She was mentally reeling. "Are you sure? Did Simon see this for himself?"

"He said he was no more than three feet away when it happened."

"Is he sure they were blind?" Even as she said it, she felt a little stab of shame. Simon was not a man without faults, but Deborah knew that Simon's word could be trusted. He neither lied nor exaggerated. His word was as solid as Mount Arbel.

David didn't answer that. He understood that this was her way of trying to take in what he had just told her. "He opens the eyes of the blind, Deborah. This doesn't prove he is the Messiah. I know that. We have had men and women of faith with the power to heal before. But—" He hesitated for only a moment, and now there was pleading in his voice. "But if he heals the sick and opens the eyes of the blind," he said, "isn't that reason enough to at least listen to him?"

She stood again, still gazing deeply at him. Finally her head bowed slightly. "I would like to go and hear this man with you, David."

He had to contain himself from shouting out. "Good."

"If what you have told me is true, I want Simeon and Ephraim and Rachel to hear as well. Find Leah. See if she will watch Esther and Boaz so we can all go together."

"Yes." He was on his feet eager now. "I will."

"It will take me about another quarter of an hour to prepare the bread; then I can leave it to rise. Go and find them. Let's go hear this Jesus of Nazareth for ourselves."

He turned and started for the door, then stopped. "Thank you, Deborah."

She looked up, her eyes troubled. "I still have many questions and even more doubts, David. He may be a man of faith, but . . . don't get your hopes too high."

"They're not."

"You know that I can't be anything but honest with you."

He smiled. "I wouldn't have it any other way."

She smiled back, but it wasn't with much humor. "Sometimes I wonder," she murmured.

II

It was a beautiful spring day in early May. At six hundred feet below sea level, the air around the Sea of Kinnereth was getting oppressive in the daytime now, but Jesus had chosen the site for his teaching well. The people had gathered on the side of a prominent hill between Capernaum and Tabgha. As happened each day, as the afternoon temperature began to climb, the hot air would begin to rise. The cooler air on the highlands would then begin to flow downward, creating a pleasant breeze. By sundown it would be stiff enough to whip up whitecaps on the water's surface. For now, the breeze was just enough to make the afternoon sun on their backs feel good.

Deborah and David sat together, with Simeon, Ephraim, and Rachel on either side of them. They had gotten there early enough to find a thick patch of grass and weeds, which gave them comfortable seating. They were facing uphill, though here near the top the ground was not very steep. From this height—probably two hundred feet above the level of the water—the entire length of the Sea of Kinnereth was visible. It stretched about twelve miles to the south and five to six miles from east to west. The air was hazy with the humidity, but one could still make out the shape of the shoreline. It was because it was shaped somewhat like a harp, a *kinnor* in Hebrew, that the lake was called Kinnereth.

Deborah was quite amazed at how many people had come from Capernaum and the surrounding areas. The hillside was almost filled, three or four hundred in all, she guessed. They sat in a wide semicircle, all facing up the gentle slope and slightly to the west. About fifty paces or so below the crest of the hill, Jesus of Nazareth sat on a low mound on the hillside that served as his bench. Simon Peter, Andrew, James, and John were all seated just in front of him. Each had his wife beside him. The place had been chosen well. The slight downhill slope and the westerly breeze worked together to make Jesus' voice clearly distinguishable even to those farthest away from him.

Deborah had decided before they left home that she would keep an open mind in this matter, in spite of her strong feelings. She owed that much to David. He had said little to her about Jesus since their return from Nazareth. That left her with a feeling of sorrow, for she knew that he conversed with Andrew and Simon Peter about Jesus often and had gone out to see him and listen to his teachings. She was determined that she would not let this come between them.

As they came toward Tabgha to the place of the meeting, moving slowly in the throngs that filled the road, they had seen Anna and the wives of Andrew, James, and John up ahead of them. David nudged Deborah and pointed. There was Anna's mother, walking beside her daughter, as healthy and normal as any of the other women. Deborah had again marveled. That was another reason she was determined to be open about this.

Once the last of the stragglers was seated, Jesus began. He spoke loudly so as to be heard, but it was not what one would call an impassioned speech. His voice was calm, and it was more like he was reasoning with them than trying to convert them. He started mildly enough as the crowd quickly quieted, giving a series of brief statements that all began with the Aramaic *ashar*, which literally meant "to go straight forward," but in common usage meant "to be blessed, to be for- tunate, or to be happy." "Blessed are the meek. Blessed are those who are poor in pride and humble in spirit, for theirs is the kingdom of heaven." At first some of his statements seemed a little odd—such as "blessed are those who mourn"—but as he went on, the several bless- ings taken as a whole made a nice summary of the happiness that came to those who chose a spiritual life.

He next talked about being a good example, using an analogy of putting a candle on a candlestick instead of hiding it under a bushel or being like a city set on a hill that everyone sees. Deborah thought that was a nice way to remind his listeners that as children of Israel they should be better than the world. At that point she reached out and took David's hand, which won her a warm smile from him. She could also tell that Ephraim and Rachel seemed impressed as well. Simeon, however, sat on the far side of them, and she couldn't see his face to tell how he was taking all of this in.

On impulse, Deborah had asked David not to tell Simeon about Peter's mother-in-law or about the blind men. Like his mother, Simeon was not very open to the idea that Jesus might be the Messiah. He too had almost refused to come to hear him teach—until David had told him it was his mother's suggestion. He was here, but his heart was not. She hadn't wanted him to come because of the sensational stories. She wanted him to hear Jesus for himself, so they could talk about it as a family later that night.

Jesus paused now, as though he had finished one thought and was deciding what to say next. He leaned forward, speaking in great earnest. "Think not that I am come to destroy the Law, or the prophets."

That brought Deborah's head up. That was exactly what the scribes and Pharisees were saying about him, that his claims and his teachings were contrary to the Law of Moses. "He has no formal learning," Aaron had thundered after the Nazareth experience, "and yet he seeks to overthrow all that Moses said."

"Truly I say unto you, until heaven and earth pass, one jot or one tittle shall in no wise pass from the Law, till all be fulfilled."

Deborah looked at David with wide eyes. That was an affirmation of unmistakable clarity and was startling, to say the least. The jot, or *yod*, was the smallest letter in the Hebrew alphabet, barely a scratch compared to the other letters. The *seraphs*, or tittles, were no more than tiny marks that helped the reader distinguish between letters. It was a common saying among the scribes that it would be better that heaven and earth pass away rather than to have the smallest letter or even one dot in the Law changed. Now Jesus had turned that saying against them. He was not calling for an abandonment of the Law. He was telling the people, if she had heard him right, that they were expected to fulfill the Law to the fullest. Wait until she told Aaron that!

Because she was thinking about Aaron at that moment, what followed next hit with even greater impact. "For I say unto you, except your righteousness shall exceed the righteousness of the scribes and Pharisees, you shall in no case enter into the kingdom of heaven."

He stopped as a stir rippled across the assembled multitude like the wind stirring the leaves of a vineyard. People turned to each other in surprise. *More righteous than the Pharisees?* Had they heard that right?

Rachel, who sat beside her mother-in-law, was staring at Deborah. "How could anyone possibly be more righteous than Uncle Aaron?" she whispered.

David was shaking his head. "He didn't say that our adherence to the Law should be greater than theirs," he explained. "He said our *righteousness* should exceed theirs. I think he's talking about what we are inwardly, not what we do outwardly."

Rachel's mouth opened in a large O, and Ephraim, her husband, began to nod slowly. So did Deborah. Now that made more sense. And then Deborah decided maybe she wouldn't mention any of this to Aaron after all.

Simeon was leaning forward too, but he had focused on something else. "Did you hear that, Mother? He spoke of the kingdom."

That was right, she thought. He had mentioned the kingdom. If there was one thing everyone seemed to agree on when they talked about the Messiah, it was that he would be a king, that he would bring forth the kingdom of God. Before she could answer, however, Jesus, who had seemed content to let the reaction to his words go for a few moments, began to speak again.

"You have heard that it was said by them of old time, 'Thou shalt not kill; and whosoever shall kill shall be in danger of the judgment.' But I say unto you, that whosoever is angry with his brother without a cause shall be in danger of the judgment.

"Ye have heard that it was said by them of old time, 'Thou shalt not commit adultery.' But I say unto you, that whosoever looks on a woman to lust after her hath committed adultery with her already in his heart."

"See," David whispered triumphantly. "He's saying that it's not enough to look at the outward commandments; it is what is in our hearts that matters. Anger leads to murder. Lust leads to adultery. That's where he wants us to focus."

Deborah watched her husband with some amazement. That was exactly what Jesus was saying, but none of them had seen it. Had he heard some of this before from Peter and Andrew?

Jesus went right on with his comparisons between the old and the new. "It has been said, 'Whosoever shall put away his wife, let him give her a writing of divorcement.'"

Deborah's head jerked up. Now there was something that had long been a source of great anger to her and one of the few things over which she bitterly argued with Aaron. In the Law of Moses it said that a man could give his wife a bill of divorcement "if she found no favor in his eyes." It also added, "because he hath found some uncleanness in her." Shammai, the great doctor of the Law, had interpreted that last comment to mean that she had been unfaithful to her husband. That Deborah could understand. But Hillel, the other leading sage of their time and the one Aaron honored and accepted, interpreted the first part of the scripture much more liberally. He said that a man had the right to divorce his wife if she displeased him in *any way*—if he no longer loved her, if she cooked a meal badly, or if he saw another woman who was more beautiful than his wife.

That infuriated Deborah. More than one woman she knew had been divorced—literally tossed out by her husband—and left to fend on her own. Some had even been forced into a life of harlotry in order to support herself and her children. It was a great evil in Deborah's eyes, and she leaned forward with intense interest now, daring Jesus to support such an insane interpretation.

"But I say unto you," he went on, "that whosoever shall put away his wife, saving for the cause of fornication, causes her to commit adultery."

Yes! She felt a burst of exultation. He was not going to stand with Hillel. Good thing. If he had she would have stood and walked away, no matter what David thought.

"Moses suffered you to write a bill of divorcement to put a wife away"—he paused, and Deborah saw his jaw tighten, and there was indignation in his eyes—"but this Moses did because of the hardness of your hearts. From the beginning of creation, God made male and female, and he told them that for this cause should a man leave his father and mother and cleave unto his wife and that the two of them should be one flesh. If they are one flesh, then they are no longer two. Therefore, what God has joined together, let not man put asunder."

Deborah wanted to shout aloud. *Yes! Yes!*

She realized that David was watching her, his eyes filled with joy as he saw her reaction. She still held his hand, so she squeezed it happily.

Whether this man was the Messiah, she wouldn't say. But her initial reluctance to listen to him had evaporated. Here were teachings that resonated within her. This was a teacher she could follow.

She was so surprised by it all that she listened with even greater attention as he continued with this pattern of comparing the Law of Moses to a new and higher law. He was talking about swearing oaths and how foolish it was to swear by Jerusalem or by the hair of your head, as if invoking those things made one whit of difference.

"Let your communications be, Yea, yea; Nay, nay; for whatsoever is more than these cometh of evil."

Again there was a burst of warmth. That was the perfect description of the man she had come to love so deeply. There were no empty promises, no solemn vows with David. If he said he would do something, it was as good as a written bill of agreement.

Again Jesus paused for a moment or two to let his words sink in and to let his listeners respond with each other. He shifted his weight on the small mound, leaning forward now as he spoke earnestly.

"Judge not, that ye be not judged," he went on, "for with what judgment you judge someone, you shall be judged by that same judgment. And with whatever measure you measure things out to others, so shall it be measured unto you. And why do you behold the mote that is in your brother's eye but cannot see the beam that is in your own?"

Deborah smiled and saw that her children were smiling too. There was a metaphor from the mind of a carpenter, she thought. A mote was a speck of sawdust, a common annoyance when something was being sawn. It was so tiny as to be almost invisible and yet could be a great irritant. But the word he had used for *beam* was a carpenter's term. A beam was one of the large boards used in constructing the framework for a house or the support for the roof.

"Will you say to your brother, 'Hold while I get the mote out of your eye' when there is a beam in your own eye? You hypocrite! First cast out the beam from your own eye. Then you shall see more clearly to remove the speck from your brother's eye."

Simeon leaned forward and looked at his mother. "Now there is some practical religion for you," he called softly. "I think I'll share that one with Uncle Aaron."

She laughed. It was interesting how many of them were thinking about Aaron and the teachings of the Pharisees as Jesus spoke.

"You have heard that it hath been said, 'An eye for an eye, and a tooth for a tooth.'"

Good, Deborah thought. Here comes another comparison between the old law and how we should really live it. The statement about an eye for an eye was one of the most famous in all the Law of Moses. Some would even say it captured the entire essence of the Law.

"But I say unto you," Jesus went on, "that you resist not evil; but whosoever shall smite you on thy right cheek, turn to him the other also."

Suddenly it was as if a chill wind had sprung up and blown across the assembly. There were soft gasps and low cries of astonishment. What was this? Turn the other cheek if you were struck?

"And if any man will sue you at the Law and take away your coat, let him have your cloak also."

Once again Simeon leaned forward so he could see his mother, but now she could see the shock in his eyes as well. But if they had been surprised at what Jesus had said thus far, what came next turned Deborah to stone.

"And whosoever shall compel you to go a mile, go with him twain."

Her hand shot to her mouth. Out of the corner of her eye, she saw a rapid movement and jerked in time to see Simeon go up to his knees, his fists clenched, his jaw tight, his eyes locked on the face of Jesus. Deborah was suddenly sick. There was only one person who could compel another to go with him for a mile. A Roman! By law a Roman soldier could stop any person—old, young, healthy, infirm—and force him or her to carry his pack for one Roman mile. The legionnaires reveled in that right and used it mercilessly as a way of proving their complete superiority over their subjects. It was insulting. It was humiliating. It was hated by every Jew who chose to call himself a Jew.

"Give to him that asks of you, and from him that would borrow something of you, turn him not away." If Jesus was aware that his words were being hurled out into the crowd like great rocks from a catapult, he gave no sign. He spoke calmly and slowly enough to let each concept sink into their minds.

Deborah pulled her hand away from David's, recoiling from the words that poured down upon them. Simeon turned, staring at her in total disbelief. She dropped her head, staring at her hands, which were now clasped together in fierce desperation, barely aware that they belonged to her. A low, angry undercurrent of sound rippled across the hillside as people turned to each other in astonishment. This was the Galilee, and he dared to preach of appeasement and surrender here?

Jesus went on. "You have heard that it hath been said, 'Thou shalt love thy neighbor, and hate thine enemy.' But I say unto you, Love your enemies. Bless them that curse you, and do good to them that hate you."

Deborah heard a sharp gasp, and only after a moment did she realize it had come from her son. Simeon was on his feet, his body as stiff as a rod, his fists balled so tightly that his knuckles showed white. Ironically, his tunic had fallen open to reveal the angry scar that ran across his chest, as if to shout to the world, "They gave me this, and you ask me to forgive them?"

"Simeon!" It was David. His eyes were wide and stricken. He was motioning to his son to come over and sit down beside him. Simeon glanced at him once, and Deborah saw that his eyes were like the ice brought down from Mount Hermon. Then, as others stared at him, Simeon spun around and started away, walking swiftly in and out among the people. As he went, first one and then another arose and followed after him. Seven or eight in all walked down the hill and out of earshot of the man who sat on the mound of dirt and taught the people.

Deborah could feel her husband's eyes upon her, but she didn't look up. It was all she could do to stay where she was. If it wouldn't have shamed David even more than Simeon had shamed him, she too would have plunged away. For now there was a horrible image before her eyes. It was not of that day in the courtyard when Simeon lay in a pool of his own blood and she and Leah were dragged away in bonds. It was of a day many years before that. She was fifteen years old. She could still feel the prick of the spear at her back, making her lift her head to watch as they drove the nails into the hands and feet of her father, then dragged him upwards and hung him on the cross, where it would take him another three days to die. This was the lesson Rome would teach the families of the Zealot rebels. And this was the enemy Jesus wanted her to love. These were the ones who cursed her and her mother and every other rebel Jew in the hated province of Judea. And she was supposed to pray for them?

She closed her eyes tightly, trying to squeeze out the image that filled her mind and the words that were hammering at her ears here on this hillside above the beautiful sea that lay behind them.

III

They ate in silence except to ask for food. Leah and Joseph watched the three of them, wanting badly to ask what was wrong but not daring to.

After supper was over, they left the dishes for the servants to clear and went up on the roof to visit in the cool of the evening. Simeon and Leah were the last to climb the stairs and were behind the rest of the family. Leah leaned close to her brother. "Simeon, tell me what happened. Why are you and Mother so upset?"

He stopped, putting a finger to his lips.

She dropped her voice to a whisper. "I'm fifteen, Simeon. I'm not a child anymore, even though everyone seems to treat me like I am. Tell me what happened."

He looked at her, realizing that she was right. She was not a child any more than Shana was a child. But he still did not want to talk about it. "Leah, I—"

"Simeon? Leah?" Their mother's voice came to them clearly from above.

Simeon pulled a face. "Yes, Mother?"

"If we are going to talk about it, we'll all talk about it together."

Leah pulled a sour face. "I'm sorry," she mouthed.

He took Leah by the elbow, and they joined the rest of the family. As they sat down, Leah looked at her mother. "Ephraim and Rachel said something happened today, I was just asking Simeon—"

Her mother raised a hand. "Please. I am sure your father would like to talk about this as well."

David's shoulders lifted and fell. "Deborah, I . . . " He just shook his head.

"No, it's all right. I don't want everyone walking around the house whispering as though Simeon and I were sick or something."

That startled Simeon a little. He was the one who had stalked off in the middle of Jesus' sermon and had been surprised when his mother had come home upset as well. Since his father and mother had returned home, no one had spoken of the afternoon's experience.

Young Joseph was watching his mother closely, sensing the emotions simmering just below the surface. She saw the anxiety in his face. "This is not something of great concern to a ten-year-old, Joseph. You are welcome to stay, but if you would rather go out and play—"

She got only that far, and he was up and away. "Thank you, Mama."

For what seemed like a very long time, no one spoke. The silence grew heavier and heavier. Finally Deborah looked at her husband. "Go ahead, David. Tell them what you thought."

He shook his head slowly. "What I think isn't important for now. I know what you and Simeon thought when he began speaking about—" He took a breath. "Look, I understand more than you think, even though I never had most of my family killed in front of my eyes, nor have I had a Roman centurion nearly cut me in two with his broadsword. I am not going to try to tell you that you are wrong for feeling as you do."

"But you don't agree," Simeon said, the bitterness still too strong in his mouth to hold back his words. Then seeing the hurt in his father's eyes, he went on hurriedly. "To be honest, I really liked some of the things he said. I'm like you in that way, Father. I like a pragmatic approach to life. That's why Uncle Aaron and I clash so often. He is so theoretical, so lofty. Jesus was very practical." He turned to Leah. "For example, he said we shouldn't have to swear an oath and invoke the name of Jerusalem, or the temple, or God. We should be so filled with integrity that we just say yes or no, and that is as good as an oath."

"I like that," she said.

"He also talked about judging others," Deborah noted, also wanting to let David know she had listened with an open mind. "He said we should make sure we correct our own faults first before we try to change someone else." She smiled at David. "I know you didn't think I was accepting anything of what he said, but I did."

She turned back to her two children. "He said when we give alms, we should do it in secret, not to be seen of men but for God. I liked that. I've always found it bothersome when we're on the Temple Mount and some rich man blows the trumpet so that everyone will take notice while he drops his money into one of the contribution chests."

"Me, too," Leah said. "They are so pompous."

Now David came in. "He said the same thing about prayer, that we shouldn't make loud prayers on the street corners so that men will think we are righteous. We should go into our closets and pray in secret. Then God, who hears in secret, will answer us. In fact, he talked a great deal about the importance of what we are inside and not just outside."

Leah shook her head. Rachel told her that Simeon had left in the middle of the sermon, but no one was talking about that. She turned to her brother. "You got up and walked out?"

"I did."

"Why?"

David raised a hand quickly. "If your mother or Simeon want to tell you that later, they can. I just want to say one thing, and then I'll say no more."

"No, Papa!"

That brought all of them around. Leah was as gentle as a dove in her nature. To hear her speak with such forcefulness was a shock.

"I want to know what Jesus said that made you so angry, Simeon. I can't understand why you are all so upset unless I know." She looked at her mother, her eyes showing hurt. "I've heard Papa talk about Jesus so much, I wanted to hear him too. So tell me."

Surprised by the intensity in her daughter, Deborah sat back. "I'm sorry, Leah. You are right. You are old enough now to be part of this."

"It's all right. But tell me now. I want to know." She looked at Simeon, but he waved her off with a jerk of his head. He was still seething, and repeating it would only make him boil again all the more.

So Deborah sighed and summed it up as quickly as she could. "The Law of Moses says that we are to take eye for eye and tooth for tooth.

It is to make sure that justice is served. But Jesus said we are to live a different law. We are to love our enemies, to bless them that curse us and pray for those who take advantage of us and use us despitefully."

She paused, but Leah only watched her, not seeming to be shocked or surprised at all by what she said. How different she was, Deborah thought. And how ironic. Normally it was mother and daughter who bonded closely together, or father and son. But it was Simeon who had inherited his mother's fire, and it burned in him like a bucket filled with brimstone. While she was close to all of her children, it was Simeon and she who were bound together with this undefinable core of passion. Leah, on the other hand, had inherited her father's gentle nature, his patience and goodness. Like Deborah and Simeon, David had a special closeness to his only daughter.

Thank heavens, Deborah thought. She did not view that part of her that she had passed on to Simeon as a blessing and was grateful she had not also given it to Leah.

"Don't stop, Mother," Simeon said tightly when she didn't answer. "Tell her the rest of what he said."

There was a pained look on David's face, and she knew it was because of the anger he saw in his son. She sighed and went on. "He also said that if a Roman compels us to carry his pack for one mile, we should offer to take it a second mile."

Finally, Leah was shocked. She stared wide-eyed at her mother, and her mouth was partially open. "He said that?" she exclaimed.

"He didn't actually use the word *Roman*," David pointed out. "Just that if a *man* compels you to go a mile, go with him twain."

There was a soft exclamation of disgust from Simeon. "And how many Jews do you know who will force another Jew to walk a mile with them?"

Realizing his mistake, David said nothing more.

Now the fire had erupted, and Simeon raced on. "He said that we should love our enemies, pray for those who mistreat us. He said if we are smitten on the right cheek, we should turn the other as well."

One hand came back, and he yanked his tunic free to show the ugly scar there. "So according to Jesus, after that centurion cut me down I was wrong not to have staggered back to my feet begging him to do it again."

"That's not what he said," David came in.

"Not in those words, but that was what he meant." He whirled back to Leah. "And that Roman tribune who took you and Mother captive—we're supposed to love him too, pray for his well-being." The words spat out like drops of molten steel.

He swung around to his father. "By the way, the centurion is back."

David started, then nodded. "I heard that this morning."

"But you weren't going to tell me."

"Simeon, I—"

"Oh, don't worry, Father. I'll not be seeking him out. Actually, it's the tribune I want. And when I find him, I won't be turning the other cheek again."

Deborah stared at her hands, pressed tightly together in her lap. One part of her wanted to leap to her feet and shout encouragement to her son. Another part of her had gone as cold as the waters from a spring. This was her legacy to him, and someday he would find the Roman officer and make good his vow. And the chances that he would not return to her were very good.

"That's what Jesus taught," Simeon hissed. He looked at Leah, but everyone knew he was speaking to his father. "That's what this new Messiah would have us do. Well, sorry if I couldn't stomach any more of it. That's why I left."

Leah looked at her mother, almost sorry that she had triggered this outburst. Silence filled the room. Simeon stood facing them, his chest rising and falling. Finally he looked directly at his father. "All right, Father. I've had my say. Go ahead. Say what you are feeling."

He didn't look up but only shook his head.

"No, David," Deborah said. "You have always taught us to say what we think. Don't be angry with us when we do."

He straightened. "Do you think that is what it is? That I am angry that Simeon speaks what is in his heart?"

"Then what?" Leah said. "I want to know what you thought, Papa."

Simeon was gradually calming down. He moved over and sat beside his mother. "Yes, Father. Leah is right. I have spoken my mind. Now I would hear what you have to say."

"I would simply ask you some questions," David finally said.

"All right."

Deborah nodded as well. "We are listening."

"Why only the right cheek?" David asked, his voice thoughtful.

"What?" Simeon felt David had totally lost him.

"Jesus said that if a person smites us on the right cheek, we should turn to him the other also. What happens if a person hits us on the left side of the face? Do we get to strike back?"

Deborah was watching her husband, her face puzzled. "I don't understand what you are saying, David."

"Think about it for a moment. If I, being right-handed, as most people are, strike you on the right cheek with my open hand, how will I have to do it?"

Finally it was Leah who saw it. She began to nod. "I have to strike you with the back of my hand."

"And if I strike you with the back of my hand?" he asked, leaving the question hanging.

Leah was excited now. "It is a great insult. It is how we show our utter contempt for another person."

"Yes," David cried. He lifted his right hand and made a quick movement, as if he were striking another person on the right cheek. "The very gesture is insulting." He turned to Simeon. "I don't think for a moment that Jesus was saying that we cannot defend ourselves from an enemy. He's not talking about a threat to our lives; he is talking about a threat to our *pride*. A blow on the cheek is not life threatening, but men have been known to kill one another over such a petty insult as a slap on the face. Well, what if we don't care what men think of us? What if all that matters to us is whether God accepts us or not?"

Deborah looked dubious, but she was thinking. There was a certain logic to what he was saying.

"Next question. How do you suppose God tailors the weather for each individual person, based on their personal righteousness?"

Leah's mouth dropped open. "Is that what Jesus said?"

Simeon glared at her, knowing exactly what his father meant by the question. "No."

David went on, half musing. "Being the Almighty God, I suppose he could make the sun shine only on those he loved and the rain fall only on those he wishes to bless."

Leah still looked bewildered, so Deborah came in, with just a trace of irritation tightening her voice. "What your father is referring to is that Jesus said that God sends his rain on the just and the unjust. The same with the sun. He used that as the reason for loving your enemies."

David leaned forward, peering at Simeon. "So what did he mean by that?"

Simeon flung out one hand. "Don't ask me. I can't make any sense out of what he was trying to say."

To everyone's surprise, it was his mother who responded.

"If you don't have an answer, Simeon, just say so. Don't be petulant."

"Never mind," David said quickly. "So, Simeon, do you consider the Romans to be human beings?"

Suddenly wary, Simeon answered slowly, "Of course."

"Do you think they are children of God?"

Simeon hesitated.

"I'm not talking about his spiritual children, those who follow and believe in him. I'm talking about whether or not God created them."

Simeon balked, sensing he was being led where he might not want to go. "That doesn't excuse for one minute what they do, Father."

"He didn't ask us to *excuse* our enemies, Simeon," came the soft reply. "He asked that we *love* them."

"Don't, David!" Deborah cried, holding up one hand. "Don't even say that again." Her lips were trembling as she tried to fight back the tears. The memories of her father had surged in again, causing her stomach to twist sharply. She didn't realize that tears now streaked her cheeks.

When David finally spoke, he did so with infinite gentleness. "I told you, I have no right to condemn how you feel. All I know is this. The last words Jesus spoke as you left, Simeon, were these: 'Be perfect even as our Father in heaven is perfect.' I believe that is the key to understanding why Jesus said what he did. God is the model for us. Only as we become like him can we ever hope to return to his presence."

He looked up. "Can we honestly believe that of all his children, God feels love only for the Jews? That he hates all the rest of them?" He shook his head slowly. "What Jesus was teaching us was not about carrying packs or praying for men who sell women and children into slavery. It's not about who we can hate and who we can't hate. It's about being like God, about being more like our Father."

He stopped, and no one spoke for a long time. Deborah still did not raise her head. Simeon was staring out the window. Finally David stood up. He started away, moving very slowly, as if burdened heavily. Then he stopped. He didn't turn, but they heard a soft exclamation of amazement. "And we thought that what the Pharisees demand of us is hard."

CHAPTER NOTES

While we know that Peter had a wife and probably a family (see Matthew 8:14; Luke 18:28–29), we do not know his wife's name. The author has given her the name Anna rather than always referring to her abstractly.

The Sermon on the Mount is given in its entirety in chapters 5–7 of the Gospel of Matthew. Mark and Luke make reference to the same teachings but do not include it all in one sermon as Matthew does. Other teachings of Christ on marriage were included here for purposes of the novel (see Mark 10:2–12).

The reference in the Mosaic Law granting the right for bills of divorcement is found in Deuteronomy 24:1. Three statements from near contemporaries of Christ indicate how casually the sanctity of marriage was treated by some men at this time. The school of Hillel said, "If the wife cooks the husband's food ill, by over-salting or over-roasting it, she is to be put away." Rabbi Akiba, who lived sometime after Christ, said, "If a man sees a woman handsomer than his own wife, he may put her [his wife] away, because it is said [in Deuteronomy], 'If she find not favor in his eyes'" (as cited in Talmage, p. 384).

Flavius Josephus, the Jewish historian, is proof that such counsel was taken to heart, for in his autobiography, he says, without a trace of remorse, "About this time, I put away my wife, who had borne me three children, not being pleased with her manners" (as cited in Clarke, 3:74).

The suggestion that being smitten on the cheek was a grievous insult comes from such passages as Job 16:10 and Lamentations 3:30.

Again for purposes of the novel, some of the scriptural passages have been paraphrased.

CHAPTER 16

FOR THE REASONING OF MORTALS IS WORTHLESS, AND OUR DESIGNS
ARE LIKELY TO FAIL, FOR A PERISHABLE BODY WEIGHS DOWN THE
SOUL, AND THIS EARTHY TENT BURDENS THE THOUGHTFUL MIND.

—*Wisdom of Solomon 9:14–15*

I
15 MAY, A.D. 30

The family of David ben Joseph of Capernaum had secured the gates to the courtyard, locked the doors to their house, finished their evening prayers, and were preparing for bed when they heard a loud pounding on the courtyard gate. David gave Deborah a surprised look. It was not unusual in the merchant business for David to have visitors after dark, but not this late. Many homes were already shuttered for the night. Knowing the servants had already retired, he slipped on an outer robe, took one of the small hand lamps, and walked through the house to the front door. He opened it and stepped out onto the stone landing. "Who is there?" he called.

"It's Shana. I've just arrived from Beth Neelah."

II

"You came down alone at night?" Deborah asked, concern written across her face.

"Yehuda and Daniel are preparing things for the beginning of the harvest. They could not leave."

Simeon, Leah, and Joseph had all come from their rooms to join their parents in the main sitting room. Shana looked around at them, her eyes lingering for just a moment longer on Simeon. Then her head came up proudly. "I am not afraid. I know the way even in the dark."

"What's wrong?" David asked. Brave or not, Yehuda would never have sent her down to Capernaum alone unless there was a serious problem.

"It's Naomi," she said to Deborah. "She has taken very ill."

"No!" Deborah exclaimed. "What is it?"

Shana shook her head. "We're not sure. High fever. She's very weak. She keeps asking for you. Teresa asked if I would come and tell you."

Deborah shook her head gravely. Her cousin was almost ten years older than she was, which put her in her mid-fifties, an age that many women never reached. She had been a widow now for almost four years and had moved back to Beth Neelah to be close to her oldest daughter. If Teresa had sent for her, then Deborah knew that this was not just a minor illness. "We'll leave first thing in the morning," she said.

"I'll go with you," Leah said.

But Deborah shook her head immediately. "The harvest season is just beginning. There is too much to do here. Your father needs all of you." She looked to David to confirm that.

Though he didn't want her to have to go alone, he finally nodded. "Do you want Simeon to escort the two of you back up to the village?"

"No. I'll take Phineas or one of the other servants."

Shana was also nodding her head. "Yes, a servant will be sufficient. Galilee is not like Judea. Our roads are safe. There is no danger."

"Can I go to Beth Neelah, Papa?" Joseph asked.

His father turned and looked at Deborah. "We can do without Joseph," he said.

She nodded. "I would like that." Then she turned to Shana. "Would you like something to eat?"

"No. I brought some bread and fruit to eat on the road."

"Then let's get you to bed. I would like to be off again at first light."

III

18 MAY, A.D. 30

For the third time in as many days, the family ate a cold breakfast together. David had finally sent Phineas and two other servants with Deborah. One of those was the cook. In their absence, Leah offered to cook something for her father and Simeon each day, but they were satisfied with bread and cheese or some dried grapes and olives. On this morning, Simeon and Leah were just finishing cleaning up the meal when David poked his head into the kitchen. "I'm going to go down to the fishing boats," he said. "Peter and Andrew took their boat out last night. I need to check on their catch."

Simeon turned. "I thought Peter and Andrew were with Jesus and not fishing anymore."

"They were with Jesus two nights ago when I last saw them. But I was walking along the shore last night and saw that their boat was gone. They still have to make a living and support their families." He paused for a moment. "If you two will gather up the books and papers here, I'll meet you at the storehouse in about an hour."

"Can I go with you, Papa?" Leah said, drying her hands on a small towel. "Simeon, you can bring the books and things, can't you?"

"Of course."

"I would like that," David said, pleased to have some company. "Let me get my walking sandals, and we'll be off."

IV

"Papa?"

"Yes?"

"May I ask you a question?"

"Of course."

They were just leaving the village and starting down the path that led to the beach. They were walking slowly, enjoying the freshness of the morning.

"Do you believe that Jesus is the Messiah?"

He answered without hesitation. "Yes."

"In spite of what he said about loving the Romans?"

He nodded. "And in a way, *because* of what he said about the Romans."

"Why?"

He peered at her, pleased to see that she really wanted to know. "The more I have thought about it, the more I have become convinced that if the Messiah is really going to bring back the kingdom of God on the earth, it can't be just for the Jews. What kind of God would choose one set of his children over another and treat them favorably while he ignores the rest?"

"But we say that the house of Israel are the chosen people, Papa. Don't you believe that?"

"Of course I do, Leah. But why were we chosen? Because we were better than other people? When you read about how often Israel murmured against God in the wilderness and the incident with them worshiping the golden calf, you know that wasn't the case. That's not what the Lord said to Moses."

"What did he say?"

"The Lord told Moses that we were to be a holy people. And then Moses said something like this: 'The Lord has chosen thee to be a special people unto him, above all the people upon the face of the earth. But the Lord did not set his love upon you or choose you because you are great in numbers. The Lord chose you because he loves you and because of the oath which he swore unto your fathers.'"

They had slowed because David was filled with earnestness now and not thinking about where they were going. "He made a covenant with Abraham that his seed would be God's people. We are his *covenant* people more than his *chosen* people, Leah. Our covenant is to serve God and bless others. That is why we are chosen. I don't think God expects us to withdraw into our own little world and look down on all others with hate and contempt."

She walked on in silence for a time, thinking about what he had said. Then she looked up at her father. "Will Mama be angry if I believe that Jesus is the Messiah?"

"Of course not. Your mother would never stop you from believing as you wish." When she just nodded, he went on. "Do you think you might believe that Jesus is the Christ?"

"I don't know. That's why I want to hear Jesus for myself." Suddenly she looked up at him and smiled. It was filled with such trust and sweetness that it caught David's breath for a moment. "But you believe he is the Messiah, Papa, and I have always believed you. That's a start, isn't it?"

He put his arm around her shoulder, unable to speak for a moment. "Yes, my sweet Leah," he finally managed. "That's a start."

V

There was no fisherman's catch to check on. When they reached the place where the fishermen kept their boats, the beach was filled with activity, but Peter and Andrew's boat was beached on shore. The net was folded in a pile on the deck. There was no sign of anyone. A few feet away, the boat that belonged to Zebedee and his two sons also rocked gently at the water's edge with no one around it. Puzzled, David looked at Leah. "Look at the net. It's dry. It hasn't been used."

"It doesn't look like the boat has been out all night," Leah agreed.

"Yet last night it was gone. And yesterday morning as well."

Suddenly from the boat itself they heard a noise. As they turned, Peter appeared, climbing up out of the hold, one hand holding a coil of rope. He stopped, then grinned and waved. "David! I was going to come and see you this morning."

"You were?"

"Yes. I have much to tell you." He smiled even more broadly. "Good morning, Leah. What brings you two out so early?"

"Well," David said, "I passed by here last night and saw that your boat was gone. I assumed you had gone fishing, so I came to see how you did."

"No fishing," he said. "We took the Master over to Gadara night before last. We returned long after dark last evening."

David nodded. Gadara was on the eastern shore of the Sea of

Kinnereth, partway down its length. He gestured toward the net. "But you didn't fish?"

"No." Peter stowed the rope, walked to the bow of the ship and hopped lightly down to the pebbled beach. He came over and grasped David on one shoulder. "It's good to see you, my friend. Come. I just had to put some things away here. Jesus and Andrew are at home. Anna and her mother are preparing breakfast. Come and eat with us."

"We've eaten," David answered, "but we shall walk with you."

"Good. I have so much I want to tell you." He looked at Leah. "And I am pleased that you would be here as well, Leah."

"Leah has an interest in the teachings of Jesus."

"Really?" Peter said, clearly pleased.

"I do. I haven't had a chance to hear him for myself, but Father has told me much about what he says. I am very taken with it." She looked up at him. "Will Jesus be teaching today, Simon?"

"Probably," he said. "We shall ask him." He gestured with his head toward town, and they began walking slowly. As they did, Peter turned to David. "Speaking of fishing," he said, sobered now, "Anna said you delivered payment the other day for another good catch."

David looked away. "I did."

"But there wasn't a good catch, David. There hasn't been *any* catch for more than two weeks now. How could there be when we have not gone out fishing?"

Leah was staring at her father, who seemed embarrassed. "It is not my privilege to devote my full time to following the Master," he said, not meeting Peter's probing gaze. "He called you and Andrew and the others to be fishers of men. Well, I would like to be part of that, so I shall pay you for a different kind of catch."

To Leah's utter amazement, suddenly there were tears in Peter's eyes. She couldn't believe it. Simon Peter? Strong-minded, totally independent, sometimes gruff, usually impetuous, and always unemotional Peter? Touched to the point of tears?

He brushed quickly at them, shaking his head, almost as surprised as Leah and David were. "Do you remember what the Savior said to us the other day when he spoke on the mount?"

"What?"

"He was speaking directly to those of us he has asked to come and follow him."

David began to nod. "About the lilies of the field?"

"Yes." He cleared his throat, getting control again, and spoke to Leah. "He told us to take no thought—to not be overly anxious—about what we would eat or drink or how we would clothe ourselves. 'Is not life more than meat, and the body more than raiment?' he said."

He sighed, deep in thought now. "I wasn't sure exactly what he meant. But then he reminded us that the fowls of the air neither sow nor reap." He grinned quickly. "Nor do they go out in boats to fish, for that matter—nor do they gather their crops into barns. And yet Heavenly Father feeds them. Then he looked right at us. 'Are you not better than they?' he asked."

Leah could see that Peter's eyes were shining again. "Think about it, Leah. As your father said, Jesus reminded us about the lilies of the field. 'They toil not,' he said, 'neither do they sow, and yet Solomon in all his glory was not arrayed like one of these.'"

Leah was enchanted by the imagery. This was the season of wild-flowers. Just a few days before, while she was out walking with her mother, she had stopped and picked one of them, totally delighted by the lustrous beauty of the petals, the perfect blend of shape, color, and smell. "Yes, what a beautiful way to put it."

Peter saw that she understood his words perfectly and was pleased. "Then Jesus simply said to us, 'If God so clothes the grass of the field, which today is and tomorrow is cast into the oven, will he not take care of you, O you of little faith?'"

He turned to David. "Anna and I talked much about my decision to follow Jesus. How would we live? Would there ever be time to fish again? What about the children? We knew we would do whatever he asked, but we couldn't see how we were possibly to make do. And then suddenly your payment arrived at the house."

David was moved too, and could only nod.

"'O you of little faith,'" Peter repeated. "When he said that, I didn't think he was talking about me."

"It is little enough I can do," David said softly.

"Well, there will be times when we still fish, I suppose, but in the meantime, know that you are doing the work of the Lord when you help Andrew and me and James and John." He took a deep breath, relieved to have that said. "Now listen, David. You won't believe what has been happening."

"What?"

He turned to Leah. "I want you to hear this too, Leah. You keep this in mind when you finally get a chance to hear the Master teach."

"I will," she said, surprised by his sudden intensity.

"There is so much, but let me start with the night before last. It had been a full day of teaching—well, you remember. You were there for part of that day." Then he frowned. "By the way, I saw Simeon get up and leave during the sermon."

"Yes," David sighed. "I'm sorry. I hope Jesus wasn't offended."

He shook his head and laughed softly. "One does not easily offend Jesus," he said. "I told him about Simeon and what had happened with Deborah and Leah."

"Oh?"

"I thought he was going to weep," Peter said softly. "He is so saddened by the cruelty we find in the world." He frowned, thinking about that, then went on. "Anyway, as we finished that evening, I thought we would just go home and have a quiet night to rest. But suddenly Jesus wanted to go over to the other side of the lake. There were still a lot of people around, trying to get to him. Maybe this was his way of getting a rest."

"He must get tired of never having time to himself," David agreed.

Peter shrugged. "Whatever it was, we did as he requested. We set off just after sundown, along with several other boats that decided to go with us. Soon it was dark, but there was a steady wind, and we were making good time. Jesus was exhausted. People had been swarming around him all day. So he went to the back of the boat, got some netting for a pillow, and immediately went to sleep."

David laughed softly. "He must have been exhausted indeed. I hate being on your boats. All that rocking and pitching."

"Exactly," Peter said. "It surprised us a little how quickly he fell asleep." Now his eyes became very grave. "As we made our way along, the wind began to stiffen. At first we were glad. It would speed us across, and perhaps we could get some sleep before daylight came again. But you know how quickly things can happen out there."

David suddenly snapped his fingers. "Night before last? I awoke in the night. The wind was howling in the treetops. I remember thinking how glad I was that you weren't fishing at that time." His eyes widened. "You were out in that?"

"Yes, and howling is a word that barely describes it," Peter said, his voice very low. "In all my days of fishing, I've seen only half a dozen times when it has come up so quickly and been so strong."

David understood exactly what he meant. The unique geographical setting of the Sea of Kinnereth created unusual conditions. When the cooler air from the highlands began its rush to the lowlands around the lake, by most evenings the wind would be stiff enough to raise whitecaps on the lake. Occasionally, conditions would be such that the winds would become a full-fledged gale. Even the most experienced fisherman had been caught out on the lake in such "storms of wind" as they called them, and more than one had drowned.

Now Peter stopped and turned to face the two of them. To Leah's surprise, he addressed her directly. "I know how your father feels about Jesus, Leah. Tell me what your thoughts are."

She thought for a moment before answering. "I haven't been privileged to hear him for myself," she began, "but I have great trust in my father's feelings."

"Good for you, Child," Peter said. "That is the key, to be willing to believe." And with that, his hesitancy vanished. "Then listen carefully to what I have to say, for this will help you as you listen to Jesus."

"All right."

"As the wind strengthened with every moment, we realized that we were in serious danger. In the first place, almost every one of the boats had many people on them, so we were riding low in the water. As the waves became worse, they began crashing over the sides of the boat, filling the holds. We were bailing water as fast as we could, but could not begin to keep up with it. The boats began to swamp."

He looked at David. "It was terrible. We had to hang on with all our strength or be thrown out of the boat. To try to bail out water under such conditions was impossible. I was trying to keep the sail from tearing to shreds. Andrew was at the rudder fighting to hold our course. The other boats were in a similar state. We were shouting and yelling—" He shook his head. "Even now it leaves me cold to think about it."

"I can imagine," David said. "I thought we were going to lose the trees in our courtyard."

Peter shook his head, his face even now still filled with disbelief. "And Jesus? You won't believe this, but through it all, he was still asleep at the back of the boat."

"No!" David exclaimed. "How could he be?"

"I don't know. The boat was pitching back and forth like a wild donkey. We were shouting and yelling. And he slept."

"What happened?" Leah said, thoroughly mesmerized by Peter's story.

"Finally, frightened more deeply than I have been in many years, and frankly a little frustrated that he should sleep through it all, I crawled to the back of the boat and shook him awake. When he opened his eyes and looked at me, even then he didn't seem to realize how desperate our situation was. 'Master, Master,' I cried. 'How can you continue to sleep? Do you not care that we perish?'"

Simon Peter passed one hand across his eyes. "I can't believe I said that to him, but things were pretty grim by then." Peter's thoughts were far away; his eyes filled with awe. "He didn't answer me. He got to his feet and made his way to the front of the boat. Then he stood there, looking out into the storm and the darkness, the waves crashing around him, the wind tearing at his hair and beard."

Peter's voice dropped almost to a whisper. "He raised one hand and spoke three words. 'Peace, be still.'"

No one spoke. Somewhere off in the willows a bird was singing lustily. To their right they could hear the soft lapping of the water against the shore. At last Peter's head came up. "You know how these storms are, David. They can come up in ten or fifteen minutes, then be gone again just as quickly."

David was staring at him. "Are you saying the storm then blew itself out?"

His head moved back and forth slowly. "No. The storm didn't blow itself out. If it had, that would have seemed like a miracle to us, but it would have been easier to explain. Storms can sometimes change that quickly."

"*Easier* to explain?" Leah asked, picking up on how he had emphasized those words.

"Yes. What happened next—there is no explanation for it."

Leah could not stand it. "What happened? Tell us."

He turned and looked out across the water, which was now smooth as a mirror, reflecting the sunlight in a blinding glare. "The moment Jesus spoke, the wind began to die. In no more than two or three minutes—two or three minutes, David!—the wind was completely gone, and it was perfectly calm."

"No!"

"Yes. He raised his hand, spoke three simple words, and the waves *instantly* began to subside, the wind stopped, and—" He gestured toward the lake. "Almost before we realized it, the water was just as you see it now."

Both hands came up to his face, and he rubbed his eyes, partly to get the tiredness out of them, partly as though to clear his vision. "Then he turned to us," he went on. "There was this gentle, quiet rebuke in his voice. 'Why is it that you were afraid?' he asked. 'Where is your faith?'"

"Incredible," David breathed. "I wish I had been there."

Leah didn't know what to say. She felt like she was staggering from a blow. "What kind of man is this Jesus?" she whispered.

Peter jerked around. "That is exactly what Andrew said. 'What manner of man is this, that even the wind and the waves obey him?'"

CHAPTER NOTES

The passage that David quotes to Leah about Israel being God's chosen people is from Deuteronomy 7:6–8.

The stilling of the "storm of wind" is told by three of the four Gospel writers (see Matthew 8:23–27; Mark 4:35–41; Luke 8:22–25). On one of the author's trips to Israel, he and his wife were crossing the Sea of Galilee in one of the tourist boats that run between Capernaum and Tiberias. It was late afternoon, and the wind had come up with surprising swiftness, raising four- and five-foot waves on the lake. As we finished reading the story of the stilling of the storm together, the boat's captain told us that just two weeks before a "storm of wind" came up so suddenly in the night that two experienced fishermen had drowned when their boat swamped before they could return to shore.

CHAPTER 17

[HE] . . . HEALED ALL THAT WERE SICK: THAT IT MIGHT BE FULFILLED
WHICH WAS SPOKEN BY ESAIAS THE PROPHET, SAYING, HIMSELF
TOOK OUR INFIRMITIES, AND BARE OUR SICKNESSES.

—*Matthew 8:16–17*

I
18 MAY, A.D. 30

"Simeon! Ephraim!" Leah burst into the small room at the back of the storehouse where her two brothers had a table filled with books and scrolls of parchment.

"There you are," Simeon said. "We were beginning to wonder what had happened to you and Father." He looked past her. "Where is he?"

"At Simon Peter's house."

"Is there trouble?" Ephraim asked, sensing that she was very agitated.

"No, no. He wants you to come. We're going to spend the day with Jesus, listening to him teach."

"What?" Simeon exploded. He thumped the table once with the tip of his index finger. "What about all of this?"

"Papa says to leave it. It can wait until tomorrow."

Ephraim looked at Simeon, obvious dismay on his face. "But Papa is the one who said we absolutely had to get the books done today."

"I know, but something happened. Peter told us this most wonderful thing. Papa says the books can wait. He wants you both to come."

Simeon blew out a long breath of frustration. "It's a good thing Mother isn't here to hear that."

"Oh, I wish she were," Leah exclaimed. "I have so much to tell her. We were at Simon Peter's house. Jesus was there. Oh, Simeon, he's not what you think. He's wonderful. So gentle and kind. So wise."

Simeon turned away, his lips tight. "So much for getting this done today," he grumbled.

Leah went around and leaned on the table, putting her face close to Simeon's. "Please, Simeon. This can wait. When you hear what happened, you'll want to hear him."

"I've heard him already." He jerked his head. "Ephraim can go if he wants."

"Simeon, please!"

"I'm not going, Leah." He turned back to the table and grabbed a quill pen. "I can't believe that Father is going to go chasing after him again and leave all of this for us."

Stung, Leah stepped back. "I have never once heard Papa complain when you go chasing off with your Zealot friends, so why are you so angry?"

That hit Simeon in a vulnerable place, for he had more than once felt guilty leaving his father and Ephraim with all the work while he went off with Yehuda and the rest of his band. "You're right," he said grudgingly. "Papa can do what he likes. But I'm not going. I am not interested."

Exasperated, she turned to her oldest brother. He hesitated for a moment, then shook his head. "I'm leaving for Jezreel soon to begin assessing the wheat crop. We've got to finish this today."

Leah understood. Ephraim half wanted to come. If Simeon had

agreed . . . "Papa said to leave it," she tried once more. When neither responded, she whirled away. "All right then."

As she started for the door, Simeon turned around again. "So what is this wonderful thing Peter told you?"

"You said you weren't interested," she shot back. "Remember?" And with that she was gone.

The room was quiet for a time; then Simeon looked at his older brother. "Mother would not be happy if she knew this."

Ephraim looked glum. "I've never seen Papa like this. It worries me a little."

"More than a little," Simeon agreed.

II

It seemed as though every single person in Capernaum and half the towns round about had come to see Jesus of Nazareth. Leah couldn't believe it. She and her father held hands tightly, trying to stay close enough to hear the Master, but it was a challenge. Capernaum had a population of about two thousand people, and there were that many more in the towns nearby—Bethsaida, Chorazin, Tabgha, Magdala—so she knew that it only seemed like everyone was here. There were probably no more than three or four hundred people following along, but in the narrow streets of the city, it became a real crush trying to stay close.

Jesus moved along slowly, aware of the attention he was drawing but paying it little mind. He hadn't stopped to do any formal teaching as yet. There really hadn't been much chance. People were constantly pressing in on him, asking him questions or simply wanting to shake his hand. Now as they reached the small open square in front of the synagogue, Jesus stopped, and the crowds flowed in around him, leaving him at the center. Leah and her father pushed in to where they were just two or three people removed from him.

The crowd quieted as they saw a well-dressed man wearing a richly embroidered cloak around his shoulders come up to Jesus. It was one of the scribes, a colleague of Amram the Pharisee. Leah didn't know his name, but she had seen him walking with the other Pharisees in town. "Master," he cried.

Leah thought he used the term of honor with a trace of sarcasm but realized that might just be her own feelings against the Pharisees. "I would follow you whithersoever you go," he said. "Tell me where you live so I can come and visit you."

As the silence deepened, Jesus looked at him steadily. Then he said, "Foxes have holes, and the birds of the air have their nests, but the Son of Man has nowhere to lay his head."

"That's true," her father whispered in her ear. "Since they rejected him at Nazareth, he has been staying in a temporary shelter on Peter's roof."

That answer clearly was not what the scribe had expected, and he backed away, saying nothing more. A woman cried out, but Leah couldn't hear what she said. Jesus turned to face her, and they could not catch his answer either.

Then suddenly a cry went up. "Leper! Leper!"

It was like someone had poured out liquid fire on the multitude. On the far side of the square, directly opposite from Leah and David, the crowd began to melt away, falling back in panic as they tried to make a path. And then Leah heard it too. The dull clanking of a bell sounded through the shouts of the crowd. In the Mosaic Law, people diagnosed by the priests as having leprosy were required to rend their clothes, put a covering over their head, and warn others of their approach by crying "Unclean! Unclean!" Because it was so easy for a voice to be lost in a crowd, it had become a common practice for lepers to also carry a brass bell and ring it loudly wherever they went.

With the crowd falling back, Leah now saw the man. He was covered in a long dark robe, white with dust and torn in several places. Whether these were from his rending it in keeping with the Law, or simply through wear, she could not tell. Leah suppressed a little shudder of horror. Even from where she was she could see the dark sores that marred the man's face. When he lifted his hand to clank the bell again she saw that it was twisted and misshapen, with patches of black. The crowd responded with angry hisses, muttered imprecations. What was he doing? A leper knew better than to enter a crowded square. "Send for the magistrate," someone blurted. "Get him out of here."

But then Leah no longer heard the crowd around her. The man was moving straight for Jesus, only ten or so paces away now, and Jesus hadn't moved. All around him everyone shrank back, revulsion twisting their faces. Jesus stood perfectly still, watching the man calmly as he came closer. Then the crowd saw what was happening, and the noise was cut off as if it had been smothered with a blanket. Every eye stared at the scene before them.

The leper shuffled forward until he was no more than five or six feet away, far too close to be in compliance with the Law. He pulled back the hood and revealed the ghastliness of his face for all to see. Leah sucked in her breath sharply, stunned by the awfulness of the man's infirmity.

"Lord," he said, obviously frightened by what he was doing and by the hostility of the people on every side of him. "Lord, if you will, you can make me clean." It was a plea that tore at Leah's heart.

For several seconds there was not a sound. Leah could see Jesus' face, which was only partially in profile to her now. He was watching the man steadily, not at all shocked by what he was or by what he had just said. Then his head nodded slowly. "I will," he said. "Be thou clean."

What followed next would stay etched in Leah's mind for the rest of her life. It was as though each tiny movement took two or three seconds to be accomplished. Jesus stepped forward as the man dropped to his knees. And then the unbelievable happened. Jesus stretched out his hands and laid them on the man's forehead. For an instant Leah thought she was going to retch. She closed her eyes and looked away as she heard a gasp of utter horror rip through the crowd.

She couldn't bear to look, and yet she couldn't bear not to. She opened her eyes again. Jesus stood there, his eyes half closed, his arms stiff, his hands still covering the terrible rawness of those open sores. And then his eyes opened slowly, and he dropped his hands to his side. Leah leaned forward, trying to see the leper's face, to see if he was as shocked as she was that he had been touched. But the moment Jesus' hands moved away, the man's own hands flew up, and he buried his face in them. A great sob—whether of pain or joy, Leah could not tell—tore from deep within him. Then his shoulders began to shake.

Suddenly Leah felt her knees go weak. Blindly she clutched at her father's arm. "Look at his hands, Father!"

David grabbed her hand, already seeing what she was seeing. Where before there had been swollen, twisted knuckles and fingers, blackened with the decaying flesh, now there were only straight, healthy fingers, knuckles perfectly normal.

A great "Oh!" swept through the crowd as the leper slowly lowered his hands, holding them out in front of him to stare at them. What he saw was astonishing to him. What everyone else saw was far more than that. His face was pink and unmarred, the flesh as whole as the day he had been born. Slowly his head raised, and he looked up at the Master. Tears sprang unbidden to his eyes and trickled down his cheeks. Now it was his hands that reached out. He grasped the hands of Jesus and clung to them as though he were going to fall off a precipice.

Jesus smiled at him. "Don't feel as though you must go and tell everyone about this," he said quietly. "Tell no man. Go and show yourself to the priest as Moses commanded. Offer a gift of thanksgiving to God. That will be testimony enough."

"Yes, Master!" It came out as an exclamation of joy. Then the man let go of Jesus' hands and threw his arms around his legs. He dropped his head and kissed the top of Jesus' sandals. "Praise be to God," he cried through his tears. "Thank you, Lord."

III

About midday Jesus stopped at the home of Andrew and went inside, probably to take a meal. But the crowds would not leave them alone. Some went in with them, while the rest pressed in around the open door, trying to hear every word he might speak. Seeing there was no way to get inside, David and Leah moved away a short distance, found a shady spot beneath a pomegranate tree, and sat down to wait for them to come out again.

David waited until Leah was settled, then smiled softly. "Well, what do you think now of this Jesus of Nazareth?"

A storm stilled with a word. A leper cleansed with a single touch. Leah's mind could barely take it all in. Finally, she realized that she hadn't spoken aloud. She smiled at him fully now, her heart feeling as if it was going to burst with joy. "Andrew said it best. 'What manner of man is this?' How can he not be the Messiah, Father? I know now why you believe as you do."

The joy that shot through him at her words almost took his breath away. "Then you believe he is the promised Christ?"

"Yes!" She laughed then, surprised at both her lack of hesitation and her enthusiastic response. "I do, Papa. It's not just the miracles. It's—" She shook her head, frustrated that she couldn't think of the right word. "There is so much power in him. Just being around him you can feel that. I've never met anyone like him before."

"Nor have I." He was deeply pleased. At last here was someone in the family who was feeling what he was feeling, seeing what he was seeing. Suddenly he wanted to share with her his experience in Bethlehem. Speaking slowly at first he went through the whole account again, just as he had done with Simeon.

To his surprise, when he finished, Leah was crying. "What a wonderful story, Papa. Why didn't you ever tell me that before?"

"I used to tell everyone. But then—" His eyes dropped. "I—I don't talk about it much anymore."

"Have you asked Jesus if he was born in Bethlehem?"

He shook his head. "I don't know if that would be appropriate. Perhaps when the time is right."

"What did Simeon say when you told him?"

"He was impressed. Moved."

"But not convinced," she said sadly.

"Well, I don't think he doubts what I told him. He just doesn't think there is any connection to Jesus."

"Why won't he even come and see, Papa?"

His head dropped slightly and pain pulled around the corners of his mouth. "Sometimes things happen in our lives of such terrible consequence that it is like lightning striking a great tree. Even though it goes on living, deep inside it is scarred and burned. What happened to your mother when she was just your age was so dreadful, so unbelievably horrible, that it has left one corner of her filled with memories that she can never erase from her mind. That she is the warm and wonderful mother and grandmother—and wife—that she is, is astonishing under the circumstances. It shows just how strong she really is inside."

"I know. I hurt for Mama when I think of what she went through, but why is Simeon so bitter? I mean, I know about that day in the courtyard. It was terrible. I still have nightmares about it. But I'm not filled with hate like he is."

David was surprised at this maturity in his daughter. These were questions he had wrestled with many times. He had no idea that she had them as well. "Well," he began, looking for the right way to express it, "as you know there is a special bond between Simeon and your mother. It is like their spirits are closer, more in harmony with one another than is normal, even between a mother and child."

Leah nodded. "You and I have that too, don't we, Papa."

He smiled and touched her hand. "Yes, we do. Because of that special closeness, Simeon's pain and anger is really an extension of your mother's pain and anger."

She was nodding slowly, starting to understand. "He told me once what was the most terrible part of that whole experience last fall."

David's eyes widened a little. "He did? What?"

"He was still conscious when the soldiers tied mother and me up and dragged us out. He tried to get up and stop them, but he was too weak. He couldn't move. He just had to watch us be taken away. He thought he would never see us again."

David was nodding slowly. "He never told me that." That explained much. "And so even though I was able to free you, that didn't change the other. The wound Sextus gave him was not the greatest damage that was done."

"Sextus?" she asked in surprise.

David looked at her, sorry that he had slipped. "Yes. Sextus Rubrius. That is the name of the centurion who struck him down that day."

"You know him?"

He sighed. "We had business dealings before all of this happened. We had become friends. He is a good man, Leah. A decent and honorable man. Did you know he gave money to build the synagogue here?"

This was a day for stunning revelations, she decided. "Does Simeon know that?"

He shook his head quickly. "No. My association with him is done now. There's no need." He turned and looked toward the crowd gathered around Andrew's house and decided to change the subject. "Leah?"

"Yes, Papa?"

David's eyes grew thoughtful. "When your mother returns from Beth Neelah, will you tell her about today? And Simeon too?"

"Of course, Papa. I want to tell everyone. It's like I'm on fire inside me, Papa. I've never been so happy. I can hardly wait to talk to Shana too."

He laughed in pure happiness. "Oh, Leah, I am so pleased you were here today. This is wonderful. If I try to talk to them . . . " He shrugged. "Well, you've seen what happens. But coming from you. Yes, that's the answer."

"I'm not sure Simeon will listen."

"He will listen. He is angry right now, but your brother is fair-minded, and he has a good sense of what is truth and what is not." He stopped, his eye drawn by a movement near the house.

Leah turned to look too. Four men came forward slowly, staggering under the load of a litter they carried. A fifth man lay upon the bed. The litter was really not much more than a straw mattress laid on some fish netting stretched between two long poles. Ropes were attached to each of the four corners of this makeshift stretcher; the four carriers had placed the ropes over their shoulders to help them carry the weight. They were moving around the perimeter of the crowd, trying to find a way through to the door.

"Let us through," one of the men cried. "Make way."

A few on the outskirts of the throng turned to look at them, but there was no way that a pathway large enough for the five of them to get through was going to open up.

"Please!" another of the men cried. "Let us through to see the Master."

Leah's father got to his feet, and she quickly joined him. They could see that the man on the litter was seriously stricken. His face was thin, almost gaunt. One arm laid feebly across his chest, the other flopped loosely over the side. As the men carrying him tried to push their way in, he started to lift his head to see what was happening, but he got it no more than an inch or two off the litter before it dropped back again. His eyes closed, and he uttered a low moan.

"I know this man," David said. "He has the palsy. I had heard that he had been stricken. It started with a severe headache and a burning fever, then he completely lost the use of his limbs." He began to move forward as he spoke, and Leah fell in beside him. "He is very ill. I am surprised they would bring him out at all."

The men with the litter had completely circled the throng and found no one willing to make way for them.

"I'm going to help," David said, starting across the street toward the house. But even as he did so, one of those accompanying the litter turned and pointed. Like almost every other house in the Galilee, Andrew's house had a set of stone steps on one of the outside walls that led up to the roof. With access to the roof from outside as well as inside the house, visitors did not have to go into the house in order to get to the flat roof, which served as patio and courtyard for many homes.

Moving swiftly, the four men carried the stretcher to the stairway. The steps were narrow, and the two men on each end of the litter had to move shoulder to shoulder to negotiate it, but in a moment they were on top of the house. Seeing that he could be of no help now, David stopped. He and Leah backed up so as to see better what was happening on top of the house.

Once on top, the men moved quickly across the roof, then set the litter down. One of the men bent down and opened a trapdoor.

"They'll never get that litter through the opening," David said. "I've been in Andrew's house. The door to the roof is too narrow."

He was right. The men lifted the litter again and maneuvered around the opening for several moments. They were clearly frustrated. Again they set the litter down. Now all four of them dropped to their knees around the opening. Then to Leah's and David's amazement, they heard the dull clunk of tile on tile.

"What are they doing?"

David was gaping, not sure he was seeing right. "They're removing the tiles to enlarge the opening."

He grabbed Leah's hand. "Come on."

Pulling Leah with him, he ran the last few steps to the house and then went up the stairs. As they stepped onto the roof, the four men were just picking up the litter again, this time holding the ends of the long poles instead of the ropes. To one side they saw a stack of tiles and some loose boards. What had a few minutes before been an opening wide enough to accommodate only one person at a time was now three times its original size. That, of course, didn't change the width of the stairs going down into the house, and for a moment the men were again perplexed. But they had come this far, and they were not to be denied. One spoke to the others, and they set down the litter again; then each took one of the four ropes and lifted the litter enough that it swung free. Staggering under the weight, they shuffled forward, straddling the opening in the roof.

"They're going to lower him down," Leah said.

Without waiting for David, she moved forward to see better. David fell in behind her. As they reached the opening, the men began to lower the litter, hand over hand, down into the house, using the ropes attached to the poles.

Because the sun was at its zenith, its rays streamed directly downward, illuminating the inside of Andrew's simple home. David instantly began to pick out faces. There was Peter, standing, his face a study in astonishment. Andrew sat at a table, his mouth half open as he looked up at what was happening. Jesus sat beside him. James and John were across the table. They were all staring upwards in complete surprise, but David saw that Jesus was laughing softly. He seemed to be the first to realize what the men were doing.

Hands reached out and caught the stretcher, then lowered it to the floor. Loosing the ropes, the four men went quickly down the stairs into the crowded room.

Now others had followed David and Leah up onto the roof and were crowding around to see better. Then Leah forgot about them as she turned and peered down into the house.

"We are very sorry," one of the four men was saying to Andrew. "We tried to get in through the door. The people wouldn't let us through." He turned and looked at Jesus. "Our friend is sick with the palsy, Master. Can you do anything for him?"

Jesus began to nod slowly. He looked up again, as though measuring the enlarged hole and all that it represented. Then he stood up and moved over to stand beside the litter. The palsied man's eyes were open. One hand fluttered pitifully as he tried to reach out and implore for help.

"Son," Jesus said in a firm voice, "thy sins be forgiven thee."

David heard a gasp at his elbow. He turned. One of the men beside him was staring down in horror. "Blasphemy!" he hissed to his associates. "Who can forgive sins, but God only?"

He spoke in a loud whisper, and with the noise of the crowd David had heard it only because the man stood beside him. But down below, Jesus turned and looked up. Had he heard the man? David couldn't believe he had. The crowd outside was shouting, trying to learn what was going on. More people were coming onto the roof and running over to try to see what was happening.

The man who had spoken glared down but said nothing more.

Standing beside her father, Leah saw that Jesus' eyes narrowed slightly. He glanced up once more, but then spoke to those around him. "Why reason you thus in your hearts?" he said. "Which is easier? To say to this man with the palsy that his sins are forgiven, or to tell him to arise and take up his bed and walk?"

David looked at his daughter as the crowd began to whisper to each other. David said nothing, but the thought that flashed into his mind was this: To actually forgive a man's sins was something only God could do. That was true. But anyone could say, "Your sins are forgiven." Who was to say whether they were or were not? But to tell a crippled man to arise? In one instant, those watching would know whether something had happened or not.

Before he could finish that line of thinking, Jesus spoke again. "But so that all of you may know that the Son of Man has been given power on this earth to forgive sins—" He turned and looked down at the paralyzed man who lay at his feet. "I say unto you, Arise! Take up your bed. Go your way. Return to your own house."

Though David was aware of the noise of the throng below them on the street, here on the roof and down in the house no one spoke. No one moved. It was almost as if no one even breathed. Every eye stared at the gaunt figure on the makeshift litter. For what seemed like a full minute (though it probably was only a moment or two), it was as if everything had been frozen in place.

Then a woman gasped. A great cry exploded from those close enough to see. The man on the litter reached out his hands and grasped the two poles firmly. In one swift move he sat up.

"Praise be!" a woman exclaimed. Those nearest the man fell back, gaping at what they were seeing. One of the four men who had carried his companion to this place dropped to his knees, reaching out to steady the man. He waved him off. And in one more quick jerk, the man was on his feet.

David felt Leah's fingers dig into his arm, but he could not take his eyes off the scene below. The man who just moments before could barely lift his head from off the bed stood before Jesus. His eyes were wide. Slowly he reached down and touched his legs, rubbing them back and forth, not in pain but in wonder.

He looked at Jesus, who smiled at him, then nodded his encouragement. The man dropped to his knees and folded up the bed. "Thank you, Lord," he said as he straightened again. He turned to his companions. "Let's go home."

As they started for the door, a roar went up. David grabbed Leah's hand and moved swiftly over to the edge of the roof above the front door of the house. As they looked down, they saw the crowd finally begin to fall back. In a moment the man with his bed stepped outside. He blinked at the brightness of the light; then, with a cry of exultation, he lifted the poles and the rolled-up litter high above his head and shook them triumphantly to the crowd.

For several seconds Leah did not move. It was as if her heart had stopped once again. Then she pulled away from her father's grasp. "I'm going to get Simeon and Ephraim here even if I have to drag them," she said. She spun away and ran down the stairs that she and her father had climbed just minutes before.

CHAPTER NOTES

The word that is translated as *palsy* in the King James Version of the Bible is the Greek *paralouomai* (par-a-LOO-oh-mai), which means to be paralytic or paralyzed (see Hastings, p. 599; Fallows 3:1282). It is used several times in the New Testament and may refer to different types of illnesses or debilitations caused by disease or injury to the brain or spinal cord. Hastings supposes this particular case might have been something similar to spinal meningitis.

CHAPTER 18

MEN WILLINGLY BELIEVE WHAT THEY WISH.

—Julius Caesar, De Bello Gallico, *iii.18*

I
18 MAY, A.D. 30

"You are so stubborn, Simeon."

"Leah, look." He stopped, searching for the right words.

"Simeon!" she cried. "Listen to me! I saw a paralytic raised from his bed. I saw a leper cleansed in one instant. Why won't you believe me? This isn't hearsay. I saw this with my own eyes."

Ephraim broke in. "Hesitate all you want, Simeon," he said, "but as for me, I'm going to get Rachel. What Leah has just told us is—well, it's incredible. If it were anyone but Leah, I wouldn't believe it. I have to see this for myself." He looked at his sister. "Rachel and I didn't say much the other day, but except for what Jesus said about the Romans, we liked what he taught. It was so reasonable." He glanced quickly at Simeon. "And it felt right." Then back to Leah he said, "We'll have to ask someone to watch Esther and Boaz. Where will we find him?"

"They were at Andrew's house when I left. If they're not there, just look for the crowds. There are hundreds of people following after him now."

He nodded, shot Simeon one more disbelieving look, and went out the door. Leah turned back to the brother who was next to her in age.

"Tell me again," he said, forestalling what he knew was coming. "You said when you first saw the man on the stretcher he was across the street from you. Are you sure he was paralyzed?"

"No, I'm not absolutely sure, Simeon," she retorted. "I was a full twenty feet away. It would be easy to make a mistake at twenty feet."

"Sorry, I was just—"

"And when Papa and I were on the roof looking down into the house, we were at least five or six feet away. Maybe we just thought the man got to his feet and rolled up his bed and carried it outside."

"All right, Leah," he said, regretting his mistake.

"No, Simeon," she said hotly. "How can you sit there and try to explain away what I saw? Maybe it was just globs of dirt on that leper's hands and face, which I mistook for sores. And somehow, while a hundred of us were all watching, Jesus magically rubbed the dirt off his face and hands without any of us seeing it. I should have thought of that. He's just a magician working clever tricks. I'm so glad you helped me understand."

He got to his feet and took her by the shoulders and shook her gently. "All right, I'm sorry. I do believe you."

"Then why won't you come?" she pleaded. "Please, Simeon. Come and see."

He was surprised at the fire in her. He had never seen her like this. Like their father, Leah was always the one for moderation. She was the peacemaker in the family. But now she was coming after him like an angry bull. And then a thought came, and he had his answer.

"Leah, who is my favorite prophet?"

She stopped in the middle of another attempt to change his mind. "What?"

"Remember when we used to play at being the kings and queens and prophets when we were children? Who was always my favorite?"

She thought for a moment, remembering, and a smile came without her being aware of it. As children she and Simeon had spent many hours reenacting the scriptural stories, taking on the roles of their favorite people. Leah had always chosen to be one of two women—Queen Esther, who saved her people from annihilation by the Persian king, or the prophetess Deborah, her mother's namesake. Deborah had raised an army and overthrown the hosts of Sisera, chief captain of the king of Hazor. Simeon, on the other hand, often picked a hero who was famous for his success in battle—Joshua, King David, Jonathan. But the one he chose most frequently was not a general at all, but a prophet. "Elisha," she said finally.

"Yes. Do you remember why?"

She started to shake her head, then stopped. "Because he had such faith."

"Yes." Now he leaned forward. "And how do we know he had strong faith?"

"Because of all the—" She stopped, her eyes widening.

"Go ahead," he urged, pleased that she had seen it.

"Because of all the miracles he worked."

"Exactly. After the mantle of Elijah fell on Elisha, Elisha worked one miracle after another. He smote the waters of the Jordan, and they parted for him. He cast salt into the bitter spring at Jericho—salt, of all things!—and turned the waters sweet as honey. He multiplied a cruse of oil for a widow, caused an ax to float on water, raised a young man from the dead."

He stopped and leaned forward, emphasizing his most telling point. "He cured Naaman the Syrian of leprosy."

Leah was on the defensive now, seeing exactly where Simeon was going with this. "Not by touching him!" she said, but it came out lamely.

"No, he had him wash seven times in the Jordan, but Naaman was cured." Now he looked triumphant. "There is no question but what Elisha was one of the greatest of the prophets." There was a long pause.

"But was he the Messiah? No. So maybe this Jesus is a great prophet and—"

She leaped on that. "*Maybe?*" she cried. "Are you trying to tell me that a madman or an imposter could do what he is doing?"

"All right, let's say that Jesus *is* a prophet. If what you say is true—" He stopped at her sharp look. "I'm sorry. Knowing that what you say is true, then I'd have to agree that he is a great prophet. But that doesn't make him the Messiah, Leah. That's what bothers me. You and Papa are so sure he is the Promised One, but he doesn't fit what the prophets have told us about the Messiah. I'm sorry, but I just can't believe he is the one we have been waiting for."

"You mean you won't believe," she said sadly.

He threw up his hands. "Can't? Won't? What's the difference? Don't try to trap me with words, Leah."

Gentle of nature or not, Leah had not grown up with two older brothers without learning how to stand her ground. "Jesus works miracles as easily as Simon Peter and Andrew pull fish from the sea, Simeon," she said quietly. "If you knew it was an Elisha who had come among us, would you still refuse to go hear him?"

She had him, and they both knew it. He looked away. "I'm right in the middle of tallying the books. When I finish I'll come and see what is happening."

Suddenly her face was filled with wonder. She stepped back, her eyes wide. "You're afraid to come."

"Don't be foolish."

"No," she said, slowly nodding now. "That's it, isn't it? If you come and listen to him and see the things he does, you just might be convinced that he is all that Papa and I say he is."

"I said I'll come in a little while," he retorted, irked now.

"Be careful, Simeon," she said softly. "If you come, you may have no choice but to believe. And then what will you do? You might even have to change the way you feel."

II

Leah found her father not far from where she had left him. Along with the rest of the crowd, he was again waiting in the street. Jesus was inside one of the homes. She reported quickly, and with obvious disappointment, about her conversation with Simeon.

Her father didn't seem too surprised. "He has to make his own choices, Leah. There's nothing we can do but invite him."

"But why is he being this way? Ephraim believed me." She looked around. "In fact, he said he was going to get Rachel and come. You've not seen them?"

"No." His eyes were wistful now. "I so wish your mother was here. Why did she have to be gone at this time of all times?"

"I don't know," Leah answered, "but I will tell her everything, Papa. I can hardly wait."

"She may be like Simeon, Leah." And then he remembered Deborah's words before they had gone to hear Jesus teach on the hillside a few days before. "Don't get your hopes too high."

Before she could answer, someone called out. They both turned to see Ephraim and Rachel coming toward them at a swift walk.

"Over here." Leah waved, then looked at her father, very pleased. "I was hoping Rachel would come. She'll believe all of this."

David only nodded, not as confident as his daughter.

As they came up, David reached out and shook Ephraim's hand; then he gave Rachel a hug. "Where are Esther and Boaz?" he asked.

"With my mother," Rachel answered. "We tried to leave them with a neighbor, but Esther wouldn't hear of it, even though she knows them well. That's what took us so long."

"I'm so glad you've come."

Ephraim looked around at the milling crowd. The streets were full, but everyone seemed to be standing around waiting. "So where is Jesus?" he asked his father.

David pointed. Across the street from where they stood was a large stone house with a courtyard behind a stone wall. "He's in there."

Ephraim's mouth dropped. "In the customshouse?"

David nodded.

"Surely he is not paying tribute. What taxes would he owe?"

David smiled quietly. "I don't think he's paying taxes or customs."

Now Rachel moved up to stand beside her husband. "Isn't this the house of Matthew Levi the publican?"

"It is," David said, suspecting what was coming next.

That even took Leah aback. "He's with a publican?"

"Yes." David smiled briefly. "Ironic, isn't it. First he forgives a man of his sins. Now he has gone into the home of what most people consider to be one of the vilest of sinners."

"Not just a sinner," Ephraim said darkly, "but a traitor as well."

The acrimony in his son's voice neither surprised nor disturbed David. It was a feeling widely held among their people. In the Roman system, *publicani*, or publicans, usually Romans of wealth and power, bid for the right to collect taxes in the various provinces. To be a *publicani* was a highly lucrative position, because whatever a person could raise above the flat assessment levied by the emperor was his to keep. Vast fortunes had been made through this system, and Rome encouraged it because it brought in the state's revenues with a minimum of effort. The fact that the system encouraged graft, extortion, and corruption made little difference to them.

Within the provinces the *publicani* would contract with local tax collectors, also called publicans, who would see to it that the taxes in each area were collected and sent on up the line. These local publicans were paid on the same basis—a flat-fee assessment—and as with their masters, they too often extorted the people for as much as they could. Hatred for the publicans was common throughout the empire, but in the province of Judea bitterness ran especially deep because not only did they rob the people, but they were seen as directly aiding in the support of a pagan regime. The depths of those feelings were best illustrated by the fact that the scribes had legally classed the publicans with harlots, heathens, and highwaymen. Their testimony was not acceptable in the courts, and their contributions to the temple or the synagogue could be refused, though often they were not. The scribes even went so far as to declare it lawful to falsify statements of assets, swear falsely, or use almost any other means to avoid paying taxes.

"Matthew is not like some publicans," David said to Ephraim. "You know that. He's always been fair with us." He frowned. "If it had been Matthew making that assessment last fall instead of Absalom, that whole thing with the Romans would never have happened."

"That may be true," Ephraim said, "but still, Father, surely Jesus knows better than to consort with a publican."

Leah said nothing but watched this exchange closely. She, too, had been shaken to learn that Jesus was in the house of one of the publicans. Then a strange thought came into her mind. How was it that her father seemed to know these various outcasts? He was friends with a Roman centurion. He defended a publican. What else was there she didn't know about him?

"Be careful, Ephraim," her father was saying. "Remember the lesson that the prophet Samuel was taught when he was sent to the house of Jesse to choose a successor to King Saul."

Ephraim was still staring at the house across the street, but Rachel had snapped around at that. When Ephraim didn't respond, she gently nudged him.

He turned. "What lesson?" he asked, his mind only half focusing on his father.

David had seen the look on his daughter-in-law's face and saw that she understood. "You tell him, Rachel."

She began to quote softly to her husband. "'And the Lord said unto Samuel, Look not on his countenance, or on the height of his stature; because I have refused him; for the Lord seeth not as man seeth. For man looketh on the outward appearance, but the Lord looketh on the heart.'"

Now Ephraim was listening, and Rachel saw the impact of the words on him. "That is one of my favorite scriptures," she said.

David spoke slowly now. "The world would define what a man or woman is by what they do, what they wear, where they live, how they make a living. God, on the other hand, says that it is what is in the heart that determines what we really are. And I can tell you this: Matthew Levi—publican or not—has a good heart, and blessed be God for that. We desperately need some tax collectors who have some integrity."

Leah's eyes were shining suddenly, and when she went to speak, her voice caught. She swallowed quickly, then took a breath. On impulse, she went up on her toes and kissed her father on the cheek.

His eyebrows shot up. "What was that for?"

"Because I like your heart too, Papa."

They said nothing more. Ephraim and Rachel talked quietly off to one side, and while she couldn't hear what they were saying, Leah was pleased to see that, unlike Simeon, her oldest brother was still open to considering the words of their father.

That was tested further, however, when ten minutes later Jesus finally reappeared. As Jesus came out of the house, Matthew was part of the circle of disciples who followed immediately after him. That sent a murmur of disapproval through the assembled crowd. At the first opportunity, David left his family and moved up beside John. They whispered together for a minute; then David fell back again.

"What?" Ephraim asked as soon as he had rejoined them. "What were you asking?"

David paused for only a moment, then spoke firmly. "Jesus has called Matthew to be one of his disciples."

"Just like that?" Ephraim said, clearly disappointed.

David nodded, looking suddenly a little depressed.

"What, Papa?" Leah asked. "I thought you were just telling us not to judge others on outward things."

He looked surprised. "That's not what is bothering me. I think it's wonderful that Matthew has been called."

"Then what?" Rachel asked.

"It's just interesting who he has called to follow after him. Andrew and Peter. James and John. Philip. Nathanael. Bartholomew. James the son of Alphaeus. Every one different from the other. He's called fishermen. He's called a Zealot. Now he's called a publican."

"A Zealot?" Ephraim exclaimed.

"Yes. He called a man named Simon a few days ago. He's not from Capernaum, so you probably don't know him. But he is a follower of the Zealot way."

"Does Simeon know that?" Leah asked.

"No." David sighed. "Whatever it is they were doing before, each of these men has now been called to follow Jesus and become fishers of men."

"Is there anything wrong with that?" Rachel asked, still sensing that something was bothering her father-in-law but not sure what.

He shook his head. "No."

But Leah now understood. *Maybe he'll call a merchant next, Papa.* She almost said it aloud, then decided it would only embarrass him. She slipped an arm through his and pressed against his shoulder, loving him more at that moment than she had in her entire lifetime.

III

Simeon saw the crowd while he was still a full block away. He slowed his step, picturing Leah's reaction when she saw him. It wasn't something he relished, particularly if there were others nearby. Deciding he would stay on the periphery of the crowd, then tell his family later that he had come, he slowed his step and moved closer to the buildings. He was not trying to hide, just be as unobtrusive as possible.

As he joined the crowd, he quickly realized that there was no way he was going to get close enough to Jesus to hear them. Fine. At least he had tried.

He fell in behind a group of rabbinical students from the *yeshiva* that was held in the main synagogue. They were in a state of high agitation, talking about forgiveness of sins and consorting with publicans. Simeon tried to make sense of it, but he caught only snatches of their conversation and quickly moved off. These young men reminded him too much of his Uncle Aaron when he was younger.

"Let me through. I need to get through."

Simeon turned. Without meaning to, he had worked his way about four or five deep into the throng now. Behind him, just coming up on the crowd, a man was calling out and trying to push his way into the crowd.

Simeon started to look away, then went cold. Like himself, the man was clean-shaven and wore his hair, which was peppered with gray, cropped close to his head. At first Simeon saw only the man's face in profile, but then he turned, calling out to the crowd again. It was as if someone had shoved a fiery javelin between Simeon's ribs. He gasped, his eyes gaping at the man before him. It was Sextus Rubrius, the Roman centurion.

The people surged in around the man, and Simeon lost sight of him. He shook his head, dazed. Perhaps he had been mistaken. Surely a Roman soldier would not venture alone into a crowd of Jews, especially here in the Galilee. Without conscious thought, Simeon pushed forward, shoving people aside, straining to see the man again.

And then Simeon was just a few feet behind the man. He was still shouting, his voice rough and commanding, and people were making way for him. Now Simeon had a clear view of his back. There was no question. This was the Roman. He was not in his uniform or armor, but neither had he tried to disguise himself as a Jew. He wore the short skirt favored by the Roman working class and a leather vest fastened with metal hooks around a cotton tunic. He wore a belt but no scabbard, either for dagger or sword.

Simeon's stomach twisted sharply. So it was true. His attacker was back in Capernaum. People cried out or muttered angrily at Simeon as he pushed hard to keep up with the man. His fists were clenching and unclenching spasmodically, and there was a sudden bead of perspiration on his upper lip. With a start he realized that he too was unarmed. That brought him back to rationality. His statement to his parents that he no longer cared about the centurion, only the Roman tribune, was now completely forgotten. The desire for revenge was like a roaring furnace.

Then rationality partially returned. What was he going to do if he caught up with him? Still breathing hard, Simeon slowed his step, falling back a little to give himself some time to think.

Others around them now realized who was calling out for them to move aside. "He's a Roman!" someone cried. "It's a soldier. Watch out." A woman turned and saw him and grabbed her child, a look of horror on her face. Rubrius paid them no mind. He clearly had an objective, and nothing was going to deflect him.

They rounded a corner and entered a wide plaza near the main well of Capernaum. The crowd spread out as they poured into the open space. Simeon pulled up short when he saw the centurion stop. He seemed hesitant all of a sudden and looked around, his head sweeping back and forth as he searched the crowd. Cautious now, Simeon moved in until he was no more than two or three feet off to one side and behind him.

Simeon tensed. The centurion had seen something. He went up

on the balls of his feet, waving an arm back and forth. "David!" he called. "David ben Joseph."

Rocking back, his jaw going slack, Simeon now saw the man to whom the soldier was waving.

IV

David ben Joseph drew in his breath quickly when he saw who was shouting and waving at him.

"Who is it, Papa?" Leah asked.

Everyone around them was turning. Just ahead of them, Jesus and the disciples had also stopped and were turning around.

"Excuse me," David said, grim-faced. He started away, moving toward the shouting man.

And then Leah went rigid. The crowd was moving back, making a path for the two men, and she had a clear view of the older man, who was coming toward her father. She had last seen that face some six months before in the courtyard of their home.

Her hand shot out, and she clutched at Ephraim's arm. "It's the centurion," she whispered.

"The centurion?" he said dumbly, not comprehending.

"Yes! The one who attacked Simeon."

One hand flew up to Rachel's mouth. "No!" she said.

"We've got to stop him," Ephraim cried, lunging forward.

Leah wasn't sure if by "him" he meant their father or the centurion, but she leaped after him and dragged him to a stop. "No, Ephraim. It's all right. Father knows him. Come on, I want to hear."

David came to a stop a few feet from Sextus, his eyes fixed on the Roman's face, hardly believing what was happening, remembering with cold dread the promise he had made to Deborah just a few days before. "*Shalom*, David," Sextus said, greatly relieved.

"And peace to you, Sextus Rubrius," he said gravely.

Suddenly the hardened veteran was fumbling awkwardly for words. "I—I heard that your son is all right now."

"Yes. Thank you. He's fully recovered."

"I am most pleased to hear that."

"I understand. Thank you."

Around them the people were moving in closer, muttering and whispering darkly. David ben Joseph, one of Capernaum's most influential citizens, was speaking with a Roman officer? David was vaguely aware of his children coming up behind him, but his eyes never left Sextus' face.

"Do you know the man they call Jesus of Nazareth?" Sextus said abruptly.

David reared back a little. "I have heard him preach." Then he was suddenly wary. "What of him?"

"I need to find him," the Roman said, anxiety noticeably raising his voice in pitch. "Is it true that he heals the sick?"

"Yes. That is true."

"My servant," he started. "You know him, I think. Jepthah, son of Abraham?"

"Yes, I do know him."

"He is very sick, nigh unto death. I thought—" His eyes dropped. "I know I am not one of your people, but when I heard that Jesus heals, I wondered if . . . " He couldn't finish.

"He's *goyim!*" someone hissed just behind them. "Jesus won't speak to him."

There was a tiny tic near the corner of one eye, but other than that it was as though Sextus had not heard. "Would you speak to Jesus for me, David? It is not for me that I ask. It is for Jepthah. And he is one of your people."

The pleading in his voice pierced through any last hesitation David had. "Yes, of course. Come with me."

Sextus fell back a step. "No, just—"

David shook his head. "Come. It's all right."

As the Roman fell into step behind her father, Leah was struck with an image from earlier in the day. The sight of a leper had sent a wave of revulsion through the crowd. Now Sextus Rubrius was creating a similar reaction, only this time there was open hostility amidst the disgust. Strangely, she felt a sudden burst of pride when she saw that her father did not respond to it one way or the other. The two men seemed deaf and blind to the muttered calls, the shaken fists, the twisted faces as they approached the place where Jesus and the others stood watching what was transpiring.

David went straight to Jesus. Again, as with the leper, Jesus did not seem either surprised or upset that David brought with him a Roman soldier. There was a look of interest, almost curiosity, mixed with the wonderful calmness that he always seemed to wear. To Leah's surprise, it was Jesus who spoke first. "*Shalom,* David ben Joseph, merchant of Capernaum. Peace to you."

David was taken aback that Jesus had called him by name. "And to you, Master," he said, stammering a little. He turned. "Rabbi, this is—" There was a moment's hesitation; then he straightened. "This is a friend. His name is Sextus Rubrius."

"*Shalom,* Sextus Rubrius," Jesus said pleasantly.

"Peace unto you, sire," Sextus answered in excellent Aramaic.

"Master," David went on, hurrying now. "Though this man is a Gentile and a Roman soldier, I would speak in his behalf. He is a friend to our people. He loves our nation and has even helped us build a synagogue."

At that Leah turned around and looked at Ephraim. Had he known that? Ephraim shook his head quickly.

Jesus nodded and looked at Sextus again. "What would you have of me?"

The centurion's face fell, his mouth twisting with concern. "Sire, I have a servant at home. One of your own people. He lies sick and is grievously tormented."

There was a brief pause, then, "I see. Then I will come and heal him."

An audible gasp exploded from the crowd. Jesus had said it as simply as if he had just been invited into the synagogue and not into the house of a Gentile, and a Roman soldier at that.

Sextus Rubrius was as shocked as the crowd. "Sire," he stammered, "I—Lord, I know your customs. I am not worthy that you should come under my roof."

Jesus said nothing, but one eyebrow lifted in question, as if to say, "Do you think that is my custom?"

Rubrius hurried on. "I am a man used to being under authority, sire. I also have men under my command. If I say to this man, go, he goes. If I say to another, come, he comes. When I tell my servant to do something, he does it." Now he straightened and looked Jesus directly in the eye. "Sire, if you speak the word only, my servant will be healed."

Now it was Jesus who seemed surprised. For a long moment he stared at Sextus, searching his face. Then he turned to Peter and Andrew and the others standing with them. "I marvel at what I have heard. I have not found this kind of faith in Israel."

Ignoring the astounded looks on their faces, he turned to speak to the crowd. "I say unto you who have witnessed this man's faith, many who are not of Israel shall come from the east and the west and shall sit down with Abraham, Isaac, and Jacob in the kingdom of heaven, but the children of the kingdom shall be cast out into outer darkness."

"What!" someone shouted. "Are you saying that the Gentiles—"

"And there," Jesus went on calmly, "those who think they are the children of the kingdom shall weep and wail and gnash their teeth because of what they have lost."

Then before anyone could say anything more, he turned to the centurion. "Go your way, friend. Because you have believed, it shall be done unto you as you have said."

Sextus, his eyes wide with gratitude, stepped back. His arm came up sharply, and he slapped his chest in the traditional Roman salute. Then he bowed his head slightly. "Thank you, sire. Peace be upon you and upon your house."

"And to you as well," Jesus said quietly. "Go in peace."

As he started to turn, the soldier's eyes caught David's. He gave the barest of nods, a fleeting smile, and then he was gone.

V

Two full blocks away, Simeon walked aimlessly, half in a stupor, his mind numbed and sluggish. Words rang out hollow and flat in his mind, over and over as though they were being struck from a blacksmith's hammer. "*Shalom*, Sextus." "*Shalom*, David." "I have heard that your son is recovered. How pleased I am to know that I did not kill him." "Yes, thank you for your tender concern. I am so relieved that your sword did not cut him in two."

He kicked viciously at a small rock, sending it skittering away. He was grateful now that he had reacted so quickly. The moment he saw his father start to turn and recognized who it was, he had ducked down behind the people and brought his hood up to cover his face. He had stayed hunched over, close enough to hear but not showing himself.

His lips clamped in tight compression as the words came slamming in again. "Jesus, this is Sextus Rubrius. He is my *friend*. This is the man who nearly killed my son, but he is my friend, my brother. Would you be so kind as to help him?"

Now he wished he had waited to hear how this self-proclaimed Messiah had answered that. Would he too embrace the Roman dog with open arms? Perhaps he would launch into another call for love and brotherhood, for turning the other cheek, and praying for those who threatened to destroy everything that was sacred. But he hadn't waited. When his father had called the centurion his friend, Simeon had turned and plunged away.

Did his mother know any of this? Was she part of this conspiracy of friendship that everyone seemed to know about but him? Then he shook his head. It couldn't be. Not his mother. But there was no question about the rest of his family. Leah had stood there looking at the man who had nearly sold her into slavery as if she was ready to invite him back into their home for supper. And while Ephraim had looked shocked at what was going on, why hadn't he done something? Why hadn't he hurled himself at the throat of this man? Had he forgotten what happened to Roman slaves? Couldn't he picture his mother in some stable, cleaning up after the cattle, her hands blistered and her fingernails black? Didn't he know what would happen to a girl as lovely and innocent as Leah? She would become the whore of some Roman dandy. Why weren't his brother and his father beating at that man with their fists instead of smiling and nodding and leading him to Jesus?

His breath exploded from him, as though he had just been struck again by the sword of Sextus Rubrius. He threw his head back. "You would have me believe that your Jesus is the Messiah?" he cried in an agonized whisper. "No, Father! How can I believe a man I can no longer trust?"

Chapter Notes

Because the Jews hated the Romans so deeply, those people of their own nation who served the Roman government as publicans, or tax collectors, were bitterly resented and held in the greatest contempt (see Edersheim, *Sketches*, pp. 55–57).

There are two accounts of the healing of the centurion's servant (see Matthew 8:5–13; Luke 7:1–10). It is Luke who tells us that some of the Jewish leaders spoke in behalf of the centurion, indicating his friendship toward the Jewish people.

In both Matthew's and Mark's list of the Twelve Apostles chosen by Jesus, there is one who is called Simon *the Canaanite* (Matthew 10:4; Mark 3:18). At first this seems odd, because in normal usage a Canaanite was one of the Old Testament peoples who inhabited the Holy Land before the people of Israel conquered it. But Luke identifies him as Simon *called Zelotes* (Luke 6:15; emphasis added). In Hebrew the word that means "zealous" is *kahna*, and one who is zealous would be *kahna'im*. In Greek the word is *zelotes*. Thus most scholars agree that the better rendering of Simon's title should be *Kahna'im* instead of Canaanite, meaning "Simon the Zealot," or "the zealous one." Since the Galilee was the heart of the Zealot movement, it is most likely that this member of the Twelve Apostles had been a follower of the Zealot movement before his call (see for example, Dummelow, p. 661; Guthrie, p. 898).

CHAPTER 19

ANGER IS BRIEF MADNESS AND, UNCHECKED, BECOMES
PROTRACTED MADNESS, BRINGING SHAME AND EVEN DEATH.

—*Petrarch*, Sonetti sopra Veri Argomenti, *XIX*

I

18 MAY, A.D. 30

"What a marvelous day this has been," Leah said, her voice touched with wonder.

Simon Peter turned to her, nodding quickly. "Every day with Jesus is a marvel, but yes, this day has been unbelievable."

They were standing together in a small group—David, Leah, Ephraim, and Rachel, along with Peter and John. Jesus was a few feet away, talking quietly with the other disciples and a few who still lingered from the crowd. He had dispersed the crowd by promising that he would be with them again tomorrow. The light was soft now, the sun having disappeared behind the western hills about half an hour before.

Leah looked at her father. "Was it really just this morning that we went down to the beach and started all of this?"

David smiled with a look of deep peace. "It seems as though we have lived a week since then, doesn't it."

"It has been wonderful," Ephraim said.

Peter turned and peered at him. "So?"

Ephraim's eyebrows lifted. "What?"

"So how do you feel about Jesus now?"

To David's great joy, there was not one moment's hesitation from his older son. "How could I not believe after what we have seen this day?"

Rachel was nodding vigorously too. "It has been wonderful. The other day when we heard him on the mount, I felt something in my heart. I wasn't sure what it was. Now I understand. It is because he is the Messiah, isn't it?"

"Yes," John said fervently. "How could any person not feel his heart come alive in Jesus' presence?"

"Alive. Yes, that is the word."

They turned as Matthew Levi walked up to join them. David smiled and reached out his hand. "We haven't had a chance to congratulate you, Matthew. We are so pleased with what happened today."

"And shocked," he said wryly.

Ephraim laughed along with the others. "Yes, I have to admit, I was shocked when I learned that Jesus had gone into your house."

"No more than I," he murmured. "No more than I."

Peter was sobered now too. "Isn't it interesting?" he mused. "Look at us. Fishermen. A tax collector. Tailors, merchants, wives, mothers." His eyes hooded momentarily. "Roman centurions. Even among those of the Twelve he has called, there is such a difference. We all come from different walks of life. Some are from Capernaum, some from Bethsaida. Judas is from Judea."

"Which one is he?" Rachel asked.

Peter turned and pointed. "Well, as you know, there are two of us called Judas, but Judas Iscariot, as we call him, is the one to the left of Jesus, with the lighter robe. He comes from Keriot down in Judea."

John was pensive now as well. "Rich, poor, learned, simple—Jesus seems not to care about what we were or where we came from before. He calls Peter *Cephas,* or the Rock. He calls James and me *Boanerges.*"

David turned in surprise. "The sons of thunder?"

There was a laugh as Peter put his hand on the younger man's shoulder. John was not yet twenty and was the youngest of the inner circle of the disciples. "When Jesus first said that, I thought, 'Of course.' These two sons of Zebedee are like a clap of thunder—strong, vigorous—" He paused, shooting John a quick look. "Stubborn as a net caught on the bottom of the lake."

John yelped in protest. "You call *us* stubborn? Did you ever wonder why Jesus calls you a stone?"

David hooted. "I've *never* known Peter to be strong-minded."

"All right, all right," Peter said as the others all laughed at that. "We weren't talking about me. We were talking about Jesus." He looked at David. "I know Deborah is up in the hill country, but I was disappointed not to see Simeon here today."

Leah's face fell. "I went and told him to come. He promised he would." She looked at her father. "Why didn't he, Papa? He told me he would."

David just shook his head. "I don't know. We'll talk to him tonight. I am so disappointed that Deborah wasn't here."

"We'll tell her," Rachel said. "Perhaps we can get her to come and listen to him again, to see for herself."

Peter looked at David. "When do you expect her back?"

He shrugged. "We got word yesterday that Naomi is doing better. Another day or two probably."

"We likely won't be here by then," he said. "Jesus wants to go to Jerusalem for the Feast of Weeks."

David sighed. "I wondered if you would be going." Pentecost, as it was known by its Greek name, or the Feast of Weeks as the Jews called it, followed seven weeks after Passover. The Greek name signified the fiftieth day, or the day following seven weeks of seven days each. It was a one-day festival only, celebrating the close of the wheat harvest. In the book of Exodus, Moses had specified it to be "the feast of harvest, the first fruits of thy labors." Though many people went to Jerusalem for that celebration, it was not anything like Passover. David's family rarely went because it was one of the busiest times of the year for a merchant.

"That's all right," John said, seeing David's disappointment. "We should be gone no more than a week. Then we'll be back here again."

Rachel spoke again. "I wish I could somehow capture the look on that woman's face after she touched Jesus' robe and was healed—I would like to show that scene to Mother. That is something I will never forget."

"And what about the joy on the face of the wife of Jairus?" Ephraim came in. "I have never seen anything so radiant as the light in her eyes."

Now it was Matthew who spoke up. "Can you speak about what happened inside the house, Peter?"

Peter looked at John, who nodded slowly and said, "I suppose with those who have accepted Jesus it would be all right."

Peter seemed to agree with that. "I'm not sure why Jesus took only James and John and me into the house."

"Was the girl really dead?" Leah asked. "Before you went in, Jesus said she was only sleeping."

Peter shook his head, his face a study in amazement. "No, she was dead. There was no question about it. Her mother had watched her draw her last breath. That's when she sent for the mourners. The girl had been dead long enough for everyone to gather. That's why there was such a crowd at the house."

No one spoke now, but every eye was fixed on Peter. "We went into the room where the young girl was laid out on the bed." He uttered a deep sigh of pain. "I thought my heart would break when I saw her. She was so innocent. So lovely. Jairus—staid, unemotional Jairus—he was weeping like a baby. His wife could barely stand, she was so distraught with grief." He stopped, deeply moved at the memory.

John went on for him, his voice very soft. "Jesus went to her bedside and reached out and took her hand. We thought perhaps he was going to see if she was really dead. But then he said, 'Damsel, I say unto you, arise.'" His eyes were wide and bright with wonder. "Immediately she awoke and sat up."

"You can imagine the parents' reaction at that point," Peter said huskily. "We all just stood there, dumbfounded, unable to believe for joy. Then Jesus told her parents to get her something to eat."

Once again the group fell silent, each person contemplating what he or she had just heard. It was Matthew who finally spoke. "He told her to rise?"

John and Peter both turned to him. "Yes, why?"

"And do you remember what he said to the man they lowered through the roof at Andrew's house?"

David answered, remembering clearly when he and Leah had been looking down into the room. "He told him to arise, to take up his bed and go to his own house."

"Yes," Matthew said eagerly.

Peter was puzzled. "So, there is a point to that?"

Matthew's eyes were shining. "Think about what has happened in just the last two days. A raging storm was stilled with a word. The blind now see. A leper was cleansed, a paralytic restored. A soldier's servant was healed without the Master even going to his home. Then there was the woman with the issue of blood, cured by simply touching the hem of his robe. And finally, this beautiful young girl is brought back from the dead."

"It has been a time like no other in the history of the world," Peter whispered.

"Well, there is one thing you have not considered," Matthew went on, his voice heavy with emotion. "When I began this day, my life was like the surface of a stormy sea. *I* was unclean. *I* was blind. I sat on my seat in the customshouse, not realizing that it was *I* who was spiritually paralyzed, that it was *I* who was spiritually dead."

The tears spilled over and began to trickle down his cheeks. He was not aware of them. "As you marvel about what you have seen, do not forget this. I stand before you now a different man. The storm in my heart has been stilled. I am healed of my sickness, cured of my blindness, cleansed of my uncleanness. I have been raised from spiritual death to new life."

He looked at Peter. "What you saw in the house of Jairus was a miracle of astonishing power. But for me, the greatest miracle of all is what has happened to my heart."

II

When Leah came back out of her bedroom, she stopped. Her father stood at the table with the small writing board in his hand. He was reading it, his face moody.

"What is it, Papa?"

"It is a note from Simeon. This is why he didn't come today."

"Why?"

"He says he has gone to Beth Neelah to see how Aunt Naomi is doing."

"But—" She shook her head. "He never said a word of that to me. In fact, he kept saying that he couldn't come and hear Jesus because there was too much to do. And now he's gone to Beth Neelah?"

David laid down the board and sighed. "Who can speak for Simeon?" he sighed. "I just wish I would have known. I would have sent a note with him to your mother."

Leah nodded. "Come on, Papa. It's too late now. Rachel will have supper waiting for us."

III

"Before Leah and I leave," David said, "there is something I would like to say."

They sat together in the main room of Ephraim and Rachel's home. The evening meal was finished. Esther and Boaz were now in bed and asleep. The three of them turned to face him more fully.

"As you probably noticed, as we were returning home, Peter and I fell behind the rest of you."

"Yes," Leah said. She had wondered what had engaged them in such earnest conversation.

"He gave us some counsel. The more I consider it, the more I see wisdom in it."

"Counsel?" Ephraim asked. "For all of us?"

"Yes. About Mother and Simeon."

Now he had their full attention. "What, Papa?" Leah asked.

"Well, I mentioned to him again how disappointed I was that Simeon and your mother had not been there today, but that we were eager to tell them all about it."

They nodded. They had already talked about the importance of that.

"Well, to my surprise, he told me something that happened the other day with Jesus."

"What?" That was from Rachel.

"They were down in Magdala. Peter said there were some Pharisees and Sadducees there. They asked Jesus to show them a sign from heaven so they would know if he came with power and authority."

Rachel gave a little exclamation of disgust. "They see what Jesus is doing, and they still ask for a sign?"

"Yes," David answered, his face thoughtful. "In fact, that was what I was thinking. Why would they do that? Why would they demand to see demonstrations of his power before they will believe? All they have to do is follow him around."

"They are too proud," Leah said. "That's all."

"But what Jesus said is a little surprising. According to Peter, Jesus said that it was a wicked and an adulterous generation that seeks a sign and that they have been given signs enough from the prophets."

"I agree," said Ephraim. "That's a good answer. What we saw today is enough to convince anyone about Jesus."

"Is it?" David shot back. "There were people there today who were angry only because Jesus forgave sins."

Leah sat back. "And there were some who couldn't get over Jesus going into Matthew's house. When I saw that I thought, 'Where were you? Didn't you see anything?'"

"Exactly Peter's point. These men demanded a sign because they don't want to believe Jesus. They already have evidence, but they refuse to see."

"Like Simeon?" Leah asked slowly.

David shook his head. "I don't know. Perhaps. But that's not all. Do you remember what Jesus said when he cleansed the leper today?" He was speaking to Leah because Ephraim and Rachel had not been with them at that point.

"He told him to go and show himself to the priest, as the Law of Moses commands."

"What else?" he prodded.

Now she remembered. "He told him to tell no man."

"Yes. Didn't you find that odd? There was a whole crowd around who witnessed this, so it wasn't as though it was done in secret. Peter told me that Jesus said the same thing to Jairus and his wife after their daughter was brought back to them. He told them not to tell anyone."

"But—" Ephraim was astounded. "There were three or four hundred people outside. The mourners were there. The girl was known to have died."

"Yes," David said again, "isn't that strange? I hadn't given it that much thought until Peter reminded me of it."

"Why?" Leah said. "Why does Peter think Jesus tells them that?"

"Well, Peter is not sure either, but here is what he thinks. And the more I've thought about it, the more sense it makes to me. If a person demands evidence of God's power before he is willing to believe, it is because he has no faith. Signs and evidence come *because* of faith, not in order to create faith. For example, think of Pharaoh. How many mighty miracles did he see? And did it change his heart? No, it only hardened it the more."

Leah's mouth had fallen open slightly. "Are you saying that Simeon and Mother—" She stopped, not sure exactly how to finish her question.

"Peter was saying that Jesus doesn't want people to believe in him only because of his miracles. He wants them to accept him, to believe in *him*, not just in what he does." He too was struggling how to put it. "As I've thought about it, I came to realize that Jesus works these great miracles because he is the Messiah. He is not the Messiah because he works miracles."

Rachel leaned forward. "Say that again."

"What we saw today happened because Jesus *is* the Messiah. Performing those wonderful things doesn't make him the Messiah. Does that make sense?"

They all three were nodding now.

"But," Ephraim said, "it *was* seeing those things that he did that convinced me, Father. I wasn't sure before then."

"I know. But you were open to him. You said yourself, you and Rachel found the teachings of Jesus the other day quite appealing."

Ephraim grinned. "Except for the things about going the second mile with some Roman soldier. I've got to admit that shook me pretty deeply, just as it did Simeon."

"All I am saying is this," David concluded. "When we see Simeon and your mother, I think we need to be a little careful about talking only about the miracles we've seen."

"But they'll hear about them," Rachel said. "The whole town is buzzing with what happened today."

"I'm not talking about trying to keep them a secret. I'm not even saying don't say anything about them. But let's be careful that we don't try to change their hearts by focusing on the miracles alone."

"I understand," Leah said slowly. "I'm afraid that's exactly what I tried to do with Simeon today. It's like I was saying to him, 'Simeon, you won't accept anything else I'm telling you, so listen to this.'"

David leaned forward, studying his hands. "There is something else I would like to say."

"We are listening, Father," Ephraim said with great soberness.

"The other day, when Jesus taught us on the mount, he spoke of prayer. He taught us how to pray, and then do you remember what he said?"

Leah had not been there, so she couldn't answer. Ephraim and his wife were not sure to what specific thing he referred. So David began to quote Jesus as best he could remember. "He said something like this, 'Ask, and it shall be given unto you. Seek, and you shall find. Knock, and it shall be opened unto you.'"

"Yes, I remember that now," Rachel said.

"And then he used the example of parents. If our children ask for bread, we don't hand them a stone. If they want fish, we don't give them a serpent. Then Jesus said that if we, who are imperfect, know how to give good gifts to our children, how much more will our Father in Heaven give good things to them that ask of him."

He stopped, and suddenly his emotions rose to the surface. He tried to speak and had to catch himself. He swallowed once, then again, and then finally went on. "I can't think of any gift I would rather have than to have your mother and Simeon come to know and feel what we now know and feel."

"Amen," Leah whispered, her own eyes suddenly glistening.

"Yes," Rachel said, reaching out to squeeze her father-in-law's hands quickly.

"Then let's not just talk to them," he said. "Let's first ask God to open their hearts to our words, to help us know what to say and how to say it, to prepare their minds so that they can hear not only what we say, but what is in our hearts." He looked up now, smiling at each one in turn. "And since we are together here now, this would be a good time to start."

"And to thank him for this day too," Leah said.

"Yes," Rachel said, on the verge of tears, herself. "Matthew is not the only one who was given a new heart this day."

"Amen," Ephraim said fervently.

"Amen," said Leah and David at the same moment.

IV

Deborah wanted to reach out and touch Simeon's cheek, lean forward and take him in her arms as she had done when he was a little boy, to make the hurt go away. But he was not a little boy any longer and the hurt now was coming out as bitter anger. He wasn't ready for a caress on the cheek. Not yet.

"Did you know about this, Mother?" he suddenly cried. The light brown eyes had turned dark, like a dust storm blowing in from the deserts of Arabia.

"I learned just the other day that your father knew the centurion and had dealings with him before—"

"And you didn't tell me?" he blurted.

"Let me finish, Simeon. I knew he had dealings with Rubrius before any of this happened last fall. He has not continued that contact since then, knowing how you would feel about it."

"Until today!" he exclaimed. "You should have seen them, Mother. That Roman soldier came up to Father like they were cousins or something. Father called him by his first name."

"Simeon, you told me that Rubrius was not asking anything for himself. His servant is one of us. Your father has known him for many years."

"Don't make excuses for him, Mother. I can't believe he would do this."

"I'm not making excuses, Son. I'm just trying to explain that it is not like your father went out seeking the centurion."

He got to his feet. "That doesn't matter! How could he do that? This is the man who nearly killed me. His own son."

"I know," she whispered. "I know. The very sight of him or that tribune would leave me physically ill."

"Yes, I know. So why doesn't it affect Father that way?" He blew out his breath. "I'm sorry, Mother, but I can't just push this aside."

"I understand, but you can't just ignore it either. You and your father are going to have to talk about it sometime."

Suddenly he remembered something and was ashamed. "How is Aunt Naomi?" He had not made it all the way to Beth Neelah yesterday because he had gotten a late afternoon start. He had stopped to sleep in a stand of forest, then rose before dawn to continue. Now it was early morning, and thus far his mother was the only one awake in the household. He had been with her now for half an hour, and in his anger and frustration he had not even thought once about the reason his mother had come here.

"Better," Deborah said, grateful that he had finally settled down enough to ask. "If she continues to improve, Joseph and I will start home tomorrow."

"I'm going to stay up here for a time."

"Simeon."

"I can't go back and face him yet, Mother. I need some time to think. Besides, I promised Yehuda we would do some things that need doing. And I have spent scarcely any time with Shana since our betrothal."

"You know this is a very busy time—"

"Ha!" he cried, cutting her off. "It's not so busy that Father and Leah and Ephraim can't all run off after Jesus. Sorry, I'm not too worried about that, Mother."

She sighed and nodded. "Perhaps I'll stay a day or two longer as well, and then we can go back down together."

"Perhaps," he said. He started toward the door. "I'm going to see Yehuda before he's off somewhere. He has no idea that I'm here." He finally managed a smile. "Thank you for listening. And understanding."

And then he went out the door. She stared at it for several seconds, then dropped her head into her hands. "Oh, David," she whispered. "What have you done?"

V

"Ho! Simeon."

"*Shalom*, Yehuda!"

"I heard you arrived this morning."

Simeon shook his head. Was there nothing that went undetected in this little village?

"Yes. I came up to see how Cousin Naomi is doing."

"This is good. I was getting ready to come down to see you."

Simeon's eyebrows lifted. "You were?"

"Yes." He reached in his tunic and withdrew a folded parchment. "This came yesterday."

"For me?"

"For us."

He walked over to his friend. "Who is it from?"

"Mordechai ben Uzziel of Jerusalem."

Simeon's jaw went slack. "Mordechai?"

Yehuda nodded, then stroked his beard thoughtfully. "He says he has a matter of utmost urgency that he wishes to discuss with us."

"Don't tell me he wants another escort," Simeon frowned.

"No. Actually, he's asking that you and I come to Jerusalem."

It was one shock after another. "When?"

"As soon as possible." He handed the parchment to his friend, and Simeon read it quickly. It was short and terse.

"He doesn't say what it is," he noted, his brow furrowing in concentration. "Why us?"

"I've thought about that all night. I think it's because he knows us. After the meeting in Sepphoris fell through, we're not only the only Zealots he's actually met, but he knows we can be trusted."

"Right," Simeon said sarcastically.

"We didn't take his money," Yehuda reminded him. "And we also saved his daughter from a great deal of shame."

Simeon grunted, not convinced. "He doesn't want us to say anything to the other leaders."

"Not yet."

Simeon pursed his lips, handing the letter back. "What do you think?"

Yehuda's head bobbed back and forth, half nodding, half shaking negatively. "They are anxious for some kind of a deal with us," he said. "I'm not sure it is ever going to work, but I suppose it's worth hearing what he's got on his mind."

Simeon nodded after a moment. "All right." Actually, he was relieved to have a reason for not going home for a time, though he wasn't going to say that, not even to Yehuda. "How soon do you want to leave?"

"Well, I slept like a baby pup last night. I can be ready in an hour. But you were out on the road, obviously—"

"I'm fine. Let's do it. I'll go tell Mother."

Yehuda cuffed him gently. "And you'd better come say hello to Shana. She's been up for an hour fretting about what she'll cook for your supper tonight. Now she's going to be very unhappy to know I'm taking you away again."

He smiled. "I was coming over right now to see her."

Yehuda laughed. "Shana is so afraid that you will find her cooking less than you desire."

Simeon looked surprised. "I think Shana is a wonderful cook. Better than you and Daniel by a bowshot, that's for certain."

"That's what I told her," he said. "But since she never had a mother to teach her how, she is convinced that she will displease you once you are married. She planned to work all day on your meal."

"You tell her that I shall return to Beth Neelah before I go back to Capernaum so I can partake of her cooking. And tell her that I have no worries whatsoever about her abilities as a wife and mother."

"I will," Yehuda said, pleased.

"Good. I'll see you in a few minutes."

CHAPTER NOTES

The surname Iscariot, given to Judas, is thought to have come from *ish Keriot*, "a man of Keriot," a town in Judea. Some think it came from *iscara*, which means "to be strangled." Since Judas hanged himself, some scholars have supposed the title was given to Judas after his death (see Clarke, 3:117).

In chapter eight and nine of Matthew's Gospel, he links together a whole series of miracles—those described in this and the previous chapter. Right in the midst of that incredible list of miracles, Matthew inserts the account of his own calling to the discipleship. In Matthew's record, Jesus said to the paralytic, "*Arise*, take up thy bed, and go unto thine house." And then it says that he *arose* and departed (Matthew 9:6–7). Just two verses later comes this: "As Jesus passed forth from thence, he saw a man, named Matthew, *sitting* at the receipt of custom: and he saith unto him, Follow me. And he *arose*, and followed him" (9:9). It was this similarity in language that led the author to have Matthew say what he does here about the greatest of all miracles.

Though they don't link them together in the same sequence as Matthew does, both Mark and Luke include accounts of these same miracles and give some additional details that are included in this chapter (see Mark 2:1–12; 5:21–43; Luke 5:17–26; 7:1–10; 8:41–56).

CHAPTER 20

SHAFTS OF LIGHTNING WILL FLY WITH A TRUE AIM AND WILL LEAP
TO THE TARGET AS FROM A WELL-DRAWN BOW OF CLOUDS.

—*Wisdom of Solomon 5:21*

I

24 MAY, A.D. 30

Miriam looked up from her writing as she heard the front entrance door below her open with a crash.

"Miriam! Miriam!"

The urgency in Livia's voice was unmistakable. Miriam stood quickly and walked to the door of the study. "I'm up here, Livia. What is it?"

She heard the sound of footsteps running across the marbled hall, then up the stairs. In a moment Livia appeared, walking swiftly toward her. Her face was red and her long golden hair a little disheveled.

"What is it, Livia? What's wrong?"

Livia came up to her, breathing heavily. "Jesus is back in Jerusalem."

Miriam visibly started. "Are you sure?"

"I was just on the Temple Mount. I saw him."

Miriam started to turn, then remembered something. "Get Levi. I'll put away my things."

By the time she had finished capping the ink bottle and cleaning the nib of her pen, the chief household steward of Mordechai ben Uzziel was standing at her door. "Yes, Mistress Miriam?"

"Levi, I've got to go up on the Temple Mount."

He nodded soberly, his eyes showing a little surprise. Normally she did not feel as if she had to account to him for her whereabouts.

"Father said there might be a meeting here sometime today. He wants me to record the proceedings."

Now he understood. "Ah, yes. Your father did mention that to me, though he said he wasn't sure if it would be today or tomorrow."

"I know. But if it is today before we return, you'll have to send someone for me."

"I understand."

"Thank you." With that she grabbed a shawl of light blue silk and threw it around her shoulders. "Come, Livia. Let's hurry."

II

They chose the route across the great western bridge that spanned the Tyropoean Valley. It was the shortest and quickest way from the Upper City to the temple. The moment they were out of her court-yard, Miriam began pressing for more detail. "Tell me more, Livia. Where did you see him?"

"At first it was just the crowds that drew me. I was by the gate of the Court of the Women when I heard some shouting over near the north porticos. Someone said it was the carpenter from Nazareth. Knowing that you would want to know, I went to see."

"Good," she exclaimed. "I've been hoping he would come to Jerusalem for Pentecost."

"When I got to where the crowd was, I couldn't see Jesus, but I quickly learned that the tumult had to do with him."

"Tumult?"

"Yes. There was a group of scribes and Pharisees there. Azariah was one of them."

Her eyes narrowed slightly. "Go on."

"There were also some of your father's party, from the Council. They were very agitated."

"Over Jesus?"

"At first I didn't think so. There was a man there. They were questioning him because he was found carrying his bed on the Sabbath."

Miriam turned to stare at Livia. "His bed? On the Temple Mount?"

There was a quick smile. "Not a bed like yours. A litter. More like a stretcher. He had it folded up and on his shoulder."

"How odd. Today is the Sabbath. You would think anyone would know better than to carry something like that on the Temple Mount. The Pharisees are always watching for violators of the Law."

"Well, that's why they were questioning him. I was going to move on, thinking this had nothing to do with Jesus, when the man said the reason he was carrying his bed was because the man who had made him whole had commanded him to take up his bed and walk."

Miriam stopped dead. "Made him whole? He said that?"

Livia nodded, eager now to share what she had discovered. "That caught my attention too, so I stayed to listen some more. Here is what the man told them. He said he had been afflicted with an infirmity for more than thirty-eight years. In recent years it had become so terrible that he could no longer walk."

She looked at Miriam now. "Do you know of a place they call the Pool of Bethesda?"

"Of course. It's down by the sheep market."

"Yes. I've heard about it, but you've never taken me there. Evidently there's something about the water in the pool."

Miriam nodded, starting to walk again. "That's right. From time to time it will bubble up. Some of the people believe that it is an angel that troubles the water. Many of the sick and infirm go there and wait. They believe that the first person into the water after it bubbles will be healed. It's really very sad," she went on. "Those poor people. Sometimes I go down there and give alms. Father doesn't know that, by the way. He thinks the whole idea of an angel in the water is ridiculous."

Livia's head was bobbing even as she spoke. "That explains it then. Everyone else but me seemed to understand what he was saying."

"What happened?"

"He said that he had been down by the pool for a long time now, trying to get into the water so he could be healed. But his infirmity was such that by the time he was able to get up off his bed and crawl down to the water, someone else would always get there first."

Miriam's eyes flew open. "I think I know the man that you mean," she cried. "He is a beggar there. Lies on his bed all the time. Gray hair, scraggly beard."

"Yes, that's him."

"They told me he has been there for years. I saw him trying to crawl down to the water once. It was pitiful. He kept asking some of the men there to help him, but no one would. I wanted to cry."

Livia reached out and took hold of Miriam's wrist. "Well, listen to this. He said he was lying there this morning as he did every day, waiting for the water to be stirred. Suddenly a man was standing beside him."

"Jesus?" Miriam blurted.

"Yes, though the impotent man didn't know who he was. He said this man looked down on him and asked, 'Would you be made whole?' The beggar thought the man was asking if he wanted help getting down to the water. He told Jesus that he had no man to help him, that when the water was troubled, he would start for the pool, but someone else was always quicker."

Miriam was partially holding her breath now. The entire land was filled with rumors of this Jesus of Nazareth and the great wonders he performed wherever he went. "Yes?"

"When Jesus heard that, he looked on him and said, 'Arise! Take up your bed and walk.'" Livia's eyes were like two great pools of blue water. "And he did."

"Oh, Livia! Then it's true. Everything they say about him is true."

"I didn't see it, so I cannot say for sure." She wrinkled her nose. "But I believed this man as he spoke. His clothes were filthy. His face was gaunt and sallow. He looked as though he had been lying on his bed for years. And yet . . . " There was a look of amazement on her face. "In spite of that, he was strong and full of life as he spoke to his questioners."

They had to step aside as a cart filled with cages of mourning doves rattled past them. They had reached the bridge and were starting across now, and the people were far more numerous.

"The scribes and Pharisees were very angry. They wanted to know who it was that told him to carry his bed. But the man didn't know. Evidently, after Jesus had healed him, he disappeared into the crowds."

"It has to be Jesus, Livia. It just has to be."

"That's what I decided too."

"Let's hurry." She dropped her hands, her face anxious. "Oh, I hope he is still there."

III

It was approaching midday by the time they came onto the Temple Mount, and the summer heat was already shimmering off the marble and limestone of the great complex. Miriam didn't hesitate. There were only a few people in the Court of the Gentiles, and these were only crossing on their way to somewhere else. The crowds were in the great porticos that lined the courtyard and provided welcome shade from the sun.

She headed directly for Solomon's Porches, which occupied the entire south end of the mount and provided the greatest space to accommodate crowds of people out of the sun. Five minutes later they found him. He was sitting on a stone bench with people crowding around him. It took another five minutes for Miriam and Livia to work their way close enough to see and hear.

A man, another Pharisee by the look of him, was standing before him. "Tell us," the man demanded. "How do you do the works that you do?" Miriam started, wondering if he referred to the impotent man.

Jesus looked at him steadily. "Truly, I say unto you, the Son can do nothing of himself, but what he sees the Father do. For the Father loves the Son, and shows him all things that he himself does. And the Father will show him greater works than these, that ye may marvel."

"What could be better than raising up a man from his bed after so many years of impotency?" someone behind them called out. "What could be greater than that?"

Jesus turned. "As the Father raises up the dead, and quickens them, even so the Son quickens whom he will."

Livia looked at Miriam, not sure exactly what that meant. "I think he's talking about the resurrection," she whispered.

"I thought you didn't believe in the resurrection," Livia whispered back.

"My father doesn't," she said in surprise. "I always have."

"Make way!" someone called out. "Make a path."

Every head turned. For a moment all they could see were two poles with cloth around them, held vertically in the air. They were moving toward them. Then suddenly Livia grabbed Miriam's shoulder. "That's the man who was healed."

The crowd fell back as the word leaped from lip to lip of who it was that was coming. Miriam inhaled sharply. There he was. The man she had seen at the Pool of Bethesda the last time she was there. In an instant she saw that Livia was right. His clothing looked as if he were ready to be buried. His face was dirty, the cheeks beneath his beard sunken, his neck so scrawny that the cords in them stood out like ropes. And yet he did not walk like a man who was sick or infirm. He moved forward confidently and with a sure step.

"There you are," he cried when he saw Jesus.

"Yes." Jesus seemed not at all surprised at this appearance.

"The Jewish leaders are very upset because they found me carrying my bed on the Sabbath. When I told them I did so because you told me to, they asked who you were."

"I am Jesus of Nazareth."

There was a curt nod. "Some thought that might be the case." Then his face softened. "I had no chance to thank you. When I realized that—" His voice caught, and he looked away. "When I realized I could walk, I was stunned. It was shameful of me not to return thanks to you."

"You have been made whole. Go your way and sin no more, lest a worse thing than this come upon you."

The man was obviously caught by surprise by that declaration, but finally nodded. He turned and shuffled away a few steps, then stopped. "Jesus?"

"Yes?"

"Take care. The leaders are raging. Some even talk of putting you to death. They see the people who follow you and fear an uprising."

The expression on Jesus' face did not change. "Are there not twelve hours in the day?" he said. "If any man walks in the day, he does

403

not stumble, because he walks in the light. If he walks in the night, he stumbles, because there is no light in him."

Again Livia turned to Miriam, a questioning look on her face. What did that enigmatic statement mean? Miriam wasn't positive, but she thought she had understood. "He's saying that he's not going to try to hide his work in the darkness just because it makes the leaders of the people angry."

"Oh."

The man with the bed moved away, and the crowd quickly closed in again.

Jesus watched them for a long moment before he spoke again. "Truly I say unto you, the hour is coming, and now is, when the dead shall hear the voice of the Son of God. And they that hear shall live, for as the Father hath life in himself, so hath he given to the Son to have life in himself."

"How can the dead hear the Son's voice? The Sadducees say that Moses did not teach that there is any life after this one." Miriam was startled to realize that she was the one who had spoken.

He turned and found her face in the crowd. For a moment his eyes held hers, and then he went on, speaking calmly yet earnestly. "Marvel not at this, for the hour is coming in the which all that are in the graves shall hear his voice and shall come forth. They that have done good shall come forth unto the resurrection of life. They that have done evil, unto the resurrection of damnation."

Miriam nodded, feeling his words settle into her heart like a healing balm. So her father and the others were wrong, just as she had felt all these years.

"You bear witness of yourself," a voice called out sharply. "Why should we believe you?"

Again every head in the crowd turned. Azariah, head of the Pharisees in Jerusalem and a member of the Great Sanhedrin, shoved aside the last of the people and stood before Jesus. When his eyes fell on Miriam, he gave a quick start; then he frowned. But then she was forgotten. Other men moved in around him, forming a phalanx confronting Jesus.

Again Jesus seemed as unruffled as if he were having a conversation with a friend. "But I am not the only witness of my words. If that were so, my witness would not be true. But what of John the Baptist? He was a burning and shining light that many of you went out to see. He bore witness of me. But there is an even greater witness than that of John. The works which the Father has given me to finish, the same works that I do, bear witness of me, that the Father hath sent me."

"What works are those?" Azariah sneered. "Show us your works."

There was an angry murmur from the crowd now. They clearly were in sympathy with Jesus and not with the Pharisees. "What about the miracle he just worked at Bethesda?" an older man asked.

Azariah whirled, his face a mask of fury. "He had a man violate the sacred laws of the Sabbath. That's what he did at Bethesda."

Jesus went on as if neither had spoken. "If you wish yet another witness, then search the scriptures. In them you think you have eternal life, but these are they which testify of me. But you do not know that, because you have not the love of God in you."

The rage in Azariah exploded. "I have spent a lifetime devoted to God. How dare you say I have no love for him."

Jesus stood now, rising to his full height. In that instant, Miriam remembered the majesty he had carried when he took the whip to the moneychangers. Even Azariah took a step back as Jesus faced him. "Do you think I will accuse you to the Father? No. There is one that will accuse you, even Moses, in whom you supposedly trust. If you truly believed Moses, you would believe me, for Moses wrote of me."

Azariah was so utterly shocked that for a moment he could not speak. His mouth worked and his beard twitched, but no words came out. Then finally they poured out of him in a stream of invective.

"Infidel! Blasphemer! You dare to invoke the name of Moses? You are not yet forty years old. How could Moses have written of you?"

Jesus shrugged. "If you believe not the writings of Moses, it is no surprise that you don't believe my words." Now Jesus turned away from him and spoke to the crowd. His eyes touched Miriam's briefly as he did so. "My doctrine is not mine, but his that sent me. If you would know if my doctrine is true, then do the Father's will. Then you can know whether I speak of myself or whether it be of God."

To that point Miriam had been caught up in the intensity of the conflict in front of her. Now his words seemed to be aimed directly at her and Livia.

He paused, looking directly at her now. "I say again, if anyone will do my Father's will, then they shall know of the doctrine, whether it be true."

Azariah was seething like a pot left too long on the fire, but Miriam was barely aware of him. It hit her with perfect clarity that this was what had been troubling her. For years she had been searching for something, looking for something deeper in her faith than what she had thus far found. She had never thought of it as doctrine, but that was exactly what it was. Her father and his associates denied the resurrection and a life after this one. In the core of her being, she could not accept that. The Pharisees had much that she found appealing, but they had turned the worship of God into a worship of the Law and all of its minutia. Surely there was something more important than that. But Jesus had just given her the key. There it was, simple and straight-forward. If you want to know for yourself, then live as God would have you live. Then you will know. How could anything be more plain than that?

A movement caught Miriam's eye. Azariah and his fellow believers had moved back a few steps and were in an urgent huddle. Then Azariah raised a hand, beckoning to someone behind them, someone out of Miriam's sight.

The crowd saw that too and turned to see what was happening. For a moment nothing happened; then a path began to open. In a moment, two men appeared. They held firmly onto the arms of a woman, half dragging her between them. The crowd went silent. Here was a completely new development.

Miriam looked at Livia, who shrugged, as puzzled as Miriam was. Then they pushed forward a little, so as to see better. The woman was obviously being brought against her will. Her dress was of common cloth and hand-stitched. Though it was clean, it had clearly seen much service. Her hair was tangled and matted, as though she had not brushed it when she had awakened that morning. Her head was down, but Miriam could see that her face was flaming red with humiliation. Tears streaked her cheeks, and her hands were clenched in tight balls.

Jesus had sat down again, but now as he saw them approaching, he got to his feet slowly. Eyes glittering with triumph, Azariah moved closer to Jesus, motioning for the men to bring the woman to him. When they reached him, they gave her a contemptuous shove. It was not hard enough to make her lose her balance, but she dropped to her knees anyway, lowering her face and covering it with her hands.

"What is this?" Jesus asked.

Azariah looked down at the woman in complete disgust, then turned to Jesus. "You say that we have no regard for the Law of Moses. Well, let us see who accepts the Law and who does not." He half turned, flinging one hand in the direction of the figure on her knees before him. "This woman was taken in adultery—in the very act!" His voice rose sharply. "Moses in the Law commanded that such should be stoned." There was another disdainful sneer. "What do you say?"

In a flash Miriam saw the brilliant cunning of Azariah and felt her stomach drop. He had just laid a most clever trap. If Jesus said she should not be stoned, then he was contradicting one of the most clearly understood and important conditions of the Law given at Sinai.

That would turn the people against him. But under Roman rule, though the Jewish Council had the right to pronounce a death sentence, only the Romans could actually carry it out. If Jesus said to stone her, then Azariah would be at the gate of the Antonia Fortress in less time than it took to say it, accusing Jesus of flaunting the laws of Rome. There weren't many surer ways to get oneself arrested than that.

She turned to Livia, stricken. To her surprise Livia had gone as white as bleached linen. She looked as though she were going to pass out. And then Miriam understood. Livia's mother had been sold off when their Roman master in Alexandria had gone bankrupt. Though she had never said so directly, Livia had hinted that her mother may have been sold into prostitution, a fate that awaited some female slaves. She had no way of knowing that, but feared the worst.

Livia saw Miriam looking at her, and her chin came up defiantly. "If she was taken in the very act," she hissed, "where is the man? Doesn't your law hold him guilty as well?"

Miriam just stared at her. She was right. She was absolutely right. The law of Moses was clear in that regard. Where was the other partner in this "terrible crime" that Azariah was presenting to Jesus?

Feeling light-headed, as though the heat had gotten to her, Miriam turned back to see how this would play out. Jesus had not moved. His eyes were on the woman, who was in a heap at his feet now. Then to Miriam's surprise, Jesus stooped down. He reached out a hand and began to trace something on the marble floor of the portico. It almost looked as though he might be writing something on the stone, but she couldn't tell from where she was.

Azariah was glaring at him. "Well," he demanded after a moment. "What say you? Shall she be stoned or nay?"

Jesus looked up. The woman's head had lifted slightly, and she was watching him through anxious eyes that were red and swollen.

Finally Jesus straightened. His eyes met and held those of Azariah and his colleagues. Miriam could not see the face of the chief Pharisee now, but Jesus was facing directly toward her. She could see great indignation smouldering in his eyes. "Let him who is without this sin be the one to cast the first stone." And with that he stooped back down again and began tracing with his finger once more.

Azariah flinched as though he had been struck a blow. He stared down at Jesus, then turned to look at those who were with him. Once again his mouth was working, but no sound came out. Miriam wanted to shout aloud. The word Jesus had used did not refer to sin in general but to the same kind of sin before them—adultery, fornication, or other forms of immorality. For years she had heard whispers and rumors about mistresses and the "little indiscretions" engaged in by the powerful men of Jerusalem, including her own father since her mother's death. That had made her sick, and she had pushed the stories aside, not wanting to think about them. But something down inside her guessed that it was true.

Then she stiffened as a revelation hit her. If the woman had been taken in the very act, as Azariah said, how did these men know of it? It was midday. Had they gone from house to house hoping to find a couple in violation of the Law so they could trap Jesus, or . . . Now the outrage in her flared into something really quite terrible. It was a deliberate trap, and this poor woman was being used as the bait.

It was one of the men who had dragged the woman forward who turned away first. He mumbled something to Azariah and slunk away. A moment later his companion followed, eyes fastened on the ground as he pushed his way through the crowd. Miriam watched in utter astonishment as, one by one, the others were shamed by that simple invitation. In Jewish law the witness whose testimony was responsible for bringing about a conviction in a capital crime was required to cast the first stone during the execution. It was a grim way to discourage bearing false witness. Now the power of his words struck her even more forcefully. "If you wish to execute the Law, then let him who is without this sin cast that first stone upon her."

During it all Jesus never looked up. He just continued to trace patterns on the stone with his finger. The woman's head was up now, her eyes wide and wondering as she saw her accusers melt away into the crowd. Finally, Azariah, fuming at the desertion of his associates, turned and walked away, muttering angrily under his breath at this sudden reversal of his careful planning.

At last Jesus looked up. He seemed surprised that the circle of men were no longer there. He stood, looking down at the woman now, whose face was turned toward him. "Woman," he said, his voice gentle and soft, "Where are those who were your accusers? Does no man accuse you now?"

There was a quiet sob, and then her head dropped. "No, Lord."

He nodded slowly, then reached down and took her hand, lifting her to her feet. "Neither do I accuse you. Go your way—and sin no more."

IV

Neither Miriam nor Livia spoke as they returned slowly back across the bridge to the Upper City. They walked in silence, completely caught up in their own thoughts. Not until they turned into the street that led to Miriam's home did Livia speak. "My family was a follower of Diana, the huntress. The Greeks called her Artemis."

Miriam turned, surprised by the abruptness and unexpected nature of her words. "Oh?"

"She was always my favorite among the gods because she was thought to be the goddess who took particular care over women—watching over them in childbirth, protecting their modesty and virtue. She herself was a virgin. In fact, when one of her fellow deities dared spy on her while she was bathing, she turned him into a stag, and the dogs ran him down and killed him."

Miriam watched her, not speaking, confused by this turn in the conversation.

Livia sighed. "Since coming to live here with you and your father, I have found much in your religion that I like."

"Really?" Miriam was both surprised and pleased.

Livia smiled faintly. "There is also much that is very puzzling."

"I understand. There are some things that still puzzle me."

They moved on, Miriam waiting for more, Livia seeming to be finished. As they approached the gate to their courtyard, Livia stopped.

"What, Livia?" Miriam gently asked, sensing there was still more beneath the expressionless face.

"I should like to be a follower of Jesus," she said abruptly. "Do you think that would be permissible?"

"Of a truth?" Miriam cried joyfully, wanting to throw her arms around her. "I too have decided I would like to become one of his disciples."

"But you are a Jew, and this would be permissible for you, would it not?"

"Livia, what you believe and whom you choose to follow is your choice. You can do what you wish."

"I know but—" She stopped as the full impact of what Miriam had said hit her. "Truly?"

"Of course," she laughed, her eyes misting. "I am so happy that you feel as I do."

"I don't understand all that he said," she said hesitantly.

"I didn't understand everything he said either, but I know how it made me feel."

Livia's eyes were large and filled with gravity. "I felt great joy when he did not turn away from that woman."

"Yes," Miriam said, remembering Livia's mother and wondering where she was now and what pitiable condition she might be in. "That was wonderful."

Livia nodded. "I shall be a follower of Jesus then," she concluded. "I shall put away Diana and try to do whatever it is that he would ask of me."

Miriam felt her throat tighten as she looked at this woman she was coming to love so deeply. "That will be enough," she said softly. "Remember his promise? If we do his will, we will come to know of the doctrine."

CHAPTER NOTES

The record states that Jesus returned to Jerusalem for a "feast of the Jews," which is not specified (John 5:1). Since Pentecost occurred in late spring and early summer following Passover, the author took the liberty of supposing it was Pentecost. Jesus' teachings about himself and the Father are found in that chapter and have been combined for purposes of the novel with events from John 7 and 8, when Jesus was in Jerusalem again several months later for the Feast of Tabernacles. The account of the woman taken in adultery is found in John 8:2–11.

Adam Clarke notes that what the King James Version translates as "He that is without sin among you" (v. 7) uses a Greek word that actually seems to specify the same kind of sin, that is, adultery or fornication (Clarke, 3:576). Thus the author's interpolation, "let him who is without *this* sin."

CHAPTER 21

ALL LAWLESSNESS IS LIKE A TWO-EDGED SWORD;
THERE IS NO HEALING FOR ITS WOUND.

—*Wisdom of Sirach 21:3*

I
24 MAY, A.D. 30

As Miriam and Livia approached the heavy wooden gate that gave entrance into the palatial courtyard of her father's house, the door swung open and Levi stepped out. At the sight of her, his eyes lit up with relief. "There you are, Mistress Miriam. I was just coming to find you."

Miriam's face fell. "Has the meeting started already?"

The steward shook his head. "No. The men have arrived, but your father isn't home yet. I was going now to find you and him and let you both know."

Miriam was relieved that they had made it in time. Her father had little patience for waiting when he was ready to transact business. She was glad that she was not the cause of any delay. "Where are they now? How many are there?"

"Just two," he said. "I asked them to wait in the courtyard."

Just two? She had gotten the idea that there would be more. "All right, Levi. I'll invite them in and let them wait in the study until you find Father."

"They're from the Galilee," he said, as if that might change her mind.

She smiled. Levi was a third-generation Jerusalemite. Like most others in the city, he viewed with pity anyone with the bad fortune to be born elsewhere. But also like most Judeans, he looked on Galileans with special distaste.

"It will be all right," Miriam said. "We'll be sure the silver candlesticks are locked in their case. Go and find Father."

Livia hid a smile behind her hand as Levi frowned. He sensed Miriam was tweaking his nose a little and didn't understand why. He gave a curt nod and trotted away.

When Miriam pushed the gate to the courtyard open, the hinges creaked softly. A man standing in the shadows by the fountain turned. As Miriam and Livia stepped inside, he lifted a hand and came forward.

Miriam stopped, shocked as she recognized who it was. "Yehuda?"

"*Shalom*, Miriam," he boomed. "And peace be to you, Livia."

Caught completely off her guard, Miriam didn't even return his greeting. "The meeting is with *you?*" Livia was staring as well.

He laughed. "A shock for us also."

As he said that, another figure came out from behind a tree. Miriam felt her heart jump a little. It was Simeon, looking at the two of them with a sardonic smile. "*Shalom.*"

Flustered to realize that her face was suddenly hot, Miriam lowered her eyes. "*Shalom*, Simeon. *Shalom*, Yehuda."

Livia was still staring at them, unable to believe her eyes. Yehuda laughed at her look. "You act as though you are seeing a charging bear, Livia."

"I—" Now her face flushed, and she had to look down as well. "I am pleased to see you both, but like Miriam, I too am greatly surprised."

"Surprised seems like an inadequate word," Simeon said, still smiling. He came forward into the full sunlight. The sand-colored eyes were teasing. "But didn't you know—the Javelin is famous for striking from an ambush because he loves the element of surprise."

"It's *you* my father is meeting with?" Miriam said again, still reeling.

They both nodded. Then Simeon looked down. "And how are your feet by now?"

Miriam looked down too. "That ointment is the most wonderful thing I have ever known. I was walking on them again in three days."

"Now we walk everywhere we go in the city and never take the litter," Livia said to Yehuda. "Miriam says that never again will she have to be so embarrassed."

Miriam shot her such a look that Simeon laughed aloud. "What is there to be embarrassed about? We are the ones who walked you all that way without considering your needs."

Miriam laughed, recovering now. This was the pleasant Simeon she had caught a glimpse of once or twice. There was no hint of the man who could fling words at you like a dagger. "Yes, you did. The least you could have done that morning as we started out was warn us it would be thirty miles before we stopped."

"Simeon is not known for worrying about the feet of those who follow him," Yehuda growled.

"How is Daniel? And Shana?" Miriam asked, turning to the older of the two of them.

"Very good, thank you," Yehuda answered. "Daniel wanted to come, but your father specified that it should be only Simeon and me." And then he gave her an odd look. "And Shana has some pleasant news. She is betrothed."

"Really," Miriam exclaimed. "Wonderful. To whom?"

There was a moment's hesitation, then Simeon raised one hand. "Shana and I were betrothed about six weeks ago."

"Oh?" Miriam caught herself, realizing that she was staring at him. She dropped her eyes. "Congratulations."

"Thank you."

Now she smiled fully. "I saw how she looked at you that night in Beth Neelah." She turned to Yehuda. "She must be very happy."

"Aye," he said. "I have tried to warn her about making a life with such an ogre as this one, but she will not listen."

Simeon ignored him. "And I, I will have to grow accustomed to having such a bear for a brother-in-law."

As they all laughed, Simeon sobered. "My mother sends greetings to you, Miriam of Jerusalem. She said you two had a most interesting talk when you were last together."

Miriam was flabbergasted at that. "We did," she stammered. "I—I found your mother to be a woman of remarkable grace and courage."

"She is that," he said gravely.

Realizing that if she stood there any longer the fact that she was greatly flustered by the unexpectedness of all this would start to show, Miriam gestured toward the house. "Our steward has gone for my father. Come in and you can freshen up and rest until he arrives. I shall gather my writing materials."

Simeon had started forward, but now he stopped. "You are to be at the meeting too?"

"Yes," she retorted, a little bite to her voice. "I keep records for my father. I remember now that you find the idea of a woman in such meetings a little disconcerting."

He instantly realized his mistake. "It's not that. It's just that your father said this meeting was to be held in utmost secrecy."

Miriam was instantly sorry she had bristled so easily. "He did? He said nothing of that to me."

Yehuda was looking back and forth between the two of them,

sensing the sudden tension. "Did your father specifically ask that you be there?" he asked.

She nodded, her mind working rapidly. At the time she thought it was unusual. Normally her father had her keep an informal record only of the Council meetings held in Solomon's Porches.

"Then he must have a purpose. Why don't we wait and see what your father says?"

"Of course," Miriam said. She started away, moving toward the house. As they reached the door, she opened it and motioned for Livia to enter. Then Simeon and Yehuda followed. As they moved into the coolness of the entryway, Simeon turned and looked at her, his eyes appraising her openly. She tried to meet his gaze but could not. "What?" she finally asked.

But he spoke to Livia. "You do not seem much like a servant any longer," he said gently.

Livia's eyes widened a little, remembering the sharp interchange between Simeon and Miriam at the springs of Ein Harod. "I told you," she said. "Miriam has never made me feel like a servant."

Yehuda shook his head. "That may be true, but Simeon is right. Something has changed between the two of you."

Miriam's head came up. "Your words were sharp but well aimed that day," she said softly to Simeon. "I am happy to say that Livia and I are—" She stopped, suddenly embarrassed to say it openly in front of Livia. They both sensed that things had changed, but they had not talked at length about it. "Livia is the dearest friend I have."

"More than that," Livia whispered. "Miriam is the sister I never had."

"Then," Simeon responded, "if my words were in any way responsible for what Yehuda and I clearly see between you now, then I am no longer sorry for what I said that day."

Miriam couldn't help it. She just shook her head. "You know what is most interesting about you, Simeon the Javelin?"

He was caught by surprise at that. "What?"

"It is difficult to tell when you offer praise and when you are launching another barb that will sting the flesh."

Yehuda roared. "Oh, yes, Miriam. Exactly so!"

Simeon shot him a withering look, then looked at Miriam. "The woman whose bow and barbs are as keen as the finest of any bowman I know should not be too quick to judge another."

II

"I have asked Miriam to make a record of this proceeding," Mordechai ben Uzziel said. He was speaking to his two guests, but Miriam understood he was giving her an explanation as well. "When we are finished, you shall read what she has recorded, and if you agree that it is an accurate record, it shall be sealed and given to a trusted associate for safekeeping."

Neither Simeon nor Yehuda changed expression, but Miriam could tell that they found this to be highly unusual.

"Once you hear what I have to say," her father went on, "you will understand. I act now without the voice of the Council. They know nothing of this, and it is my sincere hope that they never shall. However, should the need ever arise, I would like a record to substantiate that I neither acted hastily nor in a desire to profit personally from what I am going to tell you."

"We have no problem with Miriam recording what takes place," Simeon said.

She shot him a quick look, but his eyes never left her father's. "It goes without saying that we are here to listen. Our being here implies no agreement beforehand."

Mordechai waved a hand, dismissing that as obvious.

"Then speak on," Yehuda said. "You have not only our attention but our curiosity as well."

Her father leaned back. "Needless to say, Miriam and I both owe the two of you and your little band a great debt for what you did that morning in Samaria."

"A great debt," Miriam murmured.

Simeon nodded but said nothing.

"There is also another debt that is waiting to be paid," Mordechai said, scowling deeply.

Yehuda leaned forward. Simeon, oddly enough, leaned back, as though relaxing. But Miriam saw that his eyes were bright and alert, though they were not filled with trust. This reference to what had happened several weeks before was not what he had expected.

"In a few weeks a Roman column will leave Damascus. Have you heard of this?"

The two men exchanged glances, then Simeon shook his head.

"You will. There is a plan afoot to have the Zealot bands unite to attack this column."

"What Zealot bands?" Yehuda demanded.

"I have heard only one name mentioned," Mordechai said smoothly. "Is there a Gehazi among your leadership?"

Simeon hesitated. The names of the various members of the Zealot leadership were not a closely held secret, but neither were they bandied about lightly.

"It doesn't matter," the Sadducee said, seeing the look on his face.

Simeon decided there was no harm in confirming what Mordechai already seemed to know. "Yes, Gehazi of Sepphoris is looked upon as one to whom the rest of us are willing to listen."

"Well, Gehazi will likely soon call you together and tell you much of what I am telling you now. The Romans are currently gathering a large collection of arms in Damascus. These are destined for Pontius Pilate and the garrison at Caesarea. When I say a large collection, we are talking a thousand of the finest Macedonian bows, twenty thousand arrows, javelins, swords, even a battering ram or two, and some catapults. It seems that Pilate fears the possibility of a Jewish uprising."

Miriam saw the astonishment on the face of the two Galileans, and the sudden eagerness as well. A thousand bows, and the arrows to fill them? Now there was a prize to tempt any rebel group. What she couldn't believe was that her father was telling them this.

"The Romans will also be bringing down gold and silver to help finance Pilate's aqueduct project. They say it could be as much as ten talents."

Simeon whistled softly as his mind calculated quickly. The Roman *denarius* was the wage for a day laborer for one day. It took a hundred *denarii* to make a *mina* and sixty *minas* to make one talent. Thus, with one talent one could hire six thousand workers for a day! Ten talents was a major fortune. "Go on," was all he said. There was interest, but there was also considerable caution as well.

"All of this will be guarded by a full cohort," Mordechai said. "Perhaps more."

"A cohort!" Yehuda exclaimed. That could be up to six hundred men, and they would be heavily armed and very wary. That was not good.

"I think that only a fool would attempt to attack the Romans and take what they carry, but then, as you know, in my opinion you Zealots are famous for being fools."

To Miriam's surprise Simeon laughed easily. "Please, no flattery, Mordechai. It always turns Yehuda's head."

Her father went on, ignoring the sarcasm. "It is no secret that you and I disagree vigorously on what actions should be taken to deal with the situation in our country."

"Indeed we do," Simeon drawled. "So why would you bring us here to tell us this?"

"In the first place, none of this is my doing, nor is the situation in my hands. I have only learned about it by accident. When we came north to try to meet with your Zealot council, we hoped to sign an agreement that you would not provoke the Romans at this time."

"I know why you came north," Simeon said, his voice taking on an edge now. "That still doesn't answer the question."

Miriam's father held out his hands, examining his perfectly manicured fingernails for a moment. "I have had information come into my hands that the Zealots will be approached with knowledge of this Roman column in hopes that they will join in a partnership to attack it."

"A move that you would vigorously oppose."

"Normally, yes. But there is one small detail I have not shared with you as yet." He paused, letting the moment build. "The person who has this information to sell to the Zealots and who wishes to strike an alliance with you goes by the name of Moshe Ya'abin."

If a stone had dropped through the roof at the moment, it would not have left the other three in the room more stunned. Simeon's jaw went slack. Yehuda let out a single curse. Miriam rocked back, her eyes filled with horror. "No, Father!"

He turned to her and smiled kindly. "Yes, Miriam. The very one." Now his eyes went hard, and his voice became grim. "I have been searching for a way to reward our friend for interrupting our trip to the Galilee, but he is as slippery as the sands of Arabia. But in searching for his whereabouts, I came across this information—for which I have paid dearly," he added.

"Go on," Simeon said. He was poised on the edge of his chair, every muscle in his body rigid.

But it was Yehuda who broke in. "Ya'abin is too shrewd to take on the Romans. His way is to choose the weak and the unwary."

"That it is," Mordechai agreed instantly. "And so he seeks to make an alliance with the Zealots, for you have the muscle and the nerve that he lacks."

Simeon's eyes were angry. "The Zealots will have nothing to do with that snake. He is an adder waiting to strike."

Mordechai smiled sadly. "Somehow it is Ya'abin who has all the information on the movement of this Roman treasure." He held out his hands, his voice bland. "Surely even you are not so naive as to believe that your fellow partners in rebellion will turn away from such an opportunity. Even if it means taking the adder into their bosoms."

Simeon gave a soft grunt. He turned and stared out the window, pressing his fingers together as he thought.

Miriam's father waited. Finally Simeon came back to him. "And your part in all of this?"

"Ya'abin is shrewd. He would love to get his hands on some of those weapons too, but if he carries them back to Judea, he will have to move slowly and he will leave a clear trail. That is more risk than he is willing to take. So he plans to offer your people a simple trade. He will take half the gold and head south immediately on horseback, leaving the rest of the hoard to you to divide among yourselves."

Again Simeon nodded. Mordechai was right. Ya'abin was too shrewd to let himself become too vulnerable.

There was a faint smile on the face of the wealthy Sadducee. It held both confidence and bitterness. "But let's suppose that a small band of you, say one led by the famous Ha'keedohn, were to forgo the looting of the weapons and follow after Ya'abin . . . " He stopped and sat back.

Yehuda began to nod after a moment. "We get the money Ya'abin is carrying, which would be our reward for saving you and your daughter, and you get your revenge."

"I was confident that you could quickly see the implications of this situation." Now again his voice went cold. "I don't want you to kill him. Just take his share of the gold as your own and disarm him and his band. I'll see to it from there."

"You're going to bring the Romans in on it?" Simeon said softly.

"The Jewish courts would never have the courage to convict a bandit like Ya'abin. He has too many friends with daggers in their tunics. But I think crucifixion would be a most fitting reward for a man of his nature, don't you?"

Miriam shivered. She still had nightmares about that day in front of her tent, and she too was eager to see the man responsible for it brought to justice—but crucifixion? It was a fiendish way to die. The Romans had perfected it to the point where a man could live for as long as five or six days on the cross, suffering horribly, gradually perishing from shock and thirst and loss of blood. This was a side of her father she had never seen before, and it frightened her how easily that word had fallen from his lips.

"Ya'abin will not be sleeping, of course," her father went on. "He will watch his back trail carefully. It will not be easy to surprise him."

"If it was easy," Yehuda said dryly, "we assume you would have called on the children of Jerusalem to do it."

Miriam wanted to both laugh and scream at such bravado. They were like boys playing a game, each trying to show the other just how brave they could be. But what they were talking about was deadly and final if something went wrong.

"I have nothing more to offer you in the way of help except for this information," Mordechai said. "But I have absolute confidence in that information. If the price is right, even the most trusted of lieutenants can have their heads turned. When Gehazi calls you all together, Ya'abin will put forth his plan. Go along with it; then wait for your opportunity to strike. You shall have your vengeance—and a healthy cash reward as well—and I shall have mine."

"What?" Simeon said dryly. "No offer of a little gold now to entice us to accept your offer?"

"Would you take it?" Mordechai shot right back.

Simeon acknowledged that with a brief nod. "Thank you for not insulting us."

"We are not in agreement on how we save our country,"

Mordechai said, "but I think we can agree on one thing. It is time for someone to crush the adder's head. I have shown you where he shall be and how to do it. Now it is up to you."

Simeon got to his feet abruptly. "We thank you. Yehuda and I shall give this careful thought. If things prove to be as you have said, you shall have your revenge."

Mordechai stood as well. "If you would wait a moment, you can read Miriam's summary of our meeting. Except for one thing. There shall be no names in the document. Not yours. Not Ya'abin's. If any of this, even a whisper should leak out, it would be disastrous."

"We understand."

"Good. Once you see that the document is accurate, it will be sealed and put away for safekeeping."

"I have full confidence in your daughter's record," Simeon said.

Miriam looked up quickly at that, but there was no sarcasm in his voice. For once it was a compliment without any hidden messages. She continued to write swiftly.

"I am not sure how this protects you," Yehuda said, standing to join them. "Why not just tell Pilate all of this and let him take Ya'abin for you?"

Simeon had already seen down that road. "First, because Mordechai is not confident that the Romans can catch Ya'abin. They will be like a great ox chasing after a rabbit."

"A great and stupid ox sometimes," Mordechai said bitterly.

"And there's something more," Simeon said, watching Mordechai closely. "If we successfully steal the Roman gold and help ourselves to a cache of weapons such as Mordechai has described for us, Pilate will surely have to respond. And unless I have underestimated our benefactor here, Yehudah, Mordechai ben Uzziel hopes that the Roman eagle will swoop down and solve the problem of the Zealot rebels once and for all. Thus the Great Council in Jerusalem no longer has to worry about it."

Miriam, who was listening intently to all of this as she wrote furiously, gasped softly. She saw it the instant Simeon said it. That was exactly what her father was thinking. To her horror, her father only laughed. She heard the contempt in it, but there was also genuine respect for the young man who stood before him. "That would be a tragedy," he said blandly, "but of course, you are willing to take that risk because a confrontation with Rome is exactly what you have been waiting for. Am I right?"

Simeon looked over at Miriam. "If I have your word that your record of this meeting shall not be altered, Yehuda and I shall take our leave. There is much we have to consider."

There was a sharp intake of breath. "You have *my* word on that," Mordechai hissed.

"I do. If I have Miriam's as well, then we shall be doubly sure."

She was staring at him, hardly believing what he had said and what that implied. "I will see to it," she said.

"Then *shalom* and farewell, Miriam of Jerusalem and Mordechai ben Uzziel. We shall drive Ya'abin into your clever snare, and we shall both be satisfied. As for the Zealots and Rome, that will play itself out as it will."

As Simeon and Yehuda were ushered out the gate and into the street, Yehuda turned to his leader. "You agreed to all of that pretty quickly, my friend. Are you sure we can trust this man?"

"I am sure we can trust his motives, and make no mistake, he wants his revenge on Ya'abin. I don't doubt that. His pride was struck pretty deep that day. But he's worked this all out very carefully in his mind. He is not doing us a favor. He thinks this will destroy us."

"He does not know how strong we are," Yehuda said. "Nor do the Romans. If we can unite all of the Zealot bands—and such an opportunity as this could finally be the thing that will unite us—we can field two thousand men or more."

"The fat ones who rule on the thrones of Jerusalem have lost all touch with the hearts of the people. So let them sit in their velvet halls and their marbled palaces and make their little plans. It is time, Yehuda, and as you say, this just could be the opportunity we have been waiting for."

Yehuda gave Simeon a long sidewards glance. "You seem particularly happy about this."

Simeon turned, grinning happily. "Yes. This is what we have been waiting for, Yehuda. This could be the spark that finally ignites us in a common cause. Even my father says that if the Zealots could unite, not even the Romans could stop us."

Yehuda was nodding. It was an optimistic outlook, but he felt that surge of excitement too. Mordechai was right. With the arms they would seize in this attack, the Zealots would finally be strong enough to take on even a full Roman legion in direct battle. And all it would take would be one victory, and the whole nation would unite behind them.

Then he noticed that his friend was still grinning broadly. "There is more?"

Simeon smiled thinly. "Let me ask you two questions, old friend. First, this Roman column will be of such significance, who do you suppose Pilate will choose to put in command?"

Yehuda frowned; then suddenly he clapped his hands. "His most trusted officer, the Tribune Marcus Quadratus Didius."

"Second question. The road from Damascus to Caesarea passes directly through Capernaum. Who else would you expect to accompany that column?"

"The centurion Sextus Rubrius," Yehuda said, astonished that his friend had seen that far down the road so quickly.

"Yes," Simeon finished quietly. "Mordechai ben Uzziel will not be the only one who tastes the sweet honey of revenge out of all of this."

III

25 MAY, A.D. 30

"Mistress Miriam?"

Miriam turned. Levi was standing at the door of the library. "Yes, Levi?"

"There is a man at the gate of the courtyard. He requests an audience with you."

She laid down the scroll that she had been reading. "A man?"

"Yes, Mistress Miriam. The Roman officer from Caesarea."

Miriam visibly started. "Really?"

His face showed no expression, a trait that Levi had mastered many years before, long before he had become the chief steward. "Yes. He says he has a meeting with your father, but when I told him he had not returned home as yet, he asked if he might see you."

"I—" It surprised her how quickly her heart had started to flutter. She almost leaped up and raced across the room, but Levi's face stopped her. She kept her face calm. "I shall see him in the courtyard. Livia is not here right now, so I would appreciate it if you or one of the other servants could be present, but at a discreet distance, of course."

"Of course," he said, relieved now. "Very good."

"Show him into the courtyard. Tell him I shall be down shortly."

Levi bowed and backed out. Miriam stood still until the door shut again; then she exploded. She raced across the room, darted through the other door, and raced up the stairs to her bedroom, frantically deciding what would be the best thing to wear. She was glad that Livia was not here to chide her for her girlishness.

IV

"Why, Tribune Didius. What a surprise."

He smiled, and she saw that there was the faintest amusement hiding beneath the deep green of his eyes. "I thought it might be."

"I understand you are looking for my father."

He laughed softly. "Among others," he said. Her eyes were drawn to the cleft in his chin, which made him seem so masculine and strong. That was one thing she liked about the Roman style. When a man kept his face clean-shaven, you could see all of his features clearly. And Marcus Didius had features that were very pleasing to look upon.

"Please, come and sit down. Father should be back shortly."

She moved over to where the tiles ended and a series of octagonal stones provided a walkway into the garden. The meticulously designed and scrupulously maintained garden occupied the whole north half of the courtyard in front of Mordechai's mansion. A few feet into it, beneath a fig tree, a three-tiered fountain caught the sunlight and filled the air with the soft sound of murmuring water.

"How exquisite," Marcus said, moving to the fountain and touching its marbled basins, which were sculpted into the soft lines of seashells.

"You should like it. Father had it shipped in from Rome."

"Ah. Your father has a keen sense of the beautiful."

She cocked her head. "How do you know I did not pick it?"

For the first time his calm assurance slipped a little. "I just assumed if he—"

She laughed lightly. "He did. I've never been to Rome."

He smiled, realizing she had baited him just a little. He sat down on the marbled bench she had indicated, and she took a large wicker chair that faced him.

"Would you like to go to Rome sometime?" he asked.

"Oh, yes. They say it is wonderful."

He nodded gravely. "Whatever else people may say about Octavian Augustus, or Augustus Caesar as you would have called him, he did much to beautify our city, especially in the area around the Roman forum. He liked to boast that he found the city stone and left it marble."

"Father says it was so wondrous that he could scarcely believe it."

"Then we shall have to talk with Pilate about having you and your father invited to Rome by Tiberias."

Miriam had to stop her mouth from falling open.

He smiled when he saw her expression. "Your father is making a great contribution to peace in this land, Miriam. Caesar is always appreciative of men like that."

The memory of yesterday's meeting with Simeon and Yehuda popped into her mind. What would Pilate say if he knew about that? That gave her a chill, and she pushed it away.

Marcus grew more thoughtful now. "Your father invited me to have supper with you again tonight, something I would very much like to do, but I have just received word that I am to return to Caesarea the moment I finish with your father."

Her face fell. "I promised to show you around the Upper City the last time you were here, remember?"

"I remember well and was going to hold you to your word." His shoulders lifted and fell in resignation. "Unfortunately, though I much prefer your company to that of our noble governor—" He shook a finger at her. "And don't you ever dare mention that fact to him—duty is a merciless taskmaster."

"Then we shall just have to make it another time." She smiled warmly. "I love all of Jerusalem, but this part of the city is marvelous, especially at night when there is a full moon, as there will be tonight."

"And I would consider it an honor to return the favor and show you Caesarea by day or by night."

"I would like that very much. I love that city."

Now he was suddenly businesslike. "I have news for you."

"For me?"

"Yes. I located a slave hunter who has had a lot of dealings in Alexandria."

She leaned forward eagerly. "Really? Wonderful!"

He shook his head. "Not so wonderful. He was able to locate the papers for the names that you gave me. The news is not good."

Miriam went very still. "What?"

"The mother of your servant girl died within a year of her sale to her new master."

Her head dropped, and there was a hot burning behind her eyes. "And what of her father and younger brother?" she asked in a low voice.

"Her father was sold to a shipowner who runs grain ships between Rome and Egypt. The ship the man was on ran aground off the coast of Cyprus last year. There were no survivors. As for the brother, who was twelve at the time, he was sold as a household slave to a family in Sicily. That is good."

"Good?" she cried, horrified to think how a family had been ripped apart because of the foolishness of their patron.

He seemed a little surprised. "Yes. Household slaves are generally treated well. The slave hunter has sent off an inquiry to see if the boy is still with that household. There are some grounds for hope."

Suddenly ashamed for her outcry, she reached out and laid a hand on his. "Thank you, Marcus. You are right. The news is not good, but at least it is not all bad. And now Livia will know."

"So you will tell her?"

She hadn't considered doing anything else. "Shouldn't I?"

He shrugged. "Sometimes the truth is more painful than not knowing."

Considering that, she finally shook her head. "I would rather know. Then I could put it behind me."

"She's your servant."

"What was the charge?"

"For what?"

"The slave hunter. Surely he doesn't make those inquiries for free."

He chuckled. "This one was a little strange. He said the only cost would be a walk in the moonlight in the Upper City of Jerusalem."

Her eyes widened; then she laughed lightly. "I don't believe you."

He slapped his hand across his chest, a sign of making an oath. "That's the truth. And he asked if I might collect the fee for him. I swear by the gods that—" He stopped, his face suddenly flustered. "Oh, I'm sorry."

She laughed again. "It doesn't shock me that you swear by your gods, Marcus, as long as you don't expect me to."

He looked greatly relieved. "Nevertheless, I shall try to be more careful in the—"

They turned as the sound of hinges squeaking caught their attention. Miriam's father was just coming in from the street. Marcus immediately got to his feet. "There's your father."

Miriam stood too and started back for the main courtyard. "Hello, Papa."

He was a little surprised at the sight of her company but then immediately recovered. "Marcus, I'm sorry for being late."

"No apology necessary, Mordechai. Your daughter is a most charming hostess."

He came over and gave her a quick hug. "So she has not been rude to you?"

She poked him in the ribs, and he yelped in pretended pain.

"I have a hard time believing that Miriam is ever rude to anyone," Marcus said nobly.

"Then you haven't seen her before the third hour of the morning."

"Father!"

He kissed her on the cheek. "I didn't mean it." Then to Marcus. "You're staying for dinner?"

He shook his head and explained the new development.

"Then I won't detain you further. Miriam, could you get us some wine and bring it to the library in about five minutes?"

She nodded, surprised that he had not called one of the servants. Then she understood that her father wished to be alone with Marcus.

"Yes, Papa." She watched them walk away, then started for the wine cellar, which was around the back of the house, where the wall of the courtyard and the trees provided the greatest shade.

V

As Marcus took a chair, Mordechai walked to his desk. He retrieved a small metal key from a chain around his neck and opened it. He pulled out a drawer, then pressed a hidden latch. The door swung away to the side. Reaching deep inside the desk, Mordechai pulled out a rolled parchment. He looked at the seal, still fresh from when Miriam had pressed the hot signet stamp into the red sealing wax yesterday afternoon. She thought he had taken it to a trusted member of the Council. Instead, he had brought it only this far.

He handed it to Marcus. "Don't let Miriam or anyone else see this," he said. "Give it to Pilate. It will help him see how things are progressing."

Marcus took it and shoved it inside his tunic.

"There are still a few details to work out, but I am satisfied that things are going forward as planned. Tell the governor that I shall come to Caesarea to report personally when things are finalized."

"He asked that I remind you that he will need sufficient time to make the arrangements. It is not a simple thing that you are asking."

"I understand. I shall come the moment things are finally in place."

Marcus tapped his chest where the scroll was hidden. "I suppose this does not reveal any names."

Mordechai smiled easily. "No."

"I didn't think so."

There was a knock at the door. "Tell the governor that things are going exactly as I had hoped," he said in a low voice. "In another few weeks, I think we will have his little Galilean problem solved." Then with a pleased smile he turned and looked at the door. "Come in, my dear," he called.

VI

"Papa?"

Mordechai looked up from his papers. "I thought you were in bed."

She gave him a quick look of disbelief. She never went to bed before the second watch.

"Come in."

She did so, taking a chair in front of the desk on which he worked. "I have something I need to talk to you about."

He pushed the papers aside and sat back. "Say on."

She hesitated, then took a quick breath. "I have done something without your permission."

As she began to tell him about asking Marcus to find a slave hunter who could locate Livia's family, his eyes narrowed, and for a moment she thought he would be angry. But when she finished sharing Marcus's report that day, he merely grunted. "I see." And then his next question completely took her by surprise. "Do you find Marcus attractive?"

"I—well, I—" She was stammering and blushing hotly.

He laughed. "I think that's answer enough. And there is no question about how Marcus feels about you. When you are in the room, I can hardly get him to look at me."

"Father!"

"Well, do you think I am too old and senile to notice such things? After all, I have trotted out a dozen possible suitors for you in the last year or two, and you brush them aside as though they were ants trespassing on your table. I am past forty now. I wish to see our family carried on."

She was so flabbergasted she didn't know what to say.

"Marcus comes from a powerful Roman family. They have great influence with the emperor, I am told."

"He said he was going to have Tiberias invite you and me to Rome to thank you for your efforts in bringing peace to our land."

"Really?" he said, genuinely pleased.

But Miriam was still in shock. "You would have him become a suitor, Father? He isn't Jewish."

Mordechai gave a nonchalant shrug, as if Miriam had mentioned that Marcus had a mole on one cheek or something. In that instant Miriam saw that though her father was one of the most powerful of the religious leaders in Jerusalem, religion really meant very little to him. That realization suddenly filled her with a deep sadness.

"Well," he went on, not noticing the expression on her face, "we shall have to see what develops. Is that all you wished to talk to me about?"

She had to fight to recover her thoughts. Her mind was still reeling from what had just happened. "No, there is something else. I—It's about Livia, Father."

"Yes?"

"She has become much more than a servant, Papa. She is my dearest friend."

He frowned momentarily, then nodded. "I understand. Unfortunately, you are so bright and so mature, you haven't found many friends among the spoiled children of the elite, have you?"

Again she could barely hide her amazement. He never spoke to her about suitors or her friends—or lack of them. He rarely spoke to her at all about her personal life. She went on, hesitant now. "Knowing that Livia's parents are gone and that she has no family, I have been thinking. I would like to adopt Livia as my sister."

"What?" He had been only half listening, but that jerked him back in a hurry.

She rushed on, anxious now to have it said. "I'm not asking you to adopt her, Father, for I know that would have implications for inheritance and all of that. But you have given me my own funds. I have invested them and seen them multiply. I would pay for everything, and anything she receives would come from me."

His brow was deeply furrowed, and the lines around his mouth were deep and rigid. "Miriam, think what you are saying."

"I have thought, Father. I've thought a lot about it. We are so close. I love her as though she were my sister, Papa."

"I know, and that's fine, but—"

"No, you don't know. We are so much alike. Like yesterday, when we heard Jesus of Nazareth. We both—"

The look on his face cut her off. "You heard this Jesus yesterday?"

"Yes." Now she realized she may have made a serious mistake. "Livia heard that he was on the Temple Mount. We were there when Azariah brought that woman."

"The fool!" he spat. Then his eyebrows shot up. "So that's what he meant?"

"What?"

"He said there was something about my family I ought to know. When I asked him what it was, he said it could come later. He saw you there, didn't he?"

"Yes, I—"

"And he thinks he can use that against me," he said to himself. There was a mirthless laugh. "What an old hypocrite. And what was he thinking, trying to act on his own with that woman without the voice of the Council?"

"It was terrible, Papa. They were using that pitiful woman as though she were a block of wood."

He brushed that aside. "I don't want you having anything to do with Jesus, Miriam. Do you hear me?"

"But, Papa!"

He leaned forward and slammed his fist down. "I mean it, Miriam," he bellowed. "You've flirted with this and that in religion over the years, and I've held my tongue. But I will not have you listening to this madman from Nazareth."

She couldn't believe what he was saying. "Madman? Father, he's not. What he says makes so much sense. And what he did for that woman yesterday was one of the most wonderful things I have ever seen.

"Enough!" he roared. "This man is threatening everything we've worked for, everything we have built up so carefully."

"Jesus?" she asked, completely incredulous.

"Yes! The people fawn over him as if he were some great prophet. Mobs follow him wherever he goes. You know what that does to the Romans. If we don't stop him, he could be like Samson and pull everything down on top of our heads."

Miriam felt the coldness shoot through her. She remembered the words of the impotent man when he had found Jesus yesterday. *Take care. The leaders are furious with you. Some even talk of putting you to death.* "What do you mean you have to stop him?" she half whispered.

"Miriam, I will say nothing more of this man. Nor will I have you speak his name in this house again. Do you understand? I have powerful enemies who would love to know that I cannot control my household."

Somewhere down deep in her, a coldness began to spread. "Are you telling me what I can and can't believe, Papa?"

He shot to his feet. "I am telling you what you will and will not do," he thundered. "I will not hear one more word! Not one! Now you are excused."

Miriam got slowly to her feet, dazed and bewildered. In her eighteen years of life, she had never seen her father like this. And she could never remember him raising his voice in more than mild irritation at her. Her chin came up, and without a word, she turned and walked quietly to the door.

As she opened it, he spoke again. "And there will be no more of this nonsense about Livia, either. If I have to, I shall find another servant to take her place."

CHAPTER 22

I

27 MAY, A.D. 30

"It is so good to have you back home, Deborah."

"It is good to be home again."

"I am glad that Naomi recovered. I was afraid that the reason you were there so long was that there might have been a funeral."

"No, I—" Deborah stopped. "I wanted to be sure she was completely better."

They were lying together on the bed, the cover thrown back. The windows to their room were open. Moonlight filled the room with soft light, and the breeze coming off the Galilean highlands was finally taking some of the day's heat away.

David sighed in contentment and laid back, putting his hands beneath his head and looking up at the ceiling.

"David?"

He turned his head. "Yes?"

"I need to talk to you about Simeon."

He nodded. When she had arrived just an hour earlier, he had been surprised at her reticence to say more about their son than that he had gone to Jerusalem and that when he returned, he would probably stay in Beth Neelah for a few more days. "Go on."

And so she told him. She told him why their son had left Capernaum so abruptly. She told him about the hurt and the anger, the sense of betrayal, the bitterness not only against his father, but for Leah and Ephraim as well, because they had tacitly taken their father's side in this. Through it all, David said nothing. He turned on his side to face her again, watching her face in the moonlight, seeing the pain there, and feeling the unspoken condemnation.

"I don't know what you are going to do, David," she said in conclusion. "The damage that has been done may be irreparable."

For a long moment he said nothing. He had a pain of his own, and it was greater than just for his son, though that had settled in over him like a shroud. Finally, he took a breath and began. "The other day when you and I talked about Sextus Rubrius, I made you a promise. I told you that I would not have any further association with him."

"Yes," she whispered, her voice husky now. "Yes, you did."

"Deborah, I—" Again his breath came out in a sigh. "As you know, our people have come to develop deep feelings of animosity and mistrust toward the Gentiles."

"This isn't just a Gentile, David. This is the man who tried to kill my son."

"*Our* son," he gently corrected her. Then he went on quickly. "Part of those feelings developed out of a response to God's commandments to avoid partaking of the influences of the world. Part of it came because somehow we thought being the chosen people made us superior in some way to everyone else."

She came up on one elbow. "David—"

"No, hear me out, Deborah. Then you can say what you have in your heart."

She nodded and lay back again.

"Some of the more extreme rabbis have taken this charge to keep ourselves separate from the world to ridiculous lengths. For example, one has even said that if you see a child fall in a stream of water, if it is a Jewish child, you are under moral obligation to try to save it. If it is the child of a Gentile, however, you may save it if you wish, but there is no moral imperative."

There was great dismay in his voice. "Have we become so spiritually blind, so utterly bankrupt? I didn't go out seeking Sextus Rubrius, Deborah. Neither did he come looking for me. His servant was gravely ill. He couldn't bear to stand by and do nothing. When you think about it, it is astonishing that he would come seeking out Jesus—a Roman soldier coming to a Jew for help! When he saw me there in the crowd, he saw a face that he knew, someone who might help in a time of great need. Would you really have me turn away under such circumstances? Would you have me leave the child to drown in the river because it is the child of a Gentile?"

Deborah didn't answer. She had begun this conversation on an accusatory note. Now she and Simeon were the ones being questioned. And what was worse, she knew he was right. Simeon's bitterness had deeply affected her, but she knew in her heart this was not a deliberate betrayal on David's part.

"I will try to explain all of this to Simeon," he continued, "and I shall do so as gently as I can. I do understand his anger. I do understand the pain that both of you feel. But I must say this. If Simeon cannot see why I did what I did, then there is something deeply flawed in our son, and I grieve to think that he has come to this point."

"David, I tried to tell Simeon that you had not initiated this contact." She took a deep breath. "You know what cut him most deeply? When you called Rubrius your friend."

He sat up. "But he was a friend, Deborah. I was sick when I learned what he did to Simeon. I hated him bitterly for a time. How could he have done that? After all we had done together." He began to rub his eyes. "And yet . . . Sextus is an honorable man, a good man. Are we so nearsighted that we see goodness only in those of our own kind?"

"I'm just telling you what Simeon said," she answered dully.

"Simeon evidently turned around and left when he heard me say that. He didn't get to see what happened next."

"Does it matter?"

"It matters very much," he answered softly. And then he explained about Sextus and his conversation with Jesus, about how he felt unworthy to have Jesus come into his house, and about giving orders and having them obeyed.

"It was later that afternoon," David went on. "Another servant from the household of Sextus came to report to Jesus. He told us that when Sextus returned home, he found his servant completely healed. Amazed, Sextus inquired of the others in his household at what hour his servant had been cured." There was a brief pause. "It was the exact hour when Jesus told Sextus that his request for Jesus' help had been granted."

Deborah said nothing. Here it was again, the question of Jesus. It seemed to loom up before them every time they talked, every time they were together. He was a miracle worker. He was a fraud. He taught like no other teacher. He was mad. She was so weary of going back and forth, up and down.

"You need to know, Deborah, that while you were gone, some amazing things have happened. I saw them. Leah saw them. Ephraim and Rachel were there to see some of them as well."

Her breath came out in a long, soft sound of weariness. "I'm not surprised."

"You probably sensed tonight that something has happened to Leah."

Deborah's head came around. She *had* noticed that. Leah had been . . . What? It was like she was bursting to tell her mother something, but held back. When Deborah had commented on it, her daughter had laughed awkwardly and said they would talk in the morning. "What about Leah?" she asked slowly.

"She is completely convinced that Jesus is the Messiah."

Her mouth tightened as the impact of his words hit her. "So that's what you've been doing while I've been gone," she said. It came out with more bitterness than she had intended.

"No, Deborah. That is what has been happening while you were gone." He paused, then said, "Ephraim and Rachel too."

She jerked up to a sitting position, turning to face him. She stared at him, but words didn't come.

"I know what you're thinking, but I did not initiate this. Leah and I went for a walk down to the boats and things just started happening from there."

"So now it's Simeon and me against the rest of the family?" She couldn't believe what she was hearing.

"Is that how you see it?"

The pain in his voice sent a jab of shame through her, but she was too hurt to respond to it.

"Leah wants desperately to talk with you about it. Rachel too. But they won't unless you ask them. If you don't wish to hear, they'll know that and won't say anything."

"I—"

"But if you don't want to hear any more about Jesus, then you'd better go back into the hills, Deborah, because the whole town is on fire with what has been happening. Don't talk to Anna, because she has no question in her mind. And if you see Andrew's wife, you'd better turn away because she was there, and she'll want to tell you what happened too."

She pulled her knees up, hugging herself, trying to shut out his words.

"Deborah, know this much. You can no longer ignore Jesus. You can't simply dismiss him because he offended you with his teachings about the Romans."

"If I can't accept his teachings, how can I accept *him?*" she cried.

"I'm not trying to convince you. I really mean that. I am just saying that you can no longer pretend he is just another man out trying to gather a following. Talk to Anna. Talk to your daughter, to your son and his wife. Listen to what happened, to what they saw and heard. Then you'll know why they are convinced that Jesus is not just any man."

She said nothing. Her mind was in turmoil. She felt sick at heart. If Simeon came home to this, he and his father would never be reconciled.

"There's something else you need to know, Deborah."

"Not tonight, David," she sighed. "Haven't you told me enough?"

He went on softly. "Day before yesterday, I was alone with Jesus for a few minutes. So I asked him a question."

She thought she knew what that question was. *Are you the Messiah?* But she was wrong.

"I asked him if he had been born in Nazareth."

Her head turned slowly. A sudden prickling sensation raced through her body.

"He said no. He said that though both his father and mother were from Nazareth, because of some unusual circumstances he had been born in Bethlehem."

She just stared at him, her eyes wide in the dimly lit room.

"His parents went to Bethlehem during Passover because of the call for the Roman census. Both are of the lineage of David, so they returned to the city of their ancestors."

Now he seemed far away from her, lost in his memories of that time. "He said that by the night they reached Bethlehem, Mary's time had come. Mary is his mother's name."

He stopped again, and Deborah found that she was holding her breath.

His voice became very quiet and very somber. "They could find no lodging there, so a kindly man made a place for them in a stable."

"And that's where he was born?" she whispered, feeling as though her head was whirling.

"Yes."

"Did you tell him your story first?" Deborah asked, grasping for something to steady herself. If David had told Jesus of his experience first, then it would be easy to—

"No. Nor did I tell him afterwards. In recent years, I have spoken to only three people about that night, Deborah—you, Simeon, and now Leah. I haven't even told Peter."

That cut off her next question. If Peter had known, perhaps he had told Jesus. Then she shook her head. Was she so desperate to avoid the truth that she would do anything to sidestep it?

"I also asked him how long ago that was," David finished softly. "He said it was thirty years ago this last Passover."

II

For a long time after David's breathing had steadied and deepened, Deborah lay on the bed, staring up into the darkness. When she was finally sure he was asleep, she slipped carefully off the bed, found her robe, and tiptoed out of their room. She padded noiselessly down the hall, eased through the main door, and went out into the courtyard.

For almost an hour she sat in the moonlight, staring at nothing, barely moving as she tried to sort through the tumble in her mind. After going back and forth a hundred times, she eventually came to this. She either had to reject David's experience of thirty years before or decide that he was lying to her now, or she had to accept the possibility that Jesus of Nazareth was what her heart and mind could not believe was true—he was in truth and deed the promised Messiah. That was her choice—simple in one way, terrible in another. How could she in honesty to herself simply dismiss David's incredible experience in Bethlehem thirty years earlier? She had never doubted him before. Had Jesus somehow learned about the experience shared by the shepherds that night, and was he capitalizing on it to pass himself off as the Messiah? She shook her head. It was possible, but so remote, so unlikely.

And yet, again and again her eye was drawn to a spot in front of the fountain. The moon was low in the sky, and the fountain was in shadow, but she didn't need to see with her eyes. The stains on the tiles there were so vividly etched in her mind that she needed no visual reminder of them. What of that? she cried out in her mind. What of seeing her son struck down in front of her eyes. Or what of her father? What of her mother, who died in a cold and dreary cave because her heart had been shattered by the terrible events that had overtaken their family? If Jesus—who spoke of love and forgiveness and going the second mile—truly was the Messiah, what of all that? What of justice? What of evil unrestrained?

Deborah looked up, staring at the moon and the stars that surrounded it. Then she moved from the bench and dropped to her knees. For a long time she didn't move; then finally her eyes lifted again to the heavens. "O God," she whispered. "What is happening? What am I to do?" She drew in a deep breath. "I would be honest with thee. I would do thy will. But I cannot see the path thou wouldst have me walk. Help me to open my heart to the truth. Help me to find the way."

She stopped, wondering what more to say. What more was there? Then her head bowed. "Help me find peace. Amen."

III

"Esther, do you want to go to the market with Granmama?"

Esther was seated on the floor, playing with some strings, forming them into endless patterns. She looked up, her four-year-old eyes gravely considering the invitation. She looked first at her mother, then at Deborah.

Deborah crouched down beside her granddaughter. "Granmama is going to buy some food for supper, Esther. Why don't you come with me?"

It was as though she had spoken to a rock with eyes. There was not the slightest change of expression, not on her face, not in those eyes that were the color of the rich, dark earth.

Deborah smiled and looked up at Rachel. "How does she do that? How can she not show the slightest reaction? It's as though I weren't even here."

Rachel shook her head. "I don't know. She is so funny sometimes." Then she came over to her daughter and squatted down to face her. "Esther, if you don't want to go, that's all right. But Granmama would like to have company. And you could help her carry things."

Esther blinked, still quietly taking the measure of them both. "What about Boaz?" she finally said.

Her mother shook her head. "Boaz is still asleep, Esther. And besides, he's not a big boy yet. He's too little to help. But you're not. Will you go and help your Granmama?"

"I'll hold your hand tight," Deborah said, wondering if that was the cause of her hesitancy. She was always uncomfortable around people she did not know.

Finally there was a slow nod. "All right."

"Wonderful." Deborah stood up.

Rachel took Esther's hand and pulled her up as well. "Go get your sandals. You can't go out with bare feet."

Esther turned and trotted out of the room. Deborah looked at Rachel. "It's no wonder both her grandfather and I spoil her so much. She is adorable—those large eyes. They make her look like she's twenty-five."

"Well, she loves you, that's for sure. She won't even go to the market with Ephraim."

"I'll keep her right with me. We'll be fine."

IV

"You pick the ones you think are best."

Esther looked up at her grandmother to see if she was really serious.

"Go on. You like rolls. Which do you think we should get?"

Seeing that she really meant it, Esther turned back to the table where the baker had spread out his offerings. Her mouth puckered up in concentration; then she gravely pointed to some small round rolls on top of which the baker had put honey, letting it soak into the light brown crust.

"Good choice," Deborah said. She nodded at the baker. "We'll have ten, please." She opened the smallest of the cloth bags she carried, and he began to place them inside. When nine were in, Deborah reached quickly for the last one. "We'll keep this one out," she said. She paid him, then split the roll in two, handing the top half to Esther.

"Thank you, Granmama," she said in a little voice, eyeing the baker to make sure he would not be displeased.

"You're welcome, my little almond blossom."

She took her free hand, and together they continued, moving from stall to stall in the busy marketplace, munching on the roll as they walked. They bought some sunflower seeds from a young boy; ginger, pepper, and marjoram from the spice man; and some carrots and radishes from a vegetable farmer.

"Oh, look, Esther," Deborah said a moment or two later. "The first of the melons are here." She was pointing to a vendor three spaces down. He had no table, but he had a pyramid-shaped stack of watermelons on the ground in front of him. Behind him, a small cart was filled with more of the same. A woman was arguing loudly with the man over the price. Since it was the very first of the season, Deborah was sure the prices would not be very reasonable. As Deborah and Esther reached them, the woman shook her head and walked away empty-handed, grumbling aloud about greedy people.

The farmer looked up at the two newcomers and pulled a face. "Some people would rob the food right out of my children's mouth."

Deborah smiled to herself. The street hawkers and the fruit and vegetable vendors were all the same. They haggled fiercely. If you did not immediately pay the asking price—which was always about double the fair value and which they had little expectation of getting—you were accused of stealing food from their children, forcing them to let their aged grandmothers go without a roof, or taking the clothes off the family's back. It was the way of their people, and their love of bargaining went back as far as Abraham, if not further.

Deborah looked for any sign showing the price. There was none. Not a good omen. "How much?" she said. Esther, holding tightly to her hand now, had ducked in behind Deborah's skirts and eyed the man from behind that point of added safety.

"Half a shekel each."

"What?" Deborah cried, pretending shock and dismay.

"First of the season," he noted, gesturing with a waving hand. "You won't find any others in the market on this day."

"For half a shekel I could grow my own and support my family in addition. And besides, they are small." And they were. The melons were round and barely larger than a loaf of bread.

"Lady Deborah," he said, his voice as smooth as olive oil, "you have better things to do than to work all day in the blistering sun, raising calluses on your lovely hands, having your fair skin burned red as the flesh of the melon and your fingernails filled with dirt." He held up his soiled hands to prove his point. "Why then would you begrudge a hardworking man a modest and well-earned living?"

She laughed. He was good at this. It was all said with a mournful expression and great pathos. The fact that he knew who she was didn't surprise her at all. David was one of Capernaum's most prominent citizens. The wife of David therefore had a certain prominence of her own. The only bad thing was that he knew she could afford to pay whatever he asked. That would not work to her favor.

Deborah looked down at Esther. "This early they won't have much flavor."

Esther nodded gravely, as if she had already come to that same conclusion. The man gave the cry of a wounded bird. "Ah, Lady Deborah. Why do you speak so?" With a movement that was so quick that it startled Esther, he reached under his robe and withdrew a long knife. Esther shrank back, but he wasn't looking at her at all. He grabbed a melon from the top of the stack, placed it on a board beside him, and split it open with one fluid movement of his hand. He quickly sliced a piece the thickness of his finger and held it out to Esther.

She retreated deeper into the folds of Deborah's skirt, peeking out after a moment to eye the man with considerable misgiving. Deborah took the piece from him and nibbled one part of it. It was good, better than she had hoped. She didn't let that show on her face, of course.

She reached down and held it out for Esther. "You try it," she said. "Tell me what you think."

Tentatively, Esther took it from her grandmother and took one bite, then another. Again her expression gave nothing away.

"What do you think, Esther? Is it good?"

She gave the briefest of nods.

"Ha!" the vendor sniffed. "At least one woman in this family has a sense of taste. Come, Madam, I give you a very good deal."

"We'll take four," Deborah said. She began to reach inside the small leather pouch where she kept her money, then stopped. "For one shekel."

"*What?*" the man cried. "Would you rob a man in broad daylight? Three for one and a half shekels, and that is still the cruelest of thievery."

"Actually," Deborah said slowly, ignoring the jibe, "I don't really need that many." She sighed. "In fact, I don't have that much room in my bag. And they are so heavy." She looked at Esther. "Perhaps it is better if we get nothing today."

Esther shook her head slowly, her eyes showing her disappointment.

That delighted the man. "When your husband and sons return home tonight," he said unctuously, "they shall sing your praises for bringing them fruit from the fields of Shaul of Genneseret. I would wager, in fact, that I shall receive a visit from your husband before morning. He shall ask if he can sell my melons throughout the whole of Galilee."

She wanted to laugh but held her peace. Here was one grand charlatan. Then finally she began to nod. "Three, then, for one shekel," Deborah said, "and only because my granddaughter has believed your wild rantings and has taken pity on you."

"Done," the man said with a sudden grin.

Deborah sighed. She had offered too much, or he would never have agreed so quickly. The man began to reach for a melon. Deborah held up her hand. "Oh, no," she said. "My granddaughter and I shall pick them."

He harrumphed a little but waved his hand, inviting them to proceed.

Deborah explained to Esther how one could tell which melons were the best by thumping them. The lower the pitch, the better the taste and the juicier the fruit. That was a revelation to Esther, and she joined her grandmother in this new game with the first indication of any emotion. She thumped each one enthusiastically, cocking her head and listening intently. When Deborah indicated that the one Esther picked was probably the best of the lot, for the first time she saw that hint of a smile that was more noticeable in her eyes than on her face. They picked two more, and Deborah paid the man gladly. She had won a minor triumph with her little sober sphinx, and if she had been robbed in the process, it was worth it.

They set the melons aside beneath the farmer's cart, promising to return for them in a little while. They were heavy, and Deborah did not want to carry them with her everywhere they went. They walked on happily, Esther finally more talkative. She would answer in simple words or phrases when Deborah asked her questions, but otherwise was content to take in everything with that same grave expression.

They left the area of fruits, vegetables, and dry goods and started down another street where the butchers and the fishmongers had their tables. They had barely approached that area of the market when Deborah saw a crowd of people ahead, blocking most of the street.

"What is it, Granmama?" Esther asked, pulling back a little.

"I don't know. Just some people. Maybe it's a fresh catch of fish." She took her hand more tightly. "Come on. Pampa loves his fish fresh, and since Andrew and the others have stopped fishing, we have to buy them like everyone else. Let's go see."

Esther moved in closer to Deborah, who squeezed her hand as they walked, but Esther did not protest. She carried the sack with the bread, while Deborah carried their other purchases in her other hand. As they reached the outskirts of the crowd, Deborah tried to see over their heads to what was there. It wasn't fresh fish. The people were in a large semi-circle around the wall of one of the houses. Deborah knew this area well and knew there was a stone bench there. She could see that someone was seated on it, his back half to her.

"What is it?" she asked a woman just in front of her.

She turned. "It's Jesus of Nazareth."

A frown creased Deborah's brow. So he was here in Capernaum again. She hesitated, tempted to turn away. Deborah was still battling with herself inwardly. She had not found the peace she sought. Part of that was her fault. That she knew. She had not talked to Anna, wife of Simon Peter, or the other women she knew. She had told Leah she wasn't ready to talk about what had happened to her. Not yet. She still regretted that in a way. The pain and disappointment in her daughter's eyes had made her almost weep. Gratefully, David seemed to understand. When Ephraim had started to raise the subject of Jesus at supper the first night after her return, it had been David who had stopped him with a look.

But she had not been able to avoid hearing everything. The whole town was buzzing with news of Jesus. One could hardly go out without hearing a conversation about him—he had done this, he had taught this, he had been here. Mostly it was talk of the miracles. Some of it she dismissed as exaggeration and rumor, but some things she had heard from actual eyewitnesses. She had overheard a woman at the well who had been one of the mourners at the house of Jairus. She had seen that little girl, the woman said. She had seen her laid out on the bed, no life in her. And then she had seen Jesus come out of the house, and moments later Jairus and his wife and daughter followed them. Deborah had left then, without her water, her mind reeling.

She turned and looked at the man sitting on the bench. David was right. She could not simply ignore this any longer. Postponing it day after day wasn't helping her either.

She looked down, squeezing Esther's hand. "Hold my hand tightly, Esther. Granmama just wants to see for a moment."

That was unnecessary counsel, for with all the people close around them, Esther was clinging to her now.

It took Deborah three or four minutes to make her way through the crowd, angling in a way that would bring her to where she could see Jesus' face and not just watch him from the side. As they neared the front of the crowd, she saw Amram the Pharisee and several of his associates. They were standing directly in front of Jesus, who was seated on the bench. Peter and Andrew stood on each side of Jesus. Deborah then saw John and James in the crowd a few feet away.

When she reached the place where no one was directly in front of her, Deborah brought Esther around to stand in front of her so she wouldn't get lost in the press of people. A woman beside her, who had a boy about Esther's age, looked at her and smiled. "The Pharisees are trying to make Jesus look foolish," she offered. She seemed amused by that concept—as if such a thing were possible!

Nodding, Deborah turned to look at the cluster of men confronting Jesus. It was obvious that Amram and his colleagues were quite agitated. Amram was stroking his beard in quick, jerky movements. "By what authority do you speak as you do?" he demanded.

Peter stepped forward. "Do you not hear what is happening?" he said, clearly irritated. "The blind see. The sick are healed. Evil spirits are cast out from those who are tormented. What more authority do you need than that?"

Deborah suddenly started. Standing in the group of Pharisees with his back to her was a familiar figure. She leaned forward, and then he partly turned. It was her brother, Aaron. She peered more closely, finding that hard to believe. He was here in Capernaum and hadn't even let her know?

Then she was pulled back into what was happening. Amram raised one hand and shook it at Peter. "He casts out devils by the power of Beelzebub, the Prince of Devils."

Peter's face darkened, and he looked as if he was going to erupt, but it was Jesus who spoke. To her surprise, his voice was of perfect mildness. "But how could that be?" he asked. "If a house is divided against itself, it will fall. If a kingdom is divided against itself, it will fail."

"What is that supposed to mean?" one of the Pharisees snapped.

"You say that I cast out evil spirits by the power of Beelzebub, but why would Satan give me power to work against his own kingdom? If Satan is divided against himself, his kingdom cannot stand."

Amram and those around him were caught completely off their guard with that simple answer. Aaron was fuming, speaking in sharp angry hisses to the man standing next to him. It was clear they had no response to that.

"And," Jesus went on, speaking more to the crowd now than to his antagonists, "the Pharisees themselves believe that they have been given the power under the Law to exorcise evil spirits." He turned back to Amram. "If you cast out evil spirits, do you do it by the power of Beelzebub as well?"

For a moment Deborah thought Amram was going to explode right there. His eyes glowered in outrage.

"When a man is strong and well armed in his palace," Jesus continued, "then his goods are at peace. But when a stronger man comes, he overcomes that man and takes the armor in which he trusted and spoils his goods."

Deborah's head came up slowly. Suddenly Amram and Aaron were forgotten. That was a remarkable statement. Was Jesus saying he was stronger than Satan? She started to shake her head, hardly able to believe that, but then stopped when Jesus went on.

He lifted one hand and extended his finger, as though he were going to shake it at them, but he didn't. He just pointed. His voice became firm and strong. "If I, with the finger of God, cast out evil spirits, then why do you doubt that the kingdom of God has come unto you?"

The crowd gave an approving murmur. Though many of them believed that the Pharisees were probably closer to carrying out God's will than the aristocratic Sadducees, they were nevertheless pleased to see them taken down a notch in their arrogance and pride. And there was no question that the crowd's sympathy was with Jesus right now.

Amram whirled, pulling his robes around him. "We do not have to listen to such babbling," he snorted. "Come!" He strode away, hissing at the crowd to make way for them.

As they passed by Deborah, Aaron finally saw her. He was at first startled at the sight of her; then his eyes narrowed. He hurried over to her. "What are you doing here?" he said in a low voice.

"I've just gotten here," she said, taken aback a little by his anger. "I saw the crowd and wanted to see what was happening."

"The man is unbelievable! Absolutely unbelievable!"

Irritation flashed in Deborah. "Good morning, Deborah," she said in a sweetly mocking tone. "How nice to see you. I've just come down from Sepphoris and have dropped by your house to say hello. And by the way, hello to my niece, Esther."

The woman beside Deborah snickered. Aaron's face was red. "Oh, I—we—well, we did just arrive this morning. They've called a council to discuss how we should deal with this Jesus and—"

The same lady broke in. "Why don't you just listen to him. He is a wonderful teacher."

"If I wished to speak to you, Madam," Aaron said haughtily, "I would address you directly." He sniffed and turned back to Deborah. "I will be here several days. I was going to come by this evening."

Deborah softened a little. "Did you bring Hava and the children?"

He shook his head, surprised that she would even ask.

"Do you have a place to stay?"

"No."

She touched his hand. "Supper will be at sundown."

He nodded curtly and spun away, hurrying after the others, who were disappearing into the crowd.

Deborah felt a tug on her skirt. She looked down. "Why is Uncle Aaron angry, Granmama?" Her dark eyes were wide with concern.

Laying a hand on her cheek, Deborah smiled. "He's not angry, Esther. He's just a little upset right now. It's all right." She squeezed her hand. "I think it's time to go home, don't you?"

Her head bobbed quickly, gratefully, but before Deborah began to move, the woman beside her grabbed her son's hand and pushed forward. "Jesus," she called, "will you give my son a blessing?"

Surprised at that, Deborah turned back. She saw that with the departure of Amram's group, the crowd was moving in closer around Jesus. She felt Esther go rigid as the people began to push in around them. Deborah slipped the handles of the bag over her arm and lifted Esther up.

Other women were bringing their children forward too. Several had babes in arms. "Touch my son, Master," one cried. "Please bless my baby," said another. "Here, this is little Joseph. Will you bless him?"

Peter and Andrew moved forward, holding out their arms and trying to hold the crowd back. "People," Peter said loudly, "please give the Master some room."

The woman with her boy had reached the fisherman by now and tried to duck around him. Simon Peter quickly blocked her way. "Good woman," he said, "your child does not need a blessing from Jesus. Young children are without sin."

"Peter."

He turned at the sound of Jesus' voice. "Yes, Master?"

"Suffer the little children to come unto me."

Peter was clearly caught off guard with that. "But, Master, I—"

"Suffer them to come," Jesus said gently, "for of such is the kingdom of heaven."

With that Peter stepped back, making way. Andrew did the same. To Deborah's surprise, it was the children who moved in. They swarmed around Jesus, delighted to be given an open invitation.

Deborah was amazed at what she saw next. Jesus remained seated, reaching out to take a hand or touch a face, laughing and smiling in delight at the response of the little ones to him. A little boy of about three, with a dirty face and a mop of tangled black hair, edged in close. Deborah couldn't determine if his mother was with him or not. He watched Jesus in wonder, too shy to move forward but obviously wanting to be noticed. And then Jesus saw him and held out a hand. Slowly the boy came forward. Jesus leaned forward, scooped him up, and deposited him on his lap, laughing at the boy's startled expression.

That brought Deborah up with a jerk. She looked at Esther, who was watching what was happening with eyes as wide as the melons they had just bought. "Would you like to go see Jesus?" Deborah asked on impulse.

Esther turned away sharply. "No!" she blurted.

Esther held her more tightly. "That's all right," Deborah said. "You don't have to. And Granmama is right here. It's all right."

Greatly relieved, Esther seemed to relax. She turned back to watch.

Jesus raised a hand and said something to the children. They quieted quickly, and the crowd did the same. He reached out with his hand and ruffled the hair of the boy on his lap; then he looked up at the faces of the surrounding people. "My disciples have asked me, who is the greatest in the kingdom of heaven? Well, I say unto you, unless you be converted and become as these little children, you shall not enter the kingdom of heaven."

People turned to look at each other in surprise at that pronouncement, but no one spoke.

"Whosoever humbles himself as this little child, it is that person who shall be the greatest in the kingdom of heaven."

The little boy had turned and was watching Jesus as he spoke. He reached up and touched Jesus' beard, as though to see if it was real.

Jesus smiled and put an arm around him. "Whoever receives one such little child as this, receives me." Then his expression grew somber. "But I warn you, whosoever offends one of these little ones, it would be better for them if they had a millstone tied about their necks and they were drowned in the depths of the sea."

Then, brightening again, he gave the boy another hug and let him slide off his lap. He stood up, preparing to leave, and the crowd fell back again. As his eyes swept the crowd, they suddenly stopped on Deborah and Esther. When Esther saw that he was looking at her she shrank back a little, but to Deborah's surprise she did not turn away. She continued watching Jesus with unblinking intensity.

Jesus smiled and beckoned with one hand for her to come to him.

When Esther realized it was her that Jesus was beckoning to, she gave a quick shake of her head.

"It's all right, Esther," Deborah said, suddenly wanting Esther to share in the gentleness of what she had just witnessed. "He won't hurt you."

Again there was the brief movement of her head. Deborah looked at Jesus and shrugged helplessly. Jesus only smiled; then, gesturing to Peter and the other disciples, he began to move away.

Suddenly Esther was squirming in her arms. "Down, Granmama!"

Deborah let her slide to the ground, grateful to have the weight removed from her arms. Then to Deborah's utter astonishment, Esther broke free from her grasp. She darted away, weaving through the people.

"Esther!" Deborah moved quickly after her granddaughter, fearing that she had panicked and would run blindly into the crowd.

As Deborah cried out again, people turned. They were already making way for the little girl who was threading her way through them. Now hearing Deborah, they opened a path for her as well. As they did so, Deborah saw her granddaughter run up to Jesus, whose back was to them as he moved away. Deborah was dumbfounded as Esther reached up and tugged on the back of Jesus' robe.

In surprise he turned and looked down. A smile instantly filled his face when he recognized who it was. He bent down as though to speak to her, and Deborah got her second shock. Esther threw her arms around his neck and kissed him on the cheek. Jesus was momentarily startled; then, with genuine pleasure, he took her in his arms.

Deborah reached them just as Jesus lifted Esther up, unable to believe what she was seeing. Jesus looked at her as she came up. "You are Deborah, wife of David the merchant." It was a statement, not a question.

"Yes."

"And this is your granddaughter?"

She nodded. She was a little overwhelmed to be so close to the man who had been the cause of so much turmoil within her. She was also disarmed by the great warmth she saw in his eyes.

Jesus looked at Esther. "And what is your name?"

"Esther," she said without hesitation.

"Ah," he said soberly. "You are named for the great queen who saved her people."

Esther nodded gravely.

"I—" Deborah had to start again. "This is astonishing. She is usually so shy around people."

Jesus was still looking into Esther's eyes. "Then I consider it the greater privilege," he said. "Thank you for that sweet kiss."

A tiny smile played around Esther's mouth. It was an expression that Deborah knew well, a signal that the sphinx was happy inside but trying hard not to let the world know.

Jesus turned to Deborah and searched her face. She fell back a step under the intensity of his gaze. It was as though he were probing her very soul.

"I—" she started, faltering.

He smiled and let Esther down to the ground, but his eyes never left Deborah's. "Except *you* become converted," he said softly, "and become as this little child, you cannot enter into the kingdom of heaven, Deborah, wife of David of Capernaum."

With that he briefly laid a hand on Esther's head, then turned and walked away. The crowd immediately surged in behind him, and he was lost to Deborah's sight.

Deborah stood transfixed. A great rush of peace had swept over her, and without realizing it, tears sprang to her eyes. She felt a little hand reach out and take hers. Through blurred vision Deborah looked down.

"I like Jesus, Granmama," Esther said. It came out with such complete purity and innocence that Deborah had to take in a quick breath.

Then she dropped to her knees and threw her arms around her granddaughter. "Yes," she whispered, holding her tightly. "I do too, Esther. I do too."

V

It took only a moment to realize that the house was empty. Not surprised, he left again, headed up the street to Ephraim's house. Joseph was playing outside with two other young boys. On seeing David, he waved happily. "*Shalom*, Papa."

"Hello, son. Is Mama inside?"

He shook his head.

"Where is she?"

With the careless shrug that was so typical of a ten-year-old, Joseph answered. "I don't know."

David went inside. Ephraim's house was much smaller than his parents', with a courtyard that was only about twenty feet square. As he stepped inside, David saw Esther and Boaz sitting on the tiles playing together. Esther jumped up. "Pampa!"

"Hello, little one." She ran to him, and he swept her up and gave her a kiss. "Is Granmama inside?"

She gave a quick shake of her head.

"Oh." He set her down again, a little puzzled.

"I saw Jesus," Esther said.

He had already started toward the house. He stopped short. "You did?"

She nodded gravely. "With Granmama."

"Where?"

She flipped her head happily. "We bought melons, Pampa! I picked the best ones. I know how."

"That's good, Esther. Where did you see Jesus?"

Now she was suddenly shy. "I gave him a kiss."

He just stared at her.

With that, she ran back and sat down beside Boaz, who had barely acknowledged the presence of his grandfather. Just then the door opened, and Leah and Rachel stepped out. Leah came over to him and gave him a quick hug. "I thought I heard your voice."

"Where's your mother?"

Leah gave him a strange look. "Didn't she come to see you?"

"No."

The two women exchanged looks. "Then I think she's down by the water," Rachel said. "You'd better go find her."

"What's wrong?"

Rachel smiled. "Just go find her."

VI

When Deborah finished, David reached out and touched her cheek, caressing it with the back of his fingers. "I can't believe it."

She laughed softly through her tears. "Neither can I. I was so confused, David. So upset. Then in one instant I knew. It was as if everything was suddenly new within me. And I had this great calm inside. I've never felt anything like it before."

She lifted a hand and laid it over his, pressing it against her face. "I'm sorry I doubted you, David. I am—"

He shook his head quickly. "Don't," he whispered. "This is enough. This is more than I dared hope for."

She sat back. "Even my father, David. Suddenly the terrible pain is gone. I don't know how, but I know that everything is all right with him and Mama. That somehow God will make things right."

"Yes. That's it, isn't it? Somehow God will make things right."

Her face saddened. "What about Simeon? What will he say when he finds out that we've all turned against him? Or at least that's what he'll think."

"I don't know," he murmured. "I've never prayed for anything as earnestly as I am praying for him right now."

Her eyes widened. "Were you praying for me too?"

"Of course."

The tears brimmed over again. "Thank you."

He slid over beside her and put his arm around her. "If God can change your heart so completely, then maybe he can change Simeon as well."

Struck by that thought, she began to nod. "Yes. It is a miracle what happened to me today. And all because of Esther. If she hadn't gone

462

up and kissed Jesus, I would have turned away." She moved in closer against him. "Let's pray for Simeon now, David, before we go back."

He nodded, still filled with wonder at what was happening. "Yes, I would like that very much."

CHAPTER NOTES

Beelzebub, which is one of the names given to Satan in the New Testament, is actually *Beelzebul* in almost all of the original manuscripts. Beelzebub was the Philistine god of the flies. Some scholars believe the Israelites, making a play on words, changed that to Beel*zebul,* the god of the dung heap (see Fallows, 1:255–56). It is a fitting title for him who presides over all moral corruption and filthiness.

The account of Jesus with the children is recorded by three of the Gospel writers (Matthew 18:1–6; 19:13–15; Mark 10:13–16; Luke 18:15–17).

CHAPTER 23

EXCEPT A MAN BE BORN OF WATER AND OF THE SPIRIT,
HE CANNOT ENTER INTO THE KINGDOM OF GOD.

—*John 3:5*

I

30 MAY, A.D. 30

"Your brow seems weighted with the troubles of eternity tonight, Simeon."

Simeon's head came up in surprise.

Shana smiled softly. "Is my company so burdensome?"

They were sitting on a stone bench beside the watchtower that overlooked the family's olive groves in Beth Neelah. Daniel and Yehuda were working a short distance away. They were close enough to serve as chaperones but far enough away that the two of them could have some privacy. Even though Simeon and Shana were now betrothed, it would be highly improper for them to be alone together until after the formal wedding.

Simeon reached out and took her hand, holding it in both of his. "Your presence is like a spring of water in the desert, Shana. It soothes my spirit and brings me peace."

Her eyes, black in the last light of evening, warmed with pleasure, but her countenance did not brighten. "I fear that your face does not support what your tongue is telling me."

He exhaled slowly, wearily. "I'm sorry. As you have probably guessed, Yehuda and I bring back a troublesome problem from Jerusalem." His shoulders lifted and fell. "And then there are the thoughts of what awaits me when I return to Capernaum in the morning."

She was instantly contrite, even though she had only been teasing him. "Oh, Simeon. It will be all right. Your mother will have told your father by now about what happened when you saw the centurion. You can make peace with him. He has such a good heart."

"It is not my father's heart that is the problem."

She squeezed his hand back. "Does the fact that you have different feelings about the Romans require that you do not speak to each other?"

"No, but I—"

"Then put the differences aside. Be reconciled with him. I know he will welcome that."

He looked at her for a long moment, then began to nod slowly. "Yes, you are right."

"Your mother will help. Before she returned to Capernaum, she told me that she is greatly concerned about the two of you."

"I will do it," he said, a touch of hope returning to his voice. "Thank you."

She smiled shyly. "What is a wife for if not to be strong when her husband needs it?"

"You will make a wonderful partner, Shana. I wish I could say the same for your betrothed."

"I shall make do," she teased.

He didn't smile. "The paths that lie ahead will not always be easy for you either, Shana. There is much to do. There will be danger for Yehuda and Daniel."

"And yourself?"

"Yes."

"Then I shall stand with you in that danger. That is what your mother did with her mother and father. It is what my mother did with my father. Would that we could always choose the paths we follow."

"I know, but the Law of Moses excused a man from battle if he was betrothed or during the first year of his marriage so his bride did not have to risk becoming a widow. Unfortunately, as Ha'keedohn, I can hardly ask others to go where I do not lead them."

She touched his cheek briefly. "If it is concern for me that darkens your brow, then I feel I have failed you. You know I am with you in what has to happen. If it will free our country at last, then let it come. The wife of the Javelin will gladly be a full part of whatever is required."

He looked at her in wonder. These were not simply empty words borne of a desire to please him. She felt the Zealot spirit to the very core. His mother had been right. Shana might worry when her husband and brothers went off to battle, but she would hand them their bows and their swords without adding guilt to their quivers.

He let go of her hand and stood up, suddenly filled with passion. "This is the time we have been waiting for, Shana. The Lord has put into our hands an opportunity to bring about the thing we have dreamed about for all these years. This is the answer. *I know it!* I can feel it like fire in my bones. Within the next few weeks, we shall see great things come to pass."

"Then my heart is filled with joy that I stand beside you while history is made."

They heard a sound to one side, and they both turned to see Yehuda walking toward them. He came up, smiling ruefully. "This is a time for courtship, Simeon. You look as though you are preaching a sermon about hellfire and the perils of *Gehenna* to my sister."

Simeon was still looking at Shana. He smiled softly. "Your sister needs no sermons from me," he said. "It is I who would be taught of her."

"She has taught me many things as well," Yehuda said gruffly, laying a hand on Shana's shoulder in a gesture of simple affection.

"I am sorry that I must go down to Capernaum, Yehuda," Simeon said, changing the subject. "There is much to do, and it is not right that I leave you and Daniel to do it alone."

"Daniel and I will be fine. We will leave in the morning and begin to gather up the men." Shana looked up at her brother in surprise. He ignored her questioning look. "You have to settle this with your father. We will be ready when you return."

"We have neglected our duty," Simeon said with some remorse. "Other than our little clash with Moshe Ya'abin a few weeks back, our little band of brothers has had little to do. I have not set the proper example in maintaining the sharpest edge. But I shall return the day after the Sabbath. Then we shall work them hard to get them ready."

"What is happening?" Shana asked, her eyes wide.

"I'll tell you all about it later," Yehuda said. "Now it is time for Simeon to sleep. He must leave before the sun lightens the eastern hills." Then to Simeon he added, "Old Mordechai, the cunning and shrewd one, thinks he has worked this all out to his satisfaction, but he has opened a door that not even the Great Council of Jerusalem will be able to shut again."

"That's just what I was saying to Shana," Simeon exclaimed. "The day for which we have prepared all these years is finally near at hand."

"Yes. Go down to your father," Yehuda urged. "Let the feelings between you die. When the victory is won in a few weeks, what will Sextus Rubrius matter any longer?"

Simeon smiled fully for the first time. "You are right, my friend. In a few weeks, what will it matter at all?"

II
31 May, a.d. 30

David ben Joseph walked quickly, trying to keep up with his youngest son.

"When did Simeon return?" David asked again, even though that had been his first question when Joseph burst into his office at the storehouses.

Joseph turned, trotting backwards as he faced his father. "I came immediately. He's not been home for a quarter of an hour yet."

"And he asked specifically for me?"

Joseph frowned. That was a question he had already answered as well. "Yes. Mama was going to come find you, but Simeon said I could run faster."

"How is he?"

Even though he was only ten, Joseph understood the deeper meaning behind that question. "He's fine, Papa. He doesn't seem angry."

"Good."

David didn't ask more questions but only increased his pace to stay up with his son.

III

"I'm sorry, Father," Simeon whispered as they held each other in an embrace. "I'm sorry I let my anger carry me away to blindness."

"It is I who am sorry."

Simeon released his father and stepped back, glancing at Deborah. "Mother has explained what happened. I understand now that you had no choice but to respond. The Roman was asking for help for one of our own people."

David was watching his son's eyes closely, scarcely believing that what he had been dreading for days now was so easily resolved. "I did not seek him out, nor do I have any plans of maintaining any kind of relationship with Sextus. We both understand that it is better this way."

"I appreciate that, but it is all right, Father. I was in the wrong." Simeon gave a sardonic smile. "Sometimes my temper burns more fiercely than a jar of pitch. You have warned me before that if I am not careful, it may consume me someday."

Deborah was watching her son as intently as was her husband. Was this the same man who just a few days before had so utterly rejected her attempts to help him understand what had happened and why? What had occurred in Jerusalem that wrought such a change of heart? In one far corner of her mind, she felt a tiny flicker of suspicion, but she was so relieved to have this moment over with and so easily that she pushed it aside.

Leah got to her feet and came to her brother. She threw her arms around him. "Welcome home, Simeon. I missed you."

He looked at her in surprise and tipped her chin up so he could see her face. "You're not still angry that I didn't come that day after I promised I would?"

"But you did come," she said. "Or at least you started to." She blushed slightly. "I must admit, I was somewhat upset with you when you didn't appear that day."

"You will have to tell me about everything that happened. I think I am finally ready to listen."

Leah's eyes were suddenly shining. "Oh, Simeon, it was an incredible day. I'm bursting to tell you all about it."

Deborah stood as well. She went to her son and slipped an arm around his waist. "There is much we all have to tell you, Simeon," she said softly. "Much has happened in the family since you went to Beth Neelah and then on to Jerusalem."

He smiled, having no idea what she was referring to. "I'm ready to hear it all," he said gallantly.

Strangely, his mother seemed saddened by that. "Ephraim and Rachel are part of this too. We shall have an early supper; then we can talk."

IV

It was well into the third watch of the night, perhaps an hour past midnight. The courtyard was dark, lit only by the light of the stars overhead. Simeon lay on the wooden bench, his hands beneath his head, staring up at the sky above him, though his eyes did not see. He had risen from his bed more than an hour before, far too troubled to sleep, and slipped quietly outside to try to sort through the tumble of his thoughts.

It was as though he had stood at the foot of one of the steep cliffs in the wilderness of Judea, hoping for a cooling rain shower, and had been struck by an avalanche of rocks and earth instead. That his father had come to accept Jesus as the Messiah was no surprise whatsoever. Simeon had expected nothing less. After Leah's passionate plea that he come and see Jesus for himself on that "day of miracles," as she called it, neither was it a great shock when she announced that she stood fully with their father in this matter.

Then the avalanche had started to rumble. Rachel had started it, jumping in immediately after Leah finished. When Simeon realized that she was telling him that she too had come to believe in Jesus of Nazareth, he got his first real shock. He was still reeling when Ephraim began his story. While Simeon was trying to assimilate that and all it meant—Ephraim had been as skeptical as Simeon when he had left the storehouses!—his mother began. She spoke of Esther and the marketplace and of a powerful change of heart.

Simeon blew out his breath, starting to get angry all over again. Tomorrow the family was going down to the seashore. There they would be baptized and officially become disciples of Jesus of Nazareth. He could hardly believe what he was hearing and could not, no matter how hard he tried, bring himself to do anything more than stare at them when they asked if he would come with them, not to be baptized, of course, but to share in their hour of joy.

He grunted and stood up, the tiredness seeping deep into his body. Yet he knew there would be little sleep this night. He could handle the change that had happened. He could even reconcile himself to the idea that he stood alone now in the family. What he could not shake out of his mind were the other things he had heard last night. This was what troubled him the most.

Leah called it the "day of miracles." As she began to describe all that had happened that day when she had come to try to persuade Simeon and Ephraim to go with her, Simeon remembered what he had said. He had brushed it all aside with the analogy of Elisha. Jesus might be a great prophet, but that didn't make him the Messiah. Now he wished he could really believe that Jesus was only one more in the long list of great prophets.

They had talked for almost an hour, each one recounting this aspect or that of what Jesus had done. These were not tales from strangers or the latest gossip from women doing their washing at the water's edge. This was his family, and they had seen these things with their own eyes.

Further, these things had not happened in some far-off place to people no one had ever heard of. Simeon knew the widow named Ruth, wife of Yohanan the weaver. For years it had been common knowledge in Capernaum about her "condition," as everyone called it. You could tell just by looking at her that she was gravely ill. As a boy, Simeon had asked his mother what "issue of blood" meant. Only later did he come to understand the concept of a gradual but relentless hemorrhaging that sapped her energy, drained her color, stole her life one drop at a time. He could still remember clearly how Ruth had frightened him as a young boy. Her face was so gray, so pale. For twelve years she had lived with that terrible condition, spending every extra shekel she could eke out on doctors who could not even offer her much comfort, let alone a cure. Simeon's mother told him that she had spent the day with Ruth just two days before. She was whole, filled with life, still rejoicing in the miraculous change that had come upon her. And all of this after simply touching the hem of Jesus' robe.

Simeon had been to the home of Elah ben Reuben in just the last six months. He had gone with Leah and his mother to take a loaf of bread to Elah's wife. They had just learned that Elah had been struck down in the prime of his adult life. First had come a raging fever, then the loss of all power in his limbs. The palsy had left him totally unable to stand. Simeon had stood by awkwardly, trying not to stare in horror at what life had handed to Elah ben Reuben. Now Elah was back in his shop, working every day from sunup to sundown. How could Simeon possibly doubt the story Leah told, as she described watching Elah stand up in response to the command of Jesus, pick up the bed on which he had been carried into the house, and walk out into the street with it?

It went on and on. Jesus had stilled a raging storm with a single word. He had commanded a dead maiden to rise from her "sleep," and she had come back, much to the embarrassment of the professional mourners. Water was poured into pots and came out as the finest wine. Joachin the leper was now living back in his home, the home that he had been forced to leave four years before when the dreaded disease came on and he was pronounced unclean. Jabez the beggar, who had been blinded as a young boy, had started work in a wheelwright's shop as a new apprentice. In a few years, he would become a master wheelwright.

What manner of man was this? That was what kept sleep from coming to Simeon, son of David, this night.

And what of his father's Bethlehem experience? David had quietly told Simeon last night that he had finally gone to Jesus and asked him about his birth. He *had* been born in Bethlehem exactly thirty years ago this spring. He *had* been born in a stable and cradled in a manger. How many could say that! And yes, his mother *had* told him about the shepherds that had come to pay homage to his birth that night. How did you dismiss that out of hand?

He groaned softly and dropped his head in his hands. But if Jesus was the Messiah, the Anointed One of which the prophets spoke so clearly, why wasn't he acting like it? Why did he speak of loving your enemies and turning the other cheek? Simeon had never accepted his father's explanation of the "suffering servant" Messiah. On this matter, Simeon's heart was with his Uncle Aaron. The Messiah was the Deliverer. God would send a king to rise up and overthrow their oppressors. It had to be! Their people had suffered long enough.

Absently he began to rub at his chin, feeling the stubble there. It had been two days now since he had last shaved. He would have to shave again soon. It was possible in the days that were coming that he might have to pass himself off as a Roman, or at least pass through their lines without arousing suspicion, as he had done on more than one occasion in the past.

Suddenly he slapped his leg. He was staring into the night, his eyes wide and astonished. He shot to his feet. Simeon had deliberately chosen to go clean-shaven some time ago, with his mother's encouragement—even though most of his countrymen let their beards grow full and rich. He had made that choice so he could pass among the enemy undetected, though he had to admit that he now preferred it, especially in the summer's heat. Was that his answer? What if Jesus *was* the Messiah but was not ready to reveal himself publicly as such? What if he were hiding his true intentions until the time was right?

Simeon spun around, looking up at the darkened window where his father and mother slept. What was it his father had said when he told him the story of Jesus changing water to wine in Cana? When Jesus' mother asked him to help, he had told her, "My hour is not yet come."

Simeon almost felt dizzy as the pieces began to fall into place. Jesus was no ordinary man. That could no longer be denied. He was remarkable in such a way that the very word could not describe him. Not even the greatest of the prophets had ever done what he was doing. And because of that, he was building himself a tremendous following. Simeon had seen for himself the crowds in the streets, the multitudes on the mount who had come out to hear him preach. Normally such crowds would have drawn the Romans like a carcass drew vultures in the desert. If there was the slightest talk of rebellion, of resistance, Rome would respond with brutal efficiency, and that would be the end of the matter.

But what did the Romans care about some local religious movement? By policy they did not interfere with the worship of their conquered peoples unless that worship contained a threat to Rome itself. Some country preacher who called on people to love their enemies, to forgive everyone, to live in peace and harmony wouldn't even raise an eyebrow. It was brilliant. Simeon could picture in his mind some legionnaire sending in a report to his superior. "Nothing of concern here. The man is even telling the people to carry our packs twice the required distance." *What if you even helped a Roman centurion by healing his sick servant?* That would snuff out any and all suspicions once and forever.

It was like he had just awakened from a deep, restful sleep. His mind was alive, racing with excitement. This resolved the dilemma. This answered the questions. Jesus *was* the Messiah. He had to be. Bethlehem and the manger. The incredible power. The swelling popularity. And if he were holding back, just waiting for exactly the right moment to—

Simeon had begun pacing back and forth in his excitement. Now he stiffened, as if he had just been struck with a bolt of lightning. A few days ago Mordechai ben Uzziel had extended an opportunity that could change history. Simeon and Yehuda had both felt that keenly. *Like fire in my bones!* Those were Simeon's own words.

His mouth opened, and he gave a soft exclamation of pure astonishment. This Roman column, with its massive collections of armaments, was the spark that would finally unite the various fires of rebellion into one great blazing torch. What better moment than that for the long-awaited Messiah to step forward and proclaim his leadership?

The idea was so stunning that it nearly took his breath. He stood there, feeling as though his whole body was being jolted by some unseen power. *Yes!* He raised a fist to the sky in triumph. *This is the answer!* Now he understood.

He wanted to race into his parents' room and shake them awake. "I will come to your baptism, Mother," he would shout at her. "I will come and listen to Jesus and watch him with newly opened eyes. Yes, Father. Peter and Andrew asked me to come and see this Jesus for myself. Well, I shall! I shall!"

He turned his face to the sky, his heart singing with joy. "I thank thee, O God," he whispered. "I thank thee for opening my eyes and helping me to see thy holy will."

V

1 JUNE, A.D. 30

Deborah and her son were seated together on a grassy spot about fifteen paces from the shoreline, where the waters of the Sea of Kinnereth lapped softly against the pebbles. The grass was no longer green. The last rains had been several weeks ago now, and except for the forested areas, the Galilee had turned from green to golden brown. Leah and Joseph had the two children of Ephraim and Rachel down at the water's edge, looking for the tiny seashells from which necklaces and bracelets and brooches were made and sold in the villages around the lake. The rest of the family members were standing with a small group down by one of the boats. Peter and Andrew were there, along with their wives and families. At the moment, David was talking with Peter's mother-in-law, Anna's mother. Ephraim and Rachel were in deep conversation with Zebedee and his family. Deborah had been in that group up until a minute or so before. Then she had noticed Simeon standing awkwardly off to one side and had left to come and give him company.

He looked around and gave a sardonic grin. "So much for a quiet baptismal service for just the family and a few friends."

She smiled and nodded.

Supposedly only a few had been told about this, but that seemed to make no difference. Wherever Jesus was, a crowd quickly followed. The man from Nazareth was a little farther down the beach, cornered by a small group of men who were speaking earnestly to him. Even as he watched, Simeon saw another clot of people appear on the path that led to the main part of town, hurrying to get there before something important happened.

Not that Simeon was displeased. In fact, just the opposite was true. With his new perspective, this was actually quite gratifying. Not even Judah of Gamla, his mother's uncle, had garnered a following like this, and he had been the most charismatic leader to rise up in Israel in more than a hundred years. One had only to whisper the name of this carpenter and it was like the very rocks themselves rose up to follow after him.

Simeon looked up as he realized that his mother was staring at him curiously. He forced a light smile. "What?"

"Are you *sure* you are all right?"

"I'm fine." When Deborah raised one eyebrow slightly, he laughed. You didn't hide anything from this woman. "I was awake for a long time last night, thinking about what all of you told me about Jesus."

"And?"

"And I decided that you and Leah and Father are right. Jesus is no ordinary man. I determined to come and listen to him for myself, hear more of what he has to say, and then decide."

She gave a momentary look of surprise, instantly replaced by hope. "Really, Simeon?"

"Yes, Mother. I want to know. After hearing what he has been doing, I would be a fool not to at least hear him."

There were sudden tears in her eyes, and she reached out and laid a hand on his arm. "That's wonderful!"

He felt a sudden stab of guilt. He didn't want to mislead her. "I'm not sure yet, Mother. I'm not making any promises."

A fleeting smile came and went. "Did you know those are almost exactly the words I used with your father a few weeks ago?"

"Really?"

"Yes. If you are willing to ask, that's enough. That's what your father and I have been praying for."

That startled him a little. They were praying for him?

Then she cocked her head quizzically. "What happened to you in Jerusalem?"

Caught off guard, he fumbled for a moment. "It was—It turned out to be a very interesting meeting."

"Interesting?" Her tone told him that she knew he was being evasive.

"Yes, and significant too. I can't say more now, but soon I'll be able to explain everything."

"Will there be danger?"

He looked away, unable to answer her untruthfully.

"Oh, Simeon," she whispered.

"Everything is going to be all right. Just give me a week or two, and then you won't have to wonder any longer." He decided to change the subject. "You're really sure this is what you want to do?" He motioned with his head toward the water.

"Without question." Her voice was barely a murmur, and yet it was rich with conviction. "I wish I could describe to you what happened that day in the marketplace. In one instant my heart was completely changed." She turned to look at where Esther was swishing her hands back and forth in the water, her face completely somber as she concentrated on her task. "Thanks to that precious little one."

Simeon nodded. Last night, as his mother had described what happened with Esther and Jesus, he thought he had understood what she had been trying to tell him. But this morning, as the family came to the beach, Jesus had been talking with James and John and Philip. The moment Esther saw him, she wiggled out of her father's grasp and darted over to tug on Jesus' robe. He instantly turned from the men, dropped to one knee, and whispered something to her. She giggled and kissed him on the cheek. Then she trotted back to her father. Like the rest of the family, Simeon adored this little dark-haired, dark-eyed enchantress. Like the rest of the family, he worked hard every time he saw her to win her acceptance. To see it given so openly and so spontaneously had left him a little misty-eyed as well. "I understand," he said.

"You understand what?"

They both turned, then stood, as David came over to join them.

"We were just talking about Esther and Jesus."

Simeon's father bobbed his head, then took his wife's hands. "Are you ready?"

"Oh, yes, David. I've never been more ready for anything in my life."

"I think Jesus is too," he said. He lifted one hand and pointed off to their right.

Jesus was coming toward them. Seeing that, Rachel called to Leah to bring the children; then she and Ephraim and the rest of the family came over to join David and Deborah and Simeon.

Jesus was smiling as he came up. He clasped David's hand in a firm grip. "This is a wonderful day, my friend."

"Indeed, it is." David half turned and took Simeon's arm. "Jesus, this is our second son, Simeon."

"I know." It was said simply as his eyes probed Simeon's.

"I—I have heard much of you," Simeon said, a little disconcerted by the directness of his gaze.

Jesus smiled quietly. "Have you now?"

Before Simeon could answer, Esther began pulling on Jesus' sleeve. He looked down, laughed softly, and scooped her up. "What is it, little one?"

"Can I be babatized too?" Esther said.

He chuckled as he enfolded her in his arms. "Young children such as yourself have no need to be baptized until they are older. You are pure and innocent. Would that all who seek to enter the kingdom of heaven were like that, young Esther."

That seemed to satisfy her. But then her eyes fell on Simeon. She swung back to Jesus. "What about Simeon? Can he be babatized?"

Simeon visibly started. "I—"

Jesus didn't even look at him. He pulled her close and whispered something into her ear. She turned and stared at Simeon, her mouth forming a large O. Laughing softly, Jesus set her down again, and she moved back to stand by her mother.

"You have won her heart," Simeon said, not sure what else to say. "And she does not give it that easily."

"All the more reason to treasure such a gift." Then Jesus' gaze intensified. "You are the one they call Ha'keedohn, the Javelin, are you not?"

Startled, Simeon nodded.

There was the hint of a smile in his eyes now. "And what I said that day on the hillside offended you somehow." It was a statement of simple fact and not an interrogation.

Simeon did not know what to say. He had wondered if Jesus had noticed him shoot to his feet in the middle of the sermon and bolt away. He felt his face flush a little, but Jesus did not wait for an answer. He turned back to Simeon's parents. "I have asked Peter to baptize the two of you and young Joseph." He swung partially around. "And I have asked Andrew to baptize Ephraim and Rachel and Leah. Is that acceptable to all of you?"

They were all nodding. "Of course," Ephraim and his father said at the same moment.

Peter took a step forward. "I would consider it a special privilege, David."

"We are the ones who are honored, Peter," Deborah answered for the both of them.

Jesus stepped back, extending one arm, indicating that they should move down to the water's edge. But just as they started to move forward, there was a commotion off to the left. Everyone's head turned. Coming from the direction of Capernaum, a small group of men was hurrying toward them. At the head was Amram, leader of the scribes and Pharisees in the town. Then several of the family gasped. Directly behind Amram was a familiar figure. It was Deborah's brother, Aaron.

Jesus stopped, content to wait while they approached. Simeon thought he detected a slight tightening around Jesus' mouth, but he could not be sure. As the group stopped a few feet away, Aaron gave a cry, pointing toward Deborah. "What are you doing here?" he demanded.

Color flooded across Deborah's face. Everyone was staring. "I am going to be baptized, Aaron," she said, her voice surprisingly calm. "The better question is, what are *you* doing here? I had no word that you were coming down from Sepphoris."

"I heard that you were thinking of becoming a disciple of this man." He flung out his hand contemptuously in the direction of Jesus.

"He came to see if he could bring you back to your senses," Amram hissed. "To save you from a terrible mistake."

To Simeon's surprise, it was his father who answered, and his voice was taut with anger. "This is a family matter, Amram. We don't need any help."

Deborah had not been deflected by that. She was still looking at her brother, her eyes sorrowful. "So you *just* arrived?"

That knocked him back a bit. "No, I arrived last night."

"And you didn't come to me and share your concerns in the privacy of our home? Is that what I deserve from the brother I raised as though he were my son?"

"I—"

"Have I or David ever given you cause to think you are not welcome in our home?"

"How can he feel welcome in a home where the light of faith has been snuffed out?" Amram exclaimed.

Simeon jerked forward. Ephraim's hands balled into fists. The rudeness of the man knew no bounds. But it was Jesus who reacted most swiftly. He stepped forward so that he was standing just a foot or two away from the chief Pharisee. He never said a word, and because his back was to them, Simeon could not see his expression or tell if his eyes were filled with anger. Jesus was a good handspan taller than Amram, and the shorter man flinched and stepped back, as if he were about to be struck. Jesus never moved, but after a moment Amram's eyes could no longer meet his gaze. He turned away, muttering something under his breath.

"Good-bye, Aaron," Deborah said softly. "Thank you for caring about my eternal soul. I know you mean well."

"It is not just Mother and Father you need to pray over, Uncle

Aaron," Ephraim said, his voice trembling. "Rachel and I are going to be baptized today as well."

"As am I," Leah added softly, as Aaron's face went even redder than before.

"Aaron," David said, stepping forward. "If you wish to stay and observe, you are welcome. If you wish to discuss this matter further, Shabbat begins this evening. There will be a place set at our table for you. Now it is time for us to proceed."

"It is you who has poisoned the mind of my sister," Aaron cried. "I hold you accountable."

"He has filled my mind with understanding, Aaron," Deborah cut in. "This is my choice. My decision." Her chin dropped. "Good-bye."

She turned away, her head high, her eyes shining. David turned as well and took her hand, and together they started toward the water.

"You don't know what you are doing," Aaron shouted.

"Come, Aaron," Amram broke in, clutching at his arm. "We are too late. They are beyond hope."

As quickly and noisily as they had come, the group turned and bustled away. Jesus watched them for a moment; then, completely unruffled, he also turned and waved a hand at Peter. As the fisherman moved forward to join David and Deborah, Deborah stopped. When she came around to face Jesus, there were wet streaks down her cheeks. "I am so sorry—" she started.

He raised a hand, cutting off the rest. Then he turned his head and watched the retreating figures for a moment. When he spoke, it was not just to Deborah but to the assembled crowd. "You need not fear them which can kill the body but are not able to kill the soul. Rather, fear him which is able to destroy both soul and body in hell."

There was instant quiet. Everyone leaned forward, straining to hear. Finally Jesus' eyes came back to Deborah. "Some think that I am come to bring peace on the earth," he said slowly.

Simeon felt a sudden jolt.

"I am not come to send peace, but rather a sword."

Yes! When he had least expected it, there it was. There was no innuendo, no veiled message here. Simeon wanted to whoop for joy.

Deborah looked suddenly bewildered. Simeon's father was clearly startled as well.

Jesus laid a hand on Deborah's shoulder, peering deeply into her eyes. "I am come to set a man at variance against his father, and the daughter against her mother, and the daughter-in-law against her mother-in-law."

Simeon rocked back a little. What was this?

"I tell you now that a man's foes shall be they of his own household. And you must know that he that loves his father or mother more than me is not worthy of me. He that loves a son or a daughter more than me is not worthy of me."

Suddenly Simeon's exultation died away. This was a reference to Aaron. Jesus was telling his mother that in spite of the pain, she had made the right choice. The disappointment was as sharp and as bitter as the joy had been sweet just moments before. And yet, what did Jesus mean about not sending peace?

Simeon's thoughts were cut off as Jesus stepped back from his mother and looked directly at him. "And he that is not willing to take his cross and follow after me is not worthy of me. He that tries to save his life shall lose it; and he that is willing to lose his life for my sake shall find it."

Once again, in an instant, Simeon's emotions swung sharply in the other direction. He stared at Jesus, letting the words ring in his mind. Now he understood. He had been so confident, so sure that it was he, Simeon the Javelin, Ha'keedohn, who would create the opportunity for Jesus to step forward and claim his kingdom. Here was a stinging rebuke. Who was Simeon of Capernaum to decide when the Messiah would carry out his work? Did the whole mission of the Great Deliverer depend on a single man or a single band of men?

There was more there too, and it was deeply sobering. The kingdom was not going to come in peaceably. It *would* require the sword. And some would die. Some on the side of right would die. The charge to take up your cross was a grim reminder of what awaited anyone captured by the Romans before the battle was fully won.

He bowed his head in shame. *I stand rebuked. I hear what you are saying. I wish only to be an instrument in your hands.* His chin lifted, and he looked squarely into the face of the man who watched him steadily now. "I understand," he said in a low voice.

At first there was no response; then finally Jesus nodded. Then he motioned to Peter.

As they gathered at the water's edge and the women helped his mother remove her outer robe and her sandals, Simeon noticed Esther standing quietly by her mother. He sidled over and bent down.

"Esther?"

"Yes, Uncle Simeon?" Her eyes were grave.

"What did Jesus say to you?"

"He said Esther doesn't have to be babatized."

"I know. But after that? What did he say when you asked if I could be baptized?"

She looked surprised. "Jesus said not to worry. You will be babatized in a little while."

CHAPTER NOTES

The people who were on the receiving end of Jesus' various miracles are rarely identified in scriptures. Nor are we typically told where they were from. The blind, the lepers, the woman with the issue of blood—the Gospel writers give us only the briefest glimpse into their lives. The purpose of those writers was not to call attention to individuals but to testify of the mission and power of the Redeemer. But, on reflection, we know that they were real people. We know they must have had family and friends and employers and neighbors. Surely we can assume that their lives were profoundly changed by their momentary contact with the Savior and that those changes affected many others around them. Even though the names and other details are "fictional," the author chose to supply them here as a reminder that while some things were not recorded, they were still reality.

The testimony of Jesus about the division that his teachings would bring to families and the need to take up one's cross and follow him is found in Matthew 10:28, 34–39. To have that teaching occur during the time of a baptism, however, is not based on scripture.

CHAPTER 24

DO NOT TRUST THE HORSE, TROJANS. WHATEVER IT IS,
I FEAR THE GREEKS, EVEN WHEN THEY BRING GIFTS.

—*Virgil*, Aeneid, *ii. 48*

I

2 JUNE, A.D. 30

They lay together in the near darkness, Miriam on her huge bed,
Livia on a small couch pushed alongside it. The great house of
Mordechai ben Uzziel was dark and silent. They had heard the last of
the servants retiring more than an hour before, and there was no
longer any light coming from Mordechai's study at the bottom of the
stairs. The only light in the house came from a quarter moon through
the window. And still they talked, sleep nowhere close for either of
them. Miriam had spent most of the day checking her father's books
and accounts, but after their supper, which welcomed in the Sabbath,
her father had retired to his study to work. So Miriam and Livia had
gone to their room and spent the evening together, reading and talking. Her father had no qualms about lighting a fire on the Sabbath, so
they could have lit lamps, but they chose not to, letting the darkness
gradually envelope them and leaving them only the choice of talking.

In the solitude and quietness, Miriam told Livia what Marcus had learned about her family from the slave hunter. They wept together then, arm in arm. After the tears for her mother and father, Livia brightened somewhat, encouraged by the news that her younger brother might still be found.

After a long silence, Miriam decided to share something else with Livia. Speaking slowly, she told her about her desire to adopt her as her sister. Now the tears were of a different kind. Livia buried her face in her hands and sobbed, deeply moved by Miriam's love. Originally, Miriam had planned to tell of her father's reaction so Livia would understand why they might have to wait for a time to begin the proceedings, but after seeing Livia's joy she did not have the heart to do it. Miriam had already determined that she would move ahead swiftly and quietly, before her father learned about it. Once it was done, he would grumble a little, perhaps even throw one of his truly frightening furies, but then it would go away—especially if she said nothing more about the preacher from Nazareth. She understood now that it was Jesus who had set off her father's rage, and Miriam had been foolish to use that moment to bring up the subject of Livia.

"Tell me what you are thinking."

Miriam reached out and grasped Livia's hand. "I was thinking about you being my sister," she said happily. "I've always wished I had a sister."

There was no response, and Miriam sensed a sudden change of mood. "What?"

"I've been thinking about that," Livia said slowly. "I cannot fully tell you what it means to me that you would say that, Miriam."

"But?"

"But I don't want you to do it."

Miriam came up on one elbow. "Why?"

"Because your father won't like it."

"I . . . Why do you say that?"

"Because if I officially become your sister, then in some way that makes me eligible for part of your inheritance. Is that not right? That will greatly displease your father, and rightly so. I have no right to any part of what your family has."

Miriam felt a sudden lump in her throat. What other servant would not be rubbing their hands together at this point and counting the possible benefits that might come?

"I already think of you as my sister," Livia said, her voice soft with emotion. "I don't need to be adopted to make it reality."

"I know that," Miriam responded, "but I want others to know you are not a servant any longer. I want to share what I have with you. I didn't earn it either. How can I be so blessed and not share it with someone I love?"

"I want you to promise me that you won't say anything about this to your father."

"Livia, I—"

"Promise me."

She sighed. "All right, I won't." One part of Miriam was relieved, though her relief was stained with guilt as well. This would solve the problem of having to confront her father again. It was better to let him think she had accepted his decision. And Livia was right. If Livia was officially adopted, that would have implications for her father's will, whether Miriam waived them or not. And if they ever found Livia's brother, her being adopted would only become more complicated.

To Miriam's surprise, Livia stood. "Thank you, Miriam. Now I had better go to my own room."

"But—"

"If one of the servants found me sleeping in your bedroom and not in the servants' quarters, your father would be furious."

"All right. Are you sure you want to come to synagogue with me tomorrow?"

"Yes. It feels good. I like to be there." Livia reached out and touched Miriam's shoulder briefly and then was gone.

II

A quarter of an hour later, Miriam was still seeking sleep. There was not the slightest heaviness in her eyes. With her concern about Livia settled for now, her thoughts turned to Jesus. She constantly inquired whether or not he had returned to Jerusalem, but the answer was always the same. No one had seen him or heard from him in the city. Rumors surfaced continually that he was in the Galilee, perhaps even in Capernaum. She thought about Simeon and his mother and wondered if they knew of Jesus or had gone to hear him.

If Jesus did come back to Jerusalem, what would she do? She sensed that the clash that had erupted between her and her father over Jesus was much deeper than mere irritation at her previous flirtations with religion. He had a deep disdain for anything pious, but something about the man from Nazareth had unleashed feelings much deeper than that in him, and it troubled her.

Her head turned as she heard a soft sound. She raised her head, listening intently. It sounded like the outer gate to the courtyard. Surprised, she got to her feet and padded silently to the window. Her bedroom window looked over that portion of the courtyard that held the greater part of the garden. From there she could also see the main entrance to their compound. In the light of the quarter moon, most of the area enclosed in the walls was dimly lit. She stood for a moment, peering into the darkness, wondering if she had imagined it. Then she leaned forward. There was a lighter patch in the outside wall. The gate was standing open.

That was puzzling. Had the wind blown it open? She shook her head. There was no wind at the moment, and her father left very strict instructions for the servants to secure the gate each night. Then a movement caught her eye. She stiffened, her heart suddenly pounding.

A dark shape slipped through the gate, followed immediately by a second. Someone was inside the courtyard now. Instinctively, she drew back, even though she knew that no one could see her in the darkness. Suddenly memories of the attack on their camp in Samaria rushed in upon her, and she felt herself go cold. Were they under attack again? Surely not here in the city. Then a voice spoke in the darkness below, and relief washed over her.

"Everyone is asleep. I think it's best if we stay out here."

Her body sagged, the tension easing away. It was her father's voice. It was all right. He hadn't gone to bed after all but was out on some business once again.

She put her hands on the windowsill and leaned way out, trying to identify his guest. The second figure was as tall but not as thick as her father's rotund shape, but she could not tell who it was. She heard the murmur of another man's voice, but not loud enough for her to tell who it was.

Then once again she stiffened, this time in pleased surprise as the voice spoke more loudly. "And how is your daughter?"

She almost cried out. It was the voice of Marcus Didius. So that was her father's guest! He must have just arrived from Caesarea. That would explain the lateness of the hour. She frowned then. It would be strange if her father had invited him to stay the night. Mordechai would open himself for great criticism from some members of the Great Council if he actually let a Gentile sleep in his home. Then she remembered his first words. *It's best if we stay out here.* Marcus had come as a visitor, not a guest.

Miriam whirled and walked swiftly to the large cabinet in which she kept her finest dresses. In a moment she had slipped off her sleeping robe in exchange for a long dress of Egyptian silk that was dyed a deep scarlet and set off her dark eyes and black hair to perfection. She chided herself a little for the rush of excitement she felt, knowing that the courtyard would be dark and Marcus would barely be able to tell the color she wore. But that didn't change her mind, of course. She ran a brush through her hair quickly, picked up her slippers in her hand, then slipped out the door and moved quietly down the stairs so she would not awaken any of the rest of the household.

III

Mordechai led the way to an arched stone arbor behind the fountain, which was covered with grapevines. Two stone chairs stood beneath it. Here even the faint light of the moon disappeared into the shadows. They slipped into the deeper darkness, and both of them sat down. Mordechai looked around one more time. He didn't like the idea of meeting here, but the message had been too urgent, and there was no time to make other arrangements. When they were settled, he looked at the tribune. "Pilate must be feeling some sense of urgency to send you out so late at night."

"Actually," Marcus said, ignoring the implied barb about the lateness of the hour, "I got here shortly after sundown, but the governor insisted I wait until the city was asleep before I came to see you."

Mordechai grunted, accepting that. Yes, to have a Roman officer come to his house while it was still light would not have been wise at all. Things were coming to a critical stage now. He wished no attention at all at the moment.

"And how is the governor?" he asked.

"Filled with questions," Marcus answered sardonically. "Filled with many questions. I am here to learn some answers."

IV

Miriam came down the back stairs that led directly into the garden. Careful not to make any noise—Levi, the chief steward, had his room just down the hallway—Miriam let herself out, shutting the door quietly behind her. She stopped to listen, her eyes searching the darkness. Where had they gone? Wondering if her father had taken Marcus into the house after all, she stepped forward on the marble tiles. Then she heard the murmur of voices off to her left. They were just beyond the fountain, probably beneath the arbor.

Suddenly demure—it just would not do to come bursting in upon them—she slowed her step, her mind searching for a reasonable explanation as to why she was out walking in the garden at midnight. She smiled. It didn't have to be convincing, just reasonable. She moved quietly forward, trying to catch the clear sound of their words so she could break in at a natural breaking point.

V

"Is everything in order?"

Marcus reached up and slipped off the hood of his robe. He had come without his uniform, but even then his instructions had been clear. No one was to know who was visiting the home of Mordechai ben Uzziel, leading member of the Great Council of Jerusalem. Now, even though the night air was cooling rapidly, he was still sweating from being covered during his swift walk through the city from the

Antonia Fortress. He ran his fingers through his hair, smoothing it back. "Everything is in order. I leave in the morning for Damascus."

VI

Miriam stopped short, disappointment coming as sharply as a blow. So Marcus had not come to have her fulfill her promise to show him more of her city. Her mouth pulled down in a pout. Though she had told herself a hundred times that the differences between her and this Roman officer were deep and profound, she still found the thought of being with him exciting and stimulating. How ironic that of all the men she knew, only two stirred any interest in her. One was betrothed and soon to be married. The other was from a world so far removed and so alien to her own that she could scarcely fantasize about it. She threw her shoulders back, petulant and irritated. She would march forward and confront her father, ask him why he had not given her any warning that Marcus was coming. But even as she started forward, what she heard next stopped her cold.

VII

Marcus leaned forward, peering at the wealthy Jew in the darkness. "Pilate and I found it interesting that the handwriting on that scroll you gave me was a woman's."

There was an answering chuckle. "I thought you might."

"It was Miriam's writing, wasn't it?"

"Yes."

"Is that wise? I thought this whole matter was of the utmost secrecy and that no one except the three or four of us could know."

"Miriam knows only a fraction of the whole picture. I needed a way to convince a couple of the parties that I was sincere. The two in question know Miriam. They have confidence in her."

"And how did you explain the fact that she was making a record of all this? That seems a little strange for a man as careful as you."

"I told them that if what I was doing ever came forth, I needed a way to convince the Council that I was not undertaking this sharing of information for my own personal gain."

"And they accepted that?"

He sounded somewhat irritated in his response. "They did. I don't do things without carefully considering all the possibilities." Then, "How soon will you start back for Caesarea after you reach Damascus?" Mordechai asked.

Marcus answered without hesitation. His instructions from Pilate were to fully brief their co-conspirator. "It will take us four days to reach Damascus. I'll need one day to rest the men and get things in order. We'll leave after that. By then the moon will be about half-full, and that's important. Will that give you enough time to set things up as you need?"

"Yes. My party awaits only the signal that it is time."

"It is time that the governor knows who this party is. He is quite insistent, in fact."

Mordechai had expected nothing less. Now that the time had come, he knew Pilate wouldn't play any more games with him.

"I should like to know how Pilate plans to spring the trap," he finally said. "For that, I shall give you the name."

Marcus felt a burst of irritation. Was this man bargaining with him like a common street hawker? But he had his instructions. "Fair enough. The plan is simple. Right now, two maniples of legionnaires have left Caesarea. Not even their commanders know the real reason for their movement. They have been told very plausible stories about their assignments. One is in the vicinity of Mount Carmel, supposedly to guard against a rumored attack on the new aqueduct there. The other is on the south side of the Joknean Pass, undergoing battle drills.

"The night I reach Capernaum on my return trip, the two groups will receive orders to march under cover of darkness into the mountains on both sides of the Joknean Pass. They will muffle their swords and armor. The cavalry will be given cloth coverings for their horses' hooves. They will stay off any roads and known paths. We have already had scouts out to find acceptable routes. If any person should happen to see them, he will be detained and held until the affair is brought to completion. The armies will make camp in the heavy forest on both sides of the pass, no later than an hour before dawn. There they shall wait in hiding—without fires, of course—through the entire next day. By the following night, when I enter the pass with the column of wagons, they will move in closer, no more than half an hour's march from the place of ambush."

Mordechai could tell that Marcus was enjoying this and suspected that this was, for the most part, his own plan. And it was brilliant. No wonder Pilate had confidence in him.

"On the same day that I leave Capernaum, the governor will also leave Caesarea with yet another maniple, supposedly bound for Antioch to greet the legate of Syria, who is coming down to Tyre." Marcus smiled at that little subterfuge. The legate actually had no plans to travel anywhere that Marcus knew about. "Pilate's group will reach the western entrance to the pass just as darkness falls. There they shall wait until the time is right."

"So," Mordechai said in open admiration, "you will have a great three-pronged pincer in place."

"Exactly. My column will approach the Joknean Pass just as darkness falls. This will let the rebels think they can attack us under cover of darkness and yet still have the rest of the night to carry off the weapons. But in reality, we shall have a little 'accident'—all very believable, I assure you—that will delay us for some hours just outside the entrance to the pass. The Zealots will be watching *us* very closely, allowing the two maniples to move into position without being noticed. By midnight everything will be in place." He smiled thinly. "Wouldn't want the rebels to slip away now, would we?"

"And what if any of these maniples is discovered by the rebels before the trap is sprung?"

Marcus shrugged. "That would spoil everything as far as getting the Zealots; but if that were to happen, I will simply change the route of march, go straight to Ptolemais, and bypass the Joknean altogether. Pilate will neither risk those arms nor ten talents of gold unless the chances of success are high."

"Pilate is not thinking that he'll try to send something besides the actual arms, is he? Such as straw or empty boxes? He promised he wouldn't."

"He seriously considered it," Marcus admitted. "But we both agreed that there will be too many spies in Damascus. No, I'll be bringing the real thing."

"Good," Mordechai said dryly. He had known all along that Pilate did not like the idea of having something go wrong and letting those huge quantities of munitions fall into Zealot hands.

He leaned forward. "When the Zealots first strike, that will be a critical time for you and your men. My man knows that he is to bring the fighting to a halt as quickly as possible, but if you surrender too easily, the others will suspect something is wrong. On the other hand, if you put up too much resistance, you are going to lose more men than is necessary."

Marcus waved his hand impatiently. "Yes, yes, Pilate understands all of that. He has given me very strict instructions."

Mordechai made a shrewd guess. "I think that Pilate is less

concerned about losing a few men than he is about losing his weapons and the gold. Is that a fair statement?"

Marcus responded with a grunt but said nothing more. Wasn't that the way of most politicians? What were a few lowly legionnaires to them?

Mordechai chuckled softly. "My daughter would never forgive me if something were to happen to you, Marcus."

Marcus leaned forward until his face was close to the Sadducean. "I am not sure *Pilate* would ever forgive you if something happened to his lead tribune, Mordechai ben Uzziel." Then he, too, laughed easily.

Mordechai felt a sudden cold wind touch his brow. He understood very well what had just been said. "Everything has been carefully planned," he responded. "But this venture is not without risk, Tribune. I hope the governor remembers that."

"We all understand that," Marcus snapped, "and the governor is willing to take that risk if we can eliminate the Zealots once and for all. But everything had better go as planned up to the point of the actual battle. From there on, we'll be responsible."

"Excellent."

"I have one question that still troubles me."

"Which is?"

"How can you be sure the other Zealot leaders will agree to let your man be the one to escort us out of the canyon? Once we surrender our weapons, we will be very vulnerable."

"There are two answers to that. First, since it is my man who brings the information to the Zealot council concerning the column, he can dictate the terms. He will insist that he be allowed to lead you away."

"If I were a Zealot leader, I would be suspicious of that."

"They would be *if* he were a Zealot, but he is not. This is what makes the whole thing work. He is a Judean. Though he would love to get his hands on those weapons, he can't afford to burden himself with them. Getting them back to his home territory would leave *him* exposed and vulnerable."

"A Judean?"

"Yes. So his plan will be as follows. He will take you and your men and half the gold, leaving the other half of the money and all the weapons to the Zealots. He will lead you out of the pass and turn you loose on the coastal plains to troop back to Caesarea with your whipped tails between your legs." Mordechai was making this as clear as possible. What he had engineered was intricate and delicate and extremely dangerous. If anything was going to go wrong, it would likely be over this very question. "As to the second question, What's to keep them from slaughtering you and your men once you surrender your weapons?"

"The thought had crossed my mind," Marcus said, his voice droll.

"It will be a temptation. They hate you and all you stand for."

"Really?" Marcus drawled.

"But they're not ready for a full confrontation yet. A massacre would trigger the wrath of every legion that marches under Rome's banner. They are too cunning to make that mistake."

Marcus was satisfied. He had only one more area of questions. "And this man of yours? He obviously knows much more about the whole plan than the Zealots. Does he know about the trap we've set?"

There was a hoot of derision. "Of course not. Do you think I am a fool?"

"So why? Why is he willing to trust you?"

"Because he thinks I am the one who learned what you Romans are up to. Also, in addition to the ten thousand shekels I have already paid him, he thinks he will walk away with five talents of gold out of this."

"That's what is in it for him? What does he think is in this for you? Why would he put his life in your hands?"

"Simple. He is convinced that this will strike a terrible blow either to you Romans or to the Zealots. Either way, the Council wins, or so he thinks. Also, either way opens up the field for him if Rome and Galilee enter a full-scale war again."

Marcus nodded. He could see he was not the only brilliant strategist here. "When he learns that you have betrayed him as well, you will have made a dangerous enemy."

"How much danger can there be from a man hanging from a cross?" came the calm answer. Mordechai didn't feel that he needed to add that he had made doubly sure that Moshe Ya'abin would not escape the clumsy hands of the Romans.

"And this man's name?" Marcus asked, standing and preparing to leave.

"It is a name that will surprise you."

"I am rarely surprised anymore."

Mordechai hesitated, caution still making him nervous, but then he spoke. "His name is Moshe Ya'abin, the one they call the Judean Fox."

For a long moment there was silence; then Marcus smiled. "You were right. You surprise me."

"There are not many I would trust with this kind of treachery," came the sarcastic reply. "But he has few equals in that department."

"No wonder you want him crucified. I shall suggest to Pilate that you receive a special invitation."

"You are most thoughtful, Marcus, but in actuality, I leave at dawn for a trip to Alexandria. I feel it would be wise if I were not in the city once things begin to unfold, to allay any suspicions."

"Are you taking Miriam?" he asked. This was something he hadn't expected.

"Oh, no. This will be for business reasons. Everything here must appear in order. I have already left her a letter." He stood too, ready to be done with it. "I shall return in less than a fortnight. I trust there will be news of a terrible tragedy in the Galilee awaiting my return."

"I trust there will," Marcus said. Out of habit, he slapped his arm against his chest in salute, then spun around and walked swiftly out the gate. Mordechai followed along slowly after him, waiting until he was gone to secure the lock on the gate once again.

VIII

"Livia. Wake up!"

Livia gave a soft moan and pushed the hair back from her eyes. "Miriam?"

"Wake up, Livia. I have to go to the Galilee."

That did it. She shot up to her knees. "The Galilee?"

"Yes! Immediately."

"Are you mad? It's the middle of the night."

Miriam sat down beside her, gripping her shoulders. She quickly told her what had just happened. Livia's eyes widened until they were like great circles in the faint light. "So that whole thing with Yehuda and Simeon was a trap?"

"Yes." Miriam fought to keep her voice low. She was filled with horror and loathing. "My father planned it all, Livia. He used me. He's using Simeon and Yehuda to destroy the Zealot movement." She got to her feet again. "How could he do this? Simeon and Yehuda saved our lives. His life! I think even if he had gotten the money, Ya'abin wouldn't have let us go."

She began pacing, greatly agitated. "They've set up a massacre, Livia. I can't let that happen. Even if he is my father. We've got to warn them."

"How?" Livia's face had gone as pale as parchment. "You can't go to the Galilee alone. It's too dangerous."

"I have no choice. They'll be destroyed. Yehuda. Daniel. Shana.

The Romans will wipe out entire villages, just as they did before. They'll go after Simeon's family."

Suddenly she saw a solution. "I'll make my own way. I can't let Father know. You'll have to say I went to see my cousin Lilly in Joppa or something. I can make it as far as Jericho tonight."

Livia shuddered and leaped off the bed. *"Ma'ale Adummim?* You would go through there at night?" If she had been shocked before, now she was shaken to the core.

Miriam couldn't meet her eyes. Actually she had already considered that, and it left her terribly frightened. Jerusalem sat astride the central highlands of Israel, perched on the ridge top at about twenty-six hundred feet above the level of the sea. Jericho was at the north end of *Yam Ha'melach,* the Sea of Salt, thirteen hundred feet below the level of the Great Sea. In a distance of no more than fifteen miles as the raven would fly, the road from Jerusalem to Jericho dropped almost four thousand feet. It was barren, desolate, and dangerous. It had originally been named *Ma'ale Adummim,* the Red Way, after several bands of brightly colored rocks along the road. But *Ma'ale Adummim* had taken on new meaning now. It was so frequented by highwaymen and bandits that it had literally become the Red Way, the Way of Blood.

Miriam looked away. "What choice do I have, Livia? They saved our lives." She bit her lip. "I can't believe my father is working with Moshe Ya'abin. Even if he is trying to destroy him. How could he do that?"

Livia was fully alert now. "We must have an escort. Even for two of us, it would be extremely dangerous."

"We?" Miriam echoed. "You are not going."

Livia's eyes narrowed. "You are not the only one who owes a debt to Simeon and Yehuda." Then a tight smile appeared briefly. "Besides, you are completely daft if you think you are going to leave me here to try to explain all this to your father when he returns."

Then she was all business again. "There is a man in the market-place. I have heard him speak of his sons who hire out as guards for those who can pay."

Miriam's heart gave a little leap. "Really?"

"Yes. I am sure it shall cost us—you!—dearly."

"I don't care. Offer them whatever it takes."

"I shall go there at once, while you begin to pack." She shook her finger at her. "But we are not leaving tonight. I will not let you do it, even if you have me beaten."

There was a steel-hard determination in Livia's eyes, and Miriam realized that she truly meant it. She suddenly wanted to cry.

"If we leave at first light, we can still make it as far as Beth Shean and—"

"No," Miriam broke in. "We will not go by way of Jericho. With an escort, we'll go through Samaria. It's still dangerous, but it will save us many hours." Finally she was thinking rationally. "If we wait until Father leaves in the morning, then we can go and be back before he even knows we have left."

"What about Levi? What of the other servants?"

So much for thinking rationally, Miriam thought, her heart falling. She began to pace again, her hands plucking at the soft fabric of her dress. Then she stopped and whirled to face Livia. "No, this is not the way. Father *will* find out." Her face paled. "He can never know, Livia. If he learns what I have done to him . . . " She could only shake her head. Livia would not be the only orphan in this house.

"Then what?"

"Marcus said he leaves for Damascus in the morning and that it will take him four days to reach there. We can make it to Capernaum in two. That gives us some time to work things out more carefully."

Livia nodded. She was greatly relieved to see that emotions were not the primary thing driving Miriam any longer.

"It is the Sabbath. If we suddenly try to leave in the morning, Levi

502

will be very suspicious. But I have talked recently about going to see Lilly and her husband, Ezra, in Joppa. I'll tell Levi I've decided to do that since Father is gone for a time. We could travel with a caravan—there are always some going to Joppa—so Levi doesn't worry."

"Joppa is a long way from the Galilee." Joppa was directly northwest of Jerusalem on the coast of the Mediterranean Sea.

"Yes, but we could go from there up the *Via Maris*. That has so much traffic, we can hire a carriage and no one will notice. And Lilly will keep our secret." Miriam's face fell. "Especially if she knows what it will mean if Father ever learns that I have betrayed him."

"Oh, Miriam! I am so sorry for all of this."

She straightened and took a deep breath. "We must sleep. Tomorrow will be the longest day of my life. I don't know if I can act natural."

"Well," Livia answered, her mind working swiftly now too, "we have no choice if we are to fool Levi."

Miriam sighed wearily. "We have to make it look natural. We just have to."

CHAPTER 25

PUT UP AGAIN THY SWORD INTO HIS PLACE: FOR ALL

THEY THAT TAKE THE SWORD SHALL PERISH WITH THE SWORD.

—*Matthew 26:52*

I

2 JUNE, A.D. 30

Simeon stopped in surprise halfway down the hallway that led into their summer kitchen, the room at the back of the house that got the most shade. It had been another night with little sleep. Sunrise would come in about half an hour, and the room was filled with a soft and diffused light. His parents sat close together in the semidarkness, and as he peered at them he saw that they were holding hands. He could hear the soft murmur of their voices. He stopped. He was barefoot and still in his night robe, and they had not heard him.

His face softened at the sight of them. His father's hair and beard were only now showing the first signs of graying, whereas many other men of his age were completely gray. His mother's hair, on the other hand, straight and full and pulled back and tied at the nape of her neck, was almost completely gray and had been for some time now. He had often wondered if that was the result of the bitterness of her early life and the burden of grief she had carried for so many years. One eyebrow lifted. Or had the gray hair come from worrying about her middle son, who prowled the hills and put his life at risk?

He almost turned and went back to his room. He didn't want to talk about yesterday. He had spent most of the night trying to sort through his thoughts and had finally given up. At sundown Shabbat had begun. The beginning of the Sabbath day and the Shabbat meal together were traditionally a time of great joy in a Jewish home. The Sabbath was welcomed as if she were a visiting queen. Simeon felt a little stab of shame. His presence had certainly dampened that. He had been poor company and finally excused himself right after supper and went to his room. Nor had his guilt been helped when from his room he heard the sounds of laughter and celebration as the family rejoiced together once he was gone.

As he now stood in the predawn light, his mother looked up, somehow sensing that someone was there. Instantly her face was wreathed in a warm smile. "Simeon! Are you awake already?"

There was no choice now. He smiled back and walked into the room.

"*Shabbat tov*, Simeon. Good Sabbath, Son." His father motioned for him to sit.

"Good Sabbath, Father." He bent down and kissed his mother on the cheek. "*Shabbat shalom*, Mother."

"*Shabbat shalom*," his mother answered, searching his face. "Did you not sleep well?"

He shrugged diffidently. "All right." He moved around the table and sat down. "No Uncle Aaron?" He was sure he knew the answer. Aaron had not appeared in time for supper, and Simeon was pretty sure he would have heard him had he come in later.

A shadow fell across his mother's face as she shook her head slowly. "No. I didn't expect he would." Then she forced a smile, obviously not wanting to talk about that further. "You didn't eat much last night," his mother noted. "Would you like me to get you something?" It would be cold, of course, for no fires would be lit on the Sabbath.

"No, no. I'm fine. I'll wait for the rest of the family." He took a quick breath, deciding that the sooner he got it over with, the better. He turned to his father. "I know this is a terribly busy time, Father, but I have to return to Beth Neelah. I'm not sure when I'll be back."

His mother's countenance fell, but his father was not overly surprised. "So soon, Simeon?" his mother said. "You've barely been home."

"I know, but there are things that must be done, and I have left too much for Yehuda and Daniel to worry about. I'll probably leave after synagogue services." He pulled a wry face. "Especially if Uncle Aaron is not here to lecture me about violating a Sabbath day's journey."

His father gave him a warning look as he saw his mother wince. Instantly contrite, Simeon reached across and touched her hand. "It will be all right. Aaron will get used to the idea of you being a disciple of Jesus. Just give him some time."

She shook her head but said nothing.

"Simeon?"

He turned to his father.

David hesitated, his mouth showing lines of concern.

"What is it, Father?" He thought he knew. He thought he was going to talk to him about Jesus. He was wrong.

"I know you are trying to save us pain by not telling us what is going on, Simeon, but your mother and father are not as out of touch with things as you may think."

He tried to hide his surprise but did not succeed. "What do you mean?" he managed.

"I know about the Romans in Damascus. That's why you went to Jerusalem, isn't it."

Simeon could only gape at him.

"Oh, I don't know the details. In fact, I'm guessing about some of it. Day before yesterday, Esau of Gaza brought down a caravan of spices from Damascus. He said there is word of a huge store of Roman arms going to be shipped to Caesarea shortly." He shrugged. "Then yesterday word came down from Sepphoris. You forget that I sit on the council here. They're calling for a meeting of all the Zealot leadership. They want me to come."

Still reeling, all Simeon could think of to say was, "And will you?"

He shook his head. "That is not the answer."

Simeon jerked forward. "How can you be so sure, Father?"

"Because I know this is not the way to solve our problem."

A burst of irritation swept through Simeon. "And what if it is? What if this is all that Jesus has been waiting for?"

Both of his parents registered shock. "Jesus?" his mother finally said. "You think Jesus will be part of this?"

"No." He took a quick breath. "But what if he's waiting for the right time to proclaim himself? What if he's waiting until our people can finally unite in a common cause?" He looked at his father. "You said it yourself, Father. You said that if we could ever once become as one, we wouldn't need the Messiah. We could drive out the Romans by ourselves."

"I said that?"

"Yes! And it's true." Now his words came tumbling out. "Suppose Jesus knows that if he reveals himself too early, the Romans will move in to stop him. But when the time is right—"

The incredulous look on his mother's face stopped him. "You think that?"

He nodded, suddenly not as sure as before. "I know he teaches love and peace, and I accept that too. But remember when he taught us how to pray? He told us to pray that God's kingdom would come. And yesterday, you heard what he said. 'I come not to bring peace, but a sword.' I think he's giving a few veiled hints to tell us that when the time is right, he'll step forth and claim the reins of leadership. He will proclaim himself as the promised Messiah."

"He has already proclaimed himself as the Messiah," his father said softly.

Simeon's breath exploded outward as he shook his head. "Not in the way I'm talking about! Maybe, Father, just maybe I am the one who is right this time," he said hotly. "Maybe it's *you* that heard wrong."

"Simeon—"

But he rode right over his mother's soft warning. "What if that's the reason Jesus told us we had to carry a soldier's pack for an additional mile? What Roman is going to worry about a man who teaches submission? And by the way, I think that is why Jesus was willing to help your Sextus Rubrius. What better way to assure the Romans that he isn't a threat to them?"

"Ah, Simeon."

The pain was so evident in his father's voice that it made Simeon wince. He stiffened and sat back. "You're not going to try to stop me, are you, Father?"

Their eyes met and locked; then his father slowly shook his head.

"I have to go, Father. I'm sorry, but I have to."

"I know. But revenge is a seductive mistress, Simeon. Be careful that you do not go for the wrong reasons."

"I'm not after revenge," he cried, "I'm after justice! I want Pontius Pilate to know that there is a price to be paid for extorting exorbitant and wrongful taxes." His eyes hardened. "I want to teach a Roman tribune that there is a God who watches over his children and who does not ignore the brutality and viciousness of evil men."

"And you are to be the instrument of that justice?" his father asked sadly.

"Well, why not?" he shot back. "Didn't God use Gideon and

Joshua and David as instruments to punish those who would destroy our people? Isn't that how he works?"

"Oh, Simeon!" his mother exclaimed. "What have I done to you?"

He swung around in surprise. "*You?*"

Her eyes were swimming now. "It was *I* who set your feet on this path. I am the one who put the sword in your hand and the hate in your heart."

Anger flashed up. "No, Mother. It was you who gave me the courage to do what is right. Jesus said that yesterday too. If we don't have the courage to die for him, then all will be lost."

She just shook her head and looked away. Painful silence filled the room. He was pleading as he spoke again. "That *was* what Jesus said yesterday, Father. You heard him."

David gave a deep sigh. "Yes, I did. I heard him, but I didn't hear what you heard."

Simeon stood up, sorry that he had come down, sorry that it had come to this. He hadn't intended it this way. He had wanted to have a quiet Sabbath with his family, then slip away. He had hoped that the next time he talked with his parents, he wouldn't have to explain anything. They would see for themselves.

"I would like to say one thing," David said, looking up at his son.

Simeon let out his breath in a long, soft sound. "You know I will carefully consider anything you say, Father."

"There have been many who were valiant servants of God who have taken the sword in defense of the kingdom, Son. And not just men. Your mother was named for one who led Israel in battle and won a great victory. That is not what concerns me."

"Then what?"

"Perhaps there was never a more valiant and brilliant warrior than King David. Goliath was only the beginning. He united the tribes of Israel and ushered in the golden age of Israel. But—" He stopped, and again pain played around his mouth and in his eyes.

"But what?" Simeon asked, not wanting to ask but unable to stop from doing so.

"Do you remember what the women used to sing about David that so infuriated King Saul and eventually led to their estrangement?"

Simeon felt a sudden twitch. He knew instantly what his father was referring to. "'Saul has killed his thousands,' he quoted softly, 'but David his tens of thousands.'"

"Yes. That's how he made the kingdom of Israel into a world power."

"But?" Simeon asked again, knowing there was a purpose in this.

"But there is one story that is often lost in all of that. As David consolidated his power and gained wealth, he went to the prophet Nathan. 'I live in a palace,' he told him, 'and the Lord still has nothing but a tent for his house. I should like to build a temple to the Lord.' Do you remember what happened?"

Simeon sensed that this was going in a way that wasn't going to be what he wanted to hear. "Yes. Nathan at first was pleased, but that night the Lord told him that David would not be privileged to build the house, that one of his sons would."

"That is correct. In the writings of Samuel and the book of the kings, we are not told why the Lord said that, only that it wouldn't be David's privilege. But in the chronicles, we are told the specific reason."

Simeon felt a touch of shame. He should know this as well as his father, but he had no idea what was coming.

"I read this again just last night before going to bed," David said slowly.

"What does it say?"

"According to the chronicles, David called Solomon to his side one day and told him that it had been his plan to build a house to the Lord, but that the word of the Lord had come to him saying, 'Thou hast shed blood abundantly, and hast made great wars. Thou shalt not build an house unto my name, because thou hast shed much blood upon the earth in my sight.'"

He was looking at the floor as he quoted softly, and Simeon was grateful that he was, for his face was burning as though with fever.

His father said no more. There was no need. "Father," Simeon started, choosing his words with great care. "I have never rejoiced in warfare, nor in the shedding of blood as some do. But there are times when evil men leave us no choice but to take up the sword."

His father got slowly to his feet. "I know what you are, Simeon, and it gives both your mother and me great satisfaction. You are a son the likes of which few parents are privileged to have." Suddenly there were tears in his eyes. "We know that you must do what you must do, but go with God, Simeon. I do not want to put doubts in your heart. I do not desire to make your hand hesitate when the time comes to strike. But open your heart to his voice. Let your hands carry out only *his* will. Promise me that, and I shall say nothing more."

Simeon looked at his mother. Her eyes were filled with tears now as well. Finally he looked back at his father. "I will," he said simply. "I would have it no other way."

David stepped forward and put his arms around his son. "Then go with God, my son. And may he watch over you in whatever is to come."

II

Simeon hung back as his family saw Jesus and some of the Twelve standing outside the synagogue and went up to greet him. After this morning Simeon had nearly decided not to go. He had almost volunteered to stay home with Esther and Boaz instead of having Rachel leave them with a neighbor girl. But he didn't. He was grateful there had not been a greater confrontation between him and his father, and he also knew that if he left now it would only add to his mother's sorrow. So he went. Now he started to slip around the crowd. He would go in and save a place on one of the center benches for himself, his father, and Ephraim. It was obvious the synagogue would have standing room only again this morning.

To his surprise, Peter saw him and moved quickly to intercept him. "*Shabbat tov*, Simeon."

"*Shabbat shalom*, Peter." They gripped hands and shook them firmly.

"And how are things this morning?" Simeon asked him, afraid Peter had something in mind.

Peter shook his head. "Other than the Pharisees, everything is fine."

"Not Aaron?" Simeon asked quickly.

He nodded sadly, glancing sideways at Simeon's mother.

"What did they do?"

Peter blew out a disgusted breath. "We went out early this morning. Jesus wanted a chance to be alone with the Twelve, to have a chance to teach us. As we were coming back, the first of the crowds were waiting." He shrugged. "Jesus doesn't seem to mind, but it would be nice to have some time alone with him now and then."

"So what happened?" Simeon asked.

"We were coming through a field of wheat. We hadn't eaten breakfast before we left, so we were getting a little hungry. Since it is the time of the harvest and the heads are ripe, some of us started breaking off the heads of grain and rubbing them between our hands in order to get the chaff off. Then we ate them."

"Don't tell me," Simeon said, remembering how the Pharisees warned even a tailor not to stick his needle in his robe lest he forget and be guilty of carrying his "tools" on the Sabbath day. "They accused you of harvesting."

Peter nodded, his mouth twisting. "How did you guess?"

"I have Uncle Aaron as my teacher," he said sourly. "Remember?"

"Well," Peter continued, "the minute they saw what we were doing, it was like someone had dropped a dog in a litter of cats. They were dancing and spluttering like crotchety old mares. 'Why do your disciples do that which is not lawful on the Sabbath?' they demanded of Jesus."

"And how did he answer that?" Simeon was curious now.

"It was interesting, actually. He told them that the Sabbath was made for man, not man for the Sabbath. And then he said that the Son of Man is Lord of the Sabbath and that we had not done anything wrong."

There it was again. Simeon was struck once more with how eminently reasonable Jesus could be. Simeon liked that very much. If it just weren't for all of the other questions. He shook it off, determined not to get that chain of thought started again this morning.

"Good for him." Simeon motioned toward the door. "We'd better go in or we won't get a seat."

"Yes. I'll get the others."

III

The main synagogue in Capernaum was much larger than the tiny one in Beth Neelah or even the one in Nazareth. Capernaum was a large, prosperous town, and it required much more space to accommodate those who came each Sabbath. It seated close to three hundred people, but even then it filled quickly, and the latecomers had to stand around the perimeter or look through the windows to try to hear. As in all synagogues, the men and women were separated by a wooden latticework partition. It was open enough that Simeon saw that his mother and Leah and Rachel had found a seat near the back. Simeon recognized many of the people he saw, but numerous strangers were there as well—from the surrounding villages, he supposed.

Then he frowned. Coming through the door was Amram and several others of the scribes and Pharisees. Uncle Aaron was with them. Aaron glanced once in their direction, sniffed loftily, then refused to even look at them again. He studiously avoided looking in the direction of the women. Through the lattice Simeon saw the sadness in his mother's eyes as she watched her brother turn away. Simeon's anger deepened when one of the officers of the synagogue made those along the front row give up their seats to the latecomers.

Saddened for his mother, angered by Aaron, he turned his mind to other things. After a few minutes, Jesus entered and was also shown to a seat near the front—probably at the insistence of Jairus, a ruler of the synagogue, in gratitude for what Jesus had done for his daughter a few days before. Simeon watched him settle, noting the hostile looks from Amram and his group, the curious looks of those who were strangers to this synagogue, and the pleased looks of those who had chosen to be his disciples.

Then Simeon let his thoughts take him to other places. In a short time he would be off for Beth Neelah. He was anxious, glad that the time had finally come for action. This had been a frustrating visit home. Up there, he would know exactly what he was doing. The air would be cooler and clear of the daily haze, and that would do the same for his mind. He would gather his men, and they would begin their preparations. He wouldn't allow himself to wonder whether things were going to work out as he hoped. Only time would tell him that.

Through the recitations of the *Sh'ma* and the *amidah*, the eighteen benedictions, Simeon tried to stay focused, but he was not overly successful. He counted up the men that Yehuda and Daniel were even now gathering in to their band, assessing their strengths and weaknesses. He would have to decide how best to utilize them when the actual raid got under way. He took mental inventory of their weaponry, noting what had to be mended, made, or purchased. He laid out in his mind what training would be most critical and where it could best be done. He thought of Shana and smiled inwardly. She was not torn with questions. She loved him and desired only one thing, and that was to stand at his side and make him happy.

When Jesus stood up and a sudden hush fell over the congregation, it caught Simeon by surprise. All shuffling and movement of feet stopped as Jesus covered his head and moved to the *bima*, or central platform. By tradition he ascended the platform on the side nearer to his seat. When he finished, he would descend on the farther side. Totally attentive now, Simeon watched as the carpenter from the hill country of Galilee moved to the wooden lectern that was in the center of the *bima*. This was called the *migdal etz*, or "tower of wood." From that position, whoever was teaching stood with the scriptures laid out before him. So Jesus was going to teach.

The hush seemed to deepen as Jesus reached his place and looked out upon the congregation. Then, to Simeon's surprise, he did not look down and begin to read from the scroll that was on the stand. Instead, he turned until he was looking directly down on the group that included Amram and Aaron. That they were angered that he should be standing in the spot of the teacher was evident from their eyes. That they were taken by surprise when he turned and looked at them was clear from the way they suddenly began to squirm in their seats.

"I would ask a question," Jesus said, his voice low and rich and calm. He paused, letting the moment build in tension; then he turned to his left and looked at a man who sat near the end of one of the long stone benches. This was a man Simeon did not know. He was probably from Bethsaida or perhaps Chorazin. "Rise up and stand forth," Jesus commanded the man.

Everyone watched as the startled man got slowly to his feet. His face had gone suddenly crimson. Instantly there were gasps of surprise and shock as the congregation saw the man's right hand. Both arms hung loosely at his side, and both of his hands were visible. But both hands were not the same. The left was normal, but the right hand was a shriveled, twisted shadow of what it should have been. Sometime long ago, whether at birth or through some terrible disease, the hand had been stricken. It was withered to where it looked like the hand of a skeleton. The knuckles bulged grotesquely. The skin of the fingers and thumb was stretched tightly over the bones. The sinews along the back of his hand showed like strips of rope on a fisherman's net. Simeon was close enough that he could even see that the fingernails were dark and gray, indicating the lack of life that lay beneath them.

When the man realized that everyone was staring at his hand, he slipped it quickly into his robe so that it was no longer visible, then stared numbly at the floor.

Jesus' voice jerked everyone back around. He was looking at Amram and his colleagues again. "Tell me. Is it lawful to do good on the Sabbath day?"

Amram flinched, and Peter's words just minutes before came back to Simeon. The confrontation that had started in the wheat fields was not over, not for Jesus.

"What say ye? Is it lawful to do good or to do evil? To save life or to kill?"

The group of Pharisees did not so much as blink. There was no movement, no expression, except for a cold, hard anger in their eyes.

Jesus shook his head, indignation tightening his jawline. "What man of you, should he have a sheep and it fall into a pit on the Sabbath day, would not lay hold on it and lift it out?"

There was only one answer to that. The Law of Moses allowed such. It was commonly referred to as the "ox in the mire" rule. To work to save the life of a trapped animal was acceptable on the Sabbath.

Jesus gripped the podium and leaned forward, his lips compressing into a tight line. "How much more then is a man better than a sheep?"

He began to nod. "Yea, I say unto you, It *is* lawful to do good on the Sabbath. I am grieved for the hardness of your hearts." Then he moved again, turning away from the Pharisees to the man who stood with bowed head and flaming face before him.

Simeon realized that he was holding his breath. The tension in the room was so real he could taste it, feel it. The women were all on their feet now, faces pressed to the lattice partition.

"Stretch forth your hand," Jesus said, his voice so low it was barely heard.

The man visibly jerked. His head came up. He stared at Jesus, his eyes beseeching, pleading to let him sit down again and become anonymous as he had been before. Jesus smiled then, and nodded. "Stretch forth thy hand."

Suddenly the man's eyes widened. He audibly took in a breath. He looked down, then back up to stare at Jesus in wonder. And then slowly, as if he were in a trance, he withdrew his hand from the sleeve of his robe.

A prickling chill shot up Simeon's back. The hairs at the back of his neck were standing straight up, and he felt as though someone had just exploded a jar of boiling hot water inside his body.

"Praise be to God!"

Simeon had no idea who had cried out. Maybe it was even him. Like everyone else in the room, he was gaping in utter astonishment. The man raised his hand in front of his face and turned it back and forth, his jaw slack, his eyes like huge brass plates. Where before there had been shriveled flesh and skeletal sticks, now there were long slender fingers, knuckles that were barely discernible. The skin was healthy and firm. The fingernails showed a rich pink beneath them.

The synagogue exploded into a cacophony of sound. Everyone was on their feet. People were shouting and crying aloud. Women wept for joy. Suddenly the man was inundated as men pushed in to see more closely. Simeon fell back to his chair. A young lad of about fourteen reached out and grabbed the man's hand and began to pinch it with his fingers, even now unable to believe what his eyes were seeing.

In a dumbfounded haze, Simeon turned to look at Jesus, but the man from Nazareth had already stepped down from the *bima* and was moving back to his seat. And then through the din, a man's voice registered in Simeon's mind. "The man violates the Law of Moses! He violates the holy Sabbath!"

It was Amram, his face a mottled patch of fury. He was shaking his fist at Jesus. "How dare you flaunt the law in our synagogue? You exceed yourself." He turned to those around him. "Away with this man!"

Simeon could only stare. Had Amram not seen what Simeon had just seen? How could he even find words, let alone words of condemnation? And then Simeon saw Aaron. He was not on his feet. He sat still on the bench. His face was white, his eyes filled with shock, as though he had just seen a spirit dancing before his eyes.

In three steps Simeon went to him. He reached out and shook his shoulder roughly. "Aaron!"

The head came up slowly. For a moment he didn't seem to recognize him. "Did you see that?" Simeon cried. "Did you see what happened?"

Aaron's head didn't move, but Simeon saw it in his eyes. He saw the astonishment, the shock, the awe, the utter disbelief. Yes, Aaron *had* seen it. Simeon thought about the hurt this man had brought to his mother's eyes yesterday. "What do you do with *that*, Uncle?" Simeon shouted at him, barely making himself heard over the din. He shook him again. "What do you think of this Messiah now?"

Aaron got to his feet, still half in a trance. Simeon's father had come over now. Aaron looked at the two of them; then finally his eyes focused on Amram, who was still raging at the crowd. "Leave me alone!" Aaron cried, jerking free. "Go away! Leave me alone!"

CHAPTER NOTES

The scripture Simeon cites about King David is found in 1 Chronicles 22:7–8.

Matthew, Mark, and Luke all record the story of the healing on the Sabbath day in the synagogue in Capernaum (see Matthew 12:1–3, 9–13; Mark 2:23–28; 3:1–5; Luke 6:1–10). All three also indicate that this healing closely followed the criticism leveled at Jesus and his disciples for "threshing" on the Sabbath. Matthew and Mark suggest both events happened the same day. All three evangelists note the reaction that followed. Matthew says, "Then the Pharisees went out, and held a council against him, how they might destroy him" (12:14). Mark adds that this was done in partnership with the Herodians, a group that supported bringing the family of Herod back into power, and who, incidentally, were normally bitterly opposed by the Pharisees (see Mark 3:6). Luke adds that "they were filled with madness; and communed one with another what they might do to Jesus" (Luke 6:11).

CHAPTER 26

THE GODS PLAY GAMES WITH MEN AS BALLS.

—*Titus Maccius Plautus*, Captivi

I

6 JUNE, A.D. 30

"Take your marks."

The twenty-eight men up and down the line bent forward, hands reaching, fingers splayed out, every sinew as tightly strung as their bows.

"Ready?" Yehuda glanced at Simeon, who nodded curtly.

"Go! One. Two. Three. Four."

As Yehuda began to count, the men jerked up their bows. Hands flew to the quivers strapped across their backs. Fingers snatched the shafts and brought them down, nocking them onto the strings in one fluid movement. At the count of three their bows were up and drawn back until the metal tips of the arrows touched the wood. At four, one eye closed and the tips of the shafts moved slightly, honing in on the targets thirty paces away.

"Five!"

Twenty-eight arrows flashed away, filling the air with a soft hum, like a hive of far-off bees. Almost as one, twenty-eight missiles thwacked into the straw sheaves that held up the painted targets.

"Again! One. Two. Three."

Simeon watched in pride. On their first attempt at this, the day after he arrived back in Beth Neelah, their firing had been good but ragged. Now it was as though one mind controlled twenty-eight bodies. The rhythm was smooth and perfectly controlled. Here and there he saw a shaft miss the mark, disappearing into the trees behind, but the targets now bristled, and there were more than half in the center circle Daniel had painted for them to sight on.

When all seven arrows had been loosed, Simeon stood up. "Excellent!" he shouted. "This is the band I remember. Good work, my brothers."

He smiled as Yehuda turned and came over to where he was standing. The men started to laugh and call out to one another as they walked toward the line of targets. The Javelin was pleased at last. That was a good omen.

"They are ready," Simeon said happily. "With men as good as this, it doesn't take long to bring them back up to their peak."

Yehuda frowned. "Will they be so disciplined when the air is filled with Roman arrows?" he growled.

"They are not untested," Simeon said, still half-teasing, a little surprised at Yehuda's pessimism.

"None of us has been tested as we shall be if things develop as we hope."

That sobered Simeon, and he nodded. "True, my friend, but when the prize is of great worth, the costs rise to meet it."

Yehuda sank to the ground, and Simeon followed suit.

"You are worried," Simeon said after a moment.

"I don't like the idea of depending on information from a fox who is more jackal than fox."

Simeon nodded, knowing exactly what he meant. The word had

come from Gehazi. The Roman column in Damascus was loading up and preparing to leave. Soon all the Zealot bands would be called to come to Sepphoris. There the man with the detailed information on the exact movements of the Roman column would share his knowledge with the rest of them, and they would prepare the ambush based on that knowledge. Other than Gehazi, only Simeon and Yehuda knew that the man they would have to trust was Moshe Ya'abin. That was enough to leave any reasonable man filled with worry.

"We have the added advantage of knowing that, so far, everything Mordechai ben Uzziel told us is correct. That gives us an important safeguard."

"There is too much treachery here, Simeon," Yehuda grumbled. "Mordechai betrays Ya'abin because he wishes to get his revenge, but at the same time, he hopes that this will lead to our downfall as well. Ya'abin betrays the Romans. The Romans hope to annihilate the Zealots. I don't like it."

"I have considered that carefully," Simeon answered soberly. "And it well may be. But by the time the column reaches Capernaum, we will know exactly how many men they have and how well protected they will be. Even if they have a full cohort, they don't know we can field twice that number against them. The fools. They cannot believe we could unite and put more than a thousand into the field."

"It is not the two thousand that I hoped for."

"Only because Gehazi demands but the best of our men. I would rather have a thousand of the best than two thousand where half are incompetent or untested."

"Agreed, but I still don't like it."

Simeon turned and peered at his friend and most trusted lieutenant. "Enough that you want to sit this one out?"

The black beard twitched for a moment as he bit his lip; then he shook his head. "No, we shall see it through. But I don't like it."

"You and I shall take it upon ourselves to watch Ya'abin very closely. If he is up to something, we will know it before he can carry it out."

"Are you really going to hand him over to the Romans?"

Simeon shook his head. "Mordechai would like that, for he hopes that the Romans will snatch you and me in the bargain. No, we shall only drive that thieving Judean fox into the Roman net. They can take it from there." His eyes were hooded and clouded now. "We will have other scores to settle in addition to Ya'abin."

"Amen," Yehuda rumbled.

They were quiet for a time, both lost in their thoughts. Then Simeon stirred. "I am going back down to Capernaum this afternoon." Yehuda's head jerked up, but Simeon went on quickly. "The men are ready. You and Daniel can see to the few things that still need to be done until I return. I'll be back by late morning day after tomorrow, in plenty of time for the meeting."

Yehuda turned and watched their men. They had gathered in a circle and were checking their arrows for damage before returning them to their quivers. "Is this all because of Jesus?" There was no mistaking the touch of disgust in his voice.

"I have to know, Yehuda. There's no question about him being the Messiah. I have to know if I am right about his plans, or if my father's feelings are correct."

"And you think Jesus is going to tell you?"

"I'm not going to ask him directly. I don't feel comfortable with that. But if I can get Peter aside, or even Andrew or James or John, they'll know." He turned and looked out across the valley below them. "If Jesus is just waiting, and we are about to present him with the opportunity he needs, think what that will mean, Yehuda. After all these years of delay, think what that will mean."

"It's a fool's mission," his friend said darkly.

"If you had been in the synagogue you wouldn't say that, old friend," came the soft reply. "I saw that man's hand, Yehuda. In one instant it was restored to perfect wholeness. *One instant!* No ordinary man, not even the most extraordinary leader, does things like that. Jesus has to be the Messiah."

Yehuda just grunted. Simeon's account had troubled him, but he wasn't yet convinced. If you had asked him to give an explanation, he couldn't have done so, but he trusted his feelings, and this did not feel right.

Simeon got to his feet. "Will you tell Shana? I think I'll start down now. I'll see her before we leave again for the meeting."

"Shana will be fine. She is worried, of course, but Shana will be fine."

"You told her everything?"

"Only that we are going out again, but she is strong, Simeon. You don't need to hold back from talking with her."

That surprised Simeon. "It is hard for her to know that we shall face danger, so it is easier for us not to talk about it." His shoulders lifted and fell, and he turned and looked at the men. They were moving back to their places along the line, preparing for the next drill. He changed the subject. "They are good men, Yehuda. This will turn out. You will see."

II

7 JUNE, A.D. 30

It took Simeon until well after dark that day to reach Capernaum. Fending off any questions from his family, he had a quick supper and went to bed. Early the next morning he left before breakfast, grabbing a small bag of dates and a handful of almonds.

He stopped at Peter's house, but Anna said that he and Jesus and the rest of the Twelve had also left early, even before the sun had risen above the hills of Gadara. Jesus wanted more time alone with his closest disciples. No, she did not know where they were going.

At Andrew's house it was the same. At Zebedee's, the old fisherman told Simeon that his sons, James and John, had stopped by briefly the night before. They had said something about possibly going to Bethsaida, which was three or four miles to the east of Capernaum.

Frustrated but determined, he set out, inquiring along the way, knowing how Jesus drew people after him. No one had seen him. Not in Bethsaida, not on the road between. Discouraged, he set his face west again. In Capernaum again, word was that Jesus had been seen going west. He went on, staying clear of any contact with his family. Two miles farther, just as the sun reached its zenith, he got his first encouragement at the little village of Tabgha. A farmer selling vegetables alongside the road told Simeon that Jesus and his disciples had passed through about two hours before. No, he didn't know where they were going, but they were still headed west.

On Simeon trudged, bending his head to the blistering heat and the hot wind that came in from the south. As he reached the Plains of Kinnereth, a broad area of rich farmland yet another two or three miles farther on from Tabgha, he finally had success. Some women were working at a threshing floor—a large, stony area where neighboring farmers brought their sheaves of grain and put them beneath the threshing sled. With the threshing done, the women now stood with wooden pitchforks winnowing the grain. In smooth, even strokes, they picked up a forkful of the grain and tossed it up against the wind. The straw and chaff blew away in a golden white cloud, while the heavier grain fell to the ground.

"Do you know by chance of a man named Jesus of Nazareth?" he called to them.

"That we do," one of the young ones called back, smiling prettily at him. "Our fathers and husbands have gone after him just now, in fact."

"Would you know where they might have gone?"

Two of them turned and pointed. Squinting against the afternoon sun, he saw immediately what he had not seen in the distant haze. Another half mile on, a gentle hill rose out of the plain. As he peered more closely, he could see that a gray mass covered much of it and that it was moving slowly.

He turned back. "It looks as if you may be the only ones who have not gone after him," he smiled.

"True that is," the young one answered back. "And as soon as we are finished here, we shall join them as well."

He waved and walked on, staring now at the mass of people he could see out ahead of him. It was amazing. They were out and away from any of the villages, but the moving mass covered most of the hillside.

By the time he reached them, the crowd had basically stopped moving, settling down on patches of rock or areas of vegetation. As Simeon made his way slowly through the throng, it quickly became obvious that the name of Jesus was on everyone's lips. He had said this. He had said that. Had this person listened to him teach before? Had they heard how he had cleansed the temple in Jerusalem? He had done this. He had done that. It was no surprise that what Simeon overheard most was references to Jesus' miracles. He had healed a blind man. He had touched a leper and made him clean. Did they know about the daughter of Jairus, ruler of the synagogue in Capernaum? She had been raised from the dead. Simeon stopped as a man then asked those around him if they had heard about the other time Jesus had raised someone from the dead.

Simeon couldn't help himself. He turned aside and walked over to the man. "I overheard what you said. Who told you this?"

The man was about his father's age but obviously of the working classes. His beard was dirty and tangled. One tooth was rotted away, the others stained brown. His tunic looked as if he had wiped his hands on it many times. "No one told me," he answered proudly. "I saw it with my own eyes. I was no more than five or six paces away when it happened."

"Tell me."

"Are you a disciple?" the man demanded, peering up at him suspiciously, taking note of the fine quality of Simeon's tunic.

He hesitated for a moment, then nodded.

That satisfied him. "It was amazing. Jesus was coming to our village. I had heard he was coming to Nain and went out with many others to hear him. We were just approaching the gate when we heard the shrieking and wailing of mourners. A moment later a funeral procession came through the gate on its way to the graveyard. There were five or six men carrying the casket on their shoulders, followed by the rest of the people."

Simeon nodded. The scene the man described was typical. "And the casket was open?" Unless there was disease or a terrible accident, the body was always left uncovered until the actual burial.

"That's right," the man said. He looked around, noting that a small group was moving in around him so they could hear too. He beamed proudly. "When Jesus saw that it was a young man who had died, he asked those of us from Nain if we knew him. We did, of course. We told him it was the only son of a widow woman." His face fell. "It was very sad. The dead man was the only means of her support."

"So what happened?" a woman standing behind him asked.

"That seemed to affect Jesus quite deeply," the man went on, his eyes moving back and forth to take in the different members of his audience. "Then, to our surprise, Jesus stepped forward and touched the casket. The men who were carrying it stopped immediately. I thought he just wanted to look at the body."

"But he did more than that," Simeon prompted.

"He certainly did. He spoke to the dead man. 'Young man, I say unto you, Arise.' And he did." The man shook his head, wonder in his eyes all over again. "The widow's son sat up and began to speak." He chuckled. "That made a few women scream, I'll tell you. There that young man was, sitting up in his coffin and talking away just like he had come into your house and taken a chair."

Simeon turned away, not waiting to hear the rest. He moved up the hill quickly, swinging his head back and forth as he sought for any sign of Jesus or Peter. He no longer wondered why the crowd was so huge. Jesus was emptying villages from twenty and thirty miles away.

To Simeon's surprise, Jesus was not teaching when Simeon finally found him. Or rather, he was not teaching the multitudes. A small group of men and women had gathered in around him, and he was talking earnestly with them. To Simeon's relief, Peter and Andrew were off to one side, seated on a low outcropping of rock. They looked weary and just a little frustrated.

The moment Peter saw Simeon, he jumped to his feet and went over, beaming happily. "Simeon! What a welcome surprise. I thought you were up in the highlands."

"I was."

"Are you looking for your folks? I don't think they're here today. Your father had some loads of wheat coming in."

"Actually, I was hoping to find you, Peter."

"Really? Is something wrong?"

Simeon gave a quick shake of his head. "No, I just had some questions."

The fisherman broke into a broad grin. "You sure it's me you're after?"

Simeon laughed. "I don't want to trouble Jesus. There are so many others. But you know what he believes, what he teaches."

"You flatter me, Friend, but I will do my best."

"Can we walk?"

"Of course." He turned and called back to Andrew. "Simeon and I are going to walk for a few minutes. We'll be back."

Andrew waved, and they moved away.

For almost a minute, Simeon said nothing. He moved toward the outskirts of the crowd, wanting to be able to talk freely without people turning to watch them. As he looked around, he said to Peter, "There are so many."

Peter shook his head. "We've never seen it quite like this. The crowds grow larger every day."

"This would be enough to start a major rebellion," Simeon said, watching Peter out of the corner of his eye.

He laughed shortly. "It wouldn't be much of an army. First sign of rain and I think they would all run for shelter."

Simeon laughed at the jibe, then quickly sobered. "If they had the right leader they could be trained," he said, keeping his voice light.

Peter stopped, peering at Simeon. "Was that a question?" he said.

Again Simeon had to laugh. Peter always said he was nothing more than a simpleminded fisherman, but anyone who knew him knew better. His mind was quick, his insights shrewd, his understanding of human nature keen.

"Just ask me straight out, Simeon," Peter said. "I saw that you were troubled the other day at the baptism."

"All right." He took a quick breath, relieved not to have to skirt around the issues, hinting at what he wanted to know. "You believe Jesus is the Promised Messiah, yes?"

"Yes. Without question. Do you?"

"I do now."

"You mean after yesterday?"

"That, and after all my family told me has been happening."

"Good, but it's not enough to be convinced because of the miracles, Simeon. I cautioned your family about trying to use those as a way of convincing you to believe."

"They didn't." Or did they? Leah had been pretty excited about what she had seen. Then he brushed that thought away. He didn't want to be deflected. "So what does that mean to you, Peter?"

"What does what mean to me?"

"The fact that Jesus is the Messiah. Do you think he has come to deliver us from Rome?"

Peter reached up and began to stroke his beard. "I'm not sure."

"You're not sure?" The disappointment hit him hard.

"No. Sometimes he speaks about overthrowing the world, about overcoming the powers of darkness and evil and I think, 'Yes, he is the Great Deliverer for whom we have been looking.' Other times . . . " He lapsed into his own thoughts, not looking at Simeon any longer but gazing out across the waters of the lake, now barely discernible in the afternoon haze.

"Other times he talks of love and forgiveness?" Simeon supplied.

"Yes, exactly."

"I heard him say that we were to love our enemies and forgive those who treat us spitefully. But that doesn't seem to be the main message he has for people."

That won him a sharp look. "You haven't heard him that much, Simeon."

He quickly corrected himself. "Does that seem to be his main message?"

"I don't know if I would say that is his main message, but—" Peter stopped, his brow furrowing. "For example, the other day I asked him about forgiveness. I, too, was a little troubled by what he had said. When he gave us the model of how we should pray, he said, 'Forgive us our debts, as we forgive our debtors.'"

"Yes, I remember that."

"Well, I had been thinking about it. Knowing that he expects us to do more than the normal, I asked if we forgave someone seven times if that would be enough."

"*Seven?* The law requires only three times, and that's if they come asking for forgiveness."

He pulled a face. "I know. I thought I was being vastly generous. Do you know what he said?"

Simeon shook his head.

"He looked directly at me and said, 'I say not unto you, until seven times, but until seventy times seven!'"

A stunned gasp exploded from Simeon's mouth. Seventy times seven? His mind automatically did the calculations. "*Four hundred ninety times?*"

Peter shrugged. "That's what he said. I think what he really meant was, 'Why are you counting?'"

This did not fit Simeon's theory of what Jesus was about, which showed on his face. Peter pointed to another rocky place. "Sit down, Simeon. You need to hear what followed next."

"He said more?" The dismay in his voice could not be hid.

"Yes, he then gave a parable. A really astonishing parable, the more I've thought about it. He said that the kingdom of heaven is like a certain king who decided to take an accounting of his servants. When he had begun to reckon with them, he met with one who owed him ten thousand talents."

Simeon had been staring at a line of ants carrying tiny seeds in a sinuous line around the bottom of the rock. His head came up sharply. "Ten thousand talents!" For a working man, one talent was a major fortune. A hundred talents would be beyond his wildest dreams.

"It's a staggering sum, isn't it. Well, Jesus went on to say that when the servant did not have sufficient means to repay the debt—obviously!—the king commanded him to be sold, along with his wife and children and all that he had, and payment to be made."

"Oh, that would help! What's the price of a slave now? Thirty pieces of silver. Even if the man had a large family, that would barely be a tiny dimple of what he owed."

"That makes what followed all the more astonishing. The servant fell down at the king's feet and pleaded with him saying, 'Lord, have patience with me, and I will pay thee all.'"

A mischievous grin stole over the apostle's face. "Do you have any idea how much patience the man is asking for?" He didn't wait for Simeon to answer. "Even if he paid him back at the rate of one talent per week—an incredible sum!—it would still take nearly two hundred years!"

"This can't be a true story," Simeon said. "It's more like a fable."

"He never said it was true. He just said that the kingdom of heaven was like this story."

"So did the king agree to this fantastic proposal and give the man some time?"

Peter shook his head.

Simeon pounced on that. "I knew it."

"No," Peter said, his voice soft with awe. "He forgave the man the debt. Took it off the books. Totally forgot the whole amount."

Simeon started. "Jesus said that?"

Peter seemed pleased to see that Simeon was a little dazed by this too. He had been. The story had left him spinning. "But that's not the end of the story."

"Say on," Simeon said, no longer trying to predict what was coming next.

"But that same servant had one of his fellow servants who owed him a debt as well. He owed him a hundred denarii."

"After ten thousand talents, a mere pittance."

Peter went on without responding to that. "Well, this servant laid hands on his fellow servant. He took him by the throat and demanded that he repay the debt. And this fellow servant fell at the first servant's feet and besought him, saying . . . " he paused for effect, "'. . . *Have patience with me, and I will pay thee all.*'"

Simeon was transfixed. "The same words he had used with the king."

"Exactly. But the first servant would not listen. He had no mercy on him. He called for the officers and had his fellow servant sent to prison until he paid the hundred denarii back."

"After the king forgave him of ten thousand talents?" Simeon blurted.

"I was so angry by that point," Peter said with a rueful smile, "I had forgotten that this was only a story. But Jesus went right on. The king called the first servant back before him. 'O thou wicked servant,' he said." Peter stopped again. "Isn't it interesting? He didn't call him a *wicked* servant when he owed him ten thousand talents. Only now does he use that term. 'I forgave thee all that debt,' the king said, 'because you desired it of me. Should you not also have had compassion on your fellow servant, even as I had pity on thee?'"

"I would say so," Simeon said, not realizing that he, like Peter, had become so caught up in the story that he was responding as though it were real.

"And then came the lesson," Peter concluded. "Jesus looked right at me then. 'So likewise shall my Heavenly Father do also unto his children,' he said, 'if they from their hearts forgive not every one his brother his trespasses.'"

Suddenly Simeon felt his face burning. Peter surely knew about Simeon and what had happened when Jesus healed the servant of Sextus Rubrius. He was close enough to their family that he surely knew of the fire that burned in Simeon's heart every time he thought of Marcus Quadratus Didius. Was this the whole point of Peter telling him this?

But Peter seemed lost in his own thoughts. "I've thought a lot about that, wondering what he meant. Do you know that the one debt is six hundred thousand times larger than the other?" He didn't wait for an answer. "Do you realize that though a man could carry a hundred denarii in a pouch in one hand, a talent would be like half a large sack of grain? And it would take a column of men almost ten miles long to carry ten thousand talents!"

"Then why?" Simeon blurted. "Why is Jesus so fixed on forgiveness? What is he trying to teach us?"

Peter was staring at the ants now too. He reached down and formed a little ridge in the dust with his fingertips. The nearest ant faltered for a moment, then went right up and over the top. Finally he looked at Simeon. "How many times do you suppose a person sins in his life? I mean, if you count every *thought*, every *act*, every *word* that makes us less like God—which is a pretty good definition of sin, I suppose—how many times do you think we trespass against God?"

Simeon was so dumbstruck by the question he didn't answer. He just stared at Peter.

"A thousand times, maybe?" Peter's eyes narrowed. "*Ten thousand times?*"

"Maybe more, in some cases," Simeon whispered.

"If God is willing to take such debt upon him, forgive it without requiring full payment, then how can we go before him in the judgment and say, 'But Lord, Micah hurt my feelings. Ezra wronged me when he stole my cattle. Baruch took my wife away'?"

Simeon shot to his feet. "All right," he burst out, "I understand what you're saying. But isn't God a god of justice too? Someone has to make things right. What I need to know is, will Jesus be the one to do that when he brings in his kingdom? Will he take the Sextuses of the world, and the Roman slime who sell women and children into debauchery and slavery—will he take them and throw them into prison until the uttermost mite is paid? Tell me that, Simon Peter. Is that the Messiah I believe in?"

Peter just stared back at him, caught completely aback by the ferocity of Simeon's sudden anger.

"You want to know what my question is, Peter? Well, I'll tell you. I want to know if Jesus will step forth and lead the armies of Israel if the right moment comes. I want to know if he will be *that* Messiah, for that is the Messiah for whom I am looking."

Peter got slowly to his feet. "I do not know, Simeon. I am still like a child at his feet. Every day he teaches us new things, reveals more of his mind to us." Then he slowly began to shake his head. "But I do not think so."

"Why?" It was an anguished cry.

"About a week ago, while we were up north near the base of Mount Hermon, he spoke of coming in glory to his Father's kingdom. I can remember thinking that he was going to tell us that he was the very thing you just described."

"But he didn't?"

"No. Suddenly he started talking about going to Jerusalem. He said he had to suffer many things of the elders and the chief priests and the scribes." There was a long pause, and Peter's eyes grew hooded and dark. "He told us he was going there to be killed and then to rise again the third day."

Simeon rocked back. "Killed?"

"I know," Peter said. "That was exactly our reaction too."

"If he is the Messiah, how can he talk about being killed?"

It was as if Peter hadn't heard him. "I don't know what he meant. And I haven't dared ask him." He reached out and grasped Simeon's arm. "Why don't *you* ask him. I would like to know how he will answer you."

Simeon just shook his head. Suddenly he was too tired to care anymore. Killed in Jerusalem. What kind of madman's talk was that?

"Come, my friend," Peter said, pointing up the hill. "It looks as though Jesus is ready to teach again. Perhaps we shall both learn something from what he says today."

III

Simeon didn't hear much of what Jesus said. He listened for a time and realized that Jesus was not saying much that was new or startling. Some of it he had heard before. So he gave free rein to his mind to try to sift through what he had heard, like the women winnowing out the grain from the chaff. Surely the Messiah had not come to die. That was how Simeon had started his thoughts, but immediately he began to question that premise. Was he to live forever? The prophecies didn't say that. So he *would* die at some point. But violently? Against his will?

Then he visibly started. That's what they had said about Judah of Gamla, his mother's uncle. When he led the uprising of the Zealots some thirty years before, which for a time looked as if it would successfully drive the Romans from Israel, everyone had said God would protect him. His work was so important, how could God let him die? But he had. And violently.

And yet, from his death had been sown the passion that still breathed life into the Zealot cause. Could that be it? What if the uprising began and then Jesus united all the factions of divided Israel behind him? That would make him the prime target of the Romans. They would do anything to eliminate him. Cut off the head and the body dies. That was as true of revolutions as it was of serpents.

Simeon's thoughts were pushed aside as he realized that Jesus had finished speaking. He stood and stretched, and people all around him were starting to stand up and shake out the kinks as well. Glancing up at the sun, Simeon realized it was late in the afternoon. He had spent the whole day trying to find Jesus and was no closer to finding answers than when he had started.

Peter stood and moved over to stand beside Jesus. "It has been a long day, Master. The hour is late. We should send the people away so they can return to their homes before it is dark."

Jesus looked around on the vast throng before him. "I have compassion on the multitude," he said. "Many have had nothing to eat today. They need bread."

Peter looked at Andrew and the others in quick dismay. "But Master," John spoke up, "we are here in the wilderness, away from any of the villages. Where would we get sufficient bread to feed a multitude such as this?"

"Yes, Lord," James said. He was a little older than John but not quite so free to speak his mind. "It is late in the day. Let us send them back to the nearest villages to buy bread for themselves."

Jesus shook his head slowly. "I will not send them away fasting, lest they faint along the way. Let us give them food to eat." He turned to the disciple called Philip. "Go and buy bread for the people."

Philip fell back a little. "But, Master, even if we were to buy two hundred denarii worth of bread it would not be sufficient for this multitude, even if everyone took only a very little."

Simeon was listening carefully to this interchange, touched by Jesus' concern for the people and yet struck with the irrationality of thinking they could somehow solve that problem out here. He was suddenly aware of his own hunger. He had eaten nothing since early morning, when he had had a handful of almonds and a few dates.

Jesus looked around at those whom he had called to be his followers. Simeon could not tell if there was disappointment in his eyes, or just thoughtfulness. "How many loaves do you have?"

Peter held out his hands, palms up. They had eaten the last of their bread some hours before. Andrew turned and pointed. "There is a young boy with five barley loaves and two fish. But what is that for a multitude such as this? The people, including ourselves, have emptied their baskets already."

"Bring it forth," Jesus commanded. Then to Peter and the others he said, "Have the multitude sit down. Have them sit in companies, fifty men in each, along with their wives and children."

As the other disciples rose quickly and began calling out to the multitude, Simeon watched in astonishment. There were no more protests from the Twelve. Did none of them dare point out to Jesus that five loaves and two fish wouldn't begin to feed even one group of fifty? Obviously not. Andrew walked swiftly over and spoke to a lad of about Joseph's age. The boy listened, nodded cheerfully, and retrieved a basket. In a moment Andrew returned and handed the basket to Jesus.

Jesus waited patiently while the great crowd divided itself. He said something again to Andrew, who responded by retrieving some of the baskets they had brought with them—ten or so in all—and brought them back to Jesus. All of them were empty except the one the young boy had given to them.

The people were seated in rough circles that spread out in every direction across the hillside. Now all quieted as Jesus took the basket with the small loaves of bread and two smoked fish from the Sea of Kinnereth. He raised it high and closed his eyes. Many closed their eyes as well, but Simeon could not take his gaze away from Jesus. Peter's story had hit him hard, but strangely enough, it was not as disappointing as this was turning out to be. Could a man who was the Messiah be so blind that he could not see the problems he was about to create for himself? If the food was not sufficient for all, then it was better that none were to get any. Feeding a handful would create only unrest and grumbling. In a crowd this size, that could easily become unmanageable in a hurry.

He saw Jesus' lips move and heard the word "thanksgiving," but nothing more was audible. Finished, Jesus knelt before the empty baskets and began to break the loaves into pieces, distributing them between the empty baskets spread out in front of him. He then gestured to the apostles. They stepped forward, their faces clearly registering some of the same fears that Simeon was feeling. One by one he handed them a basket, and they turned and moved away.

Simeon was a little surprised to see how much Jesus had put into the basket intended for his own group. The group was not as large as some of the others, and yet the basket was filled with three half-loaves and half of one of the fish.

Simeon decided he would not partake. He could wait. Part of life as a Zealot was learning to go without food when necessary. He would leave his share for others, especially the women and children. It was Peter who carried the basket to Simeon's group, and he started at the front. When he reached Simeon, who was near the back, the basket was still half full. Simeon stared, surprised. He had seen a couple of others hesitate, but Peter had given them a sharp look, and they had finally partaken. Simeon had expected nothing but small fragments by the time the basket reached him. But there was still plenty remaining. He looked up. "Eat!" Peter commanded.

Simeon took one of the half-loaves and broke it in two. There were only three or four others still waiting after him, and seeing that half of one fish was still left, he broke off a piece of that as well.

He had begun to eat, grateful to get something in his stomach finally, when he noticed Peter again. He was standing in front of their group, staring down at the basket. Simeon stopped, wondering what was wrong. Peter looked up, and his eye fell on Simeon. He held up the basket, tipping it a little so Simeon could see the contents. It looked no less filled than when he had started. Completely surprised at how much was left, Simeon looked around, feeling suddenly guilty. So the others had just pretended to take their share.

His eyes swung back to Peter, who had turned to Jesus now and was holding out the basket for the Master to see. Jesus smiled, nodded as if he had expected nothing less, then motioned for him to go to the next group.

It was then that a tiny shiver ran up and down Simeon's spine, for one by one the rest of the Twelve were finishing with their groups and holding up baskets that were still full for Jesus to see.

For the next fifteen minutes, any thought of eating was banished from Simeon's mind. He sat frozen in his place, watching what was transpiring. One by one the apostles would take a small basket of food, with three or four half-loaves of bread and part of a single fish, and start it around one of the seated groups. They would stand there, their eyes wide with amazement, as the basket moved from hand to hand and everyone partook. As Simeon watched closely, he saw that each person took a portion of food before passing the basket on. Yet when the basket was handed back up to the apostles, it was as full as when it had begun.

Simeon felt almost as if he had been transported out of his body and was watching, from high above, so far-off that he perceived but did not understand. Yet there was no mistake. Again and again the baskets were handed to the people. Hands reached out. The loaves were divided and shared. Strips of fish were torn off and put into waiting mouths. Again and again and again the baskets moved on as full as though no one had touched them.

Through it all, Jesus stood watching, quietly supervising to make sure all were being served. The crowd had come to realize what was happening too. At first there had been an excited murmuring. Now a total, awestruck silence had settled over the multitude. The only sound was the soft whisper of the breeze.

Finally it was done. Peter returned first, his face pale and filled with wonder. He handed his basket, still as full as when he had begun, to Jesus. Jesus nodded and set it down on the ground before him. Next came Philip. Then Nathanael and Andrew, Judas, Simon Zelotes, James and John. Each brought a basket; each basket was set beside the next on the ground. Mesmerized, Simeon counted each one as it was placed beside the other. When twelve baskets were lined up together, he finally looked up.

Jesus glanced at the baskets one more time, each filled as full as that sent up by the young boy to begin with. He nodded in satisfaction. "Return to your homes, good people," he called out, raising his hands. "And give thanks to God for his glorious mercies."

IV

Simeon had almost reached the bottom of the hill, moving slowly, still trying to make his mind comprehend what it had just witnessed. Twice he almost stumbled because his eyes were not seeing what lay on the path before him. He heard the sound of running feet and turned. Peter was coming down the hillside at a dead run. "Simeon!" he called. "Wait!"

Simeon stopped, turning fully around. All around him people were streaming slowly back down toward the roadway that ran along the northern shore of the lake. They, too, were strangely subdued, and few spoke. Peter slid to a stop, puffing heavily. He bent over for a moment to catch his breath. When he straightened, he looked deep into Simeon's eyes. "You came to get certain questions answered today, didn't you?"

Simeon could only nod.

"And now you have more than ever before."

"More than my mind can fathom." He turned and looked back up the hill, nearly empty now. "I did a rough count, Peter. I counted the groups. There were about five thousand people here today."

"I know." He smiled, and his expression was filled with astonishment, wonder, weariness, and bewilderment all at once. "I know." He paused for a moment. "There is something else you need to know, Simeon. About Jesus."

"What?"

He shook his head. "I want you to go to Nazareth sometime while you are in the highlands."

"Nazareth?"

"Yes. Ask for Mary, the widow of Joseph the carpenter."

"Jesus' mother?"

"Yes." He gripped Simeon's arm, fingers digging into the flesh through his sleeve. "Ask her about her son, Simeon. She has your answers. Go and talk with Mary."

CHAPTER NOTES

The account of the raising of the widow's son in Nain is found in Luke 7:11–16. Peter's question about forgiveness, and the parable of the unmerciful servant that followed, is found in Matthew 18:21–35. The feeding of the five thousand is one of the few events of Christ's ministry recorded by all four Gospel writers (see Matthew 14:15–21; Mark 6:33–44; Luke 9:12–17; John 6:5–14).

Since Joseph, Mary's husband, is never mentioned as part of the family once Jesus reaches adulthood, most scholars assume that he had died by this point.

CHAPTER 27

I

7 JUNE, A.D. 30

To Simeon's great surprise, just before midday, while he was still some ten or so miles away from Beth Neelah, he saw a familiar figure striding down the road toward him. The figure recognized him at the same moment and shouted out, waving a hand enthusiastically.

As Yehuda reached him, his face was wreathed in smiles. "Simeon! But this is wonderful. I was on my way to Capernaum to find you."

They gripped each other's hands. "You were coming for me?"

Yehuda nodded, the smile fading. "Yes. Word came this morning from Sepphoris."

"The meeting has been called?" Simeon exclaimed.

"Yes. For tomorrow before sundown."

Yehuda wasn't looking at Simeon and thus didn't see the shadow fall across his countenance. "So the Romans *are* coming?"

"Well, you and I are not supposed to know anything at this point, of course, but I assume so. All Gehazi said in the message was that something very big was up."

"Any idea how soon?"

"We know from our own sources that a large column of Romans is scheduled to leave Damascus this morning."

Simeon said nothing, his mind working it out from there. Damascus was just over fifty miles from Capernaum and about seventy from the Joknean Pass. It would take a column with wagons two days to reach Capernaum and another day to make it to the pass. So three more days and it would be too late to make any more decisions.

Yehuda was watching him closely. "Is something wrong?"

Startled, Simeon forced a smile. "No, I—I was just figuring it out in my mind."

"Come then," the big man said, slapping Simeon on the shoulder. "The men are all at Beth Neelah. They have been working hard. They're anxious to show you that they are ready."

II

As Livia watched Miriam, she was reminded of a caged tiger she had once seen at one of the gladiatorial games. Miriam padded back and forth in the confined space, her head high, her eyes showing the nervous energy that drove her. The two rooms they had secured at the inn at Ptolemais were small, with only a tiny window that looked out onto the courtyard where their animals were stabled.

She stopped, whirling to look at Livia. "I can't stand this any longer," she cried. "We have to go tonight. I'm going to talk to Ezra again." Ezra was the husband of Lilly, Miriam's cousin. He was their escort on this journey.

Livia didn't move except to shake her head. "You know he's right, Miriam. We can't be making this last part of the journey at night, especially with Romans in the area. They'll detain us, and then you will be too late."

Miriam made an exclamation of both disgust and frustration. She came over and threw herself down on the bed beside Livia. "What if we're still too late? What if after all this we are too late?"

Livia sat up, pulling her knees in so she could face Miriam squarely. "We are not going to be too late." She held up her hand, her fingers extended. "Figure it out. You said that Marcus told your father it would take four hard days of marching to reach Damascus, right?"

"Yes. And those four days are past," Miriam cried.

Livia went on calmly. "That was in the evening, the beginning of the Sabbath, when Marcus came to the house. He said he was leaving the next morning."

"Yes," Miriam was listening in spite of herself. She wanted to be convinced that Livia was right.

Livia began ticking off her fingers as she talked. "So let's say that the next day, which was the Sabbath, is day one. We stayed in Jerusalem that day and got things ready to go."

"Right."

"Day two"—she pushed another finger down—"we left for Joppa. Day three, we arrived at Lilly's house."

"So Marcus is almost to Damascus now!"

"Almost, but not until day four."

Miriam threw up her hands. "And day four we sat in Joppa all day. Why did I let Lilly talk me into that?"

Livia gave her a stern look. "So Ezra could secure us a horse and carriage and food for the journey. So Ezra could get someone to watch his shop so he could go with us. So two very frightened women didn't have to make this trip on their own. So your father will never find out what we are doing."

"All right, all right. I got that lecture from Lilly already."

"Well, I'm glad someone was thinking clearly." She smiled to soften her words. "Now we're to day five, the day we left Joppa, but Marcus arrived at Damascus on day four, or night before last, right?"

Miriam nodded.

"Day five we made it a little past Caesarea and stopped for the night. Day six—today—we came on here to Ptolemais."

Miriam frowned. Originally she had figured only two days from Joppa to Capernaum, going the shortest route through the Joknean Pass. It said something about her mental state that she had not remembered there were Roman patrols prowling about on both sides of the pass now. They had orders to detain anyone who saw them. Ezra refused to take that risk, so they had taken the extra day and continued up the coast to Ptolemais. From there the road to Capernaum would not come close to the Roman lines. Miriam's despair rushed in again. "But by now, Marcus is on his way to the ambush site."

Livia sighed and shook her head. "If he's marched his men for four full days, he can't turn around and leave Damascus the very next morning. He's got to take one day to rest. At least. Maybe two."

"No, just count one."

"All right, so yesterday, day five, he rests. Even if he left Damascus this morning, he couldn't be to Capernaum yet. You said it was fifty miles. That's a minimum of two days' march, probably three with wagons. So the very earliest he could reach Capernaum would be tomorrow."

"All right," Miriam said begrudgingly, accepting Livia's measured calm. She could feel the tension in her begin to lessen a little.

"It's twenty-five miles from here to Capernaum. Ezra says if we leave at first light, we can be there before sundown." She smiled, more brightly than she was feeling. "We are not too late. That will give us a full day to tell Simeon and Yehuda and warn them off."

Miriam sighed and reached out for Livia's hand. "If we ever get through this, I swear I'm going to go to bed for a week."

Livia smiled and nodded, lying beside her friend. "There's nothing more we can do, Miriam. We've got to get some sleep now."

"There is one more thing we can do, Livia."

"What?"

"We can pray that it all works out." She sat up, taking both of Livia's hands. "Will you pray with me, Livia?"

There was a sudden lump in Livia's throat. "Don't sisters pray together all the time?" she asked softly.

III

8 JUNE, A.D. 30

"You have done well," Simeon said. "They *are* ready."

Daniel's face broke out in a broad grin. "Can I tell the men you said that?"

Simeon nodded. "Just don't praise them so much that they get lazy again."

Laughing, Daniel turned and trotted away. Simeon looked at Yehuda. "I mean it. The men are as ready as they'll ever be, thanks mostly to you and Daniel." He pulled a face. "I'm afraid I haven't been much use to you these last few days."

Yehuda pulled at his beard, looking at his old friend through narrowed eyes. "What's going on, Simeon?"

Simeon pulled around. "What do you mean?"

"You know what I mean. Where are you?"

Simeon feigned ignorance. "I'm right here." He laughed, trying to brush it off. "What are you talking about?"

"Even Shana commented on it last night. You're a hundred miles away, Simeon. You have been ever since we got back from Jerusalem. And frankly, that worries me."

Simeon bristled a little. "When the time comes, I'll be there. You know that."

"Do I? I've never seen you quite like this before. You want to talk about it?"

He started to shake his head. No, he definitely did not want to talk about it. And yet . . . if all went as planned, tomorrow they could be depending on one another for what might prove to be their very lives. He sighed. "Sit down. You're right. There has been a lot on my mind lately."

It took him a full half hour. He started with the day on the hillside when he had listened to Jesus and grown so angry he had walked away before the sermon was over. He told him about his father's experience in Bethlehem and what Jesus had said that confirmed that it was he who had been born that day in a stable. Yehuda already knew about the situation with Simeon's father and Sextus Rubrius, so Simeon passed over that lightly and focused on the "day of miracles," as Leah called it. He told him about his mother's change of heart and how it had come about.

When he came to the day in the synagogue when Jesus called forth the man with the withered hand, Simeon's voice slowed and his uncertainty became obvious. When he started explaining what had happened yesterday with the crowd of five thousand hungry men and their families, he stumbled and faltered, searching for words that would convey what he was feeling.

Finished at last, he shrugged and sat back. "So that's where I am. I don't know what to think anymore."

Yehuda leaned forward, his arms on his knees, his eyes staring at the ground. "Do you think he is the Messiah then?"

Simeon did not hesitate. "I don't want to, but—" he exhaled wearily. "But yes. I believe that he is the Christ."

Yehuda's eyebrows lifted slightly. "So what does that mean?"

Simeon threw out his hands in frustration. "What does that mean? If he *is* the Messiah, Yehuda, you tell me what that means. It means, *he is the Messiah!*"

"What does that mean for you as Ha'keedohn?" Yehuda answered evenly. "What does it mean for you and what is about to happen?"

Shaking his head, Simeon got to his feet. "That's what is so troubling. I don't know anymore. I was so sure that this whole thing with the Romans was the answer. We would get the arms. We could do something that would finally unite the people; then Jesus would step forward and lead us to the final conquest."

"And you don't think that anymore?"

"I'm not sure." The irritation boiled up. "Is that all you're going to do? Sit there and fire questions at me? Tell me what *you* think. Do you think a man who can take five small barley loaves and two fish and feed five thousand men plus some women and children is someone to ignore? What do *you* think, Yehuda? Is he the Messiah, or isn't he?"

Yehuda straightened. His expression was not a happy one. "Maybe others in the crowd had food you didn't know about. Maybe—"

Simeon's look stopped him cold. "That doesn't work, Yehuda. There is no natural explanation. *I was there!* I saw basket after basket come back full after hundreds and hundreds of people had been taking food out of them. Don't try to solve this problem by turning your back on reality."

Yehuda flared right back at him. "Well, I *wasn't* there, so I can't answer your question."

"You think I'm making this all up?"

"Of course not." He stood and faced Simeon. "I believe you. I have to because I know you would never lie to me. But at the same time, I can't believe it. Give me some time to think about it."

Simeon's anger evaporated. "Yes, that's exactly where I am. I can't believe it, and yet I cannot *not* believe it."

"So? We're going to a meeting this afternoon, and tomorrow we'll very likely be facing battle. You tell me what all this means to you so I don't have to worry about it anymore."

"About *it?*" he cried. "You're not worried about *it*; you're worried about *me*."

Beneath the beard, Simeon saw his friend's mouth tighten into a thin line. "I'm worried about a leader who may hesitate when there is no place for hesitation, who will equivocate when decisiveness is critical."

Simeon almost shouted at him. "I want to believe as I did before, but what if I'm wrong? What if Peter and my father are right and Jesus is not the Great Deliverer we're looking for?" He reached up with both hands and rubbed his face, suddenly very tired. "What if he didn't come to serve as the Messiah we've been wanting? What if what we are about to do is terribly wrong?"

Yehuda just shook his head. "How can it be wrong to fight against something evil? Come on, Simeon. Have you forgotten so soon what your mother's family and my family went through? Do you just look away and hope things will be better?"

"No, I—"

Yehuda rode him down. "If this Jesus can lead us to victory, then I stand right behind him. If all he's going to do is sow doubt and fear and hesitation, then I want no part of him."

They fell silent, both breathing hard, both surprised at the passions they had triggered in each other. Finally Yehuda sighed. "Peter told you to go to Nazareth and see if you could find your answers there. Well, do it."

That surprised Simeon, and his eyes showed it.

"Go. We'll have to leave here for Sepphoris about the seventh hour if we are to be at the meeting before sundown. That leaves you time enough. You go and find your answers."

"Are you sure?" Simeon said, feeling an immense relief. Nazareth might be the solution.

"I'm sure, Old Friend," Yehuda said gravely. "You find your answers, because if you don't, I'm not sure I want you leading us into whatever it is that's waiting for us tomorrow."

IV

Simeon had seen the mother of Jesus once before, on that day when he and his family had traveled to Nazareth from Beth Neelah to attend synagogue services and Jesus had been taken out in a rage and nearly killed. But Simeon had seen her only through the latticework partition that separated the men and women, and even then his focus had not been on her but rather on her son. So now he studied her as she sat across the table from him, waiting for him to continue.

He could see the resemblance between mother and son, especially in the eyes. Mary's were wide set and full of expression. They carried in them that same gentleness and wisdom that Simeon found so compelling when he watched Jesus. She looked about the same age as his mother, perhaps a little younger. Then he realized that she had probably been married at sixteen or seventeen, the normal marriage age for most girls in the smaller villages. Since Jesus was thirty now, that would make her two or three years older than Deborah. Perhaps Mary looked younger than she was because, unlike his mother's, her hair had only the first touches of gray.

He took a quick breath, realizing that she was watching him, waiting for him to speak. "I apologize for barging in without sending word first."

She smiled. "If Simon Peter suggested that you come, no additional word was needed. He loves my son, and my son loves him."

"I know." He hesitated, not sure exactly how to begin, but then, seeing the openness on her face, he decided that the only way to get his questions answered was to tell her of the turmoil within him. So for the second time that day he talked through his recent experiences. Much of his account was greatly abbreviated from what he had told Yehuda. Other things—such as his terrible experience with Sextus and the Romans—he skipped altogether. Simeon did explain about his involvement with the Zealots, and summarized the conclusions he had come to about what role Jesus might play in the Zealots' plans. Only as he came to the feeding of the multitude did he describe in detail what had happened. She seemed pleased to hear of it but wasn't as surprised as he had expected her to be.

Simeon finally stopped and sat back, strangely relieved to have unburdened himself to her. To his surprise, when he finished she only nodded. And waited. She knew somehow that all of this was just a prelude to why he had come.

Realizing it was time to ask his questions, he leaned forward, studying his hands. "I don't want to ask anything that would offend you or that is inappropriate."

She smiled. "I appreciate your concerns, but let me be the judge of that."

"All right." He drew in a deep breath. "Is your son the promised Messiah?"

"Yes." It came out softly but without a moment's hesitation.

The breath exploded from him. "You know that for certain?"

"Without any question. I'll explain why in a moment. But I think you have another question—something else that's troubling you."

"Yes," he said, surprised at her discernment. "Yes, I do."

"Then ask that one first."

"Has he come to deliver Israel from the bondage of Rome? Is he just waiting for the right moment to step forward and claim the kingdom?"

A shadow seemed to momentarily darken her expression, so her answer again caught him unexpectedly. "Yes," she said in that same firm voice.

It was all he could do to restrain himself from reaching out and grabbing her hands and shaking them. "*Yes?*" he exclaimed.

She nodded. "Yes. The answer to your questions is yes. But the answer to your real question is no." She smiled quietly when she saw his consternation. "Has my son come to deliver Israel from bondage? Yes. He has come to deliver *all* the world from bondage. Is he waiting for the right moment to step forward and claim his kingdom? Yes, but not in the way you think. He is not waiting for you or the Zealots or anyone else to raise an army and invite him to take his rightful place at its head. He is not the kind of deliverer you and so many others expect."

Simeon fell back, her words puncturing the euphoria as quickly as it had come. "Are you sure?" He didn't know what else to say.

"I should like to tell you why Simon Peter asked you to come to me; then I will let you decide if I am right or not. I do so with some reluctance, for I fear it shall only bring deeper questions and more unrest to your soul."

"I want to know," he said after a moment. "If Jesus *is* the Messiah, then I want to know what that means. For me. For Israel."

Again she nodded. Then her hands came together, and she began. "First of all, you have to understand that I am still learning about my son and what he is. I know that sounds strange coming from his mother, but when you hear my story you will better understand.

"It all began thirty-one years ago this summer. I was living here in Nazareth, the village of my birth. At that time I was betrothed to the man who would become my husband. His name was Joseph the carpenter."

"I too am betrothed," Simeon volunteered. "To a girl from Beth Neelah."

"Good, I wish you happiness." She went on, now more slowly.

"One day I was alone in my house. I don't even remember what I was doing. Suddenly I realized that there was a brilliant light in the room."

That brought Simeon fully alert. "A light?"

"Yes." Her eyes had a faraway look in them. "At first I was frightened. Then, even more terrifying, I saw a man standing in the midst of the light." She shook her head at herself. "No, not in the midst of the light. He was the *source* of the light. It emanated from him as though he were the sun itself."

Simeon felt the same prickling sensation up his back that had come when his father told him about his experience on the hills outside of Bethlehem. "An angel?"

"Yes. You can imagine. I was a young girl. I was alone. I was so startled, I nearly bolted from the room. But then the angel spoke to me. 'Hail,' he said. 'Hail, thou that art highly favored. The Lord is with thee. Blessed art thou among women.'"

Her eyes glowed, the wonder of that day back upon her. "As his words filled my heart, I was troubled at his saying. What manner of salutation was this? I wondered. Then he called me by name. That surprised me. I can remember thinking how strange it was that he knew who I was. And again, what he said was very strange. 'Fear not, Mary,' he went on, 'for thou hast found favor with God.'"

She stopped, and her eyes came back to rest directly on Simeon. As he met her gaze, he saw that there was a challenge in her eyes, and he wasn't sure why. "I want you to listen very carefully to what I am about to tell you, Simeon."

"I'm listening."

"What the angel said next was so stunning, so shocking to me, that I could hardly believe what I had heard."

He knew he should stop interrupting, but he couldn't stop himself. "What? What did he say?"

"He said, 'Behold, thou shalt conceive in thy womb, and bring forth a son, and shalt call his name Jesus. He shall be great,' the angel went on, 'and shall be called *the Son of the Highest*.'" She stopped, watching him intently. "Do you understand what I just said, Simeon? He said that my son would be called the Son of the Highest."

He nodded. He was missing something, and he wasn't sure what.

She seemed disappointed that he reacted so calmly. "Then the angel told me that the Lord God shall give unto him the throne of his father David."

"The throne of his father David?" Those words leaped out at him.

"Yes. I am of the lineage of David. So was my husband, Joseph."

"But that's a Messianic promise of kingship. The Messiah is to inherit the throne of David and become a king over Israel again."

"Yes, he is."

Now she had Simeon's complete attention. "What else did he tell you?"

"He told me that he would reign over the house of Jacob forever, and of his kingdom there should be no end.'"

"So *that's* how you know?" Simeon blurted. His spirit soared. This was wonderful. That ended any question left in his mind. An angel had declared it to her. And his kingdom was to have no end.

"Yes," she said quietly, "that's how I know that he is the Messiah. But let me tell you again, the first thing that the angel told me was that this son I was to bear would be called the Son of the Highest."

"Yes, the son of God. So? Aren't we all children of the Highest?"

She smiled faintly, tolerantly. "I didn't understand at first either. Of course, I was still reeling from the very experience itself. But there was something else. I still am not sure how I knew this, but as he spoke I knew with complete certainty that he was not talking about some future event. He was telling me that I was going to conceive a son very soon."

"Immediately after you were married, you mean."

"No. I was to conceive immediately."

Simeon gaped at her. "But—" he fumbled for words, afraid that he was moving into a highly personal area. "You said you were only *betrothed* to Joseph. How soon were you to be married?"

"Not for several months." She nodded, very slowly and with the greatest of gravity. "That's right. The angel was saying I would conceive *before* I was married."

Simeon looked away, so perplexed he was at a loss for words. Was she suggesting what he thought she was suggesting? That the angel was asking her to somehow violate the vows she had made?

She watched him struggle with it, waited quietly, not helping out. Finally, when he shook his head in complete befuddlement, she smiled faintly and went on. "As I look back on that day, I realize I should have stood in absolute awe. Here was an angel from the presence of God, in *my* house, speaking to *me!* I should have asked him a thousand questions, but when I realized what he had just said, that I would conceive a son, all that came out was, 'How shall this be, seeing I know not a man?'"

Simeon had frozen into place. "And what did he say?" he whispered.

She straightened, her voice suddenly filled with power. "The angel answered and said, 'The Holy Ghost shall come upon thee and the power of the Highest shall overshadow thee. Therefore that holy child that shall be born of thee shall be called *the Son of God.*'"

It was as if the very house held its breath. No sound penetrated through the open doorway. Nothing moved. Time itself seemed suspended.

"Yes, Simeon. I am saying exactly what you think I am saying."

"But—"

"Joseph was the father of all my other children, but he was *not* the father of Jesus."

Unconsciously, his hand came up, and he began rubbing at his eyes.

Her face softened, and she laughed softly. "Don't ask anything yet. Let me finish."

He could only nod numbly.

"By that point I was barely hearing anything any longer. I was in a daze. Then the angel told me that my cousin Elisabeth had conceived a son in her old age and was with child. I already knew that. It was the talk of our whole family. Her husband was a priest in Jerusalem. An angel came to him in the temple and told him that Elisabeth was to bear a son, even though she was many years past the time of child-bearing. And then the angel looked at me in such a way that it felt as though his eyes pierced every pore of my body. 'Remember,' he said, 'with God, nothing is impossible.'"

Simeon stirred, but she held up her hand quickly. "I felt so humbled by then that all I could say was, 'Behold the handmaid of the Lord. Be it unto me according to thy word.' When I said that, the angel immediately departed."

She rushed on, anxious to lay it all out for him. "I left the next morning for Judea to visit with Elisabeth. I wanted to see her, to see this miracle for myself. I stayed there for three months, until she was delivered of a son." She paused. "By the way, do you know what they called him?"

Simeon, surprised that it would matter, shook his head.

"They called him John. He later came to be known as the Baptist."

He jerked forward. "John the Baptist?"

"Yes, he and Jesus are cousins. But that's another story. Some wonderful things happened while I was with Elisabeth, but that's not important now. What happened next is important. When I finally returned to Nazareth, three months had gone by." She blushed a little. "Not being married, perhaps you may not understand the ways of women, but as time passed, it was no longer possible to hide the fact that I was with child." There was sudden pain in her voice. "Remember, I was betrothed to Joseph, who knew nothing of any of this. I don't know who first noticed. Perhaps it was one of the women at the well, perhaps someone in the market. What does it matter? The first pointed finger became a hundred; the first whisper became a constant murmur."

"And no one knew what had happened to you?"

"No one except my own family." She shook her head. "Nazareth is a small village. Small villages are so close they can be merciless. The assumption was that something had happened while I was in Judea. Poor Joseph. How it must have cut him when he heard."

"You were still espoused?" Simeon asked, his voice low. He was thinking of his own situation and what he would think if word came to him that Shana was with child. The very thought left him sick inside.

"Joseph was a good man, Simeon. A just man. As you know, under the Mosaic Law a person guilty of fornication can be condemned to death. At the very least, Joseph could have dragged me before the Council and had me publicly humiliated and condemned. And what could I have said in my defense? That I was a virgin carrying a child? That God himself was the Father?" There was a sorrowful laugh. "I'm sure that would have put an end to all the talk.

"Fortunately, Joseph was not willing to destroy me publicly. He decided he would just quietly give me a bill of divorcement and be done with it. While he was still brooding about what to do, an angel came to him one night and—"

"The same angel?"

"We think so, though we can't be sure. Anyway, an angel of the Lord appeared to him too. 'Joseph, thou son of David,' he said, 'fear not to take unto thee Mary as thy wife, for that which is conceived in her is done by the power of the Holy Ghost. She shall bring forth a son, and thou shalt call his name Jesus, for he shall save his people from their sins.'"

Simeon felt as if he were two people, one listening intently to this woman's story, the other a long way off watching a tableau being reenacted. "So what did he do?"

"This will tell you a lot about the man I was privileged to marry. It was the middle of the night when the angel came to him. He rose immediately and did as the angel had bidden him. We were formally married before morning."

Simeon was trying to picture all of this in his mind. "I'll bet that stopped the rumors short," he said in soft sarcasm.

There was a fleeting smile. "Right. All it really accomplished was that Joseph now got the blame instead of some unknown person in Judea." Her shoulders lifted, then fell again. "Anyway, six months after I returned I brought forth my firstborn." She hesitated, once again her eyes fixed on Simeon. "Not *our* firstborn. *My* firstborn. We didn't consummate our marriage until after Jesus was born."

There it was again in stark, unmistakable, inescapable words. "So the father of Jesus . . . " He had to stop. He couldn't even bring himself to say the words.

"Yes," she exclaimed. "The father of Jesus is God the Father. My son is literally the Son of God."

It was too much for him to grasp. He dropped his head in his hands, staring at nothing as he tried to take it all in. There was never even the slightest question about whether what she had told him was true. He could no more doubt this woman than he could doubt his own mother.

Smiling now at his confusion, she said, "When my time came, it was nearing Passover. That was the year of the census called by the Romans. We had to go to the city of our ancestry for registration so—"

He jumped in quickly and finished her sentence. "So you went to Bethlehem."

She stopped. Now it was she who was surprised. Simeon quickly told her about his father's experience.

"He was there?" she asked. "He was one of the shepherds who came that night?"

"Actually, he was not one of them, but he was with them. And yes, he was there."

"I would very much like to meet your father, Simeon. I had no idea."

"I'm not sure even Peter knows about that," he responded.

They both lapsed into silence, lost in their thoughts. Finally Mary looked at him. "If you have to be in Sepphoris, you're going to have to leave soon."

He glanced at the window, measuring the shadows cast by the sun. She was right.

"I warned you, didn't I, Simeon of Capernaum? I warned you that what I had to say would only bring greater questions, more unrest to your troubled mind."

"But—" he threw up his hands. "The Son of God? How can such a thing be?"

She took no offense. She understood exactly what he was feeling. "Even now, after thirty years, I still can scarcely take it in. But think about it for a moment. If what I tell you is true, doesn't that make it easier to understand what he does? He stills a storm with a single word. He makes the blind see and cleanses leprosy with a touch. A withered hand becomes whole in an instant." She peered at him more deeply. "Five loaves and two fishes multiply endlessly until five thousand are fed, leaving more at the end than there was at the beginning."

"Yes, I see that. But a *man* who is the Son of God? Why?"

Mary became very sober, and her eyes were also troubled. "I have told you that I do not yet understand everything. But this much I can say. The angel told both Joseph and me that we were to call him Jesus. As you know, *Jesus* in its Hebrew form, *Yeshua*, means Savior. But Simeon, Jesus did not come just to save us from Rome. He came to save the world from *sin*. All of us. Every soul."

She let that sink in for a moment, then pressed on. "It would take a great and charismatic man to be the Messiah for which you are looking, Simeon. Such a man comes along only once every few generations. But what if you are talking about a Messiah who saves *all* men?

Who redeems us not just from political bondage but spiritual bondage of every kind? Who somehow offers himself as a ransom to pay the debt of all the wrongs of all time so that we can return to live with God? What man could work such a work as that?"

And then, in one flood of understanding, he saw it. His head came up slowly, and he began to nod. "No man could work a work such as that." He breathed in deeply, tingling in every pore. "It would take someone who was *more* than just a man."

CHAPTER NOTES

The details about Mary's conception and the nativity of Jesus are given in such detail by Luke (see chapters 1–2) that some scholars believe Mary must have shared the story with him so that it could be recorded for all generations. Matthew includes the story of the angel's visit to Joseph (Matthew 1:18–25).

The author took the liberty of speculating about some of the feelings Mary may have had about those experiences, but did so based on the information that is included in the scriptural record or that is known about Jewish customs and practices at that day.

CHAPTER 28

THERE IS A SNAKE HIDDEN IN THE GRASS.

—*Virgil*, Eclogues, *iii*.93

I

8 JUNE, A.D. 30

When Simeon left the village of Nazareth, he struck out on the road back to Beth Neelah, but a mile out of town he turned off the road and plunged into the heavy pine forests that covered the long stretch of the Nazareth Ridge. His step slowed, and he breathed deeply, soothed by the rich smell of the pines and the soft crunch of the needles beneath his sandals. Angling to the right, he worked his way through the trees until he came to the edge of the hillside. For a long time he stood there, drinking in the spectacular panorama. There before him lay the vast richness of the Jezreel Valley. Off to his left in the distance, Mount Tabor jutted upward from the flat plain like a half-buried catapult stone—round, majestic, completely separate from everything around it.

Far below him the green patches of melon and vegetable gardens stitched together the browns and golds of the wheat fields, some already harvested, others waiting for the scythe and the sickle. His eyes picked out signs of life here and there. An entire family was going through a melon patch, carrying the fruit to a cart to which a donkey was tied. Half a mile away, several women were bent over with sickles. Behind them, sheaves of grain stood at attention like rows of soldiers waiting for a command to march away. To his right, along the line where the fields gave way to foothills, he picked out a shepherd boy at the head of a sprinkling of white and black dots—the white, the thick wool of sheep; the black, the long hair of goats used to weave the tents the nomadic tribes lived in.

He moved over to the shade of a large oak tree and sat down. Though he knew that even at this moment Yehuda and Daniel were probably anxiously watching the road for him, he pushed the thought away. He lay back, closed his eyes, and, word by word, began rehearsing in his mind all that Mary, the mother of Jesus, had told him.

II

Sextus Rubrius, centurion in charge of the detachment of the Tenth Legion Fretensis, currently on assignment at the garrison in Capernaum, stepped inside the tent of his commanding officer and saluted sharply.

"Ah, Rubrius. You're here."

"Yes, sire. We just arrived."

Marcus Quadratus Didius, Rubrius's commanding officer, flicked a hand at his aide, who bowed quickly and backed out of the small tent. When he was gone and they were alone, Marcus motioned to his fellow soldier. "Take off your helmet. Sit down." He picked up the silver pitcher on the collapsible table beside him and poured a goblet of wine. He handed it to the centurion as he settled into one of the camp chairs across from his commander.

"You made excellent time, sire," Rubrius said. "We didn't expect you for another two or three hours. The messenger said—"

"I know," Marcus responded quickly. He was pleased that Rubrius had come this early. He had feared it might be close to the ninth or tenth hour of the day before Rubrius came to see him, for that was when Marcus had expected to arrive himself. "We pushed hard from Damascus yesterday, made more than thirty miles."

"I thought you would be staying in Capernaum, sire. We've got things in readiness there."

Marcus shook his head. "No. Here on the Plains of Kinnereth we're five miles closer to our destination." He grinned ruefully and lifted his own cup. "Besides, you were the one who taught me that Capernaum is not the best place for a Roman to spend the night."

Rubrius smiled too. "Yes, sire. We do try to keep a low profile there." He took a drink, then leaned forward. "Do you plan to go all the way to Ptolemais tomorrow then?"

Marcus pulled a face and shook his head. "We're not going to Ptolemais. We'll take the Joknean Pass straight on to Caesarea."

Sextus lowered the cup slowly. "The Joknean? Is that wise? Ptolemais is farther, but it's a much safer road. With the wagons—"

Marcus cut him off. "Drink your wine, Rubrius. There is much I have to tell you."

A quarter of an hour later, Sextus's cup was still barely touched. Now, however, deep lines had appeared around the corners of his eyes, and his mouth had pinched in a little. "So the Zealots know we're coming," was all he could think of to say when Marcus finished.

Marcus nodded, letting him assimilate it all.

"The men won't like the idea of surrendering. Not without a real fight."

"That's why we've cut back to only two hundred men—two-fifty with what you've brought—instead of the full cohort. Our source in Jerusalem is saying the Zealots will have about double that. That should make it a little easier to convince the men that surrender is our only option."

"And what if the Zealots don't honor their agreement to let us pass once we've laid down our arms? We'll be in a terrible trap, sire. The Joknean Pass is not a good place to fight."

"We're going to turn and run only until the rest of the troops arrive. The governor and his maniple will be bringing enough weapons to rearm us; then we're going right back into the fray." His lips pressed together. "Only the officers are to know any of this, of course. I want our soldiers to be angry. We've got to convince these rebels that they've totally humiliated us and we're on the run."

"It's a . . . risk," the centurion said after a minute.

Marcus sensed that he had almost said "terrible risk." "It's all been carefully orchestrated, Rubrius. And this is not a suicide mission. If we can catch the Zealot leadership and deal them a shattering blow, we'll set their movement back ten years. Twenty years."

Though it was clear that he still did not like what he had heard, like all good officers, Rubrius accepted what was decreed.

"Brief the other officers," Marcus said, obviously ready to conclude. "If those other maniples are discovered, we'll get word of it. If no messengers come by tomorrow afternoon, then I want to be at the entrance of the pass at least an hour before sundown."

"But you said—"

"Yes, I know. I said that the other maniples won't be in place until about midnight." He lifted his cup one last time, raising it in a toast. "We want the *lestai* to see us clearly while it's still light. Get their appetites up. Then we'll have our little accident, which will delay us for several hours. That will give the rest of our force time to get into place."

"Yes, sire. I'll go alert the others."

"Don't worry, Sextus," he said, calling him by his given name for the first time. "All of this has been very carefully orchestrated." Then he felt a little foolish for telling a man of Sextus's wisdom and experience not to worry. "Not that we have any choice. Pilate wants this very badly."

"I can understand why," Sextus grunted. He almost added, "But it is not the governor who is going into the pass to get it." But of course he did not.

III

It was more than an hour later. Simeon stood at the edge of the steep hillside, absently throwing rocks down into the trees. Time and again he tested the questions that tumbled over and over in his mind against the new truths he had discovered, but he couldn't make them fit.

Then, as he was remembering what Mary had said about the village and their reaction to the news that she was with child, one of her comments jumped out at him. "What was I to tell them? That I was a virgin with child?" At that, a passage from Isaiah leaped into his mind. It was something he had not thought about for years, but as a young boy in the *yeshiva*, his teacher had made him and his classmates memorize a passage from the prophet because of its Messianic significance. Now the words roared in his mind like a clap of thunder.

"Therefore, the Lord himself shall give you a sign: Behold, a *virgin* shall conceive, and bear a son, and shall call his name Immanuel."

Simeon drew in his breath sharply. *A virgin shall conceive.* He sat down slowly, unmindful of where he was. Now the memories came back sharply. The word in Hebrew was *ha'almah*, usually translated as the maiden, or the virgin. The old teacher, a rabbi of short temper but deep wisdom, had pontificated on that word at some length. It was, according to the rabbi, a passage that had triggered much disagreement.

That it was Messianic in nature no one disputed. Exactly what was meant by the woman whom Isaiah designated as *ha'almah* was not as clear. Some, the rabbi explained, believed that Isaiah was talking about his own wife and some future child of his, but that didn't make sense. First, Isaiah never had a son called by that name. Second, though *'almah* was occasionally used to refer to a married woman, typically it was reserved for a woman who had come to maturity and was now ready to be married.

What if he literally meant a virgin, an unmarried woman? He was staggered by the thought. Had Isaiah actually been shown Mary seven hundred years before she was born?

And then the second insight slammed in. "And she shall call his name Immanuel." Simeon rocked back. *Immanuel.* The name meant "God with us." *God with us!* He had never before considered the significance of the name. Many proper names incorporated the Hebrew word for God, which was *El.* Daniel meant "God is my judge," and *Joel,* "the Lord is God." Though not terribly common, Simeon knew more than one woman who, inspired by Isaiah, had named her son Immanuel. It was not the name that electrified him. It was the context. "My son is the Son of God," Mary had stated, her words ringing like steel on stone. And Isaiah said, *And she shall call his name, "A God is with us."*

His mind was rushing like a torrent over a precipice. He leaned back, closing his eyes, feeling almost dizzy. At first his mind had recoiled at Mary's words. The concept was so utterly unexpected, so completely fantastic.

Then a second passage blazed into his consciousness. It too was from Isaiah and was the passage his Uncle Aaron had quoted that night when they were debating whether the Messiah was to be the Deliverer or the Suffering Servant. "For unto us a child is born. Unto us a son is given. And the government shall be upon his shoulder." That last phrase had been the point Aaron had emphasized. Now the rest of the passage sent chills racing through Simeon's body. "And his name shall be called Wonderful . . . the *Mighty God*." He let out a long, low sigh of complete wonder. The Messiah was to be "the Mighty God."

Any thought of Yehuda or Sepphoris or Moshe Ya'abin and the Romans was long since banished now. If Jesus was literally God's son, born of a mortal mother, yet sired by a divine Father . . . For a moment he bowed his head, wanting to ask if such a thing could truly be so. Almost instantly, his head came up again. He didn't have to ask. *I know!* As those incredible words had poured from Mary's mouth, Simeon had known they were true. He wanted to doubt. He *needed* to doubt. But he knew. He fully understood that now. He looked up and spoke to the sky. "I know that Jesus of Nazareth is the Son of God. *I know it!*"

Suddenly shame washed over him like a crashing surf. The memory of that day on the hillside when Jesus had been teaching came back to him. He had not liked what Jesus had said. In fact, he was infuriated. *I was sitting at the feet of the Son of God, and I turned my back and walked away.*

IV

With a start, Simeon looked up through the trees. Sunlight filtered softly to the forest floor. It was late. He could see that the sun would be setting in less than an hour. Astonished that hours had passed, he looked around. Had he slept? He shook his head. He was not at the edge of the hill any longer. He had been walking. He no longer even knew for sure where he was. He had walked and walked, his mind like a raging furnace, alternating between wonder and shame, astonishment and bewilderment.

Sometime during that time, he had wrestled with the question of Sextus Rubrius and Marcus Quadratus Didius. It had been one thing to thrust aside the call to love your enemies and forgive seventy times seven when Jesus was nothing more than a wandering teacher from Nazareth. Not so any longer. If it was the Son of God asking him to turn the other cheek, to pray for those who would despitefully use him, to go that second mile, Roman or not—that was a very different matter indeed. The parable of the unmerciful servant blazed into his mind with new power and meaning, and he went over it again and again. Then he remembered with sharp pain Peter's questions. *How many times do you suppose a man sins in his lifetime? A thousand? Ten thousand?*

A low sound of anguish broke from his lips. "But what of tomorrow, O Lord? What do I do about tomorrow?" There was no answer to that, of course. And then he did something very unusual.

Traditionally when Jews prayed, they lifted their eyes skyward and spoke to God directly. It was a unique way of acknowledging that God viewed them as his children and not just creatures spun off a divine pottery wheel. But now Simeon did not look toward the sky. He found a fallen log and sank down to his knees beside it. He lowered his head and closed his eyes.

"O God. I thank thee this day for the miracle that has been mine. I thank thee for putting the thought into Peter's heart to send me to Nazareth." He paused. "I thank thee for what I have learned from this woman, chosen of thee to be the sacred vessel for thy beloved Son. But I am in anguish, Father. Thou knowest the circumstances that lie at hand. I have gathered good and faithful men to participate in this contest with our enemy. I know that our cause is just, yet I also know that I can no longer be driven by hate. In times past thou hast called on thy servants to rise up and smite their enemies and drive them from the promised land."

He stopped, wondering if he had the right to let his thoughts roll out so freely. Yet this was the turmoil he had to resolve. *I have to know!*

"O God, it is I who have brought these good men to this place and time. Can I simply turn away and leave them to face this battle alone?

They do not know what I now know. Could it be possible that I might be an instrument in thy hands to bring about a greater purpose?"

He stopped. There was nothing more. He was spent, exhausted, totally drained. The only remaining plea came from his heart. "I beg of thee to hear my cries, O God, and give me peace."

For a long time he stayed there, bent over the log in the silence of the forest, his eyes staring at the ground but not seeing. And then as his soul gradually quieted and the turmoil subsided, a voice came into his mind. It was not audible. At least he did not hear it with his ears. And yet he instantly recognized it. It was the voice of his father, David. Strangely, as the words came slowly and distinctly, burning into his mind as though etched with an iron drawn red-hot from the fire, Simeon realized that though his father had made reference to this scripture, he had not quoted it directly as it was being quoted to him now.

"And David said to Solomon, My son, as for me, it was in my mind to build an house unto the name of the Lord my God. But the word of the Lord came to me, saying, Thou hast shed blood abundantly, and hast made great wars. Thou shalt not build an house unto my name, because thou hast shed much blood upon the earth in my sight."

Only after another long time did Simeon finally get to his feet. With heavy heart, he glanced up at the sky to get his bearings, then turned to the right and started for the direction of the road that would take him to Beth Neelah and then on to Sepphoris.

V

Simeon stopped, his hand raised before the door, drew in a deep breath, then knocked softly. Immediately he heard the scrape of a chair. A moment later the door opened, and Shana was framed in the light from the lamp behind her. Her eyes widened in surprise.

"Simeon?"

"*Erev tov*, Shana. Are Yehuda and Daniel back yet?"

She shook her head, clearly bewildered. "But I thought you were with them."

"I was supposed to be. Something came up." His mind was working swiftly. The sun had set almost three hours ago. Sepphoris was about two hours' walk from Beth Neelah. "So they haven't come back from the meeting yet?"

"No." She leaned forward slightly, her large, dark eyes filled with anxiety. "Is everything all right, Simeon?"

He nodded absently. "Yes. The meeting probably went longer than they anticipated."

She bobbed her head in a nod, causing her long, dark hair to dance in the light. "Perhaps. Is everything all right with *you*, Simeon?"

How did he answer that question? He forced a smile. "Yes. I'm just working some things out." He turned his head and looked down the street of the village. "I'll start down the road to Sepphoris and meet them."

"Simeon? I—"

But he didn't want to talk. Not yet. "I'm sure they're fine," he broke in. "We'll be back in a little while." Not waiting for a response, he turned and walked swiftly away. Just before he turned the corner into the main street of Beth Neelah, he looked back. Shana was still silhouetted against the lamplight in the doorway. He raised one hand and waved, then went on, not waiting to see if she waved back.

VI

With full dark upon the land, Simeon didn't see the men until he was only thirty or forty paces away from them. When he saw there were two of them, he called out immediately. "Ho, Yehuda. Is that you?"

"Aye."

Taking a quick breath, Simeon strode forward to meet them, dreading what he knew lay ahead. Daniel came forward quickly, moving out ahead of his brother. "Simeon. What happened to you?"

"I was delayed. It's a long story."

In the light of the half-moon he saw Yehuda give him a sharp look as he came up and joined them. Simeon rushed on. "Let's keep walking. I'll bet you're tired and anxious to be home."

The three of them fell in together, starting back the way Simeon had just come. "Did you come through the village?" Daniel said. "I hope Shana kept supper for us."

"I saw Shana for a minute, but she didn't say."

"She'll keep it," Yehuda grunted. "She always does."

"So," Simeon said quickly, wanting to keep control of the conversation, "how did it go?"

"About as expected," Yehuda answered.

"Ya'abin was there?"

"He was," Daniel said. "In all his devilish smoothness."

"Did he recognize you?" Simeon asked the older brother.

"Almost instantly," Yehuda answered. "I pretended shock and outrage at seeing that this was the man with whom we were going into partnership. Gehazi finally had to intervene to keep us from coming to blows."

"Good, good. It's important that he doesn't suspect that we know anything."

"Right." It was said with heavy sarcasm.

Simeon glanced at him quickly, then away again. "And is everything as Mordechai said it would be?"

"It looks like it." Yehuda's voice was cool.

"Any word on where the column is now?"

"They passed Capernaum sometime after midday."

Simeon nodded. The commander in him had taken over, and he was assessing the information as it was shared with him. "Anything else?"

Yehuda started to shake his head, but Daniel answered first. "Ya'abin made quite the point about getting the soldiers to lay down their arms as quickly as possible so there isn't a massacre. That didn't set too well with the rest of the group."

Simeon nodded. That too was as Mordechai had described it. "And Gehazi agreed?"

"Gehazi seems to accept whatever Ya'abin is telling him."

"What's wrong, Yehuda?"

He strode on, his head down, his shoulders hunched. "Something's not right. Ya'abin seems pretty confident that once we jump the column, if we show enough firepower and offer them a safe withdrawal, they'll lay down their arms and let his group lead them through the pass and let them go."

"And you don't agree?"

"I don't know. You can say a lot of things about the Romans, but they're not cowards." He shook his head. "And yet, if they stand and fight, we could be there half the night."

"Do they have a full cohort?"

"No, and that's another surprise. The reports coming in say they have less than three hundred men."

"And we have?"

"Over a thousand," Daniel said, much more confident than his older brother. "When their commander sees that, even his knees will start to tremble. They'll have to surrender or be massacred."

The older man gave Daniel an incredulous look. "Romans don't *have* to do anything, little brother."

"What is it, Yehuda?" Simeon asked. Whatever was troubling him, it ran deep. "We've known all along this carried considerable risk. When the prize is that sweet, the risks become more acceptable."

"Oh, so it's *we* now, is it?"

Simeon slowed his step, looking away. So here it was at last. For a split second his mind considered and rejected half a dozen ways to deflect the question. But that wasn't fair. He turned and looked up at the man who had stood by his side for more than three years now. "You're right. It's not *we*. I'm not coming tomorrow."

"What?" Daniel cried.

But Yehuda only nodded, his face grim.

"I can't. Now is not the time or the place to try to explain why. When this is all over, I'll come back and tell you everything."

"You can't just leave us," Daniel exclaimed, his voice going up a notch. "The men are depending on you. You're the leader they trust."

"The men have a leader every bit as good as me in Yehuda. He knows everything I know and more." He looked fully at Yehuda now. "Under the circumstances, he will be better than I could be."

Daniel threw up his arms, turning to his brother for help. But Yehuda said nothing for a time. They strode along in silence for almost a full minute; then Yehuda asked Simeon a simple question. "You are sure of this?"

"Yes. I'm sorry. I don't have a choice."

He gave a scathing look. "You always have a choice."

"Not once you commit yourself to a certain path."

He grunted and looked away. "Nazareth did it?"

Simeon nodded glumly. Then after a moment, he went on. "I'm going down to Capernaum tonight. I need to see my parents." In a way it was like a burden had been lifted, though his heart was still torn with sorrow. "I'll stop by and tell Shana, then go on from there."

Yehuda was shaking his head before he even finished the sentence.

"What?"

"Shana knows very little about any of this—the meeting, yes, but not about tomorrow. Not about you and your questions. Not about Nazareth."

"What is all this about Nazareth?" Daniel broke in.

Both men ignored the question. "You go on down to Capernaum," Yehuda said, his voice completely cold now. "Sort things out. Then we'll decide if Shana needs to know more than she does now."

Simeon walked on, searching for something he could say to help Yehuda see, and knew that there was nothing. "I understand," he said quietly. He stopped. Daniel stopped too, thinking there was more to be said, but Yehuda went on, and after a hesitant moment, Daniel ran quickly to catch up with him.

"May God be with you tomorrow, my friends," Simeon called softly. "And may your hand be strong."

Yehuda didn't turn, but his voice floated back to him. "And God be with you, Ha'keedohn. May your heart find peace in the path you have chosen."

CHAPTER NOTES

The Messianic scriptures from the Old Testament that Simeon deals with in this chapter are Isaiah 7:14 and 9:6. The passage about King David is found in 1 Chronicles 22:7–8. The explanation for the original Hebrew in the Isaiah passages comes from Keil and Delitzsch, 7:216–21, and Fallows, 2:855.

CHAPTER 29

NOR IS ANYTHING DONE UPON EARTH APART FROM THEE;

SAVE THAT WHICH THE WICKED DO, BY THEIR OWN FOLLY.

BUT THINE IS THE SKILL TO SET EVEN THE CROOKED STRAIGHT.

—*Cleanthes, Fragment 537*

I

8 JUNE, A.D. 30

Miriam was first to hear Ezra's sandals on the gravel, and she leaped to her feet. A moment later his dark shape appeared in the moonlight, striding toward them. Livia was up as well, coming to stand beside Miriam.

He was shaking his head before he even reached them.

"*No?*" Miriam cried.

"The gates are barred. The local Council has a guard there. No one is allowed entry into the city until morning."

"They have to let us in," she exclaimed. "I have money. Surely—"

"I tried that. The man nearly arrested me when I even suggested we would be willing to pay if he would let us through."

Miriam fell back against the carriage, feeling the hope whoosh out of her like someone had just stepped on her stomach. All because of one small stone. She closed her eyes to stop the tears from springing forth. She was so tired. So close to emotional collapse.

As planned, they had left Ptolemais before sunup, turning east. Their progress had been a little slower than they had hoped—after three days on the road, the horse was getting tired—but they were moving along well. Then just at midday, as they passed over a particularly rough stretch of road, the horse had driven a sharp stone into his left front hoof. Ezra noticed the animal limping immediately and removed the rock, but the damage had been done. In another hour the horse could barely hobble, let alone pull the carriage. Finally Ezra had unhitched the animal, and the three of them walked back to the nearest village. By the time they had purchased a new animal and returned to the carriage, they had lost a full four hours. Now it was into the second watch, and the gates to Capernaum were shut.

"Come," Ezra said gently. "You and Livia try to get some sleep in the carriage. We'll be at the gate the moment it opens in the morning."

Miriam looked away, fighting the great desire to throw herself onto the ground and just bawl.

"There's one other thing," Ezra said, smiling.

"What?"

"I asked the guards if they knew anything about a Roman column headed west."

Miriam's head came around slowly. "And?"

"They said a large company of soldiers coming from Damascus with thirty or forty wagons passed through this afternoon and are camped about five miles west of here."

Miriam's heart leaped within her. "Then we're not too late?"

"No."

Livia took her hands and squeezed them tightly. "I told you," she said. "You need to listen to me more carefully."

II

Deborah looked up with a start at the sound of someone pounding hard on the outside gate. She was bent down over the small cooking fire, stirring ground wheat into boiling water. She straightened, cocking her head. Leah was at the table, grinding more grain on a flat piece of basalt stone. They were alone in the kitchen this morning since David had the servants helping at the warehouse, and they were sleeping there.

"Someone's at the gate," Deborah said in surprise. She glanced out the window. It was light now, but the sun was still half an hour from coming over the eastern hills.

"I'll get it," Leah said, setting the grinding stone aside.

As she stood, they heard footsteps coming rapidly down the stone stairs from the bedrooms upstairs. "I heard," David said as he appeared. He was wrapping his sash around his tunic and pulling it tight. He hadn't stopped to put on his sandals.

"Who do you suppose it could be this early?" Deborah asked.

"You stay here. I'll see who it is."

But Deborah didn't stay. She wiped her hands on her dress and followed him to the main door of the house. When David stepped out into the courtyard, she stood where she could see through it to the gate.

"Who is it?" David called as he reached the heavy wooden panel. "Who's there?"

"Ezra the sandalmaker. From Joppa. I'm looking for the house of David ben Joseph, merchant of Capernaum."

David turned and shot Deborah a puzzled look, then began undoing the bar. They didn't know any sandalmakers from Joppa. That was nearly a hundred miles from Capernaum. Deborah stepped forward a little farther, peering into the soft morning light. David finished removing the heavy bar, then opened the gate and stepped back. Immediately a man passed through the opening and began conversing with David in low tones. The light was not bright, but it was sufficient for Deborah to discern that she had never seen this man before.

Then a sharp gasp was torn from her throat. A second figure came through the gate. This time it was a woman, and she was standing so the morning light illuminated her face. "Are you David ben Joseph?" she asked, breaking in on the two men.

"Miriam?"

Deborah's soft cry spun Miriam around. For a moment she didn't see where the voice had come from. Then her eyes picked out the figure standing at the doorway to the large house. "Deborah!" She darted forward. "Oh, blessed be the Lord. We've found you."

III

Deborah was numbed into silence. At first she had cried out in soft horror again and again as Miriam, the daughter of Mordechai ben Uzziel of Jerusalem, poured out her story. With each new revelation she felt as though a vice was squeezing down on her heart and lungs, making it more and more difficult to move or to breathe. Ezra and Livia sat back, content to let Miriam take the lead. Occasionally, as David pressed Miriam with questions, Livia would remind her mistress of this point or that which she had forgotten.

Finally it was over. Miriam's eyes dropped. "I am so sorry," she said, speaking to both of them.

"For what?" David cried. "You are not behind this."

"But it is *my* father. And I was unwittingly a part of it. He used me to convince Simeon and Yehuda to agree to all of this."

Finally Deborah found voice. "There is nothing to be sorry for. You have taken a terrible risk in order to warn us." Then her face softened. "Actually, it is Simeon and I who owe you an apology."

Miriam's face showed lines of fatigue, and there were dark circles beneath her eyes. Those words took her by surprise. "For what?"

"Back when we first met at Beth Neelah, I suggested that you lacked what we in the Galilee value most highly."

"I remember. Thank you," she murmured. Then again the pain was on her, and she swung around again to David. "You have no idea where Simeon is?"

David was as pale as the flour Leah had been grinding on the stone. He shook his head.

"He's in Beth Neelah," Leah said. "With Yehuda. Or at least, that's where he was going a few days ago."

A shadow passed across David's face. "I'm afraid it's already begun. We may be too late."

Ezra stirred at that. "No." He explained quickly what the guards had told him about the Roman encampment.

Hope sprang into David's eyes. "Then perhaps—"

A noise brought them around. Young Joseph came into the kitchen, still in his nightshirt, rubbing sleep from his eyes. Deborah motioned for him to come to her. She took him and sat him down beside her, whispering for him not to interrupt.

"We have to assume," David went on, speaking to Miriam, "that the Romans will leave this morning for the Joknean Pass. That's about twenty-five miles from here, which means this whole thing is going to happen tonight. If we leave immediately, maybe we can get to Beth Neelah and try to find Simeon and Yehuda before they leave for—"

"Papa?"

Deborah turned and shook her head sternly at her youngest son. "Joseph, I told you. You must sit quietly now. Don't interrupt."

"But Mama, Simeon isn't in Beth Neelah."

Everyone turned in complete surprise. "He's not?" David exclaimed.

"No, he's upstairs in bed."

David shot to his feet. "What?"

"He came in early this morning. I heard him go into his room, but he made me promise to let him sleep for awhile."

Miriam was staring at Deborah. "But how? The gates to the city were locked."

Deborah was suddenly soaring. Simeon was here? Then he was safe. She barely heard the question.

"But Simeon never uses the gate," Joseph told her.

David was nodding. "One of our warehouses backs on the city walls. There's a small doorway there. We use it all the time at night."

"Get him, Joseph," Deborah said, giving her son a gentle push. "Get Simeon and have him come down quickly."

IV

Simeon adjusted the girth of the saddle, then jerked it down hard to make sure it wouldn't slip. Satisfied, he turned around. David and two of their servants were finishing the harnessing of the team of horses that would pull the carriage. Phineas, their chief servant, was putting a basket of food in the netting at the back.

There had been no question about going on foot. Getting to the Joknean Pass would require nine or ten hours of walking, and that was unacceptable. Their whole success now depended on them reaching the place where the Zealots were gathering before everything began to unravel. So David had sent Simeon to the livery stable to secure two riding horses for him and Simeon and a team of horses to pull Ezra's hired carriage. That would cut the journey down by two or three hours, which they hoped would be enough. Almost an hour had passed since they had heard the first pounding on the gate.

Simeon heard footsteps and turned to see his mother, Miriam, and Livia come out of the house. His mother was pulling a light silk shawl up over her head to protect her from the sun.

He gave the horse a final pat and turned to meet them. "Mother, I still don't like this. This is not going to be any place for women."

Deborah just smiled and walked on past him. "We've already made the decision, Simeon."

He turned to his father. David shrugged. "Miriam has to start back for Joppa or else her father is going to learn that she is not there. We can't send them by way of the Jordan Valley because that takes them through Jerusalem and someone might see her. Nor do I feel safe sending them down through Samaria. Ptolemais is the best route."

"I'll not be letting them get anywhere close to where you're going to be," Ezra spoke up.

"I agree," Miriam shot right back, "but we are going to find a place that's safe, and we are going to wait until we find out what happens." She glared at Simeon. "If you think I've come all this way only to go back to Joppa and stew and worry for the next three or four days waiting to hear the news, then you are not thinking clearly."

"Miriam and Livia have earned the right to know what comes of this," his mother said. "Besides, you need them for another reason."

"We do?"

"Yes, you really *aren't* thinking clearly. As you start trying to decide what to do, you're going to have a hundred questions. If you'll remember, Miriam is the only one who can answer those questions."

Miriam smiled triumphantly. "But thank you anyway for trying to protect us from any harm."

Once the women were settled in the carriage, Simeon mounted up and prepared to move out in front. As he rode up beside the carriage, he caught a glimpse of Miriam's face. She looked haggard and very tired. Livia was equally exhausted. He stopped the horse. "I haven't stopped long enough to say thank you to you two," he said without preamble. "Now it is Yehuda and I who are in your debt."

Miriam shook her head quickly. "Only if we are not too late."

"What you have done is incredibly brave. I apologize for anything I may have said the last time you were here about your being a coddled woman of Jerusalem."

She was startled; then she cocked her head, giving him a stern look. "You never said that in my presence, Simeon of Capernaum. Which means you must have been talking behind my back."

"I—well, I mean—" He was fumbling badly.

Deborah chuckled softly. "I am afraid both Simeon and I said things about you that now prove to be an embarrassment. Please accept our regrets for being hasty to judge."

"I do." Then the lighter mood disappeared as quickly as it had come. "My father is not a monster. He loves our country. He thinks this is the way to protect it."

"Unfortunately," Simeon said, without malice, "sometimes those with the best of intentions are the ones who frighten you most deeply."

David was mounted, then urged the horse forward, motioning for the others to get started.

As the carriage began to roll, Miriam called out to Simeon before he went ahead to join his father. "I know that you deeply disagree with my father. So why are you here in Capernaum and not up in the hills with the rest of the Zealots?"

Deborah turned in her seat. "Yes, Simeon. You still haven't explained why you are here."

He slowed the horse to keep pace with the wagon, his face a study in contrasts. Finally he shook his head. "I'll explain everything when this is over, Mother. I have much to tell you. I'll only say this much: Do you remember that day when Father was trying to warn me about going out against the Romans?"

"Yes."

He saw that his father had turned in his saddle and was listening too. "Do you remember what he said?"

Deborah nodded again. "He talked about why King David couldn't build the temple."

"Yes, it wasn't that he had gone to war. It was because there was *too much* blood on his hands. Well, yesterday the scripture he cited came back to me with great force. I had been struggling to know what to do." He seemed a little embarrassed. "I was off by myself, praying about it, actually."

He turned his gaze on Miriam. "When that conversation came back to me, I thought that might be my answer. I thought the Lord was telling me that if I joined in this attack with the rest of the Zealots, I would end up with too much blood on my hands. Even if it was Roman blood, I knew I couldn't do that any longer."

Deborah was staring at him, hardly believing what she was hearing. David slowed his horse to a walk and came back beside his son. "You thought it *might be* your answer?" he asked softly.

Simeon nodded. "Yes. That's when I told Yehuda I would not go with them." He looked away. "And so I abandoned them."

"And now?" his father prompted.

"Now I think I see better what the Lord was trying to tell me. That warning was not just about Roman blood; it was about Jewish blood as well. Galilean blood. The blood of good men who have been duped into thinking this is the way to hasten the coming of the Messiah, just as I was duped into thinking that."

He saw that his mother's eyes glistened in the sunlight. He couldn't meet her astonished gaze. He could only shake his head in sorrow. "And now I pray to God that Miriam's coming has been in time. If not, then my hands will be stained with the blood of the very men who thought their lives were safe in my keeping."

V

In the first two hours they made only one brief stop, resting their horses at the top of the long incline out of the Kinnereth basin. On the road again, Simeon and David rode alongside the carriage. Simeon had Miriam start from the beginning once more to tell everything she could remember about what she had overheard. He listened in silence, interrupting only once to encourage her to take her time and try to remember every detail. When she was finished, he thanked her, then motioned to his father. They rode out ahead, horses side by side as they discussed what strategy they would undertake as they tried to prevent a major tragedy from unfolding.

It was not as simple as it sounded at first. For one thing, Moshe Ya'abin would be close at hand. If Mordechai had set this whole thing up with the Judean outlaw—which was an inescapable conclusion after what Miriam had heard—then he must not learn that he had been discovered. Ya'abin knew enough to ruin everything should he become suspicious. Gehazi was going to be a problem too. Stubborn as a piece of knotted oak, shrewd as a weasel, and fearless as a lion, he would be wary of this new information. Nor would he simply pack up and ride away, not when there were forty-some wagons filled with arms.

One conclusion David and Simeon quickly came to was that Miriam's name had to be protected in all of this. Not even the slightest shadow could fall upon her. She already knew that if her father learned of this, it would cause a breach between them that would be irreparable. What she hadn't yet thought through was that if the

Romans learned who had betrayed them, not even her father's influence would be enough to save her. Simeon had explained that to Ezra as plainly as he could, but Ezra was no fool. He may not have seen all the implications, but he had already determined that he and his wife would do whatever was necessary to provide a believable cover story for Miriam's absence from Jerusalem.

Several times as they continued onward, Simeon would wheel his horse around and ride back to the carriage to fire questions at Miriam; then he would return to his father, and they would drop into deep conversation again. When they stopped briefly to water the horses about the fifth hour of the day, Deborah quietly took Simeon aside. "Miriam desperately needs rest," she said. "She's mentally, emotionally, and physically exhausted. Can you leave her alone for a time so she can sleep?"

"Of course." He had planned to do that anyway. The first beginnings of a solution were starting to form, and he needed time to work it out in his mind.

When they started again, Deborah put a small pillow against her shoulder and insisted that Miriam lean against her and try to sleep. Livia was in the second seat and had a place to lie down. Surprised and pleased, Miriam did so, but to no one's surprise, sleep would not come. She was strung more tightly than the trip wire used to snare a rabbit or a fox. Sensing how much she needed to get her mind onto other things, Deborah began talking softly. She told her about their family, about Esther and Boaz, about the son and daughter-in-law Miriam didn't know. She spoke of David's work as a merchant and about life in Capernaum.

Amazed at how comfortable she was feeling with this woman, Miriam began to talk as well. She told Deborah about her own mother, who had died some years before, leaving Miriam alone. She spoke briefly about her father and their life together, but that carried too much pain, and she went on to other things. She explained about

Livia and what had happened between them since Simeon had appeared that morning in Samaria. She started telling Deborah about the city that she loved so much.

As she spoke of the temple and how she and Livia loved to walk through the courtyards, Miriam had a sudden thought. "Have you heard of Jesus of Nazareth?" she asked. As she spoke, Miriam was sitting back against the seat, her eyes closed against the bright sunlight, so she did not see Deborah jerk around to stare at her. "Yes, I have heard of him," Deborah said carefully.

Eager now, Miriam sat up and told Deborah about the morning when Jesus had driven the moneychangers from the temple courtyards. She told her about Nicodemus and what he had learned and how neither of them knew exactly what Jesus meant about being born of the water and the Spirit. When Miriam finished telling Deborah about the woman who had been taken in adultery and brought forward by the scribes and Pharisees and how Jesus had dealt with her, to her astonishment she saw tears in Deborah's eyes. "Do you know of this man?" Miriam asked in surprise. "Livia and I have determined to join his followers, but we have not been able to find him."

For the next hour, as they drove along together, they were barely aware of the world around them. Livia had sat up and was listening carefully as well. The grim circumstances that brought them together out in the highlands of the Galilee were forgotten for the moment. Deborah started at the first. She told Miriam about David's experience thirty years earlier. She recounted how excited he had been when word had come about John the Baptist. Miriam half turned in her seat to watch Deborah's face and sat without moving as she told about that day in Nazareth when Jesus had announced he was the Messiah, and about the sermon he had given on another day and the anger it brought her and Simeon. She told of what had happened to her family on the day of miracles while she had been visiting her cousin Naomi in Beth Neelah.

They wept together without shame when Deborah told Miriam about little Esther, about how shy and reserved she was, and what had happened that day in the market when Esther had run up to Jesus and given him a kiss.

Miriam wiped at her eyes, no longer tired, the tension in her completely gone. "Thank you, Deborah," she said quietly.

"I can't believe it. You wish to be his disciple too."

"With all my heart."

"And I as well," Livia said from the backseat.

Miriam reached out and took Deborah's hand. "I wish I could return to Capernaum and meet Jesus."

At that, Ezra, who drove the horses and had said nothing at all during the conversation, shook his head. "We must get you back to Joppa and then on to Jerusalem."

"Yes," Deborah said. "There will be another time."

Ezra turned to Deborah. "I too would like to hear more of this Jesus."

And so as Simeon and his father talked of more sobering things, Deborah told her three listeners everything she could about Jesus, about what he said, what he did, the miracles he had worked.

When Deborah finished, Miriam was filled with joy. "And I thought we were coming to Capernaum only to find Simeon and warn him."

Deborah turned to look at her fully. "Do you remember the words of the Psalmist, Miriam? 'Behold, he that keepeth Israel shall neither slumber nor sleep. The Lord is thy keeper. The Lord is thy shade upon thy right hand. The Lord shall preserve thy going out and thy coming in from this time forth, and even for evermore.'"

"Yes, I love that passage."

"Well, I know now that it was the Lord who brought you and Livia and Ezra here today. And now we all know why."

VI

"Miriam asked me a question a few minutes ago, Simeon."

Simeon was about to take a bite from the small loaf of bread he held in his hands. He lowered it again and looked at his mother. "What was it?"

They were stopped near a small spring about a hundred paces from the road. It was past midday, and their stop would be a brief one.

"She asked me if you were a follower of Jesus."

It was hard to tell who was the more startled at that, Simeon or his father. David stared at Miriam for a moment, then turned to watch his son. Miriam quickly explained, summarizing what she had told Deborah about her experiences in Jerusalem.

Deborah then spoke up. "I have told Miriam that we were all baptized a short time ago. Except for you, Simeon."

Ezra looked back and forth between them, clearly curious as to how this was going to turn out, but Simeon didn't see that. Nor did he see the questioning look on his parents' faces. He was staring at the ground, his eyes hooded and unreadable.

"*Are* you a follower of Jesus?" Miriam asked. "Your mother isn't sure how to answer that."

He looked up. "No," he said softly.

Now it was Deborah who was startled. That was not what she had expected at all, not after what he had said that morning. "But—"

Simeon faced his mother squarely. "Has Peter told you about what happened the other day on the Plains of Kinnereth?"

"About the multiplication of the loaves and the fishes? Yes, he told us. Your father and I were so disappointed that we were not there."

"Did Peter tell you that I was there?"

David leaned forward. "You were?"

"Yes." Simeon offered a quick and silent thanks to the big fisherman. He wasn't going to pressure Simeon into anything, not in that way at least.

"You saw that yourself?" his mother said, her eyes wide with wonder.

"I sat no more than ten or fifteen feet away from Jesus." His voice was still low, barely audible.

"And yet—" His father stopped, not sure what to say.

"There's something else you need to know." He took a quick breath. "I went to Nazareth yesterday. I spent more than a couple of hours with Mary, who is the mother of Jesus."

Deborah stared at her son in astonishment. "Why didn't you tell us? What did she say?"

Simeon shook his head. "When we return and things are at peace, I would like very much to tell you and Father everything. It was—" He stopped, searching for the right way to say it; then he shook his head again. "I'm still trying to take it in."

Miriam could not restrain herself. "You speak as though you believe that Jesus is the Messiah, yet you say you are not one of his followers. I don't understand."

"I don't believe that Jesus is the Messiah," Simeon said, sitting back on his heels, watching his father's face carefully. Then, even as the disappointment filled David's face, Simeon went on. "I *know* that he is the Messiah. And he is more. I know that as well."

"Really?" Deborah cried.

"Yes, Mother."

"But—" Miriam was fumbling. "How then can you say you are not one of his disciples?"

"I am just learning what it means to accept him," Simeon said sadly. "Even now I wonder if I can go in the way he would have me go. Perhaps when this is over, I will have a chance to ask him if he will teach me what it means to be a true follower."

Deborah stood, tears streaming down her cheeks, and walked to her son. As Simeon stood to meet her, she took him in her arms. "Why didn't you tell me, Simeon? Why didn't you tell me?"

"That's why I came home last night, Mother. I came down to tell you and Father that I had found my answer."

VII

It was approaching the tenth hour of the day when they reached the place where the road forked and two hand-painted wooden signs were nailed to a post. The sign pointing to the right said Ptolemais; the other, Caesarea. Simeon reined his horse around and rode back to the carriage. Ezra reined in, and the three women straightened.

"There's a grove of trees over there," Simeon said to Ezra. "Wait there for us. Stay out of sight of the road."

"We will."

"From here you can see across the valley." He lifted an arm and pointed. "See where the line of hills begins, about five miles away? There's a cleft there. That's the entry to the Joknean Pass. If you look closely along the base of the hills to the right, you can see some wagons."

They were all peering, and suddenly Miriam gasped. She could see dozens of wagons, small specks against the darker hillsides. "Is that the Romans?"

Simeon nodded but still spoke to Ezra. "They're still more than an hour away from the pass. If you see them turn and start coming back this way, leave immediately. Head for Sepphoris. I showed you that road a few miles back."

"Yes, I understand."

David swung down from his horse and went over to the carriage. Deborah got out and went swiftly to him. "Oh, David, be careful."

He held her tightly for a moment, then kissed her softly on the lips. "We will, my Deborah. Pray for us."

"Every moment until you return," she answered huskily.

"And Ezra and Livia and I as well," Miriam cried.

Simeon dismounted and moved to the carriage. "Again, Miriam of Jerusalem, we express our deepest gratitude for you and Livia, and for your courage. When this is all over, I would like to speak with you more about Jesus."

"I don't know when," Miriam said, "but Livia and I are going to come back to Capernaum as soon as we can so we can hear him for ourselves."

"Then," he said with a nod, "we shall see you then."

He turned to his mother and gently took her in his arms. "It will be all right, Mother. We think we have worked out a way to see this through."

"I couldn't bear to lose you, Simeon. Especially now."

"You're not going to lose me," he said. "But we both know that this has to happen."

She bit her lip but nodded. "I know."

He kissed her on the cheek. "I love you, Mother."

"And I you," she whispered fiercely. "Go with God, Simeon."

"If God will have me," he said wistfully, "that would be my deepest wish."

CHAPTER 30

IACTA ALEA EST.
[THE DIE IS CAST.]

—*Julius Caesar*, Divus Julius, *xxxii; spoken at the crossing of the Rubicon*

I

9 JUNE, A.D. 30

Daniel leaped to his feet and gave a low cry. "It's Simeon!"

Yehuda spun around.

"I told you he would come!" In spite of their strict orders to stay concealed, Daniel left his place of hiding and ran through the trees like a deer.

"*Shalom*, Daniel," Simeon said, gripping his hand as he slid to a halt.

"I told them you would come. I told them not to give up."

Simeon turned as Yehuda came up as well. "Hello, Old Friend."

Yehuda nodded gravely, then reached out his hand and clasped Simeon's arm tightly. "*Shalom*, Simeon. Welcome back."

Simeon started to say something, but suddenly his throat choked off and he could only nod.

Yehuda turned in surprise as a second figure appeared, and he saw it was David. He stared for a moment, then gave Simeon a questioning look.

"Many things have happened," Simeon said quickly. "You were right. Ya'abin has a game of his own. We have just learned of it. Where is Gehazi? We have to speak with him right away."

"He took up the first position just to the east of us," Yehuda replied. "I'm surprised you didn't see him when you came through."

"We saw evidence of many, but they let us pass without challenge when they saw it was us."

A noise behind them brought them around. A man was coming toward them. Simeon stiffened as he saw who it was.

"Well, well," Moshe Ya'abin sneered, "so the mighty Javelin finally found his courage."

"If you think it was lack of courage that delayed Ha'keedohn," Daniel retorted hotly, "you are not only a fool but a craven coward as well, for you besmirch the name of a man who knows no fear."

"Mind your tongue, young pup," Ya'abin snarled, "or I shall have to cut it out."

Yehuda straightened to his full height and leaned forward. "Would you like to settle our differences now, before the Romans come?"

The ferret-faced thief only laughed. "You speak empty words, big one. You know that Gehazi would cut out both our hearts if we started something now. When all of this is done, there will be time enough to settle old scores." He looked at Simeon. "All of them."

"There are many scores to be settled this day," Simeon agreed easily. Then he turned his back on Ya'abin. "Tell me where to find Gehazi," he said to Yehuda. "The Romans even now are approaching the pass. I must speak with him."

"I'll show you where he is," Ya'abin said, stepping forward.

Simeon whirled on him. "If Gehazi wants someone to leave his position," he said coldly, "then Gehazi will give you that order directly. I can find him without your help." He swung back around to Yehuda.

"There's a large outcropping of rocks three or four hundred paces from here," Yehuda said. "His men are there. They'll take you to him."

Muttering to himself, Ya'abin spun around and stalked away. Glancing over his shoulder, Simeon frowned. "Watch him closely, Yehuda. The man is a viper."

"We will," Yehuda said. "We already have one of our men close by their position."

"We have to go," Simeon said. "I will return as quickly as possible, but I wanted you to know I was here."

"I never doubted it," Daniel said, shooting his brother an accusatory look.

"This is where you belong," Yehuda murmured. "We will pass the word. The men—and not just our band—will be happy to know that."

II

Gehazi listened intently; the only sign that what he was hearing was being processed was in the darkening of his eyes and the lowering of his brow.

"Where did you learn all of this?" he demanded when Simeon finished speaking.

"From a source with which I would trust my life," David answered. "Beyond that, we cannot say. You surely understand that. If the Romans learn about this, they will hunt that person down without mercy."

"And what if this itself is a trap?" he shot right back. One hand came up to rub his beard, showing the tips of two fingers missing. It was a sharp reminder of who it was that stood before them. Gehazi was as old as David, perhaps even older. He had been one of the young warriors of Judah of Gamla, Deborah's uncle, the man who had started the entire Zealot movement. Thirty years ago, Gehazi had been quick enough and brave enough to escape the Roman snare when so many others had been caught. Since then, his life had been dedicated to continuing the cause Judah had begun. He had performed so many feats of courage that he was now the acknowledged leader of the Zealot movement and the only one capable of uniting the various bands under one head. The two fingertips were a gift taken by a Roman centurion who had caught Gehazi one night and tried to make him reveal where the rest of his band was hidden. If one looked closely into his beard, one could see a jagged scar across his jaw he received when, two days later, he killed that same centurion and made his escape.

"Make no mistake," Simeon jumped in, "there is a trap, but it is not of our informant's making. Those two Roman maniples on our flanks will begin moving into position as soon as it gets dark. While you are blithely taking control of the wagons, they are going to swoop in like a hawk on an unsuspecting mouse."

"I already have sentries posted in all directions."

"And you think they'll stop a full maniple?" Simeon cried. "Come on, man. Think! There's going to be a disaster here tonight."

Gehazi's eyes narrowed dangerously, and David reached out and took Simeon by the shoulder. He pulled him back and stepped into his place. "There's a way to know if this is true," he said.

Gehazi pulled his glare away from Simeon and looked at David. "I'm listening."

"The Roman column is no more than a mile or so away from the entrance of the pass. If they keep coming, they will be to your position just as darkness closes in."

"The perfect time for us. The moon rises early tonight."

"Yes," Simeon shot back. "The perfect time. Perhaps too perfect."

David went on quickly. "If our information is correct, the other maniples are hiding about two hours from here. They will start moving into position as soon as it's dark. By midnight they will be close enough to spring the trap, but until then they won't be close enough to help."

"By midnight we'll have those wagons rolling, and there won't be anyone left for the Romans to find."

"That's just it," David exclaimed. "That's why the commander of the column has to delay entering the pass. There's going to be an 'accident' of some kind, something that will look natural but will stop them in place for several hours. By midnight you will still be waiting for them to reach your position." He didn't have to go on from there.

Gehazi took that in.

"Knowing that, you could hit them wherever they stop. However, they'll see you coming, and you'll lose the element of surprise. They'll have time to form a defense, and as you know, the Romans fight best when they have room to maneuver."

"You'll still be trying to get control of the wagons by the time midnight comes," Simeon said quietly. He realized that his father's approach was right. Calm. Rational. Show Gehazi how limited his options were.

Gehazi leaned back, his dark eyes moving back and forth between the two of them. "Even if you are right, I am not simply going to turn and run, not when there are forty wagons filled with armaments out there that we desperately need."

"What if we can get you what you want without a bloodbath?" Simeon said, calm again now. "It won't be all that you want, but it will be more than you'll get if the Romans do as they intend."

"And how do you plan to do that?"

Simeon told him. He spoke slowly and simply. Gehazi alternately frowned, grunted, spluttered angrily, and finally nodded. He didn't like it, but he saw it clearly. Finally, when Simeon finished, he didn't speak for some time.

David waited for a few moments, then spoke in a low voice. "Save your men to live for a day when *you* can choose the field."

"All right," he said after another long pause. "Supposing I accept your proposal. Just how do you make it work?"

David sighed. "With your approval, my son and I are going to pay a visit to the Romans."

III

Tribune Marcus Quadratus pulled in his horse and stood up in the stirrups, feeling the stiffness clear down to his toes. With the exception of one day's rest in Damascus, this was his seventh day in the saddle. He longed now for the time when he would be back in Caesarea. He already had it all planned out. He would spend his first full day at the baths, alternating between the pleasantly cool pools in the *tepidarium,* the shockingly cold waters of the *frigidarium,* and the scalding temperatures of the *calderium.* The steam would open his pores and cleanse his body of the accumulated sweat, grime, and impurities. He would end the day by having one of the well-trained slaves rub his body down with oil, massaging it in until he was totally rejuvenated.

He settled into the saddle again as a wagon rattled by him, bringing him back to the present. He was a little surprised that he had let himself get so carried away in his thoughts. He looked around. "Rubrius?"

Up ahead a figure turned and came trotting back to him. "Yes, sire?"

"Isn't that the pass just ahead?"

"Yes, sire."

"Isn't it about time then?"

Sextus Rubrius turned again, squinting into the sun, which hung above the hills to the west of them. "Can you see that low ridge of rock up ahead about two hundred paces?"

Marcus leaned forward, shading his eyes. A spine of rock covered with a few scraggly bushes ran across the line of their approach. He could see where the road had been cut through it. "Yes."

"We thought that might be the best place. The road is narrow, and one wagon will block it. The surrounding ground is too rough to take wagons around it."

"Good. Don't use the first wagon. That looks too convenient."

"No, sire," Rubrius said without expression. "We thought the third one might be best."

Marcus finally smiled. "I'm tired, Sextus. I should know better than to doubt you."

"Thank you, sire."

"You can feel their eyes on us, can't you?"

"Oh, yes," the centurion answered grimly. "For most of the day now."

"Then make it look good."

"Yes, sire." Sextus saluted, then trotted back to the front of the line.

Marcus watched as he took up position on the left side of the third wagon. To their left the plains stretched out until they disappeared in the haze. It would be difficult to have someone watch them from that direction. On their right, though, there were patches of trees and brush that marked the first beginnings of the foothills. That would be where the watchers were. That's why Rubrius had chosen the opposite side of the wagon.

Marcus spurred his horse forward to get closer. He wanted to watch how it was done. Rubrius was as wily as an old she bear. There would be no slipups with that man.

The four quarternions went through the cut, followed by the first wagon and then the second. Now Marcus saw the wooden mallet in the hand of his centurion. He was peering at the wagon wheel. Half an hour earlier he had sawn the rim of the wheel partway through and marked it with a daub of whitewash. Where the road passed through the cut, the soft dust became rocky for about twenty or thirty feet. As the wagon reached that spot and began to rattle and shake on the harder road base, Sextus swung the hammer hard, smacking the wheel directly on the spot he had marked. There was a sharp crack, and spokes and pieces of rim went flying. The wagon lurched forward, then jerked sharply to the left as the axle dropped and dug into the roadway. The driver, totally unaware of what had been planned for him, screamed as he was thrown off the seat and onto the back of the nearest horse. He bounced off and scrambled to get clear of the flashing hooves.

Marcus grinned. "Perfect," he said under his breath. "Absolutely perfect."

IV

Ten minutes later Marcus turned his head and bawled out as loudly as he could. "Where is that wheel?"

A man appeared, carrying a small wheel. It was obviously not a match for the one that had collapsed. "Sire," he cried, "we thought we had another wheel to match. But this is the only one we have left."

"What?" Marcus began to curse, swinging his riding whip at the air.

"We'll have to repair the other one, sire. It will take several hours."

"Idiots!" he screamed. "Centurion!"

Sextus leaped forward. "Sire?"

"Find out who's responsible for this mistake and have him flogged."

"Yes, sire." Then Sextus dropped his voice. "Did you see him, sire?"

Marcus had to catch himself from turning around. "No. Where?"

"In those trees to the right. Close enough to hear. He's just slipping away now."

"Off to report?"

"That's my assumption, sire."

"Perfect," he said again. Then with a smile, "Don't drive the men too hard. I want to be here for at least four more hours."

Sextus grinned too. "Yes, sire. I think I can arrange that."

V

"Sire?"

Marcus looked up. He was seated in the shade of the fourth wagon, and his eyes had drooped shut. He was alert instantly. It was one of the noncommissioned officers, a squad leader. Marcus got to his feet quickly.

"There are two riders coming in, sire."

Marcus grabbed for his helmet. "Are the men on alert?"

"Yes, sire. We have two full squads deployed. The riders don't seem to be armed."

Marcus strode forward and was pleased to see that Sextus and the other two centurions were already out ahead of the lead wagon. Off some distance, coming directly down the road toward them, two men on horseback were coming at a steady lope.

"Deploy the archers," Marcus barked. "And I want spearmen around the front wagons."

The officers sprang to obey, and men raced into position.

Still the riders came on, as if they had the road all to themselves.

"No one fires until I give the signal," Marcus warned.

"Hold until the tribune gives the command," Sextus bawled at the bowmen who had scrambled up behind the rocky spine on both sides of the road. Then, suddenly, he gave a low exclamation of surprise. He leaned forward, raising a hand to shade his eyes. Then he slowly turned.

"What is it?" Marcus asked, seeing the expression on his centurion's face.

"I think it's David ben Joseph and his son Simeon, sire."

At first that meant nothing to Marcus; then he went rigid. "Of Capernaum?"

"The same, sire."

VI

Marcus paced back and forth, the fury in him raging so hot he could barely speak.

Simeon watched in faint amusement. "By the way," he said sarcastically, "the breakdown was masterful. The man who watched it was totally convinced it was an accident."

Marcus stopped, his jaw working. There was no question. This was not a bluff. These two knew everything, even down to the planned delay at this point.

"Who dares to betray Rome in this manner?"

Simeon hooted derisively. "I could personally name hundreds who would jump at the chance," he retorted. "If Rome were nearly as frightening as Rome thinks it is, it would make your task a great deal easier."

"Simeon."

He turned at his father's soft warning. The very sight of the Roman who had dragged his mother and sister off in bonds had left Simeon almost shaking. His determination to put all of that terrible day behind him as Jesus demanded was nearly forgotten now. He got hold of himself and moved back a step. "Sorry, Father."

David stepped forward. They were speaking in Aramaic so that only Sextus and Marcus could understand what was being said. "Mordechai of Jerusalem and your governor have together hatched a brilliant plan," he said. "If it had worked, the Zealots as we know them would have ceased to exist. Unfortunately, all of that brilliance is now undone, and you find yourself in a very precarious position. The question now is how to minimize the loss and prevent a massacre."

"So you've come as our *benefactors?*" Marcus sneered. "Do you think I don't remember who you are, and how much cause you have to hate me?"

"That is past and has nothing to do with what is happening here," David said calmly. Then more earnestly, he went on. "What are your choices? Mordechai is a clever man and a cunning one, but he made one major miscalculation. To this point, the various Zealot groups have been badly fragmented, unable to mount even a minor campaign where they might cooperate long enough to win success. Mordechai thought if he presented sufficient temptation, he could entice the Zealots to unite so you could fall upon them. And he was right. His problem, however, was that he thought there would be maybe four or five hundred men at best."

Marcus was listening intently in spite of his determination to treat these two with utter contempt. They were right. Mordechai had told him that if the Zealots were able to muster five hundred men, it would be a miracle. With his own two hundred and fifty and three additional maniples lying in wait, they would outnumber them more than two to one.

David watched him, guessing what was going on in his mind. "Mordechai badly underestimated, Tribune. Currently there are over a thousand men waiting for you inside the pass."

Marcus's head came up very slowly. Then he turned to the other officers, who were watching this interchange with anxious and angry eyes, not sure what was happening. He spoke to them in Latin.

"Rubrius, you stay. The rest of you get back to your men. Have them throw up a defensive perimeter around the train. Move!"

As they jumped to obey him, his anger flared again, and he swung back on the two Jews. "Do you think you can make us turn tail and run by coming in and scaring us with empty numbers? I could have you nailed to a cross and let your friends see what happens to men who think they can trifle with Rome."

David turned to Sextus. His face was grave. "I give you my word, Sextus. We speak the truth. Even at this moment Gehazi is preparing to send men out to intercept your hidden maniples. They will not be able to stop them, but they will delay them long enough that there will be no help for you. Not before morning."

Sextus nodded gravely.

"And," Simeon came in, watching Sextus carefully, "you know as well as I that if the word gets out that we have a column of Romans pinned down here, people will pour out of the villages like ants from an anthill that has been kicked open. What is now a thousand will become two thousand, three thousand. You won't stand a chance."

"Why do you talk to my centurion?" Marcus exploded. "I am in command here."

David turned slowly. "Because Sextus knows that what we say is true. I am a man of my word, Marcus Didius. Mordechai badly underestimated our capabilities. Don't you make the same mistake."

Rubrius looked at his commanding officer, his leathered face showing open concern. "David ben Joseph is a man of honor, sire. I cannot speak to what we should do in these circumstances, but if he says there are a thousand men, then—"

"Would you be a Jew, Rubrius?" But even as he lashed out at him, Marcus knew his centurion was right. Even *he* believed that David ben Joseph spoke the truth.

Simeon watched the man he had hated for so long and realized that he could put that hate aside. Simeon commanded men. He had faced terrible risks and made assessments of what it would take to conquer. Now he could think of this man in that role and feel sorry for him. "It would seem that you have three options at this point. Go ahead and enter the pass, knowing that no help will be forthcoming. If you do, you will be cut to pieces. Or you can choose to make a stand here." He shook his head. "Your position is hardly a defensible one, Tribune. Or—"

"You lecture me on tactics?" Marcus shouted. "A Roman creates his own defensible position."

"Or," Simeon continued without reaction, "you can try to retreat, try to cut your way back through to Ptolemais, and see what it is like to have all of Galilee turn against you."

Marcus stood there, his chest rising and falling, fighting back the rage so he could think clearly. "And you have some wonderful solution for us, I suppose." It came out as bitter invective, but behind that there was also a question. These two had ridden into camp like conquering kings. They had something more in mind than they had told him so far.

"It's simple," David explained. "You surrender your arms immediately. Gehazi will withdraw from the pass and stand back half a mile away from this position so you can see, first, that he has the number of men we say he does, and second, that he has withdrawn."

"You would have me stand and watch while my enemy surrounds me?"

"He won't surround you," Simeon said wearily, beginning to wonder if they were going to fail. "He'll stand off to the north of the road. Go ahead and put up your defensive perimeter. Prepare anyway you like for the possibility of betrayal."

"Half the wagons will be left here for Gehazi," David said. "You take the other half with you and head for the pass."

"Half!" Marcus roared. "Just like that? We'd like twenty wagons, sire, filled with arms, if you please. And thank you very much for your kindness."

David went on, unruffled. "Gehazi was just as furious at that suggestion as you, Tribune. He is sure he can take them all."

Marcus sniffed in disgust. "Ask for one wagon, and perhaps I shall consider your offer. Do you think we have no courage to face this fight?"

"No one questions your courage or that of your men," David said sadly. "Will it take rivers of blood to prove that what is needed here is wisdom and not courage?"

Simeon went on quickly. "If you surrender your arms, we swear with an oath that you will be given safe passage through the pass and set free. We know that was your intent anyway, but this way you won't have to lose any men doing it. As you know, Ya'abin is to get half the gold for his part in this. Gehazi has agreed to let him take all of it. He will be waiting in the pass to escort you down to the Plains of Sharon."

"As you also know," David came in, seeing that despite Marcus's anger their words were having an impact on him, "Mordechai has arranged a little surprise for Ya'abin as well. He'll walk straight into the arms of your governor, and none of the ten talents will be lost."

Rubrius stepped forward. "If Gehazi is sending men out to intercept the other maniples, Pilate will not be able to get through to us."

David turned. "We did not tell Gehazi about the third maniple. He knows only of the two on each flank."

"You swear that?" Rubrius said, obviously caught by surprise by that announcement.

"I swear it," David said evenly. "On my life." Then he turned back to Marcus. "What will it be, Tribune? Gehazi knows about your little subterfuge with the wagon wheel. He is even now poised to sweep down upon you. Nail us to the cross. Delay us even another ten minutes and you will no longer have any choice." He rubbed wearily at his eyes. "And many men will die here."

"Pilate will have *me* on a cross if I give up twenty wagons filled with armaments," Marcus said, half to himself.

"Better he lose twenty than forty," Simeon shot back. "And he can save two hundred and fifty men in the bargain. Surely he won't fault you for a choice like that."

When there was no response, Simeon's own anger flared. "Come on, Tribune! Those other maniples are not going to be here before morning. You don't stand a chance."

"Don't throw your men into the fire as if they were worthless rags," David pleaded.

For a long time Marcus was silent. Then he looked at David. "Ya'abin is set to escort us out of the pass?"

David felt a little thrill of exultation. Marcus was considering it. "Yes, just as originally planned."

Marcus turned to Sextus Rubrius. "Centurion?"

Sextus seemed to have expected the question. "We can fight. We *will* fight; you know that. But they are right, sire. Our original intent was to surrender our arms and lure them into the trap. Now there is no trap."

"Go on."

The grizzled old veteran looked first at David, then at Simeon, and finally back at his commander. "I think if we try to make a stand, we will be annihilated."

Marcus stood there for a long time, staring westward to where the sun was now low above the hills, throwing the entry to the Joknean Pass into deep shadow. At last he turned to David. "We will not surrender our weapons. We march through the pass with the twenty wagons *and* our own personal weapons."

David and Simeon were both shaking their heads. "Gehazi will never agree to that," David explained. "He's already suspicious of this whole setup. You come marching in with your weapons and he'll unleash everything he's got against you."

"And what if your word isn't good enough?" Marcus said. "How do we know we won't march into that pass and still be ambushed? If we are to be annihilated, I choose to do it with a sword in my hand."

David nodded, sadly. "All I can give you is my word. Though Gehazi is your sworn enemy, he has made an oath. If you lay down your arms and leave him twenty wagons, you shall not be attacked in any way."

Marcus looked at Sextus again. The centurion nodded briefly. He took a deep breath and made up his mind. "Agreed. Let's get on with it."

As David and Simeon turned and started for their horses, Simeon leaned in and whispered to his father. "I'm going to rejoin Yehuda and keep our band in place to watch that thief Ya'abin. We've got less than thirty men. The tribune will never notice if that many aren't here."

David nodded. What neither of them saw as they whispered to each other was that Marcus had moved up swiftly behind them. As they reached their horses, he whipped out a dagger from his belt and shoved it up against Simeon's back. "Stand still, or you die!" he cried.

Simeon's hands shot skyward.

Marcus threw an arm around his neck and pressed the dagger more tightly against Simeon's tunic.

David looked on in dismay. "What is this?"

Marcus held Simeon tightly. "You ask that I accept your word in all of this, David ben Joseph, and so I shall. But I shall have more confidence that you will not betray me if I hold your son until we see this thing through."

David's face was stricken. "Is this how Romans honor their agreements?" he exclaimed.

"This is how we ensure that our agreements are honored," Marcus hissed. "Now go!"

Simeon arched his back, trying to escape the prick of the dagger's tip. "Go, Father. There's no more time. I'll be all right."

David hesitated for only a moment, then swung up into the saddle.

As he wheeled his horse and gave spur to it, Simeon half turned his head. "And when am I to be released, O noble tribune? When you deliver me to your governor as your apology for losing twenty wagons of arms?"

"What Pilate does with you when we have reached safety is not my concern. Now move."

Simeon turned his head the other way. "Father!" It was a cry of agony and pain.

For the second time since he had come to the province of Judea, Marcus Didius made the mistake of letting his attention be diverted away from the second son of David ben Joseph, merchant of Capernaum. He turned to see if David had heard the cry. As he did so, Simeon lunged forward, breaking the grip around his neck. At the same instant, he swung both elbows back with all the force he could muster. They caught Marcus squarely in the ribs. If it had not been for his leather breastplate, he would have gone down with a punctured lung. As it was, he fell back, gasping for breath, arms extended, the dagger flying from his hand.

Swifter than the flight of an arrow, Simeon snatched the dagger up. He threw his foot behind the tribune's legs and shoved hard. Marcus hit the ground with a heavy thud. Even as the men looking on reached for their swords, Simeon had the point of the dagger at Marcus's throat. "Sextus! If anyone moves, the tribune dies."

"Stand!" Sextus roared. But his sword came out, and he came forward a few steps.

"*Again*, Sextus?" Simeon asked softly. And then he forgot the centurion. He looked into Marcus's eyes, his chest rising and falling as he took in deep breaths, fighting for control again. Marcus stared back at him, shock and fear twisting his face.

For several seconds time seemed suspended. Then reason slowly came back to Simeon's eyes. "I would ask you a question, Tribune," he said, panting heavily now.

Marcus didn't move.

"Suppose I came to your family's home in Rome. Suppose you couldn't pay the price of the extortionists who levied your taxes. And suppose that I took your mother and your sister and sold them into slavery. Given the chance, what would you do to me?"

"I don't have a sister." He spit out the words through clenched teeth.

Simeon's eyes widened in surprise. "And that's your answer?"

Marcus shook his head a tiny fraction.

"What would you do?"

Defiance now filled Marcus's face. "I would kill you," he whispered. "I would kill you without hesitation."

Simeon suddenly straightened. "Yes, you would, wouldn't you."

The dagger slipped from his hands and plopped softly in the dust. "Do what you will, Marcus Didius. I am going with my father."

Without haste he walked to the horse and took the reins in his hand. Marcus scrambled to his feet, snatching up the dagger again. Sextus leaped forward to stand beside him, but Marcus did not move.

"I can take him!" cried one of the bowmen, sighting down the shaft at Simeon's back.

Marcus didn't turn but only held up a hand. Simeon grabbed the saddle horn and leaped aboard as the horse shot forward. As he leaned forward over the horse's neck, urging it into a hard run, Marcus pulled back his tunic and slowly slid the dagger back into its scabbard.

He turned to Sextus. "Call in the men. Tell them what is happening and why. I want to be ready to move in half an hour."

CHAPTER 31

ACCEPT WHATEVER IS BROUGHT UPON YOU, AND IN CHANGES THAT
HUMBLE YOU BE PATIENT. FOR GOLD IS TESTED IN THE FIRE, AND
ACCEPTABLE MEN IN THE FURNACE OF HUMILIATION.

—*Ecclesiasticus, or the Wisdom of Jesus, the Son of Sirach 2:4–5*

I

9 JUNE, A.D. 30

Moshe Ya'abin watched as his men finished loading the small bars of gold into their saddlebags. It gave him great satisfaction to watch as the leather sagged heavily against the horses' flanks. Then the smile faded as he turned back to face Ha'keedohn. "So we shall have to wait for another day to square our accounts? Just like before."

"It is not just like before," Yehuda said darkly. "The last time we saw you, you were scurrying up a hill with your tail between your legs."

"That's enough, Yehuda," Simeon said. "A dog doesn't understand what it is that makes him a dog. It's just part of his nature."

Ya'abin lunged forward, but Eliab, his lieutenant, caught him by the arm. "There will be another time," he said. "The Romans are here. We must be going."

"Why is Gehazi so anxious to have us gone?" Ya'abin said, turning to look up the narrow canyon. The first of Marcus Didius's column was just coming around the bend into view. "Could it be that there are more than ten talents, and someone is anxious that we do not learn about it?"

"You know what your problem is, Ya'abin?" Simeon said. "You always judge others by yourself."

This time the ferret from Judea broke free. He whipped his dagger out and threw himself at Simeon. It was not unexpected, and Simeon easily sidestepped it. As Ya'abin swung around, he came face to face with Daniel, who had his bow drawn back to where the tip of the arrow touched the wood. "I would like it very much if you would try that again," Daniel said softly. "Very much."

Ya'abin stepped back, his mouth twisting. "I don't think there are other Romans coming. I think the Javelin just wanted an excuse to sidestep a battle so that he would not have to prove his courage."

"There are twenty wagons of arms right there," Simeon said, taunting him with an easy smile. "The Romans are not armed. Why don't you hang around here and find out for yourself if we speak the truth or not."

"Come on, Ya'abin," Eliab pleaded. "I don't like this. Let's get out of here."

Simeon turned on his heel and walked away without another word. Yehuda followed, but Daniel backed up slowly, the arrow still steady as a rock on Ya'abin's chest. When they reached the trees, he let the arrow fly. It slammed into a tree trunk no more than five feet from Ya'abin's nose. A laugh of pure delight echoed through the narrow pass.

Ya'abin swore and started forward, but again his lieutenant grabbed his arm. "We must go."

Ya'abin stopped, his fingers clenching and unclenching. Finally, he turned. "Something's not right here, Eliab."

"I agree; so let's get out of here."

Ya'abin didn't move. His eyes were darting back and forth as his mind worked feverishly. "I think our friend in Jerusalem has had a hand in this. Even the Javelin seems pleased that we are willing to take the Romans down the canyon."

"What are you saying?"

He turned, watching the column approach their position. The soldiers had seen them, and the Roman tribune had called them into closer formation. He just shook his head. Then he turned to Eliab. "I think it only fitting that we create a little surprise of our own."

"What?"

"If Ha'keedohn is right and the Romans knew all along about our ambush, then our fat one in Jerusalem had something to do with it. That would explain how he knew so much about the movement of this column. He got it from the Romans themselves."

"Then the sooner we're back in Judea the better."

"But suppose something went terribly wrong," Ya'abin went on, half musing now. "I'll bet old Mordechai might come in for a little share of the blame, don't you think?"

Eliab had no idea what his leader was talking about. "I suppose."

"And as for our friends, the Zealots? Well, can you think of anything that would enrage the Romans more than having one of their cohorts massacred after they had been promised safe passage by the Jews?"

Now Eliab was gaping at his leader.

Ya'abin uttered a hard laugh. "And can you think of anything more likely to take the Romans out of Judea, leaving the field open for us, than a full-scale war in the Galilee?"

Ya'abin spun around, his mind made up. "Pass the word among the men. We'll wait until the moon comes up so we can see what we're shooting at." He glanced up at the sky. "Quarter of an hour. No more." He chuckled happily. "When I give the word, I want them to gradually surround the column. You tell 'em I said *no* survivors."

Eliab licked his lips nervously. "Yes, Captain."

II

Sextus Rubrius moved up beside his commanding officer. He came up behind the horse like a wraith, keeping the animal between him and the men who rode at the front of the column.

"Yes, sire?"

"Something strange is going on." Marcus spoke in a voice barely above a whisper. Just behind them on the other side of the road, one of Ya'abin's men marched along with his head down. Marcus didn't want him to overhear.

Sextus nodded. "The way the men have changed position?" he asked, just as softly.

Marcus nodded, keeping his eyes straight ahead. When they had first met their escort, Ya'abin formed his men into two main groups, one at the front of the column, one at the rear. There were only a couple of men in between, just enough to give warning if the Romans got out of line. But in the last fifteen minutes, one by one the lead group had fallen back and spread out up and down the line. They stayed clear of the soldiers, but they had definitely spaced themselves out more strategically. "What about those in the back?" Marcus asked.

"Same thing. Some of them are up in the trees, moving along parallel with us, but they're spread out all up and down our line."

The old familiar prickle started up Marcus's neck.

"Sire?"

"Yes, Sextus?"

"I cut the lashings on the fifth wagon just before we joined our escort. The canvas is still on, but we can easily get inside now. Unfortunately, there's nothing but swords inside, but—"

"But swords are better than bare hands," Marcus finished for him, immensely relieved to hear that. "Good work, Sextus. All right. Fall back and quietly alert the men. I'll try to distract the enemy a little."

As Sextus slowed his step, Marcus reined his horse sharply to the right, nearly running into the man walking there. "Hey!" he shouted in Aramaic. "The men are getting tired. How about stopping for a time?"

At the head of the long line, Ya'abin turned in his saddle, startled by the sudden cry. When he saw Marcus on his horse, he turned back around. "You'll be stopping soon enough," he called over his shoulder. "Now shut up and get back into line." Marcus heard him say something to the man riding beside him; then both laughed.

"Once the moon's fully up," the other man shouted, "we'll be able to see better. We'll stop then." Again both roared at their private little joke.

The prickle quickly moved from Marcus's back to his stomach and became a hard, tight knot. So much for the word of a Jew!

III

Simeon said nothing more. He fell silent, moving through the forest as quietly as possible, no more than three or four feet away from Yehuda. The moon was just making its first foray into the upper branches of the trees, but it was not yet enough light for Simeon to see his friend's expression.

"When are you going to tell the rest of the men?" Yehuda finally asked.

"Tomorrow, when all of this is over with." Simeon turned his head, trying to read Yehuda's face. Here and there, all around them, dark shadows moved in the same direction and at the same pace as he and Yehuda. These were the very men they were talking about—good men, brave men. "They'll accept you as the leader without question," Simeon added.

"Did you think *that* was my concern?"

Simeon shook his head. "No."

"I know you want me to say that I understand all of this," Yehuda went on. "But I don't. I don't know how to explain what you've seen or heard, but I think you're being duped. I think that you're going to find out that this Jesus proves to be nothing more than a puff of wind on the water. One minute he's here, the next he's gone, and someone else will take his place."

A great sadness moved over Simeon. What he and Yehuda had shared for the past three years was difficult to describe. Other than his own family, Simeon was closer to this man than anyone else on earth. "I understand," he said. "I wish there were some way that I could help you see and feel what has happened to me, why I'm done with this now. I—"

He stopped, his head jerking around. One of the men on his left was waving frantically. "Someone's coming!"

Instinctively, Simeon and Yehuda dropped into a crouch, reaching for their bows. Then a second cry came. "It's Daniel!"

They straightened, cutting an angle toward the man who had called out. As they reached him, they saw a figure coming toward them, darting back and forth through the trees. "Over here," Yehuda called softly.

In a moment Daniel was with them. He stopped, bending over to catch his breath.

"What is it?" Simeon asked, feeling a sudden coldness.

"Ya'abin!"

"What?"

"I'm not sure. Something's wrong."

Yehuda took his younger brother by the shoulders and straightened him to face them. "What is it, Daniel?"

He blurted it out between gulps of air. "I wasn't sure at first. Too dark to see. All together, then spread out."

"Who was spread out?"

"Ya'abin's men." He shook his head. "All up and down the line. Ambush."

Yehuda gave a low whistle, but it wasn't necessary. The rest of the men were already gathering in around them to hear Daniel's report. "They plan to ambush us?" Yehuda demanded. "I didn't think they even knew we were following them."

"Not us." Daniel turned and looked at Simeon. "The Romans. I think they're going to kill the Romans."

Simeon fell back a step, his face filled with horror. "Are you sure?"

Daniel was finally getting his breath. "They've stopped the column. I heard Ya'abin shouting something about taking a rest. But his men are moving into position all around the column. Several were stringing their bows. Others have their swords out."

Simeon started moving. "Come on. We've got to stop this."

"No!"

Stunned, he swung back around. Yehuda had planted his feet. "This isn't our fight, Simeon."

"It is!" he cried. "My father gave his word that if they surrendered their arms, the Romans could go in peace."

"And your father kept his word. This isn't his doing."

"You would massacre men who have laid down their arms?"

"No! This isn't my doing either. This is Ya'abin's doing. But neither will I risk the lives of good men to save the lives of the very ones who came out here to destroy us."

Simeon turned and looked at the others. There was no telling what they were thinking in the dim light. "Stay then," he said bitterly, "if you have no more honor than that!"

He turned and started running, stringing his bow as he ran.

"Simeon!" Daniel's low cry pierced the glade. Then he spun on his brother. "You'll let him go alone?"

Yehuda was staring after the disappearing figure as well. He uttered a low curse and leaped forward. "Let's go!"

IV

"Stand where you are!"

Marcus turned to look at the man who was confronting him. "I have a sick man back in the column. I need to see to him."

The man turned his head, trying to see his chieftain, looking for direction. Marcus kept edging forward. He motioned with his hand for the others to do the same.

"I said don't move!" The man's voice had gone shrill.

"We're just going to—"

Off to the right, someone shouted. "Now!"

The soft whir of a shaft came almost instantly. It whacked into the wagon just above Marcus's head. Just ahead of him there was a cry of pain, and he saw a man spin around, clutching at his throat.

"To the wagons!" Marcus screamed, leaping forward. He felt a brush of air go by his ear. There was a solid thud and a soft gasp. He turned to see the legionnaire directly behind him doubled over, an arrow stuck just beneath his left arm. He looked at Marcus, his eyes filled with surprise, then toppled over.

"Form a line! Stay together!" But his words were lost as a mighty shout went up. Figures came crashing down the hill, swords flashing in the moonlight. Somewhere behind him there was a terrible shriek of pain. To his right another man jerked convulsively, then bounced off the wagon and went down.

"Here!"

Marcus looked up to see a dark figure atop one of the wagons. He saw a glint of metal; then a sword in its scabbard came flying past him. It was Rubrius. He was pawing at the canvas, pulling it back with one hand and jerking out weapons with the others. Marcus felt something hit his shoulder. There was a dull clank as a sword hit the ground. In an instant, he snatched it up and whipped it out of the scabbard. "Legionnaires. Over here! Get a sword!"

A movement in his side vision brought him around. A man with a thick beard was bearing down on him, his hand held high and filled with sword. Marcus sidestepped, then thrust hard. His attacker screamed and rolled away, one hand grabbing at his stomach.

In the moonlight figures darted back and forth in a dark blur. Pitifully few of them wore helmets, a marker of his men. Everywhere he looked, Marcus could see other shapes lying on the ground, some writhing back and forth, others perfectly still. There were screams and shouts and cries. Swords clanged, horses neighed wildly. Something bumped against Marcus's leg. He looked down and saw a soldier cowering beneath the wagon. He grabbed him by the edge of his armor and jerked him violently to his feet. "Get a sword!" he bellowed, pointing up at Sextus.

He could see others of his men pressing in, grabbing the swords that were pitching out in every direction and littering the ground. Perhaps fifteen or twenty of his men were with him now, backing up against the wagons. "Form a line! Form a line! Stay together!" His throat felt raw, and yet he could barely hear himself over the din.

He looked up again. "Sextus! We're being cut to pieces. See if you can get more of the men together." He grabbed the man he had pulled to his feet. "Get up there and keep those swords coming."

Sextus scuttled across the pile of weapons and leaped to the ground. He had a sword in his hands and ripped it from its scabbard. The greatest attack was coming from the right side of the column, so he ducked quickly to the left. He tripped and nearly stumbled on a fallen legionnaire and wondered if it was one of his century. As quickly as the thought came it was gone. He ran in a crouch, screaming at the top of his lungs. "There are swords in the next wagon. Form up. Keep your backs together. Legionnaires, swords two wagons up. Get up there. Stay low!"

He found three men cowering behind one of the teams and waded into them with the butt of his sword. "Get up there. Third wagon up. Get a sword. Move!" As he kicked at them, they broke into a run. He whirled at the sound of running footsteps. Whirling, sword coming up, he saw a small man with a sword slide to a stop at the sight of him. "Come on!" he shouted in Aramaic. "Come and get me."

The man fell back, and Sextus rushed at him, swinging the double blade in a vicious arc. He made it only two steps when an arrow came out of the darkness and drove deep into his upper thigh. He grunted and went down on one knee. He dropped his sword and clutched at his leg, gasping in pain. The little man stopped, eyes wide, then with a shout of triumph raised his sword and moved in again. Sextus fell forward, rolling and grabbing for his sword at the same moment. He braced himself for the blow even as he tried to ward it off.

As the man raised both arms high, there was a soft thud, and the air whooshed out of him. The bandit stumbled forward, his eyes wide open, his teeth clenched. The sword fell from his hands, and he sank to his knees. He stared at Sextus, his eyes not seeing, then pitched forward to the ground. To Sextus's utter astonishment, he saw an arrow buried in the man's back, the shaft still quivering.

V

Simeon whipped out another arrow from his quiver, nocked it even as he raised the bow, and took aim. There was a bowman on a horse, facing the line of wagons, taking aim. Simeon let his arrow fly. In the light of the half-moon he couldn't follow the flight of his arrow, but a moment later the man gave a cry and pitched sideways off his horse.

Simeon turned as someone came pounding up beside him. It was Daniel. "Watch for helmets," he shouted as Daniel dropped to one knee and loosed off his first shot. "Everyone else belongs to Ya'abin."

"Archers! Take your marks!"

Simeon felt a rush of joy as he recognized the bull voice of Yehuda. He turned to see him waving his arms at the figures that were running with him. And then, just as they had drilled so many times back in Beth Neelah, Simeon's men spread out, dropping to one knee to form a single line.

"Ready?" Yehuda bellowed. "Go!" Off went the first volley of arrows. All up and down the line of darting figures below, men screamed or went down without a sound.

"One! Two! Three! Four!" Even as he counted, Yehuda was reaching for the next arrow and nocking it in the string. "Five!" Again there was one simultaneous rush of air as more than twenty arrows shot out into the night.

VI

Moshe Ya'abin saw three of his men go down almost as one and whirled in shock. He had been watching the Romans arm themselves, yelling and screaming at his men to cut them off from the wagon filled with swords. He stared, kicking his horse forward. Then it hit him. There were arrows protruding from his men. This was not from the Romans.

He threw himself off his horse and dropped into a crouch.

"Attack!" he screamed. "On the hill." He rolled away as an arrow thudded into the ground a foot away from his face. "Eliab! On the hill! Get some fire up there!"

Thirty paces away, Marcus had just reached Sextus Rubrius and was taking him under the arms when he heard Ya'abin's shouts. "Attack?" he exclaimed. He laid Sextus down again and peered up into the trees. He could see nothing, but suddenly arrows flashed in the moonlight and four more of Ya'abin's men went down.

"They're not shooting at us," Sextus said, gritting his teeth. "Someone killed the man who was about to kill me."

Marcus's head came up with a snap, and he shouted aloud. "It's the other maniple. They're here!"

"No!" Sextus turned himself enough to reach out and snap off the arrow buried in the dead man's back. "Look. It's not Roman."

Marcus stared at it, not understanding. "Then who?"

"I don't know," Sextus said grimly, "but they're our only chance."

Marcus saw instantly that his officer was right. The tide of the battle had suddenly shifted. Ya'abin was screaming for his men to fall back. Several had turned and were shooting up the hill at their unseen enemy. Two more cried out, and one went down.

Suddenly Marcus realized that the Judeans had forgotten all about his men. He leaped to his feet. "To the swords, legionnaires. Move! Move!"

VII

Simeon was on his feet, peering down at the scene below them, trying to make out what was happening. He heard Ya'abin's voice and knew instantly who it was. "Get Ya'abin!" he shouted.

"Go! Go!" Yehuda yelled, waving at the men. "Stop those men on horses."

Simeon started forward. "Come on, Daniel. I want Ya'abin."

Daniel sent off one last arrow and leaped to his feet. "We did it!" he cried. "We did it! They're on the run."

Simeon grinned at his exuberance, then bolted down the hill, taking great leaps over the undergrowth as he dodged through the trees. But suddenly he realized he was alone. He slid to a stop, whirling to look back up the hill. "Daniel?"

He was nowhere. Looking around wildly, wondering if he had passed him in the darkness, Simeon called again. "Daniel!"

"Simeon?" It was like the cry of a child.

He turned and raced up the hill, trying to retrace his steps. And then he saw him. Daniel was sitting up. His bow was still in his hand, though his quiver was twisted at a crazy angle over his shoulder. Then Simeon drew in his breath sharply. An arrow was protruding from Daniel's stomach. Simeon flung his bow aside. "Daniel. I'm here."

His head came up. There was a look of bewilderment in his eyes. "I didn't see it, Simeon."

"It's all right. Here, lie down." Simeon put a hand behind his back and winced as Daniel groaned between clenched teeth.

"Let me see." Simeon pulled back the tunic, exposing the flesh. The arrow was low in the abdomen and buried at least half a handspan into the flesh. If it was barbed . . . He pressed his fingers gently around the wound. Daniel screamed in agony.

Simeon shot to his feet and cupped his hands to his mouth. "Yehuda!" He listened, but there was nothing but the sounds of the battle down below. He could no longer hear his men running through the trees. "Yehuda!"

Daniel clutched at his leg. "Don't leave me, Simeon."

He dropped back down beside him. "I won't, Daniel. I'm here." He laid a hand against his cheek. "I'm here."

As he bent over him, in the moonlight Daniel's eyes were filled with tears—of pain, of surprise. "Why, Simeon?" he whispered.

Simeon took his hand and pressed it to his breast, rocking back and forth. "It's all right, Daniel. Hold on. Hold on."

VIII

"Fall back! Fall back!" Ya'abin was screaming at his men, cursing and swearing at this turn of fate. Figures came running toward him, staying low, weaving in and out to provide a more difficult target.

"Let's get out of here!" Ya'abin leaped to his feet and grabbed at his horse's reins.

"What about the wounded?" Eliab cried.

"Leave them!"

He didn't wait to see if anyone else followed him. He threw himself into the saddle and dug his heels in the horse's flanks. In a moment those who were still able had grabbed their own mounts and raced after him, leaving a cloud of dust as they pounded down the narrow road that eventually led out of the Joknean Pass.

A quarter of a mile farther on, Ya'abin gave a cry of alarm and pulled his mount to a sliding stop. The others almost overrode him before they also got their horses stopped. "Someone's coming!" Ya'abin shouted, pointing down the road to where three running figures could be seen in the moonlight.

"It's Shaul!" a voice cried. "It's the sentries."

Ya'abin swore. He had totally forgotten that he had sent three men down the road to watch for any trouble. He started forward, but Shaul's terrified cry stopped him short again. "Ya'abin! Romans coming!"

"They're not coming," he snarled. "They're behind us."

Shaul raced up, his eyes bulging. "No! A whole column. They're coming up the pass."

Ya'abin's jaw went slack.

"How far?" Eliab blurted.

"Ten minutes, maybe less. We've got to get out of here."

"Mordechai!" Ya'abin hissed.

Eliab turned and stared in amazement. "You think it's Mordechai?"

A stream of curses poured from the bandit's mouth. "Yes, this is Mordechai's doing." But as quickly as the fury had struck him, it was gone again. He swung down. "Leave the horses. Into the hills."

"What about the gold?" one of the men cried.

"Leave it!"

"No!" That came from several of the men. With half their numbers now down, they had already been calculating how much more of a share they would get.

He swore at them again. "We've got Romans coming up the road and another full maniple somewhere in the hills between us and Judea. You want the gold, you stay with your horse. Me, I'll get mine later from Mordechai ben Uzziel."

He slapped his horse on the rump and darted away, plunging into the trees on the south side of the road. That was enough for his followers. In a moment the horses were gone and the road was deserted.

IX

Yehuda stepped out, waving his arms. "Whoa! Whoa there!" He moved quickly to block the horse's path. Three horses had already raced by them with empty saddles. This one they cut off. "Easy, Boy," Yehuda soothed, coming up slowly. The head reared back and the eyes were wild, but the horse stood its ground. Yehuda took another step and grabbed the reins, then pulled its head down again.

"It's all right, Boy," he said, rubbing its forehead. "Who do you belong to anyway?" Rubbing his hand across the trembling flesh, he moved around to the side. He didn't even have to reach inside the saddlebags. The moment he felt the heavy weight there, he knew what it was. "It's one of Ya'abin's," he said. "And the gold is still here."

That brought exclamations of astonishment. "Why?" someone asked. "Why would he leave the gold?"

He shook his head. "I don't know, but I don't like it."

"Listen!" another hissed.

They turned. It took a moment; then the sound was unmistakable to every one of them. It was the clatter of many hooves on stone.

"Ya'abin's coming back," one of them cried.

Yehuda held up a hand, his head still cocked to one side. "No," he exclaimed. "There are too many." Then his heart went cold. Now he understood why Ya'abin had left his mounts and fled. "It's the Romans." He whirled. "Into the trees. Get out of here as quickly as you can. We'll see you back in Beth Neelah, if not before."

"Where are you going?"

"I'm going to find Simeon." He took off running hard back up the canyon.

They had come less than half a mile in pursuit of Ya'abin, so Yehuda was back at the place of ambush in five or six minutes. He pulled up short. The column stood quiet and deserted in the moonlight. The only movement was from the teams hitched to the wagon and two or three riderless mounts. Feeling a sudden uneasiness, Yehuda took down his bow and nocked an arrow in the string as he moved forward slowly. There were bodies everywhere. Romans, Judeans. One horse was down and wheezing badly, an arrow in its chest.

He spun around as he heard a soft moan. Three feet away, one of the Romans stirred, then groaned. In an instant Yehuda had the arrow trained on him, but he didn't move again.

He approached the first wagon, totally baffled. Ten minutes earlier this had been a nightmare scene. He lowered the bow and cupped a hand. "Simeon?"

He heard a soft sound. Yehuda whirled, but saw no one. "Simeon?" he called again.

"Put down your bow," a voice said just behind him. "Put it down or you die."

X

Simeon jerked up when he heard Yehuda's voice from below. As he got to his feet, his shout of relief died in his throat. He could see Yehuda clearly in the moonlight. His hands were held high, and he was very stiff. And then Simeon saw why. He had been so focused on Daniel that he hadn't noticed that all activity down below had ceased. Now, suddenly, figures were stepping out from behind wagons and trees everywhere he looked. And as he watched, he realized that on most he could see the soft gleam of moonlight on metal helmets.

A plumed figure moved forward, and Yehuda's hands were jerked around behind him. Simeon couldn't see it, but he knew his wrists were being tied. He bent over Daniel. "Yehuda's in trouble," he whispered. "I'll be back."

Daniel stirred but did not open his eyes. Simeon picked up his bow and began moving quietly downhill, slipping from shadow to shadow, his eyes never leaving Yehuda's figure. No one was looking up the hill anymore. Other than the small group of men with swords who now surrounded Yehuda, all the rest of the survivors were busy arming themselves from the wagons they had brought into the pass.

Then Simeon froze in place. The others heard it too—the sound of many horses coming. He heard Marcus barking orders, and as quickly as they had appeared the Romans below him melted into the night again. Simeon pressed in behind a large pine tree, praying that Daniel wouldn't awaken and cry out. The sound of the horses was rising to a dull rumble. They were just around the bend.

Simeon shook his head in great despair. He didn't have to wait to see who it was. He knew as surely as he knew there was no way he could now do anything for Yehuda. He turned and moved silently back up the hill.

Simeon broke off the shaft as close as he could to the wound, then shouldered Daniel, careful to avoid jarring him more than necessary. As Daniel groaned, Simeon looked one last time at the scene down below. The line of Roman cavalry stretched back around the bend. In the light of the moon, he could see the large red plume and red cape of the man who sat on a horse at the head of his troops. He didn't have to wonder who it was. As he quietly moved deeper into the trees, he clearly heard the voice of Marcus Quadratus Didius floating up to him on the night air, confirming what he already knew. "Governor!" Marcus called out with great relief. "We thought you would never come."

CHAPTER 32

AND JESUS SAID UNTO HIM, NO MAN, HAVING PUT HIS HAND TO
THE PLOUGH, AND LOOKING BACK, IS FIT FOR THE KINGDOM OF GOD.

—*Luke 9:62*

I

10 JUNE, A.D. 30

It was just at dawn that David and the two men from Simeon's band found them. Simeon was moving slowly along a narrow path through the forest, staggering under the weight of the man he carried over his shoulder. The three men rushed to him. As they reached him, Simeon looked up, barely recognizing them. "Father?"

"Yes, Son. We're here."

"Daniel's hurt," he mumbled.

David motioned to the other two to help him, and they gently lifted Daniel off.

"Careful!" Simeon cried. "He's in a lot of pain."

David looked up. Daniel's face was cold, his body already stiffening. "Not any longer, Simeon," he said softly. "Daniel's at peace now."

Simeon blinked, not sure he had heard right, staring down at the still form at his feet. He slowly sank to the ground and buried his face in his hands. "I'm sorry, Daniel. I'm so sorry." Then he looked at his father. "Tried to find the horse. Couldn't. Had to carry him."

"Gehazi took our horses, remember?" his father said gently. "When you went with Yehuda and your men, Gehazi said he was taking the horses."

Simeon's shoulders began to shake convulsively. "Couldn't find the horse," he mumbled.

David sat down beside him and put his arms around him. For a long time he just held him, feeling the trembling in Simeon's body. When the suddering began to subside, one of the men reached out and touched Simeon's shoulder. "What about Yehuda?" he asked in a gentle voice.

Simeon's head came up. He wiped at the tears with the back of his hand. "Romans took him." Again the anguish twisted his mouth. "Tried to get to him. Too late. Pilate. The governor. Hundreds of soldiers." He turned to his father, his eyes pleading. "I tried to get to him."

David nodded. Then he took him by the shoulders and shook him gently, trying not to show how shocked he was by his son's appearance. He also understood why. In addition to the tragedy of the night before, he was on the verge of sheer exhaustion. He had slept only an hour or two the night before and none at all this night. In the last two days he had traveled nearly fifty miles, much of that on foot. From the appearance of things, he had been carrying Daniel through most of the night.

"Simeon, listen to me. We have to move. There are soldiers everywhere. There is great danger."

Finally his eyes began to focus, and a semblance of rationality began to return. "Mother?"

"She's on her way back to Capernaum. Some of your men are taking her home. Miriam and Livia and Ezra, with an escort, left for Ptolemais in the night. They're all right."

"Have to get Daniel to Beth Neelah." His face crumpled again as a new thought hit him. "Shana. Oh, Shana!"

The two men with David looked at each other; then the one turned to David. "We've got to move," he whispered.

"Simeon, listen. We're going to have to bury Daniel here."

"No! Beth Neelah."

"There are Romans everywhere to the east of us. We're going to have to go west and make our way around them."

His head came up, and he gripped his father's arm. "Ya'abin! He was trying to kill them all."

"I know." He gestured with his head. "Your brethren told me all about it. You stopped a massacre, Simeon."

He straightened, coming back to himself. "What about the others? Gehazi? The others?"

David shook his head in disgust. "Gehazi got greedy. Instead of sending out men to intercept the Romans, he decided he would just get out of there before the Romans came. He was still going through the wagons when Pilate and Marcus, now totally rearmed, came out of the pass." He sighed, the weariness heavy on him as well. "They didn't get much, but they got away. The Romans are trying to hunt them down now."

The other man was motioning to David. "We have to go!" he mouthed.

David stood and pulled his son up to stand beside him. "Come. Let us put Daniel to rest, and then we must leave."

II

Marcus stepped inside the tent and immediately stiffened to attention. "Tribune Marcus Didius reporting as requested, Excellency."

Pilate stood immediately and came over to him. He laid a hand on his shoulder. "Marcus, Marcus. Stand down. It's over." He laid a hand on his shoulder. "You have saved us from a major disaster."

The relief hit him like a blow to the stomach. He had come expecting to face Pilate's rage.

"Come, sit down. Did you get any sleep?"

"A little."

As they moved over to a table, Marcus took off his helmet and sat in the chair the governor indicated. Pilate flicked a finger, and a slave jumped forward and poured two cups of wine, then immediately left.

"I talked with your centurion, and—"

"Sextus? How is he?"

"In a lot of pain. The surgeons dug the arrow out. He'll probably limp for the rest of his life, but he's a tough old veteran."

"One of the best," Marcus said fervently.

"He told me everything." His eyes went hard. "Have you given any thought as to who betrayed us? Do you think it was Mordechai?"

Marcus shook his head quickly. "No." He took a sip of wine, savoring the taste as it washed out the dust and grime and a long sleepless night from his mouth. "No, Mordechai had as much to gain as we did." He blew out his breath. "I can't fathom who it might have been. Mordechai took every precaution." Then his jaw tightened. "But I plan to find out."

"Have you seen the reports yet?"

"No, sire. I came directly here as you requested."

He turned and picked up a piece of parchment. "Most important, we've recovered all the gold except for three or four bars, and we think they're on a stray horse somewhere. They're looking for it now."

"Ya'abin?"

"No. I've sent one of the centuries out looking for him, but I'm sure he's well into Judea by now."

Marcus's fingers tightened around the goblet. "That's one I should like permission to pursue myself," he said.

"All in due time," Pilate said impatiently. "He lost seventeen of his men, and we captured twelve more, most of them wounded."

"And our losses?" he asked quietly.

"Twenty-eight, with about that many more wounded. That was a brilliant move to cut the cover off the wagon so you could get to the swords. You could have lost many more than that."

Marcus could hardly believe that he was being praised. Last night he had been sure he had endured the greatest disaster of his career. "That was Sextus too, sire. He was everywhere."

"Yes, yes. I'm going to see that he is rewarded."

"What about the arms?"

"How many wagons did you bring?"

"Forty-one."

"Then we lost only four. Thanks to my timely arrival and the fact that you had rearmed yourself, we caught those bandits totally by surprise. They scattered like ducks before the fox."

The relief was more heady than the wine, and Marcus sat back, marveling at what was happening.

"There's one thing I don't understand, though," Pilate said.

"What is that, Excellency?"

"Your centurion said that the Jews were the ones who stopped Ya'abin from completely annihilating you. Is that true?"

"Someone did." Marcus had been mulling over that very question much of the night.

"Do you know who?"

"We captured one of their men, sire. If he is to be believed, it was the man they call Ha'keedohn, the Javelin."

Pilate grunted. "Any idea why?"

His eyes were hooded as Marcus remembered the prick of Simeon's dagger against his throat. "No, sire, I don't," he finally answered. "I wonder if it wasn't some kind of a mistake."

III

12 JUNE, A.D. 30

Simeon straightened as Shana came around the house, escorted by one of Simeon's men. She turned and murmured something to him, and he nodded and backed away. She came on more slowly now, her head high, her back stiff.

"*Shalom*, Shana."

"And peace to you, Simeon." The word *peace* was said with soft bitterness.

"Any word of Yehuda?"

She nodded curtly.

"In Caesarea?"

"Yes. He and the others they caught are to be crucified next month."

He expected no less. "I won't let that happen, Shana. I—"

Her chin came up sharply. "Just as you couldn't let the Romans die?"

He shook his head. There was nothing to say to that.

"Why, Simeon?" she cried. "Help me understand why." Her eyes were glistening, but there was as much anger as sorrow there.

"I can't," he said sadly. "I can no more help you understand what happened and why than I could make Yehuda understand why I had to do what I did."

"And what about Daniel?" It burst from her in a cry of agony. "Did you help him understand before he died?"

He looked away. Daniel's last question was still in Simeon's mind like a never-ending echo. *Why, Simeon?* After a moment he reached in his tunic and withdrew a scroll. "I brought the bill of divorcement as you requested. It's been witnessed and signed."

She stared at him for what seemed like an eternity, tears trickling down her cheeks, then stepped forward and took it from him. "I'm sorry," she whispered.

"I know. I understand. I am too."

Her eyes held his for several seconds; then she turned and walked swiftly back to the house. Simeon watched until she disappeared, then turned his face to the east and started back for Capernaum.

IV

13 JUNE, A.D. 30

"Simeon?"

He looked up from the scroll he was reading to where his mother stood in the doorway.

"There's someone here to see you."

He set the scroll on the bed. "Who is it?"

She just shook her head. "I think you'd better come and see."

Puzzled by the gravity of her demeanor, he followed her downstairs and to the front door. She stopped there, pointing. "He's outside in the courtyard with your father."

Simeon went out. As he started across the courtyard he saw his father and another man with their backs to him, conversing in low tones. As they heard his footsteps, they both turned. Simeon stopped dead.

"*Shalom*, Simeon of Capernaum," Sextus Rubrius said quietly.

Simeon could only stare. He was not in his uniform but wore a simple tunic and hooded outer robe.

Sextus looked at Simeon's father. "I won't stay long." Then he looked at Simeon. "I just had one question I had to ask you."

A little dazed, Simeon nodded.

The Roman reached in a fold of his tunic and withdrew something. At first Simeon could not tell what it was. Then as Sextus held it out, Simeon's eyes flew open in surprise. It was the upper half of an arrow.

"Does this belong to you?"

Baffled, Simeon took it and peered more closely at it. Then he nodded. Those feathers were distinctive. He had glued them into place with his own hands. "Yes," he said, completely astonished. "Where did you get this?"

"I took it out of the back of the man who was trying to kill me."

The image of a man with a sword, both hands raised high, standing over a fallen Roman, flashed into Simeon's mind. "That was you?" he cried.

"That was me."

Only then did Simeon see that the centurion had a walking stick in one hand and that he leaned heavily upon it. Reeling, his eyes lifted to meet Sextus's gaze.

"When you decide what it is you want to do about your friend, Yehuda," Sextus said, "I would like to be of help."

With that, he nodded at Simeon, then to his father, and turned and started for the gate, limping noticeably as he made his way across the paving tiles.

V

14 JUNE, A.D. 30

Simeon rapped on the door sharply, then stepped back. He heard the shuffle of footsteps inside; then the door opened. "Good morning, Anna."

Peter's wife looked up at him in surprise. "Good morning, Simeon."

"Is—" But before he could ask, Peter appeared behind his wife.

"Simeon, what a pleasant surprise. We heard that you were supposed to get back yesterday."

"Yes, I arrived late last night."

Peter sobered. "Did you speak with Shana?"

He nodded.

"Your mother said she asked for a bill of divorcement," Anna said sadly.

"She did. Can you blame her?" He took a quick breath. "Is Jesus staying with you?"

Peter nodded. "He is, but he left early this morning."

Simeon's face fell.

Peter smiled gently. "He said he was going for a walk down by the seashore. It's still early. If you go now I think you might still catch him alone."

"Thank you."

VI

They walked slowly along the pebbled beach. From time to time Jesus would stoop down, pick up a handful of rocks and then flip them one by one into the water, watching them plop softly and disappear.

Finally he turned and looked at Simeon. "Peter told me of all that happened."

Simeon nodded, not surprised. The whole town seemed to know of the disaster that had struck the Zealots. "Did my mother tell you about the woman called Miriam?"

"Yes. When I next go to Jerusalem, I hope I shall get to meet her and her servant girl."

"She is very worried about her father."

Jesus flipped another pebble away and watched as the ripples spread outward across the smooth surface of the water. "Do you remember what I said that day of the baptisms when your uncle came down and spoke harshly to your mother?"

Simeon's eyes lifted. He had thought of that yesterday and wished he had remembered it soon enough to share it with Miriam. "I do."

"'Think not that I am come to bring peace on earth,'" he said, quoting himself softly.

Simeon picked it up from there, quoting as best as he could remember. "'I am come to set a man—or a woman!—at variance against his or her father. And a man's foes shall be they of his own household.'"

Jesus nodded his head in acknowledgment. "The word of God is like a two-edged sword, Simeon. It is quick and powerful, piercing even to the dividing asunder of soul and spirit."

"Why?" he burst out. "I thought that choosing to follow you would bring joy. That's what my mother said."

"Do you feel *no* joy, Simeon, son of David?" came the soft reply.

"No!" he cried. "I have never felt such agony of spirit in my life."

"Then why do you not turn away?"

That brought his head around. "Because I know who you are," he whispered.

Again Jesus gave the briefest of nods. "My mother sent word that you had come to see her."

"Yes. She is a remarkable woman. She told me the story of the angel." He paused, then shook his head. "The Son of God? I don't understand what that means."

Jesus smiled gently. "Does it surprise you that the finite mind cannot fully comprehend the infinite?"

"No, but if I could, I would like to understand at least a small portion."

"You already understand more than you realize."

Simeon threw up his hands. "Will it always be this way?"

"What way is that, Simeon?"

"Will it always be this hard? Following after you?"

"And if it is, what then? Will you turn away?"

That caught him up short. Would he? *Could* he? Finally he shook his head. "No, I don't think so."

He murmured in satisfaction. "That is good, for no man having put his hand to the plow and looking back is fit for the kingdom of God."

Simeon kicked at the rocks, sending several skittering away. "I am not sure that I am fit for the kingdom of God."

Jesus stopped and turned to face him fully. "That day on the mount, when I was teaching the people, you rose and stalked away."

"Yes, I'm sorry."

He brushed that aside. "You did not hear the final things I had to say."

Now he had Simeon's full attention. "What else did you say?"

"I spoke of the day of judgment. When it comes, there will be many who think they serve God but who will be surprised, for not everyone who says unto me, 'Lord, Lord,' shall enter into the kingdom of heaven."

Simeon gave him a long look, considering his words. "Then who will?"

There was a pause, then, "He that *does* the will of my Father which is in heaven."

"But the Pharisees claim they are doing God's will. My Uncle Aaron is convinced he is doing more to please God than any of the rest of us. The Sadducees claim their beliefs are the most correct. The Zealots are sure *their* way is the right way. How do you know?"

"Many will say in that day, 'Lord, Lord, have we not prophesied in thy name? and in thy name have cast out devils? and in thy name done many wonderful works?'" Jesus stopped and turned to face him again. "But I will profess unto them, 'I never knew you.'" His face grew sorrowful. "'And you never knew *me!*'"

For several long moments there was no sound but the twitter of birds off in the brush and the soft lapping of the water against the shore. "Here is what you would have heard had you stayed that day, Simeon. 'Whosoever hears these sayings of mine and *does* them, I will liken him unto a wise man who built his house upon a rock. And the rain descended, and the floods came, and the winds blew, and beat upon that house, and it fell not.'" His head lifted, and his eyes bored into Simeon's. "Why? Because it was founded upon a rock.

"'But those who hear my sayings and do them not, them shall I liken unto a foolish man who built his house upon the sand. And the rain descended, and the floods came, and the winds blew, and beat upon that house; and it fell, and great was the fall of it.'"

The turmoil inside Simeon's mind was still there, but it was subsiding. The words of this man had a way of calming even the most turbulent of seas. "I wish to build my house upon that rock, Master," he said quietly.

"And if you were to know that if you do, the way might even lead to the cross, Simeon, son of David, what then? Will you then turn away?"

Simeon pulled back his shoulders and met his gaze squarely. "I cannot."

Jesus leaned forward, peering deeply into his eyes. "And why is that?"

His answer came simply and without hesitation. "*Because I know who you are.*"

Jesus laid a hand on his shoulder and smiled serenely. "That is enough."

CHAPTER NOTES

The scripture about putting one's hand to the plow comes from Luke 9:62. The reference to those who will be saved in the kingdom and the parable of building one's house upon the rock are the concluding part of the Sermon on the Mount (see Matthew 7:21–29).

BIBLIOGRAPHY

Bahat, Dan. *Carta's Historical Atlas of Jerusalem: A Brief Illustrated Survey.* Jerusalem: Carta, the Israel Map and Publishing Co., 1973.

Blackman, Philip. *Tractate Sabbath: Being the First Tractate of the Second Order Moed.* New York: Judaica Press, 1967.

Bloch, Abraham C. *The Biblical and Historical Background of Jewish Customs and Ceremonies.* New York: Ktav Publishing House, 1980.

Brandon, S. G. F. "The Zealots: The Jewish Resistance Against Rome A.D. 6–73." *History Today,* 15 (September 1965): 632–41.

Carcopina, Jerome. *Daily Life in Ancient Rome: The People and the City at the Height of the Empire.* New Haven, Conn.: Yale University Press, 1940.

Clarke, Adam. *Clarke's Commentary.* 3 vol. Nashville: Abingdon, 1977.

Dummelow, J. R. *The One Volume Bible Commentary.* New York: Macmillan Publishing Co., 1908.

Edersheim, Alfred. *Sketches of Jewish Social Life in the Days of Christ.* Grand Rapids, Mich.: Wm. B. Eerdmans Publishing Co., 1979.

———. *The Temple: Its Ministry and Services as They Were at the Time of Christ.* Grand Rapids, Mich.: Wm. B. Eerdmans Publishing Co., 1958.

Fallows, Samuel, ed. *The Popular and Critical Bible Encyclopædia and Scriptural Dictionary.* 3 vol. Chicago: The Howard-Severance Co., 1911.

Farrar, Frederic. *The Life of Christ.* Portland, Ore.: Fountain Publications, 1964.

Guthrie, D., J. A. Motyer, A. M. Stibbs, and D. J. Wiseman, eds. *The New Bible Commentary: Revised.* Grand Rapids: Wm. B. Eerdmans Publishing Co., 1970.

642

Hastings, James, ed. *Dictionary of the Bible*. New York: Charles Scribner's Sons, 1909.

Josephus, Flavius. *Antiquities of the Jews*. In *Josephus: Complete Works*. William Whiston, trans. Grand Rapids, Mich.: Kregel Publications, 1960.

Keil, C. F. and F. Delitzsch. *Commentary on the Old Testament in Ten Volumes*. Grand Rapids, Mich.: Wm. B. Eerdmans Publishing Co., reprinted 1975.

Mackie, George M. *Bible Manners and Customs*. New York: Fleming H. Revell Co., n.d.

Mathews, Shailer. *The Messianic Hope in the New Testament*. Vol. XII, The Decennial Publications, 2d ser. Chicago: University of Chicago Press, 1906.

Ritmeyer, Kathleen and Leen. "Reconstructing Herod's Temple Mount in Jerusalem." *Biblical Archeological Review*, November/December 1989, 23–53.

Schürer, Emil. *The Jewish People in the Time of Jesus*. Nahum Glatzer, ed. New York: Shocken Books, 1961.

Shelton, Jo-Ann. *As the Romans Did: A Sourcebook in Roman Social History*. 2d ed. New York: Oxford University Press, 1998.

Talmage, James E. *Jesus the Christ: A Study of the Messiah and His Mission according to Holy Scriptures both Ancient and Modern*. Salt Lake City: Deseret Book Co., 1957.

Vincent, Marvin R. *Word Studies in the New Testament*. 4 vols. New York: C. Scribner's Sons, 1887–1900.

Wight, Fred H. *Manners and Customs of Bible Lands*. Chicago: Moody Press, 1953.

Wright, George Ernest, and Floyd Vivian Filson, eds. *The Westminster Historical Atlas to the Bible*. Rev. ed. Philadelphia: The Westminster Press, 1956.

Zimmerman, Michael A. "Tunnel Exposes Areas of Temple Mount." *Biblical Archeological Review*, May/June 1981, 34–41.

ABOUT THE AUTHOR

Gerald N. Lund is the author of several historical novels. He has done extensive graduate work in New Testament studies at Pepperdine University in Los Angeles and studied Hebrew at the University of Judaism in Hollywood. His love for the Middle East and its people has taken him to the Holy Land more than a dozen times as a tour director and lecturer.

JERUSALEM AT THE TIME OF JESUS

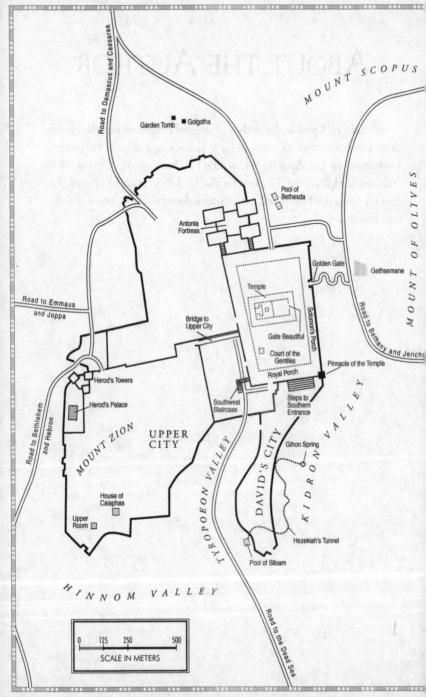

Road to Damascus and Caesarea

MOUNT SCOPUS

Garden Tomb ■ Golgotha

Pool of Bethesda

Antonia Fortress

Golden Gate

Gethsemane

MOUNT OF OLIVES

Temple

Road to Emmaus and Joppa

Bridge to Upper City

Solomon's Porch

Road to Bethany and Jericho

Gate Beautiful

Court of the Gentiles

Royal Porch

Pinnacle of the Temple

Herod's Towers

Southwest Staircase

Steps to Southern Entrance

Herod's Palace

MOUNT ZION

UPPER CITY

TYROPOEON VALLEY

DAVID'S CITY

KIDRON VALLEY

Gihon Spring

Road to Bethlehem and Hebron

House of Caiaphas

Upper Room

Hezekiah's Tunnel

Pool of Siloam

HINNOM VALLEY

Road to the Dead Sea

0 125 250 500

SCALE IN METERS

THE HOLY LAND AT THE TIME OF CHRIST

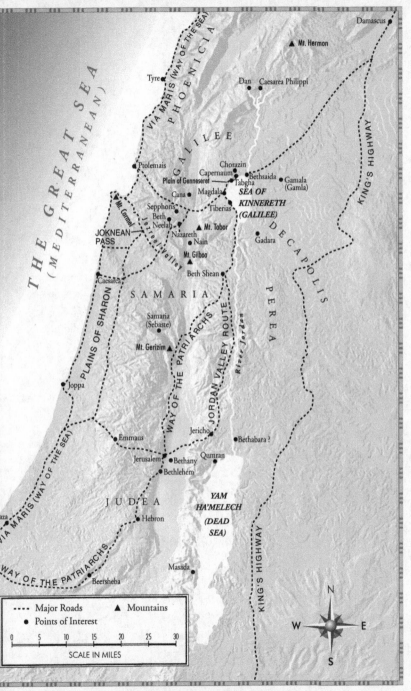

THE GREAT SEA (MEDITERRANEAN)

Damascus

▲ Mt. Hermon

Tyre

VIA MARIS (WAY OF THE SEA)

PHOENICIA

Dan Caesarea Philippi

KING'S HIGHWAY

GALILEE

Ptolemais

Chorazin
Capernaum ● Bethsaida
Plain of Genneseret Tabgha ● Gamala (Gamla)
Cana Magdala
SEA OF KINNERETH (GALILEE)

Sepphoris
Beth Neelah
Tiberias
Mt. Carmel ▲
Jezreel Valley

JOKNEAN PASS

Nazareth ▲ Mt. Tabor
Nain
Gadara
▲ Mt. Gilboa

DECAPOLIS

Beth Shean

Caesarea

SAMARIA

PEREA

Samaria (Sebaste)

WAY OF THE PATRIARCHS

JORDAN VALLEY ROUTE

River Jordan

▲ Mt. Gerizim

PLAINS OF SHARON

Joppa

Emmaus

Jericho
● Bethabara ?

Jerusalem ● Bethany
Bethlehem ● Qumran

VIA MARIS (WAY OF THE SEA)

Gaza

JUDEA

● Hebron

YAM HA'MELECH (DEAD SEA)

KING'S HIGHWAY

● Masada

WAY OF THE PATRIARCHS

● Beersheba

- - - Major Roads   ▲ Mountains
● Points of Interest

0   5   10   15   20   25   30
SCALE IN MILES

N
W   E
S

Note: Beth Neelah is a fictional village. All other sites are authentic.